THE L

AND

TRIAL AND
RETRIBUTION

Also by Lynda La Plante in Pan Books

The Talisman
Bella Mafia
Entwined
Cold Shoulder
Cold Blood
Cold Heart
Sleeping Cruelty
Royal Flush

Prime Suspect
Seekers
She's Out
The Governor
The Governor II
Trial and Retribution II
Trial and Retribution III
Trial and Retribution IV
Trial and Retribution V
Trial and Retribution VI

LYNDA LA PLANTE was born in Liverpool. She trained for the stage at RADA and worked with the National Theatre and the RSC, before becoming a television actress. She then turned to writing – and made her breakthrough with the phenomenally successful TV series *Widows*.

She has written nine subsequent novels, *The Legacy*, *The Talisman*, *Bella Mafia*, *Entwined*, *Cold Shoulder*, *Cold Blood*, *Cold Heart*, *Sleeping Cruelty* and *Royal Flush*. Her original script for the much-acclaimed *Prime Suspect* won awards from BAFTA, British Broadcasting and the Royal Television Society, as well as the 1993 Edgar Allan Poe Writer's award.

Lynda La Plante also received the Contribution to the Media award by Women in Film, a BAFTA and an Emmy for the drama series *Prime Suspect 3*. She has been made an honorary fellow of the British Film Institute and was given the BAFTA Dennis Potter Writer's Award 2000.

'The mistress of suspense'
Daily Express

'True La Plante style . . . a fast-paced romp through the worlds of horse racing and internet fraud'
Daily Mail

LYNDA LA PLANTE

THE LEGACY

AND

TRIAL AND RETRIBUTION

PAN BOOKS

The Legacy first published 1987 by Sidgwick & Jackson
First published by Pan Books 1988
Trial and Retribution first published 1997 by Pan Books

This omnibus edition published 2004 by Pan Books
an imprint of Pan Macmillan Ltd
Pan Macmillan, 20 New Wharf Road, London N1 9RR
Basingstoke and Oxford
Associated companies throughout the world
www.panmacmillan.com

ISBN 0 330 43268 0

Copyright © Park Productions Ltd 1987 and La Plante Productions 1997

The right of Lynda La Plante to be identified as the
author of this work has been asserted by her in accordance
with the Copyright, Designs and Patents Act 1988.

1 3 5 7 9 8 6 4 2

A CIP catalogue record for this book is available from
the British Library.

Phototypeset by SetSystems Ltd, Saffron Walden, Essex
Printed and bound in Great Britain by
Mackays of Chatham plc, Chatham, Kent

THE LEGACY

ACKNOWLEDGEMENTS

I sincerely thank:

Elaine Causon for her unrufflable diligence and ability to understand my spelling.

Ruth Halliday, my researcher and friend, whose enthusiasm opened new vistas, and so can be partly blamed for the length of the book.

The Lonsdale Sporting Shop in Beak Street, London. Micky Moynihan for his introduction to the world of boxing. Billy Aird, Timmy Driscoll, Bob Paget, Alex Steene for their friendship.

Terence Stamp for his knowledge of seventeenth-century furniture.

The late Patricia Phoenix who was my friend.

Jake 'the rake' Woodly, his *manushi* Eda, his *docha* Tina, and his dreams.

Richard La Plante, my husband, for trying to keep me fit and strong enough to carry the weighty volumes.

My family who will recognize shadows of themselves.

Susan Hill and Rowena Webb of Sidgwick and Jackson.

Lastly, I would like to thank Sonny Mehta, Tess Sacco, Ian Chapman, Brian Davies, Alan Gordon-Walker and Felicity Salmon at Pan Books. But mostly I give my thanks to my editor. Caroline Upcher continued to give me confidence throughout the writing of *Legacy* . . . I dedicate *The Legacy* to her with my sincerest thanks, my love and friendship.

THE LEGACY

PROLOGUE

EVELYNE JONES sat at the kitchen table, the tip of her tongue pressed to her top lip as she concentrated on her handwriting. The house was silent, everyone asleep, and the kitchen was lit only by firelight. She wore an old shirt of her Da's, and her long, skinny body was hunched over her work, her bare feet one on top of the other for warmth. Evelyne's waist-length thick red hair was braided into a single plait down her back. Small wisps of curls clung to her forehead.

She yawned, stretching her arms above her head like a ballet dancer. Her thin frame, without an ounce of fat, was more like a young boy's, and she was so tall, too tall for her age, head and shoulders above the rest of the girls in her class at school.

Hugh Jones, Evelyne's father, caught his breath. She hadn't heard him come down the stairs to stand in the darkness, watching her. Everyone said that poor Evie Jones was no beauty – so tall and thin – her best feature was her wondrous hair. Some had even said it should be ironed, it was like the fan of a concertina. But at that moment Hugh thought she was the most exquisite creature he had ever set eyes on; he couldn't move, she held him mesmerized by some magic.

Slowly Evelyne became aware of him, and she turned to give him the sweetest of smiles.

'Oh, Da, I love the family so, I love you all so much.'

'Ay, well, that may be right, but you should be a-bed . . . get yourself up, gel, now.'

She brushed past him and gave him a tickle in the ribs, and he caught her to him, held her tight. He could smell the soap on her face and neck, and kissed the white, white skin. His voice was muffled with emotion.

'We all love you, too, gel, with all our hearts.'

Slipping past him she went up to bed, but he remained standing, unable to move. His Evie, his darling child, had been untouchable for that single moment. He was so used to seeing her in her worn clothes, doing the household chores. She was just a little girl, like the other girls in the village, but that moment struck like a warning bell, telling him that Evelyne, his daughter, was different.

BOOK ONE

CHAPTER 1

DORIS EVANS looked through the compositions handed in by her class. They were, as usual, grubby, the cheap exercise books food-stained and dog-eared. Coal dust from the small hands made the texture of the paper gritty. Page after page of misspelt, blotched, childish dreams. Their subject was, 'Choose a character from history, one you would like to have been.'

The stories were similar – in many cases too similar – and Doris suspected that Lizzie-Ann Griffiths had been making herself a few halfpennies. Ninety per cent of the girls from her class fancied being Gaiety Girls, but they all spelt it 'Gayity'. Doris sighed and corrected the scrawled lines. So much for history.

Doris saved Evelyne Jones' compositions until the very last. Neat, meticulous handwriting on clean, flat pages – the girl kept her notebook in a brown paper bag. At the top of the page Evelyne had printed the date, February 10th 1909, and the title: 'I am Christina Georgina Rossetti'. Then in the same perfect handwriting the composition followed. The young girl discussed her love for her brothers, Dante Gabriel and William Michael, but what was so remarkable was that Evelyne had interwoven her feelings for her own brothers around her fictional self. She compared her own family's education to that of the Rossettis. It caught the teacher's imagination. Doris was taken aback at the depth of feeling and Evelyne's sophisticated use of the English language. She wrote about what it was like to be part of the Pre-Raphaelite movement. Evelyne was ten years old.

Doris was so fascinated she didn't even correct the spelling. She turned page after page, until the final paragraph moved her to tears. Evelyne had copied down two lines from one of Christina Rossetti's poems: Remember me when I am gone away, Gone far away into the silent land, followed by a few lines in which she said that, for many in her village, there would be no distant land, just the blackness of the mine, the blackness of death hanging over them. The blackness never stopped the laughter, the love, but so many lives were lost, and too easily forgotten.

From the schoolroom window, Doris stared down into the village. It was growing dark, and the few streetlights twinkled. In the half-light Doris could see the groups of miners gathering and moving towards the pithead for the night shift.

A hawker led his pony and cart through the village, crying that his apples were cheap, just threepence a pound. Grey house crouched close to grey house, each opening directly on to the street; there were no gardens, no colours to relieve the grey. Doris sighed. Even the leaves were grey, never green, and the berries black before they were red.

Doris hugged her brown coat around her, closed up the school and walked down to the village. It was strange to think that only a few hundred yards from here was that wondrous valley sheltered by mountains, their lower slopes covered with the darker greenness of trees,

8

the upper by the lighter mountain grasses and ferns which seemed to reach up to meet the sky. Then there was the river, curving across the width of the valley, coursing slowly along the ten miles that separated the village from the sea at Swansea. Doris' heart often ached to have all that beauty so close, and yet their houses huddled, cramped together with the massive furnaces, the coal slags and trams looming above them, the colliery dominating and overpowering the village.

The miners felt differently. To them, God had been extra kind, because just below all this beauty He had placed seams of coal, anything from eighteen inches to eighteen feet wide, and beds of fireclay and iron ore. But for Doris, man had come and defiled the beauty. Man had blackened nature with his meddling, and she hated the coal. She hated the constant threats of pneumoconiosis, 'black lungs', and nystagmus, the wandering eyes, that the men lived under, their poor, bent knees and 'beat' elbows. Doris had good reason to hate the mines – she had been widowed by them. Her treasured wedding gown was still kept in tissue paper. Her neat house was scrubbed every day and the gleaming brass in the rarely used kitchen dazzled the eye. The brass candlesticks, the strip of brass on the mantel, even the brass rod above the grate shone. The tiny, immaculate house seemed held in suspense, waiting for the warmth of a family, waiting to come alive, for life to breathe through the flower-papered walls. The big tub hung at the kitchen door ready for her man, even his tools were cleaned and polished, but Walter Evans was never coming home. The house remained a glittering monument.

Doris threaded her way through the dark streets, hearing the odd murmur of greeting from the young men who remembered her teaching. She kept her head down, her nose wrinkled against the slight wind that stirred the coal dust. In some of the back yards she could see washing still hanging. The kind of household that left its washing out was the kind that didn't care. Only on certain days could the washing be done, for unless the wind blew from the north-east it would quickly be covered in coal dust. Windows were always closed unless the north-east wind blew. The cries of the miners' wives were often heard as they belted their daughters either for not putting out the washing in time or for not bringing it in.

The men were coming off from the day shift. As Doris passed them she could hardly tell one from another. With their blackened faces and clothes they looked much like the coal they mined. Many would need to get the dust from their throats with a few pints before departing homeward for their baths. Doris made a small detour around the pub to avoid the ones who had already downed a few too many.

Doris knew them all, and as she passed they called and smiled. Mrs Griffiths, Lizzie-Ann's mother, yelled to Doris, her raucous voice grating on Doris' ears as she asked how her brood were coming along. Doris nodded to her, said that they were doing well, knowing Mrs Griffiths had already decided that they would leave the following term. Over the years Doris had tired of trying to make them understand how a few more years of education would benefit the boys. It had always proved pointless. They just followed their fathers into the mines as soon as they had enough education to sit the qualifying test, usually by the age of thirteen or fourteen. Some slipped in even younger.

The village women never tired of discussing Doris Evans, who even after thirty years was still an outsider, and always referred to as 'poor thing'. Some of the women, too young to remember, thought it was because she was widowed and without children, still living alone after all these years. Many whispered that, unlike everyone else in the village, Doris never took in lodgers although she had four rooms. Little Evelyne Jones had been right, oh so right, thought Doris. Memories fade fast. Heartbreak surrounded the village, every family was touched by it, so why should they remember hers?

The bakehouse smelt wonderful and Doris, who had left her tin of dough there in the morning, now collected her fresh bread. She paid her penny and carefully folded the linen over the bread tin. The short distance from the bakehouse to her front door could ruin the bread, covering it with coal dust so that it tasted gritty. She noticed that already her hands and coat had a fine film of dust on them. She blew her hands clean, then hurried on down the dark street.

Halfway down her street Doris met John Prosser, Tom Clapham, Rees Griffiths and Danny Tanner carrying Jack Carlick between them. Jack's blackened face was screwed up with pain, and he moaned softly. Doris pressed herself against the wall. She had taught so many of these boys and so many of their names were listed on the church walls, for explosions and fires down the mine were an annual occurrence. When the men moved on, she found the back of her coat smudged with soot from the wall.

A group of small children, clutching their farthings, were clustered around Ernesco Melardi's ice-cream cart. They should have been tucked up in bed, it was almost six, and Doris tut-tutted at them hanging around playing tic-tac. They saw her and waved, and Doris gave a sharp nod of her head. She could hear the children

11

sniggering and whispering behind her but she didn't turn back. 'Droopy-Drawers Doris' was their favourite name for her this week.

It was the sound of a child's screeching voice that made Doris catch her breath. It was sweeping over her again, and she only just managed to open her front door before her head began to thud with one of the blinding headaches that beset her so often. Doris was back in Clydach Vale again, her head thudding, her ears filled with the sound of the rushing water. She clung to the edge of the polished kitchen table. Twelve years ago, and yet it was as if it were happening at that very moment . . .

Again she heard the children's voices, the screaming hooter as the warning went out. The school had been flooded with water from an abandoned coal level. Doris had waded through the slime, searching, calling out the children's names. Three tiny bodies had been found in the playground, and then little Ned Jones was found curled up like a baby in the corner. Further on the boy's mother cradled her six-month-old baby girl in her arms, her pitiful body covered in mud. It had been so long ago, but Doris' vision of the children never dimmed. She stumbled to the rocking chair by the fire, and closed her eyes. It usually began with the memory of the children, then Doris would hear again the sound of clogs clattering on the street, the high-pitched voices calling, 'Mrs Evans! Mrs Evans!' Doris rocked herself back and forth, the clogs came closer . . . oh, so much closer . . . The fists banged on her door. The smell of the brass polish made her nostrils flare, her eyes water, and the memories swept over her, like the tears that rolled down her face.

They had been married only days, their honeymoon

just a weekend in Swansea, and then Walter had returned to the mines. They said he had been in good voice, they'd heard him singing as the cage came up, then he had collapsed and no one could revive him. The doctor said the work had drawn all the moisture from his body and because it was not replaced he had died of dehydration, just like five others that same year.

The rocking chair creaked, Doris sighed, and the pain in her head began to fade, her thin lips moved as she smiled to herself and sweet memories now eased the pain.

Doris' father was an inspector for the Cardiff Railway Company, and often at weekends he would get tickets for his family to travel around and see the countryside. He was proud of his eldest daughter; Doris was going to Cardiff University to study English. She was artistic and shy and loved to do quick charcoal sketches as the train puffed and chuffed its way across the valley.

On one of her sketching trips she had met Walter and fallen in love. Her father did not approve of the friendship. He considered the illiterate miner to be far beneath his clever daughter. However, when her father fell ill, Doris had no option but to leave the university to take care of him. Her mother had died when she was a child and there was no one else.

Once Walter had travelled all the way to Cardiff to see her, but he had been refused entry to the house by her elder brother. He, like his father, felt Walter was not good enough for her. It was not until Doris' father died that she was free to marry the patient miner. By this time her brother had qualified as a doctor and had met a well-connected girl. After a terrible argument, Doris had packed a bag and travelled to the village. She knew she would never be happy living with her brother and his snooty bride-to-be. She had wasted no time telling them, had even said that they had aspirations above their station. Doris chuckled, she could still hear herself . . .

'Father only worked the railways, he was nothing special, my Walter's good enough for me,' and off she had marched with the small legacy her father had left her, determined to marry her man.

It was the legacy which had enabled Doris and Walter to set up straightaway in their own home, which was unheard of in the village. They did not need to live in Walter's parents' house as so many newly-weds had to. They chose carefully every bit of furniture, each piece of linen, discussed the crockery, the glasses. Walter's family became hers.

She went to Swansea to choose her wedding dress. It was one of the finest the village had ever seen, cream lace-covered satin with lace cuffs and frills at the neck, the veil and train stretching a good six feet behind her. It was decorated with small seed pearls, and she had embroidered shoes to match. Walter had helped her choose the dress. The gossips had whispered that it was unlucky and it was.

Three days later Walter was dead, and Doris was alone in the immaculate house. The wedding dress lay spread out across the bed. She hated her father, blamed him for not letting them marry earlier, at least she would have had those few precious years with her beloved husband. Nor did she ever forgive her brother and his wife. Dr Collins, as he now was, never even sent a wreath. The letter had been short and written by his wife: 'Perhaps it is for the best, he was never good enough for you and we could, I am sure, accommodate you for a while until you find a place of your own here in Cardiff . . .' Doris never replied. Dr Collins, for all his snobbishness, still lived in the old family house. Half of

14

it had been left to Doris and she had every right to move back, but she didn't.

The memory of those two full days and nights were all she had to last her a lifetime. And, sadly, they had lasted. Doris had begun to teach in the village school a year after Walter's death. Her sweetheart, her husband, was with her in every corner of the house, and she needed no one else . . . 'poor thing'.

CHAPTER 2

EVELYNE HAD not been still since she had returned from school. She had slipped a pinafore over her skirt and rolled up her cardigan sleeves. Her thin arms were red raw from the cold, and yet she was sweating. Her pale face shone, her red hair clung in tight curls around her neck and the long braid down her back was loose. She tucked the wildly curling strands back and picked up the heavy buckets, puffing with the effort. As she tipped the water into the pans and the kettle, it splashed out, soaking her, drenching her bare feet which were filthy from the coal-dust-filled streets. She carried the empty buckets outside and waited in line to refill them as she did every day, every week, every month. Come five o'clock the line of village girls and women was always a hive of chatter as they met to collect water for their menfolk's baths. All their families worked in the mines and every night was bath night.

Lizzie-Ann wiped her button nose on the sleeve of her threadbare cardigan. She grinned at Evelyne.

'You back again? Well, well, Evie Jones, you'll make a fine wife.'

She wrinkled her face and pointed to her black eye, a real shiner that made her wide pansy-coloured eyes appear ever larger. Lizzie-Ann was the prettiest girl in

16

the village, and she knew it, she was a holy terror. Laughing, she said, 'Is it any blacker? Me Mam hit me so hard I near fell off me feet. "Oh," she said, "you little bugger, not brought in the washing, and Lord love me it's covered in coal dust."'

Evelyne smiled shyly and moved a step closer to the tap. She loved to hear Lizzie-Ann's prattle, and knew they'd all be laughing in a minute.

' "I'll be leaving your coal dust, Ma," I says, "because I'm going to London to join me auntie, ohhh I'm following in father's footsteps, I'm following my dear old dad." '

She swished her skirts and danced up and down, her piping voice off key, but everyone began to giggle. Seeing she had an audience she began to do the can-can.

'Come on, Evie, kick yer legs up, come on gel . . .'

'Will you really be going to London, Lizzie?'

'Didn't I just say I wuz? Oh, look, there's Dirty Jed, I'll bet a farthing I'll get a lemon sherbert outta him for showing me knickers.'

Evelyne poured the water from the buckets into a big iron pan balanced on the coal fire. Will grinned at his little sister as he stripped off his working clothes and she ducked under his arm to fill the tin bath. She loved bath time – loved the laughs and the warmth of the big old kitchen. Will was a strapping lad with curly, dark auburn hair, and black as his face was it still couldn't hide his rosy cheeks. He had a tooth missing where he had fallen down in the pit and it gave him a cheeky little-boy look, but he was a devil when it came to teasing her.

'Look at her stick legs, Mike,' Will said to his younger brother, 'it's a wonder they don't snap.'

17

Evelyne slapped him with the newspaper she was laying on the floor. Clouds of coal dust filled the air as the boys dropped their work clothes into the box and Evelyne pushed it under the table. Mike gave her a friendly pat on the bottom.

'An' she hasn't got a bum either, but I love 'er, I love 'er.'

Mike always tried to be like his brother Will, but in truth he was as reserved and shy as Evelyne. Today had been his first day down the pit, and he was so tired she had to hold his hand to help him step into the bath. He moaned as he squatted in the water.

'Give us a yell, gel, when he's through. I'll be out in the yard.'

'Won't you help me get Mike clean, Will? You'll have time before supper to go a-courting.'

They all knew that Will was stuck on Lizzie-Ann, but, good-natured as ever, Will nodded, picked up the old sheet and ripped a piece off. He touched Mike's back, which was raw from rubbing against the coal surface, and noticed that his elbows were bleeding and there were lumps on each side of his head.

'You did well, our Mike, now get yerself clean. Do it this way.'

He twisted the piece of sheet into a point, dipped it in the water.

'We do our faces first, mind, roll the corner into a point, wet it, and stuff it into yer eyes, then yer nose and ears . . . always do this first, while the sheet's clean.'

Mike prodded and sneezed and coughed, his skin felt as if it was crawling.

'Aw, put yer back into it, lad, or you'll not get the muck off . . . Evie, give him a hand, he's so tired out he's lost his strength.'

When she had helped Mike get clean, Evelyne rushed

out to refill the buckets. The kitchen was steaming and five times she went to the tap. She never blushed to see her naked brothers, nor were they shy at her scrubbing their backs with a pumice stone. They bawled at her for being too rough, splashed her when she was too gentle. She had seen her Ma bathe her Da since she was able to toddle, and had shared bath-time duties since she was strong enough to carry a bucket of water.

Mike stood up, dripping, and held out his arms for the sheet that served as a towel. She wrapped it around him and held his warm body for a moment. He was much younger than her other brothers, and his face puckered as he stepped out of the tub. Blood was running down his legs in rivulets from his knobbly knees, and Evelyne looked up into his face.

'You all right, Mike? Shall I get the disinfectant?'

'No, I can't stand the stinging.'

Sighing, Will eased his body into the water.

'My God it feels good, don't it, Mike? Ahhh, this makes it all worthwhile, will you soap me back, gel?'

As she rubbed his back, she could feel the scars under her fingers. Mike sat huddled by the fire and watched her, and she gave him one of their secret, intimate smiles. He looked down, his long eyelashes looked as if they were resting on his cheeks.

'Did Lizzie-Ann ask about me?'

Evelyne scrubbed and soaped, her skirt sopping.

'She did mention that she couldn't sleep for thinking about a certain person with no front tooth. Could that be you, our Will?'

'Is that the truth, gel? Aw, yer having me on, but if you get the chance tell her what a fine-looking man I am naked.'

With a mock gasp of shock, Evelyne slapped him. He stood up and took the towel from her, wrapping it

19

around his waist. He was indeed a fine-looking boy, even with the tooth missing.

Evelyne busied herself setting the table and pouring away the dirty bath water. Will brushed his hair, saying he would just parade on the front doorstep for a while.

'Will you get dressed, Mike, lovey, you don't want to catch cold now?'

Mike looked furtively around to see if Will had left the room then turned back to the fire. His voice was soft, lilting.

'It's so black, Evie, it's indescribable. You push your hand out to feel it, and it goes right through the solid blackness. There is no gleam of light, no shadow. It is so black – like a massive weight on you, all around you as hard on the eyes as bright light.'

He was worn out, and afraid, she could feel it, but it was unspoken. He did not look at her, knowing that she knew. He was only three years older than Evelyne.

'Will, Will, supper's on the table now, come on.'

Evelyne set down the steaming bowls of stew, the big chunks of fresh bread. The two boys ate hungrily, washing the food down with gulps of scalding tea. There was a jug of ale, too, and that went down fast, but the dust stayed deep in their lungs. They were still eating when there was a rap on the back door.

'I were just passin' an' wondered how yer Mike got along on his first day?'

Old Peg-Leg Thomas hobbled in, grinning a toothless smile, his hand already out for a mug of tea. He gasped and heaved for breath, but he rolled a cigarette as soon as he had sunk into the most comfortable fireside chair.

'Who's yer butty-mum?'

Mike wiped his mouth and told him it was Danny Williams.

'Ahhh, now there's a good butty-mum . . . yer know, if yer get allocated a butty that don't know the ropes then yer can spend maybe two years learning what should've been taught yer in the first week, an' there's the truth. Good butty, Danny Williams, knows what's what, you got a good lad ter teach yer . . . is there another drop of tea fer me?'

Evelyne wiped her plate with some bread, washed it, and refilled it from the stewpan. She poured a fresh mug of tea and loaded a small tin tray.

Her mother, Mary, was lying in the big double bed. Hanging from the ceiling and all around the room were sheets drying and the men's work clothes washed for the following day. The bedroom was above the kitchen, so the big fire kept the room hot and stuffy. Mary was dozing, her thick black hair loose, her cheeks flushed, and Evelyne saw she was sweating. Softly, she put the tray down, and went to the washstand, rinsed a cloth and crept quietly to Mary's side. Evelyne mopped her mother's brow as gently as she could, but Mary stirred, opened her eyes and smiled. Evelyne helped her to sit up.

Mary was in her ninth month, and very ungainly. The baby made a huge mound in the centre of the bed, a mound that didn't seem to belong to the woman who carried it. Mary's once-strong arms were thin, her hands bony, as was the rest of her body apart from her belly. It was as if all her strength and energy had been drawn from her and given to the unborn child. Evelyne propped up the pillows behind her Ma, and Mary leaned back. As Evelyne put the tray carefully on the bed, she noticed the tea and bread she had brought earlier had not been touched.

21

'How's our Mike, he get on all right, Evie?'

Evelyne nodded and began to tidy the room, patted the drying sheets.

'Are you feeling any better, Ma? You not been sick?'

She watched as Mary used both hands to lift the mug of tea.

'You eat the stew if you can, Ma, you need your strength.'

'Get along with you, Evie Jones, treating me like I was a baby.' Mary lifted the spoon and tried to eat but couldn't, she felt too exhausted. 'Spend some time with Mike tonight, it's always bad on their first day. I'll maybe finish my supper later . . . have you been in to see little Davey?'

'I'll go to him now. You try and eat, Ma, there's not too much salt is there?'

Mary put her hand out to take her daughter's, gripped it tight. 'You're a good daughter, and the stew's just perfect . . . I'll have a little rest now.'

She felt so weary, and her eyes closed. She was more than worried, she'd not felt as bad as this even with little Davey.

Little Davey was in his cot, his nappy wet, his shining face red and blotchy. He banged his rattle against the sides of the cot. Evelyne picked him up. The sheets were sodden, she'd have to wash them out in the morning. She put Davey on the floor while she changed the bedding and grabbed him just before he crawled out of the door, laid him on her knee and took off his wet things. The little fellow lolled in her lap, sucked her arm. She held him close, smelling his baby smell, his soft, downy hair. Little Davey was always happy, gurgling away, but his lolling head and drooping mouth revealed that he was spastic. The full extent of his problem was not yet defined, old Doc Clock putting it down to Davey being just that bit backward. Davey was three years old, but he could not walk by himself or say more than 'Da-da-dada' . . .

By the time Evelyne had cleared the table and washed the dishes, filled the kettle for the tea caddies in the morning, it was nine o'clock. She made sandwiches for her brothers, packing them in their tins. The mines were plagued with rats so all food had to be carefully packed. She then washed the rest of her brothers' clothes. They had already gone to bed as they had to be up at four for the five o'clock shift. Their beds would be taken by their Da and their eldest brother Dicken when they came home from the night shift.

It was after ten before Evelyne had a moment to sit alone by the big kitchen fire. Her eyes were red-rimmed from tiredness, she could hardly see her school books. She read by the firelight, careful not to get dust on the books that Doris Evans had lent her. This was Evelyne's favourite time, the only time of the day or night when she could be alone. She treasured it, hungered for it, and used it. This was when she did her writing, when she could dream her dreams.

Mary woke and tried to ease her bulk into a more comfortable position. She sighed, this was one she could well do without, especially with Davey as he was. As she turned she saw Evelyne standing by the bedroom window. She said nothing, just lay and watched her daughter brushing her hair.

'You awake, Mama?'

'I am, lovely, I was just looking at you. Like a mermaid you are.'

Evelyne slipped into the big bed beside her mother.

'It won't be too long then I'll be back on my feet.'

Evelyne snuggled closer, loving the smell of her mother. She kissed Mary's neck then looked up anxiously.

'I'm not too close, am I? I don't want to make you uncomfortable . . . can I feel your belly?'

Mary laid her daughter's hand on her stomach, so she might feel the baby kick.

'Can you feel him? He's a big one.'

Gently, Evelyne ran her small hand over the swollen belly, then she yawned and her eyes began to droop.

'Goodnight, Mama, sleep tight, mind the bugs don't bite.'

Mary eased her body into a more comfortable position and Evelyne's hand slipped away as she fell into exhausted sleep. Mary stared at the ceiling, imagining mermaids reaching to her from beneath crystal-clear water.

'I've never even seen the sea.'

Her own voice startled her, as if she had spoken to herself from the grave, and she was enveloped by an overpowering sense of loss. She sighed a deep, shuddering sigh, and two tears, like dew on a flower petal, slipped down her gaunt cheeks.

In the cold light of dawn Mary could just make out the fading photograph of herself. She was not alone, she was standing arm-in-arm with Hugh Jones on their wedding day. The love she still felt for Hugh couldn't warm her. Her whole body felt as if it was growing colder and colder. 'Where did I go?' she wondered. 'When was I last just Mary? Not Ma, not wife, but Mary.' She couldn't remember, and the harder she tried the deeper became her sense of loss. She wept because she couldn't remember herself, could hardly remember a time when she wasn't tired, when she wasn't carrying or worrying about one child or another. Had her whole life just been rearing children? Cooking, washing, baking? When was the last time she had been up the mountain?

The pieces fell together in her mind like a jagged jigsaw puzzle. The blazing colours, the flowers . . . Mary remembered, oh, the mountains . . . the green fields, the clear, ice-cold water. Havod, the wondrous gardens at Havod, the peacocks. Then, like a picture postcard she saw herself as she had been before all these worn years. She was so free, so carefree, and she was laughing . . . her big, blown-up body felt light . . . she was running like a hare, running on long, strong legs, a bunch of wild flowers in her hand, throwing them up into the bright, warm, blue sky, they were cornflowers . . .

Then there was Hughie Jones. She saw him as he had been all those years ago, so tall and golden they had nicknamed him 'The Lion'. Hugh was the one she had set her sights on, although he was a real lady-killer with all the girls chasing him. But Mary had been the one, the only one, to give him not so much as the bat of an eye in church. She had felt his eyes on her, and when they all congregated outside the Salvation Army Hall she had turned to her friend and in a voice just loud enough for Hugh to hear she said, 'Well, I'm going for a walk, going up the mountain.' No one had wanted to join her, they talked of going to play the piano and have a sing-song. So Mary had gone to the mountain alone. She knew he was following her, way behind and below, but she behaved as if she was completely alone. She found a secluded spot, bathed in warm sunshine, and lay down with the flowers around her, the blue sky and bright sun above. He was close, she could feel him coming closer, but she kept her eyes tight shut. She knew when he sat down only a few feet away, but still she kept her eyes closed. It seemed an age, and when eventually she opened them he had made a crown of cornflowers, and handed it to her. She slipped it on her head and they looked into each other's eyes.

It was not done for a girl to make the first move, or even be out for too long a time with a young man, a young man who hadn't even been courting her, a young man who had hardly said two words to her, let alone one with the reputation of Hugh Jones. They said not a word – he just sat there and she lay back with the crown of cornflowers on her head. Her hands were at her sides and she could feel the cool grass between her fingers. She began to wonder if he would speak at all, or if he would just get up and walk away. When she opened her eyes he was leaning up on one elbow, staring into her face.

She smiled, but he continued to stare as he slowly threaded his fingers through hers. Still keeping his distance from her, his huge hand covered hers completely . . . then he lay back and closed his eyes, holding her hand tight. Mary raised herself on her elbow and looked at his handsome face. His hair was a thick, curly mane, blond, yet his eyelashes were almost black. She bent closer and closer, and in one sudden move he pulled her on top of him, held her face and kissed her. She had expected him to be rough, to kiss her like Joe Scuttles had when he grabbed her on New Year's Eve. Hugh's kiss was sweeter, and so gentle her body ached to pull him tighter to her. He laughed, his eyes twinkled, and the dimple in his chin deepened. Then he stood up, scooping her in his arms and carried her to the steep drop of the mountainside and she clung to him. She knew he was teasing, but he took her closer and closer to the precipice.

'Marry me, Mary, or I'll throw you over the mountainside, because if you don't I'll not let another man touch thee. You belong to me.'

Mary clung to him, burying her face in his big, broad shoulder and kissed his neck. There had been no need to speak of love, no courtship, no arguments with the families. They were destined for each other.

The village said that Mary had tamed the wild lion. Stories of what Hugh Jones had been up to, and with whom, were passed around and several girls wept themselves into puffy, red-eyed misery. The prize had been caught by Mary, the quiet one – a dark horse if ever there was one, with her big brown eyes and lanky legs. She'd never even said as much as two words to the lad. The truth was there'd been no 'taming', simply a mutual recognition that they belonged together. Everyone said it wouldn't last without even a few weeks' courtship for them to get to know each other. Of course, some said she had to get married – the wild one must have got her in the family way – but that wasn't true either.

Eventually even the most sceptical had to button her mouth, because the couple seemed so contented, so happy, with no need of the social life of the village. They kept themselves to themselves, and were the envy of many other couples. Hugh Jones never stopped off at the pub on his way home from the mine with the other lads. He would be up and out of the cage faster than anyone else as soon as the hooter sounded the shift's end. At home he would be building, sawing, painting, and if anyone so much as hinted that he would go back

27

to his old ways, Hugh's temper would flare up and no one in his right mind ever wanted that. Memories of Hugh with his shirtsleeves rolled up, taking on any comer at fist fighting, even the gypsy travellers, were as clear as day. Hugh had been the source of much gossip in his wild days, but the gypsy fight was the one the village remembered best.

No one could recall the reason, it had been so long ago. It was a blazing hot day in August when, as Peg-Leg Thomas remembered, three gypsies had called on Hugh's invalid father. They had come to exact some kind of vengeance and they weren't just any old travellers, they were from the Romany clan that sold the pit ponies to the mine. They would arrive in midsummer every other year, with their wagons and trailers and roped lines of ponies. Once they had set up camp the women would go from house to house selling pegs and ribbons. Some, with their bright skirts and headbands, would be invited in to read the tea leaves or the worn, red palms of the miners' wives.

It was always an occasion, and if they were there on a Sunday, they would set up a small fair. The children were warned not to go too near to the camp or the gypsies, as no one could ever really trust them. On this particular Sunday, according to Peg-Leg, three gypsies, all wearing their smart suits and brightly coloured neckerchiefs, walked down Elspeth Street. Their arms were linked and they knocked any passer-by out of the way with a shrug. It was whispered that the man in the middle was descended from the Romany king himself. Proud, their black eyes expressionless, they were the real *Romantishels*. They seemed almost to skip, their steps as light as if walking on air. Peg-Leg said you could always tell a gyppo by the spring in his walk.

It was typical of the Jones family, no one could get

out of them the real reason for the visit of the three cocksure, highstepping men. All they did know was that Hugh was taken from his house, not exactly held between the men, but walked by them up to their camp. A few of the village boys followed, but kept well back because they could see trouble brewing, like a small cloud in the air.

They saw Hugh Jones being led to one of the very ornate caravans, taken inside and then brought out again. All the gypsy men formed a circle around him, and the one who had walked in the middle of the threesome took off his jacket. Hugh threw his own worn jacket to the ground and adopted a boxer's stance. Quite a few of the older men from the village had joined the watching boys. They all had to admire Hugh. He seemed fearless with his fists up, his face grim, and yet he could have been no more than sixteen or seventeen. For all his youth, Hugh was a lot taller than his opponent who was a grown man and, by the firmness of his muscular body, also a fit one.

The villagers watched Hugh Jones take one hell of a thrashing. Time and time again he was knocked to the ground, but every time he got up again, although his nose was bleeding and his eyes cut. Nor did his opponent fight clean – there were kicks, and Peg-Leg swore he saw the gypsy snarling and snapping as if he was trying to bite Hugh's ear off. There was no outright winner; the fight went on for a full hour until both men sank to their knees in exhaustion. Hugh had been picked up by two youths and flung out of the camp. His pals slunk down and helped him up, and only when they had put a safe distance between them and the camp were there raised fists and defiant yells, before they hurried away with the bleeding Hugh. And, by God, Hugh was at the pithead that night, bloody nose and all. They tried to wheedle out of Hugh why he had taken such punishment, but he wouldn't say a word. A couple of the boys even tried bribes, but he shook his head. It was a private matter.

The gypsies moved on and soon the incident was forgotten, unless Peg-Leg was in one of his story-telling moods or had a few beers too many. Of course, Hugh Jones always came out as the champion, taking on five men – sometimes six or seven – which only built up his legend as a great boxer. It was always murmured in the ear of anyone who crossed Hugh, 'Eh, watch it, remember the gyppos.'

So when Hugh had insisted on staying by Mary's side for the birth of their first child, the account of the fight Hugh had with Doc Clock brought out all the old stories again, and Peg-Leg drank quite a few free pints down the pub. Hugh's workmates shook their heads in amazement. 'Imagine wanting to be there at a birth,' they muttered, 'dear Lord, what was the world coming to . . .'

Hugh had been at Mary's side for the birth of his eldest three sons: Dicken, the first, then Will and Mike, but for Evelyne's and little Davey's births he had been on the night shift so he had missed their deliveries. The neighbours whispered that perhaps if Hugh had been there when Davey was born, he wouldn't be the way he was.

Hugh Jones, Mary's man, lover, husband; the crown of cornflowers had married them on top of the mountain. The taste of that sweet kiss had long since gone, but now the memory of it filled her with a new strength, and she was fifteen again. She knew he'd find her, would come running to her with his big strong arms open wide, to scoop up her tired body and hold her close to his chest. The lioness was exhausted, her brood grown, but the lionheart wouldn't fail her.

Evelyne woke from a deep sleep, sat up and felt for the warmth of her mother.

'Ma?'

She wrapped a blanket around her and crept down the stairs. As she pushed open the kitchen door she almost cried out. Mary was dressed, pulling on Hugh's heavy coat, wrapping a long, woollen scarf around her neck.

'Ma, where you going? Is it time? Shall I go call Nurse Thomas?'

Evelyne rushed over to her mother, but when Mary turned round her face was so flushed and her eyes so bright that Evelyne drew back.

'I'm going to see the mountains, Evie, I have to go up to the mountains before it's too late. Don't try to stop me, don't call the boys, I beg you . . . I'll be back soon, you'll see.'

Evelyne ran back upstairs to get into her clothes, and she heard the door slam. She ran to the window. She was frightened. Something was wrong and she knew it. From the bedroom window she could see her mother's bundled figure as she hurried up the street, helping herself up the hill with her hands against the brick walls of the houses. Evelyne woke Will, shaking him, shouting that their Ma had gone out.

Will sat up and rubbed his head. Evelyne was already shaking Mike awake, and the boys scrambled out of their bunks and ran to the window. Mary was way up the street now.

'What's all the fuss, our Evie? Ma's all right . . .'

The hooter sounded for the end of the night shift,

31

and it was only minutes before the sounds of the men returning home would fill the street. Evelyne ran to the pithead looking for her father. She knew something was wrong – knew it but didn't know what to do. As the cages full of black-faced men were cranked up Evelyne ran from one group to the next. Dai Thomas pointed over to Hugh, and Evelyne ran towards him. He was well over six foot two with broad, strong shoulders, and he stood out from the rest of the men. His back had never buckled over, he still stood upright, and with his shock of greying red-blond hair he looked more the grizzled lion than ever.

With Hugh was his eldest son Dicken, tall as his father. They were just climbing out of one of the cages when Hugh saw Evelyne running towards him. He thought automatically that Mary was having the new babe and waved to her, his mouth and gums glowing pink in the blackness of his face.

'Da, come quick, Ma's gone up the mountains, and she's too near her time, she was strange, she shouldn't have gone walking, not now, not at this time.'

Hugh and Dicken began to run, and the word spread quickly. Soon they were joined by Shoni 'Bully' Thomas, Rees Jones, and Willie 'Black Pipe' Keenan. Still black-faced, covered in dust, they ran down the street. The day-shift men were leaving home and as word sped through the street, several of them dropped their tools and went to join the search. This meant a lot, for the day men would lose out on a day's wages if they didn't turn up at the pithead on time. Dicken, Will and Mike followed their father, all of them running out of the village towards the mountain.

In the early morning the mist had been thick over the mountain-top, but the sun began to cut through and it slowly lifted. Echoes of the men's voices rang round and round as they called out for Mary. It was a strange sight, the searching, black-faced men calling to Mary as the clear, beautiful day began.

'Oh Christ, man, where is she? *Mary!*'

Hugh Jones was beside himself. He thrashed at the bramble bushes, calling his wife's name, his face streaked with sweat. He turned to the men, told them to go back, not to lose a day's work because of him; he and his boys would find her. The men eventually turned back to their work or their beds.

The whole village was agog. What on earth was Mary Jones thinking of – a woman in her condition going up the mountain – she must have lost her mind. They discussed it avidly at the water taps, over the clanking of the buckets. They would occasionally look up beyond the village, not that they could see anything, but Mary was up there somewhere. Their menfolk down the pit talked about it and, like their wives, they were only too ready to recall stories of people lost up in the mountains, men who had run wild up there after being too long underground.

Hugh Jones was exhausted. He sat on a rock, his sons around him. They had never seen their father so distraught: he clung to Dicken and began to weep. The boys were scared. Why had Ma suddenly upped and left them in that condition? It was so strange. Their safe, strong Ma, where was she?

Evelyne kept on searching and calling, climbing higher and higher. Surely Ma could not have got this far, she must be below, they must have missed her. Evelyne looked down and could see her Da and her brothers way below like small black dots . . . .

'Ma . . . *Mama* . . . *Ma!*'

Evelyne's voice echoed round the mountain. Mary was standing staring down at the river. There was a puff of smoke where a train had just passed below a bridge, a little train chugging on down the valley.

Evelyne called down to the men that she had found her mother, and they climbed up the mountainside towards her. Mary stood frozen, eyes staring vacantly into space. Hugh reached his daughter's side and Evelyne pointed to her mother, his wife . . . His face was almost clean of soot, whether from sweat or tears she couldn't make out. He edged towards Mary, speaking her name, so softly the children could hardly hear him. They watched, bewildered, as the huge man moved closer and closer, saw him take hold of his wife, rocking her gently in his arms.

'Gave us a proper scare, you did, Mary. Had the whole village out looking for you. Did you not hear us calling you?'

He turned back to his children, told the younger boys to go to the pithead and see if they could still get on the shift, the others to go home.

They began to wander down the mountainside, turning to look back up at their parents. They saw their father still holding their mother tight, so tight as if he was afraid she would throw her swollen body over the precipice. As they went further down the slopes, the two figures on the mountainside sat down, their arms around each other, their heads close, like young lovers.

Dicken could see his little sister getting anxious so he made light of it.

'You know our Ma, Evie, she's just wanting to have Da to herself.'

Evelyne smiled, then went and sat on the front doorstep and waited for hours. She saw Mr Williams' dog wander past with his shopping bag and little leather purse, saw him trot into the butcher's and collect the meat. Clever little dog, went by the main street there,

34

but round by the back cobbles when he'd got the meat. That way he was sure none of the other dogs would steal his owner's chops.

At midday Evelyne woke little Davey and fed him, then sat and played with him on the doorstep, and still her mother and father had not returned.

Dr Jones came by, with his gold watch chain. Doc Jones only had the chain, no one could recall him ever having a watch on the end of it. So he very rarely knew the time and was known as Doc Clock because of it. He'd heard about Mary, and said to tell them he'd drop by to see if everything was all right.

Along the street net curtains twitched aside. Hugh and Mary, entwined in each other's arms, walked slowly down the narrow, cobbled road. They were like young lovers – twice Hugh stopped and cupped his wife's face in his big hands and kissed her upturned face.

Evelyne saw her big Da carrying her mother up the stairs. Mary was weak, and her cheeks were flushed bright pink. When Hugh came down again his daughter had already filled the tub with water for him. He said nothing, but began slowly to wash his face and hands, soap his hair. He bent his head as Evelyne scrubbed his back, and when he stood up from the tub his massive, muscular body looked like a warrior's; there were deep scars and gashes across his back, arms and thighs. His body was still as strong as a young man's, his thick grey hair stuck up in waves like a mane.

Evelyne kissed his back softly and he squeezed her hand. Oh, how she loved him. He was not a man of many words, never had been, but he had held them all together. The boys, all of them, adored him.

'Your Ma wanted to go up on the mountains, that's

where we used to do our courting. She's all right now, just very tired. Take her some hot tea, there's a good girl.'

Evelyne prepared the tea, and just as she was about to take it up her father stopped her, took from the pocket of his old work coat a tiny wild flower, and stuck it in her hair.

'Stay a while with her, until I'm home. That woman up there is part of me, understand, child? We just found a bit of our yesterdays . . . you get so you forget she was a rare beauty. Today she was just as beautiful again, I had almost forgot.'

Mary lay in the bed, her eyes closed. Evelyne placed the tea beside her and lay down close to her mother, took her hand and kissed it. Mary turned her huge, swollen body to face Evelyne. They smiled at each other as if they had an intimate secret. Mary looked into her daughter's face, traced her high, strong cheekbones with her worn, rough hands.

'You're a good girl, Evie, I'm sorry to frighten you all so, I didn't mean to, but I just had to go up there one more time.'

As young as she was, Evelyne seemed to understand. Mary held her daughter's hand and whispered to her, made her promise on God's Holy Bible . . .

'Don't let the mines take your youth. You get away from here, Evie, don't stay too long. It'll soon be time for you to go, find yourself someone from outside, promise me, Evie?'

Evelyne promised, but she was unsure exactly what her mother meant.

She left her mother sleeping and went downstairs to give her brothers their dinner. They had just come back

from the day shift. Will was laughing and shoving Mike
. . . it seemed that Lizzie-Ann had said 'yes', and she
and Will were going to be married. Only half listening,
Evelyne gathered that Will planned for Lizzie-Ann to
move in with them until they saved enough money for a
small house of their own. So much for Lizzie-Ann and
London.

Mike's back was worse, the cuts deeper, and he said
it was his own fault because the rocks were jagged and
he couldn't remember to keep his body crouched. His
knees were in a terrible state, and his clothes were
sodden.

Evelyne washed the boys, fed them, washed their
clothes, washed out little Davey's sheets. It was night
again, and she was so tired her arms ached, too tired to
get her school books out. She sat in her mother's
rocking-chair, close to the big, blazing fire. Evelyne and
Mike were left alone. Mike subdued, his eyes red-
rimmed, unused to the coal dust. His hands and nails
were already becoming ingrained with black. Evelyne sat
and listened to him, he needed so badly to talk to
someone – not the lads, they already knew what he was
saying, they had all been through it, but for Mike it was
all new, all disturbing.

'My legs were cramped all day, Evie, I got no skin
left on the backs of my hands. An' with the dust in your
lungs you can't stop coughing, an' it's burning inside
your eyes. My skin is smartin', flying bits of coal cut into
your face . . . see, I'm in one of the lower surfaces, an' I
got to shovel on my belly.'

Evelyne listened like an old woman, nodding, darning
the men's socks. All the while she was alert for sounds
from Davey or her mother. Mike started to tell Evelyne
about the pit ponies. Mike had always loved the outdoor
life, running up the mountain to school, and he loved

animals, especially horses. Mike continued in his low, lilting sweet voice, like a musical whisper, telling Evelyne about how the horses were treated in the pits.

'Poor devils, Evie, they work sixteen hours or more straight, they often have no water. One dropped this mornin' from exhaustion – just dropped, Evie. I mean, it's not all the men's fault, sometimes you've got to take a horse out again right after it's been workin', so the poor bastard's dead on his feet before you start your shift. You got to whip him to make him work.'

Mike went on about the conditions, and Evelyne listened quietly and continued her sewing. Mike was in tears as he told her how some of the horses had to work in tunnels that were too low and, like him, they couldn't remember to keep themselves bent down, so they ripped their backs open on the jagged rocks. But they were whipped into such a frenzy that they kept on opening up the old wounds.

'After the first time through the squeeze the horse knows it's cut him, so next time he's forced through he wants to go fast, but if he goes too fast and the handler loses control, the tram full of coal can tilt and spill out its contents . . . so the men put chains through the horse's mouth to pull him back . . . and there he is, poor little bastard, with his back ripped open, his mouth chained, tortured . . .'

Evelyne looked up. Mike was on his feet, tears smarting in his eyes. He was talking about the pit ponies, but it was himself he was really talking about. And the more he talked, the more he upset himself. He ended up clinging to Evelyne and crying like a child.

'I can't go back, Evie, I can't, I hate it, I hate it, I'm scared all the time, Evie, I'm scared, and they keep on tellin' me terrible stories.'

Evelyne heard little Davey cry out, and she had to pry

Mike's arms from her and scramble up the stairs to look after the boy ... she heard the scream from Mary's bedroom as she reached the child's door. It was Mary's time. Hugh had already left for his night shift, he would miss this birth too.

They always said buy yourself a good dark suit, you'll need it, and every man did have one good dark suit besides his working clothes. The dark suit was necessary because there were so many funerals.

Will, Mike and Dicken were all dressed and ready. They sat in the kitchen waiting for Evelyne to come down. Mrs Pugh had taken Davey until they came back from the service.

There was only one coffin for mother and child, and flowers around the simple wooden box were from all the villagers. The family had asked them to pick wild flowers – cornflowers. Two horses pulled the hearse through the streets, and the grieving family walked slowly behind up to the church. It was a good turnout, everyone spruced up and wearing their Sunday best. Funerals usually took place on Sundays, as the mines were closed and no one lost a shift.

Mary Evelyne Jones and her son were buried where they could always see the mountain.

Evelyne had been a calming influence throughout. A rock, as they all said, astounding for one so young. There was quite simply no one else to run the house. No time even to grieve, and she wept into her pillow at night, quietly so as not to wake anyone. Evelyne would never forget her father's face as he watched the cornflower-strewn coffin lowered into the ground. He had been so silent, so isolated that no one dared interrupt his solitude. But there at the graveside he had roared out his grief, like a wild animal. The cry echoed round the mountain and chilled those standing at the graveside. Evelyne had held on to his hand, held it so tightly her nails cut into his palm.

That night his sons had taken him down to the pub and they had all got so drunk that Evelyne had to put each one to bed. Her father's head lolled, his eyes unfocused, as she helped him to undress. Sadly, the drunkenness persisted. Mike and Will would come straight home as usual from the mines, but Hugh would remain in the pub until closing time. Dicken waited to help him home, help put him to bed. No one tried to stop him: it was as if they knew he was trying to ease the pain, the agonizing pain of life without his darling Mary.

CHAPTER 3

SIX MONTHS passed and Evelyne did not return to school. There was always so much to do at home. Little Davey was dependent on Evelyne and the menfolk had to be cooked, washed and cared for. Lizzie-Ann had married Will and moved in until they could afford a place of their own. Evelyne put away her school books; her Christina Rossetti days were over.

Doris Evans had never been one to poke her nose in to anyone's business. She had once, she'd gone to see Mrs Reece Mogg, wanting their youngest son to stay on at school. She'd been shown the door so fast, so the story went, she'd left her brown lace-up shoes behind. However, she had thought about it for a good few weeks, and she had decided she would try one more time, this time with Evelyne Jones.

Doris dressed very carefully, in her brown hat, her brown skirt, and matching coat, set off by a nice cream blouse. She also put on her coral crêpe blouse, but felt the cream more suitable.

Doris stood on the Jones' front door step, thought it looked quite clean considering. She lifted the brass knocker, thinking it could do with a good polish, and tapped lightly, then rapped louder. She could feel inquisitive eyes boring into her back, net curtains flicked aside across the street. Her mouth went dry, her carefully rehearsed speech of introduction slipped away from her. She was about to leave when the front door was inched open.

'Evelyne, is that you? It's Mrs Evans, from the school.'

Evelyne had little Davey balanced on her hip, a duster in one hand, and her face was streaked with dust. Doris flushed a bright pink.

'Do you think I could step inside for a minute? If it's not convenient I can come back.'

The door edged open wider, and Evelyne coughed as she swallowed backwards. Her eyes watered, and Doris had to pat her on the back.

'Would you mind coming into the kitchen, Mrs Evans, only I was just feeding little Davey?'

Doris followed her along the corridor. The smell of stale beer, cigarettes and cabbage made her nose wrinkle with distaste. Davey gurgled and threw a soggy, nasty-looking crust of bread at Doris' head. A lot had changed since Mary's death, and gossip about the Jones family was rife. Mike, the youngest boy, had run off to join the army, and Will, so rumour had it, had got Lizzie-Ann in the family way so they'd had to marry. The house was bursting at the seams.

'Er, well, Evelyne, you certainly seem to have your hands full. Should I come back another day?'

With her free hand, Evelyne lifted the kettle and put in on the fire.

'Will you have a cup of tea, Mrs Evans?'

Side-stepping a teddy bear, Doris picked it up and turned to put it on the dirty table, cluttered with crockery.

'Oh, I don't want to put you out.'

Evelyne smiled and went to sit Davey on a chair, looked around the room, then at Doris.

'Would you mind just holding him while I make the tea?'

Poor Doris could hardly stand the smell of the child, and his nappy was sopping wet, but she held on to him and perched on the edge of a chair. It was a mistake, she knew it, and the girl looked terrible. She'd aged years in a matter of months, if that was possible. Her once clean, shining hair was dull and uncombed, and her face was so pale she looked ill. Evelyne was all thumbs, dropping the tea caddy; and she was so aware of the filthy state the kitchen was in that she tried to clear everything into the big stone sink.

'I won't bother with tea, Evelyne, but don't you think he should have a clean nappy on?'

Evelyne flushed and grabbed Davey, so embarrassed she was near tears. Always a sensitive woman, Doris was just as embarrassed and made things worse by sitting awkwardly, perched like a brown crow.

Evelyne laid Davey over her knee and removed the dirty nappy, dropping it in a bucket. He gurgled and laughed, drooling as she washed his bottom. And all the while Doris coughed dry little coughs, and kept opening and shutting her mouth. Her hand was sticky and she took a small lace handkerchief from her handbag.

'My Mama died, and I . . . well, I've been meaning to come and see you.'

Doris looked at her as she sat with her feet neatly crossed, her knees red and her bare feet so filthy Doris wondered when the girl had last bathed.

'Yes, I know. Did you get my note?'

'I should have written, I'm sorry, Mrs Evans.'

Doris stood up and straightened her hat. 'It's about

43

your writing that I've come, Evie . . . Evelyne. Your last composition was good, more than good, I still read it. And the reason I'm here is to see if it would be possible for you to return to school.'

Evelyne tugged at a loose strand of hair. 'I can't do that, I've no time to come to school.'

'But you are more than good, child, it's a sin not to finish your education.'

At that moment Davey put a piece of coal in his mouth, sucking it. Evelyne bent down and took it from him, threw it on the fire and picked him up. She buried her face in the small boy's neck and to Doris' consternation her thin shoulders began to shake. Doris realized she was crying.

Although never one to show her feelings, Doris suddenly rose to her feet and wrapped her bony arms around Evelyne. Doris smelt of mothballs and her pale eyes were wet with tears.

'I understand, I understand, you have the boy to care for, and the menfolk, but . . . here, don't cry, child, here . . .'

She handed Evelyne her tiny handkerchief, and didn't even mind when Evelyne blew her nose on it. She poured the tea and handed it to Evelyne, patted her head, and it all came out in a gush.

'I know times are hard, but what I've been thinking is that if you have a few hours of an evening, when the little boy is sleeping, then you could come over to my house. It's quiet, and all my books are there, and if you would like . . . well, what I'm saying is that I would be prepared to give you private tuition, I don't want paying for it, but I would like it if you could manage just a few hours.'

She felt her hand gripped tightly, and the girl kissed it hard.

'Oh, Mrs Evans, I would like that so much.'

'Well, then it's settled, whenever you say – when it's convenient to you.'

With little Davey in her arms, Evelyne walked Doris to the door. Doris was excited, she chucked the baby under his chin and laughed when he tried to bite her, a strange, high-pitched squeak. Then she was gone.

Evelyne had to shake her father awake, Dicken was waiting to go on shift.

'Da, Mrs Evans came by today and said I could have private lessons.'

Hugh swayed and stumbled as she helped him dress. He hadn't even bathed the night before, he had got so drunk coming back from work.

'You do as you wish, Evie . . . where's Dicken? *Dicken?*'

Hugh left the house with his eldest son. Evelyne went back and began to clear up the kitchen, the broken beer bottles. The new lodger arrived back from his night shift, looked in for only a moment, then went into Dicken's bed in what used to be Davey's room, the little lad now sleeping with Evelyne. They'd had to take a lodger as lately the household was always short of money – the tin on the mantel always empty. Evelyne owed money at the baker's, the pie shop, the hardware store. Things had most certainly changed. The Jones family had never been in debt before. With them being such a big family, and mostly men, there had always been wages coming in.

Hugh still worked the mines along with Dicken and Will, but Will needed his wages for Lizzie-Ann, and they were saving as best they could. But Hugh was getting a bad reputation as a drunkard. Poor Dicken not only did his own job of shovelling, but he hacked the coal face too, his father's job. Hugh was perpetually drunk, but Dicken never confronted him – he worked without a word of complaint. He went to the pub with his father, watched him waste the hard-earned money that rightly belonged to Dicken, but he could say nothing. The Old Lion was losing his roar, his shoulders were bent and his face was always filthy. At night he staggered home, leaning on his eldest son for support.

Dicken was worn to a frazzle, and he knew the managers were beginning to talk. The 'measurers' had been round – the men who counted the coal trams and picked over the contents to see if there were any stones or clay clods making up extra weight. The miners were paid by the tram-load so if the loads were down so were the wages. The wage for boys under fifteen was one shilling and sixpence a day, and over fifteen it climbed up by a few pennies a day. A twenty-one-year-old boy, even when married like Will, still only received three shillings a day.

The miners' wages were scaled according to the job. There were truck-weighers, coal tram-weighers, engineers, stokers, tenders, strikers, lampmen, cogmen, banksmiths, rubbish-tippers, greasers, screeners, trimmers, labourers, small-coal pickers, doorboys, hitchers, hauliers, firemen . . . but the élite, who worked the big veins of the mines, were the colliers, the men who hacked and chipped away at the coal. They worked in teams of two, and were completely dependent on each other. One hacked and chipped, one shovelled and filled the trams behind them, as they burrowed like moles deeper and deeper into the face. If the shoveller sat down, too lazy or too tired, then the chipper would have to lay off too. Dicken had been working for both himself and his Da. He knew it would be found out and could not continue. That night, as they came up from the cradle, the manager called them over. They went into the office and stood, caps in hand, like guilty schoolboys. The manager, Benjamin Howells, was sorry – he didn't like doing what he was going to do. He had known Hugh Jones since he was a boy, he'd been at Dicken's christening in the chapel.

Ben spoke in Welsh – maybe he thought it would soften the blow – but it hammered down anyway. Hugh was given his employment cards and Dicken, of course, stood by his father and wanted his. Ben tried to reason with him, but Dicken was adamant so Ben handed them their cards and the week's wages kept in hand, and the two men walked out. Ben sighed. What a waste to see a man like Hugh go to pieces; it was tragic. And the worst of it was, it looked like he was dragging that fine boy down with him.

Dicken and his Da were both getting drunk, drowning their sorrows. They called for drinks all round, banging on the bar for their pints. Dicken rose to his feet, weaving, and began to sing. He had a clear, high tenor, and stood with legs apart, eyes closed, while his beautiful voice soared.

Mike pushed open the bar door and stood framed in the doorway, looked first at his brother then his father. His boots were so highly polished you could see your face in them. He swung his haversack down and Dicken lurched into his arms.

'Mike, is it you, lad? Mike . . . Da, will you look who's back, an' all togged out in his fine uniform.'

Hugh fell off his stool and climbed up, gripping the edge of the bar for support.

'A drink, get a drink for my lad, the soldier boy.'

Mike could smell Hugh's breath – he reeked and his clothes were stained and filthy. He shook his head and looked at Dicken.

'Mun, he's drunk out of his mind.'

Mike soon discovered that since his Ma's death their father had rarely been sober.

Evelyne checked the stew and left the pan half on the stove. She knew they would be late again. She had hoped to go and see Doris, but she had not had even a minute to herself for weeks. Lizzie-Ann was no help in the house; if there was work to do she swooned.

'Oh God, I can't, Evie, not in my condition. A woman in my condition should not lift nothing heavy, I don't want to have a baby like little Davey, now do I?'

While poor Evelyne washed and scrubbed, Lizzie-Ann sat with her feet up. It was true she made Evelyne laugh, especially when she put flour over her face and blacked her eyelids and lips like Theda Bara. She could do endless movie-star impersonations.

'You know, soon as I've had this baby, I'm going to London,' she would say.

The lodger, a coloured gentleman, fascinated Lizzie-Ann. She would ask him to turn his palms over and then shriek with delight at the pinkness of them. Josh Walker was a kind-hearted man whose family lived in Leeds, like many coloureds who had arrived in the village. There was hardly a house left in the village without a lodger of some kind, Italian, Indian, black . . . well, there was one house. Doris Evans kept her four rooms to herself. The war, everyone said, was taking their men and replacing them with outsiders.

*

48

That night Dicken and Mike carried their Da home between them. Evelyne was so happy to see her brother that she forgot about going to see Doris. Somehow she made the stew go round, pushed her worries away. Tomorrow was another day and she'd manage to get a little meat from the butcher.

'Evie, want to walk awhile with me?'

Mike smiled, slipping their mother's old shawl around his sister's shoulders.

'I'll be gone by morning, going to France. I'll write to you, and send you pretty things . . . oh, Evie, Evie, come here.'

She went into his arms and held him tight. She loved him so, she thought her heart would break.

'Dicken's coming with me. Now shush, it has to be, they lost their jobs at the mine, this way he'll be able to send money home, and me too . . . but what of you? You're so thin, and I swear you look older, older than you should . . .' Mike could not say how he really felt, how sad he was to see his sister so gaunt, so pale. It was obvious to him that she was working herself into an early grave.

'It'll be for the best, Evie. With me and Dicken gone it should ease the burden on you. You have a lad? Someone that's courting you?'

She hung her head as she walked alongside him, flushing bright red. 'Be off with you, Mike, there's no boy interested in me, an' I'm too young yet even to be looking.'

Mike pulled her to him and kissed the top of her head.

'You are special, Evie. Tell you what I'll do, I'll bring a handsome soldier home for you on my next leave.'

The two boys were dressed and ready. Evelyne slipped

into the kitchen, afraid they would go without saying goodbye. Dicken ruffled her hair, but he was close to tears. 'Take care of Da for us, we'll be back.'

Mike smiled and blew her a kiss, as hand-in-hand with Dicken she walked them to the door. 'Evie, think about seeing that schoolteacher. You'll have more time now, promise me?'

She smiled but couldn't speak, she was too close to tears.

'Goodbye, darlin', and God bless you.'

She watched her two brothers walk down the cobbled street, their arms about each other's shoulders. Will came and stood behind her, put his arms around her, 'So they've gone. Da was too drunk to understand last night; I'll tell him.'

Deep down he knew his own days at home were numbered, he could be called up at any time.

Six months had passed since the schoolteacher's visit, and Evelyne popped a note through Doris' door. She had worked out how many hours a week she would be able to spend with Doris, although it had not been easy to arrange. Lizzie-Ann refused to take charge of little Davey so Mrs Pugh had promised to look after him.

'I don't know why you bother learning, Evie. Find yourself a boy, that's what you should be doing.'

Evelyne looked at Lizzie-Ann. She was wearing only her bloomers with one of Will's shirts over the top, her belly sticking out.

'I've no interest in boys, Lizzie-Ann . . . if you could turn your charms on at the bakery I'd be grateful, we've no bread.'

'I'll do me Theda Bara for that old bugger . . . well, go on, if yer going.'

A plate of sweet, home-made biscuits and a glass of warm milk were waiting for Evelyne, and Doris had been back and forth to the window to see if she was really coming. All her precious books were laid out neatly on the table with a clean notebook, ready for work to begin.

Evelyne tapped the polished door knocker. She was acutely self-conscious about her appearance; her hair needed washing, her cardigan was darned and thread-bare, even her skirt was torn at the hem. She wore a pair of her mother's shoes, three sizes too large, and she went pink with shame when she noticed that her heels were black with soot.

'Well, dear, better late than never. Now come in, wipe your feet on the mat.'

She stepped on to the gleaming linoleum in the narrow hall, her heart pounding, hardly able to say a word. She had never seen such lovely, gleaming furniture. There was a sofa covered in velvet with crocheted white cloths on the head rests, and there was a lovely rug in front of the fire.

'You could eat your dinner off your floor, Mrs Evans.'

They sat at opposite sides of the table and gradually became more relaxed. Evelyne soon forgot her shyness and turned the pages eagerly, clapping her hands when she discovered a word she had not heard of before. She thumbed through Doris' heavy dictionary.

'And how, Evelyne, would you spell chameleon? Look it up . . . now remember, it might not begin with a "k", it could be a "ch", so search for the word . . .'

51

The wall clock chimed nine and Evelyne looked crestfallen.

'Never mind, dear, we can continue next time.'

Evelyne found herself watching the clock in the kitchen waiting for Mrs Pugh to take little Davey, and then she was off, running as fast as her legs would carry her. Doris was always ready, standing at the door, biscuits and milk waiting on the table. She would dearly have loved to open her thin, bony arms and hug the child. Evelyne delighted her so, but she was too shy.

'Oh listen, Mrs Evans, I know it by heart now. All night I practised just as you told me . . . "From her celestial car the Fairy Queen descended, and thrice she waved her wand, circled with wreaths of amaranth. Her thin and misty form moved with the moving air, and the clear silver tones as thus she spoke, were such as are unheard by all but the gifted ear".'

Doris watched as Evelyne stood with her arms held up, her wondrous red hair wild from running, her cheeks flushed.

'That was very good, dear, now drink your milk, and remember descend is "s" before "c".'

She nibbled her thin lips, watching Evelyne eagerly thumbing through the dictionary. She had received a letter from her brother more than two weeks ago, and had spent sleepless nights over it. His wife had died – not that that had disturbed Doris in any way, far from it – but he had invited Doris to stay. He had said it was time they forgot their old wounds. And she did, after all, own part of the house.

'Evie . . . Evelyne dear, I'm going to Cardiff.'

Seeing the desperate, haunted look on her young pupil's face made her swallow hard.

'Oh, will you be gone long, Mrs Evans?' The child's thin hands clenched and unclenched. She was fighting back the tears at the thought of losing her precious lessons.

'Not long, but I was wondering if your father would give his permission . . . of course, I would pay your train fare and any expenses . . . would you like to come with me? Just a weekend trip? We could see the museums. Would you like to come?'

Evelyne was up and out of her chair, hugging Doris so tightly that she could hardly catch her breath. Evelyne's kiss was frantic, but then she raised her fist and bit her knuckles. 'I don't think it would be possible, but thank you ever so.'

Doris had confused herself, she had not really intended asking the child. Yet now it seemed imperative that she should go. The life flooding through her tired, empty shell was turning Doris into a new woman.

'Well, I won't take no for an answer, and here, look, I've a few things put by for you.'

Rushing into her immaculate bedroom, Doris pulled open a drawer, even pushing aside her wedding dress as she searched through her neatly folded clothes and wrapped a selection in brown paper. Knowing the child possessed only the poor things she stood up in, she told Evelyne she had no need for them any more.

Evelyne carried the brown paper parcel up to her room and inspected the skirt, cardigan and blouse Doris had given her. They were nearly new and smelt of mothballs. There was not a single darn or hole and even though they were old-fashioned and not a very flattering colour, Evelyne thought they were fit for a queen.

'Well, will you look at her, Will, if she doesn't look a lady! Now, don't you worry, Evie love, we'll take care of everything, and if you don't hurry you'll miss the train.'

Evelyne kissed everyone, checked that Lizzie-Ann knew what to do for little Davey, and gave her so many instructions that they almost got into a fight. Doris wouldn't come in, but stood on the doorstep with her overnight case. As the two went down the street Lizzie-Ann stared after them, then slammed the door. She turned on Will.

'There'll be no livin' with her when she gets back. Wish to God I'd never got meself married, I'd be in London by now, and that's where I'm going, you mark my words.'

Good-natured as ever, Will said nothing, didn't even mention that he'd received his call-up papers that morning.

CHAPTER 4

DORIS HAD packed a small picnic for the train, and they shared it as the train puffed its way across the valley. Evelyne was more like a child of six than a fourteen-year-old, pointing out of the window, moving from one side of the carriage to the other, unable to keep still for excitement. She smoothed her skirt with her hands, mimicking everything Doris did, acting the lady.

'Now, Evelyne, pack everything neat and tidy, don't leave any rubbish on the train. We'll put it in a bin when we get to Cardiff.'

Evelyne would have eaten the brown paper wrappings if Doris had asked her, she was so thrilled. She grew quieter as the train slowed its pace and moved into the siding at Cardiff Central Station. In clipped tones fit for a sergeant major in the Salvation Army, Doris barked orders to Evelyne.

'Tickets, handbag, case, exit up ahead, keep close by me . . . now then, we have to get a tram to Clifton Street.'

When they were seated on the top of the tram, Evelyne turned her head this way and that, her heart thudding in her chest.

'Oh, Mrs Evans, look at the castle, it is just beautiful,

55

and the grass, is it not greener than at home? Oh, look, look at the motor vehicles!'

Some of the passengers sniggered as she shouted in excitement.

'Evelyne, dear, you don't need to shout, I am right next to you, not in an open field . . . speak softly, child, it's not ladylike to shout.'

As they got off the tram Evelyne clung tightly to Doris' hand and almost got them run over, she was so unused to the traffic.

'Taxi . . . Taxi . . .'

Evelyne clapped her hand over her mouth to stop herself shouting out. She had never seen a taxi like it. It had red leather seats, and the driver wore a peaked cap. They got into the back seat and Doris rapped on the glass partition with her umbrella.

'Clifton Villas, number thirty.'

The taxi drew up outside one of a row of bow-fronted, Victorian houses, with white steps leading up to the front door and more steps leading down to the servants' entrance behind the basement railings. Evelyne followed Doris like a lamb, waiting quietly as she lifted the ornate brass knocker. A maid in a black dress with a frilly white apron and cap ushered them through a dark hallway leading to what looked to Evelyne like a palace. There were paintings and china everywhere, chiming clocks, and the drawing-room furniture was covered in velvet, everything in rusty, autumn colours.

'Doris dear, how good to see you, come in, come in.'

Doris kissed the pale lips, identical to her own, and the dapper little Dr Collins gave Evelyne a formal bow and adjusted his pince-nez as he ushered them in. He spoke so quietly that Evelyne could not catch everything he said, but he was so clean and fresh in his starched white collar. It was obvious he and Doris were brother and sister, Dr Collins was so like her, but Evelyne watched Doris change in front of her eyes. She became stiff and formal, and after their initial greetings they appeared to have nothing to say to each other.

'Would the gel like tea, Doris?'

Evelyne stood rooted to the spot, staring down at the rose-patterned carpet. The house was carpeted everywhere, she couldn't believe it. Her feet sank into the pile, into two dusty pink roses.

'Sit down, Evelyne, and say hello to Dr Collins.'

Evelyne perched gingerly on the edge of a velvet sofa, feeling its softness beneath her hands. She swallowed, about to say, 'How do you do', but he went over to the fireplace and rang a bell beside it. Evelyne noticed the pretty rose-patterned tiles around the fireplace.

'You keeping well then, Doris? Tea, Minnie, straight-away.'

Minnie bobbed a small curtsey and scuttled out, leaving the door ajar.

'Your practice well, is it, dear?'

'Well, it keeps me on my toes, ya know . . . glad you could come, makes a nice change, and young David will be pleased to make your acquaintance. He's a fine chap, fine boy . . . ah, good, tea.'

The tea was wheeled in on a trolley. There were small cucumber sandwiches, little cup cakes, and a big currant cake with a frilled collar. The maid poured the tea and handed plates and napkins. Evelyne found it very diffi-cult to balance her plate, napkin, teacup and saucer, and looked to Doris for help.

'Get the gel a side table, Minnie.'

Minnie brought a small table to Evelyne's side then picked up the sugar bowl.

'You take sugar, Miss?'

Evelyne nodded and waited, then realized that the

maid was waiting for her to help herself. She was all thumbs and picked up what she thought was a spoon, but it seemed to be two spoons in one.

'Use the tongs, child, don't use your fingers.'

Just as she had her mouth full the Doctor spoke.

'So this is your young protégée. And how do you find Cardiff, Evelyne?'

Evelyne swallowed and gulped and spluttered as the sandwich went down the wrong way. Doris moved quickly to her and patted her on the back, concerned.

'You must never speak with your mouth full, dear.'

Dr Collins consulted his fob watch and stood up, saying he had to make his rounds. Evelyne couldn't help but think how much Doc Clock would have liked that watch.

'Ahh, this sounds like David . . . yes, he's here,' the Doctor beamed with pride, standing at the bay window. 'He's got some high-society friends now, Doris, he's at the university. Oh, I wrote, yes, I remember I told you, well-connected people, be good for his profession, going to be a lawyer, did I tell you? Ah, yes, I suppose I did . . . yes, his mother would have been proud of him, God rest her soul.'

Doris crossed herself, and Evelyne looked from one to the other. She had not thought the doctor could ever have been married or have a son.

There was a bellow from the hall.

'Minnie . . . *Minnie*! *Minnie*! Anyone call for me while I was out?'

They heard laughter, then the double doors of the drawing-room were flung open. David Collins made his entrance like an actor. His blond hair shone like silk, his perfectly tailored grey suit hugged his tall, slender frame. He was very self-assured, his ice-blue eyes twinkled. 'Aunt Doris, well I never, Pa mentioned you would be

58

arriving, do forgive me for not being here to welcome you.'

Unaware that her mouth had dropped open, Evelyne stared. He could have been a prince, she had never in her life seen a man so handsome. He bowed over Doris' outstretched hand and kissed it, then turned his attention to Evelyne. He had no trace of a Welsh accent.

'And you must be Elaine, how do you do?'

As Evelyne half stood, her plate in one hand and cup and saucer in the other her cake rolled off the plate and landed by his highly polished grey kid boots.

'Absolutely the place for Mrs Darwin's cakes, my dear. *Minnie*! Come along, gel, and bring a dustpan and brush . . . now, Pa, can I get you more tea? Aunt?'

David dominated the room – lifted the mood as if the sun had suddenly shone in through the windows. He wore a delicate perfume, like lilies, that filled the air.

Doris rose from her chair. 'Well, if you'll excuse us I think we'll have a little sightseeing tour, and a wash and change before dinner. Evelyne, dear, have you finished?'

Flushing, Evelyne put her china down on the tray, and stood with head bowed, so tongue-tied it made her desperate to visit the bathroom. Doris took her arm and pulled her towards the door. David watched them leave, waiting until the door closed behind them, then looked at his father with raised eyebrows.

'Are they staying long?'

Dr Collins dabbed at his mouth with his napkin, 'Just the weekend, just the weekend.' David flipped his silk handkerchief out of his pocket and flicked a cake crumb from his boot.

'Is the skinny child an orphan? Smells quite dreadful, and one couldn't really say she was frightfully clean.'

After ringing again for Minnie to clear away, Dr Collins went towards the door.

'Couldn't spare a fiver, Pa? Bit short, only I have to take a couple of chaps to dinner this evening.'

'I would like it if you dined at home. Doris hasn't been here for many years. It would show a bit of respect.'

David whistled, irritated, then sprang to his feet.

'Okie dokie, but between you and me, it's no wonder Mother kept her at arm's length, what?'

At times Dr Collins loathed his son's supercilious attitude, but then he could be so charming the doctor gave him whatever he wanted, as did everyone else.

David turned abruptly, moving like a dancer, swept out of the room and bounded up the stairs two or three at a time. Evelyne was standing at the top, on her way to the bathroom, carrying a fresh white towel. They almost collided.

'Sorry, Elaine, bathroom's second door on your right.'

She didn't have the nerve to correct him, just blushed and scuttled past. At the bottom of the stairs Mrs Darwin stood smiling, her big red face glowing.

'Now then, Master David, will you be having dinner at home?'

'I will, Mrs Darwin, light of my life . . . oh, Mrs D, will you make sure my shirts are not folded, just put on the hangers, can't stand the creases . . . thanks awfully.'

Mrs Darwin shrugged her shoulders and plodded back down to the basement, passing Minnie.

'Prince Edward himself wants his shirts not folded, he'll be wanting me to press his socks next.'

The marble bathroom was like a wonderland. Evelyne touched the white bath, the washbasin, and gasped with delight as she turned on the taps. Hot and cold water!

60

What would Lizzie-Ann have to say, hot and cold, and a toilet of their own with a cord that flushed it.

'Evelyne, dear, have you run your bath? Don't be too long, we won't have too much time for sightseeing.'

In his room, David sighed. 'Sightseeing' . . . dear God, he hoped none of his friends would show up during his aunt's stay.

Doris and Evelyne spent the rest of the afternoon in the museums and wandering around the castle. Everything was a wonder to Evelyne. They were both tired when they returned so Doris suggested they take a little nap before dinner. Evelyne was loving every minute of it. Her small single bed with its crisp white sheets was heaven, and she dozed blissfully. She was still snoozing at dinner-time, and Doris woke her. She was embarrassed to see that Doris had changed. She had only one clean blouse.

'Shall I wear my other blouse, Mrs Evans?'

'I don't think so, dear, the gong has already rung, and you'll need it for tomorrow . . . just give your hair a brush, would you like me to do it for you?'

Doris had never brushed a girl's hair before, and she was not much good at plaiting it. At the end of all her hard work it looked as if it still needed brushing.

'Thank you, Mrs Evans.'

Doris gave her a small, tight smile, patted her and then straightened her cardigan.

'Well, shall we go down? Don't eat too fast, dear, don't speak with your mouth full, and keep your voice lowered, no need to shout, all right?'

The meal was an agony of uncertainty for Evelyne, and she spoke not a word, terrified she would choke or be caught with her mouth full. Her bread crumbled so much that she kept glancing at Doris and picking up each crumb from round her place setting. She watched Doris coping with the lukewarm soup, moving her spoon away from her and then sipping from the side of it, and followed suit. It tasted like her mother's gravy.

'So, Aunt, how is village life? Do you not miss Cardiff?'

'I don't, David . . . Evelyne, have you finished your soup?'

The main course consisted of roast beef, carrots, peas, and small, crisp roast potatoes.

'Do start, dear, don't want it getting cold.'

Evelyne began to eat and felt David's half-amused stare making her go hot and cold. She could feel her legs sticking together.

'You are to be a lawyer, David?' Doris asked her nephew. 'Congratulations.'

'Well, I will no doubt be called up. Bit of a nuisance really, in the middle of studies, but then one has to do one's bit. Wretched business, this war.'

The pudding was served, a chocolate sponge with thick, bright yellow custard.

'You know, I really must go to the valleys one day. Spent last vacs in London, met some of Mother's relatives there, jolly nice people.'

'She was a good woman, miss her you know, Doris,' put in Dr Collins. 'She ran the house like clockwork, didn't she, David?'

'So, Elaine, tell me how you like Cardiff?'

'Her name's Evelyne, and she's a very clever girl, my best pupil.'

Evelyne couldn't meet his blue eyes. She bit her lip, loving the sound of his voice.

'I do apologize, you should have corrected me before, Evelyne . . . so, Ev-e-lyne, you are still at school?'

Every time Evelyne opened her mouth to speak Doris butted in until David laughed, a lovely, chuckling laugh.

'Good God, Aunt, can't the gel speak for herself?'

'Mrs Evans is teaching me private.'

'Oh, I see . . . oh I say, Pa, did I tell you I'm playing polo? Charlie Withers said I could use one of his ponies, rather chuffed about it, actually. You know Freddy Carlton's always said I should try my hand . . . did you know Lord and Lady Carlton, Auntie?'

Doris pursed her lips, dabbed them with the napkin.

'No, when I was a girl I didn't mix in those exalted circles, but I have seen pictures of their estate. Your grandfather did their gardens, when he retired from the railway.'

Doris' quiet reproach to her nephew went over Evelyne's head. She was happy to listen to him talk, and when his attention was directed to his aunt or his father it gave her the opportunity to study him. He had a habit of running his fingers through his silky hair, then tossing his head slightly. He wore a large gold ring on his little finger. Evelyne had still not spoken more than two sentences when everyone rose and went into a small sitting room. It was cosy and informal with a huge, round bowl of fresh roses on the table. The maid wheeled in the trolley with coffee and small, round peppermints covered in dark, home-made chocolate. Evelyne slipped one into her pocket for little Davey, and tucked her worn shoes as far out of sight beneath her skirt as she could.

The fire was stacked as high as it could be and made the small room hot and stuffy, but it was a pleasant stuffiness. Doris sat next to her brother and talked with him in whispers. Evelyne had never tasted coffee before and she found it bitter but nice, like a cross between hot chocolate and very strong tea. She nearly spilled it as she sensed David standing beside her. Evelyne was too shy to look up, and all she could see was his grey trouser-leg and soft leather boot. Her blush was even worse than at supper.

'Would you care for another?'

David held out the peppermints and smiled. Evelyne was sure he had seen her pocket one, so she shook her head and felt her hair begin to come loose from its braid. She tried frantically to push it back, but the harder she tried the more the strands worked loose.

David picked up the family photograph album and carried it to the table, moving the roses aside and laying it on the crushed velvet cloth. He gave Evelyne a look to join him. She sat next to him with her hands clasped tightly in her lap, knowing her hair was all over the place and feeling her rough skin above the worn shoes, but she never once turned her face towards him, seeing only his hands with their long, tapering fingers, and the immaculate cuffs of his shirt. The village boys seemed so rough and unkempt in comparison. David wore his hair slightly long, whereas they had to keep theirs short because of the coal dust, and Evelyne had never seen hair with such a sheen on it, even on a girl.

At bedtime Evelyne scrubbed her face, neck and arms, then spent a long time washing the face cloth so it wouldn't look grey. She unfolded her mother's old, greyish nightgown that had once been white and pulled it over her head, then folded all her clothes neatly, and unlocked the door.

She tiptoed along the corridor and heard Doris below saying goodnight to her brother. About to enter her bedroom she caught sight of David's half-open door opposite. She couldn't help herself, she stared. David was sitting on the side of his bed wearing only his grey trousers and boots, nothing on the top at all. He was leaning forward, reading a book, and running his fingers through his hair. Evelyne knew she shouldn't be standing there, but she couldn't move, she wanted to touch his soft, clean white skin. She had never felt like this in her life before. She was used to seeing and touching male skin from bathing her menfolk, but this was somehow different, she didn't know quite why, but she had a pain in the pit of her tummy, and her whole body felt hot.

There were footsteps on the stairs, and she turned quickly, dropping a shoe. Mortified, she grabbed it and heard David's door close as she scurried into her room. Oh, dear Lord, had he seen her watching him?

Evelyne pretended she was asleep as Doris crept around the room and then slipped out to the bathroom. The darkness was lovely, lying between clean sheets with clean smells all around her. She snuggled down into the bed but couldn't sleep, because David's face kept floating in front of her eyes. Oh, she had so much to tell Lizzie-Ann!

Evelyne did not see David again. Their visit had passed quickly, and they were about to depart for the railway station. Evelyne stood with clasped hands as Dr Collins handed Doris a parel, saying it contained a few things that had belonged to his wife that he would like her to have.

As Dr Collins waved them on their way, David came down the stairs, yawned and asked if they had gone.

'I think you should have made the effort to come down, not good enough, you know.'

David shrugged, 'I doubt if we'll be seeing her again,

and even if we do I hope she won't bring that dreadful child with her. I mean, what on earth possessed her to bring the girl?'

The Doctor studied his fob watch, 'Doris was always one for picking up waifs and strays – look at that chap she married. Illiterate, you know, broke up the family. Now I must be off on my rounds, will you be home for supper?'

David was always irritated by his father, the way his father referred to dinner as supper, it wasn't done.

'I'll be dining out at the Carltons'.'

'You know, son, it's all very well you mixing with these chaps, but you must never forget your roots, don't get above yourself.'

David swiped the top off his egg so hard it shot across the table. 'Don't get above yourself . . .' David had every intention of getting above himself, out of his dreadful house, away from his father's penny-pinching ways.

'Goodbye, Father, have an enjoyable day,' he muttered.

When they were on the tram, heading home across the mountains, Doris opened the small parcel. She sighed, knowing she would never wear the dead woman's bits and pieces of jewellery. There were also a couple of woollen cardigans and a shawl.

'You know, I never got on with my sister-in-law. Her name was Eleanor, and she was cruel to my dear husband, mocking him. I always said I would never visit while she was still alive, and now . . . well, did you enjoy it, Evelyne?'

'Oh, yes, Mrs Evans, I loved every single minute of it, and I'll never be able to thank you enough.'

Rewrapping the parcel, Doris murmured that she

would give the clothes to the poor. Evelyne half hoped that Doris would give them to her.

'Could you make use of these ribbons?'

'Oh, yes, thank you Mrs Evans, thank you very much.'

Doris sighed and looked out of the window. The break had done her the world of good. She looked back at Evelyne who was carefully winding the ribbons round her finger.

'We'll make it a habit, I think, yes, I think it would be good for you to spend more time at the museums. Perhaps we can even go to the theatre.'

Evelyne grabbed Doris' hand and kissed it.

'Oh, thank you, thank you, Mrs Evans.'

Her whole slender body trembled with pleasure. Just think, she would be going back to that palace of a house and, even better, she would see him again – she would see David.

Evelyne knew there was something amiss the moment she let herself into the house. It was dark, cold and silent. The kitchen fire was almost out, and she stoked it quickly, disappointed to find no one at home, and worried.

'Da, I'm home . . . Da?'

She ran up the stairs, bursting to tell her news, pushed open the door.

'Oh, Da, I had such a time, such a wonderful time.'

Hugh was lying on the bed, holding Davey's small, well-chewed teddy bear. He raised himself on to his elbow. He looked ill, his eyes were red-rimmed, but he was sober.

'Has Lizzie-Ann not been looking after you?' Evelyne asked, 'I dunno, I leave you for no more than two days . . . does Mrs Pugh have little Davey, I'll go and pick him up, I've built up the fire . . .'

Hugh moaned and lay down, put his arm across his face, and his body shook.

'What is it? Has something happened? Da?'

He gripped the small toy and his face crumpled. He sobbed.

'Aw, Christ, gel, I was drunk, I was drunk . . . he was up here, an' I heard his hollerin' and I went to bring him down, down to the fire . . . he was in my arms . . . halfway down I fell.'

Evelyne was on the bed, pulling at his arm, 'Where is he, Da? Where is he? I'll go to him, I'll go to him.'

Hugh reached out and pulled her down to lie beside him.

'I fell, Evie, I fell . . . I fell on the little chap, and God help me, I've killed him.'

She moved away, staring, her eyes bright with tears.

'Ah, no, you didn't . . . you didn't . . . *Davey, Davey!*'

Hugh couldn't stop her, he sobbed as he heard her running through the rooms calling out the little boy's name. She gripped the side of his empty cot and called for him, all she could remember was his funny, fuzzy head, his drooling, soft mouth . . . and he was always so happy . . .

Lizzie-Ann, her belly even bigger, stood at the door.

'Oh, Lizzie, Lizzie, poor little Davey.'

Lizzie-Ann's face puckered, a child carrying a child herself, 'Maybe it was God's doin', he wasn't right in the head.'

Evelyne wiped her tears with the back of her hand. All her stories, all the things she'd wanted to tell Lizzie-Ann meant nothing now. She could even detect the envy, see it in the puffy, pretty face, the huge, searching pansy eyes. Little Davey was far from her thoughts. 'You have a good time?'

'No, not really . . . I brought you back some ribbons, they're on the kitchen table.'

Lizzie-Ann whooped and rushed to the kitchen, leaving Evelyne standing by the empty cot. She touched the chewed, sucked sides, and thought it could be put to use for Lizzie-Ann's baby.

Later that night Hugh was heard thudding up the stairs. He was drunk as he had been on the night he had fallen and killed his little boy. He was struggling out of his filthy old working jacket, stumbling against the bed. Evelyne slipped into the room and he straightened up while she took his clothes off him. The bed smelt terrible, the sheets and pillows stained with beer and vomit. The huge man was so broken, so pitiful . . . he held out his massive, gnarled hand to her, she slipped her own into it, although she didn't want to stay in the squalid room. Poor little Davey, his whole life just a few silly words, Da da-da-daaaa . . .

The next Sunday they buried Davey. Only a few villagers turned out to follow the sad, small family to the churchyard. They couldn't even afford a hearse. Hugh was sober, and he carried the tiny coffin in his arms as if it was a precious box of eggs that would smash if he jolted it.

Over the tiny grave Hugh swore he would never touch another drop, so help him, and as the rain started the big man went down on his knees and wept. There were no cornflowers this time, as it was winter.

Evelyne was drained, but she knew her Da depended on her and didn't give in. She stood, straight-backed, her arm ready for Hugh to lean on. Will wouldn't meet her gaze, he was ashamed, like his father. The little boy who had been left in their care now lay alongside their Ma and the baby with no name.

CHAPTER 5

THE BIRTH of Lizzie-Ann's daughter was a noisy affair. Red-faced, bawling her lungs out from the very beginning, she started as she meant to go on. She was christened Rosie.

They now had two lodgers, and Evelyne worked part-time in the bakery. They paid her a proportion of her wages in bread. Will still worked in the mines. It was 1916, and the fear of conscription hung over every household. Every day saw another boy leave for the Front, and lorry-loads of workers were brought to the mines, which caused ill-feeling and fights among the men. Uniformed soldiers were a common sight, some on leave and some new recruits. The village was being torn apart.

Doris had taken Evelyne to Cardiff three times. She treasured these trips, but she rarely discussed them at home as she knew Lizzie-Ann was secretly jealous. Fussing with the baby, she would make snide remarks, 'Oh, off again, are we? Well it's all right fer some, others have more important things to be doing than traipsin' to Cardiff. What ya do there that's so special?'

Evelyne would quietly continue with the housework.

'We just go round the museums, spend time in the library.'

'Very borin' if you ask me. Are there nice young men there? You should be thinking of looking, you know, being so tall you won't find it easy.'

Evelyne never mentioned David, but then she had not seen him since her first visit, and it was not until her fourth trip that she saw him again. He strode into the lounge. He was now a captain in the Artillery, and wore his gold-buttoned uniform with dashing flair, his greatcoat slung round his shoulders and his riding boots highly polished. 'Well, my dear aunt, oh, and your little friend, well, what a surprise.'

If David was aware of her infatuation he gave no sign, and spoke to her as if she was a child. Alone with his father he was less than enthusiastic.

'Good God Pa, I've only got a few weeks at home and *they're* here. That girl positively reeks of carbolic.'

David was enjoying his new status, as he had his time in France. He had not as yet seen any fighting, but the social life was exhilarating, and he did cut an exceptionally elegant figure. He was determined to flirt with all and sundry, setting about it like a military campaign, and was extremely annoyed when his father suggested he give Evelyne a tour of Cardiff.

'All right, Pa, but then I've done my bit, I *am* on leave, you know.'

Evelyne gasped as David carefully tucked the blanket around her knees. She had never been in a private motorcar before, only in a taxi and on a tram, and here she was in David's sports car. He wore goggles and

72

drove carefully, but to Evelyne it seemed very fast, nearly thirty miles an hour. Whenever anyone got in the way, David would hoot at them. He even let Evelyne squeeze the large, squashy rubber bulb of the trumpet-shaped horn, it was wonderful. Evelyne was like a child. The wind had brought a lovely colour to her cheeks and her hairpins had slipped out as usual. She wore no scarf, and her hair tumbled down, blowing in the wind. At first she held on to it, but then she laughed and let it fly free. In spite of himself, David enjoyed the little trip, and found 'Carbolic', as he called her, quite sweet in her gawky way. Occasionally he pointed out features of the city to Evelyne.

When they arrived home David removed the blanket from around Evelyne's knees, folded it and helped her out of the car. Her face was flushed, and she smiled, it had been the happiest day of her life. His gentle grip on her elbow thrilled her right through and made her head buzz. She wasn't sure why he felt he had to help her through doors and up stairs – she wasn't frail or any-thing – but she liked it.

'Care for a glass of sherry?' He handed it to her with a flourish, 'Drive did you the world of good, got some colour into your cheeks.'

Evelyne was so nervous that she spilt her sherry. The thimble-shaped glass was so small and she had difficulty in raising it to her lips.

'Here, allow me.' He handed her his handkerchief and she dabbed at her mouth. 'If you will excuse me, I must bathe and change.'

David swept out, leaving Evelyne to finish her sherry and look forward to dinner when she would see him again, but the sight of the two places set at the table made her heart drop like a stone. David was dining out,

73

murmured the Doctor, who then spent the remainder of the meal reading the *Cardiff Gazette*.

Later, Evelyne slipped in between the cool sheets and lay listening to the night sounds. From beneath the pillow she drew out the handkerchief with his initials, the one he had given her when she spilt her sherry. She would keep it as a memento, a keepsake of her love.

At breakfast David fairly glowed. He stood up smartly when Evelyne entered, sat down again and whacked the top off his egg. Doris was too ill to come down, in fact she felt so bad she had decided she couldn't return to the valley until the following day. Evelyne wanted to sing with joy, another whole day here with her love. David noticed that she was wearing exactly the same clothes as on the previous day, and there was a piece of newspaper sticking up from her shoes.

David ate ravenously, and more and more toast was brought in in a silver toast rack. He swamped it with thick butter and marmalade, and Evelyne couldn't believe her eyes. He took so much that sometimes he even left some on the edge of his plate. He poured tea, munched and chatted, then laughed as he noticed that Evelyne could eat just as fast as he could. In fact he reckoned she had wolfed down two more slices than he had, and joked that she must have been at the Front along with his men. Evelyne flushed with embarrassment, making a mental note not to eat so fast.

David excused himself and walked out to the hall, and Evelyne heard him pick up the telephone. He caught her staring and closed the dining room door, but she could hear the low murmur of his voice and then his laugh. The door swung open and he lolled against the jamb, smiling. 'Care for another little drive?'

All Evelyne could do to stop herself bursting into song was to pinch herself. She had never known such delight, and being tucked up in the motor, feeling his hand brush her thigh even though it was covered by at least three or four layers, made her shiver. David smiled into her upturned face, then cupped her chin in his immaculate, white-gloved hand.

'Comfortable? Think we'll have a spin in the country.'

David had arranged to meet a friend, Captain Ridgely, at a small country inn. The inn was frequented by officers on leave, and a number of rooms had been set aside for their private use. Captain Ridgely had assured David he would enjoy himself, and that he had two exquisite creatures for him to meet. Desperate to ingratiate himself with the social set, David accepted, believing he would be meeting acquaintances of Ridgely's. Evelyne, of course, had no idea she was being used to cover any potential gossip.

David drove Evelyne out past the castle and into the country, and they had to shout above the roar of the engine. They passed the railway station, leaving the town behind them, and headed along narrow lanes between the fields.

Evelyne sat smiling, taking sidelong glances at her beloved's beautiful face. Eventually they drew up at an inn with small tables covered with checkered cloths under the shade of a huge oak tree. Again he helped her out, and guided her to a secluded table. He snapped his fingers at a rotund man wearing a big white apron, turned to Evelyne, 'Sherry? Or would you prefer something else?'

Evelyne sat with her sherry under the tree. David excused himself and entered the inn; just like the men from her village, they always left their womenfolk outside. Making sure she would be able to see David if he came out, Evelyne went for a short stroll.

The fields smelt wonderful, the sun was warm and lovely . . . she sniffed, stretched, twirled, and up bubbled a laugh of perfect happiness. It took her by surprise and she wanted to shout out. Why was it she never had anyone near when she had things to tell them? She walked on across the fields then turned to stroll behind the inn. It was part of a farm complex and she could see the cows being led into the milking sheds. How little Davey would have liked to see these cows, big fat ones, browns and blacks . . .

A car similar to David's roared through the farmyard at the back of the inn. Evelyne stared down the hill as a uniformed officer, accompanied by two women, entered the inn. The women were laughing and clinging to the soldier's arm. Evelyne was so busy watching the car that she didn't see the big cow pat right in front of her. Splosh! In went her shoe, and it was such a shock that she slid forwards, lost her balance and slithered down the embankment. Evelyne had cow dung on her skirt, her knees, and her left hand – and her right shoe, the one with the newspaper inside, was covered in it. The silk scarf had slipped from her hair and was mucky too. Almost in tears she squelched towards the brook that circled the field. She took off her skirt and, dipping the hem into the icy water, rinsed it out. Then she put the whole of her shoe in. It was stinking so she picked up a stick and scraped the muck off. She smelt her hands, noticed that the cuffs of her blouse, the one Doris had given her, were covered too, so off it came . . . she was trying to clean her shoe, her skirt and blouse all at the same time, and it was disastrous. The next thing she knew she had toppled over and was sitting waist-deep in the brook.

David had already downed half a bottle of wine, and was growing impatient. The room was stuffy and smelt of stale beer and cigarettes. He was about to leave when the door opened and there stood Ridgely, with a wicked smile and a blonde on either arm. 'Now, gels, I want you to meet a *very* dear friend, and more than that, I want you to make him feel very special – after all, he *is* on leave, so let's not waste any time, eh?'

David had to turn away to conceal his astonishment. The blondes wore nothing but lacy panties and stockings beneath their coats. Ridgely came to his side and nudged him in the ribs.

'Get what you pay for? Nothing like these two in France, I assure you . . . this one's on me, old chap.'

David took another covert look at the two girls who had sat down and were casually sipping wine, waiting.

'Which one is mine?'

'Both, I'll be back in an hour.'

Flamboyantly, Ridgely kissed each girl, then with elaborate winks and gestures he left them. David gulped his wine and before he had put his glass down one of the girls was unbuttoning his uniform.

Ridgely tiptoed into the adjoining room, locked the door behind him, and crept to the dividing wall. Moving a picture aside he peeked through the spyhole. He would have a jolly story to tell the lads at the barracks tonight.

Evelyne had spread her skirt out flat in the sun, her blouse on a thorn bush. Her left shoe was all right, but the right one was very squashy and still smelt dreadful. She crept to the hedge and peeked over, looking for David, and sighed with relief that he was not there. Dear God, please don't let him find me this way, not in my mother's old shift and a cut-down vest of my father's. Please, dear Lord, I'd do anything, but don't let him find me this way. Make the sun hot to dry out my skirt and Doris' hand-me-down blouse or I will kill myself. The square silk headscarf David had given her was drying on the grass, but it was full of wrinkles. Evelyne's hair had tumbled down, all the pins flung everywhere in her panic to wash her clothes free of the cow dung. She wished she'd at least brought a comb with her. The water had made her hair curl and frizz, it was sticking out like a bush and she knew it. Her nails were full of dirt and her knees were scratched.

Freedom Beshaley Stubbs approached the field where his stallion was. It was his own *gry*. The farmer had allowed Freedom to field him separately from the ponies. The *gry* was a wild one, with a temper, but Freedom believed he was a racer and intended to keep him, not sell him with the rest of the pack. The camp was six miles from the farm, and they were moving on. Freedom didn't want his stallion broken in yet. Any travellers seeing him might try for him, the horse was a rare one. This way, keeping him wild, only Freedom could handle him and would break him when he was ready.

Apples and crusts bulged in Freedom's jacket pocket, and as he came close to the gate he saw the great beast toss his head, his black eyes flashing. In one movement Freedom legged it on to the gate, and sat on the top bar. He called the stallion 'Kaulo', the Romany word for black, and black he was. The horse pawed the ground, snorting.

'*Choom, choom*', Freedom whispered, meaning 'kiss, kiss', and the stallion moved slowly towards his master, tossing his powerful head. He nuzzled Freedom's open palm, got his apple and crust of bread, and then as if playing a game he backed away. Freedom was too fast for him, he grabbed the flowing mane and jumped, heeled his beauty forwards and they galloped around the wide, open field.

Evelyne lay back, the brook bubbled and gurgled, and she looked up into the bright clear sky. The sound of horse's hooves seemed to come from beneath her, underground. She sat up, waded across the brook and stood on tiptoe to look into the distant field.

The black-haired boy and the stallion galloped round and round and, bareback, the boy seemed to be part of the horse, his hair as black as the stallion's gleaming coat. The boy wore a red neckerchief and an old striped flannel shirt. Evelyne knew at first glance that he was a gypsy – she had seen them come to the village often enough with their ponies to sell to the pits. She and her brothers had never been allowed near the camp, their Da decreeing that his children would not mix with the gypsies ever. No matter how they had pleaded with him they were not allowed even to go to the fairs. They had cried bitter tears because all the other village children had been allowed to go, but on this one subject Hugh Jones was adamant.

Evelyne shaded her eyes, watching the boy riding, and tutted like a little old maid. Those wild gypsy boys would never come to anything. Maybe her Da was right, they were a bad lot and always thieving, so everyone said. She closed her eyes – oh, how very different her David was, now *there* was a gentleman.

She waded back across the brook and felt her clothes, they were almost dry. She began to think about David, he had certainly been inside the inn a long time. She stared over the hedge, saw the black car drive away. Funny, there in the field was that gleaming black horse, and down below in the yard by the inn the gleaming black motor. Evelyne mused, she'd prefer the motor if ever given the choice.

Her sodden shoe had shrunk, it fitted her now, but still smelt quite terrible. She stood up and stamped her foot, then bent down to pick up her skirt. She turned, looked back again – it had disappeared. She scratched her head, then walked round the bush to see if it had slipped down the other side.

Freedom was stunned. It was her hair, he had never seen a colour like it. She was the palest *manushi* he had ever seen, with hair of *sonnikey*. He gaped, then swallowed hard. She was looking at him, staring, and she had the eyes of a sea witch. They stood for a moment, frozen, his dark eyes brooding, his olive skin clear, not swarthy, his high cheekbones giving him a look of arrogance. His mouth was wide, and just as Evelyne was about to scream he smiled, showing the most perfect strong, white teeth. She was no longer afraid when he smiled, but she was still in her drawers, so she covered herself with her hands.

'Are you not chilled swimmin', gel?'

Evelyne put her hands on her hips and pursed her lips with anger. This common gyppo was standing on her skirt. All thought of behaving in a ladylike fashion left her.

'I am not swimming. I was . . . excuse me, would you mind leaving? I am not dressed.'

Freedom chuckled, but made no move to leave. He cocked his head to one side, looking her up and down which made her blush and grow so hot she didn't know what to do. But she couldn't just leave because he was still standing on her skirt.

'That's my *gry*, yonder, the stallion.'

'What?'

'I said that's my stallion yonder. I've a right to be in the field, are thee from this part?'

'No, I'm not, would you please go away?'

Freedom gave her a twinkling smile.

'I shall scream, please go away.'

But still he stood on her skirt.

'Get off my skirt, please, you are standing on my skirt.'

He hopped away, then with deliberate movements he picked up the skirt and shook it, held it out by the waistband as though for her to step into it.

'It's best thee dress yerself, gel, there's many a-wandering around these parts . . . here, give me your hand.'

Angrily, she took his hand and stepped into the skirt, then moved back sharply and began to do up the small buttons.

'Thank you.'

81

'It's my pleasure.'

David's voice echoed up from the inn's courtyard, calling her name. She backed away from Freedom but still he made no effort to leave. He lolled against the trunk of a tree, his eyes never straying from her face for an instant.

'Evelyne . . .? Evelyne . . .? *Evelyne?*'

She turned and ran a few yards, stopped to look back. He was still there. He cocked his head to one side and kissed the tips of his fingers. He repeated her name, and she tossed her head, glaring, her golden-red hair swirled around her, and then she was gone. Like a monkey, Freedom climbed the tree until he was perched high up in the branches. He watched her running down the courtyard and could see the uniformed figure pacing up and down impatiently.

By the time Evelyne, out of breath, reached David, he was irate. He could not believe the state she had managed to get herself into. Her hair was loose, her clothes, dreadful to start with, were creased and damp. As he inhaled angrily he caught the stench of cow dung. He gestured for her to climb into the passenger seat, not even bothering to open the door for her, then slammed the car into gear with a crashing, grinding noise. The car jolted forward so fast that Evelyne was pressed back against the seat.

Hearing a peal of laughter, Evelyne turned, looked back at the inn to see a blonde girl standing at one of the top windows. She was in her underwear, and even from this distance Evelyne could see her thickly painted red lips.

'Coooeeee, David . . . coooeee, lovey . . . David . . .'

David looked up at the window, and to Evelyne's

horror the girl blatantly bared her breast, flicked her tongue out at David and shrieked with raucous laughter. Evelyne couldn't believe her eyes – she looked at David, then back at the inn. An officer in uniform was now standing behind the blonde woman, and he too was roaring with laughter.

'Who's that, David? Who is that terrible woman?'

David snapped, his face furious, 'That is a cheap whore, a paid woman, a prostitute, a tart, a common slag . . .'

'But why was she calling you?'

'How the hell do I know? Shut up, I don't want to talk about it.'

He ground his teeth, his mouth set in a thin, tight line. He felt dirty, the women had wanted more money, although he knew Ridgely had paid them already, and it annoyed him. They were just like the whores in France, out for every cent they could get. He felt unclean, used, and wanted to get home for a bath as fast as he could. He hadn't really enjoyed himself, it was all bravado – the Ridgelys of this world, rich as Croesus, loved the tarts, the whores, but David didn't. He made up his mind he wouldn't go with another. They were all the same. Worse was the humiliation, because Ridgely had told him he'd been watching his performance, and it would be all round the barracks in no time.

'I saw a gypsy boy . . .'

David looked at her, through her, and muttered something inaudible as he swerved the car round the gatepost of the inn.

Freedom remained high up in the tree. He whistled softly, then watched the sports car bouncing across the cobbled courtyard. He screeched like a bird, high-

83

pitched . . . Evelyne saw him just as he swung down from the tree and raised his arm, waving to her. She turned away quickly, annoyed at herself for wanting to take another look. David swung the car along a track running beside a field, then out into a narrow lane.

'Do we have to go so fast?'

David said nothing, but he slowed down. The weeds and brambles on either side of the lane scratched against the sides of the open car, and Evelyne held her hands up to protect her face. When she took them down again she saw Freedom on his stallion, galloping through the fields alongside them. He rode bareback, clinging to the horse's mane, urging it forward and jumping the hedgerows, keeping up with the car, he was going so fast . . . Evelyne stared, it frightened her, the black horse, the boy so dark, his shoulder-length hair streaming out behind him. She gasped, clung to the windscreen – ahead of the horse and rider was a high, fenced hedge. He would never make it, he couldn't, it was too high. She screamed.

Freedom urged the *gry* on, felt the muscles straining beneath him, and then they were flying through the air. He let rip with a shout of sheer exhilaration, pure joy . . .

'*Stop! David, stop . . . stop!*'

The car screeched to a halt, almost in a ditch.

'What is it, what?'

But horse and rider had disappeared, there wasn't even the sound of hooves.

'Evelyne, for God's sake what's the matter? Did we hit something?'

'No, no, it was nothing, it was no one.'

Freedom stood with his arms wrapped around his stallion's neck, their lungs heaving as though they were one. The horse tossed his magnificent head, snorting, and Freedom laughed.

'Did thee see her, Kaulo?' Isn't she *rinkeney*, eh boy?'

Minnie the housemaid had run a steaming bath and was hovering at the bathroom door. She had been given instructions by the doctor himself to clean the girl up because she smelt so much. Minnie felt sorry for her, and even more so when Evelyne had stripped off – she was like a skeleton, and her ribs could be seen clearly. As for her undergarments, they were not even fit to clean the brass with.

Doris still lay in the darkened room with an icepack on her forehead. She had not touched her food, even the slightest noise seemed to pain her. Dr Collins sat with her for a while, taking her temperature. He was not too worried, saying it was just a migraine.

'But I feel so ill, and sometimes I just go dizzy, like a fainting fit, and the pain moves from one side of my head to the other.'

The Doctor pursed his lips, hissed softly and looked, as always, at his fob watch. 'Well, you rest up, don't worry about the young gel, perhaps if you could eat a small meal . . . I'll get Minnie to bring you something on a tray.'

Doris murmured that she didn't feel well enough to eat, and the strain of talking made her head worse as if thousands of tiny hammers were beating against her eyes.

*

Evelyne slipped into the hot, soapy water, her face pink with embarrassment at seeing Minnie pick up her clothes as if she had fleas, and holding them from her at arm's length.

'I fell in a cow pat, but I washed them.'

Minnie murmured that judging by the smell, she'd brought the cows home with her. The problem was that Evelyne had no change of clothes and even if Minnie washed them, they'd never be dry before dinner. Minnie soaped Evelyne's back and bony shoulders, then went to the door, locked it tight, and leant over the bathtub, speaking in a whisper.

'I'll bring you some things, but don't say nothin' about where I got 'em from, all right lovey?'

She nipped out of the bathroom and was back within minutes with a neat pile of fresh white underwear. There was a camisole with a small frill round the neck, a pair of satin bloomers with elastic at the knees, and a petticoat.

'They was the Mistress's, but he don't know what's in the wardrobe. Me an' cook have delved in there a few times, see, everything's just left in the drawers, terrible waste.'

Evelyne blushed with shame at Minnie stealing from the Doctor's dead wife.

Unlike the rest of the house, there was warmth and friendliness in the big basement kitchen. Mrs Darwin, the cook, was a round, fat woman who bellowed with laughter when she saw Evelyne in the huge bloomers, and gave her a wet, motherly kiss. Evelyne's hand-me-downs were steaming on the fireguard and an iron sat on the burner ready to press them.

The front doorbell chimed and Minnie rushed out. They had visitors and the Doctor asked for tea to be served right away. Evelyne watched the fat Mrs Darwin move like lightning, setting the tea tray, wrapping a gold frill around the cake, cutting tiny cucumber sandwiches, everything done fast and efficiently.

Evelyne, not wanting to get in the way, sat quietly by the fireside, taking it all in.

'He wants you in for tea, lovely, he's asking where you are.'

Mrs Darwin threw up her hands in despair. How could the girl go up in her bloomers, her skirt wasn't ironed yet. Minnie fetched the ironing cloths, laid them on the edge of the kitchen table and began to press the skirt. Mrs Darwin tried to tidy Evelyne's hair, but she'd never before had to cope with such length and such thickness, and in the end decided to put it in a long braid down her back, whipping out the ribbon from the frilled camisole and tying it in a bow. At the same time Minnie helped Evelyne into the freshly-pressed skirt, and banged the iron over the blouse.

'Shoes, where's the girl's shoes, for heaven's sake, Minnie?'

Evelyne was painfully self-conscious, Minnie's shoes were too tight and made high-pitched squeaking noises as she entered the drawing-room. Dr Collins rose to his feet and introduced Evelyne to the two guests who were sitting, straight-backed, on the velvet sofa.

'This is the young girl I was telling you about, this is Evelyne ... Lady Sybil Warner, and her daughter, Heather.'

The pair looked so regal, Evelyne wondered if she should curtsey. Lady Warner shimmered with rows and rows of multi-coloured beads, amber and ivory, draped across her ample bosom. Her daughter, dressed in oyster silk with a matching hat, had unfortunate buck teeth, which made her appear to smirk. Evelyne shook the outstretched, beringed hand, then squeaked her way to a chair.

'Lady Sybil has very kindly invited you to a soirée this evening, Evelyne, and as Doris is no better, I er . . . well, I . . .'

Evelyne had not the slightest notion what a soirée was. She gave the Doctor a perplexed look as Lady Sybil spoke in a very high-pitched warbling tone, as if savouring each trill and tremor.

'We all have to do our part for the war effort, and I am sure you will enjoy yourself. Some of the boys are from the hospital, some are on leave, always good to have a new dancing partner . . . Heather?'

Heather blinked, startled.

'Come along, dear, we must be on our way.' Lady Sybil rose majestically to her feet, 'Thank you so much for your advice, I will make sure Heather remains on your diet . . . so nice to meet you, *Eevaleen*.'

Heather gave Evelyne a doleful look as she followed her mother. Just as Lady Sybil and Dr Collins reached the hall, David arrived home. He removed his hat with a sweeping gesture.

'Lady Sybil, I must apologize for my lateness, but I was held up at the barracks.'

'Don't apologize, David dear, quite understandable, and we shall be seeing you both this evening. Heather, say hello to David. Thank you again, Dr Collins, come along, Heather.'

Evelyne craned forward to see them depart and then went over to the window. A Rolls-Royce was parked outside, with a uniformed chauffeur holding the door open. She could hear David and his father talking in the hall.

'Don't tell me, Pa, you are actually socializing this evening?'

'No, no, I'm on duty, but Lady Sybil kindly invited Evelyne.'

'What?'

'Yes, most kind, Doris isn't well enough to travel, it'll be a nice outing for the girl.'

'Outing? Outing? Father, it's a dance, really, you might have discussed it with me.'

'You weren't here . . . where are you going? David?'

David looked into the drawing-room and met Evelyne's startled gaze. He cocked his head to one side.

'Well, it appears Cinderella's been invited to the ball.'

The next moment David was running up the stairs calling for Minnie to run his bath. Soirée, dance, now a ball – Evelyne couldn't make out what on earth they were talking about. Dr Collins walked in and caught her bewildered expression. He felt sorry for her. 'Pay him no attention, you'd like to go, wouldn't you?'

Evelyne chewed her lip. Just thinking of spending an evening with David made her so excited she couldn't speak. The Doctor opened his wallet and coughed, a nervous, ticklish cough.

'Don't suppose you brought a party frock with you, so, Minnie . . .?'

Minnie was just rushing up the stairs after David.

'I'm just going to run Master David's bath, he's already had one today so I don't know how hot the water will be.'

'Minnie, will you take Evelyne out and get her a frock to wear for a dance?'

The Doctor handed Minnie a folded note and then glanced at his fob watch, murmured that he must be off and scuttled out. Minnie looked at the five-pound note and her jaw dropped.

'Lord love us, look how much he give me! Get your coat, lovely, I'll be two minutes.'

Evelyne hadn't even had time to thank Dr Collins, it had all happened so quickly. She squeaked up the stairs after Minnie, who disappeared into the bathroom to run David's bath.

Evelyne was buttoning her coat when she saw David coming out of his room, barefoot and wrapping his dressing gown around him.

'Well, well, appears we are going out together tonight.'

Evelyne swallowed, unable to look into his teasing, smiling face. As she passed him he quickly tugged her hair. She stopped, but he continued down the corridor to the bathroom.

Minnie was waiting for Evelyne at the foot of the stairs.

'Come on, hurry, I don't want to be caught by Mrs Darwin, she'll find something for me to do and we need all the time we can get. Come on, we'll go out the front way.'

Evelyne followed her out and as the door closed behind them, Minnie snorted.

'I never known a man take so many baths, ever so particular, isn't he?'

David was actually in rather a good mood. The chaps had ribbed him quite a lot about his afternoon at the inn, but he was now very much 'in' with the 'in' set, and everyone had been impressed with Ridgely's account of David's prowess with the two ladies.

He lay in the perfumed, soapy water. His skin tingled as he scrubbed himself hard with the loofah, worried that he may have picked up some disease from the tarts. He shivered with revulsion, remembering their bodies: he couldn't understand why on earth Ridgely and the other officers enjoyed these prostitutes. They revolted him, but the improvement in his reputation made it worthwhile. He set about scrubbing himself with renewed vigour, perhaps he would find someone more to his liking at the Warners' dance.

Evelyne and Minnie took the tram into the centre of Cardiff. They didn't go to any of the big stores with the elegant models in the windows – they went down a back lane into a small second-hand shop run by a Jewish family. Minnie assured Evelyne that this was where all the posh people who had fallen on hard times sold off their dresses, and they were sure to find something at half the price they would pay in any of the fashion houses. The added bonus of this arrangement was that, as Minnie knew one of the shop assistants, maybe they would get a few shillings off their purchases.

Jeremiah Goldstein's tailoring establishment and pawn shop was a back street hovel. Rows and rows of suits hung on racks, and there were shirts stacked to the ceiling. Minnie knew everyone in the shop, and Evelyne wondered how many of the doctor's wife's clothes had found their way here.

Minnie's friend was named Clara. They kissed and joked with each other, then Clara opened up an Aladdin's cave of ball gowns, feather boas and sequins. There was a smell of body odour in the room, of stale perfume clinging to the garments. Clara walked around Evelyne, looking her up and down.

'She's a right bugger to fit, our Minnie, she's all skin and bone for one, and then there's her height. She's not a dainty one, that's for sure.'

Gown after gown was taken down from the rails. Whether they were too short or too long they all looked dreadful. Clara disappeared and came back with her arms full of bridal gowns.

'Eh, she's not getting married, our Clara, they won't do. For Gawd's sake, she just wants a dancing dress, a lovely frock that swings when she moves . . .'

Clara ignored Minnie and held up a cream satin. She pulled the dress over Evelyne's head, at the same time giving Minnie instructions to go to her cousin Bertha 'what does all the ladies' hair in the salon in the main street'.

The bride must have been as tall as Evelyne, the dress was the first one that was the right length. None of them had any thought about what fashion was now in, they wanted something long and swirling. Clara was snipping round the back with a large pair of scissors, then she whipped out a box of pins. She snipped some silk orchids off a peachy-coloured dress and started pinning them round the neck.

'Have to hide her salt cellars, you could balance a teacup on those bones . . .'

Evelyne was covered in pins, and still trying on shoe after shoe. Eventually, buried beneath a pile of feather boas, they found a pair of cream satin shoes with lavatory-shaped heels. They made Evelyne that much taller, but Clara assured her the hem would drop a bit anyway.

By five-thirty Evelyne was so tired she wanted to go to sleep, but there was no rest for her. She was bathed and perfumed, keeping the noise down all the while so as not to disturb Doris. Minnie said Evelyne would not have time to eat, she would need all the time until eight o'clock to get herself dressed up.

Bertha, her mouth full of hairpins, brushed and braided, twisted and curled the mass of golden-red hair.

92

By seven-thirty Evelyne's hair was still not quite ready, but the dress hung waiting for her to slip into it. Mrs Darwin had whitened the shoes slightly, as you could tell they had been worn. Minnie suddenly jumped up, panic-stricken, they'd forgotten to get Evelyne a cloak, how could she travel there in an open motor without a cloak, she'd freeze to death.

Minnie disappeared to poor, dead Mrs Collins' wardrobe, which was becoming remarkably sparse. She returned with a glum face saying there was only the black mourning cloak Mrs Collins had worn for funerals. Mrs Darwin told her to fetch it, it wasn't the wrapping that counted, it was what was inside, and no one would notice, they'd whip some of the black ribbons off it.

Finally, Evelyne was ready, and Minnie, Bertha and Mrs Darwin stared. It was a shame, there wasn't one item of jewellery on the girl, but they'd done it, she was ready, and she could be taken for a lady any day of the week. Evelyne looked at her reflection and her mouth trembled. This wasn't, couldn't be, Evelyne Jones . . .

Bertha sat on Minnie's bed, picking up hairpins and tiny ribbons. Minnie came in and ran to the window.

'She's going now.'

Bertha joined her at the window and they stared out, watching the car slowly draw away from the dark pavement.

Doris clung to the window-frame watching her sweet Evie leave the house. She looked so beautiful, and Doris felt so proud. Weak and tired out, she held on to the furniture as she made her way back to bed, replaced the icepack on her brow and sighed. She began to daydream

93

of her wedding day, of her beloved Walter. That was what Evelyne had looked like, a bride.

There was a sweeping gravel driveway, and several other cars already parked by the house. Evelyne's head was spinning, she had never seen such comings and goings. The mansion was white, with pillars and huge trees on either side. Lamps illuminated the garden and the lake, and on the velvety lawns the bushes were thread with tiny glass candleholders all in different colours. She had to pinch herself to believe she wasn't dreaming.

David waited at the bottom of the steps with a look of irritation on his handsome face as Evelyne stumbled out of the car. He sighed, knowing this was a mistake. She'd almost fallen flat on her face and they weren't even inside yet. Together they walked up the steps to the main entrance. The double doors stood wide to reveal a marble hallway with more footmen and guests milling about. Music drifted from a ballroom with gilt-edged glass doors, flowers arranged on pedestals at least four feet high exuded their perfume into the air, vying with the fragrances of the laughing, chattering ladies. The sights, the smells, textures and ambience of wealth overpowered Evelyne. Her heart seemed to jump in her chest, her breath came in short gasps, and tremors shook her body. Only the gentle touch of David's hand on her elbow gave her the assurance that this was real, not a dream from which she would soon awaken. But her over-riding emotion was terror. Behind the masks of smiles, the bows of the footmen, the fleeting glances from the other guests, Evelyne felt they could see right through her – they could see she didn't belong, she was an outsider.

A small, sweet, white-haired woman was taking care

of the guests' cloaks. She darted forward to help Evelyne with hers, then with a tiny wave of her hand she directed her to a powder room with a row of gilt-edged mirrors and small velvet piano stools. At least, that was what they looked like to Evelyne. Several girls sat or stood around chattering and powdering their faces, touching the flowers in their hair, dabbing themselves with chiffon hankies dipped in crystal bottles of cologne. Their bracelets jangled and their diamonds glittered. They greeted each other in squealing voices, flinging their arms around each other. Kisses were exchanged, and admiring remarks about each other's frocks.

One of the stools became vacant, and Evelyne sat down and mimicked the actions of the girl next to her. She was like a tiny china doll, with pale blonde, curly hair, wide blue eyes and rosy cheeks. She wore the palest pink gown, and her tiny feet were encased in satin shoes. She turned for a moment, giving Evelyne an icy stare that swept from the top of her head to the scrubbed, second-hand shoes. She continued talking to her friends as she stared, then turned back, leaned slightly forward and cupped her hands to her tiny rosebud mouth. Her friends tittered and two other girls leaned back slightly to stare at Evelyne.

David hovered outside, waiting for her. He saw everyone coming out and wondered what on earth Evelyne could be doing in there. Then his look of impatience changed. Leaving the powder room was an angel. Lady Primrose Boyd-Carpenter couldn't help but notice David, who was one of the most handsome men she had ever seen. As she passed him she gave him a tiny smile. David's heart lurched in his chest and, forgetting Evelyne, he turned and followed the vision in the floating pink. She appeared to be very well-known, everyone acknowledged her. Officers kissed her hand as she made her way slowly towards the ballroom. Twice she turned back, aware that David was following, then she was surrounded by a chattering party of people. David caught the arm of his closest friend, Captain Freddy Carlton.

'Freddy, who is she, who is she?'

Freddy laughed, raised his eyebrows.

'Not for you, old chap, she's already taken, that is Lady Primrose Boyd-Carpenter.'

'Introduce me, you have to introduce me, I'm in love.'

Freddy beamed, his round, good-natured face glowed above his solid frame.

'So am I, and I was there before you, she's mine, so don't you dare move in. I've been after her for months.'

David leaned against the wall, watching Freddy, full of himself, easing his way through the crowd to Lady Primrose's side. She turned her heart-shaped, perfect face to smile up at Freddy, then stood on tiptoe to kiss his cheek, slipping his hand through his arm. David could have sworn she flicked a knowing look at him as she began to introduce Freddy to her party of friends. The titles rolled, Lady this, the Honourable that, and again David could have sworn that her wicked, twinkling smile was for him alone. He was besotted.

Captain Ridgely, already flushed with champagne, breezed up to David. 'Lovely little thing, isn't she, but I'm here to tell you it's a kiss on the cheek from that quarter. Place your hand on that type of gel's knee and all hell gets let loose.'

David pointed towards Lady Primrose, 'Line me up there, Ridgely, and you'll be my friend for life.'

Ridgely snorted. 'You must be joking, that's Lady Primmy, old boy, her family owns most of the mines in these parts. Besides, Freddy Carlton's got a pash for her, look at the drooling idiot. Her family no doubt already has it arranged, ya know, titles and money always marry each other . . . you, having neither, don't stand a chance . . . oh, I say, this is more my line, look what's hovering yonder.'

David turned to see poor Evelyne standing awkwardly at the powder-room door. Angry at Ridgely's insinuation that Lady Primrose wouldn't even consider him, he snapped.

'That's unfortunately with me, some wretched charge of my aunt's, if you want her, for goodness' sake take her . . .'

At that moment a fuzzy blonde swept into Ridgely's arms and demanded a dance. He departed, giving David a lewd wink.

'Another time, what?'

David sighed and walked across to Evelyne. Begrudgingly, he gave her his arm and led her towards the ballroom.

The next disaster was the dancing. It had never occurred to Evelyne that at this sort of dance they didn't do jigs, and gallop around like they did in the Salvation Army Hall. David led her to a small couch and told her to sit there while he fetched her a glass of champagne. He then disappeared into the throng of dancers. Most of the young men were in uniform, and everyone seemed to know everyone else, calling out, waving, and whizzing past on the dance floor.

Evelyne sat waiting, looking and waiting, and eventually David came back to her side with champagne in a delicate, fluted glass.

'Don't gulp it, Flamehead, just sip.'

Lady Primrose danced past, giving David another flickering, darting glance, and he turned and gazed after her pink, floating figure. Then he moved away without another word, and Evelyne wrinkled her nose as the champagne bubbles fizzed, but she quite liked the taste. It was sharper than lemonade, and icy cold, and she drained the glass and sat twiddling the stem.

David danced past with Heather Warner. The girl was sweating, swathed in tulle and net, and while she looked like a powder puff, David made her feel like the most important girl at the dance. He leaned close, feeling her plump, jelly-like body quiver.

'Tell me, Heather, that girl in pink, is it Lady Primrose? Only I am sure I know her family . . .'

Heather trod on his foot as she peered round, then blinked up into his handsome face.

'Yes, Lady Primrose Boyd-Carpenter. She's very pretty, isn't she?'

David smiled into the buck teeth and held Heather closer, placed his cheek against hers. She sighed, her frustrated passion mounting. 'Oh, she's all right . . . I must say, you're very light on your feet, Heather.'

The poor girl nearly swooned, unaware that David was slowly manoeuvring her closer and closer to Lady Primrose, until she was forced to introduce him.

'Primrose, this is David Collins, David, Lady Primrose Boyd-Carpenter.'

David bowed, kissing the delicate, white-gloved hand, and asked if he would be permitted a dance. Lady Primmy excused herself to Freddy, who was glowering at David, and they moved off to the centre of the floor. She was so fragile, so delicate, and he held her as if she were precious glass, he couldn't take his eyes off her. She smelt so fresh, her hair shone and her wondrous eyes sparkled, and dancing with her was like twirling a feather. Neither of them spoke, they just looked into one another's eyes, then smiled as Freddy huffed and puffed past, pushing Heather around as if she were a wheelbarrow.

A butler approached Evelyne with a large silver tray, and bent low towards her. She wasn't sure what he wanted, and she looked, licked her lips and placed her empty glass on the tray. He still waited, so she took another full one and smiled her thanks.

At the far end of the dance floor sat a group of uniformed soldiers. Two of them wore arm bandages, one had a large pad on one eye. Another sat in a wheelchair. They seemed out of place, holding the fluted glasses with care, afraid to drop them or snap them in their big fists, as they watched the dancers gliding past. Evelyne could tell they were as uncomfortable as she was.

Lady Sybil Warner looked over at Evelyne then searched the ballroom for David. The poor girl was still sitting alone on the sofa. Lady Sybil weaved her way towards Evelyne. More beads and feathers than ever floated around her, she was like a ship in full sail. 'Now, dear, are you enjoying yourself? Come along, come along, let me introduce you to some young men, can't have you sitting all alone, now can we? Follow me, come along.'

She introduced Evelyne to the young soldiers. Her feathers tickled their noses and she got everyone's names wrong, but they were all so nervous they didn't like to correct her. Evelyne sat and tried to think of something interesting to say, but nothing would break through her headful of pins and bows.

'Would you like to dance, Miss?'

Evelyne bit her lip, then hedged, and finally admitted

it – she actually couldn't dance. The soldier boy laughed, throwing back his head.

'We all thought you was a duchess sittin' over yonder, too good for the likes of us. Yer can't dance, girl, is that true?'

Evelyne nodded. These lads weren't the same as the young officers on the dance floor, they were her own kind, like her brothers.

'Well, I've never done this fancy two-and-two-step, but can you polka?'

Evelyne nodded, she could do a polka all right. Lizzie-Ann had taught her that. So they waited for a polka and now they were talking freely to her and asking questions. They came from different parts, but they all had families working the mines.

As the boys talked Evelyne's eyes kept straying to the dancers. David was dancing yet again with Lady Primrose, they looked perfect together. Heather appeared with small beads of sweat along her upper lip, her dress stained at the armpits.

'Are you enjoying yourselves? Food will be served in a moment.'

'Would you like to dance, miss?'

'Pardon?'

'Dance, you want a dance?'

Heather licked her rabbit teeth, nonplussed, and stuck out her arms. The young soldier, wearing heavy boots, guided her on to the floor. All the boys sniggered and whispered about her teeth.

'Always the way, ain't it, eh? All this money an' she got a face like a buckin' bronco, she looks like she's been eatin' too many of these toffees her family makes.'

Evelyne knew she shouldn't but she couldn't help laughing with the lads.

One boy, the boy in the wheelchair, didn't smile, he

sat staring into the dancers as if they weren't there. His eyes were glazed, dead, empty. Evelyne moved to the seat next to him. The boy seemed hardly aware of her. A red-haired soldier with bright red cheeks moved along to sit beside Evelyne.

'He'll not talk, he's shell-shocked, he don't know where he is, been like it for two days since they brought him home.'

Four more soldiers pulled their chairs closer, forming a protective circle with the vacant-eyed boy in the centre. They started to talk as if they needed to, the dancing and the champagne were all very well, but they had seen things, terrible things, and none of them wanted to go back. Their stories gushed out like rivers in flood, and Evelyne listened. She wanted to hold them in her arms, she felt their fear and confusion, and thought of Dicken and her darling brother Mike; they had gone off to a war she knew nothing about. The more the lads talked about what they were up against, the more Evelyne feared for her brothers. War was a long way from this elegant house, the orchestra, the young, dashing men in their cavalry uniforms. Evelyne realized that many of the so-called officers had never been to the Front. They were all show, like peacocks, in their braid and polished boots.

'Wait 'til they see what the Germans are like, lot of them won't be dancin' then, be lucky if they still got their legs.'

The tight group was suddenly aware that couples were drifting into a large side room where a long trestle table had been laid out, the weight of the food bending the legs. Food! The lads rose in unison, then they remembered they were with a lady and turned back, but she grinned at them. She stood up and moved to the silent one, bent over him, touched his face. The lads moved off towards the food and Evelyne took hold of the silent boy's hand.

'Would you like something to eat, lad?'

The vacant eyes stared towards her – so empty they frightened her. Slowly the boy lifted his hand. It was a strange move, his hand wavered, moving to her face. Then she felt his rough hand touch her cheek. She held his hand and kissed his fingers. The sad-eyed boy was so helpless, so cut off from reality, and his mouth moved, he was trying to speak. She moved her head closer.

'Mama . . .?'

Evelyne piled up a plate with chicken and ham, sweet rolled things with bacon wrapped around them, and tiny sausages on wooden sticks. The plate was so full, she dared not heap on any more. She was unaware of anyone watching her, of the nudges and the smiles or of David's eyes, bright and angry. He was ashamed, it looked as though the girl had never eaten in her life. Lady Primrose at his side ate with delicate, bird-like movements. She smiled up at him with her rosebud mouth.

'Do tell me, David, who on earth is that creature, and where exactly did you find her?'

David was very angry and flushed with embarrassment, he glared at Evelyne and then turned his back on her.

'My aunt works in a school in one of the mining villages, she's some sort of orphan, one has to do one's bit.'

Lady Primrose muttered, 'Poor thing', and her sweet voice trilled, agreeing that of course one simply had to do one's bit.

Several of the guests watched the tall girl in the flowing gown as she walked straight back to the sad, vacant-eyed boy in his wheelchair. They watched her place the napkin across his knee. Then she sat next to him and gently fed the boy with her own hands.

If anyone felt guilty they didn't admit it, but they remembered then the reason for the dance. It was not for flirting and courting, it was to give the boys who had come from the Front a night to remember. They were aware that the number of boys actually from the Front was exceedingly small, but then they knew mostly young officers anyway. Lady Primrose murmured, and it was hastily passed on, that Evelyne was a poor orphaned soul and all the gels there would react the same way if the officers they danced with came home wounded.

The ballroom had become very hot, the hundreds of candles and the great chandelier in the centre of the room shimmered and cigar smoke hung in a haze from the small smoking room. David seemed to have disappeared. The red-haired soldier pressed his face up against the window and rubbed the condensation clear as he gazed out into the garden.

'Eh, there's a big bird yonder with a long feathered tail!'

Two more of the boys scrambled up to stare out of the windows. They were becoming a trifle rowdy, having discovered that there were spirits to drink. Evelyne excused herself, she could feel her dress sticking to her body and could hardly breathe in the heat of the room.

There were several couples standing outside the gilded doors that opened on to a flower-strewn balcony overlooking the gardens with steps that led down either side to the velvet lawns. Evelyne was grateful for the cool night air and breathed deeply; no smoke, no soot here, the air was fresh and clean. She wandered down the garden, bending to smell the perfume of the roses, pure sweet fragrances in comparison to the ladies' scents.

The peacock screamed and it made Evelyne jump, then the bird swung its head and turned. As if dancing for her, it spread its tail, the colours shining in the twinkling lamplight. She laughed, thrilled by the sheer beauty of the bird, and moved closer and closer, and was suddenly knocked right off her feet by the most enormous dog she had ever seen. She sprawled face down, and the dog licked her cheek.

A small, rotund gentleman in rather ill-fitting evening clothes came rushing round the rosebushes. Red-faced, puffing with exertion, he made a grab for the dog's trailing lead and landed with a thud next to Evelyne.

'I apologize profusely, Madam . . .'

The dog stood over him and licked his face, making the gentleman's snow-white hair stand on end. Evelyne was on her feet first, and helped the gentleman to his feet. He bowed, and with one hand holding the dog's lead he apologized again, but his eyes twinkled and his arm was jerked back and forth. He whispered that he was just giving his friend a spot of exercise before he had to parade like the peacock he'd just scared off.

The gentleman's manner was so warm and friendly that Evelyne found herself automatically linking arms with him, and together they walked around the wonderful gardens. He pointed out various flowers to her, he knew almost every one by name. He asked her name, repeated it, and then wanted to know all about her and where she came from. Evelyne told him, and when she started to explain about her gown, and Bertha and Minnie, the laughter shook his whole body, his right arm still constantly being jerked by the massive St Bernard.

'But you *can* polka, is that right? Well then, may I

ask you to give me the honour of a polka, or would you like me to give you the fastest dancing lesson? I'm not what you might call a light one on my feet, but by God I can and would love to waltz with you.'

There on the lawn, with his dog tied to a privet hedge and instructed to sit, the white-haired gentleman began to teach Evelyne the simplest one-two-three waltz step. He kept up a funny commentary about 'Now you move back, now you come forward, not on my foot, young lady, turn yourself around, that's a girl, by God you're light on your feet, just like a fawn . . . round you go again . . .'

The strains of the orchestra drifted down to the lawn as they danced, the old gentleman with his head full of white hair, and the tall skinny girl in the old-fashioned gown.

The St Bernard was then dragged off, and Evelyne returned to the house. She examined her face in the powder-room mirror. Her skin was shining, her cheeks rosy from the fresh night air, and Bertha's coiffure about to tumble down from its hundreds of pins. The orchestra stopped playing, and two girls rushed out of the room. The attendant peeked around the door.

'He's here, he's here himself, be quick or you'll miss him.'

Evelyne rushed to the door, not really knowing who it was she might miss.

A crowd had gathered at the ballroom doors. Sybil Warner was on the bandstand, and to thunderous applause she introduced Lloyd George himself. Evelyne could just see his shock of white hair above the heads of the group listening by the door. He gave a short, rousing speech, thanked Sybil for her efforts, and toasted 'The Boys in Uniform', wishing them God's luck and telling them to enjoy themselves while they could. Then he turned to the waiting orchestra, and in his enormous, mellifluous voice, demanded to know if they could play a polka, he was exceedingly fond of the polka . . .

Lloyd George stepped down from the bandstand, and searched the faces of the guests. He caught sight of Evelyne and gave her a bow, held his hand out to her as the orchestra struck up a polka. He led the blushing Evelyne to the centre of the ballroom, whispered to her that she was doing just fine, and they danced. For the first few bars they danced alone on the huge floor, then other couples joined them. Lady Sybil complained to David, her nose completely out of joint, that she should have opened the dancing with Lloyd George, it was outrageous. David didn't seem to hear her, he just stared at Evelyne. How in God's name had *that* come about? Captain Ridgely passed David and whispered to him from the side of his mouth.

'Old boy certainly can pick 'em, what? Stunning-looking gel.'

David glanced at Evelyne and raised one eyebrow slightly.

'Takes all tastes, old chap, but then he is notorious for his rough side, gel's an orphan from the valleys.'

Captain Ridgely murmured that Lloyd George wasn't the only one who liked a bit of rough. He nudged David and winked.

'I did a good turn for you, what you say you arrange something for me with that delicious redhead, is it a deal? What you say?'

David glanced at Evelyne; she made no impression on him whatever, the common touch left him cold. However, David wanted to keep on the right side of Ridgely, and he gave him an equally lewd wink and returned the nudge.

David could see Lady Primrose talking quietly with

106

Freddy Carlton. Now there was someone who really interested him. Not only was she virginal, beautiful and wealthy but, to add icing to the already delicious cake, she was titled. David leaned close to Ridgely and whispered. They both glanced at Evelyne and then put their heads together again.

The dance seemed to end all too quickly, and Lloyd George moved off towards the soldiers, sat with them and talked and listened earnestly. As he got up to leave he touched the top of the sad-eyed boy's head. He didn't look back at Evelyne until he reached the main doors, then he smiled to her, and with a wave of his hand he was gone.

The orchestra began to move out of their seats, and a band of colourful gypsy men and women entered the ballroom. The women wore bright skirts and headbands, and were decked out in gold jewellery. They smiled and 'entertained' their audience, but their eyes were unfathomable. Smiling lips, friendly gestures, and yet there was an untouchable air to them. They remained aloof, distant.

The fiddlers played well, walking around the room while waiters served tea and brandy. Some guests were already departing, others sat talking. A large group, mostly women, moved into the card-room, where two gypsy women prepared to read fortunes from palms and Tarot cards. There was no need to cross their palms with silver, as Sybil had settled an overall price with them before their arrival. The soldiers were leaving, returning to their barracks, hospitals and rest homes.

Evelyne searched in vain for David, and strolled out on to the balcony. It was very late now, almost eleven-thirty. She was tired, and her mind was full of the events of the evening. She kept biting her lip to stop herself smiling. She had danced with Lloyd George himself! In actual fact, Evelyne had not the slightest idea who he was but she, the outsider, had been the centre of attention for one moment . . . she wished Lizzie-Ann or her Da could have seen her. There was so much to tell them, they wouldn't believe it. She wondered if she would be allowed to keep her frock. If so, she'd give it to Lizzie-Ann. Evelyne just knew it was her style, she'd just die for it.

Evelyne didn't notice the boy, she hadn't heard his step, and he scared her. He was staring up at her from the grass below, head to one side, and he didn't look away when she looked down. He kept his eyes on her face. Black, cold eyes . . . then he smiled, and she remembered him, it was the gypsy boy from the field.

Freedom moved up to the balcony steps, stealthily like a cat, his back to the white stone. His hair gleamed black as his eyes, and they never left her face. His gaze was magnetic, she could feel him, closer, closer, and his eyes were drawing her to him. He stopped two steps below her, and then he whispered, 'One two three, one two three . . .'

For a moment Evelyne didn't know what he meant, then he rocked his body as if dancing, and she knew he must have watched her practising on the lawn. He climbed higher and there was now only one step between them. He lifted his hand towards her, his eyes still staring intently into hers. 'Read your palm . . .'

Evelyne leaned forward slightly, her hand towards him, palm up. He lowered his head, keeping his eyes raised to hers, and kissed the centre of her palm. She curled her fingers and tried to draw her hand away, but he caught it and held it tight.

A woman seemed to spring from the darkness. Her

head was swathed in a shawl, partially hiding her face, and she wore a long, dark skirt and heavy gold necklace. Her voice was soft, but sharp.

'Freedom . . . Freedom . . .'

He turned to the woman, gave her a hard look, almost vicious. Releasing Evelyne's arm, he glanced at her briefly, then turned and moved lightly down the steps, following the woman into the darkness of the bushes. But before he was out of earshot he heard a voice call.

'Evelyne!'

David stood at the balcony doors, his face set with anger. He had seen the incident. He moved to Evelyne's side and gripped her elbow tightly.

'I've been searching for you everywhere. Come inside, we're leaving.'

Lady Sybil joined them as they entered the ballroom. Patting David's arm she asked if they had both enjoyed themselves, surely they were not going to leave before the last waltz.

'I insist that you stay for just a little while longer, dear boy, your charge will just adore the fortune-tellers . . . come along and sit with me . . . Heather, dear, see if you can get the waiters to bring us coffee.'

David gave Evelyne a curt nod, and she went to join the girls waiting in line by the gypsy woman's table.

David could see Lady Primrose and her party leaving. She didn't even turn to look at him, hadn't even said goodbye.

The gypsy musicians were packing their fiddles into their old, worn cases. They had done their allotted time and wanted to leave. They still smiled and their manners were perfect, but they were like trained animals on display. The older of the two gypsy women looked at one of the fiddlers, and he gave a tiny sign with his hand to tell her their time was up. Two of the girls moaned that they had been waiting for ages, surely they wouldn't disappoint them now. Paying not the slightest attention, the women packed up their cards, slipping them into their worn packets, and, folding their shawls around them, they started to leave. The younger woman brushed past Evelyne, then stopped and turned back. Her skin was dark and tawny, her eyes the same as the young boy's, the boy called Freedom. She stared into Evelyne's face, touched her hair. Her hands were rough, the fingernails cut short and straight across. With a quick look at her menfolk she wavered, seemed nervous. The men waited impatiently, but she remained at Evelyne's side. One of the disappointed girls pushed forward, her hand held out, but the woman ignored it, brushed it from her as she would a buzzing fly. She pulled Evelyne's hand, unfurled the fingers and stared into the palm, the same palm the gypsy boy had kissed. The gnarled finger traced along the thin lines, and she could feel the roughness of this 'lady's' hand. She looked up into frightened eyes, eyes the colour of the cold northern seas, and for a moment she hesitated, about to speak. Then she turned and joined her menfolk.

The ballroom was virtually empty now, the servants were clearing the debris, collecting the glasses. The sweet-faced powder-room attendant slipped the black mourning cloak around Evelyne's shoulders.

'This'll be a night you won't forget, child. God bless you.'

Mrs Darwin heard the front door open into the darkened hallway. She wondered if Minnie had stayed awake to see to the couple. The stairs creaked and she lay back. They must be going straight to their rooms.

David walked ahead of Evelyne up the stairs, then put

110

his finger to his lips and pointed down, creeping on tiptoe and gesturing for her to follow him into the dark drawing room. She tiptoed after him, and they bumped in the doorway. After shutting the door David lit the gas lamp with a taper from the still-glowing fire. His face twisted into a snide smile.

'Well, my little Flame, didn't you do well? Polka with Lloyd George, kissed by the riff-raff gypsy boy, and we never had one dance together . . .'

He opened the drinks cabinet, careful not to make a noise, and took out a bottle of brandy and a glass. Evelyne's heart thudded, this was the moment she had dreamed of, alone with David, did he know she loved him, was he going to learn?

He poured a measure of brandy with care and sipped it, rolling it around his mouth, then looked at her over the rim of his glass, 'You made a great impression on a friend of mine, Captain Ridgely.' He didn't even offer her a drink. 'Yes, he was really taken with you. Comes from a good family, lots of loot . . . well, to cut a long story short, he wants to see you.'

Evelyne was puzzled. She asked who Ridgely was as she couldn't recall meeting him.

'I doubt if you will be going home tomorrow, so I said perhaps you could meet him at tea time, it'll be up to you what you want to arrange with him.'

'I don't understand, what arrangements?'

David sighed. God, he thought, she really is stupid.

'He likes you, I don't want to get involved, it will be entirely up to you whether you go to meet him or not. I think you'd be throwing away a good opportunity, he's very rich, could set you up in a little place of your own . . . and he's not a bad chap, you should be flattered, girl like you won't get many opportunities, especially if you have to stay in the valley all your life.'

Evelyne still stared, dumbfounded.

'Good God, do I have to spell it out, you could earn money, he'd keep you if you pleased him enough . . .'

Evelyne's hand swung out and slapped David hard across the face.

'Christ, what did you do that for?'

Evelyne was hurt and shaking with anger. He was suggesting she sell herself, and to one of his friends.

'Now, come along, I didn't mean any harm, no need to get yourself all upset, you don't have to go if you don't want to, all I said was I would ask you.'

Still Evelyne was speechless, staring at him, shocked, wide-eyed.

'You stupid little girl, this was an opportunity for you, I'm sorry I even bothered with you.' He walked out, leaving her confused and bewildered by all he had said, by his manner towards her. She could not remember the last time she had cried for herself – little Davey, Ma, that was different. She caught her breath as the sobs rose inside her. She wept for herself, for her stupidity, for the dream that had just been shattered. Her foolishness in believing, even for a moment, that she could be part of David Collins' life filled her with shame. She ran up the stairs to her room, remembering to creep the last few steps so she would not waken Doris.

David's bedroom door was ajar, and he was watching her as she tiptoed along the landing. Evelyne turned, caught him staring, and he gave her a strange, apologetic smile, then closed his door. The smile made it all the worse, his handsome, perfect face so far from her reach. All she wanted was to go home, home to her own people, her own class.

She cried herself to sleep, her face buried in the pillow, afraid to waken Doris. No one must know, ever, of her humiliation. Suddenly she remembered that dreadful painted woman at the window of the inn, just like Nellie Lanigan from the village, she knew the men paid money to go with her. Evelyne sobbed into the handkerchief David had once given her, and even through her tears she could smell him, his faint lavender perfume.

CHAPTER 6

THE TWO brothers died with their arms around each other, Mike and Will, but the cable Benjamin Rees brought didn't mention that, simply the dreaded words, 'killed in action'. Dicken wrote a letter from the front dated March 1917 – it took four months to reach the village, and that was when they learned how the two brothers had died.

The Old Lion seemed to bend under the weight of their loss. The drinking had stopped when little Davey had been buried, and Hugh had found work in a small colliery. When the news of the boys' death came he went straight back to work a double shift. Every morning he rose at dawn and, wrapped in his greatcoat and carrying his tea caddie, sandwiches and tools, he donned his cloth cap and silently left the house. Money was very short and there were now three lodgers who worked in the mine with Hugh.

Lizzie-Ann had been very brave. Rosie was now almost eighteen months old, a pretty little girl with rosy cheeks and curly hair. Lizzie-Ann had made considerable progress as far as housekeeping and cleaning were concerned. She was skinny again, and spent hours chalking and polishing the front step. Often she had a faraway look in her eyes, daydreaming, but she never talked

114

about London now. She was grown up, a widow with a daughter to look after, a widow and still only just eighteen.

Evelyne worked at the local brick factory, tough, hard labour from six-thirty in the morning until three o'clock. In the afternoon she went to the schoolhouse to help the new teachers. Doris Evans was still at the school, but she taught the senior girls and boys. The only house without a lodger was Doris' – she was still able to keep her four neat rooms to herself.

Poverty was everywhere in the village. The children scavenged for coal chips on the slag heaps, the men no longer sat eating their packed lunches together, laughing at what the missus had landed them with this time. They all knew they had the same, bread and dripping and tea.

Evelyne trudged up the hill to the schoolhouse. The rain was bucketing down, and she'd got soaked earlier in the day on the way to the brick factory. Her hands were raw and blistered, and she was as thin as ever. She had grown even taller, reaching five feet nine and a half inches. She was Hugh Jones' daughter all right.

The schoolhouse was cold, the small fire banked low, and the children huddled in their overcoats to keep out the freezing draughts. Evelyne helped in the junior class and also cleaned the school.

Mr Matthews, the new headmaster, was elderly, and had actually retired, but he had come to take the place of the original headmaster who had joined up. He called Evelyne in.

'Mrs Evans has not been in for the past two days, Miss Jones, will you look in on her?'

Evelyne pushed open the polished front door and called out. When she got no reply she began to worry, and went along the passage into the kitchen. It was neat and clean as ever, but empty and very cold. She hurried into the tiny living room. There were books on the table as always, but no sign of Doris. Eventually Evelyne found her lying in her clean bed with the starched white sheets. She was extremely pale and as Evelyne pushed open the door she asked, with a strange look on her face, 'Walter, is that you?' Doris didn't seem to recognize Evelyne at all as she bent over the frail, thin woman and rubbed her icy hands. She pulled more blankets from the wardrobe and laid them on top of Doris.

The coal bunker was piled high, and Evelyne took the full bucket back into the bedroom, laid the fire and lit it. Then she found vegetables in their neat trays beneath the kitchen sink and made some broth. She held the frail woman in her arms, the skinny frame wrapped in the blankets, and gently spooned the hot soup into her. Slowly, Doris seemed to come to herself, and gave Evelyne such a heart-rending look that Evelyne said: 'I'll not leave you tonight, Doris, I'll stay with you.'

She sat by the fire and read Dante's *Inferno* until Doris slept, then she banked the fire, pulled a rug over herself and went to sleep.

The following morning Doc Clock came and examined Doris, muttering that she was not taking care of herself – and with her money! He stuck a thermometer into Doris' bird-like mouth, and fumbled for the watch that wasn't there, as usual. Doc Clock, the village said, would stick a thermometer into a dead man's mouth and pronounce him perfectly fit.

Doris went very fast and as quietly as she had lived. Doc Clock said she had a brain tumour, must have had it for years. Lizzie-Ann, who always got everything wrong, told everyone that Doris had died from a brain *rumour*, and that she'd had it for years. Evelyne wrote to Dr Collins, taking the penny postage money from Doris' little leather purse. The money was needed, but there was no reply to her letter.

Evelyne had to arrange for the coffin and the funeral, since there was no one else to do it. All the while she still worked at the brick factory and up at the school. She made sure Doris' house was locked up tight, because already the coal bunker was empty and with things the way they were it was a wonder the furniture was still intact. Evelyne would shiver as she checked the house, knowing Doris was lying upstairs, cold and stiff.

Doris was buried beside her husband, Walter, in a simple ceremony attended only by Evelyne and a few villagers. In her neat handwriting, Evelyne noted down all the expenses she had paid out from the money she had found in the house, and how much was left, and sent the list to Dr Collins. Still she heard nothing back and often villagers passing the cold house would mutter, 'What a waste', the four rooms could easily be let and be making someone a few bob a week.

Lizzie-Ann ran from the post office with Dicken's letter. All the women went every day and asked old Ben Rees if there was any news from the Front. Ben used to get angry, swearing that he did his three rounds a day with the post, and if there was a letter or any news they would be the first to know, but it still didn't stop the women popping in and asking.

The pub would be lit up and the piano wheeled out when any of the boys came home on leave, only to be wheeled back again when they had to go again after too short a time. Then there would be the tears at the station and the Sunday prayers that the boys would come home.

Hugh and Rosie were sitting by the fire, playing with a bat and ball. Lizzie-Ann had gone on a date with a boy who had been invalided out of the army. He was a good-hearted boy with a bad limp, and Lizzie-Ann seemed to have some of her old sparkle back.

'Will you not find yerself a lad then, Evie?'

Evelyne laughed, and carried the washing out to dry. Over her shoulder she told him she had no time to spare for lads. As she hung out the cold, worn trousers, she remembered the night she had danced with Lloyd George. She pictured David's face and sighed. She still thought of him, almost every night and prayed every Sunday that he would be safe and unharmed. It was strange that she had received no word from David's father in Cardiff, maybe they felt it best simply to forget poor Doris.

Summer was coming on and the war still raged. The villagers found it hard to picture their menfolk fighting in another country somewhere, even harder to understand what they were fighting for. The old boys sitting in the pub said they were after the bastard Germans, and that the Tommies would 'wipe 'em off the face of the earth' – their lads could do it, it was as if only Welsh lads were over there.

Lizzie-Ann had decided to marry her young man with the limp. Evelyne made Jim feel welcome, even though it meant an extra mouth to feed in the house. He was good-hearted, and made Lizzie-Ann smile again. The wedding was a simple affair, and Lizzie-Ann wore the dress Evelyne had brought home from Cardiff. The couple had no honeymoon, they just took over the front room, and life went on as usual. At least the house (unlike so many others) throbbed with life now, a bit too much at times as they still had four lodgers. Lizzie-Ann dropped numerous hints about how awful it was that they could be so cramped while Doris Evans' house stood empty. It had been more than six months since Doris had been buried, and still no word from Dr Collins.

Evelyne hurried home from the brick factory. It had been boiling hot in there, and working right next to the kilns made you sweat your guts out. She wanted a good wash before going up to the school. Already they called her a schoolmistress, although she wasn't actually qualified, but she liked it and got on well with the two proper teachers.

Ben Rees was standing by the door, his bike propped up by the wall. He had one of the dreaded yellow telegrams in his hand.

'No, Ben . . . Ah, don't say it's for us, no, please . . . no.'

Dicken was gone, and two days after the telegram arrived they got his last letter, telling them how well he was doing, and that he might make sergeant within the month.

Hugh seemed unable to take any more pain, his whole body sagged as if the wind had been punched from his huge frame. He still struggled up every morning and went off to work, but he was so silent, so empty, it was as if his soul had already slipped from his body.

As she had done all her life, Evelyne held the last

119

tenuous threads of the family together. She had to keep on working, she had to keep going up to the school, but she no longer went to church, she couldn't, and she didn't care what wrath He sent down on her. How could there be a God who would take each and every one of her brothers, and leave them with nothing?

In August, one of the hottest Augusts ever, Evelyne prepared for another burning day in the factory. She noticed her Da had gone off to work without his tea caddie. She sighed, he'd be dying of thirst by twelve, she'd just have to be late. The sun blazed in the cloud-less sky, birds sang, the grass smelt good and all over the hedgerows the flowers were blooming. The further up the mountain she walked the cleaner the air was. The raspberries hung thick and ripe, and she ate them as she walked, thinking that on the way back she would fill her skirt with them to make a tart.

She walked down the further slope of the mountain, crossed two streams and a field of cows. Her legs were getting tired, and she realized just how strong a man her father must be to take this long trek day in and day out. The winter months must have frozen him, the rain soaked him, and then he spent all those hours down the mine. When she reached the small pithead she asked for Hugh Jones, and was directed to a shaft at ground level. Black-faced men called 'hello', and five women sitting in the sun called to her and waved. This new mine took quite a few women at the pithead to sort the coal. They were as black as the menfolk, but they were laughing and joking and soaking up the sunshine.

Evelyne edged along the coal seam. She had to bend almost double, and the blackness was just as Mike had

120

described, so thick she couldn't even see a shadow. She called out, directing her voice towards the sound of hammering and the click-click-clicking of the pickaxes.

She passed two trams being pushed out by Dai Roberts, who grinned at her and said to keep on walking, and to watch her step as it sloped steeply. The air was getting so thick she was gasping for breath as she inched her way along the tunnel – her hands were her only guide.

'Hugh Jones. *Hugh Jones*!'

She could barely draw breath and the blackness was so heavy she didn't know whether to turn back or go on . . .

'*Hugh! Hugh Jones . . .*'

As Evelyne turned a bend in the tunnel she saw her father, lit up by the flame of a single candle. His face was stricken, his eyes stared into the blackness as in a nightmare. Evelyne ran to him, knowing what must be in his mind, that he must have thought there was some other tragedy, could there be another? She was quick to shout that she'd brought his tea caddie.

Hugh held his blackened arms out to her and she clung to him. With barely enough air to keep the candle flame flickering, with no more than four feet of space to work in, the massive man had to hunch himself nearly double to chip away at the face.

Evelyne felt his powerful arms holding her as he had when she was a little girl. In the blackness the grief that filled both of them was released, and they cried together, their tears mingling with the coal dust that dominated their lives.

The war was over, and home-made paper chains were strung across the streets, trestle tables were erected on

121

the cobbles and from God knew where came buns, cakes, biscuits and lemonade for the kids.

There was hardly a family in the village that had not lost a loved one in the mines or in the mighty war that had raged across the Channel. Now the lads who had survived were coming home, and their families went crazy. They sang in the streets, they belted out the old tunes on the piano and they held hands and sang 'God Save the King . . .'

Evelyne rushed around handing out cakes, and handmade crackers with no *bang*! in the middle, but containing little gifts made by some of the old women for the children. It was a wonderful day, and everyone crowded into Mrs Morgan's to drink her home-brewed wine.

Evelyne was standing well to the back of the crowd as the home-brewed wine took effect, and the singing reached a raucous level . . . Evelyne left the stuffy house. Some older women, well inebriated, grouped on a corner, looked at her with pitying faces as she walked on up the cobbled street.

'Ah, poor thing, she'll never get herself a lad now, left it too late . . . or maybe with her being so tall she'll get one who's injured, disabled, you never know.'

Evelyne Jones was twenty-one, that was all, but her eyes mirrored the anguish she had experienced. Hugh Jones could see her striding up the hill, her lean, tough body, high cheekbones and flame red hair, her strong legs like an athlete's . . . he closed his eyes, dear God, how he wished she was one of his boys come home.

Lizzie-Ann could have given herself a miscarriage, she ran so fast. The thick bundle of letters all addressed to Evelyne Jones was in a brown paper parcel, and she had to sign for them at the post office. She signed after a hell of a row with Ben Rees, who was livid because he hadn't had a chance to snoop through them. He'd dropped his bike in fury – that bloody girl was always a little bugger, and her with another kid on the way when she was no better than one herself. Ben picked up his red bike and threatened to strangle Alfred Moggs' illegitimate grandson, half coloured he was, with black, curly hair. The little bugger had already let the air out of Ben's tyres once this morning.

Evelyne took the thick brown envelope with the red line across it and started to open it, with the entire class of nosy children peering through the glass door, the headmistress looking on, and Lizzie-Ann gasping. Before Evelyne had a chance to examine the contents, Lizzie-Ann's waters broke, and the children sniggered that she'd wet herself. The headmistress, a flat-footed woman in her late sixties, took over the class while Evelyne ran for Doc Clock.

The Doctor now had the only privately owned motor vehicle in the village. This was patted, polished, and sat in by the Doc but in the driver's seat he was absolutely hopeless. More than once he had been found still sitting in the car as it teetered on the edge of a ditch, his face concerned and puzzled, his specs dangling from one ear.

'Christ almighty, there's something wrong with it again, it turned right when I wanted to go left.'

Doc Clock arrived just in time as Lizzie-Ann gave birth in the school kitchen. He shouted that it was a boy, but when he put his glasses on he realized it was a girl.

'No, it's a girl, it's a girl.'

Lizzie-Ann, sweating and exhausted, screamed.

'Oh, Christ Almighty, I haven't got twins, have I?'

Evelyne held her hand and stroked her head, saying it was all right, it was just the one.

The Doc huffed and puffed and dropped them all home. The trip in his car made Lizzie-Ann forget the letters for a moment, but she was soon reminded when Evelyne eventually opened the package and gasped, then fainted, out cold, in the kitchen.

Doris Evans had named Evelyne Jones as her heir, leaving her the little four-roomed house, which no one had realized she'd owned outright, and two hundred pounds. The news went round faster than Mrs Morgan's radio could have blasted it. In the first version, Evelyne had had a heart attack and a daughter at the same time, but eventually the news filtered through that she had received a legacy.

When it got straightened out and the story told in the right order, there was a strange calm. The villagers whispered, spread the story from house to house, pub to pub. Suddenly the Jones family's cramped house had an aura to it. Evelyne Jones had a legacy and overnight, out of the blue, the tall schoolmistress became extremely eligible. She had money, she owned Doris Evans' house, actually *owned* it. She was now a woman of property – more than the village realized, because Doris had not only left Evelyne her house in the village, but also her half-share in the Cardiff house. There were, of course, the gossips in the washhouses that said no good would come of it, but they all secretly wished they had been a little more friendly to poor old Doris.

There was no word from David in the lawyer's letter, just a stiff, formal note from the doctor thanking Evelyne for coping with all the arrangements for Doris' funeral, and that was all.

124

Lizzie-Ann had cried and Rosie had howled, though not really understanding why everyone in the house was so emotional. Evelyne insisted they move into Doris' house. There was no question of rent, it would be theirs for as long as they wanted it.

She stood and watched the couple running in and out of each room, hugging each other, then they would kiss Evelyne and thank her for the thousandth time. Evelyne took very little from the house, just Doris' books and pens, a silver-framed photo of Doris and Walter on their wedding day, and two pairs of linen sheets and pillow-cases, a set for her own small bed and another for her father's.

Evelyne's first purchase with her legacy was a wireless, which was installed in the kitchen. Hugh moaned and muttered that he wouldn't go near the infernal noise machine. The house was quiet now, no lodgers. Evelyne and her father were alone, and spent long evenings sitting by the blazing fire. He still rose before dawn to go to the mines, and she still prepared his tea caddy and sand-wiches. Evelyne couldn't help but smile as Hugh rushed in from work and turned on the wireless. He listened intently and would talk back to the speakers. On one occasion when she was late home from school she found him standing, fist clenched, shouting back at the radio that the man was talking rubbish, let him spend some time down the mines before making these rules and regulations. Unemployment was out of control, the blasted politicians were talking out of their arses.

Hugh was so irate that Evelyne thought he would put his fist through her precious radio, but he grabbed up his cap to go out. If no other bugger in the village was going to stand up for his rights, then he would. Three sons lost in the war, and for what? He banged out of the house and marched to the pithead.

The Old Lion roared, and the men listened. It was as if new life had been breathed into him. Meetings were held in their front room. The radio became a focal point for many of the meetings, the men clustered around listening, listening to their fate, but until now not actually going out and doing anything about it . . . until now they hadn't had a leader. Hugh Jones had become that leader, and his new-found energy gave him back the respect he had lost.

The men listened to him, and gradually his work with the union became a full-time occupation. He was at the pitheads, he was in the managers' office, discussing safety precautions, he popped up everywhere, he was unstoppable. The men began to turn to him with their problems, their insurance claims, and he turned no one away. The house throbbed with life, and Hugh would stand with his back to the fire, testing out his speeches on his daughter.

Evelyne appeared contented, often at her father's side handing out leaflets. She, too, got up on the small platform and spoke for women's rights in the brick factory, the bakeries, even for the women working in the mines. They wanted better conditions, overtime, holiday pay, insurance. She worked all day at school and at night she would read, discussing the campaign with her father. They became close, a unit. After church the pair would hold meetings, gathered in the small church hall. It was after one of these that Hugh stood and looked up at the mountains, then turned to his daughter and held out his hand.

'It's a fair day, we'll walk awhile.'

They walked in silence, the climb taking their breath

away. They climbed higher and higher until eventually they sat, side by side, looking down into the valley. Hugh had never been a great man with words, not intimate words, and Evelyne could tell by the way he kept on coughing and starting to speak, then closing his mouth tightly, that he wanted to talk but just couldn't get around to it.

Evelyne lay back in the warm sun. She could smell the sweet, fresh grass. Hugh lay down beside her, coughed a few more times and then leant on his elbow and looked into her face. He loved her passionately, and he wished he could find the right words to tell her so. Hugh had never referred to Evelyne's legacy, never asked her what she intended doing with it. He looked down at her face, framed by the thick red hair coiled in braids and clipped tightly to her head. He had not seen her with her hair loose for a long time. With his big, rough hand he gently traced her chin, her cheekbones. She kept her eyes closed, not ever having had such a quiet, intimate moment with her father before. Almost afraid to open her eyes in case the moment slipped away, she kissed his hand softly.

'You're a fine-looking woman, Evie, you know that?' Still she said nothing. 'You're also intelligent, a clever girl, and a good daughter, no man could ask for a better lass. Do you not think of marrying? Or having children, gel?'

He turned to her and knelt down. His body was still muscular, his shoulders wide, not an ounce of fat on him. He could have been a young man but for the grey hair, the heavy lines in his face, that gave his age away.

'I'd like to hear the sound of a boy's voice in our house, Evie, a grandson. Lizzie-Ann's pair are real sweethearts, but I'd like a grandson. Is there no boy takes your fancy? . . . fine-looking woman like you, Evie, could take your pick, it's not natural for you to be with me so much of your time.'

Evelyne had never told anyone of David, of her time in Cardiff, and there on the mountain top it all poured forth, as if she was sixteen again. The hurt, the shame, and at long last she whispered of her obsessive love of David.

'I loved him since that first time, Da, and no one seems to come up to him. I know I don't mean anything to him, he's more than likely forgotten I even exist but I see his face every night.'

Hugh was nonplussed. All the years she had kept her secret to herself, and more than that, her shame. He turned to start down into the village. He struck his fist against his thigh.

'Go back to him, then, girl, you must get the lad out of your system, or you'll start to be like Doris herself. Go to Cardiff, but by Christ, this time you'll go wearing the finest. You have the legacy, then spend it, go and see this David . . .'

Hugh held out his hand and hauled Evelyne to her feet. He roared with laughter . . . it echoed round the mountain.

'Did you really dance with Lloyd George himself?'

Hugh brought in some pages from a magazine that he had found in Doc Clock's waiting room. He had gone with one of the men to try to get the Doc to sign a medical claim, and had torn the pages out. Evelyne laughed, they were plastered all over the table, the latest fashions. She kissed Hugh, and looked at the crumpled pages. The magazine was only eight years out of date, and the skirts were being worn almost up to the calf now.

'See, gel, dove grey is the latest colour, now get

yourself decked out in that and this David won't be able to say no.'

He took out of his pocket a return ticket to Cardiff, bought, he hastened to add, with his own money, so it was not to be wasted, and she was not to hang on to her cash like an old miser but go up to Cardiff and get herself done up.

Hugh held out the ticket as proud as Punch. She went into his arms and hugged him tight.

'Oh, Da, I love you so, I love you more than I ever tell you.'

Hugh held her at arm's length, and his face shone with love for her.

'An' I get so full of love for you, girl, all I want is for you to be happy . . .'

Evelyne delayed her journey to Cardiff until the Easter holidays, then she had no excuse. Hugh marched her off to the steam train. She took a small overnight bag and her post office savings book. Hugh had got her a list of bed and breakfast hotels for her to choose from. They were so close, so loving, and his pride in her shone out of his eyes. Some said it wasn't natural, the two being together so much, and Wally Hampton said he saw them kissing like lovers on the station platform.

'Right, gel, you go and get this David and bring him back . . .'

She could see him standing, waving his big red handkerchief from the platform . . . he remained waving until the train chuffed round the mountain.

Evelyne was scared, but realized she was happier than she had felt for years. Perhaps Hugh was right, she was becoming an old maid up at the school. She began to make out a list of all the things she would buy on her first shopping spree.

David's blond hair, his smile, his sweet lavender smell. Would he still be at the same house? Her mouth went dry, what if he hadn't returned from the war – what if he'd moved. Evelyne counted the months, the years she had been away. Time had gone fast, and with trepidation she realized her foolishness. Over four years had gone by, he could be dead, killed like her brothers, her letters to Dr Collins had not been answered. By the time the train had chuffed into Cardiff Central station she was as nervous as on her very first journey all those years ago with Doris.

'Think positively,' she told herself, and set her shoulders back as she walked along the platform, her face determined, almost haughty.

Evelyne booked into the 'Rosemount', a bed and breakfast hotel. The house had a view of the castle, it was clean, and the landlady was a kindly woman named Violet Pugh.

By teatime Evelyne had been in every single women's wear shop, and her feet ached. Millinery, shoes, gloves, suits, every item had been jotted down and priced. She was stunned at the cost of clothes, and she had by no means calculated for such extravagance. That night she made a list in readiness for her next day's shopping expedition.

The saleswoman at 'Chic fashions' sighed. God, that wretched woman was back, she wished the other assistant was free. The woman had tried on every single outfit in the shop the previous day, and bought nothing. Nor was she an easy one to dress, being so tall, and then she was thin with it – a lot of the new fashions looked dreadful on her. She forced a smile between her 'Lush Red' lips, and hovered. Out came the list and Evelyne, with a look of determination on her face, asked to try on the dove-grey pleated skirt with the matching white-collared jacket.

The shop assistant stared at Evelyne as she emerged from the changing room. She muttered to herself. 'Just shows you, you never know. Girl like that looked more like she should be sweeping the place out, never mind buying anything.'

The shoes Evelyne had set her mind on did not match the outfit. She was shown the new, fashionable high heel.

'Don't you think I'm too tall to wear two-inch heels?' she asked.

The sales assistant showed how perfectly the two-toned shoes matched her outfit.

'I'll take them, thank you, and the matching hand-bag.'

It was a rash decision, but having made it she felt tickled to death, she was going to look so elegant.

Her next stop was a small milliner's in a side-street, 'Paris Designers'. The hat was a problem, the small cloche hats were very fashionable now, but none of them would fit over Evelyne's thickly coiled hair. The sales assistant pondered and sat back, took a peek inside the bag from the well-known fashion shop that contained the suit, and rifled through the tissue paper. That exquisite dove-grey . . . to her mind it was a trifle ageing for such a young woman. She scurried into the back of the shop and returned with three large hatboxes, new stock not yet on display. She sat Evelyne down before the mirror in a cubicle. She was a tiny, grey-haired woman dressed neatly in black, her name, 'Miss Freda', written on a tag pinned to her dress. She had a strange accent and was very apologetic, yet not cloying in any way. She could see the girl's big, red hands, and just by looking at her worn clothes she knew she must have some very special occasion in mind, perhaps even a wedding. She brought a magazine to Evelyne's side, flicked through it, her small, neat white hands moving fast. She stopped at a page. The fashionable bobbed hair was very much in vogue, but then perhaps for someone as tall as Evelyne the bobbed style would not be flattering enough.

'If Madame would allow me . . .'

Evelyne chewed her lip as Miss Freda worked quickly and deftly, her nimble fingers fluttering around Evelyne's head. Down came the coiled braids, flick, flick, they were undone: a silver-handled brush was retrieved from the drawer of the dressing-table. Miss Freda, her mouth full of hairgrips, tossed and wound the hair into an ornate bun, low on the nape of Evelyne's neck. She then studied Evelyne in the mirror, her head cocked to one side, then the other, and satisfied, she opened up a large hatbox. The tissue rustled and she held up a white cloche hat with a small spray of embroidered white daisies along one side of the brim. As Miss Freda held the hat to the side of Evelyne's face, the doorbell rang and a very elegantly dressed couple entered.

'Freda, my dear, I am quite desperate. I have to go to the races, and you know that darling little rose-flowered hat we had from Paris, well, Poochie here has eaten it.'

Evelyne peeked out as the woman held out a fluffy

132

dog with an awful turned-up nose and popping eyes. Miss Freda almost curtsied and ushered the couple into another cubicle. She still held the daisy hat in her hand.

'Oh, that is a little darling, Freda, do let me try it.'

Miss Freda popped back into Evelyne's cubicle and drew the curtains, and whispered, 'She is much too old to wear this, but if it is not suitable for you, Madam, well . . .' Freda had a delightful tinkling laugh. As she spoke she placed the hat gently onto Evelyne's head, tilted the daises a little lower, stood back and beamed. Evelyne stared at her reflection. She turned to right and left as Freda held a small silver mirror behind her so she could get the full effect.

'I shall leave you to make your decision, Madame, but believe me, you look stunning.'

As Freda slipped out between the curtains, she put the price tag face down on the dressing-table.

Evelyne turned the price tag over. One pound fifteen shillings. It was far too much, she simply couldn't. One pound was almost half a week's earnings for the girls at the brick factory. She sighed, wondered if she could keep her hair in this lovely knot – that would mean saving a little on the hairdresser, at least three-and-six. She stared, perplexed, at her reflection, she adored the hat, but the price . . . it really was too much.

Miss Freda passed to and fro, discussing the weather with her clients. Evelyne heard the yap-yap of the dog, the *ping* of the doorbell and then swish of her curtains. Evelyne turned to Miss Freda, and swallowed.

'I'll take the hat, thank you.'

Miss Freda beamed and gently lifted the hat from Evelyne's head as though it were precious crystal, and laid it in the box. Out of the corner of her eye she noticed Evelyne lift the mirror, studying her new hairstyle, her fingers tracing the coils.

'It is a very simple hairstyle, no? I can show you in two minutes how to do it. The hairdressers here have no idea, all they do is snip, snip, everyone's head looks the same, or they frizz, frizz with the perms.'

Freda turned the small 'open' notice on the door to 'closed', and clapped her hands in delight as she moved towards Evelyne.

'Come, we have some coffee, some croissants, unless you are in a hurry? Come, darling, then I show you, it is very simple.'

Miss Freda's back room was piled ceiling-high with hatboxes. On a small work-table were laid out roses and ribbons and nets in different shades. Evelyne sat watching the bird-like woman as she chattered away and made up a hat right in front of her eyes.

'I come from Vienna, but I tell everyone I am French, I sell only Paris creations. As you can see this is a long way from France, no?'

From a small drawer she took a box of labels and waved them at Evelyne.

'I print them specially, but I don't think it is a lie because my hats are copies from French magazines, only the price is French.'

She covered her face like a small child as she twittered with laughter, then still talking fast she began sewing and serving coffee all at the same time. It tasted different from the coffee she had been served at David's house, stronger, thicker and sweeter with no milk.

Miss Freda taught Evelyne how to do her hair, then she brought out a small velvet box filled with tiny jars and fluffy powder puffs. She showed Evelyne how to whiten her hands, instructed her to cream them every night until they were soft. Then she tipped Evelyne's

134

chin up, stared into her face, and searched through her box, bringing out a tiny pot. She opened the lid carefully and, with the tip of her little finger, dabbed a very soft, pale-pink over Evelyne's lips ... she sat back and clucked and nodded, then, 'Oh, là là.'

Apparently quite unconcerned about the shop being closed, Miss Freda insisted on plucking Evelyne's eyebrows, careful not to make them too arched as was the fashion, just, in her words, 'tidying them up a little'. After every move she sat back, her tiny head bobbing up and down like a bird, constantly repeating, 'Oh, là là ...' She even painted Evelyne's square-cut fingernails with clear polish. Then she carefully packed the daisy hat and tied the box with ribbon.

'For you, darling, I will charge fifteen shillings.'

Evelyne tried to argue, without much enthusiasm, as even fifteen shillings for a hat that did not really come from Paris, France, was terribly expensive.

'Will you come and see me again? I would like it, I don't have many friends, you see, I came over *many* years ago as a lady's maid.'

She whispered as if afraid someone would overhear.

'First I was in Liverpool, then we travelled to Wales and I was just so unhappy that I left and ... *voilà*, here I am, *chérie* ... so you must go, but come and see me again.'

Miss Freda locked up her shop, bolting the door, and sat studying her accounts. She looked at her face in the mirror, how she hated to bow and scrape with her 'oh, là là's ... she sighed. If she didn't get more business there would be no shop, and she would have to go back to being a waitress, but never the other thing. She would never do that, and looking at herself she knew that not many men would want her now anyway. She put one of her specials on her frizzy head, lifted her chin and decided she was not that bad, not that old, thirty-eight wasn't old at all . . . then she sat at her sewing machine, surrounded by net and roses.

The boarders looked up briefly, but went back to slurping their soup. Mrs Pugh did notice the difference, and remarked to her reflection in the spotless hall mirror that the rest was obviously doing wonders for the girl. Catching sight of a spot of dust she flicked it with her finger.

'Something most definitely is . . .'

As she came out of the dining room, Evelyne passed Mrs Pugh in the hall.

'Are you not having pudding, Miss Jones? It's semolina with jam.'

Evelyne smiled and said she was too full, then went up the stairs to her room. Mrs Pugh stared after her, pursing her lips. The girl had done her hair differently, that was what it was. She hoped it didn't mean she had any funny ideas, any fancy men . . . then she marched back into the dining room.

'It's semolina, with strawberry jam,' she announced.

The two elderly boarders were fast asleep at the table.

Evelyne had a dress rehearsal in her rented room. First she practised her new hairstyle, then she sat for over an hour in just her camisole and bloomers with the hat on. She watched herself smiling . . . she had never been so preoccupied with her face or her body and she wasn't as sure about her appearance as Miss Freda was, but she certainly did look quite nice.

The following morning, Evelyne was dressed and ready when Mrs Pugh called to her that there was a car waiting for her, and she slowly descended the stairs from her rented room as Mrs Pugh stared, open-mouthed. She was dumbstruck, the girl moving slowly, slightly unsteadily down the stairs *couldn't* be Miss Jones . . . but there she was, looking as if she had stepped straight off the front of a French fashion magazine. Mrs Pugh looked up into the girl's face as she passed in a cloud of sweet perfume, immaculate from head to toe. 'My God,' she thought, 'the girl must have a fancy man, and a rich one at that.' Well, any funny business and she'd pack the girl's bags, she couldn't afford any gossip, not just as she'd got her two regulars installed, and for life, judging by their ages.

The hired car had been Hugh's idea. He'd told her, 'Don't go up in a ruddy horse-drawn carriage, they're old-fashioned. Hire yourself one of the new-fangled motors with a uniformed driver'. It had cost her one pound ten shillings, and she had the car for eight hours. Now as she stepped out of Mrs Pugh's front door she knew it was right. The chauffeur moved smartly to open the door, and even gave her a tiny bow.

Mrs Pugh almost pulled her net curtain down from the window, she was so eager to see everything that was going on. All the nets along the road flicked. Mrs Pugh could see her nosy neighbours, and tutted to herself, they were always at their windows, she couldn't understand why. That she was doing exactly the same thing never even occurred to her. The car moved slowly off and Evelyne sat back, savouring the smell of the leather upholstery and her perfume. So far so good. They drove slowly along the kerb as the chauffeur searched for the right house. Evelyne was so tense she sat forward on the edge of her seat. She knew exactly which house, it was printed indelibly on her mind, but she was taken slightly aback. The house didn't look as grand as she remembered. The brass didn't gleam as bright as hers back in the village.

She pressed back against the leather as the chauffeur walked up the path, rang the bell and waited. Her heart was beating rapidly and her lips felt dry. She licked them and tasted her rose-coloured lipstick. Her heart lurched as the door opened and Mrs Darwin stood framed in the doorway. She was nodding and speaking to the chauffeur. The years hadn't been kind to her either, she was much fatter and more flushed than Evelyne remembered her. Her chins wobbled as she nodded her head up and down, and she looked past the chauffeur towards the car. She was trying to see inside, and Evelyne pressed even further back against the seat.

The chauffeur gave Evelyne no hint of what had been said as he walked back to the car and opened the passenger door.

'The housekeeper said for you to go straight in, Miss.'

Evelyne was grateful for the chauffeur's firm, white-gloved grip on her elbow. She walked slowly to the door. It had been left ajar, but Mrs Darwin had vanished from sight. There was no sign of Minnie either. The comforting grip on her arm withdrew as the chauffeur returned to the car. She was alone, and instead of being full of confidence she could feel her body trembling.

Mrs Darwin stood at the bottom of the stairs. She gave a small bob and gestured for Evelyne to enter the drawing room. The smell of the house – the strange mixture of polish and medical spirits – sent a shudder through Evelyne, and she was again the gawky girl who had come here with Doris Evans. Mrs Darwin didn't recognize her.

'It's me, Mrs Darwin, it's Evelyne, don't you remember me?'

The big woman squinted, stared at her, and then her jaw dropped and she slapped her hands to her fat cheeks in total amazement. She went to give Evelyne a hug, then stopped, flustered. She flapped her apron, stared, turned away and stared again, and then her huge face crumpled into a strange, half-laughing cry.

'Lord above, oh God Almighty, gel, if you don't look like visiting royalty, then . . . can I kiss you?'

It was all right suddenly, and Evelyne bent right down and felt the plump, wet lips kiss her cheek.

Mrs Darwin ushered her into the drawing room. From below stairs came a terrible clatter, and Evelyne turned.

'Is Minnie here?'

Mrs Darwin shook her head and laughed. Minnie now had three little ones and lived over in Carlisle Road. She turned and thudded out, yelling at the top of her voice to someone called Muriel.

Evelyne stared around the room. It was just the same, but smaller, not so overpowering. There was even a bowl of roses exactly as there had always been, except that they were dead, the petals fallen around the bowl. She went to the bookcase and looked at the titles; she had read all these books in the years since she had last been here, while Doris was alive.

Mrs Darwin came back in, carrying a tray with cake and biscuits.

'Will you be moving in, Miss Evelyne? Only, we don't know what to do, like? Not since he passed on.'

Evelyne, turned afraid.

'What did you say?'

Mrs Darwin busied herself laying out the teacups.

'The Doctor, miss, terrible it was, him a doctor and to be so poorly, couldn't do a thing for himself at the end, you know, shocking. We had to make up a bed

139

down here for him, I mean, I couldn't carry him up and down them stairs, even though he was all skin and bone.'

Evelyne had to sit down, for a terrible moment she had thought it could possibly be David.

'When did he pass on?'

'Oh, it must be a year or more . . . now, I'll just get that ruddy girl downstairs to bring up the tea. Shocking time you know, now, can't get a good girl. Mind you, we've not been paid our wages, not a penny for months now, I was getting to me wit's end, I was. I really was.'

When she had gone out, Evelyne looked at the tea tray. The biscuits were stale, soft, and a slice had been cut off the cake where it had gone mouldy. She heard the basement door slam and went to the window. She could see Mrs Darwin hurrying down the road, wrapping her shawl around her fat shoulders. Evelyne jumped as a thin, dreadfully scruffy girl stood in the doorway and sniffed.

'I've mashed the tea. Mrs Darwin says she won't be long.'

She hovered, watched as Evelyne poured the tea.

'You bein' here, does that mean we'll have our wages?'

Evelyne stirred sugar into her cup.

'I don't know – Muriel, isn't it? I'll obviously have a lot of things to arrange.'

'I'll be downstairs if you want me, the bell don't work so you'll have to holler.'

Evelyne wanted to ask about David, but she couldn't get the words out. She began to wander from room to room. The house smelt musty, dank, and there was a thick film of dust on everything. Ghosts of the past crept with her as she quietly looked into each of the ground-floor rooms. Then she mounted the stairs. They creaked,

140

and even the banister was dusty. On all the walls were dark, empty spaces where pictures had been. The house had been stripped of every valuable ornament and there was an air of desolation to the place.

She went into the silent room she had shared with Doris. Nothing had changed but the mounting dust. She closed the door and went on to the bathroom, the memories flooding through her. Then she was standing on the landing looking towards David's room. She remembered his half-naked body, bending over to untie his boots, remembered his silky hair. There was even now a faint smell of lavender . . .

Downstairs, David walked into the hall with Mrs Darwin. She took his arm, whispered.

'Her name's Evelyne.'

David nodded, looked up the stairs. He rested his arm on the banister rail and shouted.

'Evelyne . . . *Evelyne, come down*!'

Evelyne dropped her comb and ran to the top of the stairs. She stood staring down at him, he hadn't changed, he looked just the same if not even more handsome . . . and he was smiling up at her.

David thought she was lovely, just lovely. Turning to Mrs Darwin he gave a slight shake of his head, and she looked sadly up at Evelyne. Then David leapt up the stairs two at a time.

'Evelyne . . . Evelyne, how are you?' Catching her in his arms he swung her up in the air. Close to she could see that he had grown a small moustache and he was much thinner, but his hair, oh, his lovely, silky blond hair was just the same.

'You remembered me? Oh, David, you remembered me?'

Taking her hand he bowed and led her down the stairs.

'And who could forget such a beautiful gel? Come along, I refuse to let you out of my grasp . . . my hat, Mrs Darwin.'

Mrs Darwin held out his brown bowler.

'Sir, don't you think you should tell her . . .'

'Now, Mrs Darwin, not another word.'

'It's little Evelyne, Doris' girl from the valley.'

David tossed his bowler in the air, ducked, and it landed right on his head. He gestured with both hands like an acrobat.

'Can I take her away from you for a while, you great, fat, horrible woman, eh? I want to show this creature off . . . come along, dear heart, your chariot awaits.'

Bursting with happiness, Evelyne was ushered outside while Mrs Darwin blinked back her tears. For a moment David's face changed as he looked at Mrs Darwin, hard.

'Not a word.'

Her fat face wobbled as she nodded. 'She danced with Lloyd George at the Warners' ball, sir, when Miss Doris was here.'

David snapped, his face looked pinched.

'Yes, yes, you said, we won't be long.'

Evelyne stood on the steps as David danced down them two at a time, took off his bowler hat and bowed low, opening the door of his sports car, bright red with snazzy upholstery. After helping her in, he tucked a rug round her knees just the way he used to, then he leant over her, his face so close she gasped.

'You smell like a fresh mountain flower, and so you should, I mean *you* are the girl who danced with Lloyd

George, no wonder, m'dear, it'll be the Princes of Wales next.'

David shouted to her as they careered round corners, they would have a celebration, this was a wonderful surprise. She laughed, and the sound of her laughter shocked her, it was so infrequent, the sound triggered the release of all the tensions and she didn't want it to stop.

As they drove through the city centre, David tooted the horn and waved and called out to many people driving past. He seemed to know everyone. He appeared elated, as happy as Evelyne. They headed out towards the country.

'You'll meet some of my very best friends, we'll be in time for the last race.'

The car roared up to the special enclosure at the race meeting. Everything was happening so fast, and there was a craziness to the whole afternoon. Evelyne was introduced to so many new faces, and everyone was friendly. She was accepted as part of the group; in fact, as the champagne flowed, several of David's friends showed more interest in her than in the racing. Not that David allowed his prize to be taken from him more than a few moments, he wanted to introduce her to everyone. He told them all she was an old friend, and they smiled and proffered drinks. Evelyne remembered Freddy Carlton, older, redder in the face, but he was delighted to meet again the girl who had taken everyone's heart at the midsummer dance.

David darted around, the centre of attention, especially with his strange, beautiful girl in tow. The women with their cute, bobbed hairstyles and short skirts seemed hell-bent on enjoying themselves, and when the last race was over no one seemed inclined to leave the private enclosure. Someone brought out a gramophone and couples danced on the grass or sat watching.

Having never danced to this kind of music, Evelyne remained slightly aloof, which only added to her attraction. She was also watchful of her new clothes; there was champagne flying around, sprayed from bottles all over people, so Evelyne moved further and further to the fringe of the crowd.

David stood on the roof of one of the long, shiny cars.

'Everyone, listen, listen . . . we'll all dine at Bianco's, the party must go on, I'm in love . . .' He tap-danced, jumping from one car to the next, tossing his bowler up and catching it on his head. 'Who's out of champers? Come along now, glasses at the ready, chaps.'

Evelyne felt as if she and David were royals; everyone followed him, and accepted her as being with him. They proceeded to get into their cars.

'I say, look at the posters, be a jolly good wheeze, why don't we go?'

The posters, in crude, bright red letters, were stuck to the walls on the stand. 'FREEDOM STUBBS VERSUS DAI "HAMMER" THOMAS'.

There was a rough sketch beneath the lettering of two boxers, fists up, about to fight each other. David immediately began charging around with his fists up, dodging, and tapping his friends with mock punches.

'What say we all go to the fight, it's a gyppo fair, chaps, should be jolly?'

Evelyne smiled with the rest of David's crazy antics. She felt a tap on her shoulder and turned. A face loomed from the past – Captain Ridgely.

144

'Well, well, hello there, I don't remember meeting you deah gel, do tell me where he found you? Captain Ridgely at your command, at your feet, deah, lovely lady.'

David bellowed across the grass.

'*Ridgelyyyyy . . . Get off her, she's mine!*'

David leapt to Evelyne's side and put a protective arm around her shoulders.

'She's mine, you no-good rascal . . . now, Evelyne, we are all waiting on your decision. Do we or don't we go to the fight? What do you say, eh?'

Evelyne saw that everyone was waiting, and shrugged, smiling.

'Whatever you say.'

'It's the fight, everyone, *meet at Bianco's first . . .*'

The cars began to roar out, cheering passengers shouting to each other and waving their arms and champagne bottles. David got into his car.

He leaned back, slithering lower in his seat, and closed his eyes for a few moments. Then he turned his head, still resting on the back of the seat. 'Where in God's name have you been all my life, Flamehead, especially when I needed you? Why have you taken so long to come back, my gazelle, my strange, wonderful lady from nowhere?'

The kiss she had dreamed of had not been so hard or brutal. She could feel his teeth, then his tongue pushing open her lips and licking them, then thrusting inside her mouth. She actually felt disgusted, the taste of champagne and cigar smoke was so strong. His hand began slowly to unbutton her dove-grey jacket with the white collar, her lovely Vogue suit, and he was pushing her against the side of the car . . . and her hat? He was crushing her hat! She pushed him away, and he lolled against the opposite door. He turned his face away, slapped the steering wheel with his hand, and when he looked back he frightened her. His eyes were blazing, staring straight through her, and again he hit the steering wheel with his fist. He was muttering, swearing, a jumble of words. Evelyne didn't know what to do. David began to rock backwards and forwards, banging his head on the steering wheel. His actions, behaviour frightened her, was he drunk?

'David, stop it please, don't . . . *David*! *Don't*. *Stop*!'

Freddy ran to the car and cupped David's chin in his hands.

'You okay . . . *David*? All right, old chap, eh? All right, are we?'

David shrugged Freddy's hands away. Freddy gave Evelyne a grin and then ran back to his motor. 'Everyone follow me!'

David pulled himself together, crashed the gears, then the sports car spun round and followed Freddy's car, way up in front. Evelyne clung to her daisy hat, terrified it would blow away. David was relaxed again, smiling to himself as though nothing had happened. Evelyne glanced at him and he caught it, winked at her. Everything was all right again, and she felt better when he reached for her hand, held it to his lips and whispered quietly, gently, 'Sorry flame . . . make it all up to you.'

The kiss she held in her memory now didn't seem so bad, and if he kissed her again she would open her own mouth.

'I love you, I love you, I love you . . .' but David didn't hear because it was all inside her bursting head, besides, he was singing at the top of his voice as he swung the car this way and that in a zig-zag across the road. His craziness was contagious and soon she was

146

joining in with him, standing with one arm raised, the other holding on to her hat.

'My Lili Marlene ... Ahhh ... my Lili Marleeeeeeeeene ...'

The tiny, elegant restaurant was almost entirely filled by David's party, the tables, covered in checked cloths, placed close together. A pianola played at full blast. Steaming bowls of spaghetti and chilli were promptly served and wolfed down by all, while they drank themselves into a loud, drunken state with more champagne and red wine.

The proprietor, a good-natured, roly-poly Italian, served the food, opened bottles and turned a blind eye to the damage. They would pay – this young set always did – and he could feel their madness, their desperation for fun. The men were all officers and he knew they had seen sights that had left them scarred – he knew because often they were too drunk to leave. He had sat with many of them crying drunkenly for their comrades, spilling out their nightmares to him, a stranger, a nobody.

Captain Ridgely stood up on a table, glass in hand. 'Here's to unemployment ... here's to us, *to us, the ones who made it home ... Cheers*!'

They sang, 'It's a long way to Tipperareeee, it's a long way to go ...' At first glance this party of beautiful young people seemed not to have a care in the world. It was only when one looked close that one could detect their lostness. Seemingly hell-bent on living life to the full, in reality they despaired for those they knew had no life left.

Evelyne looked hard at the women, as outrageous as their men, dancing on the tables holding their skirts high, garters flashing. One girl named Tulip had stripped off her dress and was dancing in her shift. She had bobbed hair and was very pretty.

One young chap with a lady's garter around his head seemed to be having a great time, waving a walking stick in the air. Evelyne craned her neck to see over the table then sat back quickly – he was in a wheelchair, he had no legs. As she looked around the dark, music-filled restaurant she could see that several of the boys were minus one or two limbs. The crazy atmosphere began to change, it became hotter and hotter, and Evelyne wanted to leave. David sat staring sullenly into space. She tapped his arm. 'David, I think we should go.'

He turned and stared at her as if he didn't know her for a moment, then he smiled his wonderful smile and cocked his head to one side.

'Whatever you say, darling one.'

He jumped up on to the table and yelled at the top of his voice that it was time to go. 'Come on, come on or we'll miss the fight, we can have our fortunes read, *everybody, let's rollll . . .*'

From beneath a table Tulip emerged, her lipstick smeared, pulling down her undershirt. She searched for her dress and spotted one of the boys dancing round in it. She gave chase with squealing laughs.

'Tulip, you naughty girl, come along and get your knickers on.'

She turned, and pursed her smeared, cupid's bow lips.

'I would, duckie, but I can't find 'em.'

At the reception desk Freddy Carlton swayed, a large cigar in his mouth, holding his open wallet. Tulip leaned on his arm.

'Give me some too, Freddy, I want to make a bet on the boxers, ohhh, Freddy, who's a booful boy!'

'I say, Bunny, are we splitting this or what, it's jolly expensive, ya know . . . *Bunny?*'

Bunny waved as he slithered down the wall, and Freddy handed over all he had and tossed the empty wallet over his shoulder.

Evelyne caught David's hand as he led her back to his car. He stopped, holding her at arm's length.

'What a lovely creature you are.'

Evelyne's heart was pounding. He pulled her to him, cupping her face in his hands, and gently kissed her. She moaned with pleasure, and he kissed her neck, her ear. Then he whispered.

'Where are you staying? Back at the house?'

She touched his silky hair, said she was in a small hotel. He caught her in his arms, swung her round.

'We'll go back to the house later, would you like that, my lovely?'

Choked with tears, all Evelyne could do was nod in agreement. She felt as if she would explode with happiness. David tooted the horn.

'To the fair, to the fair.'

The car roared off, leaving a trail of blue smoke in the clear night air.

CHAPTER 7

FREEDOM STUBBS sat in the back of the covered wagon as it jolted its way to the match. He sat quietly, bandaging his right hand, intent on getting the bandages tight the way he liked them. His left fist would be done by Kaulo Woods. Kaulo sat opposite Freedom and looked out of the canvas flap of the wagon, then turned to Freedom.

'I *kair'd* a lot of *wongar acoi*, I *chopped* my *vardo* for another, maybe I'll *dock'd to rardi*.' (I made a deal of money here, I exchanged my van for another, let's hope I do it tonight.)

Kaulo leant over and began to bandage Freedom's left hand. He shot a slanted look up at Freedom who was leaning back against the side of the wagon, his eyes closed. He looked as if he was going for a moonlight stroll rather than a heavy fight. His breathing was as regular as if he was sleeping. Kaulo could weigh the big hand, Freedom was so relaxed, letting Kaulo bandage between his fingers and across the knuckles.

Freedom looked at the small, skinny, elderly man hunched on his left, smiled at him, nodded and rested his head again on the side of the jolting wagon. The old man finished the bandaging, picked up his fiddle and began to play, singing softly.

Can you *rokka* Romany,
Can you play the *bosh*,
Can you *jal adrey the staripen*,
Can you *chin the cosh* . . .

Freedom clenched his fists, nodded to Kaulo that all was fine, all the while tapping his foot to the rhythm of the old gypsy's fiddle.

Two other fighters were further up the wagon, their hands, like Freedom's, bandaged and ready. They were smaller in build, dark and swarthy, and they sat hunched on the benches facing each other. Freedom always sat apart. He stood apart from them anyway, because he was six foot four. This was tall for anyone – never mind a Romany – but then it was known that his blood wasn't pure. Freedom was a half-caste. His mother, Romalla, was the daughter of a Romany king, and Freedom's birth had brought shame to the family. His mother was dishonoured, an outcast, and she had been forced to join another, non-élitist, Romany camp. Her father had refused to have anything to do with her and hadn't spoken to her since, nor had any member of her family.

Romalla was a catch to have in any camp. She was not only a princess of pure blood, but she carried the powers with her. That made her a valuable asset as a money-earner. Freedom had inherited her powers, but he didn't use them; it wasn't done for a male Romany to read hands. However, he had proved to be of royal blood even though half-caste, and was accepted by the lower ranks as a prince. This made him acceptable, and he roamed from camp to camp, even as a child, taken into many families and treated with respect. The stigma of the words *posh ta posh* – bastard – having no effect on him, at least outwardly.

Romalla was rumoured to have had many lovers, and

who Freedom's blood father was no one ever discovered. Or if anyone knew they kept quiet, not wanting to earn Freedom's *tippoty*, or wrath. He was both respected and feared, and although still only twenty-four it was likely that he would become a clan leader. Romalla had died three summers ago of a heart attack. The news was brought to Freedom by a courier carrying the charred back wheel of her caravan, all her goods having been burnt with her body. The wheel was proof she had gone and it was handed to him to roll his fortune further. Romalla had died without revealing who Freedom's father had been. All she had ever said was that he was a 'lion of a man' and one she was proud to have bedded, always implying that the man had been her choice, and one she knew would dishonour her.

Freedom was now becoming famous as a heavyweight boxer and had already made a lot of money for the travellers. The wagon entered the field where the fair was being held and the big tent for the boxing match had already been erected. A beautiful young girl was sitting on a low wall at the entrance. As the wagon rumbled through she jumped down and ran to it, directing the horses to the space allocated for the wagon. It was the best place near the exit; the best was always reserved for Freedom.

When the wagon was in position, Rawnie pulled back the canvas flap. She was a stunning Romany *dukkerin*, and she would make good money at the side shows tonight. She was decked out in all her finery, her red silk shawl wrapped around her head, her hair in two long braids down to her waist. There were gold studs in her ears with loops of gold coins dangling from them. She wore rings and bangles, and even a ruby stud on the side of her nose. Coal dust enhanced the blackness of her slanting eyes, and she would bite her full lips until they shone as red as the ruby in her nose.

She jumped aboard the wagon, pulling behind her a heavy wooden box of food and drink for the men. She always served Freedom first, she was his *manushi*, and although all the men were after her she had eyes only for Freedom. As the men ate the cooked rabbit with chunks of bread and steaming, sweet tea, Mr Beshaley came aboard.

Mr Beshaley was dressed in a smart suit with a waistcoat; it was only the scarf around his neck in place of a collar and tie that made him look different from a well-dressed city gent. He wore a gold fob watch on a chain, gold cuff links, and a gold looped earring in his right ear. His once jet-black hair was now iron-grey, but straight, not a wave in sight.

All the Romany men's hair was black, even Freedom's, coal-black and shining. They all had the same dark, tilted eyes with strange black pupils, high cheekbones and full, wide lips. Freedom differed only in his size. In every other way he looked like a pure-blood Romany.

Mr Beshaley seated himself on the bench. He opened his leather wallet and took out a wad of notes for the betting. Although he himself would not be allowed to place bets as Freedom's manager, there were many of the clan around the match who would place bets for the team. First Beshaley turned to the two fighters at the front of the wagon and discussed their impending fights with them, how they thought they would fare, even asked outright if they would win or lose. Joe shrugged, he felt that the miner pitted against him being that much heavier might sway the odds, but he wasn't going to get himself badly hurt, because he had another bout coming up the following Saturday at a fair in Glamorgan. Beshaley nodded, so they would place bets on the miner for that bout. He turned to the second, a young boy, and asked him what his chances were. Then he told them to go out and get some fresh air into their lungs. It added to the cash flow, because on their walk about the site they would keep their eyes and ears open and report back to the guv'nor. Occasionally they would also feed back bits of gossip for Rawnie to use; it was pointless using her powers in a place like this, it was too much effort.

Freedom stayed behind and listened to Beshaley, and the meeting became serious. Freedom could be up against it as his was the main event. Beshaley talked in detail about his opponent's moves in previous bouts. The man was a good stone heavier than Freedom and a dirty fighter who butted with his head. Hammer also had a habit of not shaving before an event and would get his opponent into stranglehold and rub his thick stubble hard into the man's eyes. The referee they had for this fight would probably give way to the miner and not break up the holds as he should. There were many miners in the audience to support their man, and the referee was also a collier. Three trams of miners had arrived from Llanerch Colliery and they were already drunk and causing havoc. Beshaley knew it was going to be one hell of a night.

Freedom gave no hint of how he was thinking or feeling. Beshaley drew neat little diagrams and made Hammer Thomas sound more and more like a nightmare. He certainly sounded so to Rawnie who sat silently listening and watching Freedom with her dark heavy eyes. Her heart reached out to him. She wanted to sit close, tucked in the crook of his arm the way they did when they were travelling.

'Now the last bout I watched Hammer close, he gave some heavy hits, using a kind of weaving style, half round body blows. Hammer goes for body punches rather than the face, he's a good five inches shorter than you, lad, so he can hurt, you'll have to try and take him fast.'

Out of Beshaley's pocket came a crumpled scrap of paper, and he read out a doctor's report that said Hammer had been badly cut over his left eye, the skin was still very tender . . .

'Go for the left eye, Freedom, get him blinded by his own blood, then try and bring him down before the fourth. You'll have nearly a hundred riding on you, lad, so do your best.'

Beshaley stood up and straightened his checked waistcoat. His own face showed he had been in the ring many times, his nose was flattened, and he had a scar across his left eye. He touched it for a moment and laughed, showing cigar-stained teeth, then he stepped down.

Freedom had said not a word. He clenched his huge fists and leaned back against the canvas with a sigh. Sometimes, Rawnie thought, looking at his handsome face, he doesn't even know I exist. At that precise moment Freedom turned to her and smiled, his whole face softened and a twinkle came into his big, dark eyes, and he winked . . . as if he knew what she was thinking.

It was expected they would marry, she was already nineteen and he was twenty-four, but he had never brought the subject up. They walked together often, but he had never made a serious approach to her. Once, just once, he had kissed her and she would have given herself to him, but he had turned her pressing body from him with that enigmatic smile of his, and then given her bottom a hard smack.

Rawnie knew that Freedom had been with women, all the old'uns told her so – often told her with toothless nudges and winks that it was better to have a man who knew what was what before they were joined for life to a wife.

Rawnie would wait. She knew she was beautiful, had known it from the days when she was just a little *dosha*. When they found out she had the powers handed down to her from her grandmother, she had become important in the camp and was now the main *dukkerin* (fortune-teller), and the palefaces came to her regularly with their pieces of gold. The strange thing for Rawnie was that, although she could read the hands of others, she couldn't foretell her own destiny. But she knew what she wanted – simply Freedom.

In the wagon, Freedom got up, but he had to crouch so as not to hit his head, then he jumped to the ground. He stretched his huge frame like an animal and then turned to help Rawnie down the wooden step. She felt the rough bandages and wanted to kiss his hands, but he was already walking off towards the big tent.

Crowds were gathering and a number of gypsy vans had pulled in to sell their wares. There were artificial flowers made of wood chippings, fern baskets, bottles with wooden crosses built inside, sets of doll's furniture, pegs, heather brooms and rush whips, bouquets of reed flowers, all made by the old women of the camps. Some wandered around with their heavy baskets calling out their wares, while others sold directly from outside their wagons.

Freedom walked among them and they tipped their caps and wished him luck. They had all placed their hard-earned pennies on the prince and Freedom knew it. He picked up a couple of tiny *doshas* and gave them a kiss and a pat on the head. He was waved at by members of many different clans, and he gave them his flashing smile before he disappeared into the tent to prepare for the match.

Rawnie was set up in a small booth, and already had clients waiting in line. She always had one of the lads standing by in case anyone got troublesome, but she was tough and capable of looking after herself. Rarely did she tell anyone the truth, because sometimes she saw such sadness and heartbreak in people's hands she knew it was best not to say. They only ever wanted to hear good fortune was coming their way and that they were lucky.

But this was not the case with her own people. They always wanted the truth. And if she saw sadness, loss or great pain she told them so and they would be ready to face it, but then her people were different from these palefaces. The palefaces always wanted happiness ahead and Rawnie didn't look on what she told them as lies: she contended they were no more than the white lies the palefaces would tell a sick relative, 'Oh, my, you look better today', knowing they were drawing their last breath.

The crowds were getting thicker, and above the clamour could be heard the voices of a group of Romany girls singing. The singing was very seductive, whether it was due to the witchery of their slant-eyed glances or the strange, slow body movements, turning their hands with all the clinking bracelets slowly in the air. Groups of boys stood around with gaping mouths, nudging each other. The gypsy girls were sexy all right. They would lay their hats on the ground while they danced for the crowds, and as coins chinked against each other their dancing would get wilder and wilder, like a tarantella with no accompaniment but their seductive chanting. The lamps threw shadows and caught the colours of the kerchiefs, yellow or bright red, the brilliantly coloured skirts, necklaces, gold chains and red beads; the girls were magical, captivating, their swarthy skins even darker in the lamplight, their eyes flashing, eyes that belonged only to the Romany.

Few among the crowds ever detected anything but fairground atmosphere at the gypsy gatherings. They missed the undercurrent of arrogance, or apartness. The gypsies were a naturally hostile group, it was inherent in them all and made them completely unapproachable. But years of concealing their true feelings just to earn enough to live, to eat, gave the Romany eyes a strange blankness. Tonight they appeared to want nothing more than to delight the gathering crowd, but this was their work.

From the top of the hill the fair looked more like a circus, the big tent for the boxing in the middle with the booths and caravans lined up in a circle around it. Lights twinkled and there was music playing. There were many vehicles and two open-topped buses parked in the field. David's car bounced and rocked over the churned-up grass. He hauled the brake on and a loud cheer rose up from the tent. He looked over, swore, and was out, running towards the entrance. Evelyne fumbled with the catch on the door and ran after him. He shouted for her to hurry, the rest had already gone inside. Evelyne had never been to a fair in her whole life, she would have liked to stop and look at the booths and the gypsy wares but David didn't hesitate. Another roar went up, then cheers. David turned and held out his hand for her, paid the entrance fees and pulled her inside.

The place was packed. Some people were sitting on tiered benches around the ring which was six feet off the ground and had a bright canvas around it to hide the wooden stilts. Others milled around and some even sat on other people's shoulders. Big, bright torches lit the whole area and smoke drifted up into the tent top. It was stiflingly hot, and the air was thick with smoke from cigarettes and cigars as well as from the torches. Scuffles were breaking out, fists flying, and the noise was deafening. Car horns sounded, whistles blew – the whole place was in an uproar. A man in an unbelievably loud checked suit, holding a loud hailer, stood in the centre of the ring. Behind him men were taking bets, money was being passed over heads, under arms, and two men sitting on ladders at a blackboard constantly wiped and wrote up new rows of figures in chalk.

David elbowed his way forward, and Evelyne lost her grip on his hand twice and had to push her way to his side. Her hat was knocked off and she had to scrabble for it. The daisies were looking a little ragged now, but she crammed the hat back on her head. David caught sight of Freddy and the others huddled up close to the ringside. A fight was breaking out as people at the back couldn't see over the heads of the people standing on the front benches.

David eventually fought his way through to the group. How on earth Freddy had managed to capture half a bench was beyond Evelyne, but David sprang up on to it and helped her up, flinging his arm around her waist. 'Can you see? We're just in time.'

Evelyne almost fell over, but a small man behind her propped her up, and then toppled over himself as he

159

tried to retrieve the cloth cap he had dropped. A woman hit him with her handbag and called him a dirty little bugger. He countered this with a furious glare and lewd remark about her bum being too big for his liking anyway.

The check-suited man's face looked ready to burst, the sweat running down his cheeks, 'Ladies and gentlemen, the main event of the evening!'

This was greeted by a roar of approval, and he had to wait for it to die down before he could speak again.

'In the right corner, Hammer . . .'

Hammer paraded around the ring, bowing, waving, kissing his huge, gloved hands, and eventually went to his corner where three burly men stood with towels and a large bucket. A small milking stool was placed in the corner for Hammer to sit on, but he refused, and stood pulling at the ropes which provoked more cheering and yelling.

There was obviously some problem getting Hammer's opponent into the ring. Fists were flying at the other side of the tent, men were being hauled off each other, and the screams of the man in the checked suit through his loud hailer were accompanied by howls from the crowd.

'Freedom, the Romany gypsy prince . . . FREEDOM!'

Again no one could hear any details over the crowd's bellowing, and cries of 'Boooo . . . Booooo . . .' swamped the tent as Freedom appeared. He bent low, entered the ring, and went straight to his corner. He stood head and shoulders above the men in his corner until he sat on his little stool, and then they closed ranks round him and he couldn't be seen.

A burly man in a white shirt entered the ring with a white towel over his arm. He held up the towel in one hand, a stopwatch in the other. The man in the checkered suit collapsed out of the ring to sit, hugging his loud hailer, in a state of total exhaustion.

The referee waved his towel a few more times, then turned gesturing to both boxers to come out of their corners. Hammer bounced off the ropes and up went his gloved hands as he waved to the crowd. The roars of approval and disapproval came in ear-shattering waves. The referee gestured to Freedom to come forward, and as he walked slowly towards Hammer the boos and hisses grew even louder. The two men touched gloves, and whatever the referee said went unheard as the boxers returned to their corners.

Hammer hung on the ropes again, screaming that he would take the gyppo out in three rounds, 'Three, three, not-a-one, not-a-two, but three . . .' The crowd roared back, 'Three, three, three.' The tent felt as if it would collapse as they stamped their feet in unison.

The betting rose to fever pitch before the fight could commence, and more money passed over more heads in cloth caps. The fight was held up again as someone removed a passing cloth cap and tried to take the cash, provoking yet another fight.

A small, balding man fought his way to the ringside and held up a large school bell, which he rang once at Hammer and then once at Freedom. Holding the bell high above the head for the spectators to see, he clanged it again and the fight began. The crowd went quiet as the two fighters moved closer, their corners slipping out of the ring to hang on the corner ropes. High up in the tent two men had crawled like monkeys along the ropes to get a better view.

Rawnie could hear the cheers and boos, and she packed up her little card table. All the gypsies were packing.

They knew better than to stay because if their man Freedom won, they would be the target of fighting-mad miners. They moved quickly and quietly, counting their money and collecting their children so that they were ready to move out.

Jesse Blackton lounged in his booth and jingled the money he had made. He was twenty-two years old, and with a *stardo* of petty thieving already mounting up. He had the longest coal-black eyelashes, as black as his hair which he wore in a long braid down his back. He also wore his mother's earring, a long loop, in his left ear. He was very slim, and some said that was why he was such a good thief – his tiny hands could slip into a woman's *putsi* like a small child's. His family didn't approve of his thieving and he was constantly brought before the elders. But Jesse was *Tatchey Romany*, very pure-blooded, and because of that he had been forgiven many times and taken back into the fold. Jesse hated Freedom, partly because he was a *posh ta posh* and yet took the position of a prince. Among the clans Freedom was held up as an example to the children, who were told that one day, according to the readings, Freedom would be rich and successful; he would one day be the king and lead them. Jesse had always felt that to be *his* prerogative. He could trace his ancestry on both sides back to royal blood, and his many *beebees* and *cocos* were scattered from Scotland to the East End of London and beyond to Devon and Cornwall. Jesse could travel anywhere and be greeted with respect and open arms, but he remained with the Welsh family because of his desire to make Rawnie his *manushi*, his woman. He had been after her since he had joined her clan two years ago, but she would never even give him the time of day.

Rawnie knew Jesse was after her, and often she played him along a little. She knew he was royal but, in her opinion, he didn't come anywhere near her man Freedom. As it was, Jesse stood only five foot seven, but she had to admit he was a looker and she saw the effect he had on the younger girls.

'Well,' said Jesse as he leaned casually against the tiny booth, 'did you have much *bokht* tonight?'

Rawnie jingled her purse and smiled, and asked if Jesse had done well. He said nothing, just lifted his long, silky eyelashes, and gave her a cheeky grin.

A roar from the crowds inside made them both turn. That was a roar of approval, and it meant that Freedom must be hurt. Jesse turned back to see Rawnie's frightened face. He kicked at the floor, tossed a stone on to the top of his boot and flicked it away.

'Dinna worry, he's no *lang gry*. Freedom has to have the taste of blood in his mouth before he gets his temper up.'

There was a massive swell of shouts and boos, and Jesse grinned.

'See what I mean, that'll be a few *dands* gone. Maybe he won't look so handsome after this, but he can *cour* for a *diddicoy*.'

Jesse's use of the word *diddicoy*, or outcast, made Rawnie slap him hard, but Jesse just laughed and shook his head which must have been stinging. He ambled off, turning as he went to say, 'I'll wait for you, Rawnie. You'll come to me one day.'

Another huge cheer from the tent made Rawnie shiver and she packed her belongings fast, hauling them into the wagon and then, knowing she shouldn't, she made her way towards the big tent.

She couldn't even see the ring from the back of the tent so she shoved and pushed her way closer, ducking under the sweating arms, narrowly missed by clenched fists that were boxing on behalf of Hammer. She dodged men who were so absorbed in the fight they were giving blow-by-blow accounts of it to themselves. She could hear the thudding, cheering and yelling but could still see nothing. She didn't know how the fight was going, but her little, wiry body wriggled through until she could glimpse the corner of the ring through a tiny gap in the crowd.

Suddenly Rawnie could see Freedom as he sat on his stool, drinking from a bottle of water like a baby, then turning to spit into the bucket. The sweat was dripping from his hair like tears as he leant back against the post. He was rubbed down with a white towel, water was splashed on his face, and then grease was plastered over his eyes. His face looked red, but she could see no cuts, just deep, red marks, and deeper red ones on his chest and shoulders. Then her view was blocked by a scream-ing fan as the school bell rang for another round.

Rawnie didn't even know which round they were fighting or who was ahead on points, so she began to burrow her way closer until she stood behind a bench. 'The bloody palefaces, typical,' she thought, 'they are standing right up close to the ring, no wonder the lads at the back are jumping up and down just to get a glimpse.'

Hammer was hammering blows to Freedom's upper body while Freedom ducked and weaved but seemed unable to find a break in Hammer's defence. Hammer lowered his head, almost as if he were looking at the floor, but kept his fists up and jabbed, jabbed, then he swung. Three times his heavy blows had connected, but Freedom had taken it and not gone down. Hammer was heaving for breath, hissing between his teeth, and like an old ram he thundered body blows at Freedom, but the bastard just kept on taking them.

This was the hardest fight Freedom had faced to date, and he was at a loss as to how he could get at the man at all, never mind hit him hard enough to floor him. Freedom couldn't break through Hammer's defence – his guard – his jabbing fists, like an oncoming tank.

Hammer was huge and overweight, and his punches hurt. One had nearly winded Freedom and if it hadn't been for the bell he might have gone down. Hammer was judging his man, knew he'd got him foxed, now he needed to close in, but Freedom's reach held him back. The gyppo, Hammer knew, would go for any advantage he could find. He hadn't expected the fight to go this far and he'd already lost on the betting that he'd have Freedom down in three. The lad looked as though he could go the distance. But Hammer's age was against him. He had to get the boy out because there was no way Hammer could go the full fifteen rounds at this pace. He decided to open up a little, let the boy think he'd found a chink in his defences, then he'd use his famous right uppercut.

The crowd was getting restless. They weren't getting enough action, and Hammer acted on his decision to open up. It was a fatal mistake; he had misjudged the power of Freedom's punches, and he felt his left eyebrow split open like an orange. The blood streamed down and he tossed his head like a crazed bull, trying to cut the boy up with his famous Hammerhead, when another sharp blow to his streaming left eye blinded him on that side. He couldn't see the punches coming, and as he fought on he couldn't feel them either. They were

·165·

coming fast, bang bang, one after the other – there was no let-up. The crowd's boos and hisses were telling Hammer he was losing, but he struggled on, hunched up and tried to get Freedom hemmed into the corner. He knew his eye had to be attended to, the blood was splashing over Freedom's body. He hung on, leaning his weight on Freedom, hoping to tire him and praying the bell would ring – only the bell would save his neck. But Freedom couldn't be cornered, and he couldn't be stopped.

Hammer lurched at Freedom, felt the big arms trying to push him away, but he clung on. The white towel of the referee flicked – it was now spotted with blood, Hammer's blood, and then the ref. was between them, trying to break Hammer's hold.

'Break . . . *Break . . . Come on, break!*'

The referee hauled Hammer off Freedom and gave him a warning against holding, which caused more loud boos and yells from the crowd. Hammer swayed and gave a quick glance to the man with the bell. He was sure it was time. That look was his downfall, he felt the left side of his face blow apart. He was reeling backwards, he stumbled, and the blows kept on coming and coming, then it was black, black on black; Hammer was going down, down into the mines. He was shouting for his Da to help him up, there was heavy, black, thick smoke everywhere. He couldn't breathe, his chest heaved and he screamed again for his Da, screaming that the roof was caving in. He was falling, falling down a black shaft, no light, no sound, just silence.

The huge crowd in the tent was ominously quiet, they stared in disbelief as their magnificent Hammer crawled along the canvas floor. He seemed to be crying and his knees were gone, he couldn't get himself up.

Then his body crashed, face down, the spray of blood and sweat drenching the first row of the audience.

Evelyne gasped as the red spray splashed across her suit, and she put her hands up to cover the nightmare in front of her. The huge man crying like a baby, his head split open and the cheering, screaming crowds. She heard herself shouting, and the next moment the place was in an uproar as the men clinging to the ropes high up in the tent fell, landing in the crowd. The benches started toppling as they were pushed from behind, spilling their occupants forwards on to the people in front. Bench after bench went over, trapping people underneath, screaming, fighting, writhing bodies everywhere, a mass of struggling arms and legs.

Freedom and his crew ran from the ring, pushing the avenging, clawing miners back. They were spat at, insulted, accused of cheating, rigging the match. This had happened once before at a boxing match and the gypsies knew they had to get out fast, move their wagons. The touts would collect the money and bring it to the camp; the main thing was to save themselves from the mob.

Hammer's trainer and corners were still trying desperately to revive him, shoving the crowds out of the ring. It was pandemonium as a sprawling mass of bodies fought to get out of the crush. The apparently lifeless body of Hammer was passed over heads and outstretched arms to give him air, get him out of the tent.

Evelyne clawed her way up over bodies and finally stood, screaming for David, searching frantically for him. She saw Freddy dragging benches aside and he shouted for help. It looked as though David had broken his leg.

Rawnie pushed and shoved, trying to follow Freedom, and felt her scarf being yanked off her head by an irate miner, who held it in the air.

'Here's one of the bloody gypos!'

Hands were all over her, pawing at her, ripping at her clothes. Dear God, why hadn't she listened, why hadn't she done as she'd been told? Rawnie scratched at the leering sweating faces.

With the help of two of the others, Evelyne and Freddy finally managed to get David outside. He was bent double in agony, teeth clenched. Freddy tried to calm him, giving orders to the hysterical women. The rest of their friends were gathering, calling out to each other, thankful they were safe. There was so much shouting and screaming going on that their voices were drowned.

Freedom jumped aboard the wagon where the waiting boys patted his shoulder and cheered. There were two men up front, and one of them flipped the horses' reins and the wagon made for the exit. Motor horns were blaring, and now above the yells could be heard the distinctive bells of police cars as they approached the field. The horses kicked and rolled their eyes, and Freedom climbed up front to take the reins.

The guv'nor, Mr Beshaley, ran to the wagon, his face flushed.

'Get out, get out fast, past the law, he's dead, Hammer's not come round, they think he's dead – I'll sort out the cash here, see you back at the camp.'

Beshaley saw Freedom immediately draw the horses back as if to get down. He banged on the side of the wagon.

'Get out of here, all of you . . . *Go go go*!'

The horses were skittish because of the running, shouting people and the sound of the police bells. A crowd of miners was heading for the wagons, shouting to each other. They were going to overturn the gyppos' carts. The wagon moved forward, cutting through the mob. Suddenly Jesse was running wildly towards them, waving his arms and pointing back at the tent. Freedom stood between the horses, heaving them back by their collars, handed the reins to one of the other men and jumped to the ground. Jesse's panic-stricken face was streaked with dirt from the clods of earth the miners had started hurling at them.

'She's still in there, Rawnie, she went back in there, in the tent!'

Freedom looked back in horror. The boys tried to hold him back, but he just brushed them aside and took off with Jesse running at his heels, shouting as he went, 'Get out, all of you, we'll use Rawnie's cart. . . . go, go, move.'

The wagon hurtled forwards, knocking three burly miners off their feet. They stepped out of Freedom's way, wary of him as he raised his huge fists.

Freddy managed to lay David down on the back seat of his car, then ran to the driving seat. Evelyne held on to his arm.

'He must go to the hospital, get him to a hospital.'

Freddy released her hand, 'Get a lift home with one of the others, you can't come with us, I'm taking him home, for God's sake.'

Evelyne didn't understand, and she was almost knocked over as Freddy drove the car out of the field. She stared after them. The rest of their group was

169

already moving out, their cars heading for the exits, and Evelyne ran towards an oncoming car with Tulip clinging to the running-board. The car drove straight past, leaving her standing there.

Freedom kept on the move, and when any miner approached him with clenched fists and abuse he growled like a mad dog, baring his teeth and snarling, and they stepped back.

'*Fix* . . . bloody fix, man, you cheatin' bastard!'

With one hand Freedom grabbed the man, hauled him up and threw him against a pole in the side of the tent.

'You want to take over the fight, man?'

The man's false teeth rattled in his mouth, and he held his hands over his face, terrified.

'Anyone else? Anyone else . . .?'

They backed off and let him pass. Jesse was waiting at the torn tent flap and together they went inside.

CHAPTER 8

EVELYNE SEARCHED the ground for her handbag. She put her hands to her head in despair. Her hat? She'd lost her new hat! At first she felt tearful, then her temper flared and she turned back. She'd not paid fifteen shillings for a new hat to lose it, never mind her handbag. Her hair had come down from the bun, tumbling around her shoulders, and she was being shoved from all sides, but she gave as good as she got. She stood taller than a lot of the lads she battled through. Having been brought up with three older brothers and having Hugh for a father helped. She rolled up the sleeves of her new suit, it was like the old days out in the yard of a Sunday when she was no more than nine years old. Dicken, Will and Mike were always fighting, and she'd joined in. Now she was as good as any man around her, and she punched and kicked her way through into the tent.

Jesse searched the dispersing crowd without luck, then he jumped up on Freedom's shoulders, looking for the familiar red scarf, and saw it being waved around by a group of men by the side of the ring. He urged Freedom forward like a stallion.

Evelyne felt her hair pulled from behind, and swung her fist round, belting the gormless young boy on the nose.

'Christ almighty, there's a bloody Amazon in there, bach.'

The police had imposed some sort of order now, and they gathered around Hammer's body with their notebooks out. His manager and trainer stood by, helpless. They kept looking at each other and then down at the massive bulk of Hammer at their feet.

The crowds were thinning out faster than before because the police were there and no one wanted to get booked. Hammer was carried to an ambulance and its crew worked desperately, massaging his heart and trying to resuscitate him. Eventually they were rewarded by a slight flutter of his chest, and he drew a faint breath.

Evelyne searched among the benches, lifting them up. She didn't care about her suit, it was ruined anyway, but she wanted her handbag. It had more than three pounds and sixteen shillings in it, a new comb and mirror. Evelyne suddenly felt faint, oh God, she thought, my post office savings book! She didn't care who saw her, she lifted her skirt and felt inside her bloomers, then she sighed with relief. Her precious savings – her legacy – was safe. Then her temper rose again as she remembered that her return ticket was also in the handbag.

She was now close to the ring. Its platform was on stilts, some six feet off the ground and was swathed in tarpaulins. Could her handbag have slithered beneath the ring? She pulled the fabric aside.

Underneath the ring, three lads held Rawnie down, her skirts around her head. A fourth was on top of her with his trousers round his ankles, while the others leered and encouraged him. Her face was scratched and bleeding, her mouth bruised and a tooth missing. She lay half-conscious mewing like a small, drowning kitten.

Evelyne let the tarpaulins fall back into place. 'Go away,' she told herself, 'don't get involved, get out of here, never mind the handbag, just get out, Evelyne Jones, and for God's sake do it *now*!' At the same time as the voice in her head was talking to her, someone else – not Evelyne, she was sure, but another person entirely – grabbed one of the broken bench legs and was under the boxing ring like a wildcat.

The lad on top of Rawnie had his head cracked by the bench leg, felt his hair being torn out by the roots, heard a scream like a tiger. Two of the others tried to grab Evelyne; one caught her by the hair, but she was kicking, biting, spitting, and punching with all her strength. The other tried to pull her off his mate and suddenly they all turned, open-mouthed. Light flooded beneath the ring as Freedom, his muscles straining, lifted the platform bodily upwards and tossed it aside.

Jesse took on one of the lads and Freedom, panther-like, moved towards the other three. He grabbed two of them by their necks, bashing their heads together, and knocked out the other with one punch. The boy's nose split in two and blood streamed down his face.

'You're all right now, love, it's all right, you're safe, we'll take you right now, nobody's going to hurt you any more, it's all right.'

Evelyne held the terrified, raped and beaten girl in her arms, covering her body with her own jacket. Rawnie moaned and clung to Evelyne like a child, her

173

body heaving as she sobbed. Her small body jerked and shuddered, and Evelyne stroked her hair.

Evelyne talked non-stop, saying anything that came into her mind to try and calm the terrified girl. Wood splintered around them, cries of 'Fire! *Fire! Fire!*' went up. The tent was aflame.

Jesse repeated the cry as smoke began to billow from one side of the tent, the lanterns having fallen when Freedom moved the boxing ring. He called again, but Freedom was searching one of the boy's pockets. Jesse pulled Freedom's sleeve, urging him to get out, the police were inside the tent arresting everyone in sight. Freedom still grasped the terrified boy with one hand and shook him, his feet off the ground, until his teeth rattled in his head.

'Remember me, because I'll be coming after you, each and every one of you, this is not the end of it.'

Jesse turned and gestured for them to hurry.

'Bejesus, Freedom, it'll be us in the clink if you don't get a move on.'

Freedom picked up Rawnie in one arm as if she were no more than a rag doll, and with his other hand he guided Evelyne out. They kept moving, Evelyne crouching down as she ran along behind a row of chairs. Half of her felt she had no need to flee like a criminal, but the flames were spreading behind her and the boy she had walloped with the bench leg was shouting after them, pointing at her. The smoke billowed back and masked their escape, Jesse slicing through the side of the tent with his knife.

They made it to Rawnie's wagon and Freedom helped Evelyne aboard. He laid Rawnie gently down, and the wagon jolted off, Jesse whipping up the horse. Evelyne had now lost her hat, her handbag and one shoe, her hair was loose, her stockings laddered and one sleeve was torn right out of her jacket and soaked with Rawnie's blood.

As the wagon made its way across the fields, keeping off the roads and away from the police, one of the youths was telling a detective sergeant that he had seen with his own eyes an Amazon woman with a sword, and she was beating everybody up. It was she who had given him the bloody nose, he'd not touched a soul. The youth was thrown into a police wagon and taken away to be charged with disorderly conduct. He maintained his innocence in the wagon, still persisted with his story at the police station. There had been this enormous bloody woman, like an Amazon he had seen at the local cinema. She had red hair down to her waist and was screaming like a crazy horse. One of the other boys, with his head cut open, was put into the next cell. He said nothing, but by God he'd remember that wildcat as long as he lived. Nearly broken his skull, she had.

The Amazon sat hunched in the wagon, having no idea where she was going or with whom. She watched as the big fighter they called Freedom rocked the poor girl in his arms. He talked quietly, intimately, close to Rawnie, and his soothing voice and quiet strength calmed her. She lay with her face turned away from Evelyne and began to weep softly, and all the time Freedom talked in a language Evelyne couldn't understand. She had never seen a man so gentle; it was hard to reconcile him with the fierce man she had seen fighting in the ring.

They travelled for about thirty minutes and then Jesse pulled up the horses. They were by a stream and Rawnie would want to wash. Freedom bent to lift her down.

'*Acoi Rawnie, chies so betie*, you'll wash here you're so *chiklo*, an' Jesse mun, we'll leave *gav*, the *gav mush* will be after us.'

Evelyne did not understand what they were saying. She saw Freedom lift Rawnie in his arms and then Jesse grabbed him.

To Evelyne's astonishment the men argued, the poor girl between them. Rawnie clung to Freedom's neck as Jesse tried to pull her out of his arms.

'She's ma woman, raped mun, we take revenge.'

Freedom snarled angrily, his voice hissing, '*Kek, kek.*'

Evelyne stood up and hit her head hard on the roof of the wagon. She saw stars before her eyes and slumped down again.

'Will you stop your arguing, the girl should be washed.'

They carried Rawnie to the water and she was silent, head bowed.

'Leave her with me, go, the pair of you, and let me help her.'

Jesse gave her a foul, snarling look and Freedom held him back.

'Thank ye for this, woman.'

Freedom filled a pail with water and placed it beside Evelyne. Then he took off his shirt and ripped it in two, throwing her the pieces to use as washcloths. The two men went back to the wagon, still arguing.

Rawnie sat staring, stunned, and Evelyne wet the cloths and washed the girl's face and neck, then sat down and eased the girl's skirt back to wash her thighs, and was horrified. Her legs were crusted with blood and bruised, deep blue and red marks where the boys had forced her thighs apart.

'Oh God help you, God help you.'

176

As Evelyne washed her gently, the girl laid her head on Evelyne's shoulder.

When it was done Evelyne whispered to her that there was no trace left, she was clean. She dried Rawnie with the remainder of Freedom's shirt and called out that they were ready. It was Jesse who gently scooped Rawnie into his arms and helped her up the wooden steps of the wagon.

Evelyne went to empty the pail of water. Her foot slipped and she ended up standing in the stream. Freedom appeared on the bank and held out his hand to her, and as she reached for it she slid down the bank again, ending up sitting in cold water to her waist. Freedom hauled her out with one jerk of his strong arm, but her new suit was now soaked.

'Ye'd best come back to camp and dry off by the fires.'

Evelyne hesitated, and he cocked his head to one side and waited. Then she gave a brief nod and was helped aboard. Well, she couldn't really arrive back at Mrs Pugh's in this dishevelled condition.

As the wagon rumbled and bumped its way along the rutted lanes, Rawnie sat staring into space, her hands plucking at her brightly coloured skirt. The bracelets tinkled and jangled, but she stared straight ahead, her beautiful face scratched, her lips puffy and bruised. She was calm now, her eyes impassive and distant. Evelyne supported herself on the wooden frame of the wagon as it jolted and swayed. She tried to remember what she had in her handbag, maybe the return ticket was on the dressing table at Mrs Pugh's, but she knew in her heart that it wasn't. How much money? The more she tried to remember the more she felt like weeping. Her lovely hat, oh God, fifteen shillings gone. She sat as far from the fighter as possible, aware that he kept staring at her. She felt no fear, she wasn't afraid of them, just extremely worried about her purse and the waste of money, bag, hat and shoes. She bit her lip to force back the tears, then felt disgusted with herself – that poor girl raped and all she was worried about was her outfit.

At long last the wagon stopped, and Jesse opened the fiap. They helped Rawnie down, she wouldn't be lifted but stepped down, her head high, even her dark eyes were proud, her face a mask. Caravans and wagons formed a semicircle with large tents and the site was lit up by a huge, blazing fire in the centre. Women sat on caravan steps, while cooking pots on stands around the fire sizzled and boiled.

The gypsies had done well that night and they were celebrating. Four girls danced around, flashing their skirts. In the firelight they glittered with gold and their red underskirts flashed as they clicked their heels. A fiddler started to play and an old woman beat her fists against a ribboned tambourine. As Freedom stepped down from the wagon, they cheered and a group of small children clustered around him. Jesse took Rawnie's hand and led her towards a painted wooden caravan, its shafts laid flat on the grass.

Evelyne hovered at the door of the wagon, and felt the whole camp grow still and silent as they all stared towards her, their expressionless eyes taking her in, then turning to Freedom for an answer. Freedom guided Evelyne into the glare of the fire, and she was very conscious of her appearance. She knew she must look very strange to the gathered people. Her hair was loose, her skirt filthy, she wore no stockings and her jacket had only one and a half sleeves. On top of that she was covered in mud and blood, even her face was streaked with dirt.

Freedom held her hand, guiding her firmly forward, and spoke sharply to two old women who whispered to each other. Evelyne couldn't understand him, he spoke in his strange language. Whatever he said made one of the old women step towards Evelyne and take her hand, tugging at her to follow. Evelyne was a little afraid to let go of Freedom's strong hand, but he nodded that it would be all right and to go with the old crone.

She was let into a rounded tent. Inside she could see the carved willow hoops that supported the canvas, shaped like a ribcage. The tent was large, and inside were four cot-like beds. Cooking utensils and household equipment were stacked in one corner and the floor was strewn with rushes. The tent was warm and cosy, and the old woman tugged at Evelyne's sleeve for her to follow. Opening a wooden box, the woman chatted away, although Evelyne couldn't understand a word. Out of the box came a cardigan, an old skirt and a white petticoat. Again the woman plucked at Evelyne's sleeve, gesturing for her to take off her skirt. There was a strange, musky smell to the clothes, but at least they were dry, and she began to feel a little warmer.

Evelyne could see the women scrubbing her clothes and she sighed; they looked as if they were trying to get the oil stain out, but she knew they were rubbing too hard. They should have used vinegar and brown paper, but she didn't like to move out of the tent, in fact she wasn't too sure exactly what she should do. She had no idea of the time or where she was.

Jesse was all for driving into town and finding the boys. He constantly flicked his knife, it was razor sharp and his intentions were obvious. Freedom strove to keep the peace.

'Jesse, I know, mun, what was done to her, but for us all to ride into town is madness.'

Jesse hurled the knife at a tree. It whizzed through the air.

'I'll not move out of camp until I take revenge, you saw nothin' – you did not see what they done. It scarred her mind, not just her body, mun.'

'Jesse, the men will pay for what they done.'

'Oh, yeah, you tell me how much? Go on, an' tell me how? By us going to the police when you know what they would do, clap every one of us into jail so much as look at us. We all go in *now*. We ride in, take them bastards one by one and then we ride out.'

'You go in tonight, Jesse, and they will arrest you.'

Jesse put up his fists and struck out at Freedom. He was crazy with rage.

'It's you, *mush*, they want you, the law want you for tonight's fight.'

The other men stepped in and held Jesse back. Their prince, their great warrior, made them more money than Jesse, they needed him and they needed his fights.

'He's our fighter, *mush*, so listen to what he says. It was fair, no fault of his if that bastard dies.'

Freedom gripped the furious, blazing Jesse. 'Trust me, *mush*, we'll get each one.'

Jesse wanted to weep, always they turned against him in favour of Freedom. He removed his knife from the tree.

'So be it, but I want each man dead, I want their hearts.'

*

180

Mr Beshaley rode up on his sweating horse. He shouted to the men to collect their winnings, and make it fast.

'Hammer's still alive, but the law want to question one and all, so pack up and get out, move fast, we've made good money . . . head for Scotland.'

Never one to ride with them, Beshaley heeled his horse and galloped away. He looked back once to Freedom and shouted that he would arrange a fight come next month, then he was gone.

The men occupied themselves with counting their winnings, and Rawnie's plight was forgotten for the moment. Freedom took Jesse aside and told him to get everyone prepared to move out by morning. Everyone except himself and Jesse who would repay the men who had raped Rawnie.

'How will ye do it, man, punch every miner we cross?'

Freedom smiled, and took out the wallet he had taken from one of the boys. Find one and they could get the names of the others. Jesse was so eager to use his knife – he would soon have the opportunity.

Jesse seethed inside. It was as if Freedom was always one step ahead of him, but he had to concede that it made sense. Already the men were preparing to move out, quietly taking down the tents and bringing the horses from the fields.

Freedom went to the tent where Evelyne was and stood at the opening. He could see Evelyne fast asleep, her mass of hair sprayed out across the pillow. Her white skin seemed translucent, and the soft violet shade of her eyelids fascinated him. He moved closer to the bed, and stood for a while looking down into the strange, beautiful face. He touched her hair gently – golden hair, it

181

felt soft to his touch, and then he looked again. There was something in the back of his mind, a long-forgotten memory. Evelyne woke to see his face looming above her, and started. As she sat up he smiled at her and said she had no need to fear him.

Her clothes were dry but wrinkled, and when she was left alone to change she discovered that they had shrunk. So much for expensive French labels! She went to the tent flap and opened it a fraction. Freedom was waiting, as if on guard, outside.

'I can't get into my skirt, it's shrunk.'

He turned and looked at her and then laughed, said for her to keep what she had been given. Wearing the petticoat and brown sack skirt, with her own blouse and the jacket that now had only one sleeve, she opened the tent flap. There was a blackened area where the fire had been, and all the tents had been packed away. Most of the camp had already moved on, there were just a few caravans left in line with the horses being backed into the shafts.

The last caravan in the line, with red curtains, was brightly painted, and the blues, reds and greens merged into a strange pattern all over the wagon itself.

'Rawnie wants to see you, then we will take you back to town.'

Evelyne was led over to the caravan, and she mounted the steps and tapped on the door. Jesse opened it, and with a curt nod jumped down and gestured for her to go inside.

Jesse joined Freedom, who was dismantling the tent Evelyne had used. He jerked his head in the direction of Rawnie's caravan.

'By God she's a big'un, you see the way she fought, like a wildcat . . .'

Freedom made no reply but continued to pull down the canvas.

The caravan inside was as bright as the outside, full of colours and wonderful paintings. Each panel bore a different scene, and the wooden ceiling was dark blue with moons and stars, and lanterns dangling. The brass was sparkling, polished like mirrors. Bright skirts and blouses were strewn around, and the heavy, sweet smell of musk was everywhere. A side table attached to the wall of the caravan was crammed with pots of cream and rouge. Hanging on hooks were bracelets and bangles and hundreds of beaded necklaces, mostly of bright red beads mixed with gold coins. There were boxes of gold earrings, hair slides, strange, diamond-cut stones, and amber, quaint and oriental. There was malachite and silver, and wonderful, rich, matte yellow gold, a treasure-chest of coral and jet. Evelyne gasped: there were so many colours and sparkling ornaments, it took her completely by surprise.

Rawnie sat curled up on a couch. She was dressed in a bright red skirt with layers and layers of ribboned petticoats. Her hair glistened with oils, her arms covered with bracelets, and she wore a shawl with embroidered roses. She gestured for Evelyne to sit, and seemed pleased with the effect her home had on the strange girl with the funny hair.

Evelyne had to bend slightly, the ceiling was so low, and she sat down next to Rawnie. The girl took Evelyne's hand and kissed her palm, then she removed her heavy gold earrings and handed them to Evelyne.

'No, no, I can't, please, you don't have to . . . take them back.'

Rawnie frowned, took back the earrings and reached for some beads. She held them out, and Evelyne again shook her head.

'You don't like them? What is it you want?'

Evelyne smiled and said she wanted nothing.

Rawnie's eyes filled with tears. She lowered her head, and her voice was so soft Evelyne could only just hear.

'Will you take him when you go?'

Evelyne did not understand. She looked puzzled and reached for Rawnie's hand, but Rawnie cowered back against the cushions.

'What is it, Rawnie? That's your name, isn't it? Are you afraid of me? I am ashamed for what happened to you, and I will help you in any way . . . if you want the police informed . . .'

Rawnie grasped Evelyne's arm and shook her head, said there were to be no police, they had their own ways of taking care of their people. She had to give her thanks, and Evelyne had refused her gifts; was she ashamed to take them? They were not stolen, they had been handed down to Rawnie from her mother . . . Evelyne accepted a tiny pair of hooped earrings, and as she bent to kiss Rawnie again, the girl shrank away. There seemed nothing more to say and Evelyne prepared to leave. She could hear the men moving, putting a horse between the shafts of the caravan.

She was aware of Rawnie's dark eyes staring at her, as if she could see inside her head. Then Rawnie took Evelyne's hand, her own in comparison were dark-skinned, tiny. The girl's touch was delicate, as she slowly traced the head line, the life line, her dark eyes seeming even darker as the feather-light touch traced the heart

184

line. Three times she traced the heart line and murmured, 'Mercury, Apollo, Saturn, Jupiter . . . venus, venus, venus . . . the venus.' She reached over for a lighted candle, brought it closer, and as Evelyne tried to withdraw her hand, her grip tightened. She began to drip the wax slowly into Evelyne's upturned palm until it was covered in the warm wax. Her black eyes held Evelyne as she began to spread her hand down, pressing hard, palm to palm.

Freedom looked in at the caravan door, glanced at the two women and closed the door again. Rawnie was distant, her eyes expressionless, dark pools. They held Evelyne's like a snake and then Rawnie lifted her hand away together with the imprint of Evelyne's in the wax, like a shell. She held it up against the candle flames and stared at the strange, delicate imprint.

The sides of the wagon were banged and Jesse's voice called out that they must be on their way. Evelyne stood up, nearly knocking her head on the ceiling but remembering just in time. Rawnie still held the paper-thin waxen palm to the candle flame. Evelyne was opening the door to go outside when Rawnie spoke, her low, husky voice as hypnotic as her eyes, 'He will give you two sons, strong, healthy sons, and you will lose him when the sky is full of black . . . dark birds. They fill the sky. Beware of the big dark birds, my friend . . .'

Rawnie was crying soundlessly, tears streaming down her face. She could not read her own destiny, but the faces of the palefaced woman's two sons mirrored Freedom's. She might not know it now, but one day he would be the paleface's *rommando*: she would have his heart, she already had his soul.

*

185

Evelyne turned back, but Rawnie did not look up. She was melting the wax palm in the candle flame, the tears on her cheeks like wax drops, clear, heavy drops.

CHAPTER 9

THE CARAVANS moved out. As the *dukkerin*, Rawnie travelled last. Roped to the wagon shafts was their herd of wild ponies. Rawnie stood at the door of her wagon and heard from up front the boy yelping and clicking his tongue to move her horse forward over the field.

In the distance she could still see Freedom, Jesse and the paleface woman sitting on top of the rag-and-bone cart. She sighed, so be it, she would marry Jesse, the Black Prince, if he would have her. She closed the door and flicked open the knife Jesse had given her, similar to his own. He had carved her name on the shaft. She ran her finger along the blade, then opened her palm and slit the mound beneath her thumb. The blood oozed out, became a fine trickle. Although the wagon rocked and jolted, she was able to stand still as if by magic, unaware of the movement . . . suddenly she opened her eyes wide and screamed, cursing like a witch, and the blade sang through the air to land poised in the wood of her caravan wall, twanging.

Sitting on top of the cart, Evelyne clung on for dear life. Jesse led the donkey, pulling on the reins and

187

glowering, muttering to himself. Freedom walked casually alongside, occasionally looking up at her and smiling. Twice she had almost slipped off, but each time he had been there, hand out to help her regain her balance. He had a way, this fighter, of always being there.

Jesse hit the donkey with a stick and the beast veered to the right, tipping Evelyne over. Freedom made Jesse stop the cart for a moment and got up beside her. Jesse flipped him the rein and walked on, swishing the hedges with his stick. Casually, Freedom slipped an arm loosely around Evelyne's waist and clicked his tongue for the donkey to move on. She sniffed, there was a musky, sweet smell, and at first she thought it came from the hedgerow, maybe a flower, but as she turned her head she realized it came from Freedom, that he must be using a perfume on his hair, or oil. He caught her looking at him and smiled, showing his perfect white teeth.

As soon as they entered town Evelyne jumped down, insisting she would be all right. Without a word Jesse hopped up on to the cart and took the reins again, flipped them and whacked the donkey with his stick at the same time. The cart rattled off.

'Rags, bones . . . bring out yer rags . . .'

As Jesse shouted, Freedom turned back to stare at Evelyne. He gave her a small wave and then turned to face ahead.

Not having the slightest idea where she was, Evelyne kept walking. She had not a penny to her name, and wondered if there might be a post office, then remembered it was Sunday. She sighed, no train ticket home, no handbag, and what did she look like? She was filthy, her skirt was wrinkled, her blouse torn, her beautiful suit completely ruined. She walked on until her feet ached, heading towards the centre of town.

Miss Freda stepped out of her shop, neat as ever and wearing one of her hats. She always walked past the Grand Hotel on a Sunday, showing off her creations as a means of advertising.

'Miss Freda, oh, Miss Freda . . . I've found you.'

She squinted in a short-sighted fashion and looked in the direction of the voice, then her mouth dropped open.

'Oh, oh, what happened to you, child?'

'Could I possibly borrow my bus fare, it's a three-penny ride from the terminal, only I lost my bag and . . .'

To Freda's horror Evelyne burst into tears. She looked around to see if anyone was watching, ashamed to be seen with the girl, and hustled her towards a shop doorway. Wiping her nose on Miss Freda's little lace handkerchief, Evelyne promised to come to the shop next day and repay the three pennies. Freda opened her purse and counted out the money, snapped it shut again and said she had to be on her way as she had a very important business meeting and couldn't stop to talk. From the doorway, Evelyne watched her hurry away down the street.

By the time Evelyne arrived at Dr Collins' house her heels were blistered and red raw. Mrs Darwin opened the basement door to her.

'Gawd love me, what have you been doing? Come on in, lovey.'

She ushered Evelyne into the kitchen where the maid was slumped in a chair by the fire.

Kicking the maid out of the chair Mrs Darwin settled Evelyne down with a steaming cup of tea. As Evelyne drew breath to launch into an explanation of her appearance, Mrs Darwin began to cry, wiping her nose on her apron.

'I'd have left long ago, but I've not had me wages and Master David's taken everything of value, and what *he* left that bugger Morgan's made off with. It's a shocking state of affairs . . .'

Evelyne felt the tea warming her chilled body.

'Is David at home, Mrs Darwin?'

Mrs Darwin looked at Evelyne, her jaw dropped open.

'We went to a fair last night, there was a terrible to-do afterwards, all the benches fell down and David hurt his leg. Did he come home, or is he in hospital?'

Mrs Darwin glanced at Muriel then back to Evelyne. 'He doesn't live here, not any more.' She could see the confusion in Evelyne's face and she bit her lip, concerned. 'He only stays here occasionally, see, he wants to sell this place but he can't, not without your permission, and then what with all his debts, well, the place is not what it was. He's sold off everything that wasn't nailed down. We've not been paid . . .'

Evelyne interrupted her, saying she had already said that she would see about the wages as soon as things were settled.

'Where is David living, then?'

'Well, with his wife of course. Then if he's not there he's with his friend Freddy Carlton, spends a lot of . . .'

Mrs Darwin didn't finish. Evelyne's body shook and she had to put her teacup down.

'Wife? Is David married?'

'Oh, yes, he's married all right, not that you'd know by his manner, and he's got a little boy too . . . Lady Primrose, he married Her Ladyship – oh, what would it be – three, almost four years ago.'

Evelyne couldn't stop herself shaking, her whole body trembled. Mrs Darwin stood up and bent over her. 'Are you all right, lovey? You've gone ever so pale.'

Unable to speak, Evelyne bit her lip hard, forcing herself not to faint, not to cry out, scream his name. Mrs Darwin held her close, patted her head.

'I can see by your face, lovey, something is terribly wrong. What did he do to you? Oh, dear God, what did he do?'

Mrs Darwin blew her nose on her apron and, shaking her fat head, slumped into her chair.

'We've had a terrible time with him, he killed his father, you know. Oh, it was shocking the way he carried on when he came home. See, he didn't know who he was – sometimes he would be gone for days on end and we'd have to send the police out looking for him. Her Ladyship had a shocking time of it, it's memory loss, they say, but it's terrible to see. He don't know who he is, where he is, and he never recognized his father. Broke his heart, it did, killed him as sure as I'm sitting here, shocking, terrible, shocking time.'

Evelyne's heart was hammering inside her chest and Mrs Darwin's voice droning on made it worse. She put her hands over her ears.

'Stop it, stop it.'

'But it's the truth, if it wasn't for Lord Carlton he'd be in a mental home, isn't that right, Muriel?'

Evelyne stood up and clenched her fists.

'But he knew me, he recognized me. You saw the way he ran to me. He knew who I was . . . he called my name, he did, he called me . . . he called my name!'

She sobbed, and Mrs Darwin rocked her in her arms.

'No, lovey, I went to fetch him, tell him you was here; you see, they say perhaps something from his past'll make him remember, sparking something off, like. I told him, *I* told him who you were . . . but he didn't recognize you – he didn't know you.'

Evelyne felt again the sweet kisses, his gentle kisses on her neck, her face, her lips . . . she wouldn't believe it. She shook her head fiercely, and Mrs Darwin sighed.

'Did he have his way with you?'

Evelyne turned away.

'Oh, lovey, I wish it was different, but what can I say, he used this place like a whorehouse, always bringing terrible women back here, some of them so filthy I'd have to burn the sheet afterwards. He don't know what he's doing . . . and him what used to have two baths a day.'

Evelyne downed her tea and carefully placed the rose-patterned cup back on its saucer. Always able to fight her emotions, she was suddenly icy calm, controlled, 'I'll need to see him, see about signing over my part of the house. We'll have to sell it to give you both your wages . . . Do you – do you have a telephone number where I could call him?'

Mrs Darwin nodded and led Evelyne to the hall. 'There'll be his own home, Lady Primrose's, it's her family house they live in. They had a shocking war, she lost her brother and her father, you know . . .'

Evelyne snapped, her voice hard. 'What is the telephone number?'

Mrs Darwin dialled the operator and waited for an answer. The waiting was painful. David was not at home, and a servant suggested they try Lord Carlton's home. Mrs Darwin called the operator again . . .

'Do you remember Lord Carlton, he was in the army with Master David? He married Lady Warner's daughter, poor bugger, Lord love us, what a lump . . . an' 'im such a nice looker and titled as well. Still, he's sitting in clover, lot of money and the factory's going strong. Major Warner, his Lordship, never came back neither. Some say he was killed in action, but there's those who say he stayed away, out of Lady Sybil's reach . . . hello? Hello? Here you are, lovey, you're through to the house.'

In the marble hallway, the butler held out the telephone to Freddy. 'It's Mr Collins' housekeeper, sir.'

Freddy sighed and took the receiver. 'Hello? Speaking . . . who is this? Mrs Darwin? Oh, yes, yes of course, I remember. Well, I'm afraid David's still rather poorly . . . Yes, he's here, resting. I don't really think that would be very convenient.'

Evelyne gripped the telephone tightly.

'Would you please tell Mr Collins that Miss Evelyne Jones will be calling to see him. Thank you.'

Evelyne put the ear-piece back so hard Mrs Darwin thought she'd snapped the hook off.

'Now I would like to take a bath, then I'll go straight to the Warners'.'

Mrs Darwin nodded, even said, 'Yes, ma'am'. Suddenly Evelyne frightened the life out of her.

Heather opened the drawing room doors. Freddy was standing staring at the telephone, his thoughts miles away.

'Who was that, dearest? Mummy said she thought she heard the phone ring.'

She stood staring like an owl, waiting, and Freddy sighed.

'Just someone for David, nothing.'

'Primmy's due at any moment. She called earlier to say she would be driving up from London.'

'Yes, yes I know, I'll go and tell him.'

Heather watched her husband climb the stairs. She sighed. David really played such an important part in their lives. If they weren't chasing around Cardiff looking for him, Freddy was staying at David's house or he at theirs. They had virtually made over to him one of their best front bedrooms, he stayed so often. Not that Heather ever said anything against it; far from it. It was not in her nature ever to disagree with anything Freddy wanted to do.

Just as she was about to close the door, the children's nanny appeared, dragging their twin daughters along. The little girls were very like their mother, even down to the buck teeth. They were both crying because Clarence had kicked one of them. Clarence was David's little boy and, like his father, he spent more time at Freddy and Heather's home than his own.

'Tell Clarence, Nanny, that if he doesn't behave I shall tell his mother, she will be here at any moment.'

The nanny hauled the howling children up the stairs. Trailing behind was the little golden-haired boy, his silky hair just like David's. Clarence began to shout that he wanted his mother, and was pulled away up to the nursery.

'David? You awake, old man? Just had a call from that gel Evelyne whatsit.'

David lay in the large double bed with its frills and canopy, his injured leg propped up on pillows. 'Oh,

194

Christ, that one from last night, I thought we'd got rid of her . . . I say, want a game of cards? Double or quits?'

Freddy sighed. There David sat, looking as angelic as ever, bathed, his hair shining, almost sparkling, his complexion fresh.

'Just that it could be a trifle embarrassing, Primmy called and she's on her way here. Don't think it's a frightfully good idea for them to meet, do you? You were making a bit of a meal of her, you know . . . David?'

Unconcerned, David shuffled his pack of cards. 'Can't you get rid of her for me? You know how I hate to upset Primmy . . . what on earth does she want, did she say?'

Freddy scratched his head and shrugged, muttered that it was something to do with the house, David's old home.

'You think you could sneak her up the back way so no one will know? See what she wants?'

Freddy nodded. He always did what David wanted, always had. Deep down he knew why. He would do anything to be near Lady Primrose, even if it meant taking care of her husband.

Evelyne stood at the iron gates and peered through them, up the gravel drive to the big white manor house. Without the twinkling fairy lights the drive seemed longer, and the house had lost its fairy-tale aspect. The sweeping lawns were devoid of peacocks, but the flower-erbeds and the hedges were as immaculate as ever.

Freddy met her in the drive, as if he had been looking out for here. He seemed ill at ease, nervous of her, and cleared his throat, 'Would you come this way, just follow me.'

They followed a path leading away from the front of

195

the manor, around to the back of the house that had
been part of his dreams for so many years, and in by the
servants' entrance.

Heather flicked the velvet curtains back into place. She
was spying, she knew it. David was obviously up to his
old tricks again. The girl looked positively wretched.

She went back to reviewing the firm's accounts. She
now ran the family business, Freddy paying not the
slightest attention to it, although he dipped into their
joint account freely. Heather never rebuked him, never
questioned what he did with all the 'spending money'.
She was frightened that he might tell her the truth.
What she didn't know couldn't hurt her.

Lady Sybil sat by the fire wrapped in a thick woollen
rug. She appeared weighed down by her treasured array
of beads.

'Who was that outside? I heard the gravel crunch.'

'No one, Mother, just the gardener.'

The clock chimed three.

Evelyne could hear the chimes as she and Freddy
climbed the back stairs. He had said not a word, simply
gesturing to her to follow him. As they crossed the
landing towards David's bedroom, Clarence ran from
the nursery, being chased by Nanny.

'Watch it, Clarence, don't fall over and hurt yourself,'
she warned.

The little boy ran on, disappearing from view with
the nanny calling after him. Freddy tapped on the
bedroom door and opened it. 'Here's your visitor, old
chap, don't make it too long.'

Freddy turned to Evelyne. 'I hope you'll keep quiet

about the boxing match should anyone ask you, you know there was a frightful rumpus afterwards. Police were called in to keep the rabble quiet, and David and I think it best you don't mention our presence there to anyone, all right?'

Evelyne nodded her head, and Freddy went into the bedroom. He laughed at something David must have said, then opened the door wide for Evelyne to enter.

The room was vast, and the ornate four-poster bed had a frilled and flounced canopy with more flounces round the base. A huge tallboy with a mirror on top flanked by carved angels dominated the room. A dressing-table swathed in the same fabric as the bed was covered in little silver pots, brushes, a hand-mirror, and shaving equipment in a silver rack. There were clothes draped across the back of a velvet chair, and a large tray of half-eaten food rested on a stand.

David lay back on a mound of pillows, the embroidered frills matching those on the sheet. He was wearing monogrammed silk pyjamas, and he looked as handsome as ever, just a fraction paler.

'Well, hello, Flame, come in and sit down. Have you had some tea?'

Unaware that Evelyne could see him in the mirror, David raised his eyebrows questioningly at Freddy.

'S'all right, old man, I've briefed her, she won't let the cat out of the bag . . . be back in about ten minutes, toodle-oo.'

He closed the door, and Evelyne was left standing awkwardly in the centre of the room.

'Well sit down, girl, here, next to me, but gently, the leg's really painful.'

Evelyne perched on the end of the bed and took a deep breath, hardly able to meet his smiling blue eyes.

'Suppose you met his wife? Dreadful-looking, isn't

197

she? But then poor Freddy had to take what was available, needed the cash. They run a chocolate factory you know, absolutely loaded. Still, I must say I'm eternally grateful, got me back here in no time . . .'

He had the grace to blush slightly, aware that they must have abandoned her at the boxing match. He reached over and poured himself a glass of whisky from a cut-glass decanter.

Evelyne blurted out, 'You didn't remember me at all, did you? What did Mrs Darwin tell you about me?'

David downed the drink in one and shrugged, then he told her Mrs Darwin was a drunkard, she'd just said that there was a beautiful girl waiting at the house. He gazed at the ceiling, frowned. 'They tell you about me? They treat me rather like a loony you know, because I can't remember my past. Well, my father did. If it weren't for Freddy I'd probably have been put into some kind of home. I'm all right, though, and maybe it's for the best. God knows what's hidden in the recesses of my mind, God knows.'

Evelyne twisted her hands and mumbled that she was the girl Doris had brought to the house. She bit hard on her lip, but couldn't stop the tears. David picked up her hand and pulled, making her move closer until she could smell his lavender perfume, then drew her fingers to his lips and kissed them. She moaned softly, then withdrew her hand.

'You're married, you should have told me.'

David cocked his head to one side and asked, 'Why?' He wanted to know what on earth it had to do with her. She moved off and paced the room, and slowly, bit by bit, she told him everything, even down to buying her outfit, hiring the chauffeur-driven car. He listened, put a cigarette into a holder and lit it, breathing out the smoke. He was staring into space, and suddenly, out of the blue, he spoke, not to Evelyne but to the wall, 'Did you know that the average life expectancy of a subaltern on arrival in the trenches was little more than three weeks?'

His face crumpled, like a child's, a puzzled furrow on his brow. He touched his forehead with one finger, pressing hard, and then took another drift of smoke into his lungs and turned his clear, ice-blue eyes to her. 'I'm sorry, what did you say?'

'I love you, and I've been in love with you since I was fourteen years of age.'

There, it was out, she'd said it, said everything she had intended to say, and at the finish she felt drained, empty.

'I'm very flattered, sweet girl, but tell me what did you intend me to do with this love of yours? Oh Christ, did I make a play for you yesterday? I was drunk, you know that, surely?'

Evelyne stared at him. He flicked the ash off the end of his cigarette and looked enquiringly at her. She couldn't meet his gaze. He vaguely remembered what had happened last night, and he remembered Evelyne. But he had been drunk, he excused himself. Looking at her now he couldn't believe he had made a pass at her, and all she had just told him meant nothing to him. He had absolutely no idea who this woman Doris was. His eyes narrowed, he leaned back and stared. After a moment he asked in a clipped, cold tone, 'What do you want? Well, what do you want?'

Evelyne twisted her hands, swallowed hard, and said, 'Half of your father's house is mine, Mrs Darwin said her wages have not been paid.'

'She's a liar, absolute lies, pay her every month, ask Freddy.'

'She says neither she nor Muriel has been paid. Now,

maybe they have or they haven't, I don't know, but I need to know what you want to do with the house. It's in an appalling condition. Are you going to sell it? If so, then do you need my signature?'

David yawned and said that he had not the slightest idea. Evelyne's temper was rising, her fists were clenched at her sides.

'Well, maybe the money is of no interest to you, it is to me, and I could well do with it. How much is the house worth?'

'Is that what you've come here for, money? Christ, you are all the same, money, money . . . do what you like with the house, sell it, live in it, I don't care . . . I don't care.'

Evelyne sprang to her feet.

'Maybe you don't care, but I spent money on my clothes, they were ruined, I spent money on a train ticket, my handbag, all lost at the fair *you* took me to. I own half that house, now it may mean nothing to you, but . . . I want to be paid, no more than is my right.'

David's mouth turned down like a child's. He reached for his jacket and took out his wallet, throwing it across the room.

'Take whatever you want . . . money is all your kind ever think of.'

That was it. Evelyne turned to face him, eyes blazing.

'What do you mean by that? What do you mean by "my kind"? *What is my kind? Poor, is that my kind, poor?*'

She frightened him, confused him, and he sat back in the bed, pressing himself against the pillows. He was as helpless as a child, and she knew it. She opened his wallet. There were three five-pound notes and two ten-pound notes. She held each one up as she took it out, showing him exactly what she was taking.

'Two five-pound notes, David, and one ten-pound note, I've taken twenty pounds.'

He turned away, staring out of the window. His voice was soft, hardly audible.

'Please go away, you make my head ache . . . take anything you want, I don't know what you are talking about, I really don't.'

Evelyne folded the money and told David that if he needed any papers signed he could send them to her. He turned to her, his eyes wide, frightened, childlike. He held up his arms, his beautiful face pleading. She sat down on the bed, gently so as not to hurt his legs, and he wrapped his arms around her. His silky head was close to hers, she could feel his soft skin, his sweet perfume was in her nostrils. She thought he whispered, 'Sorry', but she couldn't tell. She didn't want to hold him, but her arms lifted and she hugged him. His warm mouth kissed her innocently, then his arms tightened and his kiss became sexual, forceful.

The door opened and Freddy stood there. 'I think you had better leave . . . Come along . . . David, straighten the bed, your wife's arrived. I'll show her out.'

He stood there impatient, then stepped forward and picked up David's wallet where it had fallen. He opened it, checked inside and then looked at Evelyne. She flushed, knowing he didn't understand, and tried to explain.

'I own part of David's house, his Aunt Doris . . .'

Freddy paid no attention, he was straightening David's bed. Then he hurried to the door, pulling her by the arm.

As they reached the landing, Evelyne heard the soft, laughing voice of Lady Primrose as she caught her son in her arms.

'Clarence, yes, it's Mummy . . . it's Mummy . . . Oh, what a big boy you are, shall we go and say hello to Daddy? Yes? Come on, you show me the way.'

Freddy pushed Evelyne along the corridor towards the back staircase. Lady Primrose, beautiful as ever, appeared at the top of the stairs, Clarence pulling at her hand. She was swathed in furs and wearing a pale pink suit.

'Hello, Freddy, I got here sooner than I expected . . . all right, Clarence, Mummy is coming.'

Standing behind Freddy, Evelyne knew she had been seen. Lady Primrose gave her a cold stare, her blue eyes flickered.

'Oh, I'm sorry, I didn't know you had company. Is David alone?'

Freddy murmured that David was waiting, and that he himself would be back in a moment. Primrose called out to David as she headed for his room.

'My darling, are you all right, I drove down as soon as I got Freddy's call.'

She entered the room and shut the door behind her. Evelyne stood with Freddy in the dark little corridor and shook, her teeth chattering in her head.

'It's all right, she didn't know you, not that she would have minded, I'm sure. I'll see you out.'

He moved quickly ahead of her, guiding her down the stairs.

Lady Primrose fussed and patted the bedclothes down around David. She'd seen the girl leaving, thought maybe she was a housemaid, but she knew there would be more to it than that, there always was. She poured David's usual measure of laudanum into a glass and topped it up with water. She held it out to him, and he drank it like a good boy. Clarence sat on the end of the bed, kept on asking what she had brought him from London, until he got a sharp smack. He started to howl, so Primrose had to kiss and cuddle him.

David held up his arm for her to go to him and she sat beside him and kissed his neck and his brow, petting him just like she had Clarence.

'There, there, darling, shusssh now, you get some sleep and in the morning we'll all go home . . . Oh, who was that girl I saw a moment ago?'

David shrugged and said that Mrs Darwin had done her usual trick, told him that his aunt had brought the girl to the house before the war. She was the poor little orphan girl he'd brought to the dance when they'd first met. Primrose nodded, she remembered her vaguely, a strange, tall girl with red hair, the girl who danced with Lloyd George. She recalled that dance very clearly because it was there she had met David. They were married on his next leave, and she later became pregnant on their three-day honeymoon. A year later she had David home for good, but he wasn't the same and they said he never would be. Basically, Primrose had two children on her hands, little Clarence and her husband. Sometimes, most times, she wished she'd married Freddy, never left him for David.

'Did you remember her, darling? Did you remember the poor little orphan girl at all?'

David's eyes dropped and he shook his head, he hardly seemed to notice Primrose take Clarence's hand and lead him out of the room. As the doors closed behind them, he began to drift into a drugged sleep and all he could see in front of his eyes was an old pair of boots with newspaper sticking out of them. Suddenly, in brilliant, flashing colours he saw the dining room, Doris sitting upright with a teacup in her hand, and then a clear picture of Evelyne.

'Primmy? Primmy?'

The panic started, the terrible feeling of being on fire, the boom, boom of guns was deafening. The nightmare began again and he put his hands over his ears, began to shout, 'No . . . no . . . *No, no, no!*'

Evelyne tried hard to explain to Freddy about the house, but he was so concerned with getting rid of her that he didn't listen. He instructed a housemaid to take Evelyne out through the kitchens and the servants' entrance. In a way he felt sorry for the big, awkward girl, but then he heard the awful screams echoing down from David's room. He knew he would have to go to him, and he blamed Evelyne.

'Don't come back, this is your doing, listen to him . . . I think you got what you came for, didn't you? Go on, get out.'

Lady Primrose rushed into the drawing room. Heather and Lady Sybil could hear David's screams. Heather shut the door and put her arms around Primrose.

'It's all right, dearest, Freddy will see to him, really it's all right.'

Lady Sybil, eating tea and crumpets, muttered.

'Should be in a home, not right in the head.'

Heather gave her mother a stern look and tossed her the evening paper to read, then sat Primrose down and poured tea. The shouts and screams from David's room slowly subsided.

Freddy returned to the drawing room, giving Primrose

an intimate smile. He said David was sleeping, the laudanum had taken effect.

'That girl, Freddy, apparently Mrs Darwin suggested she visit David. I think, as it obviously upsets him so, that we really should watch out for him, don't you think?'

Freddy blushed. Just meeting her eyes made him want her. He nodded.

'Perhaps we shouldn't try any more, I'm sorry.'

Primrose gave him a sad, helpless look. Freddy made no mention of David's wallet or the night spent at the gypsy fair. He nearly dropped his teacup when Lady Sybil read aloud from the evening newspaper.

'"Riot at boxing match" . . . have you read this, Freddy? Says here a gypsy fighter nearly killed his opponent, a miner. Look, read for yourself. Says the man was almost murdered. Caused a riot, tent burnt down, dreadful to-do. Riff-raff shouldn't be allowed in the country, none of them fought in the war. If Reggie were alive he would take his twelve-bore and shoot them down.'

Freddy took the paper and agreed with Lady Sybil that they were riff-raff, he couldn't understand why anyone would want to watch them fight, *he* most certainly wouldn't. Heather smiled at him and patted his knee. He left the room, and no one noticed that he took the paper with him.

Evelyne never went back to Mrs Pugh's, not because she didn't want to pay but because she couldn't face her. The few belongings she had left there she could do without. All she wanted was to go home and forget everything that had happened. All the way home, above the noise of the steam engine chug-chug-chugging, she could hear the strains of those high-pitched voices, those posh, upper-crust voices, their secret looks and nudges, their self-satisfaction, their money. She opened her bag and counted out the notes she had taken from David's wallet, then sat back against the seat and closed her eyes. Even after everything he had done, if he wanted her she would go to him she knew it, and she was angry with herself. 'You are a bloody fool, Evelyne Jones, forget him, take the money and forget him, he's not worth it. They treated you like dirt, you only took what was rightly yours. He owed you that money, it was yours to take.'

Her heartache slowly turned to anger. She twisted her hands in her lap, folded and refolded the money. All her love slowly turned to bitterness, turned sour, and her mouth took on a thin, hard line, her face tight. By the time the train stopped at her station she was composed, her anger and pain under control. At least, she said to herself, she hadn't lost any money on this trip, in fact she'd made it.

CHAPTER 10

EVELYNE LET herself into the house and changed her clothes, bundling up the ones she had been wearing and burning them.

'Well, how did it go, lovey?'

'It didn't work out, Da . . . Now, I'd best hurry and get to the school.'

Hugh said nothing, saddened for a moment that she didn't confide in him, but he had become so busy of late that he soon forgot all about it.

Evelyne was stunned to be told at the school that a new teacher with proper qualifications would be coming for the next term. The school governors had visited during her absence and, although they appreciated the work she had done in the past, they had to have someone with proper qualifications. There was no work to be had at the brick factory, or at the coal face. Come Easter she would be unemployed, but that was Easter, and until then she would continue at the school. Her heart was no longer in it, though, and the children noticed and called her 'Miss Stick'.

*

Hugh was going from strength to strength within the union. Twice he travelled to other mines to give talks to the men, and returned jubilant that they were solidly on his side, and if the mine owners didn't bow to their demands for better wages and safety regulations, they would strike. The small house was full every evening with groups of men who would bring their problems to Hugh. Evelyne had once been pleased to be part of this, but now she withdrew upstairs to her mother's old room, where she would read until her eyes hurt.

Hugh was in good spirits. Dai Thomas had brought the local newspaper and on page three there was Hugh, wearing his cloth cap, standing rigidly straight and glaring into the camera.

As he went up the stairs, he saw the gas lamp still glowing in Evelyne's room. He tapped, and popped his head round the door. Evelyne was lying on top of her bed, wearing just a white shift, her waist-length hair brushed and gleaming. 'My God,' thought Hugh, 'if any of those buggers was to see her now they wouldn't be calling her "Miss Stick".' She looked like a mermaid. 'I got a few copies, see . . . it's me in the main photo, not a bad likeness, gel, wouldn't you say? Told me not to smile, see, so I'd look fierce, look like I know what I'm talking about.'

'It's good, Da, and you look no more than thirty, real fit and strong.'

Hugh laughed and twisted his cap round on his head, pulling a funny face. She handed the paper back to him, but he whipped out another two copies from his pocket. 'Keep it, Dai's gonna bring us a frame.'

He wanted to talk, but she put the paper down and

picked up the book she was reading. He went out, then came back again.

'Now don't start, just let me say something to you, I love you more than my own life, an' I can't stand to see you wastin' yourself, sitting up here every night, goin' up to the school every day, gettin' more an' more like an old maid, like Doris.'

Evelyne shrugged, tossed her hair and said, tight-lipped, that he had no need to worry, she wouldn't be going up to the school much longer, they were replacing her with a proper teacher. As soon as he had left Evelyne felt dreadful. She loved him so much. Why hadn't she talked with him like they used to, why had she shut him out lately? She picked up the paper and looked at the photograph, his stern face glaring into the camera. She kissed the photo and took some scissors out of a drawer.

As she snipped around the photo she couldn't help but notice the lead article on the next page, 'Police investigate two revenge murders'.

She carried the paper over to the lamp and sat down. The article stated that the two boys had been found with their throats slit open, their hands tied behind their backs. At first, they believed the motive had been robbery, but then a third boy had given himself up to the local constabulary. He admitted that he and his friends had made advances to a gypsy girl and one of the gypsy men, Freedom Stubbs, had warned them that they would take their revenge. The article requested anyone knowing of Freedom Stubbs' whereabouts to come forward.

From then on Evelyne kept every article she found, carefully hidden in her bedroom. She never mentioned the article to her father, not that she saw that much of him to talk to. He spent most evenings in a room above the pub holding meetings for the local miners. Evelyne worked at the school during the day and studied for her examinations in the evenings. Hugh no longer even needed her to help out at the meetings, taking notes and writing letters and so forth. Gladys Turtle had taken over that side of things.

'No need for you to interrupt your studies, love.'

'I don't mind, Da, really I don't.'

'Well, lass, as a matter o' fact we've got a sort of committee secretary, Gladys Turtle, from Lower North Road, nice woman, a widow.'

Although slightly put out, Evelyne said nothing. She watched from her window as Hugh met up with the 'merry widow', as Gladys was known in the village. Not that she was particularly merry, just that she had over-indulged in the sweet sherry at her late husband's funeral and passed out. She was a small, neat, white-haired woman with a shelf-like bosom, and a habit of wearing crocheted flowers on her hats or pinned to her coat collar.

Gladys had found a new lease on her boring, mundane life, working with Hugh. She had always had an eye for him, even when he was a youngster, but of course he would never have looked at her – she was no beauty like his Mary. Gladys reckoned that the way to a man's heart was through his stomach, and she cooked stews and casseroles for Hugh to take home in small pots. He would sneak into the house with them, as if embar-rassed, and Evelyne would watch him heating them up. Then he would wink at her and wolf the food down.

*

Gladys had passed by earlier, walking with Hugh – he always took her home after meetings. 'I've just walked our Gladys back, do you fancy one of her scones?'

Shaking her head, Evelyne closed her books.

'She's got a young nephew staying, nice young fella, Willie, looking for work like the rest of us. He had a good job over at Glamorgan, beats me why he gave it up. Word is, he may have got a young girl in the family way.'

Hugh coughed and stuck his finger down his starched collar.

'I was wonderin', like, maybe as she's so nice with all these scones and stews, perhaps it would be neighbourly like if we had her and this young Willie come to tea Sunday?'

'Why not, if that is what you would like, Da?'

He stood up, beaming, and shoved his hands in his pockets.

'Ay, it is, good, well, I'll leave it with you, shall I?'

Evelyne collected their supper from the fish and chip shop, and carried it home wrapped in newspaper. As she left the shop she bumped into Gladys, and cordially invited her and her nephew to tea on Sunday.

'Oh, that's lovely, I'll look forward to it.'

Not wanting Evelyne to see that she also frequented the fish and chip shop, Gladys waited until Evelyne had walked the length of the street before she went in. From behind the counter the sweating Nellie gave her a toothless smile.

'Eh, she's a right stuck-up one, that, ever since she got that wireless, come with her legacy . . . two cod, Gladys, is it?'

*

As she unwrapped the fish and chips a grease-stained headline caught Evelyne's eye, 'Third Murder Victim'. She pulled at the paper, spilling chips on the table.

'Police step up their search for Freedom Stubbs. They now believe the murders to be revenge killings, all committed by the same hand. Each victim has died in the same circumstances, their hands tied behind their backs and their throats slit. In each killing it seems the murderer knew where his victim lived and worked.'

Sunday was chapel day which meant choir practice, and Hugh went off in his Sunday suit, leaving Evelyne to prepare tea for Gladys and Willie. She baked some scones and, of course, just when she would have liked them to be the best batch she had ever made, they went flat and hard as a rock. Then she slipped down to the newspaper shop to buy a Sunday paper.

Walking back, searching through the paper to see if there was any more news of the murders, she passed a poster advertising the Easter fair. As usual the gypsies would set up their fair on the mountainside. It was always a big occasion, and being a Bank Holiday the men had an extra day off work. There would be coconut shies, hoop-la, and sometimes they built a giant see-saw for the children.

Evelyne stopped. There was a small item on the second page which simply stated that the police were no further along with their investigation. She hurried on, then stopped again. Even from the street she could smell her bread burning. She ran in with a scream of fury, but it was burnt to a cinder. As she opened the windows to get rid of the terrible smell, she saw Hugh outside with a group of miners on their way back from choir practice.

There was a hell of a row going on, Hugh standing in the centre of the crowd thumping his fist in his palm. The men were shaking their fists at him, all shouting at once.

'You bastard, Hugh Jones, we go out on strike you tell me who's gonna feed my ten kids.'

Hugh shouted back and waved his arms, 'We'll all chip in, if we don't stand united then we fall. You said yerself, mun, you not got enough money to feed yer babies now, an' yer workin', don't you understand that's what we're striking for, a living wage, mun! *We strike*!'

Some of them started to walk home, and Evelyne was about to turn back to her studies when she saw a figure on the edge of the crowd around Hugh. It was Freedom Stubbs, large as life, leaning against the wall with a half-smile on his face. Evelyne clapped her hand over her mouth and turned away from the window.

'Oh, God, it couldn't be him, not here, not in our village.'

When she looked again he had gone, as if he had vanished into thin air.

'Evie! *Evie*! Is tea ready, they'll be here by half past three lass, and the table's not laid.'

She ran downstairs to the kitchen where Hugh was already shaking out a clean tablecloth.

'Da, the gypsy fair, they're not setting it up yet, are they?'

Hugh reached down the best crockery. 'Oh, they start early for Easter, lovey. It's their big time. An' then they'll be arranging a fight as usual, Devil's Rock.'

There was a tap on the door, and Hugh gave Evelyne a startled look.

'They're here early, are we all set?'

Before Evelyne had time to answer he was opening the front door and ushering Gladys along the passage.

'Come in, Gladys, and you, Willie. Welcome, welcome.'

'Is something on fire, Hugh love? I can smell burning.'

With a frosty smile Evelyne turned to greet them.

'Here they are, Evie, Gladys you know, and this is Willie, her nephew.'

Evelyne dropped the plate of solid scones on the flagged floor and the plate smashed in two. Immediately Willie pushed forward and bent to pick up the scones.

''Fraid yer plate's broken, but the scones are none the worse.'

Hugh laughed and said it was more than likely the scones that had crashed through the plate.

Evelyne stared at Willie as he held the chair out for his aunt. She knew it was him, had known at first glance. So this was why he had left Glamorgan, given up his job, Willie Thomas was the boy she had seen on top of Rawnie, this was the lad who had torn her hair out by the roots and who Evelyne had virtually knocked unconscious with the bench leg. She wondered if he recognized her and could hardly bear to look in his direction.

'Auntie tells me you're a schoolteacher, that right, Evie?'

She busied herself passing the jam, and murmured that it was quite right. Her mind was racing. He wouldn't know her now, surely he wouldn't . . . she looked up to meet his gaze. He gave Evelyne a wink. His familiarity, calling her Evie when he had only just met her, made her temper rise. It was definitely him, the red neck, the horrid, bright red hair.

Gladys simpered coyly and looked up at Hugh, then spoke to Evelyne, 'We thought you might get uppity, another woman in your kitchen, but you've made us very welcome, Evie.'

Evelyne looked down at her plate. The scones were terrible, she could hardly get her teeth through hers. Hugh coughed.

'Ah well, I've not actually told her, we'll announce it in chapel next week, but we are unofficially engaged to be married, that right, Gladys?'

Somehow Evelyne found her voice and said stiffly that she was very happy for them. The soft, powdered cheek brushed Evelyne's, and she got a close-up view of the silly crochet work on Gladys' hat. Evelyne wanted to cry out. How could her Da want this silly woman?

Gladys insisted on staying with Hugh to wash the dishes, and Evelyne showed Willie into the front room. Willie sat on the sofa and gave her a wide smile. 'She's a good woman, Aunt Glad . . . Evie, will you sit beside me?'

'My name's Evelyne . . . so, you're here looking for work, is that right? You'll not find any, and there's the strike coming, you should go back to Glamorgan, or Cardiff even.'

He shrugged, took out a packet of cigarettes and lit one, blowing out the smoke and crossing his legs.

'Do you know Cardiff then, Willie?'

She caught his sly glance, and noticed that he flicked his ash on to her polished lino.

'I've been there, but I prefer it here.'

She was one hundred per cent sure it was him, any doubts had disappeared and she boiled with anger at what he had done.

Hugh interrupted the tense moment. 'Right, Evie,

215

will you be at the meeting? They'll be arriving any moment, Gladys is setting out the books . . . an' you too, Willie, it's important tonight.'

Hugh stood before the fire with his trousers almost sizzling.

'No man's takin' these decisions lightly, for Lord's sake, mun. You think I for one dunno what hardships we're all headin' for?'

Harry Jones jabbed the air with his finger and demanded to know if Hugh could face starving women, never mind starving kids. Hugh sighed and rubbed his hair until it stood on end. 'Jesus Christ, mun, I know that even the most tenacious strikers are giving way, but . . .'

Hugh had heard the word 'tenacious' on the wireless and now used it at every opportunity. The others stopped arguing for a moment as he explained what he meant. Harry muttered that he didn't give a bugger who was 'tenacled' or not, all he knew was his kids were starving, and he had to work to put a crust into their mouths. Hugh banged his fist against the mantel. Intensive union activity had taken its toll not only on him but on four others who were blacklisted. Again his voice rose as he told the men that there were some working with their union badges sewn into their collars for fear of the managers knowing they were members.

Taffy Rawlins twisted his cap and blurted out, 'Lot o' men tried workin' in other collieries. Soon as it was discovered they was union men, none of 'em could get taken on.'

Harry Jones rose to his feet, jabbing the air with a stubby finger. 'Ay, an' rumour 'as it, any man what's a member has 'is name circ'lated from the union roster.

216

They'll never get work, not now the strike is on, not when it's over.'

Taffy was at it again, waving his cap. 'I believe, Hugh Jones, an' there's many that says I'm right, your union is bloody destroying a man's right ta work.'

Dramatically, Hugh tore off his threepenny-piece-sized union badge and held it up above his head.

'If we don't join this union now, if we don't pull together, you'll all be no better than the pit ponies left down the mines to rot. The managers, the owners, don't give a hang whether a man dies or not, they're more worried about losing a dram than they are about any man.' Hugh's voice was earshattering in the hot, stuffy, confined kitchen. 'You lose a dram o'coal, mun, and what happens? The buggers make you pay for it. But when have *they* paid for a man's life? The proprietors know the men are weak, that they have no organization so they can do what the hell they like. The pit manager can sack when he pleases, and the poor bugger can do nothing about it, and they'd hardly pay him a penny . . . *Am I right, tell me?*'

Throughout the meeting Gladys took copious notes for the minutes. Willie paid little attention, picking his teeth with a match and yawning. Evelyne kept feeling his eyes on her but refused to return his stare.

At last the meeting broke up and Evelyne packed what food was left over from tea and slipped it to Taffy for his kids. Hugh walked Gladys home, still arguing with Harry. Willie made no move to leave with his aunt, sitting in Hugh's chair by the fire. 'I just seen there's a good film at the pictures, Evie, last show's at nine, fancy an outing?'

Evelyne folded her arms. 'My name's Evelyne to you, son, or Miss Jones. And if you want some advice I'd clear out.'

Willie looked completely unabashed. He propped his feet on the fireguard.

'That's none too friendly, considerin' we'll be related soon.'

Evelyne would have liked to swipe his gloating face.

'I've no intention of makin' a friend of you, none at all, and I don't want you in this house again, now out . . . go on, hop it.'

His piggy eyes glinted, and he slowly removed his feet from the fireguard. He looked at her, and she could almost see the wheels churning round in his flushed head.

'Way I hear it, you should think yourself lucky bein' asked out, there's not many lads left in the village. There's plenty of young girls panting to go to the pictures so don't put yourself out, Miss Schoolteacher.'

Evelyne watched the cocky boy saunter out, and she restrained herself from aiming a blow at the back of his stocky, flushed neck. As the door closed behind him, Evelyne went to fetch her heavy coat. She wrapped a scarf around her neck and slipped out the back way. She didn't want anyone to see her, to know where she was going.

The gypsies were just setting up their camp, the wagons and trailers drawn up in a semicircle, a group of men erecting the big, round living tents. A fire blazed in the centre of the ring, and a few children were hanging round, wearing cotton dresses and thin, thread-bare woollies. Although barefooted they seemed hardly to notice the cold, but they noticed Evelyne striding up the hill. She'd opened up her coat as she was warm from the long walk, and her cheeks flushed pink from the evening air.

A runny-nosed little boy with huge, dark eyes

watched her, a brooding look on his tiny face, then he put out his hand.

'Give us a penny, come on missus, just a copper, we're starvin' hungry.'

Evelyne looked down at the tiny boy already adept at begging, and showed him her empty pockets.

'Is Freedom with you, boy? I need to talk with Freedom.'

At that moment a woman with a shawl wrapped around her appeared from behind the bushes. She grabbed the child by the hair and walloped him, with a cold, angry look at Evelyne.

'There's no one of that name here.'

The children ran like hell away from the sharp-tongued woman, the little boy looking back at Evelyne. She went nearer to the camp, and now the men turned and stared with the expressionless, unnerving faces. She stood looking around, then spoke loudly, her voice echoing.

'I need to speak with Freedom, is he here with you?'

They made no reply, just turned their backs and continued working. Women passed hooded looks to one another and she saw two men talking together in sign language.

'I know he's with you and I have to talk with him.'

A grey-haired man, wearing clothes fit for a scarecrow, shuffled towards her. He came within about six feet of her and showed his toothless, shiny gums as he spoke.

'There's no one by that name here, wench. Git out of it. Listen to what I say, go away from here.'

Evelyne turned and walked out of the field and headed down the steep path, thinking to herself that at least she'd tried. She stuffed her hands into her pockets and felt the newspaper clippings, paused, looking back, and then walked on. She took the narrow path round the mountainside, beginning to think herself stupid for risking walking out this late, and so close to the gypsy camp. All her father's old warnings came back to her and she quickened her pace.

Freedom had watched her walk into the camp, seen the way she stamped her foot angrily, turned on her heel and marched out. She had snapped a dead branch off a tree and was whacking the hedges as she walked along. He sat up in the fork of a tree, watching her with his dark eyes, amused, smiling. She was an odd one, that was for sure. As Evelyne walked beneath his tree he dropped down, and she shrieked with terror. When she saw it was him, she put her hands on her hips and let him have it.

'That's a fine thing to do! You nearly gave me heart failure, you did!'

With a mocking bow, but without saying a word, Freedom began to walk along beside her. Evelyne took the newspaper cuttings from her pocket.

'I suppose you've read all these? You *can* read?'

Freedom cocked his head to one side, smiling. She only came up to his shoulder and had to look up into his face. His hair had grown longer and he had tied it back with a leather thong. He now wore a gold earring in his right ear.

'I've come to tell you to leave, the police will be here, that's what I've come all this way to say.'

With one quick hop Freedom was in front of her, walking backwards.

Still walking, she continued, 'You can't just go

around killing people, even if what they did was a terrible thing. The law must know the boy's here, and with the fair being here too, they're bound to come around asking questions.'

Freedom halted and she walked straight into him. He gripped her arm, hurting her. Evelyne looked into his face, she wasn't afraid, she never had been afraid of him, but he hurt her wrist and she jerked her hand free. 'I said the fourth boy's here in the village, and you know it, *that's* why you're here.'

Freedom took the tree branch from her hand and swiped at the bushes in anger.

'I'm here to fight at Devil's Pit, nothing more.'

Evelyne fell into step beside him, told him he was crazy, the police wanted to question him about the murders. If he came out in the open to fight, they would certainly arrest him. They had even put his name in the papers.

'So, Evelyne, you came to warn me, is that it?'

She tripped over a stone and he caught her, but she moved quickly out of reach. Flippantly, she said she was amazed that he remembered her name.

'You remembered mine, I heard you asking for me, and I thank you.'

They walked on and she asked after Rawnie. Freedom told her that she was now Jesse's woman and would be at the camp. As they walked she became aware of his familiar but strange, musky perfume, and even more aware of his cat-like litheness. He seemed hardly to make a sound as he walked, his step surprisingly light for his size.

'Have you got yourself a man yet then, Evelyne?'

She flushed and bit her lip, and he laughed softly with his little lopsided smile and slightly raised eyebrows.

'Did you ever go to an inn close by Cydwinath Farm? When we last met I thought I'd seen you before, a long time ago.'

Evelyne shook her head.

'Oh, it wasn't you, huh? See, first I saw this girl in a field – like a mermaid she was, and dressed in naught but her shift – and then I saw her again, a big society dance, it was.' He gave her his strange half-smile, his eyes twinkling, 'I was standing in the dark and it was as if she was lit up by the moon, like a moment of magic. It was a mermaid again, only, only this time she was a princess in a flowing gown, and she was dancing with an old fella with white hair, there on the lawn with not a soul to see but me.'

Evelyne stopped and bit her lip so hard her teeth almost went straight through. He looked down into her face and cupped her chin in his hand.

'I was never at a dance, and most certainly not at any farm in my shift, and I find it very ungentlemanly of you even to suggest it.'

Again he laughed, and he did a small jig then bowed low. She knew he was laughing at her, and she almost – just almost – laughed at herself.

They were coming closer and closer to the edge of the village and could see the lights twinkling from the houses. The track was smoother here and soon they would be on the cobbles leading to the main street. Freedom still walked at her side. All she needed now was for someone to see her – pray God it would not be Mrs Morgan or it would be all round the village by ten o'clock next morning. As if he could read her thoughts he stopped, bowed again, and without another word made to move away. This time Evelyne caught hold of his arm. 'Don't be a fool, mun, don't fight, don't let them arrest you, get away from here.'

222

Freedom's eyes went darker than dark, and his voice was soft but cutting, 'My people depend on the fight for their living. Money is scarce all round, but no scarcer than with us travellers.'

Evelyne told him angrily that his people would be a lot worse off if he were put in prison, which would certainly happen if the people arrested him. He turned on his heel, swishing at the air with the stick. 'They'll have to find me first.'

Evelyne let herself in by the back door. She was greeted by an irate Hugh who was worried stiff about her being so late and not letting him know where she was, and they had an argument for the first time in years. She accused him of not letting her know about his friendship with Gladys, a stupid, simpering woman if ever there was one. The stinging slap from Hugh shocked her and she lifted her fist to go for him, but he held her too tight.

'You'll take that back, you'll not say those things about her, it's jealous you are, girl, jealous, you who's too bound up in your books and readin' to find yourself a decent lad. They're all laughin' at you an' callin' you Doris behind your back. And by God, girl, you've got like her, with your mouth always turned down and your nose never out of paper!'

Evelyne countered this by telling Hugh he was behaving like a foolish eighteen-year-old, and making himself the laughing stock of the village with that Gladys. And as for her nephew! He was a pig-eyed, sweaty, revolting youth, it ran in the family. Wallop! She got another stinging blow and she backed away, scared; she had not seen Hugh so angry for such a long time.

Hugh started on about David – all that show about

223

her going to Cardiff to find the boy she loved, the boy of her dreams. It must have been all fantasy because she came back with a face like a nun's, and a tongue so sharp no one could speak to her.

'What happened, Evie? Did he turn you down? Can you blame him, look at you, you act like an old woman . . . dear God, gel, what are we doing, what are we saying? Come here, for the Lord's sake, come here.'

Evelyne went into her father's arms as if he were a long-lost lover. He held her, rocking her, kissing her hair, her neck, and saying sweet, soft things, taking back everything he had just said. She found herself kissing him back, she was so in need of love, so in need of physical contact that she was bursting inside. They were held suspended, staring into one another's eyes.

The crash of the door-knocker brought them round, and Gladys' voice, high-pitched and hysterical. Hugh let her in. It was Willie, he'd not been home since tea, and now it was one in the morning and she was worried stiff. No one seemed to know where he was.

On hearing that Willie was missing, Evelyne said that he had gone to the picture house to see the jazz film. 'Perhaps he met a girl there, Da? Wait, I'll come with you.'

She ran down the street after Hugh and Gladys, who were calling out Willie's name along the way. Lights were coming on in the houses, heads popped out of windows. Soon there was a trail of people behind them, like the children following the Pied Piper, everyone looking for Willie. Evelyne's heart hammered in her chest . . . 'Dear God,' she prayed, 'let him have met someone and gone walking.' Anything but what she dreaded.

Gladys began to shiver with cold and Evelyne took off her greatcoat and slipped it round Gladys' shoulders, forgetting the newspaper clippings in the pocket.

By the time they reached the picture house the village bobby was wobbling along beside them on his bike. Evan Evans asked over and over what the fuss was about and slowly pieced the story together in his thick brain. 'The lad's missing, is that so? We'll get a search party out.'

'What the hell do you think this is, mun? That's what we're doing.'

The manager of the cinema, Billy Jones, lived in the house next to it. They woke him by hammering on his door.

'All right, I'm comin', I'm comin' . . .' He stood on the doorstep in his dressing-gown as they explained the problem to him, then fetched a torch and a huge bunch of keys. With everyone rushing him he had trouble finding the right keys to open the door. He took so long that Hugh wanted to belt him.

'There was not a soul left in the theatre, I'm telling you, unless he went to the gents'.'

Gladys, panicking now, wanted to know if Billy had definitely seen Willie.

'Yes I did, he was here nine o'clock just before the start of the film, *It's the Jazz, Man* – best houses I've had for weeks.'

Eventually he got the door open and they spilled into the auditorium, calling for Willie.

'Now, everyone, keep back, this is police work.'

Ignoring Evan Evans, Hugh bellowed for Willie, while Billy tried to light the gas lamps.

'Which bugger's got me torch? I can't see to light the lamps.'

As they walked around peering along the rows of seats, the lights came on. Billy, up on a ladder, looked down and screamed hysterically, pointing. Hugh pushed his way through to where Billy was pointing, looked for a moment and then turned, 'Stay back, Gladys, Evie. Don't come up here, any of you . . . Evan, get the doctor.'

Gladys screamed and screamed, then fainted in a heap at Evan's feet. Evelyne moved cautiously between the seats.

'Aw, Christ almighty . . . Holy Mother of God . . .'

Willie lay between the seats. Blood from an open wound on his neck had formed a thick, dark pool which had already congealed. It was obvious from his open, staring eyes that he was dead.

Next morning the village was in an uproar. There'd not been a murder since 1905 when Taffy Ryse hammered his mother's head in, but then he was funny upstairs. Who would have wanted to kill Willie? They could all understand why Taffy had beaten his mother to death, she had been a right bitch, but Willie?

Doc Clock was limping badly from yet another car accident, and he was also getting old. He examined Willie's body and muttered that he was dead all right, which got everybody shouting at once that they'd already told the soft bugger he was dead – what they wanted to know was when it had happened. Doc Clock shrugged.

'How the bloody hell do I know – I've not been to the pictures since last year.'

*

Evan Evans was buzzing around with his notebook and a blunt pencil which he had to keep on licking. Doc Clock said he would give himself lead poisoning if he carried on. Poor Evan was out of his depth and was very swiftly pushed aside when a motor vehicle arrived with three uniformed police and a plain-clothes officer from the main station in Cardiff. They were all banned from the cinema and poor Billy was beside himself. He'd only got the film on lease and he had to send it back; if he couldn't let his customers in then how was he going to run his business?

The police searched for the murder weapon and drew chalk marks around the body before it was removed. They began questioning everybody who was known to have been in the picture house the previous night, and put out a request for any person not on their list who had been in the cinema or in the vicinity to come forward. A lot of folk, who were interested in the proceedings rather than having anything useful to say, couldn't wait to be interviewed. One of the harassed police officers was heard shouting, 'No, no, we're not interested in the week *before* the murder – just if you were in the picture house itself on that specific night or if you happened to pass it.'

Billy hovered and moaned as they closed the cinema, and begged to be allowed to open up before he went bankrupt. The police eventually conceded, and Billy opened up with a broad, white ribbon carefully hooked around five seats in two rows. He had never done such business in the whole time the place had been open. He played three shows a day with a Charlie Chaplin short in between for half-price. Not that anyone was watching the film, they were all agog at the blood-stained seat and took turns to sit close, whispering and pointing out to each other the bloodstains and the chalk marks around the spot where the body had lain. Mabel Hitchins, the pianist, drummed her fingers to the bone playing along with the films. Her neck was at a permanent angle from twisting round to tell the kids to leave the ribbons alone, they were police property.

For the three days that the murder investigation was centred in the village, Evelyne stayed indoors. She knew the police had questioned the gypsy men, and in fact seemed to have talked to everyone in the village. They mentioned nothing about the murder being one of the 'revenge killings', but there was an undercurrent of emotion among the villagers and the blame was laid on the 'gyppos'. The police were very firm, warning that there must be no vendetta between the miners and the gypsies. The law would handle the case, and once they had completed certain inquiries they would return to the village.

Hugh came home with the local newspaper and read aloud to Evelyne while she darned his socks. 'It's the gyppos, the police have been over the camp, got to be one of them, must be, police say there'll be an arrest any time now.'

The paper also stated that the murder had to have taken place during the second half of the last showing of the picture. This was because Mrs Dobson remembered selling Willie a toffee-apple. She remembered Willie very clearly because he had demanded his money back as the apple under the toffee had been rotten. The police placed the killing between nine thirty-five and ten fifteen. They also believed the weapon was similar to the one used to kill the boys in Cardiff: a thin blade, perhaps even a cut-throat razor. The gypsy camp had been searched, but they had found nothing.

Hugh shook his head and grunted, 'Be one of them vermin, sure as I'm sitting here.' He continued to read aloud from the paper, where it stated that no one at the picture house recalled seeing a gypsy at the box office. Nor had they seen any in line for Mrs Dobson's toffee-apples and coconut slices. This was also verified by Billy. Hugh jabbed the air with his finger. 'Too right, he said he wouldn't allow the buggers in his picture house anyways, not that many went in by the front door. Ask me, most of the audience slipped in the back way.'

He frowned, looking at the paper. Evelyne finished one of his socks and looked up. 'You'd think if anyone did see the killer they would come forward. It's common knowledge that most never pay at poor Billy's, though, so if they did speak up they'd have to admit they'd slipped in the back door too.'

Hugh sniffed, spat into the fire and jabbed his big finger at the paper. 'Says here they given orders for the gyppos to stay put until the police had finished accu-mulatin' their evidence, the way those lazy so-and-sos go about it I'm surprised they ever catch anyone. An' wouldn't you know there's not one man up at that camp who can't vouch for the others being up there all night, the bastards – killers, bastards!'

Evelyne had nightmares. She kept waking up sweating, going over and over the time she went from the house up to the camp. She was sure it was after nine. She remembered Gladys telling old Evan, the policeman, that Hugh had returned quickly because he wanted to hear something on the wireless at nine. The walk up the mountain would have taken her at least three-quarters of an hour. Freedom was there, she could see him clearly, dropping from the tree with that smile of his on his face. Could he really have slit that lad's throat and then laughed and joked with her? Walked almost into the village, right up past the picture house itself? The more she turned the evidence over in her mind the more she knew deep down that Freedom could not have killed Willie. Freedom couldn't because the time wasn't right, but what of Jesse? He had been at the camp, but she had not seen him. Had Jesse killed Willie? Freedom had told her Rawnie was now Jesse's woman. She knew she should go to the police – knew it, but then she would have to go through all the questions about how she knew Freedom, how she knew about the rape, why she hadn't come forward before. Even worse would be the questions about the other lads' deaths. Why hadn't Evelyne said anything before? Told the police what she knew? No matter which way she looked at it, silence was the only way out, but it was giving her sleepless nights. She prayed for the fair to be over, for the gypsies to leave, and for the village to return to normal.

The terrible scandal began to die down and the Cardiff Constabulary returned to their station, leaving the 'Super Sleuth', Evan Evans, pedalling around the village with his notebook and pencil at the ready. They had found no murder weapon, and no evidence against anyone in the village or at the gypsy camp. Willie's body was sent back to Cardiff for burial, and without his corpse the Easter festivities began to pick up in earnest.

Life was so harsh that any reason for a moment's

relief was grasped with both hands. The band marched through the streets and the choir sang their hearts out at Sunday service. Easter Monday came, and the Bank Holiday gave the village even more of a festive atmosphere; they were still poverty stricken, but the gaunt, grey, worried faces relaxed, if only for a few days. Children's money-boxes had been raided by their parents, and somehow the odd few coppers had been found for the Sunday fair.

The gypsy men were no fools, they knew they would be targets. Freedom warned them all to keep out of harm's way. Don't start anything, just let the folk spend their few coppers, read their palms. There was to be no fighting, they were in trouble enough as it was. He didn't have to say why; the hooded looks and downcast eyes were enough. The revenge was complete now.

Freedom wondered if Evelyne would come. He doubted it, but he was sure she had kept her mouth shut, but then he had known she would. He had even sworn as much to the men and women of the camp. The paleface woman was their friend, and they could trust her as they did him.

As the villagers prepared for the fair, the travellers got out their gladrags, set up their booths and tables, brought out all their wares to sell. The older women made doll's house furniture and small, carved flowers from wood chippings, which were painted bright colours. There were goldfish for prizes and headscarves hand-sewn with beads and embroidery.

The streets were filling up with families on their way up the hill to the fair. Evelyne closed her window and went down to make herself a cup of tea. She boiled a big pan of water and had an all-over wash, scrubbing her skin until it hurt, then brushed and brushed her hair. Then she went back upstairs and lay on her bed,

231

listening to the sounds of the fair drifting down, the music, the laughter. Her mouth went tight, and she wondered if they would all be having such a good time if they knew what she knew.

Hugh had gone off to a meeting in another village, and Gladys said she would wait for him to return. She couldn't think of going to the fair, not after the terrible tragedy.

'Yes, lovey, you can, it'll do you good. When I've finished my meeting I'll come and collect you, walk you up the hill, just for a while.'

Gladys was dressed and ready. She fetched the coat she had borrowed from Evelyne and hung it in the hallway to give to Hugh. Noticing a mud stain on the hem, she tut-tutted and carried it into the kitchen to clean it. Humming to herself she wet a sponge and rubbed at the mud. As she turned the coat round she felt a bulge in one of the pockets, slipped her hand in to see what it was and brought out all the newspaper cuttings Evelyne had kept so carefully. Laying them on the table she took out her glasses and began to read.

By the time she finished the last article her hands were shaking. Something was wrong, terribly wrong, and she had to have a glass of sherry to calm herself. Why, she kept asking herself, why had Evelyne cut these articles out of the papers, some were more than a year and a half old? She'd get Hugh to talk to Evelyne and ask her to her face just what was the meaning of it. Evelyne knew something, she was hiding something, and Gladys would find out what it was.

232

CHAPTER 11

MR BESHALEY felt the train was going slow on purpose. Twice he got up and looked out of the window, nearly getting his head chopped off. He checked his gold watch and drummed his fingers on the sill. A very elderly gent sat opposite him, staring into space with a pipe in his mouth. 'They dinna go as fast as they used ta, it's the strike, see, fuel shortage, it's slowin' everythin' up.' The old boy nodded, as if he had satisfied Beshaley as to the slowness of the train, and stared out of the window.

Mr Beshaley had been in London, and had not seen Freedom for nearly eighteen months. He hoped to God that Freedom had kept himself in shape, the fight this evening was very important – more important than any other fight that Beshaley had organized before.

He had been up in Scotland arranging a lightweight bout with three of his men when he had been approached by a tall, elegant man. Sir Charles Wheeler, with his cloak and cane, cut a sharp figure in the new, fashionable double-breasted suit and a brown slouch hat. He was a member of the British Board of Boxing. A gentleman boxer himself in his youth, Sir Charles financed professional boxing bouts all over England, searching out talent, and rumour had it that he paid big

233

money when he wanted a man for his own team. He had acquired a gymnasium in London, filled it with all the finest equipment, and he recruited trainers and managers from all over England and America.

Beshaley had asked for an introduction, but it had proved unnecessary, because Sir Charles had come to Scotland with the sole purpose of meeting Beshaley. Sir Charles had seen Freedom Stubbs fight and thought the boy showed remarkable promise. More than that, he believed Freedom was a possible contender for the British Heavyweight Championship. Beshaley and Sir Charles discussed the forthcoming event at Devil's Pit, where Sir Charles could see Freedom fight again. Beshaley said he owned the boy, and he too believed him to be a rare boxer. He implied that he had spent considerable sums training Freedom and that he couldn't part with him without a contract that included himself – unless, of course, he was paid enough to release the boy.

Sir Charles had known immediately that Beshaley was lying and that he no more had a contract with the boxer than Sir Charles himself had. However, Sir Charles intended to rectify that.

While Beshaley was on his way to the railway station Sir Charles' automobile had cruised past. Through the open window he had smiled at him. 'No doubt we'll catch you at the fight?'

Beshaley wanted to run after the motor and demand a lift. He swore blue murder as he paced the platform, waiting for the train. He had to get to Freedom first and sign him before Sir Charles could approach him. The damned train was so slow he feared Sir Charles and his party would get there first, before he got the chance to make Freedom sign on the dotted line. They could be difficult these gypsy boys. Even though Beshaley was part Romany himself, he belonged to no clan; in his own terms he was an entrepreneur. Far from helping Freedom further his career, if anything he had stayed clear of him since the fight with Hammer. But he had overheard Sir Charles describing to one of his men how Freedom had brought a man down with a single body punch. 'Man punches like the Devil, and he's light on his feet, best I've seen for years', and Beshaley knew it was true and could kick himself for not having signed Freedom.

The train ground to a halt and he pushed open the window.

'There'll be a blockage on the line now, sir, mark me words. Some bastard'll have laid a log on the track. It's the strikers.'

Two guards walked through the compartment and when Mr Beshaley approached them, they told him curtly that there was engine trouble and they would be on their way as soon as possible. Beshaley gave one of the men a shilling to see if they could hurry things along, he had an important appointment. The guard could hardly believe his luck, and assured Mr Beshaley he'd get the train moving within minutes.

Sir Charles adjusted his driving goggles and tried to make sense of the road map. His two companions were hunched against the wind, wearing heavy coats and goggles, their hats pulled down low. Ed Meadows was a huge man with an ex-boxer's face, his nose broken so many times it had remained flat after his last bout, the bridge pulverized. He looked up at the signpost and shook his head. They'd passed it three times to his knowledge.

'You sure you know this place, guv? Only, we been past this post three times now, an' wiv the night comin' on – I don't fancy us drivin' round all night.'

Sir Charles turned and put big Ed in his place with his upper-crust English voice.

'You'll find this lad's worth it when you see him, Ed. Now come along, chaps, let's have a good gander at the road map again.'

Ed shivered and hunched further into his greatcoat. In his twanging, cockney voice he told Sir Charles to stop at the next village and ask – it was the only way round these parts. There was more than one Devil's Pit, and they could get the wrong one.

Dewhurst, Sir Charles's valet and butler, sat stiffly next to his master in the front seat. He turned his pink face to stare up at the signpost.

'There's a village two and a half miles further on according to this, sir, perhaps it would be better to ask there.'

Ed threw up his hands in despair, 'That's wot I just suggested, but nobody listens to me. I said stop at a village, these ruddy Welsh signs don't mean nuffink.'

Sir Charles pulled his goggles down, started the motor, and they headed for the village. They were actually close, within ten miles, but the winding paths around the mountains were misleading. There was only fifteen minutes before the match was due to start.

The afternoon over, many of the villagers made their way home, clutching their small token prizes. The children began to whine, they didn't want to leave the fair and yet they were so tired they could hardly keep their eyes open. The men hung around the camp, still playing on the coconut shy and throwing 'six darts for a ha'penny'. The see-saw had done a great trade and the teenage boys were now, as the dusk fell, shoving and pushing each other to have a go for a farthing a time.

The atmosphere was becoming tense, the groups of lads hanging around and knots of older men hunched in corners, smoking. The gypsies' eyes were everywhere, and some of the men nodded to their women to pack up and get ready to put the tables away. A fortune-teller's booth swathed in canvas like a Turkish tent had been doing a roaring trade, but now only a few boys hung around outside, their hands stuffed into their pockets.

Freedom's opponent, Taffy Brown, had arrived at the campsite two hours earlier. With his two aides he had wandered around and had a few goes on the coconut shy, but he was so strong that one of the balls had not only knocked the coconut off its stand but split the stand in two. This had raised cheers from the spectators and disgruntled moans from the gypsies. The balls, bright reds and yellows, had been 'lifted' from snooker tables, and quite a few pubs would be missing them.

The younger lads drifted over to the shy, cheering Taffy on, nudging each other as, enjoying the attention, he rolled up his sleeves. His muscular arms bulged, and he moved further and further away, then went for the stall at a loping run, throwing the ball overarm as if playing cricket. The ball ripped through the canvas amid even more cheers.

Two gypsies, knowing there could be trouble, yelled that the fight was due to start at any time in Devil's Pit, which made Taffy turn and roar, arms up in the air, for his opponent to show himself.

'He's waitin' for you, Taffy, he's waitin' at Devil's Pit, mun.'

The gypsies were relieved when the miners began to drift off towards the fight.

Devil's Pit, which lay a couple of miles from the campsite, was so called because the mountain curved out in a huge arm, enclosing the dark, flat earth in jagged rocks. Not even grass would grow there. Below the pit tumbled a waterfall, the water making strange moaning sounds which all added to the eeriness of the place, as if a soul bound in the earth was trying to get out.

Some of the men from the camp had gone ahead with a wagon to prepare the site. The ring was simply marked out in the dirt with ropes hanging from crude posts at the corners. They were raking the ground flat and pulling benches from the wagon to place around the ring.

The men formed a line outside the rocky entrance. An entry fee of threepence was charged, and for this the men got a single sheet of paper which announced forthcoming events in London at the famous Premierland. It also gave details of Taffy Brown's previous bouts. Taffy had a good record, and had so far never been knocked off his feet. His manager was sure he was world champion material, but he knew Taffy had to have more experience before going to London. This match against the man who had almost killed the famous Hammer was perfect for him.

Taffy's men looked around for Freedom, but he was nowhere to be seen. They presumed he was in the covered wagon parked at one side of the dirt ring, more than likely shaking with nerves. They took Taffy back to the car and he sat with his trainer, talking tactics. Taffy wanted to know more about this gyppo, and his trainer gave him details of the three bouts he had seen Freedom fight. Two he had lost, but then it looked like a fix. The third was Hammer and the rest was history. Taffy wiped his nose with the back of his hand. 'Not quite, mun. Gimme the rounds one by one. I seen Hammer fight, he was a big bastard, this lad must have a lot of weight behind his punch. Was it a body or a head punch that floored him?'

'The lad's good, Taff, but that's not the reason we're a bit on the edgy side. We've heard Sir Charles Wheeler is goin' ter show, and we want you to be part of his stable. You know how we feel, we know you can go to the top, but we need backing, we need money. It took all we had to get these leaflets printed. We even need the few bob from this bout, but if Sir Charles sees your potential then we'll all of us be in clover.'

Taffy had heard of Sir Charles, the 'gent of boxing' – everyone on the circuit had – but to think he was coming up here to this godforsaken place was beyond Taffy's comprehension. Roberts could see him hesitate, understood why, and put his arm around Taffy's shoulders. 'Wipe him out, Taffy, that's what you're here for. The lad's got the press writin' about him, because of those murders. You drop him on the canvas and it'll be *you* they'll be writin' about, and next stop it'll be the belt. That's what you've dreamed of, isn't it?'

Taffy had more than dreamed of it – it was his one goal in life. They saw him straighten up, clench his fists, and they knew they'd have the fight they wanted.

As if on cue, the roar of a car's engine coughing its way up the hillside heralded the arrival of Sir Charles himself. He pulled on the brake and looked around the pit, shaking his head. He'd certainly been in some out-of-way places looking for fighters, but never halfway up a mountain before.

'Gor blimey, guy, you sure they're not bringing the dogs up 'ere, don't look like a boxin' match to me.' Ed sniffed and hugged his coat closer. 'Bloody cold fer Easter, ain't it?'

As debonair as ever, Sir Charles seemed entirely unruffled by his long journey. He opened his brandy flask and drained it. Already he could see the line growing at the entrance, and below them men were heading up the mountainside in force. He passed his flask to his valet who nipped round to the boot of the car to refill it. The men crowding around were uncouth, shouting and carrying beer bottles.

'I think, sir, if you don't mind, I will stay inside the vehicle. I'm sure someone will try to remove your cases.'

Sir Charles laughed, then pushed his way through the crowds to look over the ring. He was pleased to note that there was no sign of the wretched man Beshaley. It would be difficult to miss that loud checked suit.

The crowds cleared a path for Sir Charles and nudged each other, nodding to 'the toff'. Sir Charles gave Taffy a courteous nod. Taffy watched him and grunted, he'd give him his money's worth.

Freedom sat in the wagon, his bound fists ready, arguing with Jesse. Freedom was angry that he was still around, having told him to leave days ago. But Jesse had disobeyed and returned for the fight. Jesse grinned, he would steal a few wallets tonight, and one from the gent in the big motorcar. Not that he mentioned it to Freedom, he just said they needed all the hands the camp could provide – and anyway the law had left the

240

village. The crowds were bigger than expected and the takings had to be counted. Jesse rubbed his hands with glee – money, money.

Twice a boy from the entrance came with a sack of coins, tipped them into a box and rushed out again.

'Where's Rawnie, Jesse, I told you to keep her out of this.'

Jesse opened the flap of the wagon and hopped down, reassuring Freedom that Rawnie was safe, back at the camp. No one but their own had seen them return, there was nothing to fear. Freedom sighed. Jesse was a madman, he knew it, to kill the boy here in the village, in the picture house, was an act of utter madness. The police had searched every wagon, every trailer, and Freedom knew it would not end there. The law would follow them from town to town, searching, questioning. He clenched his fists, the fight far from his thoughts, preoccupied with Jesse and Rawnie. She had changed profoundly since that night at Cardiff, not that anyone could blame her after what she had been through. Freedom had detected a cold hardness in her, she would no longer come near him, curl up beside him. If anything, she would turn away if she saw him.

Rawnie and Jesse were inseparable, as if they had secrets between them, their eyes constantly gliding to each other's, giving sly, soft giggles, their hands entwined. Freedom found them unnerving when they were together. True, he had tracked the boys down for Jesse, but then he had stepped aside because, as Jesse said, it was no longer his business. It was Jesse who was exacting vengeance. He had tried to reason with Jesse and the results had caused friction within the camps. Freedom chose to move on, and joined up with various other bands. Some whispered it was because he was scared, others murmured that it was Freedom's name that was connected to the revenge killings and it was right that he should protect himself.

The Easter fair was a big money-earner for the travellers, and as there was a fight going they sent for Freedom to rejoin them. That was the only reason he was here, but it had angered him when Rawnie and Jesse appeared. He watched Jesse through the flap. He strutted around the makeshift ring, arrogant, cocksure, and the miners stepped aside. Behind his back Freedom saw them give the sign of the fist. Freedom knew the signs, and was sure there would be more than one fight tonight.

The miners already outnumbered the gypsies by ten to one, and a restless murmur was growing as they began to take their seats. It was gone six o'clock, and still the fight had not begun. The referee jumped up into the wagon, a pleasant-faced man from Glamorgan who had refereed many bouts between the gypsies and the miners. 'Now lad, keep it clean, I want no head-buttin' and no kicks, any punches below the belt an' I'll disqualify you. Make it a good fight, there's someone out there from the professional circuits watchin', so don't let's make a monkey of this, understand me?'

Freedom smiled, nodded briefly and asked if the ref. was giving the same lecture to the miner – any head-butting usually came from that side, not the gyppos. The referee checked Freedom's fists and gloves, and spoke a few words to the young lads with his bucket and stool.

'Thirteen rounds, lads, three minutes per round. When the bell goes you get into the ring, and not before.'

The crowd was now very restless, and torches were lit

242

to illuminate the arena. The beer was being swilled down, and a couple of men who had brought a crate of beer were doing a fair trade selling bottles. It was home-brewed, tasted like stewed apples, and had a hell of a kick to it, but no one minded, they were getting thirsty from shouting for the match to begin.

Hugh read the newspaper cuttings about the killings in Cardiff. Gladys was distraught, and angry.

'She knows something, Hugh. All this time she's known something and not said a word to anyone. When was she in Cardiff? Remember that time she went away and came back here like she'd seen someone die? It's the same time, Hugh, look, read for yourself.'

Like an omen, the roar of the crowds echoed down from Devil's Pit.

Evelyne was surprised to see Hugh when he burst in through the back door.

'Hello, Da, I wasn't expecting you back so soon.'

Hugh threw her big overcoat on to the kitchen table, then dragged the newspaper cuttings out of his pocket. He waved them in front of her nose. 'Come on, out with it, gel, what's all this? An' don't tell me it's just morbid curiosity, there's more to this than meets the eye, isn't there? And by God I want it, all of it! Poor Gladys is at her wits' end. This Freedom fella's fighting up at Devil's Pit right now, an' if he's the one murdered our poor Willie . . .'

Evelyne let rip. '"*Our*. . .?" *What do you mean, "Our"*? That little bugger wasn't ours, Da, he wasn't worth the worry we all had, he had it coming to him!'

Hugh stared in horror as she faced him, arms folded,

243

with such a look of fury on her face he was astounded. He threw the papers at her. 'The lad had his throat cut by those vermin and that's all you can say about it, he had it coming to him? What kind of woman are you?'

Evelyne turned away from him and he walked out, slamming the door so hard the house shook. Why hadn't she told Hugh the whole story, why hadn't she told him now? She knew it was because of Gladys, and she felt guilty. She went up to her room and from the window she could see Hugh and Gladys running up the road. If she cut across the fields as fast as she could and up the other side of the mountain, she could get to Freedom before them.

The crowd roared. The two boxers were well-matched, and both around the same weight. Even though Freedom was five inches taller, Taffy had the extra inches in muscle, his solid body straining and sweating as he threw punch after punch. Freedom was up to his old dancing tricks, as light on his feet as a woman. He seemed to be running rings round Taffy.

'Git the bugger to sit still, Taffy lad!'

They were already into five rounds, with neither boxer giving points away. They were even and both looked strong enough to go to the distance. The bell clanged and they split up, heading back to their corners. They were both filthy from the earth and coal dust they kicked up as they fought. Taffy panted and gulped at the water, spat it out and looked at Roberts.

'He's the toughest I've had yet, you buggers, he's like a ruddy fly dancing around me.'

Roberts rubbed Taffy down and he kept up a steady flow of instructions. 'Tire him, let him dance his feet off, he'll soon slow down, but don't stop the punches hitting home.'

'What d'ye mean, don't stop 'em, I'm trying hard enough and can't get at him, he's clobbered me twice.'

Roberts could see that Freedom's punch had caught Taffy's right eye, which was swelling up like a tangerine.

Throughout the break the crowd yelled, 'Tafffyyyyy-yyyy . . . Taffyyyyy . . .' No one shouted for Freedom, the gypsies sat silent and watchful. They were acutely aware of the growing drunkenness on the far side of the ring, and the echo of the men's voices combined with the gurgle of the waterfall made a horrible, rumbling, guttural noise. Like animals they were baying for blood.

Sir Charles sipped from his brandy flask, gazing at the black-haired gypsy through half-closed eyes. He watched the lean body swerving, dodging, the strong legs keeping up the strange dance steps, and wondered how long the man could keep up such a movement. He didn't seem to tire in the least, but one look at his opponent told him the big Taffy Brown was starting to tire. Sir Charles knew that the lad was waiting for an opening – knew Freedom was merely toying with the Welshman – and he was excited, grinding his teeth, a habit he had had since childhood. The lad was even better than he had been told, like a wild animal. But the most important thing about him was his intelligence. He was playing for time . . . an intelligent boxer? Unheard of!

Trying to predict when Freedom would knock Taffy out, Sir Charles turned to Ed and saw the same dazzled look on his friend's face. 'What do you think of him?'

'Gawd help us, he's beautiful, just beautiful, what I wouldn't do to get me 'ands on 'im, work wiv 'im. 'E's

245

world-class material guv, look at 'im, dancing round like 'e was fresh as a daisy.'

Evelyne raced up the path, her breath heaving in her chest. She cut her hand on the brambles as she jumped the stream, but kept on running.

Rawnie was washing out Jesse's clothes. There was no visible sign of anyone but she could hear the sound of running footsteps. She straightened up, her hackles rising. It was clearer now, someone running, and running fast . . . there was fear, and Rawnie's dark eyes flashed around the dark mountainside.

Evelyne gasped for breath and rounded the curved pathway, with still a good mile to go. She paused as another massive roar echoed down from Devil's Pit. The next moment her heart lurched as a scrawny hand gripped her hair from behind and a razor-sharp knife pricked her throat. Her legs went from under her as a hard kick from hobnailed boots cut into the backs of her knees. She fell forward, and felt her hair torn out by the roots. Screaming with agony and fear, she rolled over and found herself looking straight into Rawnie's face.

Rawnie's eyes blazed, the knife held high, and Evelyne shouted 'Rawnie! Rawnie!' As if a cloud had lifted from her face, Rawnie relaxed and backed away from Evelyne.

'Remember me, Rawnie, it's Evelyne . . . Rawnie, it's me, the girl with the red hair, look, I wear your earring, see?'

She pushed back her hair and showed Rawnie the

gold hoop earring. Rawnie stared, and Evelyne saw the small, clenched hand loosen its grip on the knife, and then Rawnie sat back on her heels and smiled.

'*O lelled thee for a jal a moskeying, an you as almost mullo mas.*'

Evelyne didn't understand and Rawnie explained, 'I thought you were a spy, you were almost dead meat.'

Evelyne got to her feet, still panting for breath. She had to find Freedom, had to speak to him. Rawnie pointed up to the mountain. Freedom was still fighting, the roars of the crowd echoed down.

It was very difficult to explain to Rawnie, but Evelyne told her of the newspaper cuttings and how they were discovered in her pocket. She didn't mention the possibility that her father could cause trouble, just that the men might turn nasty. She wanted to warn Freedom – warn the whole camp that they should leave. Rawnie laughed and asked what the papers said about the killings.

'This is hardly the time to discuss it – the fact is the villagers will believe Freedom guilty.'

Rawnie looked closely at Evelyne and then turned away, her voice soft and quiet, strange. 'Thee don't believe this to be true, but the *gav mush* do, is that so?'

Evelyne looked puzzled, and Rawnie told her that *gav mush* was the law, then she spat on the ground. She had changed so much, there was something chilling about her. Still as beautiful, but there was a nasty, sarcastic edge to everything she said. Her eyes were expressionless, then mocking, and she waded into the stream to prevent Jesse's shirt from floating away. She slapped it on to the bank, and lifted her skirts high.

'Thee washed me down that night, thee saw the marks on my body, what you say should be done to those that had their way with me? What you say, paleface? Let the

gav mush smack their filthy hands that pawed and prodded into my body? Smack their hands and say, "She was
only a gyppo whore"?'

Evelyne shook her head as the cheers carried down
from Devil's Pit, and they could have been back in
Cardiff inside that nightmare tent. Rawnie rolled Jesse's
shirt and laid it on a rock, banged it, twisted it. She
seemed in no hurry to help Freedom.

'I'm Jesse's *manushi* now, he made me *romms* him to
show he didn't care what those vermin had done to my
body. I wear his ring now, I'm Jesse's woman.'

Satisfied the shirt was clean, Rawnie shook the wet
material and then in a strange movement wrapped the
wet shirtsleeves round her waist and gave Evelyne a
slant-eyed look. Rawnie moved closer and closer to
Evelyne, her eyes hypnotic, just like the time she had
read Evelyne's palm.

'I'll tell you the *tatcho*, paleface, only you'll know,
and I can see in your *yocks* ye'll not betray me, *mande
mui*.'

Closer and closer she came until her hands traced
Evelyne's face. 'We done each one – one by one – an'
Jesse let me have their throats, look into their eyes
before the blade was drawn across.'

Evelyne stepped back, afraid of her.

'The best was the last, sucking on his toffee-apple,
and I was right behind him, just a small move and . . .'

Rawnie flicked open the razor-sharp knife and cut
through the air. She laughed delightedly at Evelyne's
shocked face, then she turned in one sweeping move,
her voice trilled '*Kushti rardi*, Evelyne', and she was
gone.

Evelyne called after her, but the girl didn't turn back.
She heard another roar of men's voices, cheering in

unison and ran towards Devil's Pit, hoping to God she could get there before her father.

Gladys hammered on the post office door, looking up at the windows and calling for Ben Rees, the postman. His wife opened a window and called down that they were all at the fair, Gladys shouted that she had to use their telephone to call the police. Hysterical, she screamed that the killer, Freedom Stubbs, was up at Devil's Pit.

By the time Gladys had got through to the police a group of women had gathered outside the post office. In murmurs and whispers they passed the name of Freedom Stubbs among them. Lizzie-Ann, always one to be in on anything going on, came rushing up. The garbled story gained detail. Evelyne Jones knew the killer, he was one of the gyppos, and he was boxing up at Devil's Pit.

'Let's get up there and warn the menfolk. We'll get the bugger even if the law can't.'

Rolling pins were hastily collected, and one woman who had armed herself with a heavy frying pan swung it around, saying she'd take first crack at the vermin. Lizzie-Ann fuelled their rising tempers, telling them that Evelyne Jones knew more than she let on. Schoolmistress she may be, but why hadn't she shown anyone what the newspapers said? She'd concealed evidence, that's what she'd done. Half the women were illiterate and would never have read the papers anyway, but, egged on by Lizzie-Ann's bitterness towards Evelyne, they went on the march, fists clenched and rolling pins at the ready, heading for the Devil's Pit.

*

Mr Beshaley was beside himself, there was not a soul at the station, even to collect his ticket. There wasn't a horse or a cart, nothing in sight, and Devil's Pit was a good five miles up the mountainside.

Doc Clock chugged by in his precious motor. He'd been up at Mrs Morgan's on an emergency call, only to discover it was her dog that was ailing. The poor animal was very old and couldn't understand that with the strike on Mrs Morgan didn't have the money to put in the purse for him to take to the butcher. He was turning nasty, hanging on like grim death to the shopping bag and biting anyone who tried to take it from him. Doc Clock's thumb was bandaged to prove it.

As if that wasn't enough, the Doc was confronted by a lunatic in a dreadful suit who demanded to be driven to Devil's Pit. Beshaley took out his fob watch and looked in desperation at the Doc. 'The fight, I've got to get up there to see the fight,' he said, 'I'll pay you whatever you ask – anything – it's a matter of extreme urgency, sir, I beg you.'

Doc Clock tooted his horn as he rounded a curve on the narrow mountain track, and smiled to himself. At long last he'd got a watch on the end of his chain. Beshaley held on grimly as the old motor bounced and swerved along the unlit track. Twice he thought they'd go over the edge, but the motor somehow weaved its way back to the centre. They could hear the cheering and shouting, and Beshaley stood up, banging on the windscreen, and bellowed for the Doc to go faster.

Evelyne stood on tiptoe at the back of the screaming crowd, but she couldn't even see the men fighting. She pushed her way through the crowd and, spotting Jesse, made her way towards him.

'Jesse . . . Jesse? Do you remember me? . . . Jesse?'

He shrank away from her, wondering if she'd seen him lift the man's wallet. His eyes narrowed and he turned to dart back into the crowd, but Evelyne caught his sleeve, and then he recognized her by her red hair tumbling down from her schoolmistress's bun. She was Freedom's paleface friend. Jesse could barely hear what she had to say over the roar of the crowd, but when he understood they weaved and elbowed their way through the men to the opposite side of the makeshift boxing ring where the gypsy men watched the fight together. He squeezed his way among them, cupping his hand to their ears and whispering, and they passed the message on.

Evelyne looked at the ring and shuddered. Freedom and Taffy were in the centre, Taffy bleeding badly from a cut below his eye. Jesse moved like a dart, in and out between the men, then he returned to her side. 'The wagon's yonder, git outta here.'

He slipped away so fast that Evelyne had no time to grab his arm, and the gypsies were quietly leaving, one by one. The combined noise of the waterfall and the men's voices was deafening, and across the ring she could see fists raised as the miners yelled, 'Take the man out, Taffy!' Over their heads she could see her father, way over on the far side, shoving his way towards the ring. His face was set, he looked vicious, and he too was shouting, but she couldn't make out the words.

The bell clanged for the end of the round, and Freedom walked abruptly to his corner and sat down, snorting through his gumshield. He was surprised Jimmy One-Eye didn't take it out of his mouth, and where was the water? Then Jimmy leaned over and cupped his hand to Freedom's ear. 'Go down, mun, first punch go down, they know who you are, all hell's gonna be let loose – police'll be here, we're gonna have to do a runner.'

Hugh was close to the side of the ring, pointing at Freedom and yelling at the top of his voice, '*Killer*! *Killer*!'

The men around him tried to hear what he was saying and Evelyne could see him making gestures, slicing his hand across his throat and pointing again to Freedom.

Taffy's corner men worked hard, rubbing the big man down, plastering Vaseline over his swelling face. Taffy was heaving for breath and trying to listen to his trainer's instructions. He gasped with pain as they painted his cut then flapped their hands and blew to dry the paint. It was smarting so badly his eyes were watering, but he could have been weeping. His hopes of the Heavyweight Championship were dimming – he couldn't even get near the bastard.

The bell clanged, and Freedom was up on his feet before the clapper was still. He looked fresh, his breathing under control but his body glistening with sweat. Taffy lumbered into the centre and hunched up, somehow he knew he was going to get it, that was it, he knew it was coming, but he wasn't going to let the gyppo get him down easily.

Freedom opened up his defences and looked as if he'd walked into the right uppercut. Over he went, falling

252

back against the ropes, which sagged under him. The crowd went berserk and Taffy gazed in astonishment at the slumped body, the ref. bending over him, counting and waving his arms. The crowd joined in as he counted.

'One . . . two . . . three . . . four . . .'

Beshaley ran from the Doc's car just in time to see Freedom take the final punch. He slumped against the rocks, feeling as if he himself had been hit, winded. Through the celebrating crowd he could make out the tall figure of Sir Charles and was about to push forward to talk to him when he saw Taffy's manager. Sir Charles was shaking his hand, congratulating him.

Doc Clock panted over to Beshaley, muttering that nobody had told him about any fight. Beshaley had paled visibly, and the Doc was concerned, but he was bodily moved aside by a group of women. 'Dear God,' he thought, 'what is the world coming to when women are watching boxing matches?' He was walloped on the back with a frying pan, and spun round.

'Oh, sorry, bach, didn't recognize you!' said the woman.

Taffy was riding high on the shoulders of two miners, and the make-shift ring was swarming with men, dancing and yelling, while Hugh Jones stood in the centre, screaming for quiet, his arms waving and his face bright red with fury. '*Quiet . . . Quiet . . . Listen to me, will you listen to me!*'

Freedom went inside the wagon while Jesse organized the hitching of the horses. Outside the wagon the noise of the men was diminishing, and one voice was raised high above the rest, a voice screaming, 'Murderer! Murderer!' The wagon rocked as the horse was backed into the shafts. Hugh Jones was slowly getting the men to listen, despite the added din of the high-pitched screams of the women who had just arrived. 'The police couldn't find him and they been lookin', we got him right here, here amongst us . . . Freedom Stubbs killed Willie, slit his throat, are we gonna let him get away with it?'

Evelyne put her hands over her ears to shut out her father's voice. She wanted to turn and run – run away from the madness echoing round the mountain like the Devil himself. She stood up and tried to get to her father's side.

'Turn the wagon over, get him out, get him out!'

Evelyne was within feet of her father, screaming at him to stop, but a clod of earth flew through the air, narrowly missing her head.

'Tell us what you know, Bitch! *Bitch*!'

Frying pans and rolling pins thudded down on heads, the women were screaming and pointing at Evelyne. A man grabbed Evelyne from behind and held her arms. 'This is the one, she's known all along . . .'

Now Hugh was fighting to get to his daughter. Evelyne pulled her arms free and lashed out at her father with her fist.

Miners swarmed around the heavy wagon, heaving together to overturn it. The horse reared and kicked, striking a man on the side of his head. The wagon rolled forward, heading directly into the crowd around Hugh and Evelyne, and the men and women sprang away in fear for their lives.

Jesse whipped up the horse and lashed out at a man who tried to bring him down from the wagon. As they careered through the crowd, Freedom leaned out of the back and grabbed Evelyne by the waist. She tried to fight him off, but she was lifted off her feet and hauled on board as the wagon bounced and rumbled through the crowd.

CHAPTER 12

H UGH STOOD in the ring, or what was left of
it, the ropes trailing on the ground. His initial
fury had subsided, he knew he had been
wrong, but he couldn't understand his daughter – his
own daughter had raised her fist to him in front of the
whole village. He stood still, shaking. What in God's
name had got into her? Suddenly he took off after the
mob chasing the wagon.

Evelyne clung for dear life to the side of the wagon,
terrified. Behind them the mob followed, running down
the mountain. Freedom yelled to Jesse to keep clear of
the camp, lead the madmen away from their people,
take to the main roads. Evelyne wept, begged to be let
out, but Freedom ignored her and clambered up beside
Jesse. The wagon rolled from side to side as the dirt
track wound and curved. The running figures were now
a good distance behind them. They passed the entrance
to the campsite, and Jesse handed the reins to Freedom.
He jumped down as Freedom whipped the horse faster,
leading the mob away from the camp. They could see
that the camp was already packed up, the caravans in
line, set to move out. Alone in the back of the wagon,

Evelyne was bruised and battered against the sides, and still she held on.

The sound of the wheels clattering on cobbles told Evelyne they had arrived in the village. The horse slowed its frantic pace and stopped.

'Stop in the name of the law, now get down, hands above your head, come on, you vermin, do like we say, get down.'

The wagon's flap was pulled open and a policeman who looked inside shouted that there was a woman on board. At the same time Evelyne heard a voice asking, 'You the gyppo they call Freedom Stubbs?'

They were already putting the handcuffs on him by the time she stepped down. He made no effort to escape, did nothing to stop them handcuffing him, and said not one word. They hauled him roughly towards the police van, and even though he made no effort to evade arrest, one of the policemen brought his truncheon down hard on the back of his neck. He slumped forward, and they dragged him like an animal into the cage at the back of the van, locking and bolting it just in time as the mob appeared at the top of the village street.

The men and women were quieter now and, seeing the uniformed police encircling the van with truncheons at the ready, they kept their distance. 'Keep on walking now, come along, get back to your homes, the show's over. Come along now, keep walking, everybody keep walking.'

Slowly, they moved in groups past the police van, their interest directed first at the van, then at Evelyne. The women shot foul looks at her, then turned their faces away.

Hugh walked to his daughter's side and laid his hand on her arm.

'Don't touch me, this is your doing, this is down to you, Hugh Jones, I'd have thought you had more sense.'

Lizzie-Ann passed by and heard Evelyne's words, and muttered an abusive, bitter, 'gyppo lover'. The other women nearby picked up the phrase, murmuring quietly but clearly as they passed the wagon, 'gyppo woman, gyppo lover.'

Hugh stood still, head bowed, and Gladys whimpered and slunk to his side. The police van was cranked up and the engine chugged into life; then it headed for the police station with Evan Evans, flushed and apologetic, hurrying alongside.

Evelyne walked, head held high, back to Aldergrove Street. She knew they were all looking at her, talking about her, and she kept her eyes straight ahead. She was comforted by the thought that behind them all the caravans would be silently moving out, at least they had not torn the campsite apart.

Hugh wanted Gladys gone; he wanted to talk in private with Evelyne, but Gladys clung to his arm. He sat her down, then folded his arms, staring hard at Evelyne. She met his gaze head on, defiant.

'Now, Evie, out with it, we have a right to know.'

In a quiet, dead voice, Evelyne told them the truth. 'I was at a boxing match in Cardiff, remember, Da, the time I went by myself? I don't want to go into the details of how I got there, but I went to a boxing fair.

There was a riot, and I was leaving, but I had to go back inside the tent for my bag, I'd lost my handbag.'

Gladys stood up and demanded to know what on earth this had to do with Willie's murder. Evelyne pushed her down and leaned over her.

'Because when I went back I saw a poor gypsy girl being raped, not by one but by four lads. An' they'd worse than raped her, they'd taken a bench leg to her.'

Gladys screeched at the top of her voice, 'You sayin' Willie had something to do with it?'

'*I saw him, he was on top of the girl* . . . it was me that pulled him off by his hair, and I'd swear to it on the Bible, you want me to swear it on the Bible?'

Gladys shook her head, repeating over and over that she couldn't believe it – not that boy, not her sister's boy, he wouldn't do a thing like that.

'He did it, Gladys, he was one of those lads, the poor girl. I'll never forget her face.'

Hugh brushed Evelyne aside. 'That's enough now, come on, Gladys, I'll walk you home.'

He helped Gladys to the door, and just as he went out he gave Evelyne a heart-broken look. She couldn't meet his eyes, the look was filled with so much hurt, why hadn't she told him?

Freedom sat in the small village gaol that had only ever housed the poor lunatic who had bashed his mother's head in. Evan Evans ponderously filled in all the forms. His prisoner was to be taken directly to Cardiff to answer the charges there. Evans had to endorse the charge-sheet accusing Freedom of the murder of Willie Thomas.

*

Doc Clock, very irate, appeared to report the theft of a golf fob watch. He was insistent, never mind the ruddy gypsy, his new gold fob watch had been stolen right off the chain he had just put it on. Evans took down all the particulars, and waited until the Doc left, before he tore up the description of the fob watch. 'He's not had a watch attached to that chain for more'n fifteen years. We should have a word with the Medical Board, he's past it, the silly old fool.'

Mr Beshaley sat in Rawnie's wagon. He swung his gold watch on its chain, fingered it and replaced it in the pocket of the checked waistcoat that matched his suit. He had used that watch to bribe people on several occasions, but he had always been able to steal it back. 'Ye think he got himself away then, do ye?'

Jesse shrugged and put his feet up on the shelf, Freedom would be all right, he murmured. Mr Beshaley pursed his lips, what a wasted night it had been, all this way and for what, to be almost mobbed. He had never even got a chance to talk with Sir Charles Wheeler – maybe to get him interested in one of his other boxers.

Rawnie, with her skirts hitched up over her bare knees, smoked a hand-rolled cigarette clenched between her teeth. Perched up on the boards she held the reins loosely between her fingers, clucking for the horses to move on, then flicked a whip across their backs. She began to sing, low, husky, as if she had not a care in the world.

Mande went to poov the gry, all around the stiggur sty,
Mush off to Mande, I takes off my chuvvel,
I dels him in the per,
So ope me duvvel dancin Mande cours well.

Inside Rawnie's caravan Jesse was held by her husky voice, he smiled at Beshaley, and lowered his thick, black eyelashes.

'Freedom always was a loser, tonight he proved it.'

He joined in singing with Rawnie, their voices as soft as each other's. Beshaley shivered, they seemed so close, these two, and he felt like an intruder. He couldn't wait to get to Swansea. The pair of them unnerved him.

Hugh climbed the stairs, heavy-hearted. He could see the gaslight beneath Evelyne's door. Before he reached the door she opened it and stood, hands on hips. 'Well, what have you heard?'

Hugh shifted his weight and mumbled that they'd taken the gypsy to Cardiff, and the word was he'd be hanged.

'What if I was to tell you he didn't do the killings, none of them, it wasn't him?'

Hugh said that was for the courts to decide. Evan Evans was in the pub telling everyone that the gypsy had said not one word, which in Evans' eyes proved that he was guilty.

'If what you said about Willie is true, then so help me God I'm for the gel, but that's no reason to slit a man's throat – *more* than one.'

Evelyne snapped that more than one boy had raped Rawnie, and turned to go back into her bedroom. Hugh caught her arm. 'Tell me how you know so much, miss? Why you had the papers, why you showed your fist to your father in front of the whole village?'

Evelyne pulled her arm free and pushed past him, back into her bedroom snapping that he'd no need to worry, she'd not been touched by any of them.

'Where you goin'? Evie?'

She kicked the door to behind her, shouting that she was going to Cardiff. Hugh kicked the door back open again, his temper rising. 'Like hell you are, you stay out of this, you've done enough as it is.'

Evelyne was pulling clothes out of a drawer and throwing them on her bed. 'It's you who's done it, Da, you, you're power-mad since you got into that union. They hang him and they'll hang an innocent man.'

As fast as Evelyne took out her clothes, Hugh stuffed them back in the drawers, his temper mounting, and he shouted that she was not to leave the house.

'I was with him, Da, the night Willie was killed, I was with him, and I'm going to say so, he couldn't have done it.'

Hugh pulled her roughly to him, his hand raised to strike her, and she stared at him, stony-faced. 'Go on, hit me if it'll make you feel better, I was with him but not in the way you think. God help me, I went up there to warn him.'

Hugh slumped down on to the bed. He couldn't understand her. He shook his head and rumpled his hair. She still opened and closed the drawers, taking out what she needed. She brought a cardboard box out from under the bed.

'Don't get involved, gel, trust me, leave it be . . . unless . . . does this lad take your fancy, is that it?'

Evelyne threw up her hands in despair. 'No, I just know he didn't do it, and I can't live with myself knowing what I know . . . Oh, Da, I should have told you before, everything, but I just couldn't, I just couldn't.'

He patted the bed beside him and she sat close to him, resting her head on his shoulder. Slowly, piece by piece, she told him about the night in the boxing tent in Cardiff. The terrible humiliation she had suffered, the

261

money she had taken from David, money she'd been so ashamed of, and at last her bitterness came to the surface. She made no sound, but he knew she was crying and he cradled her in his arms.

'Being poor, Evie, is nothing to be ashamed of, one does things in a life that're much worse.'

She looked up into his sad face and asked if he was thinking of little Davey, and he nodded his head. He still held his big arm around her shoulders, but he stared vacantly ahead. After a moment he rose and walked to the window, drawing back the curtains to look out into the dark night.

'I was quite a lad, you know, when I was a youngster. Easter fair was always a night out for the lads. She was telling fortunes in a small booth – not like they have now, it was decorated with painted canvas, sort of draped – and you paid a ha'penny for a palm reading. By God, Evie, she was a beauty, not like your ma, different, exciting to young bloods, and we was all after her. See, we couldn't lay a finger on the local gels, not without their mothers coming around with their rolling pins . . . Anyways, I set out to capture the little dark-eyed wench, all the while cocksure of myself, telling the lads I'd have her. She said I was to come back at midnight, she'd leave the caravan door ajar. Well, I had my night with her, and the next day three of 'em came prancing down the street, seems she wasn't no ordinary gyppo, but one of high blood. They dragged me out and up to their fields and all of them set on me, even the old man threw in a few punches. I was handy with me fists so I gave as good as I got, but me pals hadda carry me home.

'Next morning, black-eyed and aching all over, I made my way to the pithead, an' she was there, waitin' with a small bundle under her arm. Seemed the family threw her out, see, an' there she was waitin' for me with her bangles and beads and the little bundle tied up with string.'

Hugh turned from the dark window. He seemed heavy, sluggish, and eased his body down on to the bed and lay flat, his eyes closed. 'Maybe if the lads hadn't been gathered around I'd have acted different. I just laughed at her, Evie, told her to be on her way with the rest of her vermin.'

He leaned up on his elbow and fingered Evelyne's slip which was lying across the bed. 'Her eyes went black, like a cat's, and she lifted her hand and gave me some kind of sign, she didn't scream or shout, it was husky, her voice, that's what made it worse, the strange softness of her words . . . She cursed me, Evie, said I'd have no sons to bury me.' He put his arm across his face and his whole body shuddered as he wept, his voice muffled. 'By Christ she was right, I've seen them buried. God help me, Evie, she was right.'

Now it was Evelyne's turn to hold her father gently, wipe his tear-stained face. She said that maybe it was fate, fate that made her cross the path of the gypsies.

'I'll leave for Cardiff on the first train, Da, all right?'

The mist clung to the top of the mountain, the grey rain drizzled, making grey, cobbled streets shine. As Evelyne turned at the corner to wave to Hugh at the bedroom window, he felt a terrible sense of loss, as if he would never see her again.

Evelyne passed three women standing at the water taps. They turned their backs to her and whispered. Evelyne held her head high and walked on.

'You'll not be teaching my kids, Evelyne Jones, you dirty gyppo lover.'

A group of men leaving their house for the early shift called to her and raised their fists. 'You should know better, Evelyne Jones. Our lads not good enough for you, eh?'

Their laughter echoed down the wet street, and she hunched her shoulders as if to defend herself from their malice. She crossed the street so she wouldn't have to face another group of women who stood waiting for the post office to open. They, too, stared at her then turned and whispered to each other. She gave them a frosty smile and almost bumped into Lizzie-Ann dragging the two kids and a pramful of laundry.

Evelyne stopped, and Lizzie-Ann had the grace to blush – she had, after all, thrown a clod of earth at Evelyne the night before. 'Well, where you off to at this hour, thought a woman of leisure like you would have a lie-in of a wet morning?'

Evelyne murmured that she was on her way to Cardiff.

'Going to see your boyfriend, are you? Better make it fast before they hang him.'

Evelyne looked into Lizzie-Ann's face. Her hair hung in rat's tails, her coat was stained, her legs bare and her shoes so worn that her heels, red and raw, were showing.

'That's right, go on, take a good look at me, Evelyne Jones, nothing a few pounds wouldn't put right, but then you're such a tight bitch, you'd not a give a beggar a farthing.'

Evelyne banged her cardboard box on top of the pram and pulled Lizzie-Ann to her by the lapels of her coat.

'What have I ever done to you, Lizzie-Ann, to make you talk like this? Tell me now, I don't deserve it and you know it.'

Lizzie-Ann pushed Evelyne away, her voice rising hysterically.

'You've always been too good, haven't you? You give me a roof over me head but begrudge a shilling for food, you're a hard one, Evelyne Jones, you always were . . .'

Evelyne felt sick. She couldn't fight Lizzie-Ann, there was nothing to say. She picked up her cardboard box and turned away.

'Don't you turn your back on me, Evelyne . . . *Evelyne . . . Evie*!'

There was such desperation in Lizzie-Ann's voice, it made Evelyne turn. Old before her years, beaten, roughened, the prettiest girl in the village had gone, and in the big, pansy eyes was a terrible, heart-breaking desperation. For a fleeting moment Evelyne wanted to hold her, but the accusing voice persisted, 'Where you going? Cardiff is it? Oh, well, all right for some, go on, there'll be more than one person pleased. You should stay there, your poor Da can't get up the courage to tell you he wants to get married, go on, you won't be missed.'

A few of the women joined in, chipping in their farthing's-worth.

Evelyne was already walking away, knowing Lizzie-Ann was trailing behind.

'Take the deeds to Doris' house, take them, just like you took everything, without a thank you.'

Head high, she strode off, clutching her cardboard box in front of her. Lizzie-Ann broke down, propping her swollen, sagging body against a filthy brick wall. She cried out, but her voice was distorted with tears, 'Oh, I wanted to go to London . . . oh God, I wanted to go to London.'

*

Somewhere out of the past Evelyne heard the soft, sweet voice of her mother repeating, 'Get out of the valley, Evie, don't let it drag you down,' well, she *would* get out, and she would never come back, there was nothing left for her here.

As she paid for her ticket, her mouth trembled, and she had to bite her lip until it bled to stop herself from crying. She had only one goodbye to say, it cried in her throat, the sound of the train's steam hissing and the 'chunt, chunt' of the engine drowned her words, 'Goodbye, Da, goodbye, Da.'

BOOK TWO

CHAPTER 13

EVELYNE WALKED up the stone steps of the police station in Cardiff and stood at the high counter. The sergeant on duty gave her a pleasant smile. 'What can I be doing for you, ma'am?

Taking a deep breath, Evelyne coughed. 'I have information regarding the murders of the four boys. I would like to make a statement, and I am prepared to go to any court and swear on oath that what I have to say is God's truth.'

The sergeant rubbed his head and leant on the desk. 'And what murders would these be, young lady?'

'The gypsy revenge killings . . . my name is Evelyne Jones. I want to make a statement.'

Half an hour later, after she had related everything to the sergeant, she was taken to meet the detective chief inspector. The sergeant held the door open for her and placed a stack of forms on the inspector's desk.

'I think you'd better listen to what this lady has to say, sir.'

The inspector listened attentively to every word, nodding his head and refilling his pipe. He puffed and stared at a spot on the wall just above Evelyne's head.

'And that, sir, is the truth. I was with Freedom Stubbs

the night he is supposed to have killed Willie Thomas, and I'll stand up in court and say so.'

The inspector tapped his pipe and began to scrape at the bowl. He chose his words carefully, because asking this tall, stiff young woman if she was 'familiar' with the gypsy was a delicate matter.

'I know him only as someone who helped me on the night of the rape, that is all.'

The inspector felt she was withholding something, she knew more than she admitted, but he had to take her statement and pass it to his superiors. The statement took an hour and fifteen minutes to complete, and Evelyne's meticulous handwriting and perfect spelling impressed everyone.

'I see you've put no address down, Miss Jones, where are you residing in Cardiff?'

Unable to think of where she would stay, Evelyne bit her lip. A large poster behind the inspector caught her eye – it was an advertisement for a charity ball at the Grand Hotel.

'I'll be at the Grand, Sir.'

He looked at her for a moment then carefully wrote down the name of the hotel.

'Will Mr Stubbs be released now?'

Evelyne's innocent question made them laugh, it wasn't as simple as that. The man was charged with murder and one statement was not good enough. There were, after all, three more murders with Freedom Stubbs the main suspect in each case.

'Will I be allowed to see him?'

The men flicked sly glances at each other and then back to Evelyne, looking at her from top to toe. One of the uniformed men said it could possibly be arranged.

'Thank you for coming in, Miss Jones, and we will contact you at the Grand Hotel if we feel it is necessary.'

As Evelyne walked out of the office, she heard a chuckle behind her and the inspector speaking to one of the officers, 'I'm sure Miss Jones will be at the Grand, lads, I'm sure.'

She felt humiliated, and realized she had accomplished nothing, and they were laughing at her behind her back. She took a deep breath, decided she would have a good breakfast and think about what she should do next. She would have breakfast at the Grand, and book a room there.

When she reached the Grand Hotel she realized why the inspector had been cynical about her staying there; it certainly lived up to its name. Even the steps up to the lobby were covered with thick-pile red carpet, and there was so much braid on the uniformed doorman's jacket he looked in danger of being tied up in it permanently. He inclined his head to her, haughtily, and swung open the big brass doors with 'The Grand' painted on the glass in gold.

Once inside, Evelyne felt even more overpowered by the ornate building. The lobby was busy with residents and porters everywhere, and a bellhop loudly calling a name, trying to deliver a telegram. The head clerk Mr Jeffrey, wearing an immaculate black jacket and pin-striped trousers, looked up sharply as Evelyne tentatively rang the bell on the desk.

Evelyne almost dropped the cardboard suitcase when she saw the prices of the rooms. A heavy smell of perfume wafted past her nose, and a woman with two tiny parcels tied up with ribbon held her hand out languidly for her key. The clerk grovelled and bowed, placed a key into the kid-gloved hand and gave Evelyne a sidelong look.

'Room twenty-nine, Lady Southwell.'

Evelyne glanced down at the brochure and noted that her Ladyship had a suite on the third floor.

'Do you have a room vacant on the third floor?'

'The third floor is suites only, modom.'

Evelyne was getting hot, a flush creeping up from her toes.

'I'll have a suite, then.'

The suite was decorated in different shades of pink, the twin beds draped and canopied with tiny, fluffy pink mats beside them. The bathroom was huge, marbled, and more luxurious than any she'd ever seen in a magazine. Bath salts, courtesy of the hotel, stood in a neat row. The water smelt lovely and she stayed in the warm, scented bath until her skin wrinkled.

Her scrubbed face shining, Evelyne walked through the lobby, aware of Mr Jeffrey's scrutiny. She gave him a small, prim nod and nearly walked into a palm tree. A painted board on an easel announced the opening hours of the various dining-rooms.

'The Grand Hotel is pleased to offer guests the choice of three dining rooms . . .'

Evelyne chose the tearoom. The small tables were painted white and laid with white linen cloths, the upholstered chairs also in white, and there were potted palms scattered around the room. A trio played on a corner stand, and the few customers spoke in whispers.

Evelyne selected a table at the far side which gave her a good view of the whole tearoom and the lobby from behind one of the palms. A waitress in a neat black dress with a frilled white cap, pinafore and cuffs promptly placed a menu in front of her. The toasted teacakes and pot of tea tasted better than anything she had ever made at home, with jams in tiny individual pots. Hot water was brought to freshen Evelyne's teapot without her even asking, and she ordered another round of teacakes. She was loading butter on the hot bun when she heard a familiar voice.

'My darling, forgive me, I'm late, but I simply couldn't get away earlier, children's wretched teaparty – have you ordered?'

Evelyne peeked around the large potted palm to her right and saw Freddy Carlton just about to sit down at the next table. He seemed to have aged. His neat moustache was waxed at the ends, and he wore a pale blue shirt with a stiff white collar and narrow black tie with his brown pin-striped suit. She could just see a tiny gloved hand as Freddy raised it to his lips and kissed it as he sat down. Parting the thick leaves of the palm tree, Evelyne peered through.

'We don't have long, dearest, I have some shopping to do. I've ordered tea, are you hungry?'

Evelyne let go of the palm. Lady Primrose laughed softly, and Evelyne saw Freddy lean closer to her. She was sure Freddy kissed her, and in public!

'Is it you? I saw you from the staff door, is it you, Evelyne?'

This time Evelyne was so startled that she yelped. There in front of her was Miss Freda with a large tray of toasted scones.

'Shush, not too loud, yes it's me, Miss Freda.'

Freda beamed at Evelyne, her frizzy hair trapped beneath a frilled white cap.

'I work here now, I'm not supposed to talk to the customers, but I will bring you over some cakes . . . shusssh . . . then maybe we can meet and talk, yes?'

'That would be nice.'

Evelyne was thrilled to see Freda, but a little worried about Freddy and Lady Primrose, at the next table. Freda gave her a little wink and scurried to her customer's table, getting a stern look from a stout woman with an enormous bosom who was taking up her position at the pay desk.

While Evelyne eavesdropped on the conversation between Freddy and Lady Primrose, several waitresses passed her table, each depositing a cake in front of her with a wink. She ate her way through a piece of strawberry gateau, a cherry pie, and a large white meringue filled with fresh cream, and still they kept coming.

Rising to his feet, Freddy leaned once more across the table.

'Can we meet this afternoon? I can't bear being apart from you, it's been three whole days, will you call me and I'll arrange a room?'

'You'd better leave, darling, they'll be arriving . . . I'll call you, I promise.'

Evelyne hid behind her napkin as Freddy walked past her table. One of the waitresses blocked him from view as she laid a paper bag by Evelyne's plate.

'Freda says for you to put the ones you can't eat into this, but careful, she's got eyes in the back of her head.'

Evelyne looked at the woman behind the pay desk while the waitress cleared Freddy's teacup. She slipped three cakes into her paper bag and put it beneath the table. As she raised her head she found the woman with the huge bosom looming over her.

'Your bill, madam.'

Had she been spotted? Evelyne flushed, but the woman pivoted on her heel and made her way around the room, depositing more of the little pink slips on other tables.

Freda sidled over to Evelyne. 'Where are you staying?'

'I'm here, room twenty-seven . . . I mean, suite.'

'Here? You are staying *here*? Well, I'll see you later.'

She whizzed away through the swinging kitchen door, thinking to herself that Miss Evelyne certainly must have more money than she knew what to do with.

Holding her bag of cakes close to her side, Evelyne gave two shillings to the stern-faced woman with the bosom, and her sixpence change clattered down a chute. She struggled to get it out with one hand, afraid to lift the other to reveal the bag of illicit cakes.

'Do come again.'

Turning quickly away she bumped into Sir Charles Wheeler, who stepped aside and apologized then surveyed the room from behind his monocle. The cashier beamed and led him to a small booth, murmuring that she felt sure Sir Charles would find it suitable. He sat with his back to the room and opened a copy of *The Times*.

Evelyne pressed the lift button and waited. The brass was so highly polished it was like a mirror, and she adjusted a stray curl of hair . . . then her heart stopped.

David Collins strode in to the hotel, paused to smile at the manager, flicked his gloves off and walked towards the tearoom. He looked handsomer than ever, wearing the latest Prince of Wales single-breasted suit, a tie with a Windsor knot, and carrying a brown trilby. With an ingratiating smile the fawning cashier directed him to Lady Primrose's table.

The lift gates clanked open.

'Do you want to go up? Madam, *up*?'

The snooty bellhop doubled as lift attendant during teatime.

'Third floor.'

Evelyne stepped out of the lift and the boy nearly caught her coat as he slammed the gates shut behind her. On the carpet outside her room lay a newspaper, and looking up and down the corridor she saw that there was one outside each door. At least something was included in the price of the suite.

The headline ran in big, black print: 'Gypsy to stand trial for killings.' Ed Meadows paid his twopence and opened the paper as he made his way to the tearoom.

'Yes, have you booked a table?'

Ed stared around the room then pointed to Sir Charles' table. The cashier was aghast, the man looked dreadful in a shabby suit and down-at-heel shoes. She was about to stop him when Sir Charles laid down his newspaper, turned, and gestured for the new arrival to join him.

'Well, guv, that's the gyppo up the spout, you seen the 'eadlines, they got 'im not fer one murder but free . . . I dunno, what a bleedin' waste.'

Freda stood by the table as Ed looked over the menu. 'You got eggs an' bacon, somefink like that, eh?'

Sir Charles raised his eyebrows and turned to Freda. 'Welsh rarebit, for two please, and a pot of coffee.'

Her legs aching, Freda moved off, jotting down the order as she went. She was tired and wanted to sit down, but she had hours to go yet.

Ed leaned across the table. 'I just come from Taffy and his manager's place, the man was cut bad an' I'd say it'll open up again first bout he has, be at least five weeks

276

before he's healed up, an' he's pudgy, you know, not in good nick at all.'

Sir Charles frowned. 'You think the knockout was fixed, what?'

Ed spread his chubby hands and sighed. 'Guv, that gyppo could've 'ad 'im in round one, what a fighter, it's tragic – it's bloody tragic. Far as I could make out old Taffy was bleedin' surprised to floor the gyppo 'imself. Now, 'is manager was givin' me the old story, yer know, about Taffy's bein' famous for 'is left uppercut, but I said, I said, do me a favour, mate, the punch was a wide, open-'anded right, couldn't 'ave floored a flyweight wiv it, never mind a big'un like Stubbs.'

Sir Charles mused, fiddling with his cutlery. 'So . . . we forget about Taffy, what? He may be useful as a sparring partner, but I doubt anything else.'

'You ask me, guv, 'e's ready fer the knacker's yard. I got a theory, see the 'eadlines? Now, yer know the police was after 'im – what if he got tipped off and done a runner, like? *Hadda* go down 'cause 'e knew the law was on to 'im? That's the way I sees it.'

'Either way, old chap, we come out the losers. Pity, really felt that fellow Stubbs was champion material, damned shame, but then these gyppo fellows are not to be trusted . . . Ah, jolly good, breakfast!'

Freda placed the Welsh rarebits in front of them. Ed stared in horror. 'Gor blimey, what in hell's name is this?'

Freda put down the coffee-pot and a jug of hot milk. 'Will that be all, sir?'

Sir Charles nodded, picking up his knife and fork. 'Try it, Ed, it's quite tasty.'

Ed poked at his plate, then sighed. 'Fair breaks me 'eart. What a fighter, they'll 'ang 'im . . . We goin' back ter London then, guv?'

Sir Charles carefully cut through his toast. Yes, they would return first thing in the morning, he had some relatives he might call on. Ed looked at the orchestra and began to hum along, 'Tea for two . . .' Then he took an enormous mouthful of rarebit, chewed and pulled a face.

'Sooner the better, I've 'ad enough of Wales, Welsh rabbits an' all . . . can't taste any meat in this, more like cheese ter me.'

During her lunch break Freda went to Evelyne's suite. She took a great interest in the furnishings, then flopped down on one of the single beds, exhausted. To Evelyne she seemed happy-go-lucky as she related, with little shrugs, the story of her business failing and the fact that she was working to save for another shop. Secretly, Freda wondered where Evelyne was getting the money to stay at the Grand. Perhaps she had some cash to spare and they could go into partnership together.

'So why are you here, Miss Evelyne? Ah, I know, you are getting married, is that it?'

Evelyne laughed. 'Far from it.' She explained at length why she had come back to Cardiff, while Freda lay with her eyes closed, listening. She didn't mention Jesse and Rawnie by name, just the basic facts of Willie's murder.

'I'm a witness you see, Freda, that's why I'm here, I know he didn't kill that boy. Freedom is innocent, and I want to help him.'

Rolling over on the bed, Freda propped her frizzy head on her hands and scrutinized Evelyne. 'But it is not just one killing, is it darling? Perhaps he did not kill this Willie boy in your village, but what of the three murdered here in Cardiff? Goodness, I've read terrible things, such scandal, everyone has been frighted, it's like Jack the Ripper.'

Freedom Stubbs was no Jack the Ripper, Evelyne told her.

Recovering some of her energy, Freda sat up and swung her legs over the side of the bed. They didn't reach the floor.

'We shall go to see him, that is what we must do. But first, and I hope you don't mind me saying this, your dress is very drab, you must look smart, not like a schoolteacher, really smart . . . do you have the money for some clothes?'

Evelyne answered evasively, not that sort of money, and studied her reflection in the mirror. Freda looked her up and down, she was so thin and had grown even taller. For a small price, she suggested, she could alter Evelyne's clothes, perhaps they could buy some second-hand things.

'You will feel more confident, and I can do it very cheaply, what do you say?'

Smiling sweetly as Evelyne agreed, Freda took out a tape measure, saying that she never went anywhere without it. She departed with two pounds ten shillings of Evelyne's money, assuring her she could do wonders with it.

When she had left, Evelyne counted her remaining money. She had been 'paid' with two five-pound notes last time she had been in Cardiff, and now she was putting them to good use. As Freda had taken most of her few clothes to alter she couldn't go out, so she lingered in yet another soapy bath, her thoughts on David. She wondered if he knew what was so obviously going on between his wife and his best friend Freddy.

*

The following morning Evelyne was astonished at how fast Freda had worked. Her hemlines were up, and the new buttons on her old coat made it look quite nice.

'I will have a dress ready soon, your skirt and blouse will do for now, and perhaps if you can give me a few more shillings you can have a nice new hat.'

The desk sergeant remembered Evelyne, but refused her permission to see Freedom. Miss Freda launched into a furious speech about citizens' rights, and said that if he didn't allow Miss Jones to visit the prisoner, she would write to all the newspapers. After that they were kept waiting for half an hour, but permission was granted. They were sent to another building, where again they were kept waiting, until a tall prison warder with a set of big keys on a waist-chain approached them.

'Miss Evelyne Jones, please?'

He led her to a bare room where Freedom was sitting at a wooden table, handcuffed, an officer standing beside the door. Another officer stood outside, where he could see into the room through a small window set in the door for that purpose. Freedom had no idea why he had been brought out of his cell and sat, head bowed, staring at his hands. His hair was unruly, uncombed, and his face already dark with stubble.

As the officer left he locked the door behind him, after informing Evelyne coldly that she had ten minutes. Freedom was stunned and made to rise, but was immediately pushed back into his chair by the officer. Evelyne sat in an identical chair opposite Freedom. Now that she was here she didn't know what to say to him and could see that he was dumbstruck by her appearance. She could smell him, his heavy body odour, for the man had not been allowed to bathe since his arrest.

His shoulder-length hair was greasy and hung limp, and when he lifted his hands to move it back from his face she could see his handcuffs.

The presence of the police officer loomed over them both, and for a good two minutes neither said a word. Evelyne placed her hands, with the neat, square, shining nails, on to the table. 'I have come to say you were with me the night Willie was in the picture house. They say in the papers that you'll be standing trial for all the killings and that you'll hang.'

Freedom looked into her eyes, and then turned to look at the prison officer. His voice was so quiet, she had to lean forward to hear. 'So be it, and I thank thee for coming, God bless you.'

Evelyne leant even further across to him, trying to make him look into her face, but his head remained bowed. 'You can't just accept it, you can't, because I know you didn't . . .'

Freedom looked up, his face was hard, and now his voice was firm, though still not loud. 'You know nothing, go back to your village, *manushi*, go back, this is not your business. Forget what you know – she must never be mentioned, understand me?'

She knew he meant Rawnie, and she leant back against the wooden chair. He was prepared to say nothing, prepared to hang . . . she couldn't believe it.

'Will you do nothing? Freedom . . .' His name sounded hollow and foolish, and he turned to the officer and jerked his head for the door to be opened. The officer banged on the door with his wooden baton and it was unlocked from outside. With a hesitant look at the officer, Freedom waited to be allowed to stand.

'Do you have proof that you were not in Cardiff for the other killings? Freedom? Where were you? Freedom?'

Standing, Freedom dwarfed the prison officer who only came up to his shoulders. He didn't look back but walked straight to the door, and it was not until he bent his head to avoid the doorframe that he turned to look back at her.

His dark eyes were expressionless, black, his powerful arms bound by the handcuffs. He was like a magnificent wild beast trapped by man, unbowed and undaunted. He gave Evelyne a quick, unfathomable smile, then he was gone.

Miss Freda linked arms with Evelyne as they walked away from the prison. The girl was silent, her body stiff, her hands cold to Freda's touch. One of the prison officers had walked through the waiting room and mentioned to another that the gyppo killer had not said a word during his time in the jail.

'That his woman in there with him, is it? She'll do no good, he's for the rope and he knows it.'

Miss Freda still did not know the truth behind Evelyne's visit, surely it could not just be because she believed the lad innocent, there must be more than that.

In the middle of the street Evelyne suddenly stopped, her face angry, eyes blazing.

'They'll not hang him, Freda, I won't let them, he's like a child in there, a foolish, stubborn child.'

Together they returned to Freda's small lodgings. The room was cluttered with hatboxes, and in pride of position in the centre of the room was Freda's sewing machine. From the garret window Evelyne could see a long line of men waiting for the dole, and there were children begging in the street.

'I won't let them hang him, he's innocent, I'm going back, and I'll *keep* going back until they take me seriously and do something about it.'

Freda patted her arm soothingly and at the same time tried to measure her for a sleeve.

'I don't want a new dress, Freda, I'm sorry, I'm not going to walk away from him, I'm going to make him see sense, I have to.'

Frightened that Evelyne would ask for her money back, Freda wanted to weep. She was so short of cash that she'd already spent the two pounds ten on back rent. 'You seem so sure he is innocent – I know, don't get angry . . . I know you say you were with him, he could not have killed that boy in your village, but Evie, what of the others?'

Evelyne still stared down at the growing line of poverty-stricken, unemployed men. 'He's killed no one, I know it, there are things I can't speak of . . . but I will, I'll make him let me.'

Back at the prison, at first the warder was most unhelpful. Evelyne refused to budge, she had to see Freedom Stubbs, and it was her right. The prisoner was entitled to a lawyer. She opened her purse and took out a shilling. 'And you'll have another after I've seen him.'

She was taken to the visiting room and told to wait. At long last, after two hours, she heard the footsteps of the warder returning.

'You got two minutes and then he has to go back, I'll lose me job, ma'am, I'm trusting you to behave yourself.'

Evelyne clenched her fists, nodded her head. Another fifteen minutes passed before she heard the sound of keys turning, iron doors opening and closing, and then heavy footfalls. Freedom was ushered in, head bowed, lips tight.

'He didn't want to see you, ma'am, so much for all your trouble . . . now, *you*, sit down, I'll be right outside the door.'

They were alone, and she sat opposite him.

'We've got two minutes, so let's not waste it. Will you listen to me, Mr Stubbs? If you won't help yourself then I am going to do it, whether you like it or not.'

His teeth were so tightly clenched she could see a muscle twitching at the side of his mouth. He refused to look up.

'Now then, I have the time of the murder at the picture house, and I know for certain I was with you. Now where were you on the other occasions? I'll check out your whereabouts and try to prove you were not in Cardiff when the other lads were killed. Are you listening to me? Will you not stand up and fight? Fight for your own life?'

Still he was silent and she could feel his anger. She leaned forward, whispered, 'I'll give you my word I'll not mention Rawnie, or Jesse, I'll not ever say their names, and that's God's truth.'

Her face was close to his, her hands on the table, and he moved so fast it shocked her. His shackled hands reached over and grabbed her wrists hard, hurting her, and she was frightened.

'Woman, go away, you've no business here.'

For the first time he looked into her frightened face, and then he moaned, rubbed her wrist softly.

'I didn't mean to frighten you, girl, I'll not hurt you.'

She swallowed, he was still holding her wrists, she could see where the handcuffs had cut into his skin. She eased her hands away.

'Do you not understand? They'll say you're a gyppo lover, just like I heard them screaming at you when I was inside the wagon. You'll be treated like dirt – you'll get no respect, they'll drag your name in the muck alongside mine.'

She slapped the table between them. 'I don't care, I want to help you, can't you understand that, I *need* to help you?'

He cocked his head to one side and looked at her, repeating the word 'need' as a question. Evelyne bit her lip and felt the tears welling up. She sniffed. 'Oh, you won't understand, but I never see things through, you know? I've not even taken my examinations, I'm not a qualified schoolteacher, and then, well, last time I was here . . . I've never had the fight in me, not for myself. I'll fight for *you*, I want to see you released, I want to give you your name, Freedom.'

A tear trickled down each of her cheeks, and he lifted his hands to wipe them away, but she recoiled. 'I don't know what I'm crying for. It's you that should be weeping, will you not stand up for yourself, man? I'll stand alongside you, I give you my word, and I've got a bit of money for a lawyer.'

The key turned in the lock, and Freedom stood up. He was walking to the door of his own free will. At the door he stopped, his back to her, and his voice was so soft she could only just hear it.

'Take your fight, *manushi*, take it for yourself, there's naught ye can do fer me. Don't come back, I don't want to see you again, I won't see you . . . walk away if you know what's best, and get your teaching qualifications.'

He was gone, the visiting-room door stood open and the warder was looking at her. 'All the same, ungrateful animals, you wasted your time. Go on, love, go home.'

She handed him his shilling, and he looked at it, then looked her up and down. He shook his head. 'Keep your money, lovey, you look as if you could do with a good meal inside you, now go on, go home.'

Freda watched as the coppers, the shillings and a half-crown tumbled out on to the sewing-machine table. 'You love this man, Evelyne, is that what it is?'

Evelyne was stunned, her mouth dropped open. She had never thought of that. 'Good heavens no, he's a gypsy, Freda, but that doesn't mean he has no right to a fair trial . . . Oh, I feel so good, elated, you know. I'm doing something really worthwhile, and what's more I'm going to see it through . . . I'll be at the hotel, I'll leave the dresses and things to you, just make sure you make me look like a real lady.'

Freda was rendered speechless. She wondered if Evelyne was one of those suffragettes she'd read about, they were always going on about people's rights.

'Remember, Freda, if I look good in court then people'll want to know where I got the clothes from, you'll be back in business, what do you say?'

Freda picked up the money and was already delving into her pattern book as Evelyne ran down the wooden staircase.

Ping! went the desk bell, and Mr Jeffrey whipped round, picked up the key to suite twenty-seven and banged it on the desk.

'Will you want a table reserved for dinner, Miss Jones?'

Evelyne turned to him, and for the first time she

wasn't in any way ashamed or embarrassed. 'Not at those prices I won't, thank you.'

She was off to the lift before Mr Jeffrey could close his open jaw. Good God, she's got herself a suite and now she was acting up like she was a duchess.

The lift-boy was about to clang the lift shut on Evelyne's coat when she turned and gave him a look. 'Just you try it, lad, an' you'll get the back of my hand. Time you learnt some manners.'

Ed Meadows was tapping on Sir Charles Wheeler's door when he overheard Evelyne's remark. He turned to her and grinned.

'Good on yer, gel, cheeky little blighter, ain't 'e?'

Evelyne smiled, picked up her evening newspaper and put her key in the door.

'You from round these parts, are you?'

Evelyne had already opened her door and gave him a rather frosty look. Being friendly was one thing, but he was a little too chatty. 'I'm from the valleys, good evening to you.'

Getting no reply from knocking on His Lordship's door, Ed waddled towards Evelyne.

'I'm from London, suppose you can tell by me accent I'm not Welsh, I'm up 'ere wiv me guv'nor, name's Meadows, Ed Meadows.'

He brandished a rather dog-eared card at Evelyne.

'Boxing promotor and trainer, 'Ackney, London.'

Evelyne took the card and gave a curt nod, then realized she was behaving a little rudely.

'Evelyne Jones.'

As they shook hands, Sir Charles appeared at the door of his suite. He was dressed in a plum-velvet smoking jacket. Ed Meadows turned, then stepped back and introduced Sir Charles to Evelyne. Very debonair, Sir

Charles strode up to Evelyne and kissed her hand. 'Charmed to meet you, are you staying long?'

He wasn't frightfully interested whether she was or not, and was already heading back towards his open door. Ed beamed at Evelyne and followed the guv'nor, telling him before Evelyne could open her mouth that she was from the valleys. About to enter his suite, Sir Charles smiled. 'What a coincidence, we were there only the other night. Well, nice to meet you, good evening.'

The door closed behind them and Evelyne entered her own suite. She bumped the door closed with her behind and tossed the keys on to the bed. Typical Londoners, think there's only one valley . . . and then she pulled up, and Sir Charles' words click-click-clicked in her brain. Surely that titled gent couldn't have been to her valley . . . but it would make sense, that man . . . Evelyne fished in her pocket for Ed's crumpled card, bit her lip, and then before she could change her mind she strode out of the suite and along the corridor.

Dewhurst opened the door to Sir Charles' rooms, and stiffly enquired if she had an appointment. Behind him Ed Meadows bellowed, 'Who is it?'

Sir Charles was sitting at a small desk. There was a big fire in the grate and there were so many doors leading off the main room that for a moment Evelyne thought she had got confused, perhaps he lived at the hotel, surely he wouldn't have all this space just for one person? He fixed his monocle into his left eye and looked at Evelyne. 'Ah, yes, now what can I do for you?'

Evelyne's nerve almost deserted her, but she blurted it out as fast as she could. Had they been to the Freedom Stubbs fight? She was a friend of his and he was in prison, but he wasn't guilty and she wondered if they

288

could advise her what she could do. Her knees buckled slightly as she finished, she could feel the flush creeping up her cheeks.

Sir Charles leaned back in his chair and his monocle popped out. He swung it on the end of the black ribbon round his neck.

'Dewhurst, bring the young lady in. I'm sorry, please forgive me, I didn't catch your name . . .? Ah, Evelyne, yes, yes of course, a drink, dear? What would you care for?'

Evelyne said sherry because it was the first thing that came into her head, and Dewhurst placed a chair for her close to the desk and backed out of the room. Ed Meadows moved to stand behind Sir Charles, and asked Evelyne what she knew of the gypsy and how was she involved. 'They say he's killed four lads and you say different, that right?'

Sitting in the cosy, firelit room, Evelyne told them what she knew, took them right back to the first time when she had seen Freedom fight Dai 'Hammer' Thomas. She was taken aback because Ed Meadows kept interrupting her, asking all sorts of questions about other fights she knew of, had she seen him fight anywhere else in Wales? Did she know about the knockout in the ring the other night? Sir Charles eventually put his hand on Ed's arm and, looking directly at Evelyne and speaking very slowly, asked again why, exactly why, she had come to see him.

'Because he's innocent and I can prove it. I've offered to go into court, and I just don't think they're going to pay any attention to what I have to say, but I *know* he didn't do those murders.'

Sir Charles listened intently to Evelyne's story, then excused himself, leaving her alone with Ed.

''E's a bit of a toff, but 'e's a real gent, know what I

mean, a true blue, an' take it from me I know what I'm talkin' about, nothin' he don't know about the game, he's even bin to America, United States of America, you know, oh yeah, 'is Lordship's a real pro, was a fighter 'imself, see.'

They both turned to the closed doors, and Ed, without stopping except to swallow gulps of his frothing black Guinness, continued. 'Nineteen-o-eight there was the Aussie fella, Jack Johnson, Gawd almighty what a fighter 'e was, saw that big'un with Jim Jefferson, nineteen-ten, July fourth, you heard of the Great White Hope? I was there for that wiv 'im, 'e took us both over. But yer fighter knockin' 'em all into the corners is Dempsey, the man's a joy ter watch, a joy ter watch, I was there, an' guess who was sittin' not two rows in front of me? Special cordoned-off area – Ethel Barrymore, yes, on my life Ethel Barrymore, the famous actress, was watching Dempsey fight, bloody marvellous . . . pardon the language, miss.'

Behind closed doors Sir Charles gave quiet instructions for Dewhurst to go down to reception and ask about this Miss Jones, find out how long she'd been staying, et cetera. When he returned to the drawing room Ed beamed at him. 'My God, this gel knows about fighting, your Lordship.'

Evelyne hadn't actually said a word, but she smiled, looking into her sherry glass. Sir Charles replaced his monocle and with his long fingers he drummed on the top of the inlaid writing desk. 'Tell me, dearie, this Freedom fella, what is your relationship with him?'

She placed the glass on top of the desk and sat up very straight. 'There is no relationship, sir, not even a

290

friendship, I simply do not want to see an innocent man hang.'

She could feel Sir Charles' eyes carefully noting every-thing about her from the top of her hair to the scuffed shoes. She was glad Miss Freda had altered her clothes, at least she looked respectable, if not fashionable.

'You say you are prepared to go into the witness box? He is a Romany gypsy, isn't he?'

Evelyne nodded, bit her lip. She knew he was trying to imply that there was something between the two of them, and it made her angry.

'I don't wish to sound rude, dearie, but, well, you don't look, if you will excuse my saying so, you don't really look like most of the clientele in this establish-ment. I was wondering if you will excuse my rudeness for asking, how you are able to stay at the Grand?'

Evelyne stood up sharply, her hands gripped at her sides, her face taut. 'It is no business of yours, but I was left a legacy, and I am quite able to afford the price of this "establishment". I may not look like the so-called "ladies" I've seen parading around the lobby, but I wouldn't care to dress like them anyway, not that my legacy would run to that height of fashion. I have no other motive but to help a man whom I believe is innocent. There is nothing sexual about my friendship with him, I am only interested in justice. I am sorry to have wasted your time but I took you to be a gentleman who could possibly guide me in what I should do. I can see I was wrong, excuse me.'

Ed Meadows rose to stop her, but Sir Charles laid his elegant hand on Ed's arm again. Evelyne reached the door, turned and thanked Sir Charles for the sherry and then turned abruptly and walked out.

'Why d'yer behave like that, sir? I fink she was a true

'un moment I hear her givin' that snotty lift-boy a bollockin'.'

Sir Charles smiled, raised his whisky glass. 'On the contrary, I would say she's magnificent, she's a tigress, Ed m'boy, but we have to be very sure, I'd say that gel will make a first-class witness, and from what I've read to date the boy will most certainly need that, plus a lot more. Go and check on a chap called Smethurst, he's a lawyer, we'll need the best there is – or the best Cardiff can provide.'

From the hotel lobby, Ed Meadows asked if Miss Jones would care to have dinner with him, as Sir Charles had suggested it. Evelyne said she had a previous engagement and Ed apologized for disturbing her, but thought he should mention to her that His Lordship had already set the wheels in motion. He was hiring a lawyer first thing in the morning to act on behalf of Freedom Stubbs. He was going to pay a visit to the prison himself, and Ed added that he hoped she was not affronted by his invitation to dinner. Evelyne felt awful and would have liked to change her mind, but she knew she had nothing suitable to wear so she thanked Ed again and said perhaps another time.

Miss Freda had taken Evelyne at her word. She had been round the second-hand shops, run-down tailor's shops, bespoke tailor's, pawn shops. With an eagle eye for a bargain she bartered and argued and scrimped, and saved a penny here, twopence there. There was a dreadful pink satin ballgown that she could pull the beads from and hand-stitch instead round the collar of a fawn suit, the pinkish beads setting off the fawn of the jacket.

Accustomed to rising early, Evelyne was sitting on the window-seat with her legs curled beneath her when Freda arrived at seven-fifteen. Poor Freda looked pale, with deep circles beneath her eyes, but she had brought four garments, all finished down to the buttons. She was able to double her money on each item, but she didn't feel she was cheating Evelyne, she had cut and sewn all night long and she would defy anyone to tell what or whose they had once been.

Freda hid in the bathroom when Evelyne called down for some coffee to be sent up to suite twenty-seven, and stayed there until the waiter delivered the steaming pots.

They discussed Evelyne's outfits and talked about what sort of hat she needed to go with each. Evelyne counted out the shillings and pennies, double-checked it and handed the money to Freda, then she went into the bathroom to brush her hair. Returning to the bedroom she found Freda curled up like a dormouse on the unmade bed, so deeply asleep, she didn't even stir when Evelyne slipped the eiderdown round her tiny shoulders.

The rest of the day was spent in shopping and carefully choosing material and one pair of shoes that would be suitable for all the outfits.

Ed Meadows was waiting in the lobby when Evelyne got back, and he rushed her up to Sir Charles' suite.

Freedom Stubbs had turned down Sir Charles' offer to take over his case, refusing point-blank, although thanking Sir Charles for his time and obvious expense. Sir Charles had pulled many strings and had his motor-car waiting to take Evelyne to the jail. She must talk to him, tell him he was being foolish and would hang for it unless he accepted their offer.

*

293

Ed Meadows sat in the front of the car with the chauffeur, and gave Evelyne details of the offer, making it sound simple and, of course, to Freedom's advantage. Sir Charles wanted Freedom to sign a contract to be under his sole management.

'We reckon he could be a contender, see Evie, me and the guv'nor want to train 'im, like, get 'im ready. It's a fair contract, all the money 'e laid out for the court case, legal fees and what 'ave you, would be comin' out of whatever 'e'd earn as a boxer.'

Evelyne, clutching the contract, was led through the jail to the visiting room. This time the prison officers were cordial and called her 'ma'am'. Freedom was brought into the small room in handcuffs, but he had bathed and shaved. His hair was shining, and was braided down his neck. He sat, head bowed, opposite her, and the officer told Evelyne quietly that she could stay as long as she wanted.

One officer was left on duty inside the room, as usual, and another outside the door, but this time the room was not locked.

'Well, what have you got to say for yourself, Freedom? You know how much trouble I've been to, and Sir Charles, you can't say no, you must be out of your mind.'

Freedom looked down at his hands and pursed his lips. Evelyne leaned over and whispered that no one was concerned about anyone else, nothing had been mentioned about anyone else's involvement, no names. All they were interested in was his innocence or guilt.

'You are innocent, I know it, I can stand up and prove it in Willie's case, but you'll have to say where you were on the days when the other lads were killed.'

Freedom shifted his weight but still he would not

look up and meet her eyes. He remained silent, infuriating Evelyne.

'Sir Charles Wheeler's no ordinary man, he can help you in your boxing, all you've got to do is sign this contract an' he'll make you a contender.'

Having misunderstood what Ed Meadows had said, Evelyne had no idea what 'contender' meant. Freedom smiled, still with his head down, his eyes averted.

'You sign this and he'll take all the court costs out of what he's agreed to pay you. It's a chance for you, you can't throw it away.'

Still he said nothing, and she tried cajoling and various other approaches.

'Do you not want to box, is that it?'

Freedom lifted his head and stared at her, then turned to face the prison officer. 'Aye, I want that, I just don't want no one else to be involved.'

She knew he was thinking of Rawnie and Jesse, and she couldn't believe it. Her temper got the better of her. 'You are a fool, you know that, a stubborn fool, I don't know why I'm wasting my breath on you!'

'And I don't know why, you tell me, I don't know why I deserve this, no one has ever fought for me before, why you, what do you want?'

'Because you're *innocent*, that's why, I'd do it for any man who was about to hang when I knew he shouldn't.'

She laid out the contract and read down the detailed, neatly typed pages. She turned it over, Sir Charles was guaranteeing Freedom a wage, and a fair one as far as she could see.

'Is there something here you don't agree with, is it too long a contract, is that it?'

Freedom rubbed his head, glanced at the attentive

prison officer and then said in a barely audible voice, 'I can't read, I don't read.'

Evelyne could see his embarrassment, and she got up to ask the officer if she could move her chair round the table to discuss the contract with the prisoner.

They sat close and she whispered each clause of the contract, her finger tracing the lines. He sat, head bent, staring intently at the pages.

'He promises to give you accommodation at his estate outside London for the time you will be training until the time you desire to find your own establishment. These costs will be deducted from your wages together with the costs this case will incur. He also wants you to have a suit ordered for the trial, and . . .' Evelyne looked at him, his face close enough for her to touch. He was not paying any attention to the contract but looking at her closely, scrutinizing her face. She turned back to the papers, blushed, coughed, and started again.

'Clause four, this one down here, says you will be contracted to Sir Charles for five years, after that time you will be free either to renew your contract with him or not, as you choose. This contract is valid for all parts of the world.' As she turned the page her hand brushed against his, and he moved his handcuffed wrists further way.

'He, Sir Charles, that is, has the right to bring all contractual obligations here assigned to termination at any date he so wishes.'

She opened her bag, and the officer moved a step into the room. She held up a pen, then looked at Freedom. 'You going to sign it? You *have* to, it's the only chance you have, and I think it's a pretty fair deal.'

Freedom nodded, and with her hand guiding his he signed his initials, 'F.S.'

Evelyne promptly folded the contract and slipped it

into her handbag. Freedom looked at her with a strange expression, then he looked away and kept his voice low as he said, 'You gimme your word they'll not try to bring in my friends.'

Evelyne snapped her bag shut and nodded her head. 'You have my word, and I want yours that you'll give Sir Charles any information not concerning your friends that'll help you, will you promise me that?'

Freedom promised, and she gave the officer a look to let him know the meeting was over. She went to walk straight out, but then she stopped, bent her head towards Freedom and lightly kissed his cheek. It was a friendly gesture, there was nothing sexual and no intention of it being so. As the door closed behind her she turned back and saw him through the small window. He held his handcuffed hands over his face, and he seemed defeated.

When Freedom took his hands away from his face the tears were wet on his cheeks. He was crying, without a tremor, without a sound. His dark eyes blinked, and with one gesture the tears were gone, and he rose and lifted his hands to the officer. He was ready to be returned to the cells.

Sir Charles Wheeler brought Ed sharply down to earth. The fact that Freedom had signed their contract was no reason for celebration. They still had to prove the boy innocent and that was not going to be easy. He turned to Evelyne, checking his watch, and told her that they had a meeting with the lawyers in one hour. He didn't exactly dismiss Evelyne, but he told her he had things to do, and Dewhurst hovered at the door to usher her out.

'Have you the finances to remain here, Miss Jones? As I recall, you had only booked in for three days. The

297

case could take a considerable time to get to court and you are the star witness.'

Evelyne was in a bit of a dilemma. Basically, she did have the money, but that would mean dipping into her precious legacy, and she had always taken great pains not to touch it unless absolutely necessary. But if she said she didn't have it, would Sir Charles pay for her room, or would she be moved elsewhere?

Sir Charles took her silence to mean she did not have enough money, and with hardly a pause for breath he turned to Dewhurst and gave instructions to have Miss Jones' account at the hotel given to him. He did not even wait for her to thank him, but strode into the study with Ed at his heels.

Evelyne wanted to dance along the corridor, she could still stay here, and for free. She could have as many baths as she liked, as many cream cakes, and all paid for by Sir Charles.

The lawyer's office was dark, wood-panelled and lined with books. One whole wall was taken up with yellowing documents. The desk was claw-footed and covered in more of the same thick, yellowing documents. Smethurst swept into the room wearing his gown, having come directly from the court. His domed head was framed by a strange fringe of orange hair sprouting out at the sides, but the thickness of his eyebrows made up for the lack of hair on the top of his head. Mr Smethurst was a junior partner, but Evelyne decided that if he was a junior then the senior partners must all be really ancient.

Smethurst, Humphrey George, Esquire, had a booming voice, and his flabby hand gripped Sir Charles' in a pulverizing handshake. 'Charlie, well, Charlie, sit down, sit down old chap, you must be Miss Jones, seat, take a pew all of you, be back in a tick.'

They could hear his booming voice as he called for someone named Ethel to get the kettle on the boil for tea. He returned quickly, minus the gown and pulling on a Harris tweed jacket, almost the colour of his hair. His baggy trousers and heavy brogues were covered in mud. His Old Harrovian tie had worked its way around to the back of his neck, and the collar of his crumpled shirt stuck up. He and Sir Charles had been at school together.

'Right, I've done a bit of prelim on this, and I'm afraid things don't look too good, not good at all . . . Ahh, Ethel, thank God, I'm parched . . . tea, everyone? Oh, and Ethel some ginger nuts, there's a good gel.' He poured tea and talked constantly as it slopped into the saucers, then waved the milk liberally over the whole tray.

'Now, my gel, let's take a look at your statement, jolly well written and clear as a bell, but we have one problem the opposition will be on to like hawks . . . How long have you known this fella? Two – no, don't interrupt me, tell me when I've finished. Right, point two, you state you were at a boxing match up on Highbury Hills, right? Yes, now I have to have witnesses to that fact, witnesses to say you were not, *not*, with the gypsy people, but there under your own steam, so to speak, and that before that date you had no connection with the . . . the er . . . chap, Freedom Stubbs. These two points are *extremely* important because what they will throw at you is that you were, you are, fabricating the whole story to enable us to get the chap free . . . so I will have to ask you certain . . . delicate questions, that will no doubt be asked by the prosecution council.'

Smethurst listened attentively to Evelyne as she stated clearly that until the time of the first boxing match she had never set eyes on Freedom Stubbs.

'So tell me, what does an attractive young woman like you want to take up with this gypsy for?'

Evelyne was up on her feet and banging on the desk in fury at Smethurst's insinuations. He leaned back and raised his eyebrows. 'So I am to take it that there is no romantic connection, purely a platonic friendship on your part with this gypsy, yes? Have you ever had any form of sexual relationship with him? And, further, do you intend to do so should this lad be set free?'

Evelyne banged the desk again, saying she had never ever had such thoughts and nothing was further from her mind. All she was interested in was Freedom's innocence. 'I saw that girl, I saw the girl the lads raped, and I believe in British justice, they will not let an innocent man hang.'

Smethurst gave her a slow hand-clap and pushed his chair back from his desk.

'I think, Charlie, she'll be wonderful, and as you said, like a tigress, but I'm afraid, Miss Jones, you'll have to control that temper of yours. In the witness stand it is imperative that you behave like a lady at all times, never raise your voice – never – just answer clearly and concisely, understand?'

Suddenly he threw a question, like a dart, towards Evelyne.

'So who do you think killed those miners, hum? Any ideas?'

She swallowed and looked down at her hands, licked her lips and lifted her head to stare straight into Smethurst's bright eyes.

'I have no idea, sir.'

He chucked the pencil down and opened a drawer,

took out some toffees and unwrapped one. 'That was a lie, but don't . . . no, don't argue with me, I don't want to know, just tell me whether Freedom Stubbs himself is innocent.'

Evelyne kept her voice level, her eyes fixed firmly on Smethurst. 'He did not kill those lads.'

'Good, good, because I don't think he's guilty either. Right, let's get started, yes?' He flicked a look at Sir Charles who caught it like a tennis player and with a brief nod to Evelyne instructed her to wait in his car.

Smethurst waited until the door closed behind Evelyne before speaking. His manner changed slightly, he grew quieter, less expansive. He unwrapped another toffee. 'I think, Charlie, it's best that you let Miss Jones settle her own accounts at the hotel. By all means hand her the finances, but I don't want it known you are paying her way. Secondly, I shall check all the alibis the fellow has and then get back to you, leave the statements of Collins and Lord Carlton to her . . . Oh, and fix the gypsy up, you know, get him a suit, looks better if he's respectable, I think that's about it for now.'

As Sir Charles rose to leave, Smethurst rocked in his chair.

'You still see that chap you used to adore at school, Willoughby something-or-other? Still fond of him, are you?'

Sir Charles prodded the floor with his cane. 'Killed in action, Ypres.'

'Oh, sorry, nice fella . . . so, Charlie, you think you'll have a champion, do you?'

Sir Charles smiled softly, leaned on his cane. 'When have I ever been wrong? So, what do you think our chances are?'

Smethurst sniffed, sucked at his toffee. 'Not good, but then I have never lost a case. I'd like to get Freddy

Carlton's statement sewn up, and that other bloke, Collins. Push those through, they are rather important.'

Sir Charles already had the door open and his trilby sat on his head at a jaunty angle. He tapped his cane. 'Leave it to me . . . Thank you, Ethel, for the delicious tea and ginger nuts, good afternoon.'

Smethurst rocked backwards, then swivelled round in his chair. He thought Sir Charles was still the unfathomable gent he had been at school. The question of fees hadn't even arisen, but he was sure he would make a fair amount.

'Ethel, I think, dear heart, we'd better get the press on our side for this one, start calling them, would you?'

The case was by no means easy, and if the truth be known Smethurst felt they didn't stand a chance in hell of acquittal. The gypsy was, after all, charged with not one murder but four . . . but, by Christ, it would make headlines, and with the society mixture Smethurst knew he had a very potent cocktail.

CHAPTER 14

E VELYNE COULD feel her whole body tense up. Her mouth went dry, but there was no turning back now. The operator was on the line, and with an encouraging nod from Miss Freda she went into her carefully rehearsed speech. 'Would you please put me through to Lord Frederick Carlton's residence, the number is Cardiff five-five-four . . .'

Miss Freda moved closer, listening. Evelyne covered the mouthpiece. 'It's going through, don't get so close, you make me nervous.'

Miss Freda edged away. Evelyne went red, swallowed. 'Hello, is that you? Er, you may not remember me, but my name is . . . oh . . . oh yes, I would like to speak with Lord Freddy Carlton please . . . Evelyne Jones . . .'

'What did he say? What, what?'

Evelyne hissed, 'It was the butler, shusssshhhhh . . .'

Freddy reached for the phone, irritated. These new-fangled things were a dreadful intrusion on one's privacy. Even more so with a friend like David Collins. One was forced to accept calls from God knows who, and on reverse charges. He snapped into the phone. 'Yes, speaking . . . who is this? Who . . .? No, I'm sorry . . .'

Freddy was about to replace the phone. 'Evelyne who? Who?'

Frantic, Evelyne looked at Miss Freda. 'Oh, please don't put your phone down, sir, not until you have heard what I have to say, it's very important.'

Miss Freda was gesticulating wildly. Evelyne covered the mouthpiece.

'You don't 'ave to shout, darlink, they can hear you as if you were in the same room, don't shout.'

Evelyne started again.

'Do you recall the boxing match? With the gypsies? The night there was a . . . hello? Hello, are you still there? Oh, Freda, I can't hear him now, there's no sound at all coming out.'

Freddy glanced across the hall towards the drawing-room, hoping his wife would not appear as usual to ask who was on the telephone. He spoke in hushed tones. 'Now listen, dearie, I don't like you calling my private number, firstly, and secondly I have absolutely no intention whatsoever of admitting to being at some wretched boxing match, is that clear? Now, please do not call me again.'

As he had expected, Heather came in from the garden, carrying a large bouquet of flowers. She paused, eyebrows lifted. 'Something wrong, dearest?'

Freddy covered the phone with his hand, smiling. 'No, no darling, just a call from the club, snooker game.'

Heather smiled, knowing perfectly well it had nothing to do with a snooker game. She went in to the drawing room where her mother, Lady Sybil, sat in her wheelchair, playing patience. 'Who's he talking to?'

'Just his club, Mother, nothing important.'

Freddy waited until the door closed behind his wife, then turned back to the phone. 'Are you still there? Hello?'

Miss Freda handed the telephone back to Evelyne,

whispering that he was back on the line again. Evelyne started to shout again, but lowered her voice when Freda waved frantically.

'I said, sir, that perhaps David Collins will help, you see it is imperative that you act as my witness, my witness . . . He is charged with murder, and he is an innocent man.'

Freddy tried to control his voice. 'And David Collins is sick, you must not at any cost disturb him. I won't allow it, do you hear me? And I think you have a nerve, yes, a bloody nerve, calling here. We want nothing to do with you. Is that perfectly clear?'

Poor Freddy sensed the drawing-room door opening behind him, heard a bang as his mother-in-law's wheel-chair was wheeled out, and was almost beside himself. 'I am sorry, I really cannot discuss the matter any further, the answer is no, and please do not call again.'

He replaced the phone and strode along the hall.

'Going out, dear?'

'Yes, yes, I have to go to my club. If David calls, tell him I need to talk to him.'

Heather pushed her mother's chair into the hall, watching Freddy grab his trilby and slam out of the front door without a backward glance. Lady Sybil sniffed and rattled the vast array of beads on her chest. Her thin wrists clanked with rows of bangles.

'For someone who has never done a day's work in his life, he certainly does rush about, doesn't he? Really, always amazes me why you put up with him, dear, what on earth has he ever done for you?'

Heather sighed, sucking in her breath over her pro-truding teeth. 'He married me, Mother.'

*

Evelyne replaced the phone.

'Well, Freda, that was dreadful, he wouldn't even listen to me.'

Not one to give up, Miss Freda paced the room. 'Next we find this Tulip girl, she will also be a witness, yes? Come along, Bianco's still thrives, we will ask there.'

Tulip? Yes, the owner of Bianco's remembered her very well indeed, he could describe her in detail. He rolled his eyes lewdly and made clucking sounds as he talked.

'Do you know where we could find her?'

He sighed, sat down, and shook his head sorrowfully. 'I'm sorry, the lady is more than likely pushing up the tulips herself. She died, oh, one year, maybe less . . . but I knew her well, many nights she was here, but . . .'

They returned, crestfallen, to the hotel, and took the lift to Sir Charles' suite. As they knocked, Sir Charles swung the door open. 'Well, how did it go, dearie? You have good news?'

Evelyne sighed and shook her head. Far from it. She told him the bad news, that neither Freddy nor David would act as witnesses, and that Tulip was dead. She had never before seen Sir Charles angry. He muttered under his breath and swung his monocle about by its ribbon. He paced the room and asked her to tell him once more, right from the beginning, what had taken place. All through her story he drummed his fingers and wandered around the room.

'Freddy, or His Lordship, as he is now, wouldn't stand up in court because of the possible scandal, but the gossipmongers would like to know just how familiar he is with David's wife. I saw him, saw him with Lady Primrose, she doesn't love David . . .'

Sir Charles replaced his monocle and sat down, interrupting Evelyne's bitter tirade. 'Lady Primrose Boyd-Carpenter? Getting me rather confused, my dear. Now repeat what you just said with a little logic so I can piece it all together.'

Evelyne felt as if Sir Charles' magnified eye was boring into her as she repeated her story yet again. He threw back his head and roared with laughter, which took her completely off guard.

Dewhurst carried in the telephone from the study, trailing the long cord. 'Mr Smethurst for you, sir, I apologize for interrupting but it is long distance and rather urgent.'

Smethurst was very pleased with himself, so far the story Freedom Stubbs had told him was checking out. The killings that had taken place in Cardiff could not have been committed by their client. In each case he was in another town, and in two instances he was actually in a boxing ring. Sir Charles replaced the receiver. It was more important than ever that Evelyne's story checked out one hundred per cent. 'Now you are sure, absolutely sure, that David Collins' wife is having some sort of liaison with Lord Freddy, yes? Am I right, yes?'

Evelyne bit her lip. Never one to gossip, she hated the sound of her own voice saying it. 'Lord Freddy was engaged to Lady Primrose before David. After the war, when David came home, they married and had a son, but David had changed, and Freddy and Primrose were friendly even then. Now, well, I have seen them being very familiar actually in the tea room here at the Grand.'

'Good God, the tea room, well, well.'

She felt he was laughing at her primness, but the next moment he opened his wallet. 'I want you to purchase a very special evening gown. It's essential that you look absolutely stunning. Off you go, and remember, a *stunning* creation, I think something green to go with your colouring.'

He didn't even look at the amount he had given her, just handed her three notes. They were five-pound notes, and Evelyne didn't know what to say. Dewhurst ushered her out of the suite, and Sir Charles got to work immediately, making calls to Lady Primrose and to Freddy Carlton.

Ed rushed in, looking crestfallen. 'Gor blimey, I just 'eard, not one of them toffs will admit to even being at the fight, that's our defence up the spout, ain't it?'

Sir Charles covered the telephone with his hand.

'Ed, my old chum, don't be such a defeatist, do you really think I would give up so easily? You know the Wheeler family has relatives all over England, rather distant, of course, but I intend to pull family strings.' He listened to the telephone. 'Yes, dearie, I'm still here . . . oh, thank you.'

Ed sat on the edge of his seat.

'Hello, my dear gel, is that Primrose? Why, it's Charlie, yes, I am in town . . . oh, only just arrived; goodness, it must be so many years . . . how's your mother? Oh, she is? So sorry . . .'

Sir Charles appeared to be in the throes of one of his usual social calls so Ed made for the door, but Sir Charles stopped him.

'Ed, pass the word to Miss Jones that she is to be here in my suite prompt at nine o'clock, not a minute before, thank you . . . Hello, Primmy? You still there?

Ah, now then, I know it's short notice, but could you make it this evening? Oh, splendid, splendid.'

Finding no answer at Evelyne's door, Ed went down to reception and left a message for her – nine o'clock sharp, not a minute earlier or later. They were to dine in Sir Charles' suite. Just as he was licking his lips at the thought of a nice, frothing beer, he was called back to the desk. Sir Charles wanted him to collect a small package from a local jewellery store.

Freda had not been one hundred per cent certain about the gown, and nearly fainted at the price tag, but Evelyne was sure, and she bought it.

'Oh, Evelyne, I could make it for a quarter, no a tenth of the price, I could, I really could.'

The pair returned to the hotel, exhausted, and Evelyne collected her keys. As she read the message she turned to Freda in horror. 'It's tonight, the dinner's *tonight*! Oh, Freda, I'll never be ready!'

As tired as she was, Miss Freda worked on Evelyne like a little beaver. She laid out the long satin gown, the white gloves and the tiny, embroidered handbag. Evelyne sat in front of the dressing-table mirror in a pure silk underslip, and Miss Freda began to brush her hair, which fell to below her waist. Freda had to get down on her knees to brush out the ends. They had shampooed and scrubbed the hair until, when dry, it shone like gold.

A tap on the door sent Evelyne rushing this way and that as she was nowhere near ready. 'Who is it? I'm not dressed!'

'Miss Jones, it's me, Ed, I got somefink for yer from

Sir Charles, it's just for ternight, 'e says, but for you ter use it.'

At Evelyne's nod Miss Freda opened the door, peeked round it and took the parcel from Ed. As she shut the door he tapped again.

'It's Miss Freda, ain't it? Evelyne said you was helping her, like, are you available ternight for a few drinks, there's a good dance hall wiv a band?'

Blushing and tittering, Freda said she would be delighted.

'Oh, Evie, I have a date myself, now I have to rush . . . Oh, my hair, oh, my dress . . . Oh, can you manage without me, darling? Oh, he said to give you this, for tonight, from Sir Charles.'

Not two minutes ago Freda had been too exhausted to move. Now she leapt about like a young girl.

Evelyne was delighted to be left alone. She opened the brown paper and looked at the leather case, then inched open the lid and gasped. It contained a necklace of diamonds and emeralds with matching bracelet and drop earrings.

At eight o'clock sharp Dewhurst ushered Lord Frederick Carlton into Sir Charles' suite, accompanied by what Sir Charles at first presumed was his mother, only to discover it was his wife. The short, squat, dumpy woman wore a frightful dress, and more diamonds than the royal jewels.

'Freddy, old boy, how delightful to see you, come in, come in, and Dewhurst, champagne immediately.'

The champagne, well chilled and in tall, fluted crystal glasses, had just been served when Dewhurst announced David Collins and Lady Primrose. Freddy blushed, not expecting to see them, and quickly rose to his feet. David was obviously slightly drunk, but even so he looked as handsome as ever. He wore the new-style dinner jacket, but then he would, he had always been obsessed with fashion. Lady Primrose wore the latest fashion, a very short sequinned dress with a small cloche hat to match. The sequins on her dress were rose pink at the top, shading down to almost plum colour at the hem. She wore dark velvet slippers with a small heel, and fine silk stockings. She looked stunning, more beautiful than Freddy had ever seen her. His heart lurched inside his chest, and he had to gulp champagne to stop himself shaking.

Sir Charles went straight to Lady Primrose and called her 'Primmy', kissing her affectionately on the cheek, then took her hand and guided her into the room.

'Do you know my cousin Lady Primrose? Yes, I'm sure you do, and her husband, David Collins?'

Dewhurst slipped in and out serving champagne and then passed a trayful of tiny squares of crisp brown toast topped with caviar. He squeezed the lemon himself to ensure that none of the guests had to get their fingers sticky. Tiny lace napkins were placed on knees, everyone smiled and gradually the atmosphere relaxed.

Lady Primrose gave David a slight warning look as she saw him accepting another glass of champagne. They had had the most awful row earlier about his drinking. If it wasn't his drinking, it was his erratic, often violent moods. He had even accused her of telephoning Freddy when it was Sir Charles on the phone. He was jealous, and with such tantrums he exhausted himself. He had become more like a child than ever. She hoped he would behave himself this evening, Sir Charles being her mother's sister's son, and so immensely rich. She wanted at all costs to keep on the right side of his family. Their own finances were being depleted fast. One day she might have to turn to Sir Charles for assistance.

David leaned back on the velvet sofa and crossed his

legs. He always felt a flicker of irritation when he was announced as Mister David Collins. He was, after all, a captain, not that anyone ever remembered or gave him his rank. How he would have loved a title; still, he hadn't done too badly, he was married to one. He gave Freddy a shifty look. Rather be married to Lady Primrose without a lot of cash than be married to the homely Heather, fortune or no. He could see that Heather was wearing a couple of hundred thousand pounds around her squat neck.

Sir Charles was the perfect host, giving his complete attention to his guests. He made each one feel like the most important person in the room, but somehow he seemed to ignore David, laughing and joking intimately with Primrose, chatting about the times they had met as children. 'Remember, Primmy, the day I beat up that stable lad? Gawd, it was funny, even funnier now to think I am so closely associated with boxing. Do you ever go to any of the matches? Jolly good sport, not that the ladies enjoy it of course, it's very much a man's game.'

Sir Charles caught a slight look of panic passing between David and Freddy. He gestured to Dewhurst to refill the glasses and stood with his back to the fireplace. Freddy still sat about ten inches away from his dumpy wife, his eyes constantly straying to Primrose, who was being delightful, telling a witty story about the time when she drove to London to be presented at court. As she spoke her head shimmered and glistened with sequins. She took a cigarette and placed it in a long holder, and Freddy leapt to his feet with his lighter. He touched her hand slightly and she quickly withdrew it, promptly moving across the room to stand closer to Sir Charles who took out his fob watch and told them they were waiting for his special guest and then they would dine. He had ordered dinner to be served in his rooms, if that suited everyone. They could adjourn to the ballroom for more champagne and a twirl round the dance floor after dinner. Lady Primrose began to giggle and display her new dance steps. Her movements were beautifully co-ordinated as she danced the Charleston.

Sir Charles took the opportunity to cross the room and stand by David looking down at him and murmuring that he must get his tailor's name, he liked the cut of David's trousers. He studied this handsome man, noticing the slight, nervous tremor of his hands. 'You were cavalry, weren't you, Captain? Yes?'

David's hand tightened on his champagne glass and he pursed his lips.

'Your chaps had a bad time of it, heard your regiment was one of the first up front, dreadful carnage. I was lucky, they started bringing in the vehicles by the time I made it over there. Bit of shrapnel in the eyes, that's why I have to wear this, but I was one of the lucky ones.'

Primrose could also see the signs – David's face had paled, and his whole body was shaking slightly. She danced over to Charles and tried to change the subject. 'When are you going to get yourself married, Charlie? You've been on the society lists as a catch from the early days.'

Sir Charles laughed his wonderful, infectious giggle. 'Never found the right one yet, but that doesn't mean I'm not still huntin', ya know.'

Primrose sat next to David and gripped his hands, whispering for him to hold on, not to start it here, not tonight.

'Good heavens, Charlie, aren't we ever going to dine?'

As if on cue there was a tap on the outer door, and Sir Charles checked his watch. Exactly nine o'clock.

'My last guest, and then dearest we will dine immediately.'

Dewhurst opened the door. The whole party turned expectantly. Sir Charles took a fraction of a second to realize that this really was his little Miss Jones before he leapt to attention and bowed, his hand out to draw Evelyne into the room.

Dewhurst had not given her a second glance when he opened the door, which deflated her a little.

'Miss Evelyne Jones, Sir Charles.'

Sir Charles greeted her with his arms open wide. 'Well, my dear, do come in, I am so thrilled you could come . . . now, let me introduce you . . . Lord and Lady Frederick Carlton . . . my cousin Lady Primrose . . . and her husband, Captain David Collins.'

Freddy had the most awful sick feeling in his stomach, but he swallowed, forcing a smile. He should have known something was up, but all he did was bow and gesture for his wife to step forward.

Heather was so nervous she didn't recognize Evelyne immediately, but as she came closer to shake hands her piggy eyes widened in amazement. 'Oh, but we've met before.'

Sir Charles gave one of his infectious laughs, and turned to Primrose and David. 'Isn't she stunning? Quite beautiful, absolutely beautiful, my dear. Now, give me your hand and I think if you don't mind Evelyne dearest, we shall go in to dine straightaway.'

David bowed low over Evelyne's hand, she could smell his lavender perfume and his silky hair was the same as ever. He had not recognized her.

'Where on earth did you find this stunning gel, here in Cardiff?'

Already guiding Evelyne towards the dining room, Sir Charles was holding her hand tightly, giving her great comfort. 'Oh, I thought, dearest, you said you had once stayed with David, in his father's house, am I wrong?'

She looked directly at David and saw awareness dawning. For a moment he looked panic-stricken, flicking nervous eyes towards his wife, but she was laughing with delight at the elaborate dinner table.

'Oh, Charlie, you are so clever, what a delightful table . . . oysters, too! Oh, you are *such* a delicious man, you really are.'

Sir Charles seated everyone, putting himself at the head of the table and David on Evelyne's left. He still held her hand. Suddenly Sir Charles leaned so close she could feel his breath. 'My dear, you have surpassed yourself, you look like a queen. I shall not leave your side. Quite, quite lovely.'

David could not take his eyes off Evelyne, he was confused, trying hard to collect the jagged pieces of the picture which were gathering like a storm in his head. She was dazzling; could it be that funny girl, could it really be that girl he had taken to the fight that night? Her cheeks were flushed, the rest of her pale skin translucent. Her dark eyes, like the sea, looked even more green because of the rich colour of her satin gown. The emeralds and diamonds glittered, but it was her hair that outshone everything, like gold, so simply done, a single braid to below her waist.

Freddy looked at Primrose with beseeching eyes, but she refused to look at him, afraid David would do something embarrassing. Under the table he felt for her foot, but she pulled her satin-clad feet back beneath her chair, giving him a cool, tight look of disapproval. She found it hard not to stare at the girl, who stood head and shoulders above her. It was obvious to everyone there that Sir Charles was smitten. Only Primrose knew how very strange this was, as she had heard family rumours about him . . . well, she thought, they must be wrong.

'May I propose a toast to my dear friend Evelyne, ladies and gentlemen, will you raise your glasses?'

Dewhurst had filled their champagne glasses, and they all toasted Evelyne. Sir Charles gave the hovering waiters a discreet signal to begin serving then slipped an arm around Evelyne's shoulders and whispered in her ear, 'Don't be nervous, just follow me, do whatever I do.'

Again he was close to her, and she smiled into his piercing, unsettling eyes. He was a strange kettle of fish – she never knew where she stood with him. She would never have believed he could be so familiar, but it did give her confidence. At one point he made her turn her head so that he could straighten one of her earrings which had become entangled in a stray curl. His fingers brushed her neck and he allowed his hand to linger for a second too long, then he turned his attention back to his guests. They sat quietly, not sure how to react to Sir Charles' 'lady'. Seeing him so intimate with her made them even more uncomfortable.

Occasionally Evelyne shot a sidelong glance at David. He seemed oblivious to everything, even to his food now, and was staring, stony-faced, at the wallpaper. His only gesture was to lift his wineglass to his lips, his movements neat and delicate. When the next course arrived Evelyne had to pay close attention to Sir Charles, it was a thick lobster bisque. She watched as he used the big, round spoon from the right-hand side of his place setting, and Evelyne followed suit, using the same outward strokes, and did not once scrape the plate. The dinner seemed to go on for ever, the conversation stilted and extremely strained, David's withdrawn silence affecting them all. Lady Primrose battled on, trying to encourage the party spirit, and told them funny little stories about her two sons, Clarence and Charles, or Charlie, as he was known.

'We named him after you, didn't we, David darling? David?'

Lady Primrose smiled, but her quiet voice had an edge to it.

'David, I just said we call him after cousin Charles . . . you really must come and see the boys, will you be here long enough?'

Ignoring her question, Sir Charles signalled to Dewhurst to serve the main course. Primrose gave David a kick beneath the table. She was trying so hard, and in their precarious financial situation they really needed to keep on the right side of her rich, if rather distant, relative.

When the main course was served, Evelyne had to hide her smile as she saw Heather eating like a horse, everything before her vanishing at great speed. She made unconscious little 'mmmm' sounds of appreciation, which irritated Freddy. He frowned at her, making her peer around the table like a guilty child. Freddy's fork clattered on to his plate when Sir Charles spoke out of the blue.

'Any of you read about this gypsy chap, the one on the murder rap? Very interesting case, I have a personal interest in it.'

This game was partly at Evelyne's instigation, although it saddened her. She was being used as a pawn, and she waited expectantly to see what the outcome of the evening would be.

*

The port and brandy decanters were placed on the table, and the ladies withdrew to the sitting-room.

'Very nice dinner, Mother always says this is one of the *best* hotels ... oh, coffee, and mints, *très bon*.' Heather gave a toothy smile as Evelyne poured the coffee. 'I didn't catch where you were staying? Evelyne?'

'I have a suite here.'

Primrose began a slow dance across the room, swaying, moving closer and closer until she stood directly before Evelyne.

'Can you do the Charleston? No? Want me to teach you? Come on, try it.'

She backed away flicking her heels out and humming the tune. Evelyne sensed that Primrose was laughing at her, the baby blue eyes were spiteful, glittering.

'Thought your sort of woman had to know the latest steps.'

Evelyne continued pouring the coffee, held a cup out to Lady Primrose, who waved her hand. 'No sugar, sweet enough, be-boop-be-doo.'

She danced past Evelyne, whose cup went over and spilt down the glittering, sequinned dress. Lady Primrose didn't shriek out, she didn't move; the coffee made a dark brown stain, spreading and dripping over the beads. Her little delicate hand shot out and slapped Evelyne's face. 'I believe my husband should have done that to you a long time ago.'

The port went round for the third time, the cigar smoke swirled around the men's heads. They were relaxed, enjoying the many witty anecdotes with which Sir Charles regaled them. He played the evening like a poker game, finally delivering his winning hand, card by card. He began by moving first the decanter, ashtray

318

and his port glass to one side, and with the table cleared he leaned on his elbows on the table. 'Gentlemen, now to the business of the evening, the reason I asked you both here.'

David leaned back, smiling, the drink had eased him. Freddy, sharper and more alert, had been waiting for something. His heart beat faster.

'I want you both to stand as witnesses to Miss Evelyne Jones' statement in court next week. You were, I am led to believe, both present at a certain boxing match on Highbury Hill. The fighter was a gypsy called Freedom Stubbs.'

Freddy leaned forward, pushing his glass away. 'I am aware of the case, a murder case, but perhaps I did not make myself clear to Miss Jones. I really feel that my presence in court, particularly in such an appalling case, would be most distasteful, I have already stated my feelings on this . . .'

Sir Charles interrupted, 'Rubbish, man, your word is essential. You both instigated the evening's outing, am I not right? Miss Jones had no prior knowledge of this boxing match?'

Freddy stubbed out his cigar. 'I really couldn't say, but judging by what I know of her she's a little tramp, and the public outcry surrounding these murders would be frightful. The gel is a blackmailer, David here can tell you more . . . David? How much money did she demand from you?'

Sir Charles banged the table. 'I don't call twenty pounds a large sum, especially as the girl was more than likely owed twice that from her share of the Collins' house.'

Nonplussed, Freddy turned to David.

'You told me she had demanded more than a hundred, good God, I gave you over fifty towards it, David?'

David downed the remains of his port. His manner changed, he became surly, giving Freddy a foul look. 'The way you carry on, old chap, I'd say you owe me a hell of a lot more, you think I'm blind as well as sick? Do you? *Do you*?' He rose to his feet and lurched against the table, glaring at Freddy. 'Not your money anyway, you don't have a penny to your name, so what are you bleating about?'

Sir Charles poured more port. He spoke in a calm, conversational voice that was not raised in the slightest. 'Now, now, let's not get into a nasty argument, let's just take things easy, shall we? Whatever marital problems you both may have they certainly wouldn't look good spread across the *Cardiff Herald* . . . all that is required of you both is a simple statement saying you escorted Miss Jones . . .'

David turned his anger on Sir Charles. 'Exactly what are you implying? None of your bloody business! What marital problems? Eh? What? What's he talking about?' He was on his feet, blazing, moving round to Freddy's chair with his fist up and looking foolish and inept.

'*Sit down, David*! Sit, please, let's not raise our voices, we don't want the ladies upset . . . and I really don't want to drag my cousin into any adverse publicity.'

David sat down again like a lamb, reached for his port and downed the remainder of the glass in one gulp. Freddy looked at Sir Charles. 'The girl was brought to the fair by David, that is all I know, I had nothing to do with her, but if David agrees, then . . . David?'

David simply stared at Freddy.

'If David agrees, I will go along with whatever he has to say. David?'

There was a short burst of humourless laughter from David, then he glared at Freddy. 'I'm sure you will, always such a friend, I am not going into a bloody court and that's final.'

Sir Charles smiled his thanks at Freddy and asked to be left alone with David. As Freddy closed the door Sir Charles picked up the decanter, carried it round the table and sat close to David, who reached for the port. Suddenly, Sir Charles' hand shot out and gripped David's wrist. 'No more, old fella, I want a private chat.'

'I've got a headache.'

'Dare say you have, this won't take long . . . David, I would hate what I say ever to go beyond this room, but I want you, should I need you, in that courtroom.'

'I don't remember things, haven't you been told? You put me on a witness stand and I'll go to pieces.'

'All you have to do is sign a statement, that'll be good enough. I don't want to have to subpoena you, then you'd have to take the stand, don't make me do that . . . You know, David, you were not the only officer to turn tail, you were in the front line for six months, and your reputation was unblemished . . . I recall many officers – in particular poor old Ridgely – often spoke of you. Remember Ridgely, do you? Died of syphilis, I'm told.'

David went grey, his forehead puckered, and he turned terrible, pleading eyes to Sir Charles.

'Face it, don't be afraid, it's over, no one blames you. But sadly, there are those who can never understand. There was nightmare carnage, human carnage, to face day in, day out. It can destroy any man . . .'

'I don't know what you are talking about.'

Sir Charles rose from the table and carefully replaced the chair. He felt deep disgust for this shell of a man, a captain who had turned tail on twenty-five of his men. Not one survived. His voice was little more than a whisper. 'Oh, I think you do.'

David stared at him, like a frightened child.

'My lawyer will contact you for the statement. Now shall we join the ladies, Captain?'

Freddy had already joined the ladies. The atmosphere was decidedly chilly. A bowl of water and a cloth were brought by Dewhurst, and Freddy helped Lady Primrose try to remove the coffee stain. In furtive whispers he told her what had taken place in the dining room. 'Charles knows about us, God knows how. David's been drinking, you'll have to get him home – he looks as if he's going to throw one of his fits.'

They were joined by an ebullient Sir Charles. He gave Evelyne a small wink to say all was well, then sat with Heather, offering her the remains of the chocolates with a flourish. They discussed the family chocolate and toffee bsuiness, and he made a mental note to check out the Warner shares, perhaps buy a few. The company would be at an all-time low after the war, so the shares would be cheap.

Lady Primrose went to the open dining-room doors, then turned with a sigh, saying that she felt she should take David home, he was obviously tired. Dewhurst fetched wraps and coats, and everyone thanked Sir Charles politely. Evelyne was ignored, left sitting with her empty coffee cup. David seemed in a world of his own, his eyes vacant and a soft smile on his lips, but as they all left he turned back to Evelyne, raised his hand as though he wanted to say something. Primrose slipped her arm about his waist. 'Come along, David, the car's waiting.'

When he returned from seeing them out, Sir Charles clapped his hands.

'All went as planned, dearie, we will have their statements first thing in the morning. Now, if you will excuse me, I'm away to my bed. Dewhurst, show the young lady out.'

Evelyne stared at her reflection in the dressing-table mirror, then she tried to do the Charleston, holding on to the back of the chair. A sad, silly gesture, and she immediately felt foolish.

She replaced the diamonds and emeralds in their leather case. Like the jewels, she felt as though she had been hired for the night.

Ed Meadows walked Miss Freda home through the damp night. He was flushed from all the beer he had drunk, and Miss Freda was equally pink in the face from her numerous port and lemons.

'Well, it's been ever such a nice evenin', Freda, perhaps we could do it again if you'd like, I mean, I don't wanna be too forward. Are you walkin' out wiv anyone?'

Tittering, Freda placed her hand over her mouth. Ed grinned.

'You're a lovely-looking woman, and I've thoroughly enjoyed meself ternight, been a good time.'

Lifting her tiny hand to his lips he gave it a resounding kiss. She smiled sweetly, very much the lady. 'I would like so much to see you again, I have had a wonderful time too.'

Ed rocked on his heels, he was so tickled. 'Well then, we'll do it again, g'night . . . Oh, Freda, I'm not married or nuffink, are you available, like?'

She patted his barrel chest and he caught her to him

and hugged her expertly. She giggled and pushed him away, gave him a coy, sexy flutter of the eyelids and hurried inside.

Ed tottered back to his bed-and-breakfast hotel, singing at the top of his voice, 'I'm 'Enery the eighth I am, 'Enery the eighth I am, I am . . .'

In her cracked dressing-table mirror Freda studied her reflection. Well, she thought, he's not much, but then nor am I. She wished she hadn't lied about her age, though. She put her curlers in, creamed her face and lay down in her tiny, single bed. 'You're never too old, darling, but you'd better reel this fish in fast.'

The Rolls-Royce glided soundlessly along the dark, wet streets. David sat hunched in a corner, staring out into the night. Lady Primrose had tried to hold his hand, but he shrugged away from her. She remained close, trying not to let her thigh press against Freddy's as he, too, sat in the back of the Rolls. Heather was sitting in the front with the driver, and she spoke as if to the windscreen wiper. 'Thought it was a good meal, didn't you, dear?'

Freddy made no reply. He sighed, and Primrose looked at him. His face was haunted, he wanted her, loved her so dearly.

'I want to see a doctor, some kind of specialist, maybe it would help me,' said David, petulantly.

Primrose slipped her arm through David's and rested her head on his shoulder. He was trembling, his whole body shaking.

'Yes, dearest, that is a good idea.' Tears came into her eyes. She couldn't bear to turn to Freddy, she wanted him so much, loved him so much.

They were silent as the car drove on, the only sound the 'swish, swish' of the tyres on the wet streets.

Evelyne lay wide awake in bed. She was finding sleep hard to come by. She tossed and turned, and began to think of the village, her Da, which made her keenly aware of her loneliness. She could see Hugh's big face, and would have liked more than anything to be wrapped in his strong arms. She was twenty-four years old, and had never known what it was like to be loved by a man.

CHAPTER 15

SMETHURST AND Sir Charles sat at a small corner table in the restaurant of the Feathers public house. Smethurst was slicing his cheese with delicate precision. The port was brought to the table. Smethurst wiped his mouth with his stained napkin, lifted his glass in a toast.

'Well, here's to this afternoon's proceedings.'

Sir Charles sipped his port, noting that Smethurst had downed his glass in one. He swivelled round in his seat as Smethurst made an expansive gesture to the doorway. Standing talking to the head waiter was a stern-faced man wearing a charcoal overcoat and carrying a homburg. 'That's the opposition, old chap.' Smethurst bellowed across the restaurant, '*Jeffrey*, will you join us?'

Jeffrey Henshaw crossed to their table and introductions were made. Shaking Sir Charles' outstretched hand, he politely refused to join them. He tapped his gold fob watch and cocked his head to one side, smiling at Smethurst, 'I'd say you should be on the move, proceedings are due to start in fifteen minutes.'

Smethurst laughed, stuffed another slice of cheese into his mouth, spattering Henshaw's overcoat with flecks of it. 'Just you remember you owe me more than one favour – *Ethel Patterson*, Jeffers, *Ethel Patterson*.'

Henshaw stepped sharply back from the table, pursed his lips and tapped his homburg against his thigh. 'Listen, you old devil, you know what these committal proceedings are like, ruddy magistrates dither around and I've got a very busy day, so get those flat feet on the trot.' He gave Sir Charles a stiff bow and strode off among the tables.

'What was all that about?' asked Sir Charles.

Smethurst picked up his battered briefcase. As he placed it on the table a cheese cracker crumbled under the weight.

'I got him out of a very sticky situation with one of his clients, a Miss Patterson – very naughty lady. Well, old chap, this is it, I'll call you soon as I have a result.' Suddenly his manner was more subdued.

'You sure you don't want me along?' asked Sir Charles.

'Good God no, it could take hours. There's a hellish lot of statements to be read and witnesses to call – no, no, I'll be in touch soon as I have any news. I'm confident, we'll get the lad off, be no problem . . . unless Henshaw plays a double hand, but I have a feeling he won't. He wants the rope for Stubbs, but has to concede there's no evidence on the first three charges. Won't be as easy on the fourth murder rap, you can take my word for that . . . He's got a long list of prosecution witnesses. Well, I'm off, thanks for a splendid lunch.'

Sir Charles watched Smethurst stride off, dropping his napkin on the floor as he squeezed among the diners. He wished he could feel as positive as his friend. Smethurst's bulging briefcase, stuffed with what he had described as 'hard evidence, old bean', did not, in Sir Charles' opinion, sound good enough to get Freedom

Stubbs off three of the four murder charges filed against him.

Sir Charles had underestimated his old friend. Even Henshaw was slightly taken aback at the amount of paperwork and obvious private detection Smethurst had managed to do. Henshaw, of course, had access to the statements, but still he was impressed, and still slightly in awe of the man he had learned so much from.

Smethurst held forth, resting his elbow on top of a mound of papers. More and more were produced and waved around. The row of magistrates listened intently as Smethurst proved without a doubt that Freedom Stubbs could not have committed the three murders that occurred in Cardiff. Statements from witnesses proved that Freedom Stubbs was not even in the vicinity of Cardiff when the killings took place. A humorous throwaway line clarified his point.

'Unless my client had an aeroplane, which I assure you he did not have, it would have been physically impossible for him to have been in Cardiff on the days in question. I therefore submit that there is no case against Freedom Stubbs on the first three counts of murder, and ask for those counts to be dismissed in view of the evidence I have laid before you. There is no case to answer, sir.'

Smethurst burst out of the court. Henshaw, close on his heels, held the door open to allow his colleague to exit without getting either his briefcase or coat caught. 'Round one to you, old chap . . . but I guarantee your man will swing.'

Smethurst hailed a taxi and offered Henshaw a lift, but it was refused. The taxi passed him as he walked briskly down the street swinging his immaculate brief-case. Smethurst leaned back, patted his own bulging case and smiled. He had done his work for the dismissal of the first three counts, but Henshaw had established a *prima facie* case for the fourth murder. He was pleased with the dismissal and knew he had done well. He sucked in his breath. The contest between himself and Henshaw would certainly be interesting.

Sir Charles received the news of the dismissal by tele-phone. He wasn't elated, more relieved. Smethurst assured him he was confident the trial would prove Stubbs not guilty of the fourth murder, and confirmed that he was well ahead with his preparations. They discussed expenses – Smethurst did not come cheap. There was no question of it all being done on an 'old friends' basis, Smethurst was one of the best barristers in Wales, and his fees reflected the fact . . . perhaps they were just a little higher than usual but it was, after all, a difficult case.

As Smethurst replaced the receiver he rested his feet on his untidy desk. The first three young miners had all been found with their hands tied behind their backs, their throats slit from right to left. In all three cases they had been marked with a cross on their foreheads made with their own blood. Willie Thomas had been killed in exactly the same way, the blood mark on his forehead. Smethurst chewed his lower lip. He had been able to prove without a doubt that Stubbs could not have

329

committed the first three killings . . . but Willie Thomas was different. Smethurst prowled his office's worn carpet, ruffled his hair. Freedom Stubbs had been there, in the village. He knew how very important a witness Evelyne Jones was. Maybe Freedom didn't knife Willie Thomas, but it was going to be a hell of a job proving he hadn't had *any* part at all in the horrific murder. Smethurst's strong evidence, Freedom's alibi, depended on the jury believing he was actually with Evelyne at the time of the boy's death. Miss Jones had a lot on her shoulders.

Evelyne tried to understand, but Sir Charles had to repeat himself twice and was losing patience. The first three charges of murder had been dropped, he explained. 'Quite simply, Smethurst was able to prove there was no case against him. But he has been committed for the murder of William Thomas.'

'When? Will it be soon? How long will he have to wait in gaol?'

'Until the trial, gel, until the trial. Now we don't want you going to see him, you must have no contact with him, is that clear?'

'Yes, sir.'

'You are a very important witness, and you must behave impeccably until the trial. You can spend the time getting yourself some nice dresses, subdued, nothing too flashy, gloves and what have you, perhaps a hat . . .'

Evelyne accepted the money His Lordship gave her, money to pay her hotel bill, and for her clothes. Left alone, she couldn't stop her hands shaking, she repeated over and over to herself that the charges had been dropped. What she couldn't understand was why, if they believed her evidence, was Freedom still having to go on trial at all.

Freedom was as confused as Evelyne. Smethurst spoke very slowly, sometimes repeating himself two or three times. By now he had discovered his client was illiterate.

'But I never killed the last lad, sir.'

About to leave, Smethurst gestured to the gaoler. He looked back as the strange, unfathomable eyes searched his face. Freedom seemed childlike in his confusion.

'I'll come in to see you again – until then, keep your chin up.'

'Thank you, sir, thank you for everything you're doing.'

The police officers and warders assigned to Freedom had nicknamed him the 'Queer Fish' because he was always so silent and unapproachable. They had segregated him very early on from the other prisoners awaiting trial. Many of the men were striking miners who had resorted to stealing and poaching to make ends meet. They knew he was being charged with the murders of their fellows and they constantly jeered and catcalled in the direction of Freedom's cell. Every officer had to agree that he was a model prisoner – too good – he said neither 'thank you' nor 'good morning'. He said nothing. His black eyes frightened some of the officers, and they had drawn lots to see who would be the ones to take him back and forth to court when the day came. No one wanted to start a fight with him. Even though he was handcuffed, he still looked as if he could be dangerous.

The exercise yard was cleared for Freedom's solitary morning walk. Only he didn't walk, he ran round and round and round, running until he was sweating and exhausted. He would then be taken back to solitary for a shower. One of the warders supervising him whispered that the man was 'built like a brick shit-house with muscles standing out all over his body like a marble statue'.

Freedom knew they watched him, talked about him, and like an animal he stared back with his dark brooding eyes, and said nothing. Here, silence was his only defence against the world. No one could understand what the cell, the high brick walls and the key turning in the lock, were doing to Freedom's mind. The cell closed in on him until his only relief was to pound his fists against the walls. He wrapped them in his blankets to muffle the sound. His morning run reminded him of his stallion, the way he used to toss his head and run round and round on the training rope. He was like a roped *gry*, an animal.

When the news leaked out that three charges of murder had been dropped, the prisoners banged on their cell doors with their tin mugs, screaming at the injustice. '*You bastard, you'll hang . . . They should hang yer, you gyppo scum!*'

The press also got to hear of the murder charges being withdrawn and a small article appeared in the paper. They mentioned Freedom Stubbs by name as the gypsy being held in custody, and that he was now only being charged with the murder of William Thomas. Smethurst was furious, knowing the damage this information could cause to a jury. They could be prejudiced against Freedom before the trial began.

Tension mounted as the date of the trial grew closer. Sir Charles had spent the time staying with friends or out shooting. Ed Meadows was courting Miss Freda and they held hands like two teenagers, gazing into each other's eyes and sighing. Ed was thinking about popping the question. Miss Freda was reeling in her fish, and had already made up her mind to accept if he proposed.

Evelyne spent her days wandering around the museums and art galleries. The trial was ever-present in her mind.

Smethurst worked on in preparation for the trial. This big, scruffy man was totally dedicated to his work. His scrupulous attention to every single detail was impressive. He knew he held a man's life in his hands and, although he appeared almost buffoonish, he was an exceptionally intelligent and honourable man. He was also a kind man, and very patient.

The trial was to begin the following morning. Smethurst found a brief moment to explain everything to Evelyne.

'We begin tomorrow morning. You must not be seen talking to anyone associated with the trial. You'll be called to the stand when I am ready . . . but we'll talk again before then, just remember all I've told you and don't let him ruffle you. Answer clearly and concisely . . .'

'How's he holding up, sir? Is he all right?'

'Well he's getting a lot of stick from the other inmates, naturally, and he'll more than likely have to take a lot more. Don't you worry yourself about him . . . I take it you've not seen him, made no contact?'

'No sir, His Lordship forbade it.'

'Quite right . . . well dearie, I'll take my weary body to bed, be refreshed for the battle.'

'*Will* it be a battle, sir?'

Smethurst gave her a small pat on her shoulder, and one of his lopsided smiles. 'Trust me . . . Goodnight.'

*

Evelyne tossed and turned all night long. Early the following morning, the first day of the trial, Miss Freda and Ed peeked round her door on their way to court.

'I'll come to see you later, tell you all about it,' whispered Freda.

'Now, now, Freda, yer know that's not legal. She's a witness, you gotta stay away – maybe I'll just pop in though, eh! Ta-ta, gel.'

Left alone, Evelyne tried to read, but she couldn't concentrate for wondering how the trial was going. She prayed it would be over soon. She ordered lunch but couldn't eat anything, and eventually she sat by the window, waiting for them all to return.

The gallery was packed with spectators. They were rowdy and jocular. As the court began to fill, Smethurst swept in, his wig already at a precarious angle. Henshaw, immaculate as ever, took his position at the bar, waiting for the judge to be seated. The courtroom became hushed. There was a silent moment while both defence and prosecuting counsels took out their papers. The tension could be felt by all as they heard the sounds of keys turning in locks, and Freedom Stubbs was led up from the cells.

He dwarfed the prison officers on each side of him. He wore a neat, single-breasted suit, white shirt and tie, courtesy of Sir Charles. His long hair, as Smethurst had instructed, was tied back off his face in a thong. He was handcuffed, and he kept his head bowed, looking neither right nor left. The clerk of the court stepped forward.

Henshaw began his opening speech for the prosecution. The court listened attentively. No reference was made to any of the previous murder counts. Henshaw

334

made a blistering verbal attack on the accused man. He then proceeded to call his witnesses; miners who had seen Freedom's fight with Dai 'Hammer' Thomas, men who had heard him threaten to take revenge. Evan Evans gave a stuttering, nervous statement regarding the arrest of the accused man. Smethurst didn't let a single thing slip by him. He was in and out of his seat like a bobbing buoy, consistently attacking Henshaw for leading his witnesses, particularly in Evan Evans' case. The man was so nervous he even had a problem remembering his own address. When it was time for Smethurst to cross-question Evan Evans he bellowed, and the poor man actually jumped.

'When you arrested Freedom Stubbs did you find anything?'

'Pardon?'

'When the prisoner was arrested, did you find anything on his person?'

'No sir, we did not, but we had a damned good look. We also searched the gypsy camp, found nothing.'

'And could you tell us how the prisoner behaved? When arrested?'

'He came along quiet like, after we'd got him.'

Smethurst smiled his thanks and resumed his seat.

The next witness was yet another miner who had witnessed Freedom Stubbs' threatening behaviour after the fight at Highbury Fair. Morgan Jones revelled in the fact he had been called to the witness stand. He gave lurid details of Freedom's prowess in the ring, drawing murmurs from the gallery as he lifted his voice theatrically. When Smethurst began his cross-questioning, he kept his voice low, hardly audible, to make the witness more attentive.

'So you saw the prisoner threatening to take revenge, could you elaborate?'

'Oh yes, sir, he pointed like this, and his face was terrible fierce. He said he would get each man there, I took it to mean he would kill 'em.'

'Thank you Mr Jones, but the fight was over, was it not?'

'Yes, Dai Thomas was lying out cold, had to be hospitalized, he did, they thought he had killed him he was so bad.'

Smethurst then asked Morgan if he knew anything of Dai Thomas' present state of health. Morgan elaborated, his fist raised in a boxer's stance, telling the court that 'Hammer' was alive and well and fighting in Brighton. Morgan beamed around the court, waved to his mother in the gallery.

'Tell me, Mr Jones, why, in your opinion, was the defendant still fighting after the bout with Thomas was over?'

'Ah well, there had been some hanky-panky with one of the gyppo girls, and a few of the lads . . .'

'Hanky-panky . . .? What exactly do you mean by hanky-panky?'

'Well there had been a lot of beer flowing.'

'Are you saying there was a certain amount of drunkenness?'

'Oh yes, I'd say so . . . a few of the lads had got a bit excited . . .'

'Excited? . . . I am sorry Mr Jones, I am still not exactly clear . . . What were these lads doing?'

'Well, there was one of the gypsy girls, you know what they're like, she must have encouraged them. They were . . . having their way with her . . .'

The court buzzed. Smethurst sighed . . . 'Ahhhhhh, having their way with her! What, all of them? How many lads did you see with this gypsy girl?'

Morgan Jones huffed and puffed, rubbed his head,

and coughed with embarrassment. 'Maybe it had got a bit out of hand, but those lads paid for it.'

Smethurst ignored the reference to the boys' killings. He bellowed, making Jones gulp, 'You call *raping an innocent girl "getting a bit out of hand"*?'

The court erupted in loud boos and hisses. The judge called an adjournment for lunch.

Evelyne sat on her bed while Miss Freda tried to relate all the day's happenings. Suddenly Freda burst into tears.

'What is it, Freda? . . . Oh, for goodness' sake, tell me! Have you any idea what it's like for me, sitting here day after day, not knowing . . . *why are you crying*?'

Miss Freda gulped and sniffed. 'Because . . . because I feel so sorry for him – Oh Evie, they say he'll hang.'

Evelyne wanted to shake Freda, but she fought for control, told her that she mustn't even *think* like that.

'I've not been on the stand yet, Freda, just wait until I get my ten penn'orth in . . .'

Freda calmed down and blew her nose, while Evelyne wished she felt as positive as she sounded. Freedom was to be called to the stand the following morning.

In the early hours she woke from a nightmare, a terrible nightmare of a man swinging on the end of a rope. The man was Freedom.

Smethurst kept his eyes on Freedom and his fingers crossed as he was sworn in. He knew he was going to have to handle the man carefully. He had told Freedom to concentrate on him, to answer clearly, and above all to take care not to incriminate himself. He must make no reference to the other murders; he was on trial for the

337

killing of William Thomas, and Thomas only. The handcuffs were removed and Freedom rubbed his wrists before
placing both hands on the rail of the dock. If he was
nervous he didn't show it, but stood, head high, and
looked directly at Smethurst, as instructed.

In the gallery the women whispered and nudged one
another, and a woman's voice was heard gasping, 'It's
Valentino.'

Smethurst's voice silenced the court. 'State your
name and occupation.'

Freedom's voice rang out, sounding somehow incongruous when he said the word 'fighter'.

'You have been brought before this court charged
with the murder of William Thomas. Are you guilty or
not guilty?'

Freedom's 'not guilty' met with a low buzzing from
the court as if a swarm of bees had been let loose. The
judge lifted an eyebrow and the noise subsided.

'You are a Romany gypsy, is that true, Mr Stubbs?
And you have been working as a booth boxer and
fairground boxer for the past eight years?'

Freedom answered every question firmly. Miss Freda,
in the gallery, leaned forward to catch every single word.
She noted his strange unfathomable eyes, his face like a
mask, no one could tell what he was thinking. Not until
Smethurst mentioned Evelyne did she see a strange
reaction. His hands gripped the dock bar tighter for a
second and then relaxed.

'Would you tell the court how you met Miss Jones?'

'She helped one of the girls from my clan. The girl
had been raped and beaten, and Miss Jones helped her,
cleaned her wounds, she was gentle and kind.'

Freedom took Smethurst by surprise by continuing,
without any encouragement, 'If I am to hang, even

338

though I swear before God I did not kill the boy, I take this time to say that no woman could have behaved more kindly or with such good intentions. If there is any man in this court who says different, he is a liar.'

Smethurst could see that the judge was about to interrupt. Freedom's speech was irrelevant, and he coughed loudly. 'I am sure everyone understands. As you said, Miss Jones was very caring and . . .'

Freedom interrupted calmly, his voice as loud and clear as a bell. 'No sir, she was different. We have a word for non-Romanies, we call them "palefaces". We do not trust them, we do not want them near our camps or with our people. Because she showed us respect and was gentle to a girl that had been raped, it is not right for people to say the things I have heard outside in the streets. They are calling her a "gyppo woman" . . .'

This time the judge interrupted and told Smethurst to control his witness. Smethurst glared at Freedom. 'Please, Mr Stubbs, in your own words, tell us what happened, to the very best of your recollection. How you met Miss Evelyne Jones, and exactly what occurred on the night of the murder of William Thomas.'

Freedom explained in detail exactly how he had met Evelyne, what had happened afterwards. How, months later, he had been to the valleys for the boxing match. The spectators listened attentively. Freedom continued uninterrupted right up until the night of his arrest. Smethurst nodded, keeping a watchful eye on him, encouraging him to speak freely. Freedom finished by saying how he had been brought to Cardiff. Smethurst raised his hand to pull at his wig, a signal he had told Freedom to watch for – he was to remain silent.

Smethurst left a long pause before he raised his voice. 'Thank you, Mr Stubbs. Now, I ask you, in front of this court, knowing you have sworn on the Bible to tell the truth – did you, Freedom Stubbs, take the life of William Thomas?'

'No sir, I did not.'

Smethurst looked at the judge. 'No further questions, Your Honour.'

A low buzz went around the court as Henshaw, taking his time, stood up to begin his cross-examination. He looked with chilling eyes at Freedom. His voice was softer, quieter than Smethurst's, and the spectators all leaned slightly forward, afraid to miss a word.

'Mr Stubbs, would you please look at exhibit number four, a photograph, and tell me what the mark across the deceased's forehead means?'

Smethurst chewed his lips. Freedom was handed the blown-up photograph of William Thomas. 'Yes, sir, it's a *dukkerin*'s sign.'

'I'm sorry Mr Stubbs – *dukkerin*?'

'Romany sign, sir, a *dukkerin* is what you call a fortune-teller. It is a curse sign.'

The court murmured and hushed immediately. Smethurst sucked in his breath. His foot tapped, and he gave Freedom a hard glare. He had already said too much. Henshaw bided his time, the spectators giving him their rapt attention.

'Mr Stubbs, you say you did not kill William Thomas, a nineteen-year-old boy, a boy found with his hands tied behind his pitiful body, his throat slit, and a blood mark, a strange symbol daubed on his forehead, a Romany curse . . .'

The spectators murmured. Henshaw held up his hand for silence. Freedom appeared about to speak . . . but Henshaw continued. 'You say you did not kill William Thomas, you swear this on the Holy Bible – tell me, as a Romany, are you a Christian?'

340

Smethurst swore under his breath. The buzzing grew loud again, and the judge hammered with his gavel to quieten the court room. He warned that, unless the spectators controlled themselves and behaved according to court rules, they would be removed. But the noise persisted, and shouts began from the gallery . . . 'Liar – hang him – give him the rope . . . *The rope, the rope . . .*'

Two ushers approached the judge's bench. He leaned down to listen for a moment, then gave a tight nod of his head as he agreed to the troublemakers being removed. Several men and three rowdy women were ejected. Their voices could still be heard arguing in the corridor. Henshaw raised an eyebrow to Smethurst as silence fell once more in the court.

'I did not hear an answer to my question, Mr Stubbs. Are you a Christian?'

Freedom looked at Smethurst then back to Henshaw. 'I believe in God, and the Devil, may he take my soul if I am lying.'

Henshaw stepped up the pressure. 'Tell me, Mr Stubbs, are you or are you not the lover of Miss Evelyne Jones? Miss Jones, the only witness to give you an alibi for the night of the murder of William Thomas? Please reply to my question, Mr Stubbs. Is Miss Evelyne Jones your mistress?'

Freedom's hands gripped the dock bar tightly. 'No sir, she is not my woman.'

Henshaw turned round, shrugged his shoulders, tapped his pencil on the rail before him. This tapping was to become familiar, first the sharp end of the pencil, then the blunt end, tap-tap-tap . . .

'So Miss Jones, a schoolteacher, is nothing more than a true friend to the gypsy people. Could you tell me why, if she was simply a friend, a woman you had met on only one occasion before, why, during a boxing

341

match at Devil's Pit three days after the brutal murder of William Thomas – I am referring, Mr Stubbs, to the night you were trying to avoid arrest – why did you . . . one moment . . .' Henshaw perched a pair of half-moon glasses on the end of his nose. He picked up his notes. 'If I may quote you, Mr Stubbs, "I drove my wagon through the crowd of people and helped Miss Jones up beside me" . . . end of quote. Do you recall saying that? So would you now please tell the court why you would take hold of a woman, by her waist I presume, and lift her into a moving wagon . . .?'

Freedom was nonplussed, unable to follow Henshaw's train of thought, his complex questioning.

'Perhaps I should refresh your memory again, Mr Stubbs. We are talking, are we not, of the night the police arrested you. If she was *not* your "woman", *not* your mistress, why did you take hold of her in what I can only describe as a very familiar, if not barbaric, way?'

A woman waved from the gallery and screeched, 'He could get hold of my waist any time he likes, ducks!'

Henshaw stared at the blonde woman leaning over the gallery. The court broke into laughter and the judge again rapped his gavel sharply and called for silence. Henshaw pursed his lips, removed his glasses, and sighed. 'Again, Mr Stubbs, I have to ask you please to reply to my question. We are not here – although I must say, some appear to think so – we are not here for our own amusement. This is a court of law. I am waiting, Mr Stubbs.'

Smethurst carefully unwrapped a toffee. Henshaw had learned some of Smethurst's personal tricks, he was playing to the gallery, condoning their behaviour. It was obvious that Freedom was at a loss. He gazed helplessly at Smethurst.

Tapping his pencil with an air of martyred patience, Henshaw repeated 'Well, Mr Stubbs, we are waiting.'

'She stood by me again, sir, she said they were out to kill me because they – the villagers – believed I had done the killing. There were many men trying to push the wagon over, I took her aboard the wagon because I was a-feared for her life.'

'Are you saying Miss Jones' own people were turning against her?'

'Yes, sir, they knew she'd been with me, and that lad was dead, and in the Romany way . . .'

Smethurst closed his eyes and gritted his teeth. The court was in an uproar.

The judge called for a lunch break, and everyone filed out of the room. Freedom was led down to the cells. When he was brought back after lunch, Henshaw cross-examined him for the rest of the afternoon.

That evening Evelyne waited for Freda's usual visit. She came into the hotel room and promptly burst into tears. 'Oh, I feel so sorry for him, Evie, he looks so alone, so alone . . . And that Mr Henshaw twisted him so, made everything he said sound so bad . . . he asks one question and leads it into another, and gets Freedom confused.'

Evelyne grew more and more nervous as Miss Freda described how cold and arrogant Mr Henshaw was. They both jumped with fright as someone pounded on the door, and they heard Sir Charles' voice demanding admission.

'Now look here, this isn't on. You know you mustn't talk to the witness, Miss Freda. Now please leave instantly . . . go along, out, out – and make sure no one sees you as you leave.'

343

With a fearful look at Evelyne, Freda hurried out. Sir Charles closed the door after her. 'I shouldn't be here either.'

'How do you think it's going, sir?'

'Not good, not good at all – they're making him look like an oaf. Er . . . look here, gel, you and this fellow . . . er, you *have* been telling us the truth, haven't you?'

'About what, sir?'

'Well, this chap Henshaw's pretty sharp, and he's picked up that perhaps there's more to your so-called "friendship" with this fella than meets the eye.'

Evelyne's hands tightened in her lap. She swallowed hard. 'If I had lied to you, I would not get on to that witness stand and swear on the Holy Bible to a lie. Everything I said to you, and Mr Smethurst, was God's truth.'

'Ah, yes, quite . . . well, I think you'll be called soon. I suppose Smethurst will talk to you before then. I'd best be off . . . Goodnight.'

'Goodnight, Sir Charles.'

Evelyne lay down, hardly able to believe that after all she had been through Sir Charles had to ask her again. Her heart pounded and she began to worry. Mr Henshaw sounded even more threatening than Miss Freda had made out. He had obviously sown a seed of doubt in Sir Charles' mind.

In the morning Freedom was led, handcuffed, from the jail to the waiting police wagon. A small crowd outside hurled rotting vegetables and abuse, and spat in Freedom's face as he stared at them between the wagon's bars. They raised their fists and gave chase as it moved off. Most of them then went to join the dole queues, satisfied that they were at least better off than the gyppo. Poor they may be, but they were free.

Freedom touched a slight swelling on his right cheek.

He had been taunted so much at breakfast – not by the prisoners but by the warders – that he had lost his temper and hurled his porridge at a particularly unpleasant warder who took delight in needling him constantly. He had made lewd gestures and implied that Freedom and his kind were up to no good. Freedom was beaten as he was dragged back to his cell. The warder, still dripping cold porridge, shouted, 'They'll hang you sure as I'm standing here, and, by Christ, I'll pull the rope meself, you bastard!'

The wagon bounced and rocked over the cobbled side streets on the way to court. Freedom closed his eyes, breathed the fresh air into his lungs. As they drove through the back gates of the court yet another small group of people pelted the wagon. But a few girls stood by the gates waving flowers, calling his name. One blew him a kiss, and got a severe wallop from a man for behaving like a 'gyppo bitch'.

Smethurst was very angry. Freedom was looking rough, his suit crumpled, and there was a bruise forming on his cheek. He handed Freedom his own greasy comb and told him to do something with his hair. Clean it might be, but long strands hung loose from the leather thong. Smethurst felt sorry for losing his temper. 'The women in the gallery are on your side, lad. I wish we had a few on the jury. They'll be tossing flowers at you before the trial's over. Apparently you resemble that film actor chappie, Valentino.'

'I never been to no picture house, sir.'

An usher gave Smethurst the nod that court was about to sit, and he rushed to his chambers to throw on his wig and gown. Henshaw was already waiting, spick and span, checking his appearance in the mirror. 'So it's the big day – your girl's on the stand? Should be interesting.'

'You get copies of those two statements? From Lord Carlton and Captain Collins?'

'I did, old chap, I did. Personally I doubt if they'll help, you'd need the prince himself to step on the stand to get your chap off this one.'

'We'll see, we'll see – don't count your eggs yet. Want a toffee?'

Henshaw smiled a refusal as the judge entered, muttering about the rift-raff outside the court. Smethurst joked with the judge. 'They say my client's the spitting image of this movie star, fella called Rudolph Valentino.'

The judge snorted, 'Well, for the Lord's sake I hope the press don't pick that up, the wife'll be here next. She's seen *Four Horsemen of the Apocalypse* twice.' Smethurst nearly swallowed his toffee the wrong way as the judge swept out. '*Four Horsemen of the* what?'

Henshaw laughed, checked he had his glasses and then winked at Smethurst. 'Old boy's wife's a bit of a lady, so I've heard. Well, come on, let's get on with the show.'

Evelyne was driven to court in Sir Charles' Rolls-Royce. She was shaking with nerves and kept licking her lips because her mouth felt so dry.

At the court they were surrounded by newspaper reporters pushing forward to speak to Sir Charles. The flashes and bangs of the photographers' lights made Evelyne jump.

'May I ask you, Sir Charles, what your interest in this case might be? Please, Sir Charles, just a few words?'

'I simply want justice done, that is all. Freedom

Stubbs is an innocent man who has already spent too long in jail.'

Two police officers pushed the reporters back, allowing Evelyne and Sir Charles to enter. The massive marbled reception area of the Law Courts was daunting, and Evelyne would have found it awe-inspiring if she had not been so nervous. Voices echoed and people rushed hither and thither. She was thankful to see the familiar figure of Smethurst striding towards them.

'Ah, you're here, good, good – curtain up in about five minutes.'

'Good God, man, can't you afford a better wig, the tail's over your left ear, looks dreadful.'

Smethurst turned his wig round, only to leave the tail sticking out over his right ear. An usher was waiting to lead Evelyne round to the waiting area. Sir Charles went ahead into the courtroom as Smethurst, his gown floating around him, walked with Evelyne to a long bench.

'Now just keep calm, and remember, don't let Henshaw ruffle you. He'll try his damnedest. Shouldn't be too long a wait, and may I say you look charming.'

He strode off before she could reply or thank him for his compliment. She could see what looked like food stains down the back of his gown.

She became aware of a man scrutinizing her from the doorway. His cold eyes made her shiver, his drawn face was set and hard.

Henshaw detected how nervous she was, and knew instantly she would be putty in his hands. He followed Smethurst into the court.

One hour ticked by, then another. Evelyne paced up and down the marbled corridor. She walked to the far end and peered round the corner. There was another bench, with a number of men sitting on it, some with cigarettes in their cupped hands. Above them hung a 'No Smoking' sign in bold red letters. Evelyne returned to her bench and sat down again.

In the courtroom Smethurst was in fine form, his face flushed a deep red, his big hands waving in the air. He called for the defendant, Freedom Stubbs, to be brought into the dock.

The raised voices from the court made Evelyne's nerves even worse. Suddenly the double doors were thrown open and an usher called her name. She dropped her handbag in her haste to follow him into the court.

Evelyne's hand trembled visibly as she held up the Bible, standing ramrod straight in the witness box. 'I swear by Almighty God that the evidence I shall give shall be the truth, the whole truth and nothing but the truth, so help me God.'

Smethurst smiled at her. 'Would you state your name and occupation?'

Evelyne's voice wavered, and she got another encouraging smile from Smethurst as she answered, 'I am a schoolteacher'.

'So at the time of the murder of William Thomas you were a schoolteacher. Now then, would you, in your own time, please tell the court how you first came to meet the accused, Freedom Stubbs?'

Evelyne told the court how some friends had taken her to Highbury Hill for an evening's entertainment. At this point Smethurst interrupted her. 'I'd say that was a rather unusual evening's entertainment for a respectable schoolteacher, wouldn't you agree, Miss Jones? And just exactly *who* were these friends who suggested you go to this boxing match?' He directed a half-smile at Henshaw.

Evelyne replied, 'Lord Frederick Carlton and Captain David Collins.'

A murmur ran round the court at the mention of the high-society names. Sir Charles gasped and dropped his monocle. Smethurst had assured him that neither man's name would even be mentioned in court. He slapped his kid gloves against his hand in anger – this was really outrageous.

Evelyne was in the witness box for almost an hour before they broke for lunch. She had hardly looked at the dock, at Freedom – she couldn't. He had never taken his eyes from her face. As they led him back to his cell he tried to catch her eye, but she was being escorted from the stand by an usher.

The afternoon session began with Evelyne once more in the box. The court heard how she had helped Rawnie, but her name was not spoken. She had everyone's full attention as she explained how she had collected the newspaper cuttings, how she had seen Freedom in her village and recognized him from the boxing match. She told the court why she had gone to his camp to warn him the police were looking for him. As she stated that on the night William Thomas was killed in the picture house, Freedom had been with her, the spectators stirred and whispered. Her voice was strong, confident, as she said that Freedom could not have committed the murder. She was calm and concise throughout the ordeal, and above all spoke clearly, accurately recalling dates and times. Smethurst turned to the judge. 'At this point, Your Honour, may I say that both Lord Frederick Carlton and Captain David Collins have given statements to verify what Miss Jones has said, and they will both, if required, repeat their statements in court.'

Sir Charles gave Smethurst a furious look as he sat down.

Before Henshaw cross-examined Evelyne, he requested permission to approach the bench with Smethurst for a moment.

They spoke in whispers. Henshaw had picked up on the newspaper cuttings and he was going to find it impossible to avoid mentioning the previous murders. Smethurst gave Henshaw the go-ahead. He had been prepared for this, and it did not involve any change in tactics. He knew he could turn it to his own advantage.

Henshaw walked back to his seat and shuffled through his papers, waiting for the court to be brought to order once again. He took his time, lips pursed, carefully placing his glasses on his nose. He coughed lightly and appeared to be concentrating on his notes. In a blatantly sarcastic manner, he asked 'Miss Jones, could you please tell the court where you gained your diplomas to teach?'

Evelyne flushed and replied that she had not taken examinations, but had taught at the junior school in her village.

'So you are not, as you stated, a schoolteacher, is that correct? And at the time you visited Highbury Fair, what was your profession then?'

Smethurst jumped up and objected that the line of questioning was irrelevant and had no bearing whatsoever on the case. The judge dismissed his interruption.

'So, Miss Jones, we take it that you were not in fact a schoolteacher but a pupil, am I correct?'

Evelyne unwittingly fell into the carefully laid trap. She admitted that she had actually left school because her family needed her at home. Henshaw gave a sarcastic smirk. 'Ahhhh, I see, so now we have gone from being a schoolteacher to not even being at *school*. Dear, dear, this is all very confusing. Let us now take the reason why you were at the fair. As my learned friend stated, a boxing match is not really a fit place for a lady . . .'

Smethurst was on his feet, objecting in his booming voice. It was irrelevant whether or not a boxing match was a suitable place for a lady to be taken – indeed, if the great Ethel Barrymore frequented boxing matches he felt sure there could be no slur attached to his witness.

The judge had had enough and called Smethurst to the bar to reprimand him, saying that unless he curtailed his constant interruptions the court would be adjourned. Smethurst apologized and returned to his seat, then turned in astonishment as Evelyne blurted out, 'I may not be a lady in *your* opinion, sir, but I assure you I was invited to the fair, unaware that there was to be a boxing match. I trusted my companions and I had no reason to believe they were taking me to anything more than an innocent fair. My companions were Lord Frederick Carlton and Mr David – *Captain* David Collins. Both gentlemen, I believe. So, in your rudeness to me you are also accusing two respected men of being less than gentlemen.'

This speech caused the gallery to erupt in loud shouts and a spate of hand-clapping. The judge pounded with

351

his gavel and called for order. Henshaw's mouth twitched with anger, he shuffled his papers and was about to move on to another tactic when Evelyne, after a glance at the judge, spoke again. 'I'd also like, if I may, sir, I mean Your Honour, I would like to explain my education. It was partly private, and from Captain Collins' aunt. Mrs Doris Evans was her name, sir, and it was Mrs Evans who first brought me to Cardiff, and that is where I met Captain Collins. Just so you don't think I met him for the first time on the night of the fair.'

Henshaw snapped, 'Thank you, Miss Jones. You are implying, I believe, that you were a friend of Captain Collins' family?'

Evelyne again had the court in uproar when she agreed that Henshaw was correct, that she was a family friend, albeit a poor one.

Smethurst coughed and smiled at Henshaw behind his hand. He knew Evelyne had got him rattled, and it tickled him. Smethurst was also pleased to see the judge's obvious delight in the witness.

Henshaw was aware that he had to get the situation back under his control. 'Let us move on to Freedom Stubbs.'

From the public gallery a raucous female yelled that she'd move on to Freedom Stubbs any time they liked, and she threw down a single red rose. Again the judge resorted to his gavel to bring the court to order. He then announced a recess until the following morning and asked both Henshaw and Smethurst to come to his chambers.

Smethurst proffered a toffee to Henshaw just as the judge entered. 'Now look here, you two, tomorrow I want no more of your baiting each other out there. Just conduct yourselves and your questioning in an orderly fashion. Is it true? Ethel Barrymore goes to watch fights? Where on earth did you get hold of that?'

About to reply, Smethurst stopped short as Henshaw slammed out of the room. It was in some way an omen, a foretaste of what was to take place the following morning.

Evelyne had been in the witness box for more than an hour, answering question after mundane question, but although she was tiring she maintained her concentration throughout. Henshaw was unrelenting, eventually bringing up the fact that Evelyne had kept newspaper cuttings of the previous murders. 'You cut articles from the papers and kept them for no other reason than mere interest? I find that hard to believe, just as I find your statement that you went alone to the gypsy camp on the night William Thomas was murdered hard to believe. It was almost dark, it was, after all, almost eight o'clock.'

Smethurst had wanted Evelyne to watch every word. This time she made no reply. By not actually asking her a question, Henshaw had hoped to trip her up. He sighed, twisting his glasses around. 'We are expected to believe an awful lot, Miss Jones, that you, just an ordinary girl, climbed a mountain to a gypsy camp to warn, *warn*, a man you insist you did not know, but you go alone, taking with you newspaper cuttings regarding that man's possible association with certain murders . . .'

At this point the judge clarified that the defendant had been cleared of all charges relating to the aforementioned murders. He allowed Henshaw to ask again why Evelyne had collected the reports from the newspapers, and why she took them to Freedom Stubbs. Evelyne answered that Freedom was illiterate, he could neither read nor write, and he was not aware that he was wanted for questioning. Henshaw raised his arms and shook his head in disbelief. 'You expect us to believe this? This preposterous fairy-tale? Wouldn't the truth be rather that you were less than a stranger to the accused? I think, Miss Jones, you knew him well, more than well – he is illiterate, how did you know this? What I believe you *did* know was that the defendant was in your village for the sole purpose of killing William Thomas, is that not the real truth?'

Evelyne could hear Mr Henshaw's breathing, the court was so quiet. Smethurst leaned forward, tense now. She kept her voice to a low whisper. 'At the time I did not know whether or not Freedom Stubbs had any involvement with those other boys, but I had to find out . . .'

'Could you tell the court why?'

'I recognized Willie Thomas, and I knew there could be trouble. I wanted it to stop even though I felt he should pay in some way for what he did to that poor girl. I just wanted to warn Freedom Stubbs, that was all.'

Henshaw shouted over Evelyne's words, '*You approve of murder, is that what you are saying?*'

Evelyne's temper snapped and she pointed at Henshaw, her voice rising. 'I never said that! What I said was, that if anyone saw what they had done to that poor girl, I mean if anyone had seen Willie that night, like I saw him, on top of her, ripping at her clothes, they would believe he should be punished. I *never* said I approved of *murder*.' She gripped the edge of the witness stand. She was so angry, angry because tears were running down her cheeks. 'You keep putting words into my mouth, sir. I just went up to the camp because

354

I wanted to warn him there could be trouble and there might be a fight.'

'Mr Stubbs was there that night to do precisely that – *fight*. Miss Jones, have you at any time had sexual relations with the accused?'

All the spectators craned forward for Freedom and Evelyne's reactions to this question. Evelyne picked up the Bible and held it high. 'I am here because at the time of the killing of Willie Thomas I was with Freedom Stubbs, that is the sole reason I am here.'

'I am sure it is, Miss Jones, but you have not answered my question. Did you and the accused have a sexual relationship?'

'*No*! No, as God is my witness, I have not,' Evelyne sobbed.

Women in the gallery blew their noses and shook their heads. To them breaking down was somehow confirmation of her love for Freedom.

There was a sudden commotion as Freedom tried to get out of the dock, pushing at the guards. He shouted, 'Leave her alone! *Leave her be*!'

He was dragged from the court. A scuffle broke out on the way to the cells. The judge broke off the day's session.

Evelyne was driven back to the hotel in the Rolls. She knew it had not gone well. She was unable to talk to Sir Charles, who appeared more concerned about Freddy and David's names having been, as he put it, 'bandied about'.

After bathing and dressing, Sir Charles swept out of the hotel to dine with the Carltons. Evelyne watched from her window as he left. She felt drained, totally exhausted. Miss Freda could sense that she didn't want company, and tried to cheer her up by saying she'd done well, but Evelyne knew she hadn't.

'Oh God, Freda, I was just dreadful. I went to pieces, I said things I was not to say . . . If he hangs, it's my fault, my fault.'

Miss Freda shook her finger at Evelyne. 'I watched, all through the trial. He sits with his head bowed, his eyes down . . . but for you, he held his head high, he didn't seem afraid. So, you have faith too.'

'I wish it was over, dear God how I wish it was over.'

Freda hugged her, kissed the top of her head and whispered that if it was bad for them, think what poor Freedom must be going through.

Freedom lay on his bunk. He could hear the other prisoners singing, 'Swing me just a little bit higher, la-de-la, de-la . . .' He pulled his pillow over his head. It wasn't the rope he was afraid of, he didn't think of it, all he wanted was for the night to come down, for the silence. Only then, when it was quiet, when all was calm, could he believe that she had stood by him. He wrapped his arms around the pillow and whispered her name. The pillow stank of prison. A month ago he had been able to dream, even wonder what she would feel like, smell like, close to him in bed. This night he could not dream, could not even hope.

The following morning the papers were full of the society names connected with the murder case. There

356

was a large photograph of Sir Charles Wheeler and Evelyne pushing through the crowds.

Today was to be the summing-up, and Evelyne sat with Sir Charles on one side of her and Freda and Ed on the other. The court was packed to capacity.

Everyone rose as the judge took his seat and declared the session open. Henshaw gathered his meticulous notes, rose to his feet, his face stern. His voice rang out, 'I ask you, ladies and gentlemen, to look closely at the man standing in the dock. The defendant, a man known for his prowess in the boxing ring, a Romany gypsy, a booth boxer, a fairground fighter. William Thomas was nineteen years old, a young boy ready to start out in life. His life was brutally cut off, as brutal a killing as I have ever known. His hands tied behind his back, his throat slit, and to add insult to injury he was marked with a sign of a cross, a cross of his own blood smeared on his forehead. That mark, as we have heard in this court, is the symbol of a Romany curse. The accused man was heard, by witnesses, men brought before you in this court, to threaten – threaten revenge for an attack on one of his own people. This girl has not come forward, and we cannot ask William Thomas whether or not he did in fact rape this gypsy girl. So what do we have? We have, gentlemen of the jury, a defendant who wanted revenge. Freedom Stubbs was in the village, seen close to the picture house where this unfortunate boy was slain – seen on the actual night of the murder, and recognized by Miss Evelyne Jones, a woman with whom he was already on familiar terms, a woman we are expected to believe tried to persuade him to leave because she knew, *knew*, there would be trouble . . .'

Evelyne's heart was pounding. She gripped Freda's hand tightly. She could see the row of witnesses for the

357

prosecution nodding their heads in agreement with everything Henshaw said. She looked only once at Freedom, and it was as if he sensed she was looking – he lifted his head and gave her the faintest glimmer of a smile. She bit her lips and stared at the floor.

Henshaw continued. 'I beg you, consider the evidence that has been heard in this courtroom. This man is guilty, and he must pay the penalty. This is no Romany court, no eye for an eye or tooth for a tooth. I ask for nothing more than justice, and it is in your hands. You, the jury, must find this man guilty of murder in the first degree.'

Smethurst tossed his toffee-paper aside and began his speech in a low voice. 'Oh, my learned friend is very persuasive and, looking around this court now, right now, I feel many people have already made up their minds that the man standing there, the man in the dock, is guilty.' He swung his big, domed head from side to side, and gradually turned to look up into the gallery, not once directing his gaze at the jury. Instead, he looked over the assembled people with a faint look of disgust on his face.

'Freedom Stubbs is accused of killing Willie Thomas, a boy who, as you have heard, raped and beat one of his people. Looking around this court right now I would say that any man here, *any* man confronted with someone they loved in the state that young girl was in, would threaten revenge. That is not to say that any person would actually go through with the threatened act. The defendant was not alone when this girl was discovered. There were at least forty other gypsy men at the boxing fair that evening – perhaps one of those men *did* take revenge, but we have a witness to prove that this man

358

did not – could not, because at the time Willie Thomas was murdered she was with the accused.

'My learned friend has taken pains to point out that the witness for the defence, Miss Evelyne Jones, was more than familiar with the accused man. Is there a woman here today who would not have gone to the aid of a raped girl? Who would not have felt a certain amount of disgust that William Thomas was not punished for this crime? We *know* he was scared, we *know* he went to the Cardiff police, terrified the gypsy people would take some kind of revenge. You have heard a statement made by William Thomas to the Cardiff Constabulary stating that he did indeed play some part in that poor girl's rape. Miss Jones saw this girl, and has said, under oath, that she was raped and beaten. And what is the outcome? Her name has been blackened, she has been accused of being this man's mistress, he her lover, and both have sworn on oath that this is not true . . . I say she is a woman who showed nothing more than simple, decent kindness to a group of travellers. Miss Evelyne Jones should be *held up as an example to us all*, instead of being belittled, her education sneered at because, as my learned friend pointed out, she had not the qualifications to teach at the school. We have had a witness stand in front of you and give glowing reports of her ability – a qualified man, a man with examinations, the present headmaster of that same school . . . But more, her character is without blemish, she is a Christian, a deeply religious, honest woman. She has *not* lied to this court, and her evidence is of the utmost importance. She has stated on oath that on the night of the killing of William Thomas she talked with the accused, that at no time could he have returned to the village, to the picture house, and committed murder.'

Smethurst was building up steam, facing the jury, his voice growing louder and louder as he swung his arms around. His black gown billowed like a bird, a big, dangerous bird. 'Where is the witness to say the accused was at the picture house? Look at him, look at his face, the size of him – do you think you would forget that face? If this man paid over money for a ticket, don't you think *one* person would remember? Come forward?'

Evelyne swallowed hard, and took a sneaky look around the court. All the faces showed rapt attention. 'Dear God,' she prayed, 'let no one mention the back door, the other entrance to poor Billy's picture house, always better used than the main door.'

Smethurst was sweating, his hair sticking to his head, his face redder than ever. Now he banged hard on the bench, slapping it, punctuating his words, '*Where* is the murder weapon?' he demanded, bellowing, 'The police *questioned* every man in that gypsy camp, *searched* every wagon, and they found nothing, *nothing*! No *blood* on any of the accused man's clothes, and at *no time* after he was arrested did he try to escape. Is *this* the behaviour of a guilty man? *This man is innocent* . . . he stands in the dock for one reason, and one reason alone – he is a gypsy. Can you really believe that Miss Evelyne Jones could have an ulterior motive for coming forward? She is one of you, *one of your kind, you in the gallery*, and she had been mocked and insulted because she dared, yes, *dared* to come forward on behalf of the accused. She gains nothing, she wants nothing more than to see justice done . . . and you, the jury, if you have any reasonable doubt, then you have only one choice – only one – give this man justice, and pronounce him innocent. He is *not guilty*.'

Smethurst slumped into his seat. He had not referred to his notebook once. He sat back, exhausted.

The judge called for a recess until the following day, when he would give his summing-up. Evelyne wanted to weep – it was still, after all this time, not over.

The following morning, the judge spent two hours summing up the case. He then instructed the jury in their duty. His voice was chesty and hoarse as he patiently explained to them that they must digest all the evidence they had heard. That they must be unanimous in their verdict, and if there was any reasonable doubt in any of their minds they had no alternative but to find Freedom Stubbs innocent. The jury filed out, and the judge went for a glass of port with Smethurst and Henshaw.

Evelyne, Ed and Miss Freda waited in the corridor, afraid to leave in case the jury came back in. None of them felt like talking – they just sat with their eyes on the ushers standing quietly in a group by the entrance to the court. Evelyne wanted to scream. She clasped Freda. 'Oh God, Freda, they've been out over an hour, it must be a bad sign, it's a bad sign – Ed, do you think it's a bad sign? Oh . . .'

Ed saw the spectators streaming in through the main doors. The group of ushers broke up and began directing people back into court. 'Here we go, Evie love, this is it by the look of it. Come on, or we'll miss our seats.'

Evelyne sat down, trembling, expectant. The clerk stood waiting for the judge, the ushers closed the doors.

'Please be upstanding . . .'

The noisy clamour of everyone rising drowned the

last words as Smethurst and Henshaw preceded the judge into the court. Smethurst did not so much as glance at Evelyne, or Sir Charles, who was standing at the back of the court.

The jury filed back into their seats, the foreman obviously nervous, twisting his cloth cap round and round in his hands.

The clerk of the court waited for the judge to settle himself, then stepped up to the jury foreman.

'You have made your decision?'

'Yes sir, Your Honour sir, we have, sir.'

'And is it the decision of all of you?'

'Yes, sir, it is.'

The clerk held out his hand for the slip of paper in the foreman's shaking hand. He licked his lips. 'Please tell the court your decision. Do you find the accused, Freedom Stubbs, guilty or not guilty of murder?'

'Not guilty.'

The court erupted in one enormous cheer. Evelyne covered her face, the relief was unbearable. She repeated, 'Not guilty, not guilty,' over and over as if she could hardly believe it.

Freedom, standing in the dock, lowered his head and wept. The noise of the court was like a drum beating in his brain. A whirlwind whooshed around him, he was floating above everything, no voice was clear, no face – just hands grabbing, shaking his. He realized his hand-cuffs had been removed without knowing how. It was all a blur of confusion which climaxed in Freedom, surrounded by Sir Charles, Smethurst, Freda and Ed, walking from the court. He was free.

*

The press clamoured around them, camera flashes popped, the babble of voices asking him to look this way and that way, people screamed at him, wanting to know how it felt to be free. Crowds of women threw flower petals like a wedding party as they stood on the courthouse steps.

Sir Charles waved and smiled to the people, his arm around Freedom, then he held up Freedom's right arm as if he was in the boxing ring. The crowd went wild, chanting 'Freedom, Freedom, Freedom . . .' and still he kept feeling it was a dream, that he would wake up, at any moment he would wake up in his small cell.

Ed pushed the people away as they moved down to a cavalcade of cars drawing up outside the court. Evelyne put her hands over her face as the flashing cameras blinded her, and she was separated from the main group. In the excitement Ed turned to Miss Freda, who was crying one moment and laughing the next, and shouted to her above the din.

'Marry me, will you marry me?'

Freda flung herself into his arms and they were carried along by the crowd to the waiting cars.

Evelyne was helped into Ed and Freda's car. Sir Charles had taken Freedom in the first car, which was now drawing out of the driveway. People ran beside the car, cheering, and Sir Charles waved to them as though he were the Prince of Wales himself.

Smethurst bundled himself into the last car and leaned back, satisfied with himself.

At the hotel, reporters hung around the entrance, more hovered inside the tea-room, and the cameras popped and flashed. They clustered around Sir Charles and Freedom, all talking at once, demanding interviews with the boxer. Sir Charles dominated the proceedings, while Freedom stood at his side.

'Gentlemen, please, please stay back, we will give a press interview in the morning, please, please stay back.'

Freedom looked over the heads to see Evelyne standing to one side. She seemed as overawed by the whole experience as he was. He tried to catch her eye, but she was jostled by a group of women determined to touch Freedom.

Some large porters arrived on the scene and began to move the crowd out of the hotel. Sir Charles steered Freedom towards the lift, where the snooty bellhop, beside himself, bowed and flushed and smiled to the cameras at the same time. They were the first to get clear of the lobby.

The movement of the lift made Freedom's heart lurch, and he put out his hands to steady himself.

'Keep your hands off the sides, sir, or you'll get hurt.'

The bellhop swung the gates open and Sir Charles stood aside for Freedom to go ahead of him. Dewhurst was hovering at the door of the suite, delighted but trying very hard to remain aloof and cool, as was his place.

'Book a table for dinner, Dewhurst, take over the small private dining room. Tonight we will celebrate.'

The door to Sir Charles' suite closed as the second lift reached the third floor, and Freda, Ed and Evelyne stepped out. The pair were so brimming with happiness and excitement that Evelyne's quietness went unnoticed.

'You comin' in? We'll 'ave some champagne, double celebration, eh? You told 'er yet, Freda? Come on, let's get in there.'

Evelyne was at the door of her own suite before Freda

gasped out that she and Ed were going to be married, then Ed pulled Freda's hand and led her towards Sir Charles' suite.

Evelyne let herself into her room and closed the door, welcoming the silence, the peace. She was exhausted. She threw her hat on to the bed. So much for Freda's creations, no one seemed to have noticed her, never mind her clothes.

The bath water was running as Evelyne lay on her bed. She realized then that it was all over, she had finally seen something right through from start to finish. Freedom had been proved innocent, he was free, and instead of feeling elated she felt empty. While the trial had been on, she had had somewhere to go, something to do, and now she had nothing. She knew Sir Charles would be returning to London and, if Freda and Ed married, more than likely her only friend would be gone, too. She was alone, once more she was Miss Evelyne Jones, but now there was no 'schoolteacher' after her name. She had nothing.

She closed her eyes and tried to think what she would do with her life. The truth was, she didn't know what she wanted. She hadn't thought much of home – her Da, yes, but not the village. The verdict would certainly make some of those bitches swallow their words. They all seemed so far away, it was hard for her to believe she had only been away for a matter of weeks. She made up her mind that she would put a call through to the post office, just to see how Da was.

Evelyne had no idea that while she was soaking in the bath the papers were streaming off the printing machines. Headlines declared Freedom Stubbs' innocence, and there was a large photograph of Freedom standing next to Sir Charles. Below it was a smaller, single photograph of Evelyne. She was called the heroine, the woman who had brought about the gypsy's release from jail.

CHAPTER 16

EVELYNE MAY not have thought that anyone had noticed her clothes, but one person did, and was so bitterly angry she tore the newspaper to shreds.

Lizzie-Ann, with a charabanc full of miners' wives, was on a day trip to Swansea. They had scrubbed their best clothes, begged or borrowed their fares for the trip to listen to a political meeting organized by striking miners' wives.

The lecturer addressed the women, unaware that actually to be there some of them had spent their week's food money. Their clothes were clean, why shouldn't they be? They were proud women, women who would not in any circumstances plead poverty, and their men were proud too. They were there to prove that they encouraged their men to fight for their rights, to claim better wages, they were there to stand up for their striking men.

The naïveté of the women, their belief that, by standing up and showing others, they would be followed went sadly amiss. The report that eventually found its way back to the powers-that-be claimed that, judging by the women who had shown up at the meeting, there was not so much hardship as was believed. The women showed no signs of exceptional stress, they seemed clean and prosperous, and it was noted that since the strike the death rate in the villages had dropped. Articles were written by various people stating that the men and boys were benefiting from the open-air life. The women, free from coal dust, began actually to enjoy regular hours. Schoolchildren now had a decent meal provided by the school every day, in some cases eleven meals a week, at a cost to the government of three shillings and sixpence per child. Special supplies of clothes and boots were sent to mining villages.

The state of the women's minds was even harder to detect than their outward show of 'prosperous, middle-class women'. The papers reported that they all seemed to be in good spirits, hard-working and running relief funds, collecting money from whist drives, women's football matches, dances and socials.

None of the government officers seemed really to see these four hundred women or the miners for what they were, an embattled community fighting for its life. The more determined they were to win, the braver the face they showed to the world. As their fellows, the blacklegs, caved in under the strain of unemployment and returned to work, they were slowly breaking the fighting spirit. The ridiculous calculations of strike pay and poor relief screamed out by government propaganda nailed their coffins down.

The strike was almost over, but the women didn't know it yet. As they travelled back to their villages they had high hopes that they had accomplished much for their men. The year was 1926, and it was a sad year for almost all the families of the largest single body of workers in the country. They had lost their battle and returned to work, caps in hands, defeated.

The Rhondda contingent was on the last stage of the journey. Tired, happy and ignorant, they passed around a bottle of gin they had clubbed together to buy. As the bus careered and jolted over the rough roads, the women sang their hearts out. 'My Little Grey Home in the West . . .' For some who had never travelled beyond their village, it was a day out to remember for the rest of their lives.

Lizzie-Ann cavorted up and down the aisle, hanging on as the charabanc rounded the sharp mountain bends. She was doing her old music-hall turns. She flopped into one of the empty seats at the back and saw a clutter of newspapers, a couple of days old, crumpled up on the floor. They had been used to wrap sandwiches in Swansea. The photograph of Evelyne stared up from the floor.

'They only gone an' *freed* the bugger, he's been proved innocent . . . will you look at 'er, all togged out for a dance an' mixin' with the posh people, an 'er a dirty gyppo lover.'

One skinny woman stood up and said that in her opinion if a man was proved innocent in a court then that was the Lord's word.

'You're only saying that, Agnes Morgan, because your old man's been inside more times than you've had hot dinners, so siddown and shuddup.'

The rain started pelting down, and the bus bumped and rolled its way to the valley. Lizzie-Ann held a shredded piece of the paper. She smoothed it out on her worn skirt and studied the picture in minute detail.

Evelyne looked like a lady, standing there with a titled gent and wearing her fancy clothes. Lizzie-Ann couldn't help but compare herself, her worn, red hands, her stockingless legs and her puffy feet encased in hand-me-down lace-up shoes with thick, unflattering soles. Lizzie-Ann couldn't contain herself, she started to sob, her whole body shook, and all the bitterness and jealousy rose to the surface. 'I hate her, I *hate her guts*! It should have been *me*, it should have been *me*!'

The rain was still bucketing down as the women made their way home. Depression hung over every house in the village, and none more so than at Hugh Jones'. He stared into the fire, shaking his head. He had failed, the men had trusted him and now they were to return to work for even lower wages. He pounded the mantelpiece with his fist. 'Bastards . . . *Bastards* . . . *You bloody bastards*!'

Lizzie-Ann pushed open the back door and chucked in the torn and muddy newspaper. 'Here, Hugh Jones, read what your own's doin', whilst we're stuck here fightin' for a livin' wage, you should be ashamed of her. She'll never step over my front sill again, that's for sure.'

She banged the door shut so loud the curtains along the street flickered and faces peered out into the dark, rainy night.

Hugh picked up the paper, pressed it out flat on the table and saw his daughter's beloved face crowned with a smart hat. She was staring arrogantly into the camera. Above her was a picture of Sir Charles Wheeler, one of them rich land-owning bastards, how could she? Hugh felt a shadow cross his grave, and slowly he picked the paper up and stared at the photograph of Sir Charles

Wheeler. He was holding the arm of the boxer, Freedom Stubbs, above his head.

Hugh dropped the paper and grabbed his cap, the back door banged once more and the curtains along the street flickered. The neighbours watched the big, hunched figure of Hugh Jones walking down the street.

'Probably goin' to Gladys's.'

But Hugh went into the pub. The place was empty apart from a few old'uns, and they sat hunched with their fags stuck in the corners of their mouths, playing dominoes.

'Yaaalright, Hugh lad? I'll have a half if you're buyin', and if you're not, sod ya.'

Hugh paid them no attention. He carried his frothing pint to an empty table and sat down. The men's hacking coughs and mutterings were accompanied by dull thwacks from the dartboard. Jim, Lizzie-Ann's husband, with his skeletal frame, a cigarette hanging from his mouth, stole sly looks at Hugh, but Hugh seemed not to notice. He was drinking steadily, draining his glass and banging it down for a refill.

'Ya gel's gone off with a gyppo, we hear, Hugh boy. Like 'em big, does she?'

The toothless old domino players cackled and coughed and went silent as they fingered their empty mugs.

Eventually, Hugh lurched out of the pub, and one old boy creaked to his feet and pottered over to drain the very last dregs from Hugh's fifth pint.

'All right fer some buggers, course, she hadda legacy, that's wot's carryin' 'im.'

*

371

Gladys could smell the drink on Hugh's breath. She said nothing, but folded her arms. She'd not seen him this bad before. He had a tipple like the rest of the men, but he was well away tonight.

'Have you eaten, lovey?'

'The lad got off free, Gladys, the gypsy, they found him not guilty.'

Gladys pursed her lips.

'Well, we know who we've got to thank for that, so the least said the better.'

Gladys couldn't even say the girl's name. She shuddered as Hugh put out his big hand to her, not even looking at her. 'Come here, come here, whassamatter with you? Come here.'

Gladys wouldn't move, she muttered that he was drunk and that he knew how she hated it, the drink.

He stood up, almost stumbled, straightened up and put his cap on. 'I'll be away then, goodnight.'

Gladys bit her lip as Hugh tried clumsily to open the door. He swore, and kicked it.

'We're going to have to talk, Hugh, a proper talk, not now, when you're sober.'

He turned on her and glared, he wasn't drunk, that was what was wrong with him, he wasn't drunk. 'I don't belong here, Gladys, I never did.'

Gladys let rip, afraid of losing him, afraid of having him. She became hysterical, her voice shrieking, 'She's not coming back, Hugh, you've been waiting for her to come home. Well she's gone, and you walk out that door you'll not come over my doorstep again. She's no good, you're well rid of her.'

Hugh gave her such a look that her blood froze. 'You're not fit to clean her shoes, woman.'

Gladys burst into tears and Hugh strode out into the wet, dark street. As he turned the corner into Aldergrove

Street he quickened his pace, the lights were on in the house, the lights . . . Evelyne had come home.

He ran the last fifty yards like a young man, round into the back alley, overturning milk cans, till he burst into the kitchen.

'Evie? Evie? *Evie . . .*?'

It was Hugh that had left the gaslights burning. He laboured for breath, realizing the house was empty. Pain shot up his left arm like a red-hot poker, shooting and burning.

'Evie? *Evie*? Oh God, gel, come home.'

He picked up the newspaper, his breath heaving in his chest. The gas lamps lit the picture like a Chinese lantern, the faces alive, looking at him, and it was the face of Freedom, with the black hair, the arrogant slanted eyes and high cheekbones that made the second burning, stabbing pain rip up his arm and across his chest. He felt his arm stiffening, he couldn't bend it, he couldn't bring the paper closer to his face, his mind couldn't control his limbs, couldn't make them work. Hugh felt himself falling, unable to stop himself. His outstretched hand, gripping the paper, crashing into the dying embers of the fire. He couldn't move his hand away from the coals, the paper caught light and still he couldn't move.

Freedom's face burnt in front of him, the paper curling and browning as the flame crept slowly, slowly, towards his daughter's face. Then they were both gone, small, black flecks of burnt paper fluttered from the fire. Hugh could see her, see her with her bangles and her beads standing at the pithead, her little parcel of clothes tucked under her arm. Dark, heavy slanting eyes, black hair – the gypsy girl and Freedom were one.

*

Gladys took over the funeral arrangements and buried Hugh. The whole village walked behind the coffin. The choir and the brass band sang and played their hearts out in their farewell to the Old Lion. No one even attempted to contact his daughter; Gladys had told them all that on the very night Hugh had died he had been with her, and had disowned Evelyne. He was ashamed of her and wouldn't have wanted her at his burial. Gladys did concede to having Hugh buried alongside his dead, she couldn't do otherwise. He was with his sons and his wife.

The small headstone bore just the family names and dates. All the fragility and hardships of life, the laughter, the love, all contained in the silent, sad grave. Summer was coming, and cornflowers were scattered across the fields beyond the cemetery, but no flowers lay on this plot of freshly dug earth, there had been no one who cared enough to place them there.

The owners of the mine had already taken over the house in Aldergrove Street. They made a half-hearted attempt at tracing Evelyne who was still unaware of her father's death. It was as if there was nothing, nothing left of the Jones family but a list of names on a grave. How the Old Lion would have roared one last time with rage, but he lay with his sons, his wife, in silence.

Sir Charles had installed Freedom in one of the rooms in his vast suite at the hotel until they were ready to depart for London. They had been very busy, signing release papers, giving press interviews, settling accounts. They were now ready to leave Cardiff first thing in the morning, and Sir Charles had arranged a small dinner.

Freedom had not spoken to Evelyne since the trial, even to thank her. He had asked about her many times, but was always dissuaded from calling on her personally.

'Wouldn't look right, Freedom, remember how they questioned your relationship with her in the courtroom, I don't want you ever to be seen together, is that clear? You will be able to thank her at dinner before we leave, that will have to suffice.'

When he was not being led around by Sir Charles, Freedom sat alone in his small servant's room. He was free, but he wondered if he had simply exchanged one cell for another; his life, he knew, was no longer his own. It had been accepted without question that he would accompany Sir Charles when he returned to London. He would miss his people, miss his life, but there was nothing he could do about it.

Evelyne had dressed and changed for the dinner. She wore the dress Sir Charles had bought for her, the green ribbons in her hair, but the diamond and emerald necklace had been returned to the jeweller's. She had been just about to leave her suite when the telephone rang. The receptionist had been trying to get a call through to the village post office for her. Evelyne had tried so many times, and had asked them to keep trying, but the line was always busy. It was the only one in the village apart from the doctor's and the police station.

She ran to the phone, excited, she wanted to hear her Da's voice, knew he would make everything all right, she had decided to go home.

Sir Charles was flushed, his familiar laugh filled the room, and the champagne flowed freely. He congratulated Ed and Miss Freda, but he couldn't help thinking that Ed was making a mistake. As sweet as Miss Freda was, to Sir Charles' critical eye she was a bit of an 'old boiler'. Ed seemed overjoyed so Sir Charles assured him that of course there would be a place for Miss Freda on the estate.

Lady Primrose and David arrived. The fact that he had 'spoken up' for the gypsy had given David a new social standing. Society admired him for it, as they did Lord Frederick who was also expected. Sir Charles smiled to himself. No one would ever know how he had twisted their arms.

Lord Freddy arrived with a magnum of champagne. They had been photographed in the hotel lobby and Freddy had given a rousing speech about 'British Justice'. He enjoyed the limelight, and he shook Freedom's hand, congratulating him.

Miss Freda constantly turned to the doorway, expecting to see Evelyne, but still she didn't arrive. Sir Charles beckoned her and suggested perhaps she should fetch the heroine to share in the celebration. Freedom went to Miss Freda's side and suggested that he should go to her. She blushed, having to crane her head to look up into his face. She told him Evelyne's room number and sighed. It was all so romantic.

Freedom slipped from the room and leant on the thick, flocked wall-paper in the corridor. He felt hot and the shirt and tie made his neck hurt, as if he was still bound and cuffed. He appeared relaxed and able to take care of himself, even mixing with the people in Sir Charles' suite, but all the faces and voices, the hand-shakes and the pats on the back, combined with the camera flashes to make him feel like roaring.

Two housemaids in their black dresses with white caps and pinnies scuttled past Freedom with lowered glances and nudges. He blushed and walked down the corridor to Evelyne's door. He pulled at his collar, ran his fingers through his hair. When he knocked he found the door was slightly ajar. He was not sure what he would say to her, how he would say it, but it was to Evelyne that he owed so much, far more than to Sir Charles.

He tapped again and then pushed the door open. He had begun to think she wasn't there when he noticed the bathroom door. He moved silently across the room and pushed the door gently.

Evelyne was huddled in a corner on the marble floor, her face pressed against the tiles, pressing hard so the white, ice-cold tiles hurt her cheeks. She couldn't cry, couldn't speak, she just wanted to press her body so hard against the walls and floor that it would disappear. Freedom knelt beside her, reached for her hand. It was as cold as the tiles, and she withdrew it and hugged her arms around her. He reached to turn her face towards him, and felt her straining against him, trying to hide her face.

'What is it, *manushi*, what is it?'

He lifted her easily from the floor and held her in his arms, carried her into the bedroom like a child. She was so close, he could feel her cold cheek against his neck, and he sat down, cradling her in his arms. Cupping her chin in his hand, he looked into her face. She was like a mute, staring helplessly at him, and he didn't know what to do to help her. 'What is it? Tell me, tell me?'

Freda opened the door.

'Come, darlinks, Sir Charles is waiting, everyone has arrived.' Her face creased with worry as she saw Evelyne; 'My God, what is wrong? Evelyne . . . Evie, are you sick?'

Firmly but gently, Freedom told her to leave them alone, he would take care of Evelyne. She went straight back to Ed and whispered that something had happened, Evelyne was sick. Sir Charles beckoned her to his side. He asked her quietly where Freedom and Evelyne were, and Freda told him that Evelyne was sick, but it was all right because Freedom was taking care of her. Sir Charles' monocle popped out as he straightened up, angry.

Striding down the corridor, Sir Charles burst into Evelyne's suite without knocking. Ed followed, with Miss Freda close on his heels. His voice rose in anger, 'I want you out of here this instant, you hear me? Out! Did anyone see you come in here? Did they? Answer me, man, did anyone see you enter?'

Freedom was standing by the bed on which Evelyne lay curled like a child, her face as white as the bathroom tiles. Her hands were clenched to her sides, her eyes staring, oblivious to everyone in the room. Freedom moved silently to Sir Charles and gripped him by the shoulder, blocking his way. He hissed. 'You treat me like I was a guilty man! I done nothing wrong – I came to bring her to you, I've not laid a hand on her.'

Frightened for Evelyne, Miss Freda went to her side. It was as if she were frozen. Freedom left Sir Charles rubbing his shoulder where the pain of that grip still burned, and walked softly to the bed. 'She has grief inside her, Miss Freda, let me talk to her.'

Sir Charles gave Freda a small nod, but did not move from the room. Ed still hovered behind him. They were all slightly in awe of Freedom's contained strength, his power.

Freedom moved close to Evelyne, placed his hand on her head, then bent low, crouching down to look into her vacant, faraway eyes. '*Manushi*, let it go, don't hold it inside you, it will hurt you more. Embrace it, love it, grow from it, release your pain.'

Evelyne did not move, but her mouth quivered and she formed the single word, 'Da'.

Freedom whispered, 'Is it your father? Then see him, hold him, kiss him goodbye.'

Sir Charles stepped closer, 'If the girl's father has died, really I think we should leave her alone. Come along, everyone, please.'

He waved Ed and Freda out, and then waited for Freedom. There was a fleeting moment when no one was sure how Freedom would react to being ordered from the room. The dark eyes flashed, but then he bowed to Sir Charles' wish and walked out.

It was not in Sir Charles' nature to show emotion. He coughed, then spoke from where he stood, 'Can you hear me, dear? You have a good cry, and then if you feel well enough, join us when you can.'

Evelyne neither moved nor spoke. Sir Charles sighed, 'We leave Cardiff first thing in the morning, you are welcome to join us, I am sure I will be able to find some employment for you . . . Miss Jones? Ah, well, perhaps this is not the time to discuss it . . . but, should you need anything, you only have to call.'

Evelyne couldn't hear him, only the soft words of

Freedom cut through her pain . . . She began to picture her beloved Da. He was standing on the mountain, his arms open wide, laughing his wonderful, deep, bellowing laugh. She did not hear the door close behind Sir Charles. She knew what she had to do, and she rose from the bed as if every limb was stiff. She began to pack her clothes.

Sir Charles bade everyone farewell and surveyed the debris of the party. He sighed, he was tired out. He instructed Dewhurst to leave everything for the hotel staff, they both needed a good night's sleep before the journey.

On his way to his bedroom he passed Freedom's door. He paused and tapped lightly, inched the door open. Freedom lay sprawled across the bed, naked apart from a sheet draped across him. His long hair splayed out across the pillow; he looked like a Greek god, his handsome face more beautiful in sleep than any man's Sir Charles had ever seen. He swallowed, embarrassed at his intrusion on the sleeping man, and closed the door softly. His skin felt hot; he owned that creature, owned him, at least for the next five years.

The following morning Sir Charles and his chauffeur were packed and ready by seven. They departed with Freedom for the railway station, leaving Ed to arrange transport for all their luggage.

Freda was waiting in the lobby with her few possessions when Ed came down. He looked harassed, mopping his brow with a bright red handkerchief. It took four porters to carry Sir Charles' luggage from his suite to the waiting taxi.

'Have you seen Evelyne, Ed? Have you seen Evie?'

'I just went into 'er suite, she must 'ave already left wiv Sir Charles . . . now, don't get me muddled, love, I got a lot ter think about . . . Gawd almighty, you see 'ow much luggage I got to take charge of? His Lordship's offered her work on the estate so don't you worry yerself none, Gor Blimey, thirty-four cases.'

Miss Freda sighed, relieved to hear Evelyne was coming with them. 'He is a good man, Sir Charles, and with all of us together it will be like a family, Ed. Just like a family, won't it?'

Ed paid no attention as he ticked each pair of suitcases off the list. Satisfied all was well, he picked up Miss Freda's case.

'Well, let's be on our way, love, don't want to miss the train.'

Sir Charles was already installed in his private first-class compartment with Freedom. Ed and Miss Freda, helped by Dewhurst, settled themselves into the third-class compartment at the far end of the train. Picnic hampers, luggage, tickets, all caused such comings and goings that no one missed Evelyne. Freda and Ed presumed that she was with Sir Charles and Freedom, and if Sir Charles gave it a thought at all, he believed she was in the third-class compartment.

Evelyne had caught the local steam train to the valley earlier that morning. She could not face goodbyes. She wanted the mountain, the clean air, it was as if she couldn't breathe properly, her whole body felt constricted, tight. Hugh floated in and out of her thoughts as if she was going through her life, year by year. She could not really remember who had said, 'Reach out and love him, hold him, release the pain', all she knew was that she had to go on up to the mountain one last time.

As the train wound its slow way through the valley she began to relax, as if Hugh would be waiting on the platform for her. Her head was light and she felt dizzy. She had to make herself breathe deeply, knowing that if she didn't, she would come apart. 'Hold on,' she whispered to herself, 'you are almost home.'

The movement of the train rocked Freedom gently from side to side. He was sitting opposite Sir Charles, who had begun the journey in good spirits, pointing out views to Freedom but, receiving little or no response, he had fallen silent.

Freedom stared out of the window and chewed his lip. He wondered if he should ask about Evelyne. Sir Charles had been openly irritated when he had ventured to ask after her as they boarded the train. He had told Freedom she would be with the others.

'She's on the train then, sir?'

Sir Charles crossed his immaculately tailored legs. 'Let us get something quite clear, shall we? Miss Jones was your only witness, your only alibi. You swore in open court that there was nothing between the two of you but the desire to see justice done. If you lied, you make a mockery of everyone concerned in your release, even the verdict. Without her testimony you would, most assuredly, have been hanged. If it was ever to be discovered that you both lied, then I would feel it my duty to hand you over to the police. I don't want you seeing the woman.' He stared hard at Freedom, his eyes glinting, and was met with a black, unfathomable, hooded look.

Freedom leaned forward, but Sir Charles didn't

flinch. 'All I asked was if she was on the train, I have not had time even to say thank you. I was innocent, I never cut no man's throat . . . sir.'

'Do not worry yourself over her, I shall find her work, I think we both owe her that much.'

Freedom nodded and again stared out of the window. The matter closed, Sir Charles opened his writing-case. Freedom waited, leaning back, and through half-closed eyes he studied Sir Charles, as if willing him to sleep. The pen scratched on the paper, dipped in the inkwell . . . then the case was set aside and Sir Charles' eyes slowly drooped, his head lolled on his chest.

The moment he was asleep Freedom rose like a cat, stealthily slid the door back, and went silently out into the corridor. He made his way down the train, from compartment to compartment, until he reached the third-class section, searching for Evelyne.

Ed Meadows looked up as the door slid open and Freedom bent his head to enter. 'Hello, son, how's the toffs' section, then? Sit down, sit down, soon be time to take down the picnic hamper.'

Freedom looked at the sleeping Dewhurst, then Miss Freda. He remained standing.

'Sit down, lad, you'll get a crick in the neck.'

'I was wanting to pay my respects to Miss Evelyne, sir.'

'None of your "sirs", name's Ed . . . Is she not wiv you?'

Miss Freda looked concerned. 'We thought she was with you . . . Ed, you said she was on the train, is she not with Sir Charles?'

Ed went red, rubbed his balding head. 'I went to her rooms, like, an' she'd gone. I thought she was wiv you, ain't she wiv you? Hey, where you goin'? Just a minute . . .'

Freedom strode to the rear end of the compartments, opened the door.

'She won't be back there, lad, that's the luggage . . . Freedom?'

Ed stood up, then fell backwards as the train lurched. Miss Freda caught his arm. 'Oh, Ed, Ed, I feel terrible, I should have gone to her.'

Ed released her hand, about to follow Freedom, then turned. 'You don't fink 'e'll get off, do you? He wouldn't, would 'e?'

The train gathered speed, and Ed hung on to the strap above his head. 'He couldn't, could he? Freda, what do you fink?'

Miss Freda felt wretched, but she shook her head. The train thundered into a tunnel, and Ed felt his way along the corridor in the darkness, banging against the sides. He kept telling himself the lad was just looking for Evelyne, but his heart was pounding. God, he wouldn't run away, would he?

As the train sped out of the long tunnel into the light of day, Ed sighed with relief. He could see Freedom, way up ahead of him. He called out, but the noise of the train drowned his words. He ran on, bumping into the luggage piled high on both sides of the compartment. Freedom shouted back to him, 'She's not on the train!'

He was pulling at the stiff white collar and tie, courtesy of Sir Charles. In a panic, Ed reeled from side to side of the train, grabbing at the straps. 'Now, don't go doing anything silly, son, we can contact her when the train stops.'

Freedom slid open the big loading door in the side

of the compartment, and Ed screamed at the top of his voice.

'Don't! *Don't, for God's sake*!'

Desperately, Ed ran to catch Freedom as he stood poised at the open door, but he was still just out of reach when the train lurched and Ed had to hang on again. He could see the ground flashing past, and then Freedom jumped. Ed clung on for dear life to the side of the door, the wind whipping his cheeks, his jacket billowing out. He saw Freedom land, roll away from the wheels of the train, and in seconds he was on his feet running like a wild stallion. Trailing from the door where it had caught was Freedom's tie.

'Dear God, Freda, 'e's jumped the train, what the hell are we goin' ter do?' But there was nothing they could do, and Ed slumped down into his seat. He was beside himself. 'I'll get a bollockin' for this, mark my words, 'is Lordship'll blame this on me. Gawd almighty, the bloody fool, what he go an' do a fing like that for? What are we goin' ter do? He's just thrown away the chance of a lifetime . . . Gawd almighty, that's me out of a job, us out of a place ter stay . . . Bloody hell, what a mess.'

'He will have gone to Evelyne, she'll make him see sense, you will see, Ed, he signed the contract, didn't he?'

'He's a gyppo, Freda, nobody ever knows what those buggers're thinking. We should 'ave tied 'im up, that contract don't mean nuffink to them . . . it don't mean nuffink . . . Oh, Freda, we just lost a champion, me 'eart's breakin' . . . he's gone, he's gone.'

Dewhurst slipped his bookmark into the pages of *Crime and Punishment*. 'I think I'd better go and tell

Sir Charles, he may want me to pull the communication cord.'

Near tears, Ed watched Dewhurst bounce his way down the corridor. He gripped Miss Freda's hand. 'You watch Sir Charles get the law on 'im, they'll 'ave 'im back in a cell, the bloody fool.'

From the opposite side of Aldergrove Road, Evelyne could see her house, the lines of washing billowing in the breeze. Two children sat playing on the doorstep. She turned, head bowed, to walk up the cobbled street towards the mountain. She had to pause, leaning against a wall to rest and give herself strength to continue. Looming high above her, high above the village, the mountain rose as if fighting through the thick mist of black coal dust.

Her feet echoing on the cobbles caused a few curtains to flutter, and someone whispered, 'Evelyne Jones is back'. She hurried on, passing Doris Evans' house. Lizzie-Ann was just opening her bedroom curtains, and almost called out, but she clamped her hand across her mouth. 'Oh God, please don't say she wants her house . . .'

But the hunched figure kept on walking, looking neither to right nor left.

'She's going up to the grave,' Mrs Pugh murmured as she peered from behind her back-yard wall. All around were the sounds of the village waking, preparing for the morning shift, buckets clanking, clogs clattering. The mine spewed forth its blackened men, doors opened and slammed closed as the miners set off for their day's work. Like a shadow, Evelyne quickened her pace towards the grassy slopes, as if the clean air drew her.

'Hurry, Evie, it's bath time, come on, gel, get the water on.'

The church organist began his morning practice, squeezing out 'Onward Christian Soldiers' from the old organ. Threading her way through the soot-stained tombs, she began to run. The grass, fresh with dew, glistened, the water drops holding small speckles of coal dust like black tears. Hugh Jones, Mary Jones, the stillborn baby, little Davey, all lay together in the shadow of the mountain. Will, Mike and Dicken, all gone. The grave, so tiny, so cold and grey. There was nothing for her to embrace, nothing tangible for her to hold and feel. Drained of all emotion, she stood staring at the names of her beloved family. Nothing to embrace.

High on the mountain peak the sun broke, piercing the grey like a shaft of gold. Evelyne looked up and, hardly aware of what she was doing, began to run, higher, higher. She scrambled over bracken, stumbling, falling, but pushing herself on, upwards, higher, to the clean air, to the sun.

Freedom knew she would make for home. He had no thought for himself. He hitched a ride, then, to the consternation of the driver, jumped from the moving car. He ran the five miles down to the village, along the small, winding footpath, keeping up the steady, strong pace until his lungs were bursting. He saw the village below, pushed himself on. At the far end of the valley the mountain rose.

The streets were thronging with miners. Freedom was no fool; he knew what would happen if any of them caught him. He kept to the back lanes, his jacket collar turned up, his breath catching in his throat. He reached the corner of Aldergrove Road and saw a woman with three children slam the front door. Had he got confused? Was it the wrong street? He felt a tug at his sleeve and spun around.

Lizzie-Ann hugged her worn cardigan to her and stared up into his face. Her voice was strained, hoarse, 'She's gone up the mountain, gone crazy like her Ma.' Backing away, she took a sly look over her shoulder, afraid to be seen talking to the gyppo. She was frightened of him.

'There's nothing here for her, nobody wants her back.' She couldn't meet his eyes.

Freedom gave her a small nod of thanks, but she turned on her heel and scuttled away before he could say a word.

Gladys Turtle was out of breath when she caught Lizzie-Ann at the water taps. 'They say she's back, Evie Jones, is that right?' she gasped. 'Have you seen her? And the gyppo? Well?'

'By Christ, yer a moaning Minnie, Gladys Turtle, if I hadn't two kids an' another on the way I'd be off, now bugger off and mind yer own business.' Lizzie-Ann watched as the water spurting from the tap overflowed the bucket, ran over her worn, down-at-heel shoes, and trickled away down the cobbles. She whispered a prayer. 'Don't come back, Evie, please, oh, please . . .'

Although near exhaustion, Evelyne was still climbing, but now she gasped clean air into her lungs, heaving for each breath. Not far, not far now – she was almost there.

Her hair had worked loose, tumbling around her shoulders. She unbuttoned her coat. Soon she would be on the very peak, high above the valley.

Far below, Freedom began to climb. He couldn't see her, but he had found her suitcase by the grave. Further on he found her scarf caught in a bramble bush and held it, standing poised and still, listening, shading his eyes to look up the mountain against the sun. He threw his jacket aside and moved on, his heart thudding in his chest. Alert as an animal he could sense her, knew she was not far. He climbed higher, and suddenly fear gripped him tight. He looked down – it was her coat, cast aside. For one terrible moment he thought it had been her, his *manushi*. He called for her, shouted. Her name echoed around emptily, no Evie answered back.

'Evelyne . . . Evelyne . . . *Evelyne*!'

Rounding a shelf covered in man-sized boulders, he saw her, way above him, standing like a statue, arms up, hair blowing in the clean wind. She was turning, slowly, dangerously, her head back and eyes closed. At any moment she could fall, lose her balance. She was dancing with death.

His voice was low and soft, a whisper. 'Is it a partner you're wanting, Evie?' He was terrified she would open her eyes and fall, but she smiled, head high, facing the sun. He inched towards her without a sound, closer, until he could reach out and catch her . . . he grabbed her by her long hair and pulled her to him. She turned on him like a wildcat, eyes blazing, and struck out at him, but he held her, took the blows . . . dragged her to safety, while she scratched and fought him every inch. When he had got her to a safe distance, he gripped her by the shoulders, trapping her arms at her sides . . . 'Look, look, see how close you were, woman, you could have been killed.'

She struggled, kicked out at him. 'Maybe that's what I want, get off me, you bugger, let me alone, this is my business . . . *It's my life, God damn you!*'

He didn't mean to hit her so hard, her head snapped back and her mouth started to bleed. The shock made her still, calmed her.

'You're my life too, you'll give yourself to no mountain.'

'I'll not give myself to you either, let me go!' But she didn't struggle any more, and he eased his hold until he simply held her in his arms. The wonder of the valley spread below them, as if only for them. He picked her up, gently, and carried her to a rock, sat her down.

'What was his name? Your Da's name?'

She turned her head away from him, touched her bleeding lip . . . after a moment she whispered his name, 'Hugh, Hugh . . .'

'Well, girl, call out to him, call as loud as you can, release it, release him . . .'

She shook her head, and Freedom cupped his hands to his mouth and called her Da . . . called for Hugh.

His voice came back with the name of her father, and she felt the tears inside. She threw her head back and, as if defying the mountain, she cried out for her father. 'Hugh . . . *Da! Da . . . Da . . .*'

The echo thundered, boomed, the words meeting, joining, until the sound became a roar . . .

Freedom watched her, her face like a child's as she cupped her hands to her mouth and called to the air. He let her rise, moving closer to the edge . . . *'Mary . . . Will . . . Mike . . . Daveyyyyyyyyyyyyyyyy . . .'*

She reached out to her dead, arms spread, calling to them, and when her grief broke through he was there at her side. All the tears she had not shed when she was a child, the tears for Hugh, for her family, for all of them.

She would never remember how long she had wept, only that he was there. He cradled her, rocked her like a baby and she felt safe, secure, and slowly, gradually, she was quiet.

'I can feel your heart, *manushi*,' He laid his hand over her right breast. It felt as if it was burning through her . . . then he took her hand and laid it against his own heart. He laughed, lying back in the grass.

'You laughing at me, man?'

He took her hand, kissed her fingers. 'No, *manushi*, I'm not laughing . . . see, we gyppos, when we marry we don't need no church, no service. Some of 'em have 'em, but most place hands to hearts . . . when they beat as one, well, then they're married.'

She didn't know whether he was serious or not, because he had such a strange smile on his face. But she could feel the imprint of his hand on her breast, as if her heart were on fire. She looked into his eyes, and he drew her gently to him. His kiss was so sweet, his lips hardly brushed hers, and it was Evelyne who reached for him, pulled him to her . . . the burning in her heart spread through her whole body, and she clung to him.

He reached over and slowly undid each button of her blouse. She didn't resist, but lay still until it was undone completely, and he pulled it gently away from her breasts. Her skin was white, white, her breasts had the palest pink nipples he had ever seen . . . He bent his dark head and kissed each nipple in turn, then lay his head on her breast and felt the pounding of her heart.

He whispered, '*Manushi*, my *manushi* . . .' Gently, unhurriedly, he slipped her boots off, untying each lace and easing them away from her feet, kissing her toes, light, featherweight kisses. He unhooked her skirt, and she did nothing to assist him, lying with one arm across her face, eyes closed. He lifted her in his arms and pulled the skirt from beneath her until she was naked, and then he laid her down on her skirt. She was frightened, afraid to open her eyes, to see him, see his face. He stood up and slipped out of his trousers until he too was naked, and stood looking down at her for a moment. Then he lay next to her, she could feel his heart and she waited, but he didn't touch her. Her whole body was burning, her mouth dry, her heart pounding as if it were going to burst through her breasts.

She lowered her hand from her face and let it rest at her side. She could feel his skin. Slowly turning her body to face him, looking into his eyes, she put her hand to his heart. He smiled and laid his hand on her heart.

He made love to her gently, guiding her, making sure he didn't hurt her or make her afraid, and when he was sure of her, knew by the movements of her body that she was ready, he let loose his passion. Evelyne rose with him, moved with him, and they were insatiable, their greed for each other consuming. She made love with a rage, until she was released by an explosion inside her body that in turn released her mind. It was such an exquisite emotion that she wanted it over and over again.

She slept safe in the crook of his arm. He studied her face. She sat at peace now, and she was his. He would never let her go, she was his *manushi*, his wife.

She was shy at first when she woke, covering her naked breasts with her hands. He made her take her hands away, telling her she was more beautiful than any wild-flower they could see. To assure her of this, he gathered wild cornflowers till his arms were filled with them and laid them over her body.

'Oh, these were my Ma and Da's favourite.'

There was no pain when she said their names. Her grief had gone as her loved ones had been embraced and kissed goodbye. Then together they laid cornflowers on the grave.

'Now, gel, which way would you say London was?'

'London?'

'Aye, I'm to be a champion boxer, I signed a contract. Sir Charles said he'd give thee work . . . Come, give us yer hand, gel.'

Freedom had made a crown of cornflowers. She laughed when he set it gently on her head. Then arm in arm they walked down from the mountain, away from the grave. Evelyne's gentle, delighted laugh echoed back to them, like the soft whisper of Mary Jones . . .

'Leave the valley, Evie, promise me . . .'

BOOK THREE

CHAPTER 17

S IR CHARLES Wheeler's estate was twenty miles from Salisbury. After passing through Andover, the route then wound through mile upon mile of country lanes. Eventually, small, white, hand-painted wooden signposts directed the traveller towards 'The Grange' and along lanes only wide enough for a single vehicle, so that it seemed as though The Grange might be only one of the numerous farms buried among the fields and woods.

The arched stone entrance, with gates twenty feet high, set in six-foot stone walls, gave no indication of what lay beyond. The driveway was of gravel, raked smooth, and showed no tracks, but the hedgerows and the profusion of rhododendron bushes with their bright pink and purple blooms gave a hint of what lay beyond. The bushes gave way to a stretch of oak trees half a mile wide, their thick trunks and massive branches joining in an arch, and still the driveway continued.

After a further mile through the magical bower, The Grange itself was still not in sight until, rounding a curve, there it was, standing in such splendour it took the breath away. Hundreds of rose bushes covered immaculate sloping lawns which bordered the horse-shoe drive. A vast fountain sprayed fans of water twenty feet from the open mouths of marble dolphins. Glittering mermaids rode on the creatures' backs, hands outstretched to welcome visitors. But dominating it all was The Grange, a majestic, overpoweringly beautiful house. Six white pillars flanked the fifteen marble steps to the arched entrance. Three storey high, built in white sandstone, the house was awe-inspiring in its size and architectural proportions.

On each side were more lawns and gardens, with lily ponds and statues. Paths led to the outhouses, stables, barns and, hidden behind a bank of trees, a farm with sprawling, well-kept fields. Behind were more gardens, a man-made lake, and mile upon mile of forest and sloping hills. The Grange dominated the thousand acres surrounding it with such power that any onlooker bowed to its presence.

Also behind The Grange were staff quarters for those who worked the land. In comparison with the house, their cottages were like rows of dolls' houses. The stables were more splendid, with vast paddocks containing a herd of the finest hunters, groomed by a score of stable boys. The ground staff numbered thirty-five; gardeners, gamekeepers, huntsmen. In addition, there were more than twenty full-time staff employed to run the house. Cooks, butlers, footmen, pantry-maids, valets; all quartered on the very top floor of The Grange ... the personal estate of Sir Charles Wheeler.

Rawnie blew a circle of smoke from her hand-rolled cigarette. It drifted and curled above her head in a blue haze. She closed her eyes. She stood high on the brow of a hill overlooking The Grange. Next to her stood Jesse, chewing a long piece of grass, as handsome as ever. He shaded his eyes to look down into the paddocks below.

'Do ye see him?'

'Aye, it's him, cross the paddocks, running like a hare . . . Mun runs for 'em like one of their *grys* . . . look at 'im.'

Way below her Rawnie watched the running figure of Freedom. Behind him was a motorcar, and they could see a boy standing on the running board, shouting and waving his arms at Freedom.

With one eye on his stopwatch and the other on the road, Ed Meadows swerved the car, almost knocking the boy off the running board. He put his foot down on the accelerator, and closed the gap between the car and Freedom. 'Tell 'im to ease off, that's enough for today.'

The boy shouted, but Freedom continued to run. If anything, he picked up speed.

'Jesus God, 'e'll run 'imself ter death.'

Ed tooted the horn and drove alongside Freedom. 'Hey, hey, that's it, Freedom . . . come on, lad, ease yerself down.'

Freedom turned his head towards Ed, but ran on. He had a look on his face that Ed had become accustomed to, a strange, defiant stare. Eventually Ed drove in front of Freedom and turned the car across the lane, got out and shouted at him in a fury, hands on hips. 'When I say you've 'ad enough I mean it. You've run more'n fifteen miles and we got to go an' work out, you tryin' ter kill yerself?'

Breath hissing, lungs heaving, Freedom faced him. His long hair was dripping, and his old, rough shirt was sodden with sweat. He laid his hands on the motor, and

Ed quickly wrapped a towel around his shoulders and began rubbing him down. Freedom shrugged him away, flicked the towel out of his grasp, and stepped aside to wipe his own sweating body. 'Months I been here, mun, every day, runnin', sparrin', liftin' the weights, trainin' . . . and for what, when do I fight, mun?'

Ed's look told the young lad to move off. The boy was one of the sparring partners they had brought from London and he was standing staring at Freedom, hero-worship written all over his face.

Ed moved closer to Freedom. 'You don't talk ter me that way. You want a fight, I want a fight, but we do what 'is Lordship tells us to do, we wait. *I* tell *you* when we're ready for a bout, not you, *I'm* the bloody trainer.'

His breathing eased, Freedom tossed the towel to the boy and shrugged. His voice was quiet, his fist clenched.

'I'm ready, you know it. I been fighting years before I was brought here, I'm in the gym day in day out, an' for what? To entertain 'is Lordship's toffs when they come ta visit? I hate him always watchin' me, is that all I'm here fer? I want a fight.'

Ed knew all that Freedom was saying was right, but he could do nothing. He moved to Freedom and began to rub his shoulders, calming him as if he were an animal. 'I know, I know, lad . . . maybe we'll take it easy for a few days, huh? Maybe I pushed you too hard.'

Freedom laughed, rubbed Ed's balding head. 'I want a fight, Ed, that's all.'

As they were about to climb into the car there was the sound of an owl hooting. Neither the young boy nor Ed paid any attention, but Freedom turned, suddenly alert. Then came a whistle, soft but shrill, and Freedom shaded his eyes to look up into the woods. He cupped his hands and whistled, and again came the high-pitched, single note, like a bird.

'Gawd 'elp us, get in the car, what yer doin' now? Birdwatchin'? Come on, lad, let's have breakfast, I'm starvin' after all this exercise.'

Freedom jumped on to the running board of the car as Ed drove back to The Grange. He looked up to the woods and smiled, gave a small wave like a salute. Jesse and Rawnie knew he was aware that they were waiting, he had answered their call.

Evelyne had been up since six-thirty, eaten her breakfast in the kitchens and then begun her work in the library. Sir Charles had given her the job of repairing and cataloguing the vast collection of books. Since her arrival at The Grange, Evelyne had seen him only once, when he implied that he would employ her on condition that she have no contact with Freedom. Quietly and icily, he had told her he was prepared to make Freedom a champion, but if he discovered there was anything more in Freedom's run from the train than the desire to thank her for her part in his acquittal, he would have no option but to destroy Freedom's contract. He did not want any scandal, any repercussions or publicity in relation to the murder charges Freedom faced in Cardiff.

'He ran once, let him try it again and I will wash my hands of him, is that clear?'

Evelyne understood the veiled threat and assured Sir Charles that she would work in the house as instructed, nothing more.

She was given a small room in the servants' quarters at the top of the house. She spent her days in the musty library, ate her meals with the servants. The housekeeper, Miss Balfour, was loathed by all of them. She ran The Grange like a military camp and God help anyone who did not knuckle under her regime. Due to the nature of Evelyne's work, she was immediately set apart.

'I have always interviewed the staff in the past, Miss Jones . . . However, as Sir Charles has already instructed you in your duties, make sure you carry them out to the letter.'

The housemaids' and parlourmaids' gossip bored Evelyne, and the rules and regulations they all abided by frustrated her. The house revolved around the periods when Sir Charles was in residence, his weekend house parties. Evelyne had no chance to see any of his high-society guests. All servants, unless they were actually in attendance, were told to stay out of sight. Evelyne felt trapped. Even to enjoy the beauty of their surroundings was forbidden; they were not allowed to use the grounds or walk among the rose gardens. The gulf betweeen 'them' and 'us' was brought home to Evelyne daily.

Her frustration mounted until she felt she would explode. This was not what she wanted, to be a servant. At least in the valley she had felt free, but here she was bound by such strict rules that even to be in the main hall was a sin. But her secret meetings with Freedom would have been judged a greater sin, were they discovered.

Freedom had also had the lecture from Sir Charles, but with a difference. Sir Charles had implied that Evelyne would be dismissed if he should hear so much as a whisper of an association between them.

Freda, now Mrs Ed Meadows, had tried to talk to Ed, tried to tell him that keeping the couple apart was asking for trouble. In his heart Ed knew she was right, but it was not only the cottage and his job that were at stake, there was the future champion's career. 'You got ter do what 'is Lordship wants, Freda love, there's no way round it.'

'Ed, this is our home, Sir Charles won't even know if they come and have a little supper with us now and then, just once a week, on her afternoon off . . .'

Ed huffed and puffed, but the suppers had become a regular weekly occurrence, and it was during these evenings that Evelyne had begun to teach Freedom to read and write.

They had been at The Grange almost four months, and tension lay close to the surface. Freda could feel it and it worried her. She hoped the four of them would discuss it today, it was Evelyne's half-day off. Freda always cooked a roast on these occasions, and she had already begun laying the table. Ed paced up and down, unable to relax enough to put his carpet slippers on.

'You know he's ready ter fight, and we ain't had a word from Sir Charles. He's gettin' hard ter handle, Freda, he knows 'e's ready an' all. I just don't know what else I can do . . .'

Evelyne arrived and tossed her coat aside. She sighed, and slumped into the fireside chair.

'I've had enough of that Miss Balfour. The library's nearly finished and she snoops after me, checking that I've done this or that. Well, she'll not get me lugging buckets of coal up and down them stairs like the maids. She caught me in the drawing room, I was just looking at the paintings and she tells me I have no right to be in there. "I'm just looking at the paintings, Miss Balfour," I tell her. "You've no right to look," she says. Can you believe it, Freda? I said to her, "You don't mind if I look out of my window and see the woods, the country-side, he don't own *them*, does he?" '

Ed sighed, looking very glum. 'They do, love, they do, far as the eye can see – all his Lordship's land, he owns the lot.'

Evelyne turned to Ed with a furious look. 'Well, he doesn't own *me*!'

'As long as you are in his employ, he does.'

Evelyne paced the tiny cottage while Freda finished setting the table. Ed flicked the curtains aside, wondering where Freedom was and hoping no one would see him coming to the cottage.

'He's late, he's in a terrible mood, an' all, can't you talk to 'im, Evie? Settle 'im down, you know he's taken to sleeping outside, made hisself some kind of tent? The lads don't know what to make of him . . . where the hell is he? You got the time, Freda?'

Freda pointed to the clock, then checked to see how the chicken was cooking. Unlike everyone else, Freda was happy as a lark. The cottage, with its new curtains and loose covers, delighted her. 'Oh, he'll be here, he won't miss seeing his Evie.'

Ed sighed. That was another thing, if Sir Charles found out about those two, there would be real trouble. He was up and down, jumpy as a ferret, worried someone would find out about these weekly meetings.

Evelyne took out Freedom's exercise books, thumbed through the pages of looped, childish writing. 'He won't try half the time, you know. He should be able to read and write by now, but he won't concentrate for more than a minute . . .'

Freda tittered, waved her wooden spoon. 'His attention is too much on you, that's why, darlink.'

Ed flicked the curtains again, muttered, and sat down opposite Evelyne.

She was shaking her head, still turning the pages. 'Funny thing, he's completely ambidextrous, and he's no fool, got a wit about him, has me laughing . . .'

'What? What you say 'e's got? Ambi what? Ill, you fink 'e's ill?'

With a giggle, Evelyne explained to Ed that she meant he could write with either hand, right or left.

'Gawd 'elp me, I been assumin' he was a southpaw, but . . . Hey, wait 'til I get him in action termorrow, *ambidixious*, that what you call it? Well, I never . . . look, Freda love, I'll just go an' see what 'e's doin', all right, ducks?'

Freda raised her eyes to heaven. 'Well, at least that cheered him up . . . Evie?'

Evelyne was staring into the fire, Freedom's book still on her knee. Freda sat on the arm of her chair and hugged her.

'What is it, darlink, you want to tell me?'

Evelyne kissed Freda's hand. 'I'm thinking of leaving, Freda, I feel as if I'm being buried alive. There's a whole world out there, and I want . . . I want . . .'

'What, Evie? What do you think is so special out there?'

Confused, frustrated, Evelyne bit her lip. 'I won't know unless I try, but I want to teach, you know? And maybe I could get work that would fulfil me. Here, I'm just stifled.'

'What about Freedom?'

Tears pricked Evelyne's eyes, and she shook her head. 'There's no future for us, you must know that, and if Sir Charles knew we even saw each other . . . well, I don't have to tell you what would happen.'

Freda kept quiet, knowing Evie had to talk, get it out of her system.

'We meet on Sundays, oh, far away from this place,

up in the woods. We walk, and he's like a child. There's a wild deer, and he calls to it and it comes over, nuzzles him and takes food from his hand. He knows the name of every flower, every creature, and sometimes it's magic with him. He's so gentle, caring, and those times I love him . . . He's like no other man I've ever known, and yet, he won't educate himself, he won't better himself . . . I *have* to go away, Freda.'

Freda bent and kissed the top of Evelyne's head as Ed burst into the cottage. 'He's gone, no sign of 'im no place, the lads said they saw 'im crossin' the field at six, an' 'e had a bundle under 'is arm. He's run off . . . you better go back to the house, Evie, I'm going ter 'ave ter get a search party out.'

'Oh, Ed, don't be stupid, he will be back! He will just have gone walking, you know the way he is – he knows it's Evie's supper with us.'

'There's a gypsy camp in the field behind the woods, I got to get to 'im first. If the estate manager finds out, they'll get the law on to 'em. If they're poachin', there'll be all hell let loose.'

Evelyne's hands clenched in anger. 'Ed, he came here of his own free will, he'll not run out on you . . . for God's sake don't tell the game wardens, I'll go and find him.'

Ed gripped her by the shoulders, tight. 'You'll do no such thing, 'is Lordship's back, arrived half an hour ago wiv a whole party of society people, I don't want you gettin' involved. My job's on the line as it is, havin' you meetin' him here.'

It was Freda's turn to confront Ed. 'Ed, listen to her, she knows him better than anyone, he'll be back, you know he will.'

'*Will he*? Well, you go an' tell that bitch, Miss Balfour. He took a bundle under his arm all right, two hams, a chicken and a turkey what they was preparin' fer Sir Charles' bleedin' house guests. It ain't me settin' the gamekeepers on 'im, but Miss bloody Balfour.'

Evelyne grabbed her coat and was halfway to the door.

'Evie, darlin', I'm sorry, don't get me wrong, I trust him, Gawd 'elp me, I love the lad, but . . . I been worried sick these last few weeks. I knew somethin' was brewin', I didn't mean to sound off at you, you an' him are welcome here any time.'

Evelyne gave him a small smile, then hurried back to The Grange. From her tiny window high in the roof she could see the flare of torches as the gamekeepers prepared to search the woods. She was saddened by Freedom's foolishness, but at the same time it cemented her decision. She would have to leave.

The camp-fire was lit, piled high with logs stolen from The Grange's wood-house. There were only four wagons, belonging to travellers on their way back from the Ascot races. Sitting in a semicircle around the fire, they ate the food Freedom had brought. There was beer and Jesse had two bottles of whisky. They were all in good humour, and one of the men took out his fiddle and began to play. Strung up on one of the wagons were rabbits, poached from the estate.

Jesse was wearing a new, dark pin-striped suit, and he was proud of it, flaunting his waistcoat, amusing them all as he clicked his heels and danced to the fiddle. There were gold rings on his fingers, and his heavy earring was of gold. He clapped his hands, and his whiter-than-white teeth gleamed in the firelight. 'Will you *rokka* Romany, Freedom? Eh, ehe heyup yup?'

Freedom had been downing beer and whisky and

now he lolled against the side of a wagon. He shook his head and waved for Jesse to continue. Jesse was making them all laugh at the fine man Freedom had turned into, living like a prince and being made to run each day to beat the motor vehicle . . .

Rawnie slipped to Freedom's side. She still wore her brightly coloured skirts, her bangles and beads. Her thick, coal-black hair was braided and threaded with gold. The kohl around her eyes made them seem huge, like the tame deer that fed from Freedom's hand. But she was thin, even gaunt, and she coughed constantly. 'Are thee well, mun?'

Freedom smiled up at her and nodded, held out his hand for her to come and sit with him. She looked back at the arrogant, dancing Jesse. She wouldn't come close.

'Does he care for thee?'

She drew on the ever-present hand-rolled cigarette, releasing a cloud of smoke that all but obscured her face as she spoke in her low, husky voice. 'He does . . . are thee with the paleface woman?'

Freedom smiled, tilting his head. 'Ay, she's my *manushi*.'

A small boy with dark, flashing eyes and thick, black curly hair appeared behind Rawnie's skirts. Freedom leaned forward and the child peeked around Rawnie and gave him a cheeky grin.

'He be called Johnny . . . Johnny Mask, he's a right bugger, we call him mask because you can belt the livin' daylights out of him an' he don't ever care none.'

Freedom looked up at her as she touched the young boy's head, gently. Then Johnny ran back to Jesse, clicked his heels, and the pair danced together.

'He be Jesse's boy, a pure *Tatchey*, then there are two more *doshas*, see them, on the *vargo* steps.'

Freedom looked over at the two little girls, hand in

408

hand, watching the dancing. He stood up, watched Rawnie's sad eyes. They were not her own, she did not even have to tell him . . . he held out his arms, wanting to hold her. She tossed her cigarette aside, stepping back so he could not touch her. 'We're moving to the races, north, we'll join the clans. Jesse is leader now, but we need a strong-armed man, the fights are where the money is . . . livin' like a king, maybe ye don't need it.'

Her voice had become mocking. She rolled another cigarette, and as she lit it the flame illuminated her face, her haunted eyes. 'Will thee travel with us, Freedom? See, there's Chalida with no man beside her, she's Romanchilde.'

Chalida, sitting with the two *doshas*, was a beautiful girl with her hair unbraided to show she was unmarried. She looked up, and Freedom gave her a small bow, then turned to Rawnie and shook his head. Before he could say a word, two gypsies ran to the fire and began stamping out the flames. They shouted and pointed into the darkness, and everyone began to run this way and that.

Four gamekeepers with blazing torches were moving towards the camp through the woods. They carried shotguns, and their tracker dogs strained at their leashes. Jesse began shouting instructions. Pans and bottles and equipment were swiftly packed, and the horses were dragged from their roped pen to harness to the wagons. The poached rabbits and pheasants were quickly hidden.

The children screamed in terror as the gamekeepers crashed into the camp and released their dogs. For a moment Freedom was frozen, he couldn't believe what was happening. One of the little *doshas* was hunched by a wagon, shrieking with fear as a dog snarled and

409

snapped at her. In seconds Freedom was on his feet and at her side. He kicked the dog away and grabbed the child, lifted her into the wagon. 'Call your men off, you bastards, call the dogs back . . .'

Jesse was already fighting with one of the game-keepers. Freedom ran to a man he recognized, grabbed him by his lapels. 'You call your men off or so help me God I'll have your throat wrung, hear me . . . look at me, mun, you know me.'

Little Johnny Mask was beating back one of the dogs with a stick. Jesse had wrested a shotgun from the hands of one of the gamekeepers, and had turned it on the man Freedom held. 'No . . . Jesse, no!'

He held the gun poised, finger on the trigger. Rawnie ran to his side and placed her hand over the barrel. 'Freedom, get them out of the camp, tell them we'll move out, we mean no harm . . .'

The gamekeepers, terrified, did not need to be asked twice. They backed off, calling their dogs to their sides. Freedom held the shotgun, keeping the men back, but he stood with them, not his own people.

It took only a short while before the wagons were ready. Jesse walked up to Freedom, carrying his son in his arms. 'Come with us, brother, leave with us.'

Past antagonisms forgotten, Freedom held Jesse close, and they kissed each other on both cheeks. From his pocket Jesse took a gold coin, pressed it into Free-dom's hand. '*Kushti rardi*, brother.'

The wagons moved out, and the gamekeepers made their way back down the hill to The Grange. The men were silent, their dogs under control. Freedom walked slightly ahead of them, his thoughts with his people. As they came out of the wood he saw below him, glistening like a mirage, The Grange, lit by a multitude of chandeliers. His anger rose up and he stiffened. They had treated his people no better than dogs.

'Come on, move on, bloody gyppo, get on back . . .'

In an instant Freedom swung around and knocked the man out, took his shotgun and broke it into pieces. Then he took off so fast none of them had a hope of keeping up with him . . . the night enveloped him, and he could no longer be seen or heard.

The gamekeepers ran into the courtyard and reported to the chief warden. 'Bastard took off after his people, bloody gyppo should never have been brought here in the first place.'

Evelyne could hear them and their dogs clearly. Watching from her little window, she saw the police wagon arrive, and she turned back to her cot bed. So Ed had been right, he had run. She was feeling queasy, and she reached for her dressing-gown, slipped quietly along the corridor to the bathroom she shared with the other servants. Fighting her dizziness, she was violently sick. More than ever she felt she must leave The Grange.

As she returned to her room, she found two housemaids whispering together near her bedroom door. One of them turned to Evelyne.

'Oh, Evie, they say the gyppo fighter's run off, half-killed the gamekeepers, tried to strangle one, and him what was almost hung afore . . . *and* he stole the dinner cook was preparing for Sir Charles, what a to-do.'

Miss Balfour appeared, wearing a hairnet, tight-lipped, her skin wrinkled like a prune. 'Back to bed, all of you, now. This has nothing to do with you, back to bed this instant.'

The two maids shot into their rooms like rabbits

bolting into their holes. Miss Balfour stared at Evelyne with such overt disgust on her face that Evelyne barred her way.

'If you have something to say to me, Miss Balfour, then say it to my face.'

Miss Balfour shrank back and scurried to her room, locking the door behind her. Evelyne entered her own bedroom and gasped. Freedom lay on her bed, smiling, his feet up on the iron bedrail. She closed the door fast. 'What are you doing here? Do you not know everyone's out searching for you, and now the police are called in – are you mad, man?'

Miss Balfour could have sworn she heard a man's voice. She slipped out of her room and crept along the corridor, listened at Evelyne's door. Afraid to confront them both, she tightened the cord of her dressing gown and hurried down the back stairs.

Freedom cocked his head to one side and placed his finger across his lips to remind Evelyne to speak softly.

'Will you come with me, you don't belong here, and they keep us like prisoners . . . Come away with me? Is this the way you want to live your life? To be paid each month so they own you? So they can tell you when to eat and when to sleep?'

He began to undo his shirt, as if the sounds of the baying dogs below and the whistling of the searching policemen had nothing to do with him.

She whispered back, frantically, 'You're drunk, I can smell it, and you go back down right now. They think you've run, and poor Ed will get into terrible trouble.'

He threw his shirt aside and began to unbutton his trousers.

'Are you mad, man? What are you thinking of, here, in the house?'

His face changed, his eyes were so black they frightened her, 'They don't own me, they got a piece of paper says they do, but I'm no animal to be bought. No man sets his dogs on me.'

'You forget yourself, Freedom Stubbs. If it weren't for Sir Charles you'd be at the end of a hangman's rope and you well know it.'

'It's you that saved me, you, *manushi*, now come here.'

She backed away from him, pressed herself against the wall. 'I'm not your *manushi*, I am not your wife. You don't belong to them? Well, I don't belong to you. Now get out of here, go on, get out!'

His fist curled in rage, but she stood up to him, unafraid now.

She slapped his fist. 'That's all you know, isn't it – the fight? You don't want to better yourself – well, run back to your people, go on, run back, but don't expect me to be with you in some wretched wagon, chased off the land, run out of every town.'

In a fury he pulled her to him, but she slapped his face. He took it, smiled down at her, and she stepped back and slapped him again.

'Oh, *manushi*, is that all yer know, the fight? But my, my, you're *rinkeney* when you're angry . . . now come to me before you give me a *tatto yeck* . . . see, I got something for you.' He handed her the gold coin Jesse had pressed into his hand . . . she threw it across the room. He cocked his head to the side, then picked up his shirt and began to dress.

Suddenly she clung to his back . . . he turned in her

413

arms and cupped her face in his hands. 'Eh, woman, you twist me so, ye don't know what thee wants, listen to your heart, *manushi*, listen.'

He kissed her, slipping her nightdress off, carried her to the bed and laid her down. He snuggled his head close to her and whispered, 'They'll have a long night ahead searching for me.'

'No they won't, you're going back, go and give yourself up to them before you cause any more trouble.'

'Is that what you want?'

Miss Balfour rapped on Evelyne's door.

'Open this door this instant, I know you've got a man in there, come along, I've got Mr Plath with me, open up.'

In a panic, Evelyne reached for her nightdress while Freedom pulled on his shirt and hopped around trying to get into his trousers. Miss Balfour threw the door open. She was carrying a policeman's truncheon, and was followed close behind by Mr Plath, the estate manager. They just caught Freedom slipping out of the window. Mr Plath made the mistake of grabbing Freedom's leg, and got a nasty kick in the groin. He rolled in agony on the floor while Miss Balfour screamed, 'Help, help . . . someone help!'

Sir Charles made a hurried exit from the house to talk to the police, who were there about the poachers. He had been playing an after-dinner game of rummy, and he was still clutching his cards. His house guests gathered at the windows.

Poor Ed was beside himself, he knew it had all got out of hand. The gamekeepers were embroidering their

414

stories about the gypsy campers every time they retold it. They had been set upon, fired upon, punched and threatened with knives. 'Freedom, was 'e wiv 'em? Will someone tell me, was 'e wiv 'em?'

'Was 'e wiv 'em? Look at me throat, the bugger nearly throttled me.'

Sir Charles crossed the courtyard to speak to Ed, his cards still in his hand. 'I want him found, Ed, brought back, in handcuffs if need be. This is outrageous, do you have any idea of how much time and effort I have been putting in, trying to arrange a bout for him in London? So help me God, he can go back to jail, what on earth possessed him to . . .'

A screech from a gamekeeper interrupted him. 'Sir, oh, sir, there's a man on the roof, look, there he is!'

All eyes were raised to the roof of The Grange, and there he was dancing, singing at the top of his voice,

> *Oh, can you rokka Romany,*
> *can you play the bosh,*
> *Can you jal adrey the staripen,*
> *can you chin the cosh . . .*

Balancing, holding his arms out as if he were walking a tightrope, Freedom teetered on the roof's edge. The crowd grew silent.

'The man must be mad, or drunk, or both.'

Miss Balfour ran to join the crowd. Behind her, Mr Plath came limping, clutching his injured parts.

'This is her doing, sir, he was with her.'

Sir Charles turned to Ed. His voice was steely, and Ed's heart sank. 'When the fool comes down, give him to the law.'

'But, sir, he's done nuffink wrong, he's just 'ad a few too many.'

415

Sir Charles' face twitched, he was so furious. 'Don't play games with me, Meadows, I know exactly where he's been. His friends, so called, have been poaching on my land. He almost killed Fred Hutchins over there. Be in my study first thing in the morning, is that clear? And get all these people away, there has been enough disturbance for one night.'

As Sir Charles strode from the courtyard, there was a gasp from the onlookers. He looked up to see Freedom swinging down from ledge to ledge like a monkey. The police moved in to corner him, and he dodged and ducked as they chased him, then they surrounded him. As they dragged him away, he looked back and Sir Charles flushed as he gave him a dazzling smile.

Ed went into the barn. They had tied Freedom's hands to one of the posts. His shirt was torn, his face filthy.

'Why did you do it, lad, there's two coppers out back with black eyes, and to kick Mr Plath of all people, in the balls. He's the estate manager . . . I dunno, I don't, why in God's name did you do it? Why did you run?'

Freedom sighed, shook his head. 'If I'd wanted away, Ed, I'd not have been dancing on the roof, now would I? You tell me why they trussed me up like a chicken?'

'Sir Charles says he's through with you, you could even get sent to jail. Poachin's against the law, never mind what you done to the estate manager.'

With one movement Freedom wrenched the ropes away from the post, shaking the whole barn. He turned on Ed, and Ed backed away, terrified by the anger in those black eyes.

'You tell His Lordship I want to fight; I don't want to

be kept here like one of his stallions. They're groomed, and brushed, but spend more time than they should in their stalls. You tell him I could have killed his game-keepers, each one of 'em, and Mr Plath's lucky 'e still got anythin' between his legs.'

He swung a punch at the punchbag, splitting it in two. 'They set their dogs on children, that were wrong.'

Then he walked out, calm as ever. All Ed could think of was that punch, he had never seen one like it . . .

The following morning Ed went cap in hand to Sir Charles, beseeched him to listen before he launched into the speech he had obviously prepared.

'Last night I saw a punch, Sir, that would floor any champion in England. I saw it with me own eyes. He's wild, but he's trained every day, not put a foot out of line. Don't send 'im away, sir, find him a fight! 'E's yer champion, I swear it.'

Sir Charles listened, tapping his fingers on his mahogany desk. 'Ed, I'm a sportsman, you know that, I believe in him just as much as you, but I cannot have any scandal. Unless you control him, then I am afraid, champion or no, he'll have to go . . . if these riff-raff follow him around, then . . .'

'Your gamekeepers should not 'ave set the dogs on to the children, gyppos or not, sir.'

Sir Charles rose from his seat and stared out of the window, his back to Ed. 'How's your wife? Settled in, has she?'

'You bastard,' thought Ed. He knew exactly what Sir Charles was implying; his livelihood depended on Freedom. He and Freda didn't own their cottage, they owned nothing.

'I'd like to see how he's been doing, set up a bout in

417

the barn, would you? Then we'll discuss it later . . .
that's all for now.'

Evelyne sat on the edge of the leather chair. Sir Charles'
study smelt of polish and cigars. She watched him
carefully cut the end of his Havana with a gold clipper.

'I will, of course, give you references, but you must
understand, under the circumstances your presence here
is . . .'

Evelyne interrupted him. 'I have packed, sir, and Mr
Plath has given me my wages. You see, I had already
made up my mind to leave.'

Sir Charles studied her for a moment. Her composure
unnerved him slightly. Sitting ramrod straight, her chin
up, her green eyes never leaving his face, she was not
apologetic in any way. Suddenly he leaned forward, and
she could see a muscle twitch at the side of his jaw, 'Stay
away from him, I shall clear everything with the police
and my gamekeepers, he'll get every chance I can give
him, but stay away from him.'

Evelyne stood, her mouth trembling slightly, but she
held on to her emotions. Without shaking his outstretched hand she opened the oak-panelled door. She
didn't look back, just closed the door silently behind
her.

Freda was polishing her brass fender when a housemaid
tapped on her door. She handed Freda a letter. 'She said
be sure you get it, I got to rush now, I'm behind with
me work . . . you done this place up ever so nice, Mrs
Meadows.'

Freda didn't hear the girl leave, she was turning the

letter over in her hands. It was Evie's writing, she'd know it anywhere, with its fancy loops and curls.

Ed had warned Sir Charles to stand well back from the ring. The sweat from the boys might spray on to his grey suit.

Freedom was in high spirits, despite a slight hangover. The evening's drama appeared to have had little or no effect on him. He was unaware of how Sir Charles had settled everything, unaware how close he had been to losing his chance as a professional boxer.

Taking each boy in turn, even though he was only sparring, he gave such a good performance that Sir Charles gave Ed a wink, gestured for him to go to his side. Ed called out for the boxers to take a break, and he and Sir Charles waited for Freedom to join them.

Sir Charles leant on his silver-topped cane. 'Appears you don't think I've been pulling my weight? Not arranging a bout soon enough for you? Well, it's not as easy as that, old chap. You're unknown, a pit boxer, and they are, as you must be aware, two a penny. To gain a good rating in the game, why, you would more than likely have to take on twenty bouts before you could get any legitimate recognition.'

Freedom rolled his towel into a ball and chucked it aside. Sir Charles could smell him, like an animal, his sweating body was so close . . . he stepped back, just a fraction. 'I have been masterminding a plan for you to hit the main circuits in one swoop. I have arranged for you to be the sparring partner for the present Irish Heavyweight Champion. He will be arriving in England shortly for an attempt at the British title.'

Freedom was about to let rip, Ed could see it, so he

419

put out a restraining hand. Sir Charles continued, uninterrupted.

'They will have all the sports writers there to see this Irish champion working out. And, Freedom, it will be up to you to show what you are worth – particularly when the press are in abundance – be your showcase, so to speak.'

'Sparring partner? But I been workin' for a professional bout, that's what Ed – what *you* promised me from the word go, sparrin' ain't no professional bout.'

Sir Charles checked his gold fob watch and pocketed it before he spoke, making Freedom wait, hanging on his every word. Then he smiled, such a rare occurrence with Sir Charles that it was rather off-putting. His voice was almost sexual in its softness, its humour. 'Ahhh, but what happens, old fella, if the sparring chappie knocks out the contender – leave a bit of a gap for the main event, wouldn't you say?'

Ed gave Freedom a warning look to keep his mouth shut. 'He'll beat that Irish git wivout a doubt, if you'll excuse the language, sir.'

Sir Charles strode to the barn doors, swinging his cane. 'Let us hope he can. Ed, we leave for London first thing in the morning . . . jolly good bout, lads, well done.'

It was a few moments before it dawned, then Freedom gave Ed such a hug it winded him and he had to sit down on a bench to get his breath back.

Freda could hear Ed singing, 'Oh, we got no bananas, we got no bananas today . . . tarrah!'

He opened the cottage door and threw his cloth cap in the air, then swung Freda round, wanting to dance, but she pushed him away. Behind him, Freedom bounded in, forgetting to stop so that he cracked his head on the top of the door, but he didn't care, he was in such high spirits. 'Get Evie for us, Freda, we got some news – we're off to London and we got a fight.'

It was Freedom's turn to twirl Freda round on her dumpy little legs. 'I got her this, picked it on the way over. She was in a fair temper with me last night, so put it between the sheets . . . her book's sheets, Freda, no need to look so shocked!'

Freedom laughed and tossed the cornflower in the air, then tucked it into Freda's hand. She turned helpless eyes to Ed, but he was beaming from ear to ear. There on the table lay Evie's letter. Freda held it out to Freedom, then let her hand drop. She had forgotten Freedom couldn't read well enough yet. 'Evie's gone, Freedom, she left this morning . . . Here, she wrote to us all. She says she couldn't come and say goodbye as . . . well, I don't have to tell you, we'd all be crying. She wants to make her own way, better herself . . .' Freda couldn't go on, her face crumpled like a child's and she sobbed.

Freedom went to her, held her gently in his arms and whispered to her, 'It's all right, it's all right.'

Releasing her, he walked to the door like a man bereft. Ed tried to stop him leaving. 'Now, don't do nuffink you'll regret, son, we go to London and . . .'

Like Freda, he couldn't continue. Freedom gave Ed a heartbreaking look, then a strange, soft half-smile. He seemed so calm, his voice so soft and gentle.

'We have a saying, if you love something, set it free, if it comes back to you it is yours, if it doesn't, it never was . . .'

Freda opened her hand, and there was the cornflower. Freedom held her hand gently, then tucked the flower behind her ear. He smiled. 'Evie's favourite flower.'

Freda had never seen such open despair in a man's eyes, she wanted to wrap her arms around him and comfort him. She watched helplessly as he walked away.

'I'll go to him, go with him.'

'No, Ed, leave him, leave him a while.'

From the cottage window they watched him walk, straight-backed, across the courtyard. There was no spring in his step now, no high-stepping Romany saunter. As he reached the open fields he looked up and let out a single howl, like an animal caught in a trap. The cry chilled them both, the rooks screeched and flew from the trees like a black cloud, and then Freedom began to run, and run, until he was no more than a black spot on the horizon, as small as the birds he had disturbed.

CHAPTER 18

E D BECAME more expansive as the train pulled in
to Victoria Station in London. He was getting
back to his home territory, and he couldn't wait
to get Freedom ready to meet the Irish champion.

From Victoria Station, Ed and Freedom took a taxi
to Lambert's Gym in Bell Street, a run-down area of
Soho. The city throbbed, noisy, crowded and dirty, and
Freedom loathed it, was disgusted by it, but Ed was in
his element, 'Oh, it's good to be back, you'll love it
'ere, Freedom, come on, down yer go, gym's in the
basement.'

The gym was alive with the thudding sounds from punchbags and ten boxers working out. The walls were covered
with photographs and posters of famous boxers and
bouts. Freedom looked around, feeling out of place in
his suit and shirt. The boxers gave him only a cursory
glance and carried on with what they were doing. Ed
seemed to know everyone, waving across the gym,
thumping a young boy on the shoulder. ''Ello, son, how
ya doin'? 'Arry me boy, nice to see you, long time . . .
Jimbo, you still at it, thought you retired . . .'

Ed passed through, beckoning Freedom to follow

him, and they crossed the floor of the gym, skirted the ring in the centre and made their way to the small offices at the far end. Ed banged on the door and opened it, again gesturing for Freedom to follow.

'Jack, I just got in, any chance of a word in your shell-like? Want you to meet me new lad.'

An ex-boxer himself, with cauliflower ears and a flattened splodge of a nose, Jack Lambert was now a promoter. He wore a shirt that was minus its collar and wide red braces, and he was rarely seen without a huge cigar sticking out of his mouth. Freedom and Ed followed him into his small office at the back of the gym.

Freedom was aware of being given the once-over by the cigar-smoking man. The puffy eyes stared hard, examining him from the top of his head down to his feet. Freedom shifted uncomfortably and looked down at the floor.

'This your new lad then, Ed? He's a big'un, isn't he? He a half-caste, is he? Dark, isn't he?'

Freedom opened his mouth to speak, but Ed shut him up with a quick look, and launched into a speech that had Freedom listening intently, hardly able to believe his ears. Ed told Jack that Freedom was a fresh'un, straight out of the booths, not had a professional fight, but they wanted to try him out for starters, he was just a gypsy lad.

'You rate him, do you Ed? What weight's he carryin'?'

Ed shrugged, although he knew Freedom's weight down to the last ounce, muttered that he was around twelve, thirteen stone, so he'd have to be in the heavyweight class.

'That's my trouble, see Jack, I don't want 'im to go into a professional bout yet, 'e's not ready, what I'm after is – until I've 'ad time to work on 'im, just for a few shillings, lad's gotta eat, know what I mean – I was

424

wonderin' if you could see to a couple of sparrin' matches, anyone comin' in fer a big bout around his weight. You got a match ahead? One suitable, eh?'

Ed knew exactly which bout was due – it was Murphy, the Irish Heavyweight Champion, coming to fight the present holder of the British title. Jack scratched his head and then drummed his fingers on a page of his book. 'There is the Murphy crowd comin' in, but they'll be bringing their own spar. Doubt if they'll want a bum an' mouth round before the big bout. 'E's an Irish bog fighter, an' he's takin' on Sam Gold's boy. It's a big bout, Ed, whoever gets through will have a crack at the world title, take on Dempsey 'imself.'

Ed homed in on Jack, Murphy would be perfect. 'You got it all up 'ere, Jack, always said that, we can see how the lad fares with a champ, we'll know for sure what we got or what we 'aven't, you'll set it up then?'

Jack stubbed his cigar out, had another good look over Freedom and then nodded. As Freedom and Ed left, Jack wasn't sure if he'd been given the bum's rush himself. But then it had been his idea, so he asked the operator to put a call through to Ireland.

Ed skipped along the pavement, clapping his hands. 'The old bugger fell for it, hook, line an' sinker.'

Freedom strolled along beside him, still not knowing what the hell was going on.

'Look, son, we got you a sparring bout with the Irish titleholder, he's comin' over for a crack at the British title, right? British Heavyweight, now then, you show what you can do and 'is Lordship's gonna make sure the press'll be there, with me?'

Freedom still hadn't cottoned on, and Ed began to think that his prize didn't have much 'upstairs'. 'This is your fight, you ain't gonna spar, you're gonna box 'im right outta the ring.'

Freedom was dubious, it was a short cut, but somehow it didn't seem right to him. It was dirty. Ed snapped at him that it was life, that was all, and the best fighter would win, who knows, the Irish fighter might wipe Freedom out.

'Don't you think for one minute Murphy's a pushover, he's a fighter, and 'e's desperate to get that title, you any idea how much Dempsey took at the gate last fight, one million dollars, mate, *one friggin' million dollars*!'

After crossing town to Tower Bridge, Freedom and Ed took a bus over the bridge to the dockland area. Freedom trailed after Ed as he walked down squalid streets, up alleys, until they arrived at a small, two-up, two-down house which was squashed into a seedy row of identical houses, the street alive with noisy children.

Ed led Freedom along the passage into a small back room with two cot beds. It was a far cry from The Grange. 'Right, lad, dump yer bags, toilet's out in the yard, an' by the stink of the place the drains is clogged up. Still, maybe we won't be here for long, eh?'

Freedom stared around the squalid room, at the cracked window, grey with dirt, that looked straight out on to a high brick wall.

Unperturbed as ever, Ed was checking the blankets for bedbugs. He whistled, full of energy, and talked nineteen to the dozen. He told Freedom to unpack, but Freedom had only the clothes he stood up in and his training gear.

'I'll be two minutes, gotta ring 'is Lordship, tell 'im we're settled, like, then we'll get us some dinner . . . put

426

yer feet up, get as much rest as yer can, want you fit for Murphy, eh?'

Left alone, Freedom sat down on his bed. He didn't open his bag, or even check the bed for bugs. He simply sat, hands cupped loosely in front of him. When Ed returned almost an hour later, Freedom was in exactly the same position.

'Right, Murphy's comin' into town, you're to meet him tomorrow. I'll fill you in on how you behave. These bog Irish need a bit of handlin', and you are going ter give a performance . . . but you save the best for the press, are you wiv me? . . . like an actor? Yer know, rehearsin', savin' hisself for the opening night . . . Freedom? You listened to a word I said?'

'What happens if he don't want me to spar?'

'Leave that to me. It's sorted, now get off yer backside, I'm starvin' 'ungry.'

Ed pulled open the door and turned back, hesitating, then went to Freedom and gave him a hug, 'Eh, this place ain't much, I know that, but give us time? Best nobody knows nuffink about yer, understand? Sir Charles, he knows what he's doing.'

Freedom gave him that half-smile of his. 'Thing is, Ed, I don't think there's room in here for His Lordship . . .'

Ed cuffed him one, but didn't laugh. 'There's them an' us, that's life . . . now get a move on or I'll 'ave shockin' wind.'

Pat Murphy looked far from 'bog Irish'. He was wearing a long, camel-hair coat with a velvet collar, and a black felt hat, a satin band around the crown. He wore a carnation in his buttonhole and carried a silver-topped walking stick. Ed slithered around the edge of the room,

427

wanting to get a good look at the Irish champion without him knowing. Two men, equally well dressed, stood beside Murphy, and he towered over them. His huge chest under the tailored suit and overcoat looked a lot wider than Freedom's.

Murphy was posing for a photograph, the photographer hidden under a black cloth.

'Mr Murphy, could you please hold that pose, thank you sir, and now would it be permissible to have one of you on your own for the *Evening Chronicle*?'

Murphy smiled as his two men departed to lean against the ropes. He wore a fine leather glove on his right hand, in which he also held its mate, leaving his bare left hand to rest on the ropes. Ed could see a heavy diamond ring on his little finger. More disconcerting was the size of the man's fists – they were like spades.

'Come on then, man, let's be done with this, the bars are open.' Murphy held his pose, his white teeth gleaming in a frozen smile. He was an exceptionally handsome man and his face bore little or no sign of his boxing career. His nose was straight, his hair, thick, black and curly, hid his ears so Ed could not see if they bore telltale marks. Murphy's eyes were small and china-blue, and they twinkled as he spoke in his thick Irish brogue.

Jack gave the photographer his marching orders, and was about to join Murphy when he spotted Ed. Murphy gave Ed no more than a cursory glance as he moved with his two men towards Jack's office.

'This is Ed Meadows, he's got a good sparring partner for you, Pat.'

Murphy turned to Ed and gave him his full attention. His twinkly eyes went icy-cold as he gave Ed the once-over.

'Well, they better get him over here, I'll be needing work outs before the match, your lad good, is he?'

At that point Murphy's trainer, O'Keefe, laughed and said that his boy needed the very best, and it was lucky they had offered a sparring partner as their own had been put into hospital the night before they left. Murphy looked at Ed.

'I never meant it, stray punch, poor man went down like a lead balloon, and that's just how I intend to put the champ down, isn't that right, Paddy?'

Paddy O'Keefe nodded, raised his fist and punched the padded, camel-hair shoulders of Murphy's coat.

'Oi, watch out for the coat, it's pure camelhair, this, have you ever felt such soft material, Jack, go on now, have a feel, is it not like a baby's arse?'

They moved into Jack's office, and Ed asked when they would like his boy brought round. Murphy flicked his gloves and said he'd work out first thing in the morning, around ten o'clock.

Ed met with Sir Charles at the Pelican Club, and they ate a big fry-up together. A boxing match was taking place while they ate, not that Ed paid any attention.

'He's a champ, and 'e's flash, must 'ave made a lot of money on the Irish circuits, his face looks unmarked and he's got fists the size of shovels. I wonder if we're not pushin' our lad too fast.'

Sir Charles picked at his steak and seemed more concerned with his tomato than with anything Ed had told him. Ed sighed and tapped Sir Charles on the arm to draw his attention to the entrance. Murphy, his camelhair coat and hat taken from him, stood at the grill-room bar. 'There 'e is now, sir, look at 'im, and 'e's got the confidence of Jove himself.'

They watched as Murphy shook hands with a group of well-dressed City gents and was shown to a table.

They made a great fuss of him, and many eyes were turned towards the ringside table where he sat.

The Pelican Club was half-full of regulars, and a strange bunch they were, a mixture of toffs and betting men. Titles rubbed shoulders with gamblers, bookies and sportsmen and, thankfully, there was not a woman in sight. The club was very much a man's world, reverberating with loud laughter and men calling to each other between the booths and tables.

'Man's a heavy drinker, by the look of it, and likes the social scene, wouldn't you say? Our boy'll take him, he's not our worry, old chap, take a look at the title holder.'

Ed looked around and leant across the table, 'He here, is 'e? I can't see 'im?'

Sir Charles pushed his plate away and signalled to a waiter, and at the same time he told Ed rather curtly that the champ was under wraps until the main bout, as it should be, he was not even in London.

'You just make sure Freedom knows what to do. I want *him* under wraps until I give the word, let Murphy think he's simply a sparring partner.'

Sir Charles tossed money to the waiter to hand to the boys in the ring. Some toffs came over to the table and Ed knew he was dismissed. He got up and put his hand in his pocket as a gesture, knowing the bill was taken care of.

If Ed Meadows had ever thought Freedom was in any way difficult to control, poor O'Keefe had his hands full with Murphy. He had remained at the Pelican Club all afternoon, drinking. Eventually O'Keefe had poured him into a taxi and taken him back to the hotel, and after a few hours of rest Murphy was up again and raring to go. Fresh as a daisy now, he wanted to see the sights of London. No amount of persuasion from O'Keefe would keep the boxer resting. In exasperation he looked at Murphy prancing around the room in his evening suit, looking for his dancing pumps.

'For God's sake, you're supposed to be getting ready for the British title bout, you're not here to sightsee, and what you getting all fancied up for?'

Murphy beamed. 'Bejasus, I've got three weeks to get one night out of me system, an' I give you me word I'll not touch a drop after tonight, now come on man, let's get going.'

Poor O'Keefe was dragged off to the Hammersmith Palais to hear the Dixieland Jazz Band. Murphy beamed with delight, he clapped and sang along, 'Do-wack-a-do, boop-a-doop . . .' He was up doing the Black Bottom with a woman O'Keefe had first thought to be an old lady with white hair, but when she turned round he saw that it was the new ash-blonde colour, not white but silver. Murphy wouldn't come off the dance floor and O'Keefe sat subdued and wretched. At least he was exercising, even if it was the Black Bottom.

Ed pushed open the privy door, still buttoning up his trousers. His morning ritual had been disturbed by loud, childish sobs . . . Freedom was standing in the yard with a small, ragged boy, who was clutching a rotting, dead pigeon to his chest.

'Go on, gerrout of it or I'll tan yer hide.'

Freedom frowned at Ed and gently eased the dead bird from the little boy's hands.

'It was me pet, I've tried everyfink ter make 'im eat.'

Freedom sat back on his haunches with the little corpse in his hands. The maggots were eating its eyes out, but Freedom stroked the bird's head gently. 'I tell thee what, I'll take him with me, maybe I'll have him right as rain.'

From within the crumbling house a woman called for 'Will', and the child ran off. Ed cringed with distaste.

'You'll get disease from that, chuck it in the canal, and never mind talkin' wiv the kids, you'll 'ave 'em hangin' round yer neck . . . an' get a move on, you're meeting Murphy today.'

Pat Murphy showered and O'Keefe rubbed him down, then gave him a heavy massage.

'My God, I couldn't believe my eyes, she was a dragon, boy, woke up next to a dragon, must have been near sixty, why d'you let me do it?'

O'Keefe thumped Murphy's back, hard. It wasn't for want of trying to prize his champion away from the woman. He'd almost got a back-hander as Murphy, drunk as a lord, insisted the woman was Gloria Swanson.

Soon Murphy was togged up and waiting, ready, in the gym. He was doing press-ups in a corner while two young lads watched in awe. Then he worked out on the weights, sweating, easing up his muscles. His body was very powerful, and he stood six-foot-two in his leather-soled boxing boots. Ed reckoned he was at least half a stone, maybe more, heavier than Freedom.

O'Keefe noticed the big fella immediately and crossed over to Ed, jerking his thumb in Freedom's direction.

'This the lad, is it? He's a big'un all right, let's hope he'll be able to give him a work out, he certainly needs one. Pat, Pat, come on, into the ring with you.'

Murphy danced his way towards the ring, and couldn't keep still while O'Keefe put on his gloves. He inserted his gumshield and put his leather head-protector on, then Murphy began punching the sides of the iring. Freedom stepped into the ring, gloves tied, gumshield in, and his leather helmet strapped on. The two worked well, Freedom giving Murphy a run for his money. He also took a number of punches, and pulled back on his punches a little, and was stopped as Murphy spat out his shield.

'Bejasus, what they got here, a ballroom dancer? Can't you do anything better than this punk?'

Ed gave Freedom a tiny hooded nod, he could push a bit more. The men started again, this time Freedom was feeling Murphy's punches, fending them off, but they were like iron, the man had a lot of power behind him. Freedom stepped up his punching, gave a good body blow, only to be encouraged by Murphy himself.

'Thatta boy, come on, get your pecker up, come on, gimme a run for my money.'

O'Keefe nodded to Freedom, then talked out of the side of his mouth to Ed. 'Your lad's got promise, nice mover, needs to train up the power behind his punch but he's got promise, you're right.'

Throughout the bout Freedom was using his right fist, never giving his left space, he defended, defended, very rarely pushing Murphy. Murphy dominated the centre of the ring, moving Freedom around, on him, after him, and he didn't pull some of his punches. At the end they were both sweating profusely and Murphy threw in the towel, he wanted to rest. Ed could have swiped Freedom, he just stood in the centre of the ring, unsure what to do next.

'For Chrissakes, man,' he whispered, 'look like yer out of bloody breath, heave yer chest up an' down a bit!'

*

433

The following day's sparring match was a little tougher. Murphy was working now, and not playing around. Freedom didn't have to act, he had his work cut out trying to fend off the body punches. Murphy concentrated on the body, even after the bout he went and worked on the punchbag for a further hour.

'Well, what you think, can you take him?'

Freedom mulled the question over for what seemed to Ed to be a very long time, then he said he didn't know. He didn't think Murphy was giving full power, he was holding back. The next spar Freedom would push a few punches, but Murphy had one hell of a right hook.

'But he opens up, I've been watchin' 'im, he goes to a format, right upper, right upper, an' then he's comin' in with a body left, but he double swings and in comes that right hook. You got to get into that opening, he's wide open for a moment each time.'

Freedom raised his eyes to heaven, shook his head. 'Ed, what you think I bin trying to do, mun, he's a dancer too, you know, light on his feet for his weight.'

Ed shoved his stubby finger into Freedom's chest, said that he, Freedom, was twice the mover, and lighter.

'I'm lighter, Ed, that's for sure, I'd say by about sixteen pounds.'

Jack came out of his office and went over to O'Keefe. He had a list of reporters requesting permission to photograph the Irish champion. He also had a lot of press photographs of the titleholder from the morning paper's sports edition. On the back page, Micky Morgan stood with his fists up. Unlike Murphy, his face showed war wounds, a flattened nose, crumpled ears. His eyes were slightly puffy, eyes that glared out of the newspaper.

'Eh, Murphy, wanna see how Micky's lookin' lately? Not good, that Scotch fella really gave him a going-over, see?'

Murphy took the paper and stared at the glowering man, adding up on his fingers how many weeks had gone by since Micky's last bout. 'He was cut, wasn't he? Right eye? Lemme see now . . . I'd calculate the lad's only just got nice, clean, fresh skin over this right eye, what you say, boss? Oi, O'Keefe, what you say, doesn't look too dangerous to me?'

O'Keefe didn't even cross the room, he was winding bandages into rolls, concentrating on them. 'He's a real fighter, Pat, and he's hungry, they had a good "take" on the Scottish bout. I wouldn't think that eye worries him one jot, man's a boxer, know what I mean? That opponent was good, and dirty, thumb in the eye round one, he was also very handy with his head. Micky took him out in round five, they say the fella's still not sure what hit him. Mickey was a stoker on board HMS *Junnsanta*, word is the shovel's still attached to his hand.'

Through O'Keefe's slow assessment of his next opponent, Murphy stood with his arms folded. As O'Keefe wound down and finished rolling the bandages, Murphy turned to the assembled room.

'That's what I like to hear, man giving his boxer confidence, right, thanks a lot, an' where's that gyppo? You hear him? Tomorrow, son, put a bit of energy into it, Jack, you get the press up here, I'll give 'em something to write about, and, O'Keefe, I'll have that stoker running.'

O'Keefe looked over to Ed and gave him a wink,

then he went to Murphy and cuffed him over the head, flung an arm round his shoulder and said he loved him.

'Now you're talking, Pat, talking like a winner.' Freedom picked up his kitbag. He had not said more than a few words to Murphy or his trainer. He liked them both, liked them a lot. He was silent on the journey home on the crowded tram. He liked to sit up front on the open deck. He wore a cloth cap pulled down and a woollen scarf, his jacket collar turned up. Ed wondered what he was thinking, but he never could tell, it unnerved him.

The following morning the gym was crowded with reporters hanging around with their big cameras and tripods. They were setting up by the side of the ring. Jack, dressed in his Sunday suit, brought out all the old photographs of himself, but no one was interested.

O'Keefe had to restrain Murphy from wearing his best velvet shorts, telling him they should be kept for the fight. He couldn't, however, stop him wearing his new, hand-stitched, monogrammed robe. He was there, flaunting himself, swashbuckling up and down the gym, and he had the reporters roaring with laughter as he posed and danced about. Ed looked over to his two lads, who were standing at the far end of the gym. They looked uneasy and nervous, and he made his way over to them.

'Where in God's name is he?'

Ed threw up his hands, Freedom had gone to the toilet, what a time to go! All the press gathered and where was their man? On the throne. 'He gloved up?'

*

Freedom was standing in the dirty, broken-down toilet. His coat was round his shoulders, gloves on, and he was leaning against the brick wall. His eyes were closed and he was talking quietly to himself. 'Doing this for you, Evie, I get through this then it's the title, and you'll have all the dresses and hats you want, this is for you, Evie, I'm doing this for you.'

Ed sighed with relief when Freedom entered the gym, no one paying him any attention. Murphy was up in the ring, posing, swinging on the ropes, and yelling for Freedom to join him. 'I'm not wearing me helmet, man, I want me face to be seen in all its beauty.'

As Freedom stepped into the ring, Murphy pranced over and gave him a wink. 'Right, son, don't hold back, let's give 'em a show, get your face in the press with me, all right?'

The room was set up, all the cameras in position, and O'Keefe stepped into the ring, spouting a few words about this being just a taster for the championship. Freedom's name was not even mentioned, he sat in the corner while his two lads massaged his shoulders. Murphy was pounding the air, and was led into his corner for his gumshield to be fitted.

The bell sounded, and everyone in the room focused their attention on the ring. Murphy came out hunched and ready for the attack, gave Freedom a good pounding, flashy punching, and even while he was doing it he was still talking. 'Oh, wait 'til they see me in the papers, me mother'll throw a fit, me lovely face on every stand.'

Murphy's face altered as he felt a punch hit home hard, and this time he didn't mess around, he went back at Freedom, his eyes never leaving Freedom's face. Murphy was amused, he'd seen that look, so the boy wanted to make a show of himself, did he? Well now, he would have the lesson of his life.

The whole room picked up the new atmosphere in the ring – suddenly it wasn't a game. Ed could feel his right leg shaking all by itself, and he swallowed and looked at O'Keefe. The last thing he wanted was for him to step into the ring and stop the sparring match.

A murmur ran around the gym, people moved closer in, the cameras flashed. Ed was saying a silent prayer, over and over he was willing Freedom to find that break, that break in Murphy's defence. Murphy had Freedom up against the ropes, gave him a good left jab and was about to come in with a right, left, and his famous right, when he felt as if his stomach had been blown out. The punches came one after the other, three times the force of Freedom's punches in their previous sparring matches. Murphy couldn't believe it was happening, he gave back everything he had and his fists seemed to glance off the lad, eyes to eyes, the blue twinkle had gone, and the last thing Murphy remembered was the blackness, the blackness of those eyes staring into him, expressionless, masked, in a set, impassive face.

The room went silent as Murphy crashed, unconscious, to the canvas. Then the place was in an uproar, the reporters clamouring, fighting to get into the ring, shouting for the name, the boxer's name. Ed gave the signal and the two lads grabbed Freedom and hauled him to the ringside. Freedom shoved them aside and pushed his way through the men gathered around the still-unconscious Murphy. Ed was shouting, 'Freedom Stubbs, his name is Freedom Stubbs.' It was the name that went with the first face Murphy saw as he came round. O'Keefe was hemmed in by reporters already asking if his man would still fight. O'Keefe ignored them and tried to get to Murphy.

Freedom already had Murphy sitting up, leaning against his shoulder. Murphy's right eye was streaming blood, his face blotchy red and his lip cracked. He was dazed, but even in that condition he managed a joke, 'Well I'll be buggered, I've been beaten at me own game.'

He looked helplessly at O'Keefe, beseeching him to get him out somehow. Freedom helped the big man to his feet, he wanted to tell him he was sorry, but O'Keefe pushed him away with tears streaming down his face, and helped his man out of the ring, 'You bastard, Ed Meadows, you bastard!'

It was Murphy who broke up what looked as if it could become an ugly situation. He held his hand up and looked to Freedom. 'There's your champion, good luck, son, you certainly took all o'mine!'

Murphy's legs buckled beneath him and he was carried into the dressing room. The press surrounded Freedom.

Jack looked stunned, he stared at the departing group carrying poor Murphy out, then back to Freedom in the ring. He said it to no one in particular, to the air.

'I ain't ever seen a punch like that, not ever, Gawd almighty, what a punch.'

CHAPTER 19

S IR CHARLES swung into motion, the press had a field day, and Freedom was accepted as a contender for the British Heavyweight title. He was going to make sure his champion would be totally acceptable both socially and in the ring.

Freedom was removed from Ed's lodgings and installed in Sir Charles' small bachelor flat in Jermyn Street. He wanted to dress Freedom in the finest before he was taken to the Pelican Club or White's. Freedom went to Mr Poole, the famous tailor, for his sporting set, then to the equally famous trio of high priests of fashion – Mr Cundy, the general manager of the store, who waited on his every whim, Mr Dents, in the coat department, and Mr Allen, responsible for waistcoats and trousers. Mr Allen had to measure Freedom's inside leg twice as he couldn't quite believe how long it was, and the shirtmaker tutted and muttered as he measured and remeasured Freedom's arms and neck.

On all questions of cloth, texture and style, Freedom allowed Sir Charles to dominate him. He was unbelievably pernickety, feeling each piece of cloth and taking it to the daylight to examine it.

'Would it be possible, sir, to have a camelhair coat?'

Sir Charles didn't even reply to this, just let his

monocle pop out in disgust. The fellow would be wanting a velvet collar next.

Freedom's feet were measured for boots and shoes, and Sir Charles put pressure on the makers to complete them as soon as possible.

The Jermyn Street flat consisted of a single bedroom, a valet's room, a dining room and a small sitting room. There was no kitchen, one either sent out for food or dined out. Dewhurst was installed in the flat and instructed to make sure Mr Stubbs never ate with a serving spoon again. He was to be shown how to eat like a gentleman with the correct tableware, and to be taught about wines.

Ed was amazed to see Freedom allowing himself to be carted around like a show-horse without a murmur. Not once did he complain, and only kicked up a fuss when it was suggested that he have his hair cut. This became a major argument, and eventually Sir Charles attempted a compromise.

'All right, old chap, we'll find a happy medium – won't have you sheared, just a trim, it's frightfully long and could do with a simple trim, what do you say?'

Freedom stared gloomily at his reflection and stubbornly refused to have it cut. They couldn't say it would get in the way when he was boxing, because it would be tied back with a leather thong. Ed knew what would happen if Freedom's temper was roused so he quietly suggested to Sir Charles that the long hair could be a unique advantage in being so unusual. At last Sir Charles acquiesced, and Freedom grinned. It wasn't that he minded taking care of it, he loved having it washed, loved his head being massaged, and loved choosing perfumes to use on it.

*

One week later Freedom stood looking at himself in the bedroom mirror. After three attempts to tie Freedom's tie, Dewhurst was finally satisfied, and stood back to admire his work. He had to admit the man looked splendid, apart from the hair, of course, which went without saying. With that hair and the colour of his skin Freedom could never be taken for a gentleman. Yet somehow he looked almost regal. He now had a complete wardrobe of suits, shirts, ties, overcoats, boots and underwear.

Sir Charles rested his chin on the top of his cane and looked up as Freedom entered, then beamed. Now they could dine at White's. Ed gaped and looked with renewed interest at Freedom. He was a fine looking fella, and Ed hid a smile. The lad was certainly a looker, just like the movie idol, Valentino, no doubt about it.

'I wonder, Sir Charles, if you've had any word from Miss Evelyne?'

Sir Charles was nonplussed for a moment, and Ed gave Freedom a shifty look. 'He means Miss Jones, yer know, sir, from Cardiff, she was stayin' at The Grange wiv us.'

'You see, she was my girl, an' I'm worried about her.'

Sir Charles pursed his lips. 'Miss Jones? Is that who you're referring to, Miss Jones? Good God, man, I've absolutely no idea where on earth she is, she left weeks ago. Besides, I don't like this "my girl" thing at all. If you recall your words on oath in the witness stand in Cardiff, you categorically denied any relationship with Miss Jones, are you now telling me you lied?'

Freedom's hands were clenched at his sides, and Ed began to sweat.

'I never lied, sir, it was the truth, but that didn't mean I didn't have no feelings for her. That came after the court case, she's my wife.'

Sir Charles' monocle popped out and he had to sit down. He repeated the word.

'Wife . . .? Wife? Ed, did you know about this? I find it all very disturbing. When Miss Jones left, she made no mention of you being married.'

Ed was so perplexed he didn't know which way to turn and he could see Freedom's temper rising. 'Now, now, Freedom, that might be stretchin' it a bit far, they're not married, sir, not in a church, they did some Romany thing.'

In an icy voice Sir Charles reminded Freedom again of what he had said in court, on oath. He went on to inform him of the mounting costs of his new wardrobe, not to mention the lodgings, the training, wages for Ed and the two corner men, everything provided for Freedom on the simple condition that he box. Freedom was fighting to hold on to his temper as he faced Sir Charles.

'I reckon, sir, that I done that, and I am indebted to you, course I am – but that don't mean I am owned by you.'

This caused Sir Charles to throw his hands up in horror, it was all getting really out of hand. 'Your contract with myself is legal and binding. With reference to Miss Jones, she asked to leave The Grange the day before you yourself left. Surely if she had felt any overwhelming emotional tie to you she would have told you herself? Now, I think we really must forget all this nonsense, I have a table booked for nine-fifteen and I am looking forward to introducing you to my guests.'

He swept out, signalling for Ed to follow him. They walked a short way along the street together, Sir Charles' manner deathly cold. 'Make sure he's there, will you, old chap, maybe you should tell him what he'll be worth if he wins the title. He'll get a purse of near two

443

hundred. Tell him that and we'll see how much this wretched woman means to him.'

Ed went slowly back up in the small, gilded lift. He sat down next to Freedom and patted his knee like a father. It was impossible to know what Freedom was thinking, his face was mask-like, the black eyes expressionless, he even seemed relaxed. He stared down at his big hands and he spoke softly, as if he was miles away. 'We have a saying, an old Romany saying, that if you love something, you must set it free; if it returns to you it is yours, if it doesn't then it never was . . .'

Poor Ed didn't really know what to do. He couldn't afford to lose his job, and Sir Charles was such an odd man, Ed never knew which way he would turn. 'Freedom, lad, 'is Lordship's investin' a lot of money in you, and 'e don't want no dirty publicity 'bout you an' that murder investigation.'

Freedom protested his innocence, and Ed sighed. 'He's adamant about it, an' you know without 'im you would be swingin' fer that murder, you know that. See, you'll be meetin' all kinds of people now, society, like, perhaps even the prince himself, they can't 'ave no scandal.'

Freedom frightened Ed with his sly, strange smile. 'He won't want me, though, if I lose the title, mun, will he?'

Ed shouted at him that he would have two hundred pounds purse money if he won. 'Gawd 'elp me, two hundred pounds, you know how many years I gotta work ter make that much?'

Freedom still wore that smile and Ed was scared, not of what Freedom might do to him, but because he knew Freedom didn't really care about money.

'So what happens if we was to find 'er, and she not want you? Eh?'

Freedom moved his hands like a bird, she could fly away, do as she wanted, but he had to see her.

Evelyne had found work in a small bookshop in Charing Cross Road. The owner was an eccentric gentleman called Arnold Snodgrass. He wore a crumpled, stained suit, and was never without a cigarette hanging from the side of his mouth. His yellow teeth could be seen when he spoke in his strange, theatrical voice.

The shop was stacked from floor to ceiling with books, manuscripts and papers. The stench of cats and musty, ageing paper was at first nauseating. Evelyne was so dizzy at times she had to sit down on the stepladder.

Old Snoddy was unaware of her, as he was of the stench. 'Listen to this, dear heart, a little snippet of interest – did you know that Shakespeare, that wondrous bard, actually made up the word "lonely"? Imagine him sitting at his desk with his quill and thinking it up . . . alone . . . lone . . . lonely . . . now first play he used this new word was . . . *Coriolanus*, fascinating, what? Wonderful play . . . lonely . . .'

Evelyne picked up a volume so heavy she could only just carry it from one side of the shop to the other. She sighed, her own loneliness taking precedence over Mr Snodgrass' snippet.

The next thing she knew Mrs Harris was standing over her burning one of Snoddy's own quill pens. Mrs Harris was a round, motherly woman who cleaned the shop and back room as best she could, and she also cleaned various other shops in the same area.

'She's comin' round now, sir. What 'appened, did she

445

fall or what? It's them 'eavy volumes she's carrying round.'

Snoddy slurped his morning tea and shrugged, not interested in the slightest in the health of his assistant. He was buried in *Coriolanus*, still musing about his discovery.

'Come on, ducks, best get you home an' put yer feet up, 'e won't notice yer gorn, 'e don't know what day it is.'

Mrs Harris was shocked when she saw where Evelyne was living. 'Lord luv-a-duck, yer can't swing a cat in 'ere, and by the looks of it it's damp, shockin' . . . have you no place even to boil a cup of tea?'

Evelyne lay on her bed, wanting to cry, but she shrugged off Mrs Harris' questions. 'I'm saving my money, I want to go to night classes, get my teacher's diploma, it's all right.'

Mrs Harris looked her over and then felt her forehead. 'You're running' a bit of a fever, ducks, maybe you should see a doctor.'

Evelyne buttoned her blouse, straightened her skirt and came out from behind the screen. The doctor was writing a prescription. She sat down and opened her purse, counted out the one shilling and sixpence her visit would cost.

'You must eat fresh vegetables, get your strength up, but there's nothing wrong that rest and a good diet won't put right. I wouldn't lift anything heavy, just in case . . . this is a tonic, you should come back for regular check-ups until the birth.'

Evelyne blinked, swallowed hard. 'Beg pardon, sir, what did you say?'

*

446

When Evelyne came out into the waiting room, Mrs Harris rose to her feet, clutching her big cloth shopping bag, bulging with groceries. The girl looked worse now than when she had gone in. 'It's nuffink serious, is it, ducks?'

Evelyne shook her head, biting her lip so she wouldn't cry. Mrs Harris helped her into her coat, feeling sorry for her, 'You come round and 'ave supper at my place, no need to go back to yer work, Snoddy's got 'is brandy out so he won't know if you was workin' or not.'

Sitting beside Mrs Harris on the tram, Evelyne suddenly blurted it all out. 'I'm having a baby, that's what he told me, but I can't be, I just can't be . . .'

Mrs Harris sighed, she'd guessed as much, but Miss Jones was such a nice girl, very proper, and always so well dressed, so neat and tidy. 'Well, love, there's only one way to make one, have you been doing it? Have you got a young man?'

The floodgates opened, and Evelyne sobbed her heart out on top of the tram. She was still in floods of tears by the time they were sitting in Mrs Harris' kitchen.

'Yer see, ducks, in some cases yer can go on gettin' yer monthly bleedin' and still be carryin', how far gone are you, did he say?'

'He reckoned about five months, but I just can't be, I *can't*.'

Mrs Harris poured thick, strong tea, spooned in the sugar and eased her bulk into a fireside chair. 'Well, if yer that far gone there's no gettin' rid of it – mind you, there's some that would try . . . Drink yer tea now, don't go gettin' all upset again, we'll sort it all out . . . but yer won't be able to lift no more Shake-speare, that's fer sure.'

With seven children of her own, Mrs Harris needed Evelyne like a hole in the head. Her two-up-two-down was bursting at the seams. To help make ends meet her husband Ted worked nights at the gasworks, and during the day in a carpenter's shop. When he came home he found his missus stewing up a large pan of soup, the brood sitting round the kitchen table.

'We got a house guest, Ted. Now before you hit the roof, she's able to pay us threepence a week rent . . . She's in the family way, and she's no one else to turn to. I've put her in the front room on the sofa.'

'Gawd 'elp us, woman, how we gonna fit in? Even with threepence extra?'

Covering the table with newspaper, Mrs Harris set out the cutlery. Ted sat down at the table, sighing. He was such a good-natured soul. 'You know, ducks, you'd take in a lame donkey if he was homeless, but we got to think of the kids . . .'

His wife pulled up a chair and held his calloused hand. 'Remember our youngest, little Dora? Remember how I was all set to have a gin bath at Widow Smith's in the Hollow?'

Ted nodded, and kissed her big red cheek. Mrs Harris had been beside herself when she had discovered she was pregnant again, and had not said a word to Ted, but made up her mind to get rid of it. Ted had arrived home unexpectedly from work, knowing the kids were out, knowing she would be at home. 'Come here, you big old fool,' he had said, 'you fink after sixteen years of marriage I don't know when you're in the family way? Now, gel, it's gonna be tough on us, but we'll manage, and I've got a name, it'll be a girl if there's anything in the law of averages, and we'll call her Dora . . . now give us a cuppa.'

'Evelyne's ever such a nice gel,' Mrs Harris went on, 'an' I can leave our Dora wiv her until her baby's born, that'll save us a few coppers, won't have ter farm her out whilst I do me cleanin'.'

Ted spooned up the hot soup, dipped a chunk of bread in the bowl and sucked on it. 'An' what 'appens when the baby's born, Ma? What's she gonna do then?'

'Oh, Ted, get on wiv yer, we'll face that when it comes, an' she can read an' write, she can teach the little 'uns their schoolin' . . .'

Evelyne entered the hot, stuffy kitchen, and Ted gave her a wide smile, held out his hand. 'Welcome to the family, gel, sit down, the missus'll take right care of yer, an' we'll all fit in somehow.'

Evelyne had never known such friendliness, such warmth and love, she was once more in the bosom of a family. The seven Harris children were rowdy, scruffy, and as open and friendly as their parents. Baby Dora, just eighteen months old, was left in Evelyne's care while Mrs Harris went out cleaning.

Exhausted from a long day's hard work, Mrs Harris sat by the fire while Evelyne changed Dora's nappy, cooing and making the baby gurgle with laughter. Evelyne's pregnancy had advanced quickly, and Mrs Harris began to think the doctor could have miscalculated. Evelyne was a big girl, and looking at her now Mrs Harris reckoned the baby was probably more like seven months.

Evelyne had not said one word about the father, or what she would do when the child was born.

'Will you keep the baby, Evie, ducks?'

Evelyne rocked little Dora in her arms. 'Oh, yes, I couldn't part with him, couldn't even think about it.'

'Well, it won't be easy yer know, love, woman on 'er own, you could have the baby adopted, there's many wivout that would give it a good home.'

Evelyne pursed her lips. 'There'll be no one bringing my son up but me, I'll find a way, I'll get work.'

'You never talk of the father, an' you're so sure it's a boy yer carryin' . . . does he know, lovey? About the baby?'

Whenever Mrs Harris mentioned the baby's father she saw Evelyne withdraw into herself. She had grown used to Evelyne, the way she could clam up. 'Do you love 'im still? Is 'e a society man, that what it is?'

Evelyne busied herself with Dora, but Mrs Harris battled on. 'Only, a first-born is important to a man, an' you seem so sure you've got a son inside you, d'yer not want ter contact 'im?'

She watched Evelyne put little Dora into her crib, an old orange box, and kiss the child lovingly. Her heart went out to the girl, especially when she turned with tears in her eyes. 'I just don't know what to do, I don't, but . . . feeling the baby inside me, well, I think more and more of him, but I just don't know what to do . . .'

Evelyne did think of Freedom; every night before she slept she saw his face. Leaving him the way she had was cruel, she knew it, and the more she thought of the way she had treated him the more ashamed she was. She decided to write to Freda, tell her about the baby, but

450

ask her not to say anything to Freedom. She would want to tell him herself.

As soon as Freda received Evelyne's letter, she wrote back, knowing she shouldn't, giving Freedom's address in Jermyn Street. She also set about making baby clothes, but said nothing to Ed in her letter to him. She did as Evelyne asked, and kept the secret.

Evelyne opened Freda's letter in the park while little Dora was asleep in the pram. She read that Freedom was waiting for acceptance to fight the British Heavyweight Champion, Micky Morgan, how he had beaten the Irish contender, and that they were all on tenterhooks waiting for the promoters to give the word.

Seeing his name in writing, Evelyne's heart missed a beat. She knew she had been a fool. She touched her swollen belly, pictured Freedom's face. She could almost laugh at herself, she who had wanted a better life was now living in the slums, without a job, and wheeling someone else's baby around. Then she felt a bit guilty. Mrs Harris might be poor, but she was like a second mother to Evelyne. Poverty was all around them, but Evelyne had never said a word about her legacy. It had become an obsession with her, she scrimped and saved every farthing, and yet she had more money in the post office than the Harrises ever dreamed of. Originally it had been intended to pay for her own education, but now it would be for her son's. She blushed with shame, but then argued with herself that she paid her way, she wasn't taking the Harrises' charity, just their love.

*

Every single head turned as Freedom entered the Café Royal. Women particularly noticed him, towering over every other man, even the elegant Sir Charles went unnoticed. All eyes focused on Freedom.

Their table was very prominent, chosen for that specific reason, just as the table at White's had been the night before. The whispers spread as the diners recognized Sir Charles and knew that the handsome man with him must be his contender. The sporting sections had been full of coverage of the forthcoming British title fight, including Pat Murphy's unprecedented knockout. The venue had been changed from the National Sporting Club to the Albert Hall, and the fight delayed for two months as posters and tickets were altered and reprinted. The pre-fight sales were already the biggest in English history, and it was rumoured that tickets were scarce now and were becoming a 'must'. It was also rumoured that the Prince of Wales himself would be the guest of Sir Charles and Lord Livermore.

Much of the press coverage was down to Sir Charles negotiating long and hard with the promoters, who wanted to recoup their losses from the Pat Murphy knockout, which included billboards, posters, tickets, et cetera. With the larger showcase of the Albert Hall, the losses were soon made up. Sir Charles announced that a quarter of the profits would be given to charity, thus giving the match the seal of approval for society to be there.

The British Heavyweight Champion himself kept well out of the limelight. Sir Charles had no intention of keeping Freedom under wraps, and was betting heavily on the champion as well, intending to cover his losses should Freedom lose. He loved the fuss, the glamour and the attention, basked in it, and paraded Freedom as if he were a prize hunter on a rein. Freedom held up well, his dark eyes flashing, his smile captivating everyone. His romantic Romany origins were well publicized, and the women fluttered and pretended to swoon when he kissed their hands.

Tonight, at the Café Royal, Freedom had to stand for a round of applause as the band leader moved the spotlight on to Sir Charles' table.

Poor Ed shuddered with embarrassment as Sir Charles' generosity had not included him and he was self-conscious in his ill-fitting suits and old shirt. Realizing that the slight was intended, he stepped aside from now until the last stages of his training. He contented himself instead with reading about his golden boy in the society columns.

Freda was delighted when Ed sent for her to come to town. She had worked her fingers raw, sewing clothes for herself, hoping to be there on the big night. She set off from The Grange as excited as a child.

When Ed met her at the station she was a trifle disappointed to discover that they had to travel by public transport, and even further let down to find that they had to stay with Ed's family, who were waiting for them with tea all ready on the table. Ed's brother and his wife and kids greeted the new sister-in-law with suspicion at first, but then made her welcome. They were East Enders and, although Freda never said a word, they were obviously living from hand to mouth. She and Ed were given the front room to sleep in, and it was not until late evening that Freda had a chance to talk to Ed in privacy.

'Well, darlink, how is Freedom? Will we all have tickets for the fight?'

Ed was hesitant at first, not as enthusiastic as she had

expected. In truth, his nose was very much out of joint. Freedom seemed to have changed. Only a short while ago Ed couldn't have got him to put a tie round his neck, and now he was never without one. Freedom had also been very cold and aloof with Ed, and that hurt him. He didn't like to mention it to Freda, but she detected he was not too happy.

'You won't recognize 'im, Freda, 'e looks like a toff an' 'e's actin' like one, out every night gallivantin' around the town, showin' 'imself off to everybody. He should be trainin', night an' day. You don't see this Micky out in the clubs, no way, he'll be trainin' mornin', noon an' night.'

Freda made all the right noises and bided her time. She didn't like to mention Evelyne now.

'I'm worried, Freda, see, I know 'is Lordship, next minute the lad'll believe in 'is own publicity, believe that Sir's 'is closest friend, but if 'e loses he won't see 'im fer dust, an' 'e'll lose, Freda, mark my words 'e'll lose, 'e can't go on like this. I been round three times an' 'e's still in bed at twelve o'clock, him what was out at the crack of dawn at The Grange.'

Patting his hand and kissing his cheek, Freda assured him that she would have a word with Freedom when she saw him.

'You'll need an appointment, Freda, see if 'e can't fit you in between 'is barber an' 'is tailor.'

Often at night Freedom would walk along Jermyn Street and cross into St James's Park. Climbing over the railings he would run silently round and round, or sit for hours staring at the sleeping pelicans. Then when he had exhausted himself he would return to Jermyn Street. The running eased his restlessness, his feeling of being cooped up, of being on display, a fairground amusement. The women who pawed him only made him long for his Evie, and the pain inside him grew worse and worse instead of easing, but he said nothing, told no one.

Dewhurst woke Freedom to say that Mr Meadows and his wife had called, and would return later that afternoon for tea. Then he ran Freedom's bath and began to lay out his clothes to wear for luncheon.

Mrs Harris could tell something was up, Evie was as bright as a button. She had also washed her hair and let out her best coat. She kept on asking how she looked, did she look ugly?

'Lord love us, gel, there's nothing more beautiful than a woman with a baby in her, you got a glow . . . are you off visitin'?'

Evelyne gave a tiny smile.

'Well, you tell 'im from me, ducks, he's got a special woman, you go to him, bring 'im back for supper an' all, go on wiv you, you've waited long enough as it is . . .'

Evelyne caught the tram into London's West End. Winter was coming on fast, and she hugged her coat around her. She got off the tram outside the big store in Piccadilly, Swan and Edgar. The windows were all lit up, and one of them was filled with baby clothes and cradles. She peered into the brightly lit window. Such beautiful things, the toys, the clothes. She couldn't move away, she found herself smiling with pleasure, with excitement at the thought of seeing Freedom again. She could visualize him so clearly, in his old cap and baggy trousers, running across the fields, and she couldn't understand why she was crying, it was so foolish of her, and in a public place, too.

She bathed her face and checked her appearance in the ladies' powder room inside the store, then nervously enquired the way to Jermyn Street. She was surprised to find it in the heart of the West End, having expected it to be a tram journey away. She was directed across Piccadilly, past a very fashionable shop, and down a small alley alongside a church. So this was where Freedom was staying. Evelyne stood in Jermyn Street taking in the rows of small shops selling soap, the tailors, the barbers.

Freedom stepped down from the motorcar and held out his hand to help two women from the back of the car. Evelyne could hardly believe her eyes, was it Freedom? She inched further forward, trying to see round the open door of the car. He was wearing a long, charcoal-grey overcoat, with a wide fur collar slightly turned up around his neck, and a white silk scarf. He laughed, throwing his head back, as one of the women pulled at the scarf and stood on tiptoe to whisper in his ear.

Dodging through the shoppers, Evelyne huddled in a doorway and watched as he held out first one arm, then the other, for the women to take. They fought for his attention. Being so tall he had to bend down to listen to what one of them had to say, and she took the opportunity to kiss his cheek. Evelyne gasped and stepped forward for a better view, then dodged quickly back as the three moved towards the building. A uniformed doorman stepped out and doffed his cap to them, holding the door open wide. As they went inside and the glittering doors closed behind them, Evelyne ran the few yards to the entrance, and peered through the doors in time to see them standing by a lift.

Freedom pressed the lift button. His head was aching from drinking too much champagne, but Dewhurst would have coffee ready. He was supposed to be training, but he would make up for it in the morning. As the lift gates opened he had a strange tingling sensation like an icy hand down his spine, and he whipped round, his scarf flying, ran to the doors and pulled them open. 'Evie? Evie . . .?'

He stared along the crowded, fashionable street, then shook his head. He must be drunk. The door swung to and fro, and he returned to the women.

'Oh, Freedom, we simply must take you to tea at the Ritz, say you will? Pretty please?'

He gave her a nasty, cold stare, gritted his teeth.

'Pretty please, get in, let me show you *my* Ritz!'

The two of them giggled at his awful mood, and they cuddled close to him, clinging to his arms. They felt like a pair of monkeys to him, they loved to scratch him with their long, red-painted fingernails. Still, they helped him to forget, forget Evie.

Ted Harris heard Evelyne come in, and opened the kitchen door.

'Evie, that you, ducks? A cabbie came round wiv a parcel for you, here, see, cab all by itself, no one inside.'

Evelyne took the parcel but wouldn't meet his eyes.

'You all right, ducks? Feelin' poorly, are you?'

'I'm fine, I'll just rest, I'll see to the children's tea in a minute.'

Ted watched her hurry along the passage to her room. She was so pale, it worried him.

In the room Evelyne opened Miss Freda's gifts. The tiny baby clothes, so perfectly made, were perhaps not in the colours she would have chosen, but they were beautiful. There was a little note in the parcel, but the writing was so bad that it took Evelyne ages to decipher what Freda had written.

'In haste, darling, I will come and see you. God bless you and keep you well. Yours, Freda.'

Freda's mouth seemed to be out of control, it kept dropping open as she sat and watched Freedom lounging on the sofa opposite her. He wouldn't meet her eyes, she had noticed that right at the start, as soon as they had arrived. He was being flippant and amusing, and from his shoes to his shining hair he was so well-groomed she would never have known him.

'Lads reckon you'll be having to start work first thing Monday, Freedom?'

Freda knew what Ed was going on about, but Freedom seemed to pay him little attention. Suddenly he sprang to his feet and asked Ed if he would go down to the teashop and order something for them.

An extremely disgruntled Ed departed, leaving Freedom and Freda alone together. They sat in silence for a minute, Freedom staring down at his shiny boots and Freda looking at the curtains, reckoning the material would cost at least four or five shillings a yard. He wanted to talk to her, desperately needed to talk to someone, but he just didn't know how to begin.

Eventually he rose to his feet and picked up his walking stick, tossed it in the air and then showed Freda the silver handle. 'See, it's a boxing glove, Miss Freda.'

She looked, not that she was particularly interested. It was Freedom, he had changed, and she couldn't speak to him any more.

'Yes, Sir Charles give it to me, bought it for me, he likes buyin' things, yes he does, I reckon he got me cheap, though ... Well ta-ra, Dewhurst'll see to your needs.'

He gave a low bow and was gone.

That night, Freda agreed with Ed that Freedom had changed. She couldn't talk to him, not in the old way, it was as if he was a stranger.

Poor Ed was at a loss, 'It's the way 'e 'as of making you not know what 'e's thinkin', what 'e's feelin' ... 'e told me they was married, did I tell you that? Yes, 'e said Evie an' 'im was married, not a proper service like ours, some Romany thing they just did together – becomin' a real ladies' man now, though!'

This was Freda's moment to ask if Freedom was missing Evelyne, wanted to see her at all. 'Does he still ask after Evie, Ed?'

Ed replied in a mutter that Sir Charles had forbidden it, in case a scandal about the trial got out. ''E was on a murder charge. You think the prince an' all those society people'd be sittin' pawin' at 'im if they knew that? It's best Evie's name never crops up.'

Freda couldn't bring herself to tell Ed about Evie's letter, about the baby. If anything it would cause an even greater scandal.

*

Sir Charles was staying at the Savile Club, and Ed went to meet him there.

'He's not the same lad, guv, shows no interest, an' 'e's not comin' to the gym, I was wonderin' if you could 'ave a word wiv 'im, seein' as you're takin' 'im out an' about . . . Only, if we don't get 'im ter buckle down 'e'll lose the championship an' we'll both be left – if you'll pardon the expression – we'll both be left lookin' like bleedin' idiots.'

'Ed, what do you take me for, I've not seen him in over a week! Good God, man, I'm the first to know that a fighter mustn't, as you say, burn up his wick, tell him to come to the Pelican tonight, and you too, Ed.'

Freedom was late arriving at the club, which annoyed Sir Charles, who had checked his watch three times. There was a good snooker game going on in one of the annexes, and he saw Freedom strolling along, watching the players.

'Here he is now, Ed, leave it to me.'

When he joined them Freedom asked the waiter for a beer, then leaned back in his chair, rocking it on its back legs.

'Thinking of bringing in a sparring partner, just to work you up for the big day, what do you say?'

For a reply he got a shrug of the shoulders. Freedom seemed more interested in the snooker. Staring at him through his monocle, Sir Charles lit a cigar, puffed on it.

'Ed here tells me you're below par. That true, feeling off colour, are you?'

Again the annoying shrug of Freedom's shoulders as he murmured that if Ed had said it then it must be true. Sir Charles had had enough, he leaned forward and snapped at Freedom in icy tones, 'When you feel you can talk, please contact me. I'm afraid I have better things to do with my time than to sit here and be insulted. You may believe I own you, so be it, but I am not prepared to be treated like a pimp, pull yourself together, lad, or I will throw your contract back in your face, is that clear?' He walked briskly away from the table without a backward glance.

Wanting to weep, Ed stared sorrowfully into his beer. How could Freedom do this to him after all the love and hard work Ed had put into him? 'You just kicked me down, you know that, lad? I dunno why you done this to me, you could be the next British champion, I know it, but not this way. You're breakin' my 'eart.'

Shoving Freedom's hand away he stumbled from the table, leaving Freedom sitting alone in the pit.

Outside the club an old, bent man was sweeping the pavement, where the sawdust had travelled on the gents' shoes into the road. The old chap didn't seem to notice Freedom, and almost ran the brush over his shoes.

'Aw, sorry about that, sir, here, allow me . . . you a fightin' mun are ye?'

Taking a handkerchief from his pocket, he was about to bend down to dust Freedom's shoes. He looked up for a moment. His bruiser's face was wrinkled, and he had cauliflower ears, a broken nose.

'Hammer, it's you, isn't it? Dai Thomas, Hammer-head?'

The old boy chuckled and wagged his head, spat on his fists and held them up.

'Ay, lad, that's me all right.'

With a toothless grin he looked into Freedom's face with no sign of recognition. Freedom's heart went out to him, he looked at all the traffic heading towards

Piccadilly. 'Where can a mun get a cup of tea this time of night?' Hammer waved his brush to a small alley, and accepted Freedom's offer to accompany him there. He also accepted the steaming bowl of soup Freedom placed before him. He sucked at the bread, making loud noises as he slurped the thick soup. He wiped the bowl with his crust until it glistened. He made no reply when Freedom asked how long he had been in London. But his face lit up when the ham and eggs followed, then he turned sly.

'What are you after? Why you buying all this for me, eh?'

He raised the fork and tucked into the ham, not waiting for a reply. At least, not until he had filled his belly.

'I'm Freedom Stubbs.'

Freedom stared at Hammer, did he remember? Know him? Hate him? He could clearly recall the man as he had been, arms up in the air, swaggering in his corner all those years ago in Cardiff. The café owner slapped his fat thigh and went behind the counter, delving underneath for newspapers. 'By Christ, I thought I recognized yer. Will yer look at this, this is the man that knocked out Pat Murphy just the other month.'

'Gawd almighty, I know you, this is him that knocked me teeth down me throat, remember me always talkin' of the bout, this is the mun that did it.' Hammer seemed flooded with renewed energy, he was up on his feet, prancing around on the sawdust floor. Freedom had expected the old man to go for him, but there was no animosity, more hero-worship. He thudded round to stand by Freedom's side, his big fist came down on the shoulder of Freedom's expensive overcoat and gripped it hard. 'Now then, mun, you'll have one hell of a bout with Micky, lemme tell you, I see 'im box, oh, must be

462

four, five years ago. He was just a kid, but 'e's got hands like spades, and they hurt.'

Some old boxers sitting in the café began to take notice, pulling their chairs closer to listen. Hammer basked in Freedom's glory. 'I went down so hard they never thought I'd be comin' round, three-quarters of an hour I was out, out for more than the count, eh?'

By the time Freedom and Hammer walked back towards the Pelican Club, they had their arms about each other's shoulders, the best of friends, buddies. Hammer collected his broom from the club's doorway.

'Handle yerself well, son, don't want to see you on the other end of one of these, well, not yet, anyway. Could you see your way to getting me a ticket for the Albert Hall? I'd like to be there to see you thrash the Liverpudlian. Be a proud day for me to say I went down to the British champ . . .'

Freedom promised to send him a ticket, then he hesitated. 'Don't put yer money on me, Hammer.'

Hammer grabbed Freedom's arm, and his bent body straightened. Through globs of spittle at the side of his mouth he swore at Freedom, almost pushed him off his feet.

'That's not fighter's talk, what's the matter with you, lad? I'd have given me life for an opportunity like you got, any mun would – I know I would. What's up with ye?'

To Hammer, of all people, the man Freedom had sent sprawling, he opened up, near to tears. 'They own me, mun, me, an' I'm through, there won't be no fight.'

Hammer's chin wobbled, and tears came into his already watery eyes. He looked at Freedom with disgust,

463

thudded his fist into his own chest. 'Nobody owns a fighter's heart, mun, you throw the fight and you'll not live with yourself. Take the fancy clothes away and you're a gyppo. But win the title an' you're a champion.'

Hammer stepped aside as three gents came out of the club and slipped him a few coppers. He immediately started sweeping the sawdust-covered pavement again. Freedom walked away, he didn't look back, he couldn't.

Mrs Harris could hear Evie down in the kitchen. She pulled on her worn coat over her nightdress and went downstairs.

'All right, are you, lovey? Fancy a cup of tea?'

Evelyne turned her face away, not wanting her friend to see she had been crying. They had not spoken of what had happened in Jermyn Street, there had been no need. Evelyne had been so quiet that Mrs Harris knew something had gone wrong.

'There's nothing to say, just . . . I saw him, and, well, he's not the man I knew, and I know he wouldn't want me, I know.'

Mrs Harris put the kettle on and stoked up the fire, questioned her no further. She sighed, it looked as though they would have their guest to stay for a long time. 'Whatever 'appens, ducks, this is your home now, yours and the baby's, so put your mind at rest on that.'

Evelyne hugged the big, kind woman, and the strong arms held her tight.

'There's a good gel, you'll be all right, you'll see.'

In the cold light of dawn Freda woke to see Ed standing by the window. He was dressed, ready to go out, and she put out her hand, but he didn't take it. She watched his depressed, squat figure walking down the street. The milk cart began its round, the horse clip-clopping out of the dairy half-way down the road. She made up her mind then and there that she would go and see Evelyne. Not just for the girl, but for herself and Ed too, if Evelyne could make Freedom see sense then she would see him, whether Ed liked it or not.

Sir Charles laid a neat ledger in front of Freedom, with all the expenses calculated to date. Every item bought for Freedom was carefully listed in Ed's handwriting. Clothes in one column, food in another, lodgings, keep, train tickets – every item was accounted for. There were pages and pages of figures from Cardiff, the lawyer's and the barrister's bills from Smethurst's firm, Evelyne's hotel bills and receipts, even down to her satin dress and the rented jewellery. On the following pages were the wages paid to Ed and the two lads, their expenses and their keep. Freedom's head began to spin as Sir Charles flicked the pages over. 'Not done yet, take a look at these figures, this is just for the tickets, the posters, the press.'

Page after page was turned over, and the final amount was written in the last column. More than five thousand pounds.

'I'd say we've invested quite a large sum, wouldn't you? And I think Ed told you, you will be allowed two hundred from the purse, *if* you win the championship.'

Sir Charles flicked a small piece of thread from his trouser leg, held it aloft to inspect it.

'If you lose, the contract we have will be null and void, it's quite obvious why, and surely you must see why I have to have a contract in the first place. You win the British title and you'll have God knows how many promoters after you. Next stop America, and the fights there take ten times more money than they do here. All I have done, old chap, is to protect my investment.'

He couldn't determine what Freedom was thinking, but he assumed it was slowly sinking in. 'If I have made you feel anything less than a friend, I apologize, it certainly was not my intention. I have believed in you right from the very beginning, from Devil's Pit, you know I travelled up there to see *you*?'

Pacing the room, Freedom felt guilty, confused. He was all mixed inside.

'Ed will be waiting at the gym, what do you want to do? I am perfectly willing to listen to anything within reason . . . I will be saddened if you want to walk away, but I can't stop you. You will, of course, have to repay all the costs, and I don't think it too unreasonable, not at this late stage.'

Freedom could hardly swallow, his tongue felt dry and seemed to be sticking in his throat.

'It's entirely your decision but we can't wait, not too long. If you want to back out I shall have to find another contender, won't be easy. Then again, fighters are two a penny, Freedom; sooner you learn that the better.'

Ed made both men jump as he slammed into the room, flushed with anger. 'Fighters, maybe, but not champions. You're a bloody fool, Freedom . . . sorry, sir, ter barge in like this, but I been up all night long, an' I just can't, can't let 'im walk away.' He turned to Freedom. 'If it's Evie you want then we'll find 'er, if that's what all this is about. If it is 'er, then bugger the press, I say, and I'm sorry, sir, but sod the prince an' all. I put months of my time into this lad, an' I won't let 'im throw it away.'

Sir Charles was on his feet, his manner controlled but more angry than Freedom had ever seen him. 'One moment if you please, Ed, I am sure your theatrical entrance was meant well.'

His voice was chilling in its calmness as he glared at Freedom. 'I want the truth, Stubbs, you swore on oath on that witness stand. Tell me, it was a pack of lies, wasn't it? You killed that boy in the picture house, didn't you? *Didn't you? Tell me*!'

His control left him and he raised his stick, looking as though he would bring it down on Freedom's head. Ed gaped, but Freedom moved fast, wrenching the stick away from Sir Charles. Ed thought he would break it in two, but he held it calmly, tapping it into the palm of his hand.

'I did no killing, sir, an' what I said on that stand was the truth. I dunno why I'm acting the way I am, I can only say I'm sorry . . . I love her, sir, I dunno why she went without sayin' nothin' to me, and it's eating me up inside.'

Tight-lipped, Sir Charles picked up his gloves and told Ed to take Freedom to his woman, he would see to the press personally.

'You'll fight, then?'

'I just need to see her, that's all, mun.'

Ed sighed with relief, grabbed Freedom's coat. 'Get yerself down ter the gym, I'll get Freda to bring her to you, go on, get out.'

Freedom didn't need to be told twice. He was out of the room like lightning. Ed hovered at the door.

'Well, sir, do we go on or not?'

Sir Charles shrugged. 'As you said, we've put a lot of time and money into him, why not?'

Ed ran after Freedom. Sir Charles could see them both from the apartment window, running along Jermyn Street, dodging the passers-by. The gypsy spring was back, all right.

Dewhurst coughed politely.

'Will you be wanting anything, sir?'

Still staring into the street, Sir Charles was carefully pulling on his gloves. When he spoke his voice was matter-of-fact, with hardly a trace of emotion. 'Appears our problems were to do with the gel, young fella loved her.'

Dewhurst raised his eyebrows. Sir Charles didn't look at him, could have been talking to himself. 'Funny, ya know, I have never known that sort of love, the sort he feels for this girl, never known it . . . but I do understand. You see, somewhere in the darkened recesses of my mind, I have dreamed of him loving me – never known me treat one of my boxers with such lavish care, have you, eh?'

'No sir, I have not, sir.'

Sir Charles' monocled eye glistened with a magnified tear. He adjusted his cravat. 'Get my things sent over from the Savile, would you, shall be moving back here. Ed can arrange accommodation for him, and he will not be using my barber or my tailor again, is that clear?'

'Yes, sir, perfectly clear, I shall call them straightaway.'

Sir Charles smiled at his manservant, 'You're a jolly good fellow, Dewhurst, I appreciate you greatly . . . still, I didn't embarrass myself, did I? Does no harm to have lascivious dreams . . .'

Dewhurst bowed himself out of the room and went immediately to the bedroom where Freedom had been sleeping. Sir Charles followed him and stared at the crumpled sheets. 'Well, maybe we'll have a champion. Then again we may not, send everything here to the gym. Oh, and Dewhurst – throw the sheets out, would you?'

The door closed silently behind him, and his voice echoed from the corridor.

'I'll be at my club should anyone call.'

After folding Freedom's clothes carefully, Dewhurst got some brown paper and made a neat parcel.

Freedom worked out hard and well with his two sparring partners, but he constantly glanced at the doors, waiting. Finally, Ed reappeared. 'Freda's gone to get her, lad, now get on wiv it, we need all the time we can get . . . Come on, get on with yer work out, the press is comin' fer an interview in 'alf an hour!'

All the neighbours were staring out of their windows, peering out of their doors. Freda had arrived in a horse-drawn cab, and she knocked and knocked on Mrs Harris' door.

'What's up, somebody die? Hey, darlin', you with the ratcatchers then, are you?'

A scruffy little boy answered the door.

'Is Evie here? Evelyne, is she here?'

He couldn't understand what the hysterical little woman was saying. Mrs Harris came to the door and opened it wider. She was carrying little Dora on her hip. 'Evie? Is it Evie yer want? Well, she's gorn ter the clinic, it's in Upper Lambeth Street.'

Freda was already rushing back to the cab. Mrs Harris called after her.

'If she ain't there, try Swan an' Edgar's, she winder-shops a lot.'

Freedom had changed into his best clothes for the photographers. He seemed not to care about posing, constantly glancing at Ed and then to the doors. 'Freda not called yet, Ed? You think she's found her?'

469

Ed began to panic, maybe Evie had moved, that would be all they needed. 'Just concentrate on puttin' on a good show fer the photographers, lad, I'll nip outside an' have a look, she'll be here.'

As Ed bustled out he offered a silent prayer that Freda would find Evie, and fast. They'd got Freedom back to work, but if she didn't show up Ed didn't know how long he would behave himself.

Evelyne had walked up Jermyn Street every day for the past five days, each time pausing outside the ornate building where she had seen Freedom, and the uniformed porter had begun to raise his hat to her and smile in recognition. Today she had been about to ask him if Mr Stubbs still lived in these apartments, but at the last moment she couldn't find the courage. She turned and hurried away.

Freda swiped the tram conductor with her handbag when he tried to prevent her jumping off, shouting to her that she would kill herself. She had seen Evelyne, staring into one of the windows of Swan and Edgar. Poor Freda ran round and round the building, calling Evelyne's name frantically, but she had disappeared.

'Get yourself thinking, Freda darlink, where would she 'ave gone from here, where? Please, dear God, tell me where she is?'

She scurried among the baby clothes and toys, diving among the shoppers, but Evelyne wasn't there. Disappointed, she turned back towards the stairs . . . and caught sight of the familiar red hair. Her heart skipped a beat, and she hurried around the counter . . . and lost her again . . . no, she hadn't, there was Evelyne, bending over a cradle, touching it lovingly . . .

'*Evie! Evieeeee . . . Evie . . .*'

The reporters and cameramen were just packing up when one of the boys fell down the steps into the gym. He rubbed his shin and gasped incoherently. 'They got her, she's found her, she's coming!'

Ed shouted for quiet and ran to the boy, grabbed him by the collar. 'What . . .? What . . .!? Speak up, lad.'

Freedom seemed to cover the distance from the far end of the gym to Ed's side in one leap.

'Take it easy, mate, Freda's found her, we've found her.'

Freedom sprinted up the stairs to the street, looking this way and that, desperate, but there was no sign of anyone. Panic-stricken, he turned to Ed, who ran up and down the road shouting for Freda, for Evie. The lad joined them, saying he had just seen them in a cab, they were outside the gym not two minutes ago.

Freda held Evelyne's hand as the cabbie drove them once again around the block. Evelyne studied her face in Freda's small mirror.

'Oh, Freda, I can't, look at me, I look terrible, my hair's all down and I got my old coat on and shoes full of newspapers.'

Freda rummaged in her bag for a comb, waved her hand for the cabbie to go round the block yet again. 'Here, darlink, my comb, come, let me, let me.'

Freda tried frantically to drag the comb through

Evelyne's hair, but it was a tiny comb and there was so much hair.

On the corner stood Ed, hopefully eyeing each vehicle that passed. He spotted the cab and jumped right in front of it, making the horses shy. Diving into the back he fell into Evie's arms, kissing her as if *he* were her long-lost lover, he was so excited. Freedom reappeared and Freda and Ed ran down the road to him, Freda's feet hardly touching the ground.

'She's in the cab, go on, she's in the cab.'

The look on his face made them both want to cry, he didn't know what to do with himself. He ran his hands through his hair and tried to straighten his tie while at the same time running as fast as he could to the cab. Fascinated, the cabbie looked down from his seat, this was better than the picture houses.

Freedom bent his head into the open carriage window. Evelyne had pressed herself shyly into the corner of the carriage, her cheeks flaming red and her wondrous hair tumbling over her shoulders. Standing staring at her, Freedom could find no words. His breath heaved in his chest, and try as he might he couldn't stop the sobs forcing their way into his throat, nor could he move.

Eventually he spoke, his voice strained. 'Can I ride a while with you, *manushi*?'

He climbed into the cab and sat by Evelyne's side. He could hear Ed shouting to the driver to just keep driving, drive anywhere. The carriage jolted forward.

Evelyne took Freedom's hand and placed it on her stomach, and he gasped as if he were about to explode. Immediately she let his hand go, and turned to stare out of the carriage.

She whispered, 'I'm sorry, he's yours, Freedom.' She

472

felt his hand gently caress her swollen belly, and fraction by fraction she turned her head until she could look into his face. She placed her hand over his heart, felt it thudding, and he put his hand over her milk-filled breast. Heart to heart, they whispered each other's names.

'Never leave me, *manushi*. I died a little while you were gone.'

It was getting dark, and the cabbie began to wonder who would be paying his fare. They were still trotting round and round Regent's Park. The lovers whispered to each other, their fingers interlocked as they vowed they would never again be parted.

Chapter 20

E D MEADOWS led Freedom into the weighing-room. It was full of reporters, promoters and officials, standing around the scale. Freedom wore shorts, boxing boots and a robe, the hood pulled over his head, hiding his face.

Micky Morgan, dressed in the same way as Freedom, stood with his corner men and trainer at the far end of the room. His back was to the entrance, but as the murmur of voices died down he knew his opponent had arrived. He didn't turn, but his back straightened, like an animal sensing danger.

'Gentlemen, to the scales, please.'

Micky turned slowly, eyes down, refusing to look at Freedom as they were led to the scales. Micky took off his robe first and stepped up. The two officials looked at the pointer, conferred with each other and pushed the weights along the scale bar as Ed tried to get a look over their shoulders to see what weight Morgan was carrying.

'The champion weighing in, gentlemen, at thirteen stone ten pounds, standing at six feet one and a half inches.'

Still without even a flicker of a glance at Freedom, Micky stepped down, and his trainer immediately replaced his robe around his shoulders. Ed gave him a clinical, professional appraisal. The man was in terrific shape, his skin taut, his body muscular, and his shoulders were slightly concave – good, hunched, boxer's shoulders. There was no sign of the cut he had taken over his eye in his last championship bout, it seemed completely healed. His nose was flat, eyes hooded, and there was a slight puffiness just below the brows. One of his front teeth was missing, and one of his ears was larger than the other. As he pulled his robe around his shoulders, Ed could see his massive hands, the flat, gnarled knuckles.

The fight was by no means going to be easy, Ed knew Micky looked confident, and Ed knew he was purposely refusing to look in Freedom's direction.

'Would the contender please step on the scales.'

It was Freedom's turn, and off came his robe as he stepped on to the scales. The officials moved the weights, checking carefully, and Micky now watched closely. Freedom was one hell of a size, and his skin was tawny, unlike Micky's which was whiter-than-white. As the marker on the measuring stick was lowered to Freedom's head, Micky could see he was well over six feet tall.

'The contender, gentlemen, weighs in at fourteen stone, one pound, eight ounces, standing at six feet four inches.'

'He's a ruddy Red Indian, look at the hair on 'im, halfway down 'is back.'

Both boxers were taken back to their dressing rooms, and an hour later they were called in to the conference room. The champion was applauded as he entered. He was wearing a cheap, brown pin-striped suit, a white shirt and tie, and he was carrying a brown trilby hat. He took his seat on the platform beside his trainer and promoter, Lord Livermore, who wore a black coat with an astrakhan collar and smoked a fat Havana cigar. Sir Charles, as immaculate as ever, was talking quietly to him, and shook Micky's hand when they were introduced.

Ed ushered Freedom into the room and everyone turned to look at him. He did not warrant applause, and Ed whispered for him to take the seat next to Sir Charles. He stepped on to the platform and sat down, fingering his collar and straightening the jacket of his new, single-breasted suit, tailored in soft dove grey. Carrying Freedom's fur-collared coat, Ed inched his way in behind them and sat down, worried about falling because the leg of his chair was precariously near the edge of the platform. Lord Livermore held his cigar in front of his face and smirked to Sir Charles about his snazzily dressed boxer.

'How many rounds do you think it'll go, Micky?'

Smiling, Morgan gave a jerk of his head at Freedom and said that maybe they should ask the contender how many rounds he reckoned he could stand up for. This got a roar of laughter, and Micky posed for a solo photograph. Freedom was asked if he wanted to answer the champ's question, but he stared blankly and remained silent.

The press requested a shot of Micky and Freedom together, and the two men rose and faced each other, Micky confident and brash, smiling his gap-toothed grin. He got no response from Freedom whose dark eyes stared back, expressionless. The photographers took their time preparing their cameras, and as they waited Micky whispered to Freedom, his voice inaudible to the rest of the room, 'Goin' to mark that pretty face, gyppo, goin' to mark you, break you, gyppo, hear me, take you out in five.'

Freedom stared impassively into the champion's face, as if he hadn't heard the threat.

Ed's brother had found a house for Evelyne and Freedom, further along the terrace in the same street, not five turnings away from Mrs Harris'. The previous occupants of number twelve had fallen behind with their rent, and the bailiffs had moved them out. The house had been infested with mice and bugs so they had had to scrub and disinfect everything, and call in the rat-catcher to put down poison. This was Evelyne's first home of her own and, to the concern of all the women in the street, she had worked herself into exhaustion. Seeing her, heavily pregnant, scrubbing at the steps, had earned her the acceptance of all her neighbours. Freda and several other local women had scrubbed and washed and helped hang curtains, nail down lino, and had even brought odd bits of china to help out. They all called her Evie.

Mrs Harris was Evelyne's first proper visitor. She came walking slowly up the road, carrying a big pot of stew. ''Ello, lovey, I 'ad this on when one of the kids came round, so I didn't like to waste it . . . well, well, just think of it, you a neighbour! Well I never!'

Evelyne showed her round the scrubbed little house with pride. When she saw that Evie had got a gas stove, Mrs Harris went into raptures. There wasn't a stick of furniture yet, but the curtains were lovely, and the lino was a pretty shade of green.

'Oh, Evie love, it's a palace, a real palace, you've done wonders.'

A small crowd had gathered outside, and one of the women yelled to Evelyne at the top of her voice, 'It's the bed arrived, yer bed's come!' A new bed in this street was something, and all the neighbours were agog. The mahogany headboard met with nods of approval. The bed was enormous, and the delivery men had to be helped getting it into the house.

Freedom and Evelyne went up the narrow staircase and stood looking into their bedroom. There it was in all its glory, the special-sized bed.

'Well, I never thought I'd be a *kairengo*!'

Lying down on the thick mattress, Evelyne patted it for him to lie beside her. 'What does that mean?'

He lay down and told her that a *kairengo* was a man who lived in a house. He stared up at the ceiling, and she picked up his hand, kissed it, 'Do you not like it?'

He turned and touched her face, kissed her softly, 'It's what you want that's my pleasure. Tell me, are you happy?'

She rolled over, rubbed her belly and stretched. She told him she had never been so happy in her entire life. Up she got and swished the curtains, showing him the wooden rail, then insisted that he see everything, pulling him by the hand until he got up off the bed.

'This is our home, Freedom, and here, in here, this is where the baby will be. Mr Harris said he'd make me a cradle . . . and come on down, let me show you how the gas stove lights up. You don't need to have the fire lit, see, you turn this tap here, and you light it like so, isn't it lovely?'

Delighted, he watched her as she touched the walls,

the lino, and then brought him her notebook to show him what kind of furniture they would save for. 'We'll not get anything on tick, that way we won't get into debt, but we'll buy it piece by piece, it'll be so lovely.'

Freedom went back up to the bedroom. He didn't want to spoil her happiness, couldn't tell her the house was already weighing on him, closing in on him, and he hated it. Evelyne thought he was sleeping, but he was dreaming of the open air, the fields, riding on a wild pony. He felt her lie down beside him, and her body heat warmed him like a fire.

'Feel him, he's kicking, feel.'

He put his hand to her belly and felt the strange movements of his child inside her. He would fight for his very life in the ring, and he would give her everything she dreamed of, now he had something to fight for, his wife and his child.

Evelyne shifted to a more comfortable position, careful not to wake him, knowing he needed his sleep before the fight. Sweat broke out all over her, and the kicking, thudding, unborn child felt as if he was trying to punch his way through her backbone. 'Dear God, don't let him come now, not tonight. Stay put until after the fight.'

The morning of the fight was cold, and the snow was falling thick and fast. It was not yet five, but Evelyne could hear Freedom moving around downstairs, stoking up the kitchen fire. She felt the first spasm, it shook her body, and she bit hard on the blanket. He wasn't going to wait . . . She gasped, and the spasm subsided.

Ed banged on the front door, wrapped up and waiting to take Freedom over to the gym for a work out. Freedom was in high spirits, and raring to go. 'I done made a cup of tea on the stove, Ed, and it brought the kettle to the boil as fast as ever! You get me the tickets I asked for, Ed? I got to see they get their seats.'

Ed threw up his arms and said he'd given all the tickets out, they all had them, and he had taken one over to Hammer personally. 'You got more to worry about than ruddy tickets, mate, come on, I want you running in half an hour.'

As he put his coat on, Freedom noticed that Ed had trailed some mud in on his shoes so he fetched a cloth to wipe the lino.

'Now what you doin', Freedom?'

He could hardly believe it, there was his contender worrying about dirty lino.

'Ed? Ed, is that you? Will you come up for a minute?'

Freedom pushed Ed up the stairs and wiped the floor – he didn't want Evie getting down on her knees to do it. As Ed thudded up the stairs Freedom asked him if Evie's ticket was all right.

Exasperated, Ed leaned over the banister. 'Evie's ticket's all right, she'll be at the ringside, now will you stop maunderin' on an' get yer gear together. Gawd almighty, I don't know what's come over you.'

He tapped on the bedroom door and popped his head around, about to tell Evie she was married to a charlady, when she signalled to him to shut the door.

'The baby's coming, Ed, will you get Freda? But don't tell Freedom, I don't want him worrying.'

This was all they needed! Ed went dizzy, dear God, what a time for the baby to choose, the day of the fight! Panic-stricken, trying hard to look calm, he backed out of the room.

'I'll have to go back to the house, I've forgotten the liniment.'

Freedom laughed and said he would start walking,

Ed could catch up with him. So much for all Ed's hurrying, he was the one delaying them now. He was about to go up and say goodbye to Evelyne when Ed stopped him, pushed him down the stairs saying she was sleeping, he should let her rest. They tiptoed out, and Freedom closed the door quietly behind them as Ed sprinted down the street to his brother's house. The kids were in the middle of breakfast when he burst in, yelling for Freda. She hurried in with her hair still in curlers, already preparing herself for the big night.

'It's coming, you'd better get over there fast, it's coming.'

The children started to ask what was coming, but Freda understood immediately. 'What, now? But it's not due, not yet . . . oh my God, what a time to come!'

Still the kids asked who was coming, but no one answered. Freda rushed to get dressed.

Another contraction had Evelyne wailing with pain, wishing Freda would come. She was sweating, the hair on the nape of her neck damp, and the ache in her back agony. She felt the baby moving inside her.

Freda hurried along the street, carrying two big pots for boiling water. Evie opened the door to her, 'Will you get Mrs Harris? I want Mrs Harris here.'

Freda ordered Evie back into bed, then she fetched the pans and put them on the gas stove before rushing out to get Mrs Harris, leaving Evelyne writhing on the bed in agony.

Mrs Harris asked Evelyne how often her pains were coming, and Freda replied that it was immaterial how often – they were coming, that meant the baby was imminent. Although childless herself, Freda was suddenly an authority on childbirth. But Mrs Harris, having had seven, knew exactly what it was all about, and she shouted upstairs to Evelyne, ''Ave yer waters broke yet, love?'

Freda replied that they had two pans full, and they were just putting some more on. 'I know what to do, I read all about it for Evie. I got the water boilink,' she said proudly.

With a sigh, Mrs Harris shut the door, went to the bedroom and felt Evelyne's brow. Then she checked the sheets and shook her head. 'Yer water's not even broke yet, love, you're a long way off, when was yer last bellyache?'

Feeling better, Evelyne sat up and realized that she'd not had any contractions for quite a while.

'When they start joinin' into one, yer baby's on its way down the chute, so 'ow about a nice cup o' tea?'

On his morning run Freedom conserved his strength, running easily, relaxed, not taxing himself. Then he and Ed went to the café for a huge breakfast of steak and eggs. Freedom would not eat again until after the fight.

While Freedom was out of earshot, Ed sent one of the boys over to Freedom's to find out how Evelyne was and report back. He watched Freedom working out, holding back all the time, never pushing, and later gave him a rub down in the small massage room at the back of the gym, using his own concoction of olive oil mixed with a small amount of horse liniment and a spoonful of surgical spirit. He began on Freedom's calves and worked upwards to his back and shoulders.

'If I don't knock him out, Ed; I'll gas him!'

Ed thumped him on the back and told him to shut up and relax, he was to rest and prepare himself.

At four o'clock Freedom was sleeping in the back room, wrapped in blankets, while Ed paced the street outside the gym. This was the third trip the lad had made and still the baby had not arrived. It looked more as if Ed was the expectant father, he was so worried.

'It's not come yet, they was all drinking tea an' playin' rummy.'

Ed told him he could go to the house once more, and after that Freda could call them at the Albert Hall from the telephone in the local pub. The mere mention of the Albert Hall hit Ed like a brick on the back of his head. It was getting near the time, they would be leaving for the match in less than an hour.

'He's still fast asleep like a baby 'imself, Ed, you'd think he couldn't go out like that on the day of the fight.'

Evelyne had been in labour for most of the day, and the women were beginning to get anxious. It wasn't her they were worried about, she was strong and was taking the pains well. They were worried about not getting to the fight themselves. Ed's brother was beside himself, sitting drumming his fingers on the kitchen table and coming in every few minutes for news.

'Can you not push it out? She carries on like this an' you'll be too late ter get ter the fight.'

As cool as a cucumber, Mrs Harris replied, 'It'll come when it's ready and not before . . . now, Freda, you go an' get yerself dolled up. I'll sit wiv her.'

483

Freda came to the back door, wearing her hat and carrying her coat. One look told her nothing had happened yet. It was six o'clock, and they had to leave in half an hour, the fight was to start at half-past seven.

'They won't get into the ring prompt, like, but if we ain't there someone might get our seats, and then there's the build-up, that's all part of it, we'll miss that.'

Evelyne, the centre of everyone's problems, looked around her at the concerned faces. It was almost laughable, there they all were in their best clothes, hanging on her every utterance. Mrs Harris had tied a strip of sheeting around the mahogany bedpost for Evelyne to pull against when the pains came, but the pains hadn't been coming for the last hour.

'Go on, don't miss the fight for me, I'll be all right, and Mrs Harris'll stay with me, go on.'

Mrs Harris shooed everyone out, then went back to check on Evelyne. The rubber sheet was in place, the hot water ready, and there was a clean blanket for the baby. 'You all right, love? Just breathe easy, nice an' deep, won't be long now.'

Hammer paraded at the café wearing the proprietor's jacket, and a shirt, tie and a good pair of trousers given to him by the Salvation Army. 'I'm ringside, mun, did I tell you, look, see, ringside seat, and I'm not payin' a farthing.'

He had been displaying his ticket for days. He parted with it reluctantly at the box office, and proudly announced to everyone that he had once been knocked out by the contender.

He made his way to his seat, clutching his programme

484

and making a great show of reading it, although he couldn't read a word. Inside the programme was a photograph of Freedom, and he pointed to it, turning to anyone close at hand. 'I'd put me money on this lad, he took me out once, bout in Cardiff.'

The clamour of the crowd in the pit seats and the glitter of the society people filling the boxes made the huge hall seem to vibrate. A match was in progress in the ring, but no one was paying much attention, and many seats were still empty, most of the people not bothering to claim their seats until the main event. A murmur went up as the news spread that Prince Edward's party had arrived at the entrance to the hall. The tiered boxes were almost full and still the stragglers made their way to their seats. The first match ended in a spattering of applause, and a brass band began to play a lively march. The audience clapped their hands along with the music.

The noise drifted down to the dressing-rooms, where Ed had barred everyone but Sir Charles and the two corner men. Freedom sat on a table, hands out, as Ed carefully wound his bandages. Despite eighteen years' experience of bandaging boxers' hands Ed was meticulous, constantly asking if it was all right. Freedom looked at him, 'You don't need me to tell you, just get on with it.'

The atmosphere was tense, electric. In the main dressing room Micky Morgan's hands were being bandaged. His trainer stood behind him, massaging his shoulders, soothing him, talking quietly. 'Big crowd, not a seat to be had, His Royal's arrived, there's touts outside selling

485

tickets at five times the price, gonna be a night, Micky, your night, it's your night, Micky.'

Freedom's hands were ready, and they waited for the referee to come and check them over. He sat with his eyes closed, swinging his legs. Ed wished he knew what made Freedom tick, but he never had been able to fathom him out. He might be sitting waiting for his dinner, he seemed so relaxed.

Freda, her brother-in-law and his wife edged their way along the row to their seats. They waved to a few faces they knew, and sat down. Evelyne's empty seat was now more obvious in the crowded hall. Freda had tried to get round the back but hadn't been allowed in, they'd done all they could. The phones were all engaged. The operator had said she herself couldn't put any calls through, as there were so many people waiting.

A group of men in evening dress came walking along the passage from the dressing-rooms. The hall grew quiet as all eyes watched the ring. The band struck up a fanfare. Now they could see, way up by the entrance, the tight group of trainers and corner men, and behind them the hooded figure of Micky Morgan.

'This is it, gels, here they come.'

The corner men flanked Freedom as he progressed down the hall and up into the ring. The crowd went mad, cheering and yelling, but Freedom kept his head low, his gloved fists touching each other. Behind him came Ed, sweating, his face bright pink.

'There's Ed, there . . . see?'

The group entered the ring exactly opposite them, exactly opposite the empty seat, but for the moment it went unnoticed. The fanfare blasted again and the cheers grew even louder, nearly lifting the roof off as Micky entered. He wore a dark red velvet cape with the word 'Champion' written across the back. He bent to climb through the ropes, then stood with his fists above his head, and the crowd went wild.

Carrying a microphone on a long, thick lead, a white-haired man in tails and top hat stepped into the ring. He walked to the centre.

'My lords, ladies and gentlemen, please rise for the King!'

The band played and everyone in the hall sang in unison, 'God Save the King'. Prince Edward and his party were all standing in the royal box, and he too sang the National Anthem. He gave a small wave and then he, like everyone else in the hall, took his seat.

In the ring stood Freedom, head bowed, and Micky stared straight ahead. As the audience settled in their seats again, the boxers went to their corners. The master of ceremonies called out their weights and announced twenty, two-minute rounds. The referee, Ron Hutchinson, was introduced and bowed in the centre of the ring. He had once been a middleweight champion boxer, and was now about to retire from the police force. He had iron-grey hair and a stern-looking, craggy face.

On a podium overlooking the ring were two men with a film camera, recording the match. Ron Hutchinson went first to the champion's corner and asked if everything was ready, then crossed the ring to Freedom's corner. He actually had to ask twice, as Freedom was more intent on looking across at Freda than on what was happening in the ring.

'Her seat's empty, Ed. Where's Evie, she's not here?'

Hutchinson spoke a few words to the corner men, then made a slow circuit of the ring instructing all those close to the canvas to keep their hands away from the ring itself.

'Ed, she's not in her seat, Evie's not here.'

Ed gritted his teeth and swore at Freedom, this was not the time to start worrying about Evie.

Back in the centre of the ring, Hutchinson signalled for both boxers to come forward. Freedom was staring, concerned and preoccupied, at the empty seat. Hutchinson hooked an arm around each boxer's shoulders, and above the roar of the crowd he could be heard clearly, his voice harsh. 'I want a good clean fight, no butting, no holding. You break on my word, understand? No low punches, let's keep this professional. An' above all, obey my voice. I don't want to have to say things twice, an' I don't want to disqualify either of you for dirty fighting . . . All right, then back to your corners and may the best man win.'

As the boxers' gumshields were fitted the crowd went quiet, knowing the bell would clang at any moment. Ed whispered in Freedom's right ear as he rubbed his shoulders, repeating it over and over, desperate to get through to him. 'Evie's all right, she's fit an' she's strong, and she wants you to win, understand me, are you listenin' ter me? Evie had to stay 'ome, the baby's coming sooner than expected.'

Beneath Ed's kneading fingers Freedom's shoulders froze. 'Why didn't Freda stay with her for God's sake, mun? Is she on her own?'

Out of the corner of his eye, Ed could see the bell being lifted, the stop-watch being shown to the referee. Any moment now they were going to begin, and here was his man worrying himself sick over his wife.

'Evie said if Freda didn't come to the fight she'd never forgive 'er. She's got Mrs Harris, a doctor an' a midwife an' a nurse, so she's being taken care of . . . Now, think of the fight, son, concentrate, Freedom, get in there and go fer it.'

The bell rang, the corner men whipped the stools out and jumped down from the ring.

Micky was out of his corner like a bullet, his hands up, moving towards Freedom, and Freedom took two punches before the pain brought him round. Micky's eyes were like steel, staring into Freedom's face, and his gum protector made him look as if he was leering.

Mrs Harris knew it was time, the pains were ripping through Evelyne, and she was heaving for breath. 'Grab hold of the sheet, love, pull down, come on, grab it an' pull.'

Evelyne held on grimly to the twisted sheet knotted round the bedpost. With every contraction she held on and yelled her head off. Just by feeling her belly Mrs Harris knew the baby was big, so she heaved Evelyne on to her side, knowing her spine would take too much strain if she lay on her back.

''E's a big'un, an' 'e's on 'is way, so grip hard and press down, press him out of you every time that pain comes, press down and hang on to the sheet . . .'

Mrs Smith brought up hot water, standing by and giving way to Mrs Harris' experience. The big woman was so calm, soothing Evelyne and rubbing her back, talking quietly to her and going through each spasm herself.

''Ere we go, love, 'ere comes another one . . . and push him, that's my girl, push.'

Freedom slumped into the corner, and Ed dipped his sponge and squeezed it over Freedom's face. One of the lads dipped the gumshield in the water to clean it, and the other held it ready and gave Freedom water. He gulped and spat into the bucket.

'Is there any way we can get word if she's all right, Ed?'

The lad watched as Ed lathered Vaseline over Freedom's eyebrows and cheeks.

'We got someone standing by in the pub, anyfink 'appens they'll call us, don't worry.'

All Freedom's concentration was on Evelyne, and he was sick with worry. On the other hand, Ed was sick that Freedom wasn't fighting, he was letting punch after punch penetrate his defence. Already there were deep red marks on his chest, Micky's glove prints were all over him.

'You're buggerin' around out there, hear me? If Evie knew what you was doin' she'd get into this ring herself. Your gel's a fighter, for God's sake, you gotta win for 'er.'

The bell rang again, and Micky was up and out of his corner. His trainer was satisfied, so far Micky was ahead on every round, and he began to think that Micky would take the gyppo out in five rounds as he had bragged. All through the break his trainer said, over and over, 'You've got him on the run, and he's got no punch, he's not landed one home. Take him, Micky, go on, take him.'

*

490

Round four, and Micky certainly looked as if he was beating the contender. He began to get cocky, hissing through his gumshield, 'Whassamatter, gyppo, scared, scared? Fight, come on, whassamatter, hit me, hit me.'

So cocksure was Micky that at one point he turned to the crowd so they could see him smile. The sounds of cheering were getting mixed now with booing, so Micky decided to go for it, and moved in. Bam, bam . . . he edged Freedom on to the ropes. Freedom ducked, side-stepped, ducked, sidestepped, then threw two punches so wild that Micky got in one hell of a crack. His right hook landed on Freedom's jaw.

The crowd gasped, Freedom was off balance . . . he staggered slightly then recovered. Micky was sure the punch would have knocked him down, and was surprised when the big lad came straight back at him. The bell rang, and it was yet another round to Micky. Ed had screamed himself hoarse from the corner, Freedom wasn't using his brains, he was dancing, to Ed's knowledge he hadn't thrown one decent punch, one that had landed. 'He's wiping the canvas with you, an' you're lettin' 'im do it, come on, come on, get your temper up, fight him!'

Ed eased the elastic on Freedom's trunks as the corner men sponged and towelled him. Freedom spat water and sniffed, and again Ed lathered the Vaseline on. Freedom's face was marked on the right side.

In the other corner the trainer barked into Micky's face that this was it – this was the round. Micky heaved for breath and said it was like doing the charleston out there, but he was still heaving. The gyppo might be on the run but he was still tiring Micky. 'I'll take him this round.'

Clang! They were up again, Ed's screams going unheard beneath the roar of the crowd. Ed was screaming,

'*Body*! *Body*!' as Micky was keeping his hands high, head down. He held Freedom and they both lurched over to the ropes. Micky still held on, leaning his whole weight on Freedom until the referee split them apart. Micky was no longer hissing insults, he was moving in for the kill, and he looked as if he would pull it off until Freedom caught him with a good left jab, straight on to his old cut. Micky swore and went after Freedom, hurting now, his eye smarting. He was also worried, he'd felt that jab – not that it could have cut him down, but it could be dangerous if the old wound were to open up.

When the bell clanged, round five was evens, leaving Micky a clear four rounds ahead.

'He's like an ox, I've been hitting him hard and he just takes it, I dunno where he's coming from.'

Micky's eyes were checked and greased, his trainer giving him instructions all the time, telling him to go for the head, Freedom was open 'upstairs'. The bell rang for round six, and one of the lads ran to the dressing room to get fresh water.

Mrs Harris soaked strips of cloth in hot water and laid them over Evelyne. The heat soothed her. Mrs Harris herself had never been this long in labour . . . Evelyne lay on her side, hands slightly above her head, gripping the rope. A sudden, terrible pain shot through her, as though she was being torn in two, and she screamed through clenched teeth, screamed that she'd had enough, she didn't want him, she couldn't take any more. The relief was so sudden it stunned her, and she gasped, her mouth open wide.

'Here 'e is, love, here 'e is, come on you little bugger, and about time, too.'

She was right, he *was* big, and she had to help him in the first few moments, but out he came, and she held him upside-down by his heels, one sharp slap and the next moment Evelyne's howl was joined by a lusty yell from her son.

'Here 'e is, come on, Evie love, let go of the rope, 'e's 'ere.'

Evelyne loosened her grip and eased herself over. Mrs Harris held the baby out to her and she saw the thick thatch of black hair. His lungs were working overtime, and as Evelyne held him to her, his fists punched the air.

'He's a boxer like 'is dad, eh? Will you look at 'im, Evie, I'd say he was a ten-pounder, more . . . My God he's strong.'

Round seven, and Micky slumped in his corner. As they eased out his gumshield he gasped, 'By Christ, when he gets a punch home it hurts, how's the eye?'

Micky was confident, he knew he was well ahead on points, but the corner men had their work cut out for them because his eye was opening up. They painted it, daubed him with Vaseline, and his eyes smarted and filled with tears. He gulped at the water and spat it out.

Freedom was panting and Ed was sponging him down, drenching him with the cold water. 'That was the first time you connected, the first, and you 'urt 'im. 'Is eye's openin' up, keep on that eye, an' watch 'is right. He's got a nasty sneaky double punch, left-left-right, and then in he comes, watch out for it.'

Suddenly Freedom jerked his head away from Ed's greasy fingers and stared up at him with such an expression that Ed stepped back, 'I got a son, I got a son, Ed, my boy's born.'

Ed's jaw dropped, and one of the lads had to ram the

gumshield in Freedom's mouth as the bell was raised. Freedom was up before it rang and prancing into the ring. The lads had to haul the amazed Ed out of the ring. He wasn't sure what to think, the look on Freedom's face had completely unnerved him. He checked his watch and almost gave himself whiplash as a huge cheer broke from the crowd.

Freedom was punching now, for the first time he was showing his colours, and Micky was taken off-balance. He took a punch to his left side that winded him, and he rocked. The crowd roared, but Micky paced back and gave himself a push off the ropes. For once he was on the run, the crowd knew it, and so did Micky. Freedom was jabbing, tough, hard, tight jabs, and they were hammering down on Micky's eye. He felt it splitting, and the blood began to drip down his face; he knew he would have to keep on the move for this round. This was Freedom's first clear round, and the crowd began to sense that the fight had only just begun. They were on their feet, throwing caps in the air, and when the bell rang it was hard to hear. The sound of it was sweet relief to Micky, and his men worked double time trying to close the cut. His eye was puffing up, and his vision on the left was blurred.

Freda's hat was over one ear, she had eaten her handkerchief, and shouted so much she'd lost her voice. Hammer jumped up from his seat and swung his fist as Freedom began to perk up. The poor elderly man sitting directly in front of him felt his false teeth shoot out as Hammer's fist connected with the back of his head. The pair scrabbled beneath the seat, Hammer shouting his apologies.

'Just get me teeth, twenty-five shillings' worth there, mate.'

But the teeth were forgotten as the bell clanged for round nine.

Ed was mopping his brow with the sponge, his shirt drenched, his bright red braces sticking to him.

'Come on lad, this is it, go for it. *Go for it*!'

Micky was tough and there was no way he was going to go down easily. He knew he was still ahead on points, and he took a breather, keeping on the move, letting Freedom do all the chasing.

'Fight, mun, go on, stop doing the dance, mun, *fight*!'

Having worked so hard in the earlier rounds, Micky was warned three times by the ref for holding. Round nine went to Freedom, and the ref went over to Micky's corner in the break. His men grouped tightly around him, swearing that everything was all right, and the ref had to pry their pressing hands from Micky's cut. Satisfied that the blood had been stemmed, he gave the signal for the fight to continue.

'It's yours, Freedom, keep on his eye, it's split like an orange, hear me, get his eye.'

Round ten, and Freedom was on his feet before the bell rang. The crowd was going crazy, and fights were breaking out as the people behind tried to make those in the ringside seats sit down so their view would not be blocked.

Freedom swigged the water and tried to get his breath as Ed flapped with the towel. 'I'm hitting him with all I've got, Ed, and he's still on his feet.'

Ed massaged him and kept up a steady flow of instructions. He knew Freedom was exhausted, Micky was holding on to him at every opportunity. Freedom's face was red, but there was no broken skin, and not even a hint of puffiness around the eyes.

'You got the Prince standin' up shouting for yer in that last round, take him this round, lad, you know you can.'

Freedom smiled and said that if he won this round his son would be called Edward. Again Ed felt a chill through his sweating body, and he shuddered. Freedom talked as if he knew something Ed didn't, but the bell clanged and he had to hurry down from the ring.

Micky got a second wind, God knows from where, and lambasted Freedom. Micky's nose was bleeding and his eye was swollen so he couldn't see . . . He was flaying the air, coming back for a right hook when the jab caught him, right on the jaw, clean-cut, like steel.

Micky crashed to the canvas, tried to get up, but his legs wouldn't hold him. He clung to the ropes, trying to haul himself up, but again his legs gave way.

'*Eight . . . nine . . . ten*!'

Freedom Stubbs was the British Heavyweight Boxing Champion.

CHAPTER 21

THE LOCAL people took their new neighbours to their hearts, and Freedom became their hero. On the night he and Ed went to the Sporting Club dinner to collect the championship belt and the purse, everyone was at the door. The kids asked for his autograph, they wanted it five or six times to sell copies at school. With Edward in her arms, Evelyne waved them off like the rest. Freedom was dressed up, with a white silk scarf wrapped around his neck. The Christmas lights were twinkling and the few houses that could afford them already had trees in their windows.

When they arrived at the Sporting Club, the porters stopped them as they were about to hand their coats to the cloakroom attendant, and slowly checked their names in a register. Ed patted Freedom's shoulder, 'He's the champion, mate, what's the hold-up?'

Several evening-suited gents passing through the lobby looked curiously at them while they waited. The porter eventually gestured for Ed to go through, then he bent down beneath his desk and drew out a brown paper package which he handed to Freedom. 'I'm sorry, sir, this is for you, I can't let you go in.'

Ed, of course, puffed and huffed, said there must be some mistake, but the parcel contained the championship belt. In a temper Ed told Freedom to wait, there had to have been some mistake.

The dining room was already crowded with sporting gentlemen, drinking. Sir Charles was sitting at the top table with Lord Lonsdale himself, who had embarked on one of his long, rambling tales. The guests listened attentively as His Lordship regaled them with the story of when he had met Rasputin in Russia. Most of them had heard it many times, but the story had grown to outrageous proportions. When Sir Charles saw Ed he gestured with his arms, his cigar clamped between his teeth, and excused himself. Rising from the table he stared coldly as Ed approached him.

'I'm sorry to intrude, sir, but there must have been some mistake, they won't allow Freedom into the club.'

Sir Charles was totally unruffled and told Ed that in his opinion – and in the opinion of most of the other gentlemen present – Freedom had not acted in a sporting manner. He had insulted the Prince by not appearing at the Café Royal on the night of the championship. Ed could not believe his ears – he stared, speechless, and when Sir Charles offered him a chair he refused it and turned to walk out. Sir Charles tapped him on the shoulder, 'I think it would be a good idea if you were to commence training at The Grange during Christmas. I've arranged suitable accommodation.'

Tight-lipped and burning with anger, Ed murmured that he would relay the message to Freedom. He knew it was no message, it was an order, and he held his back very straight as he walked out through the tables full of so-called gentlemen.

He found Freedom standing outside in the snow, his prize belt stuffed in his pocket. Ed didn't know how to tell him, but he didn't have to. Freedom took one look at his face and began to walk along the pavement, 'I don't want anyone to know about this, Ed, keep it between us. It's Christmas, the markets are open, we'll go and get a few things, make it a celebration to remember.'

Near tears, Ed grinned at him, and fell into step beside his champion. He knew Freedom would not forget this treatment; he had that strange look on his face, the mask had dropped into place. Even though Ed tried to tell him it didn't matter, he knew that the insult had been taken to heart.

The market was full of last-minute Christmas shoppers and the yell of the thronging traders flogging their wares. Birds were strung up outside the butchers' shops, chilled by the snow. A man selling Christmas decorations recognized Freedom and cries of 'Champion!' went round the market. Freedom was a celebrity, and the warmth of their voices and good wishes lifted his gloom.

He stopped at a pet stall and examined the pigeons, bought one in a proper cage, then grinned at Ed, 'Get someone to take this over to that little lad from the lodgin's, tell him Father Christmas sent it.'

Freedom walked down the street followed by a costermonger's barrow piled so high with parcels the donkey could scarcely pull it. Up on top of the cart was a cradle and there were so many toys that Freedom kept stopping and handing them out to children running alongside. He had bought a table and chairs, lamps, and so much food he could have fed the whole street.

Evelyne stood at the bedroom window and stared at the strange-looking carnival as it came to a halt before the house. Freedom called up to her to look, and he stood grinning from ear to ear, his arms open wide. Ed, well-oiled and with whisky bottles sticking out of his pockets, reeled around with the lamplighter, singing at the top of his voice.

Evelyne watched from the stairs as the furniture was hauled in. It seemed there were people everywhere, yelling instructions on where to put everything, and the baby started screaming. It gave Evelyne a splitting headache. Freedom carried the cradle upstairs – it was made of carved wood with angels on each side. Evelyne had longed for the cradle from Swan and Edgar, with its modern mattress and frilled drapes. This was so old-fashioned.

'Put him in, gel, come along, let's have him.'

He stuffed a pillow into the cradle, took the baby from her arms and laid him in it. Edward howled, clenched his fists and punched at the sides. This made Freedom roar with laughter, and he dug in his pockets. He pulled out his championship belt and tossed it aside as if it were no more than a piece of wrapping paper. Then he took out a small leather case, beaming as he handed it to Evelyne.

The necklace was delicate, gold with pearl drops, and there were matching pearl drop earrings. 'Put it on, gel, let us see you. Want you to feel like a real lady, and this is just to start with, wait 'til you see what else I got for you.'

Picking up the bawling baby, Evelyne followed Freedom downstairs. Rolls of carpet were stacked in the hallway, chairs and cupboards had been dumped everywhere. Her spotless kitchen was a mess of straw and china, crates and boxes, but there was not one thing she had imagined for furnishing her home. Freedom strolled around like a magician, opening boxes and displaying his purchases. Then he sat in a big velvet chair and lit a cigar.

'Where did you get all the money for this? It must have cost a bit.'

She eased her way among the boxes while he puffed on his cigar, still beaming. She could smell that he had been drinking, and she went around looking at price tags. When she reached the mountain of food, she got a terrible sinking feeling. 'Did you get the fight money, then?'

With a wide, sweeping gesture to the room he said he had, and here it all was. Evelyne had to support herself on the edge of the new table that was too big for the kitchen. Freedom had blown the lot – everything apart from odd notes he had stuffed into his various pockets. He had to vacate the chair as Evelyne looked as if she was about to faint.

All her careful saving and scrimping, and in one night he had spent nearly two hundred pounds. More than the remains of her legacy – more than all the months of saving. She was shaking with anger and frustration, and it was then she vowed to herself that he would never know about her savings. His reckless spending shocked her to the core – that he had not discussed the money with her infuriated her and she wanted to scream the place down.

'I did it all for you, gel, for Christmas.'

She couldn't be angry with him, he looked so unhappy, his dark eyes like her baby son's. She went to him and kissed him, lied and said everything was perfect.

Later, lying next to him in their huge bed with the canopy he had chosen in a colour that clashed with the paint, she stared at the ceiling, sleepless. All she could think of was what she could have done with two hundred pounds, and she wept.

Evelyne had learned her lesson. Money meant nothing to Freedom, nor possessions. If he had a shilling in his pocket, he would spend it or hand it out to whoever asked for it. He was a soft touch, a spendthrift, and the whole street knew it. Evelyne was quite relieved to depart for The Grange as, with no money coming in, she would have had to dip into her savings. At least in the country they would be fed and Freedom would be paid for his training sessions there . . . so her savings could remain intact. She made up her mind to tell Ed that any money must be given to her, and she would dole it out to Freedom.

Freda was glad to be back in her cottage at The Grange, and in no time at all she had the kettle sizzling and a pot of stewed rabbit on the stove by the fire. Ed had his feet up, his worn slippers on.

There had been a lot of changes since they were last there, a whole new stable complex had been erected and on the other side of the yard beyond the barn were kennels for the hunting hounds. The dogs could be heard baying and howling.

'Ask me 'e's tryin' ter be like 'is Lordship 'imself, there's been some money thrown about here, you see the new gardens and the shrubberies . . . Course, it's not a patch on Lonsdale's place, but that's what Sir Charles is after.'

Freda dusted and swept, stirred the stew and told Ed to pop over to see if Freedom and Evelyne had everything they needed. Grumbling, he put on his heavy coat and went out, crossing the yard to the stables. Freedom, Evelyne and the baby had been installed in the new stable complex along with the stable hands and game-keepers. Ed looked around the two rooms, sparsely furnished with just the bare essentials, and he could tell that Evelyne was upset. Freedom had gone out to the woods and from the small window Ed could see his figure like a small dot on the white fields, running flat out.

'Well, there's one of us glad to be back here. There he goes, like a hare, isn't he?'

Evelyne snapped that she could use him indoors as she had to make up a bed for the baby, and Freedom had not lifted a finger since they arrived. He'd already had a row with the head stableboy because he had not been allowed to ride one of Sir Charles' hunters.

Ed made soothing noises while he watched four gardeners hauling a massive Christmas tree that was to stand in front of the drawing-room windows of The Grange. Sir Charles had not arrived home yet, and from the number of lighted windows in the house Ed knew all hell would be let loose as Miss Balfour organized the servants in their preparations for Christmas.

Evelyne handed the baby to him, and he cooed and chucked him under the chin. Ed looked up to see Evie, neat and tidy as ever, putting on her coat. 'Yer not goin' out at this hour, Evie. You'll catch yer death.'

'I'm just going over to the kitchens to see everybody, say hello.'

The cook, the footmen, the housemaids whooped when Evelyne entered the kitchen.

'Well, let's have a look at you, well I never, so you're married, well, well, and he's back as the British Champion, well, well.'

They opened a bottle of cooking sherry to celebrate.

'So you're back, well don't expect no special treatment from me, Miss Jones,' Miss Balfour snapped, 'And I'll thank you not to keep everyone chatting in my kitchen when there's work to be done.'

'Will you not toast my good health, and my baby's, Miss Balfour?'

Begrudgingly, Miss Balfour sipped a sherry then spoke with thin, pursed lips, 'Here's good health to you, is it a boy you have? Well, that's very nice, now if you will excuse me . . .' She left, ordering all of them to return to work. The housemaids sighed and looked at Evelyne as though she were a heroine, and she was delighted at being the centre of attention. She had two more sherries before she left with her cheeks flushed and rosy.

In the cold starlit December night with the thick carpet of snow, The Grange looked magical. Evelyne breathed in the clear air, maybe it was good that they'd all come here, away from the dirty London traffic.

'You look as pretty as a picture, I've been watching you.'

Freedom slipped his arm around her and she cuddled close.

'Happy, *manushi*?'

She looked up into his smiling, handsome face. 'I am, an' you're a *rinkeney* man all right, Freedom Stubbs.'

He roared with laughter at her use of the Romany word for 'handsome', and together they walked towards Ed and Freda's cottage. They peered like children into the kitchen and then giggled. Ed had their son on his lap and Freda was standing by giving him instructions on how to change a nappy.

504

'I don't think 'e needs one, love, 'e's just done it all over me best pants.'

The following morning there was bright sunshine and Ed talked the stableboys into allowing Freedom to ride. 'Yer know, lads, if 'e wasn't a champion boxer 'e could 'ave been a jockey, will you look at 'im with that animal, bloody marvel, my God 'e's a wonderful fella.' Ed glowed with pride and beamed at Mr Plath as he strode through the stableyard.

'Ah, Meadows, all the servants are to gather in the main hall for Christmas gift time, will you instruct your party to be in the hall on the dot of eight?'

'Now, Freda, there's no need to get all uppity, all they want is us all gathered, like. Sir Charles hands out 'is gifts to the servants, see, then we 'ave a shindig, a dance in the ballroom.'

Freda pursed her lips, furious to be classed with the servants.

Evelyne laughed, 'Oh, come on, Freda, it'll be fun, and you can get all dressed up. Of course we're not servants, well, not any more.'

Ed refrained from pointing out to the two women that while they might not be staff, both he and Freedom were employed by Sir Charles. He was too relieved that Evelyne had accepted it and even seemed bent on enjoying her stay at The Grange.

Promptly at eight, not a minute before or after, the staff lined up in the hall. It was impressive to watch, there were kitchen maids, scullery maids, ladies' maids, butlers, footmen, valets, cooks, gardeners, stableboys, dog handlers, gunsmiths. Miss Balfour stood at one end of the hall with the general house manager, the estate manager and two secretaries. In a small group slightly apart from the general household staff stood Ed, Freda, Freedom and Evelyne.

Everyone wore their Sunday best or their immaculate uniforms, and the line of more than forty people stood as though on parade. It dawned on Evelyne just how wealthy this household was, how could some have so much and others so little?

Miss Balfour shook hands with Freedom and congratulated him as if she was telling him he'd brought in muck from the stables, 'Sir Charles will be coming down any moment, he will wish you all a happy Christmas, and then you are to file past him one at a time . . .'

At that moment he appeared on the staircase, and there was a sudden hush. In clipped tones he wished every one of them a happy Christmas and a prosperous New Year, thanked them for all their good work, and hoped they would remain one big family.

Sir Charles handed Ed and Freda their gifts, polite, charming, and then turned to Freedom, who received the same cordial handshake with his neatly wrapped gift. Evelyne felt humiliated, as if she was lined up in the poorhouse, and accepted her token gift with lowered eyes, not once looking into the monocle.

'Do hope you will enjoy the dance, thank you for your service.'

'Well, *manushi*, I suppose we should go an' perform for our lord and master.'

Evelyne muttered that Sir Charles might be *his* lord, but he certainly wasn't hers.

In the ballroom a small orchestra played a waltz. Evelyne removed the heavy coat she was wearing over the satin gown Sir Charles had bought her in Cardiff, and got many admiring glances. Freda had shortened it, sewn on a few sequins to freshen it up, and arranged Evelyne's hair the way Freedom liked it in a long braid down her back with ribbon threaded through, green to match her eyes. This was the only time of year that Sir Charles actually mixed with his servants so it was quite an occasion.

Tables were laid for Sir Charles and his guests at one end of the ballroom, with pristine white cloths, silver and crystal, but they were empty as yet. A long buffet at one side was covered with cloths, and tables were ranged round the other walls for the staff. Evelyne and Freedom sat with Freda and Ed and a group of the stableboys. Ed and Freedom were sitting with their heads close together, discussing boxing as usual, and Freda gave Evelyne a little shake of her head and a shrug.

The orchestra played on, and the evening began to liven up as they all did the hokey-cokey around the room. Everyone was in high spirits, singing at the tops of their voices, 'You put your right foot in, right foot out, in, out, in out, and shake it all about . . . and that's what it's all about . . . Oh, the hokey-cokey, oh, the hokey-cokey . . . Knees bend, arms stretch, *Ra! Ra! Ra!*'

During the dance Sir Charles and his guests arrived and crossed the floor to their reserved tables. When the music ended Freda flopped down in her chair, fanning herself with her hankie, 'Oh, I'm too old, too old for this kind of dance, darlink, I must have a long drink.'

Evelyne laughed. She was flushed, too, and she

headed for the table where drinks were being served. She turned to look over at Sir Charles' table, and her heart stopped.

David Collins was standing staring across the ballroom. He was lighting a cigarette in a thin gold holder. She had forgotten how handsome he was, how refined. She was jostled along the queue for drinks, and asked for two lemonades. As she waited for them she saw Sir Charles gesturing to Freedom to join his table. Evelyne stood on tiptoe to watch as Freedom bent to kiss Lady Primrose's hand, then pulled out a chair to sit down. His back was to Evelyne and David was on his right. Freedom must have said something amusing, as the whole group laughed.

Taking a roundabout route Evelyne went back to her table, avoiding Sir Charles' group. She sat down as Freda brought two plates piled so high with food it was spilling on to the cloth. 'My darlink, eat, eat, I have never seen so much glorious food.'

Evelyne smiled, but her eyes strayed constantly to David as she sipped her drink. Lady Primrose stood up and pulled at Freedom's arm, dragging him on to the dance floor. Evelyne felt sorry for him, she didn't know if he could dance and wondered if she should go to his rescue, but that would mean meeting David.

Holding hands, Freedom and Lady Primrose walked over to the orchestra, and he tapped the conductor on the shoulder and spoke to him. Still waving his baton, the conductor nodded his head. Evelyne wondered what had been said and was fascinated to see how relaxed Freedom was, he seemed almost on intimate terms with Her Ladyship.

The orchestra struck up a tango, and on to the floor glided Freedom, his hand out for Lady Primrose to follow. She giggled and looked towards her table, then stood as Freedom demonstrated a step. A few couples stood and watched as he waited for the beat to begin the dance. He closed his eyes and stood quite still, head up, then slowly began to dance, clicking his heels in Romany style, putting the whole room to shame as he glided elegantly across the floor. After a short solo he swept Lady Primrose into his arms and she laughed, throwing her head back. Then, the show over, he began to teach her the steps.

Evelyne was so astounded by Freedom's dancing that she was unaware of David's approach until he was standing directly behind her chair. 'I don't know if I can tango, but I'm willing to try, would you do me the honour, Evie?'

Startled, she turned to him, then told him curtly that she didn't tango. He promptly sat down, insisting he could wait for a waltz. He glanced at his wife on the dance door, then back to Evelyne. 'You've not changed, not at all.'

She saw his eyes flick over her dress and she bit her lip, she knew he recognized it. He *had* changed. She could see the fine lines around his eyes and mouth, and a slight gauntness. His blue eyes were paler than ever. He still smelt of flowers, and was as fresh and clean as his starched white collar. The orchestra began a slow waltz and he held his hand out to her, smiling softly. They stood up and began to dance, Evelyne overpowered by David's closeness, his blond hair brushing her face as he held her close, manoeuvring her around the polished floor.

Freda looked at them with a worried frown and swivelled in her chair to see where Freedom was. Through the throng of dancers she could see him leaning on the back of Lady Primrose's chair. She watched him take the delicate hand and began to read her palm and suddenly realized he was a bit of a lady-killer, and by the look of Primrose she was responding to his charm.

Lady Primrose could smell Freedom's musky perfume – sweet, strange and exciting, as he was – and his touch on her hand was gentle as he traced the lines on her palm. Giggling, she told Sir Charles she didn't believe in all this mumbo-jumbo, and pulled her hand away, taken aback by the expression on her cousin's face. He was staring at Freedom, his eyes furious. When he caught Primrose looking at him, he turned away and blushed the scarlet of his monocle ribbon. It was obvious that the gypsy boxer had powers which were not necessarily confined to fortune-telling.

David didn't know what to say to Evelyne, he kept trying to think of some way to start a conversation, but then stopped before speaking. He could feel her in his arms, so close and yet so many miles away. There was so much he wanted to tell her – needed to tell her – but they danced on and he remained silent. Going back through the years in her mind, Evelyne turned around and came back again. Here she was, dancing close, very close, to the man she had believed she loved, so close that if she turned her cheek she could kiss his lips, and yet nothing could be further from her thoughts. He had shrunk, she was sure of it. She was taller than him now, and that cloyingly sweet perfume was surely not the one she used to wear. His eyes were so pale they seemed filled with tears, and as if he were reading her thoughts he suddenly stopped dancing and sighed, 'I need some air, which way should I go?

Evelyne sat on the balcony steps, feeling cold, and David took off his jacket and wrapped it around her shoulders.

'Do you remember everything now, David? How I used to come and visit you? Do you remember?'

His head twitched, his mouth working. He reached for her hand and threaded his fingers through hers, pulled her closer, 'You are the most beautiful creature, that is what I remember most – and you have filled out to perfection, to perfection.'

His free hand traced her bosom, heavy with milk for her son.

'Please don't do that.'

He smiled, kissed her neck softly, and she gasped.

'You liked it once, you like it now: excite me, excite me, set me on fire.'

She looked around; he was holding her hand tightly, hurting her fingers, pulling her close, and he forced her head back, kissed her just as he had kissed her that night in his car, forcing her mouth open with his tongue.

'No, don't, please, please . . . Let go of me, please.'

He held her even tighter. 'What's the matter with you, you liked it once, I remember. I remember that, you liked it, you loved me.'

Evelyne looked at him, amazed. How could she have been so foolish? 'That was a long time ago, David, I think we should go back into the ballroom.'

He grasped her shoulders, tight. She didn't push him away, but neither did she encourage him. She whispered, 'What do you want from me?'

'You know, what's the matter? Not good enough for

you now? Tell me, what have you set your sights on for tonight? My God, for a little slut you certainly have done well for yourself, I have to hand it to you, wormed your way in here very nicely . . .'

Evelyne drew back her right hand and slapped David's face so hard that he reeled.

'I am a married woman, with a son, how dare you make such insinuations, how dare you?'

He laughed, a humourless, barking sound, a sarcastic smile on his face. 'You are still for sale, Evie, and to the highest bidder, your type always are and you know it.'

He was about to move away when she gripped his arm. 'I've *never* been for sale, David, just poor. Is that a crime? You sicken me, for if there's anyone selling themselves it's been you . . . I loved you with a passion, a childish, naive passion that you abused, just like you abused your own friend, Freddy . . . How's your wife? You knew he loved her, and yet you had to have her. Why, David? Because she's titled? Because she had money? It's *you* who's been for sale, David, *you* . . . you're nothing. Go back to your high society, your rich friends who laugh at you behind your back!'

He backed away from her, wringing his hands. 'You know, you're terribly wrong about one thing, my wife, I love her, I always have, but she makes a fool of me . . . a public fool.' His voice was childish, pitiful, and to Evelyne's dismay he started to cry. His shoulders shook, and he stuttered through his sobs, 'We're stony broke, all my fault. I lost my way, Evie, so long ago, lost my way, you see . . .'

He lifted his hands to Evelyne, a helpless gesture, then she saw the familiar habit he had of sweeping his hair back. His signet ring glinted. 'Damned wretched business, can't seem to hold on to anything . . . my father short-changed me, ya know, should have given me a sharp rap across the knuckles, but instead he encouraged me, because . . .'

He turned away from her, rested his hands on the balcony rail. '. . . Because he wanted me to succeed. Laughable, really – get in with the right set, Mother always used to say – and here I am, cap in hand, begging from Charles because we're penniless.'

'Why don't you work? You were studying to be a lawyer.'

His voice was soft, full of pain. 'I can't remember things, hardly the best credentials for the Law Society . . .' His eyes pleaded with her, 'I don't remember, Evie, I pretend I do, but so help me God, I don't, because . . . because I'm scared. Sometimes when I have been with you I recall pictures – Mrs Darwin, my father . . .'

She knew he was lying, she sensed it, lying like a guilty child. She moved closer, almost touching him, 'David, you *can* remember. What happened? What happened to you?'

He stared at her as if cornered, trapped. He shook his head and she inched even closer. 'What did you do that made you so afraid? Tell me? You can tell me.'

She held him in her arms, felt him trembling, smoothed his hair, patted the silky hair she had longed to touch all those years before. 'You know, David, in a way you don't belong here either, you are as much out of your depth as I am. Whatever you did surely can't make you hide for the rest of your life?'

His face altered, the child disappeared. His slender grasp of reality began to slip. His mouth turned down and his face twisted in fury at her assumption that he was no better than she, as if they were of the same class. When he spoke he had reverted to his usual, over-precise speech pattern. 'I'm not hiding, duckie, what do you take me for? I know what you bloody are.' He made a grab for her breast, ripping her gown.

Neither of them had heard Freedom's soft footstep, or were aware that he had been standing close by. With one swift move he gripped David's jacket and tossed him aside.

'It was that bitch's fault, don't hurt me, please don't hurt me.'

For one moment Evelyne would have liked Freedom to throw David over the balcony, then she turned, looking for help to stop him.

Ed had been searching for Freedom since Freda had told him David and Evelyne had disappeared together. As he came around the side of the house, he saw Freedom dragging David along the balcony and ran as fast as his fat legs would carry him.

'Freedom . . . *Freedom*! Evelyne, stop him, for God's sake. *Stop him*!' He launched himself on to Freedom's back and tried to pull him off the hysterical David. Freda and one of the stable lads ran out on to the balcony and the boy tried to help Ed control Freedom, but they were no match for him, and it was not until two more lads came running that they were able to haul Freedom away from the weeping man.

David flailed his arms in the air, his voice a high-pitched shriek. 'How dare you, how dare you manhandle me, *I'll have you horsewhipped, you animal!*'

It was a grotesque, embarrassing scene, and Ed tried his damnedest to calm everyone down. 'Show's over – it was nothing, just a bit of fun. Everybody go back inside, it's over . . . You all right, sir?'

He put his arm around David's shoulders, trying to smooth his jacket, but David pushed him away.

'Don't touch me, get away from me, all of you, you rabble, *you common bastards*!'

Shaking he arranged his handkerchief in his breast pocket and smoothed his hair with the palm of his hand. 'I shall be a gentleman and forget this ever happened.'

He gave Evelyne a strange, disdainful look, turned, his head held high, and made a sad, foolish exit, still trying desperately to hold on to his dignity.

One of the stableboys looked at Ed, 'You need us, Mr Meadows?'

All eyes turned to Freedom and Evelyne. As if they were animals in a circus ring, they waited for the roar. The pair of them faced each other and the atmosphere was so highly-charged that no one dared speak. Then Evelyne walked away. She heard scuffling behind her and raised voices, but she hurried on, almost afraid to turn back and see what was happening.

Ed was trying to persuade Freedom not to ride, not at this hour of the night – it was dark and the horse could fall. The head stableboy stuttered that Sir Charles would hit the roof, and received the snarling reply, 'Bugger Sir Charles.' No one had the nerve to try to stop Freedom as he galloped off without a saddle, leaving Ed thinking, 'There's Freedom's best suit ruined,' and silently praying his champion wouldn't fall. He was doubly concerned because Freedom had taken Sir Charles' prize stallion. God help them all if anything happened to the horse, never mind Freedom.

If Ed had watched for another second he would have had a heart attack as Freedom and the horse jumped a five-foot wall and headed for the forest.

The baby was sleeping, his thumb stuck in his mouth, and his warmth and peacefulness touched Evelyne. She lifted him gently out of the bizarre cradle they had brought from London and sat by the fire, rocking him in her arms. She closed her eyes, vowing to herself that he would never have to endure the humiliation she had known. She hated being poor, being subjected to ridicule. Growing steadily inside her were seeds of loathing for the so-called aristocracy.

If only Freedom would educate himself, beat them at their own game, learn to use them as they were using him. She was even more determined that she would teach him to read and write, *make* him learn. She shuddered when David came into her thoughts. He'd called her a slut. Well, she would not waste her time on him any more, he was out of her life. She looked down into her son's face, touched his head.

'You see, Edward, David's trouble is that he got given all the opportunities a man could have, but he frittered them away. You know why? Because he won't face up to being who he is. It doesn't matter, Edward, where you come from. Titles? Half of them don't have two pennies to rub together ... You're going to be somebody, be successful, be powerful and not need anyone. You have to want it and fight for it – not with your fists, like your dad, that isn't good enough. No, you're going to have to fight for an education and I'll be right alongside you. I'll kill for you to have it, so help me God I will – you'll never be any man's servant.'

Hours later Freedom came home to find the curtain drawn across the window and Evelyne already in bed. She heard him kicking off his shoes and knew he would be scattering his clothes all over the room. She got up and pulled her cardigan round her shoulders, checked

516

that the baby was asleep, and opened the curtain quietly so Freedom did not hear her.

He was sitting by the fire, staring into the coals, his bare chest gleaming in the firelight. Evelyne curled up at his feet, squeezing her body between his knees. He didn't speak and made no effort to hold her, but at the same time he did not push her away. For a few minutes they sat in silence, and then Evelyne began to tell him, softly, everything there was to know about her and David – how much she had loved him in a childish, romantic fantasy way, and how he had humiliated and hurt her . . . how even tonight he had made her feel like a second-class citizen, because of his background, his money. When Freedom had found them David was crying like a baby because he couldn't have what he wanted, she had refused his advances. Not that he really wanted her – he never had – she was poor, something that could be bought, and thrown away when he had tired of her.

'We may be poor, but our son will have everything, and you know what everything is, Freedom? Us, you and me beside him always. He's going to have what we never had, proper schooling, education. We can have that for free, but love costs a lot more, you know that?'

He didn't really understand what she was saying, but the fact that she had told him everything about David without his asking made him reach to hold her. He was so proud of her, the fight in her. He built up the fire until it blazed and brought the mattress from their bed, put it in front of the fire. Then he took off her long cotton nightdress and laid her down on the mattress, naked in the firelight. She loved him all the more. David's weakness emphasized his strength, and she lifted her arms to him. He knelt beside her and kissed her,

517

and they made love as they had in the enchanted summer months out in the fields. Since the child's birth he had been gentle and caring, but now he loved her roughly, taking her time and time again until they lay sweating, their bodies close, so close, their love deepening, bonding them together.

'Don't ever betray me, *manushi*, not ever. It would set a demon loose inside me, and I wouldn't care what happened to me, do ye understand what I am saying, gel?'

Evelyne did, she too had felt that surge of jealousy when she had seen him dancing with Lady Primrose, and it was a new emotion. She felt she would kill if anyone ever tried to take him from her. She turned in his arms and stroked his long hair, placed her hand to his heart, 'And we must always talk, Freedom, be honest with each other, never pretend or lie.'

He lay back and thought about what she had said, about them being there for their son. It had never occurred to Freedom that he had never had a father, but then the elders of the camp acted in that role. Evelyne told him the difference, what it had been like with her Da, the closeness, the strong bond between them. She sat up and prodded the fire, snuggled down in his arms and asked him what he knew of the man who had fathered him. He could remember little, just that his mother had been very young, she was a *Tachey Romany chal*, of high blood, her father a prince and her mother the *dukkerin* of the camp. Her family had visited a village in the Rhondda and she had seen with her 'eye' the boy, tall as a tree, she said, and so *rinkeney* he had made her heart stop. She had known immediately that she wanted him. Freedom reverted to his Romany tongue as he described his mother, and the tall, wild man the village had nicknamed 'The Lion'.

518

During the telling Freedom sat up, slightly apart from Evelyne, and she suddenly clutched him, hugged him, desperately. She clamped her hand over his mouth to prevent him going any further, 'No, no, don't say any more. Dear God, don't say any more.'

He had to prise her away from him, she was that strong. He lifted her bodily, and from her face he knew something was terribly wrong, it frightened him.

'Oh, God, Freedom, what have we done?'

She wanted to scream, she covered her own mouth with her hands, afraid she would cry out and wake the child . . . she bit her hand so hard he could see her teeth sinking into the flesh, her whole body trembling. When he pulled her hand away her sobs shook her, and she tried to push him away from her.

Holding him at arm's length she finished his story for him; her voice harsh, each word bringing her pain. She told him of his mother, how she had stood at the pithead and waited for her 'lion', how the man had laughed and she had cursed him. It was Freedom's turn to freeze, how did she know – how was she able to tell something he had never told another soul?

'Oh, don't you see, don't you understand . . .'

Whatever reaction she anticipated, something akin to her own horror, never came. Instead Freedom lay back and started to laugh, a deep, throaty laugh. She stood up, stark naked, and kicked him, shouting. How could he laugh, how *could* he? He caught her foot and brought her crashing down beside him. She tried to fight him off, but he was so strong it was useless. He rolled on top of her, grasping her wrists above her head, holding them tightly, 'Tell me everything about him. Let me know everything. Am I like him? Tell me, tell me.'

'Are you not afraid – that we have the same blood?'

He released her arms, caught her to him so tightly

she could hardly breathe, 'Blood to blood, Evie, we are closer, closer, do you not see that?'

His acceptance of the fact that they were even closer, bonded by blood, was at first frightening to Evelyne. Then his mood caught her, and to her amazement she found herself laughing with him.

'No one must know, Evie, they'd not understand.' He had no need to tell her that, she knew it, and even her fears for the child of such close blood were dispersed. They picked up their sleeping baby son and held him between them, and he opened his eyes and stared up into the two adoring faces.

'Our son is near pure *Tatchey*. He'll have the powers, Evie, and look at his strong body.'

To their delight, Edward gurgled and laughed up at them, and at that moment there was magic in the night, the red flames from the fire flickering on their naked bodies.

Later, while Evelyne slept, Freedom took out a hunting knife and made a cut on his forefinger. He squeezed it until the blood formed a heavy drop, then crept to the baby's cradle. He let the blood drip slowly on to the sleeping child's forehead. The stain spread, forming a cross, and Freedom's voice was a whisper as he buried the curse his mother, the clan's *dukkerin*, had laid on Hugh Jones.

BOOK FOUR

CHAPTER 22

LIFE MOVED at a fast pace after that Christmas at The Grange. Freedom was still the undefeated British Heavyweight Champion, and British Empire Heavyweight Champion . . . he fought in Liverpool, Birmingham, Porthcawl, Edinburgh, and Manchester. Evelyne did not accompany him on these travels, but stayed at home in the East End. Freedom was a celebrity, money was not short, and Evelyne kept a close watch on the purse strings. Their house was well furnished, and some items had been passed on to Ed and Miss Freda, even Ed's brother and sister-in-law Billy and Mary Meadows. The neighbours watched with avid interest as number twelve even had carpet laid all down the stairs. There was no jealousy, they were proud, and welcomed the distinction of having a champion living in their street.

Edward was almost two years old, a handsome child, tall for his age. He was very strong, and never still, so that it took all Evelyne's time to keep an eye on him. He had a terrible temper, and threw such tantrums that their neighbours would say, 'There goes that little bugger again.' But they would smile, as everyone knew how the little lad adored his father. As soon as he saw his dad coming down the road, Edward would run out, arms outstretched and shouting with delight. Proud as Punch, Freedom would swing the lad up on to his shoulders.

Sir Charles kept a close but discreet watch over Freedom's successful career. He was determined that 'The Gypsy' would try for the world championship. It was only a matter of time until a fight was arranged in America.

They were getting close when the news came that the great Dempsey, the man known as the 'Manassa Mauler', had lost his title to Gene Tunney. Sir Charles was delighted. Tunney now reigned as World Heavyweight Champion, and his reputation was on a par with Dempsey's at his peak. The new champion appeared invincible and was taking on all challengers.

Ed Meadows arrived at number twelve, his face alight with excitement. 'Where is he . . . *Freedom*!'

The moment Freedom looked up from the table he was building and saw Ed, he knew something big was on, 'Is it America, Ed?'

Unable to speak, Ed clasped Freedom in his arms, and the two men danced around the kitchen.

Evelyne returned from shopping to find Freedom out and a dozen bottles of champagne on the table. When she took a quick look at the price, she had to sit down. She had to watch his spending all the time. When he went abroad, he always brought back lavish gifts and wouldn't hear a word from Evelyne about the cost. Neither did he discuss the fights themselves with her, avoiding her questions with shrugs and laughs. His face was still ummarked so Evelyne never really knew what it took for him to get into the ring or, for that matter, what punishment he had taken.

Freedom came back with his arms full of turkeys and fruit.

'Lord, man, what on earth have you been doing? I've already been to the shops.'

Putting everything down he caught her in his arms. 'Ah, well, this is a farewell dinner, for the street, then you'd best pack your things. We leave for America and this time you'll be with me, it'll be the trip of a lifetime.'

Evelyne hugged him, 'Is it the world championship?'

He swung her round, lifted her in the air, 'Aye, it is, and I'm going to take it from Tunney.'

'Well, you'd best put me down. Any more of this tossing me in the air and you'll hurt the baby.'

Freedom lowered her gently and cupped her face in his hands. 'We'll take Edward with us, and I'll take great care of thee . . .' Suddenly what she had just said dawned on him . . . he yelped with joy. 'Are you sure?'

Evelyne laughed and said she was more than sure, she was three months gone.

The excitement of packing and arranging for their departure made the weeks pass so fast Evelyne could hardly believe it when they arrived at Southampton Docks with Freda, Ed and a pile of luggage. There was their ship, their home for the next three weeks, looming so large it took everyone's breath away. RMS *Aquitania* was majestic, dwarfing the small group at the dockside. It wasn't a ship, it was a floating city.

A steward led them to their cabins, pointing out various features along the way. The restaurant, with an oak-beamed ceiling and leaded windowpanes, seated seven hundred people. A long gallery led to what could only be described as a high street, with shops that included ladies' and gentlemen's outfitters displaying all the latest fashions in lighted window displays. There was a huge main lounge at the end of the gallery – a glorious, stunning room, as large as a concert hall, thickly carpeted and with a magnificent domed ceiling. All the chairs and settees were upholstered in the finest fabrics. There was even a post and telegraph office, unlike any the bemused group had ever seen. Adjoining it was the library, a big, square room with hundreds of books, and there was no charge for borrowing them.

Freedom had trailed around without much interest, but when he saw the gym his eyes lit up. There were parallel bars, horizontal bars, electric – yes, electric – cycling machines, and even a riding machine that rocked backwards and forwards as if you were on a real-life bucking bronco. There were also rowing machines, fencing masks and foils, boxing gloves and punchbags. Ed and Freedom stood and stared, awestruck.

The steward turned back the bedcovers and opened some of the many wardrobes and dressing-table drawers to show Evelyne. He also told them about the full-time nursery with a nanny to take care of the child at night if the passengers had not brought servants with them. He hovered for a while, then proffered a crumpled piece of paper and asked if Freedom would autograph it for him. He was so pleased, he didn't even wait for a tip.

Freedom lay back on the bed and smiled, 'Happy . . .? You like it?'

From the massive funnels of the *Aquitania* the hooter sounded, the ship was about to sail. They went up on deck and waved to no one, just the disappearing docks.

That evening, the dining room was a hubbub of noise as they took their seats, and Freda's mouth watered as she peered shortsightedly at the menu. It was written in French and confused everyone else, but Freda prattled away, '*Turbot poché en sauce fenouil, épinards, pommes frites* . . . oh, là là, *rouget grillé beurre diable* . . . darlinks, it's just divine . . . *noisettes d'agneau Maltaise, ris de veau, côtelettes de volaille aux haricots panachés* . . . It is fantastic, darlinks.'

Ed settled for the lamb cutlets, Freedom a steak, and Evelyne, after a long explanation from Freda, chose fish. They started with caviare served on crisp toast with finely chopped onions and egg yolks. They were mightily impressed, and Freda's exuberance and obvious delight in everything was very infectious.

Freedom insisted Ed accompany him to the menswear shop where the pair of them were measured for black tie and tails. Ed did try to prevent the expenditure, but Freedom laughed, asked him how much Dempsey had received for a single fight. 'You know, lad, it were more than five hundred, and bugger me yer right. You're gonna take that title, so mister, bring that shirt with the nice pearl buttons and one for the champ here.' The more Ed talked of how much Dempsey had made, the more expansive he became, smoking a Havana cigar, flicking the ash on the assistant's head as he pinned up six inches on his new trousers.

*

They had all been invited to dine with Sir Charles, and Freedom and Ed cut quite a dash in their penguin suits as they strolled along the deck to Sir Charles' opulent stateroom. Seeing everyone shaking hands with his champion, admiring him as they sauntered along, rubbed off on Ed. He was having the time of his life.

Freda and Evelyne followed their men, arm-in-arm, laughing at the contrast between Ed with his waddle and Freedom with his cocksure stride, towering above Ed.

Sir Charles was equally enthusiastic, warmly welcoming them to his suite. 'Here he is, everyone, this is my champion.'

As usual, Sir Charles had invited a roomful of elegant guests. The dinner was very formal with four waiters hovering to look after them. Freda insisted on speaking French to the waiter who served her, which nonplussed him as he came from Bradford.

Freedom was being very attentive to the attractive blonde woman on his right. Evelyne excused herself, saying she must see to her child, and the gentlemen rose, half-heartedly. Freedom seemed unaware she had left.

On her way back to her cabin Evelyne stood for a while watching the dark sea. Strains of music drifted up from the ballroom and slowly she began to waltz along the deck – one, two three, one, two three . . . she stopped to sit in a deckchair. Suddenly the lovely, balmy night was too good to miss.

She heard Freedom's voice and rushed to the rail to look over and call to him to come and sit with her. She could see him, with the blonde on his arm, strolling along the deck below her with some of the other dinner guests, towards the ballroom. Evelyne had never felt so jealous in her life. She wanted to go down and dance with him, but she couldn't. She was fat and ugly while the blonde was so beautiful and slim, not pregnant, not so tall.

She watched Freedom's progress, inching down the steps to get a better view. There was applause, and there he was, bowing and smiling. A waltz was being played and Evelyne could see him with his arms wrapped around a small woman. She was beginning to feel furious when the couple did a twirl and she could see that he was hugging Freda in his arms. They danced towards the open deck, and Evelyne stepped into the concealing shadows on the stairs. Their voices could be heard clearly below her.

'Oh, oh, I am so dizzy, darlink.'

'Aye, well, I had to have some excuse, Freda, that woman was hanging on my arm so I couldn't leave.' They leant on the rails, looking out at the sea. 'Does the sea not remind you of my Evie's eyes, Freda? Freda . . .?'

She had slithered down and was sitting on the deck, the champagne and wine too much for her. Freedom picked her up and put her over his shoulder. Evelyne put her hand over her mouth to stop herself giggling as the blonde lady appeared. 'Oh, Mr Stubbs, don't tell me you are leaving so early.'

'I'm afraid so, ma'am, my partner here has over-exerted herself.'

'Oh, do come back, we are all going for a midnight swim.'

'Aye, well, it's a nice night for it.'

The blonde was joined by another woman and they watched Freedom stride off. 'Oh, he's so manly, Gertrude, and so strong, he really is.'

'Now, now, Mabel, he's a married man.'

529

The blonde giggled, twirled around. 'That's never stood in my way before, darling.'

Evelyne had heard enough. She bent over the railings and spoke to the astonished Mabel. 'It had better stand in your way when it comes to *my* husband, miss, or you'll get more than you bargain for.'

Mabel nearly fainted as Evelyne marched off down the deck.

When the time came to dock in New York, they stood together on the deck to watch as the huge ship eased its way into the harbour. Towering above them was the Statue of Liberty, and Freedom lifted Edward up on to his shoulders to see her. The ship's hooters screamed and streamers and confetti scattered from the top decks while a band played; everyone's excitement was at fever pitch. They had arrived in New York. Freedom slipped one arm around Evelyne, his face serious and his voice quiet.

'When we go home, Evie, I'll be world champion. I promise you.'

The wonders of America did not stop at the docks. A limousine was waiting to drive them to an airport, from which they were to fly by mail plane to Chicago. Even the garrulous Ed was stunned into silence. Sir Charles bent down to talk to them through the window of their car. 'I'll be flying with you, see you there . . . Ed, you've got the itinerary, the hotel booking and the tickets. Have to get a move on, the plane leaves in two hours.'

As they sped through the streets, they stared at the towering buildings in awe, but their sightseeing tour was short and they soon arrived at the small airstrip.

They had accepted the fact that they would be flying as if Sir Charles had said they were going by train, but when they saw the fragile aircraft on the landing strip it really sank in.

'Oh, Ed, darlink, I think I am going to faint, I do. Are we really going up in that little thing?'

Freedom hugged Evelyne to him, 'You scared, *manushi*?'

She shook her head, trying to keep hold of Edward who jumped up and down in uncontrollable excitement.

Sir Charles was elated to be flying, and as soon as they climbed on board he sat next to the pilot. Freedom held Evelyne's hand, his son on his knee, and they looked out of the single, small window. They were a little frightened, and were not reassured by Sir Charles bellowing instructions to the pilot. The faithful old Dewhurst sat with his rosary in his hands, eyes closed and praying, all through the journey.

As they prepared to land, Sir Charles strapped himself into his seat, a glint in his monocled eye. 'This is thrilling, absolutely thrilling.'

The plane bounced on to the landing strip, and they all turned a little green, but were thankful to be down and in one piece. Dewhurst's knees gave way and he had to be helped down the stairs, constantly apologizing to Sir Charles.

'Freda, I think I'm dying, oh God, I'm dying, my heart it's my heart.' Freda gave Ed a big hug and told him he could open his eyes; they had landed, everyone else had already left the plane.

'Gawd 'elp us, Freda, I feel as if I was still up in the clouds.'

Sir Charles had been driven into Chicago, leaving the others to wait for Ed and Freda with the longest car any of them had ever seen. It was silver, and the chauffeur wore a blue uniform. They climbed into the Cadillac limousine, and Ed flipped through the itinerary and instructed the driver to take them to the Lexington Hotel. Sir Charles, he noticed, had 'The State' suite in The Sherman Hotel. He still as always kept his distance, and Ed knew it would be costing more than all their rooms put together . . . but as His Lordship was footing the bill for the trip, it was his prerogative.

The journey into the city was almost as exciting as their voyage, once they had overcome their nervousness at travelling on the wrong side of the road. Immensely long cars whizzed by, drawing gasps of admiration. The chauffeur gazed at them through his mirror and when he spoke his accent made Freda giggle.

'You folks from England? Well, jeez, ain't that great, I never been outta Chicago myself; that's the state capitol we just passed.'

He asked them endless questions, while stealing glances at the 'black guy' with the long hair. He thought they looked pretty scruffy, but they must have dough to be staying at the Lexington.

When they arrived at the hotel, Ed realized he had no American dollars so he had to go to the hotel bank to change his English pound notes. Two porters carried their luggage into the hotel and the limousine drove off.

They pushed through the revolving doors after the porters, Freedom lagging behind as he struggled with several pieces of hand luggage, including his kitbag. The mahogany reception desk was immensely long and at least eight uniformed bellhops rushed around in the lobby, which was crowded with guests and potted palms.

The manager looked through the glass-fronted door of his office and pursed his lips. He could see the new guests checking in and didn't like what he saw. He made a quick call to the receptionist to tell the assistant manager to come to see him immediately.

Ed couldn't understand what was causing the delay. They were all very tired, and Edward had started to cry. Ed showed the receptionist the telegram confirming their rooms. He was beginning to get impatient as no one seemed in the slightest hurry to register them and hand over their keys.

The assistant manager, flushing beetroot red, hurried from the office, lifted the mahogany flap and slipped in behind the desk. 'I'm afraid there has been some mistake. We only have one room booked, Mr Meadows. I cannot apologize enough, but I'm afraid the rest of your party will have to find accommodation elsewhere.'

Ed was confused as he crossed the lobby to Freedom and Evelyne to tell them of the situation. The little boy was really beginning to scream now, so Ed suggested that Freedom and Evelyne take his room; he and Freda could find another hotel. He returned to the reception desk and asked for the key for his companions to take the room.

'I'm sorry, sir, that is not possible, I am afraid we cannot accept your companions, that is the hotel rule.'

What on earth was the man talking about? Ed's protests grew louder and then, to his astonishment, the assistant manager pushed a card across the counter. Neatly printed on it were the words, 'No coloureds or blacks to be allowed as guests of the Lexington Hotel.'

Ed stared at him, confused, then picked up the card and reread it. 'What's this got to do wiv us, for Gawd's sake?' Ed jabbed the manager with his finger and pushed the card forward, his voice rising as he demanded to know what was going on. He had personally sent a telegram to the hotel for two double rooms, one with a cot for a child, and now he was told there was only one room vacant and his friends couldn't move into it. Sensing an impending explosion, the manager drew Ed quietly aside and repeated the hotel policy that no coloureds and no couples of mixed race were allowed in the hotel.

'Mixed *what*? What you talkin' about, mate, we ain't black, what you think we are?'

The manager turned and flicked a look at Freedom, then turned back to Ed. Suddenly it was painfully clear, they thought Freedom was black. Indeed, because of the sunshine on the crossing, his dark skin was even darker. Ed spluttered and could hardly speak with rage. 'He's contender for the World Heavyweight boxing title, for Chrissake, he's not black, he's a gypsy! That don't make him black.'

Freedom handed his son to Evelyne and began to cross the lobby towards Ed. The next moment the place was in an uproar, as Ed knocked out the manager with one punch. Ten minutes later they were on the pavement outside the hotel, Freda in tears and Ed so angry he could hardly speak.

'We ain't stayin' in this dump, any of us, come on, we'll get a taxi an' see where there's a better hotel.'

Freedom pulled the still furious Ed aside and asked what on earth had happened in there. Ed wouldn't say, but he hailed a taxi and ushered them all into it.

They stopped at two more hotels and Ed went in alone to investigate, but at each one he was told, 'No coloureds'. While he was in the second one the cabbie, who had been staring at Freedom, realized what was going on. 'Most of da hotels around dis part of the city don't take blacks. I know a place where maybe they'll let you in, you want me to try there for ya?' He hooked his arm along the back of the seat and looked enquiringly at the party in the back. They stared at him, not understanding what he was saying. He pointed to Freedom and repeated that there was a rule in the best hotels, no coloureds and no Indians. Some even refused Mexicans. A defeated Ed returned to the cab, and now that they all understood the predicament he blushed in shame for them. 'I'm sorry, lad, I told 'em all you wasn't black, but they don't believe me.'

Evelyne was silent, but as they drove off she saw in the distance a huge hotel towering above the shops and apartment buildings. The Metropole Hotel, 2300 South Michigan Avenue.

'Driver, take us to that hotel, please, and, Ed, I want to go in this time.' She would hear no argument, even when the cab driver tried to dissuade her, implying that the Metropole, of all hotels, would most certainly refuse them. Freedom said nothing, he was so taken aback, but the driver went on ominously about the Metropole and that he would lay odds against their being allowed in, not just because of Freedom but for other reasons. Evelyne repeated her instruction to take them to the hotel and gripped Freedom's hand.

As they stopped, Ed made to get out, but Evelyne wouldn't let him move. She insisted on leaving them alone and, head high, she walked into the lobby.

'She'll get no joy in dere, pal, I'm tellin'ya, I know dis town an' I know dis hotel, ya tryin' the wrong place.'

All their eyes followed Evelyne as she walked from the cab through the revolving doors and into the ornate lobby.

Inside it was opulent, thickly carpeted, with massive

ferns and palms in every corner. There was so much brass and so many chandeliers that the whole lobby seemed to glitter.

Evelyne strode to the reception desk, a long, polished counter with racks of keys and pigeonholes for letters. She had to wait for a gentleman in front of her to sign the register, a burly, fat man smoking a cigar. The clouds of smoke rose up to form a ring around his head.

A clerk, seeing Evelyne waiting, hurried forward to attend to her.

'I wish to book two double rooms, one with a child's cot, and private bathrooms, please.'

The clerk reached for the register and thumbed through the pages.

'There will be a Mr and Mrs Ed Meadows, and Mr and Mrs Freedom Stubbs with the child. Mr Stubbs is here as a contender for the World Heavyweight Boxing Championship. I am his wife.'

The clerk murmured and leafed through his book, and the large man with the cigar turned to Evelyne and beamed. 'Excuse me, ma'am, but I couldn't help over-hearing, there's more fighters comin' in for that title. The whole of Europe's after it so I wish you luck, and may I say your husband's a fortunate man to have such a beautiful wife.'

Evelyne smiled her thanks, but she was shaking. Aware that the clerk could hear her, she told the fat stranger that her husband was the British Heavyweight Champion. 'You may have heard of him, Freedom Stubbs, he's a Romany gypsy, a prince.'

Even to her the statement sounded childish, and the big man laughed. From his back pocket he took a roll of banknotes larger than his fist, turned back to the receptionist and began peeling some off. They were fifty-dollar bills, and he was paying for his room upfront.

A doorman appeared outside and leaned on the window of the waiting cab. He told the cabbie to move on, go round the block – he could return in a few minutes but the forecourt had to be cleared. The cabbie started the engine and they did a slow crawl out of the forecourt. Coming in was a glittering Cadillac limousine, bright yellow and so highly polished that the lamps and wheels seemed to spark. The chauffeur rushed from his seat to the rear passenger door and two burly men in dark-grey suits and smart white shirts and ties hurried to the entrance. They stood like guards as the chauffeur stepped back, holding the car door open.

A square, stocky man stepped out of the limousine, wearing a pale lilac linen suit, a white fedora hat, and carrying white gloves and a silver-topped walking-stick. He didn't acknowledge the two men standing on guard, but strode past them into the hotel.

Evelyne was still waiting patiently at the desk, as the clerk took forever to flip through the register, and as the brass-framed doors swung open and the lilac clad gentleman entered, the whole lobby went quiet. The two bodyguards walked immediately ahead of him, and two more appeared from behind the potted palms, hemming the squat man between them.

'I'm sorry, ma'am, but we don't seem to have nothin' available right now . . .'

Evelyne had hoped so hard it would be all right that she was bitterly disappointed. She was unaware that a porter had been sent outside to check on the occupants of the waiting cab, had taken one look at Freedom and given the thumbs down.

She had not noticed the flurry of excitement behind her, she had been so intent on the receptionist. The man wearing the flashy lilac suit was heading for the lifts, the two thickset men making a path for him. There was actually no need, as everyone stepped back quickly as soon as they saw the group. Evelyne clenched her teeth, trying hard not to cry. She knew that by now Edward would be starving and fretful, but she thanked the clerk, and her initial show of confidence ebbed fast as she hurried towards the exit.

She was so eager to leave that she bumped into one of the two bodyguards. She barely touched the man, even apologized, but the next minute she was shoved roughly aside, with such force that she fell against a pillar. This was the final straw and she turned on the man, catching him by the sleeve. 'There was no need to push me like that, it was an accident.'

She received no reply, but another shove. As she struck the pillar again, she dropped her handbag and all the contents spilled out on to the marble floor. As she scrabbled for her things, she missed seeing the boss give his protector a nasty crack on the shoulder with his walking stick. She only became aware of him when she saw, close to the handkerchief that had fallen from her bag, a pair of highly-polished, two-toned shoes. Her eyes travelled up the lilac pants to look into the dark eyes beneath the fedora hat.

'You okay, ma'am? Want me to give you a hand . . . here, allow me.'

As he bent down, she could smell a heavy, sweet perfume. The perfectly manicured hand picked up Edward's well-chewed dummy and held it out. Evelyne stood up. She was a head taller than the man, and his chubby face beamed up at her as he asked about her accent.

'I'm from Britain, Wales.'

The fedora was lifted off, he made her a small, courtly bow. As he replaced his hat, he asked if she was a guest of the hotel. Evelyne bit her lip, her eyes filling with tears. He was so friendly, so charming . . . he took out a clean white handkerchief and handed it to her. She was deeply embarrassed, and try as she might to stop them, her eyes kept filling with tears. She wiped her face and told him the hotel was full, she could not get rooms. She was unaware that the lobby had come to a complete standstill as she talked to him.

The man swept over to the counter, and now Evelyne could see the impact he made on the porters and desk staff. Every move he made was shadowed by his attendants, and now they seemed more than cordial, bowing and scraping as if the man were royalty. She watched him talk quietly to the clerk, then he gestured for her to join him at the desk.

'They tell me your husband's gonna be a contender – I tell you what, if you make sure I get a ringside seat, I'll make sure you get the best rooms in this hotel, whaddya say, pretty lady? Is it a deal?'

Evelyne was speechless as the clerk laid two keys on the counter.

'You got a kid with you? A boy, is it? I gotta boy, see, Sonny, I call him Sonny.' A photograph was taken from his wallet and displayed with great pride, then replaced carefully so as not to crease it.

The clerk coughed nervously, and looked at his ledger. 'Well, sir, there's forty-eight and fifty-eight.'

'How's that suit ya, Mrs Stubbs? Two suites next to each other?'

Evelyne flushed and managed to say 'thank you' several times.

A nearby bellhop was poised on his toes in his eagerness to please. At a wave from the fat, manicured hand he was at Evelyne's side.

'Boy'll help you carry your bags, ma'am, don't you forget my tickets, just leave them at the desk . . .'

Evelyne almost curtsied with gratitude, and followed the bellhop out to the waiting taxi. Behind her she missed a strange, chilling scene.

The gentleman in the lilac suit leaned across the polished mahogany desk, swiftly grabbed the clerk by the lapel and pulled him halfway over the counter. 'You treat a lady with discourtesy again and you'll be found with your balls stuffed down your goddam throat, you pint-sized prick.'

The terrified clerk, released, gabbled an apology, and found himself lightly shoved against his letter-rack. 'Make sure they get first-class treatment, flowers, fruit sent up, the whole bit, okay?'

'Yes sir, Mr Capone, sir. Right away, sir.'

Capone stuffed a twenty-dollar bill in the frightened man's pocket and moved off towards the bank of lifts. His bodyguard fell into step beside him, opened the lift doors and checked it over before Capone got in. As the last grey-suited man stepped inside, the folding gate was slammed on his hand. He gasped with pain, but made no other sound.

'Check 'em out. Who's with the broad, get me the whole lowdown on 'em.'

As the lift glided up to his private floor, Capone adjusted his silk cravat in his reflection in the polished brass control panel. He was in a good mood. He began to sing. His voice was strong, not quite Beniamino Gigli, but no one would dare say he wasn't at least on a par.

CHAPTER 23

A WEEK after Freedom's arrival in Chicago there was still no fight arranged. Ed was beginning to think Sir Charles was out of his depth. He had to admit the influx of contenders for the heavyweight title didn't make bouts all that easy to organize. Sir Charles assured Ed that he was trying.

'I have to look after Freedom's interests – not quite so cut and dried as we had anticipated. There are a lot of contenders, and Freedom's nowhere near the top bracket. Thing I don't want is that he has to plough his way through every boxer arriving in the States.'

Ed sighed. Running up hotel bills, trying to keep Freedom happy, was getting him down. Sir Charles poured Ed a brandy. 'I have a meeting with two chaps who may be able to guide us. They *made* Dempsey – Jack Kearn and Tex Rickard.'

Ed's jaw dropped, his eyes sparkled. Together, these two men had taken boxing into million-dollar gates, and promoted Dempsey into that league. Word was out that they were both millionaires. Rickard had been a cowboy, a small town marshal, a prospector and a honky-tonk proprietor, and the ballyhoo he created around the fights earned Rickard, Kearn and Dempsey the nickname of the 'Golden Triangle'. Ed rubbed his hands excitedly.

If they could get those two on their side, they would be made.

Ed bounded into the hotel room. The women were out shopping, and Freedom had been left to babysit. He snapped, unpleasantly, 'Who am I going to fight? Sir Charles arranged a bout for me yet? You tell him if I have to travel for a fight, I need time to train, to prepare. You tell him this waitin's driving me spare, mun?'

Ed pulled up a chair, took out a crumpled piece of paper and began to read out the awesome list of fighters pouring into Chicago from all over the world – Knud Hansen of Denmark, Tom Heeney from New Zealand, Paolino of Spain, Luis Angel Firpo from Argentina – not counting all the American fighters who wanted a crack at the title. That list was even longer.

Ed scratched his head. Their only hope was to get Dempsey on their side and Dempsey's men in their corner. With such backing they could bypass more than twenty contenders because Sharkey or Schmeling had already beaten them. For Freedom to work his way through the list would be madness. Ed shoved the paper under Freedom's nose. 'Look at 'em, count the names . . . But 'is Lordship's gonna get some help, see the three main contenders.'

Freedom interrupted, already over-eager, ready to take all three on. 'Who are they?'

'Johnny Risco is one, then there's the European titleholder, Max Schmeling, and, last but not least, the one they say will take the title, Jack Sharkey.'

Freedom paced the room. 'Can't Sir Charles get me a bout with one of them?'

Ed shook his head, becoming impatient with Freedom's impatience. 'That's what I'm tryin' ter tell yer.

All these other boxers, they want a bout, but it can't be arranged. The top three have fought most of these geezers, can't I get it through yer brain? It's like a knockout competition, any of these names wot's listed 'ere gets through all the prelims – then, *then*, they can try for the big three.'

Freedom slumped into a chair. 'So what do I do? Sit here?'

'No, son, you get down to that gym an' work out like you never done before, 'cause you gotta be ready at all times. We get a chance of a good bout we grab it wiv both 'ands, an' we pray ter God a bit of the Golden Triangle gold rubs off on us.'

Freedom blinked. Ed could almost see the wheels turning in his head. He repeated, 'Golden Triangle', then looked at Ed. It was dawning on him exactly who Rikard and Kearn were.

'Yeah, my idols. An' Sir Charles is pullin' strings ter get 'em on our side, so do as I say an' we'll get yer a fight.'

A week went by without any news, and the hotel bills were mounting. Freedom was becoming restless, he had nothing but aggravation at the gym, where they referred to him as 'the black', and he had almost got into a street brawl. A car passed him and Evelyne as they strolled arm-in-arm, and the occupants had shouted 'white trash' at her. He had chased the car in hapless fury.

He felt caged in the hotel, and Ed worried himself sick. He recognized the signs and knew that Freedom needed a bout soon. He also needed a change of scenery.

*

At long last there was progress. Sir Charles received a cable from Tex Rickard, cordially inviting them to visit him at his villa in Miami. Freda, Evelyne, and Edward, along with all their luggage and a very disgruntled, moody Freedom, left Chicago to take up residence in a small, rented villa in Miami. The villa was right on the ocean front, and Freedom began to relax a little. Sir Charles had instructed Ed to stand by, hire a car and wait. Ed was on tenterhooks, practising driving the car up and down the drive. He almost ran his future champion down as he came out of the villa swinging his towel at the motor. 'How long, Ed? How long does he want us to wait here?'

Ed pulled on the handbrake. 'That was a bloody silly thing to do. I could 'ave run yer over.'

Freedom glowered. 'You tell me how long mun? eh?'

Ed went red in the face, shouting back, 'I dunno, do I? Why don't you get on the beach, run, spend yer time gettin' fit; just fer God's sake stop asking me when-when-when-when. It'll be *when* Sir Charles says, that's all I ruddy know.'

Freedom took off down the beach and Ed hit the steering wheel, shouting at himself now. 'When you bastard, when? . . . when?'

Ed rushed into the villa bellowing for Freedom at the top of his voice. Freda was inspecting the fridge with delight, having never seen one before. 'They're on the beach, Ed . . . Ed, just look at this, it makes cubes of ice for the drinks.'

Ed was already rushing out on the beach waving his arms in the air. Evelyne and Edward were at the water's edge, laughing at the little waves. Freedom was doing press-ups.

'Freedom . . . come on, we got to go an' meet 'em all now . . . *Now*, come on, lad . . . Here, wrap this round yer neck, don't go gettin' cold.'

Freedom took the towel and flicked it at Ed. 'That'll take some doin', mun, it's blazing hot.' He went off at a fast run towards the villa, Ed following on his stubby little legs as quickly as he could.

By the time Ed collapsed on the stairs, Freedom was already taking a shower. He could hear Freedom whistling, taking his time. Ed puffed his way up the stairs and paced up and down outside the bathroom until Freedom came out, stark naked. He was deeply tanned, the outline of his shorts showing lighter. Ed hovered at the bedroom door while Freedom dressed. It never ceased to amaze him how beautiful his lad was, like a statue, every muscle clearly defined.

'What yer doin' now? We can't keep these fellas waitin'. Gawd almighty, you do nothin' but moan about wantin' a fight, now when we got to go an' talk about it, what you doin'?'

Freedom beamed at him as he pulled on a shirt. Ed heard Freda below mixing drinks in a new-fangled machine. 'Gawd love us, git yer pants on . . . *Freda*? Don't you go cookin' nothin', we're on our way out, at least, we will be when this bloody lad gets his gear on. Now, come on . . .'

At long last they were on their way.

Ed parked the rented car outside the ranch-style house, and he and Freedom were led on to a shaded patio by Kearn himself. There, already seated with Sir Charles

545

and waiting to meet them, was the second point of the Golden Triangle, Tex Rickard. He rose to his feet and they were introduced. He was wearing a cowboy hat, tooled leather boots and a large silver and turquoise buckle on his belt. He was a big, expansive man, and a man who got immediately on to familiar terms. Ed loved him. Sir Charles was looking cool and suave in a white linen suit.

The men were drinking beer and their cigar smoke drifted up into the clear, bright sky. Ed and Tex Rickard were talking nineteen to the dozen, as they had been all afternoon, of boxers, of fights. Rickard gave a blow-by-blow account of the Tunney-Dempsey fight, the bout known as the 'fight of the long count'. The new rule was that when a boxer was knocked down, his opponent had to go straight to a neutral corner. Only then could the count begin. If he didn't move, the referee would not start the count.

'Ed, ma boy, that count must have been well over sixteen, I was out of ma goddam mind! I screamed for Jack to get into the corner – he'd forgotten, see, in the heat of the moment. Jeez, I'm tellin' ya, I wanted to get in the goddam ring myself . . . so of course, Tunney got a second wind, who wouldn't after sixteen seconds?'

Ed turned to Freedom and jerked his thumb towards Rickard, telling him to pay close attention to what the man, *the man*, was saying. Freedom leaned forward and listened as the two men began to discuss the last Tunney fight, then relaxed again. He had seen the film, knew the fight punch by punch. Freedom was beside himself. There was Ed with Rickard, apparently going over every detail of every fight that had ever taken place in the USA, and on his other side Sir Charles and Kearn talking non-stop about aeroplanes.

The real reason they had all gathered at Kearn's was to discuss a bout for Freedom, to make him a contender for the championship, but so far no one had said a word about it. In fact, they never brought the subject up at all.

Freedom was moody, his temper fraying. With a terrible grinding of gears they stopped at the villa, and as they climbed out of the car, Freedom began to question Ed. 'So when do I fight, Ed, what went on? They going to help me get a bout or not?'

Ed puffed on a Cuban cigar, a gift from his new friend, Tex, and waved his hand majestically. 'These things take time, son, got to be worked out, an' Sir Charles is going ter have ter give them a percentage of the gate, see, so we don't want ter rush fings. They want ter see you work out tomorrow at a friend's place ... Anyway, did I tell you what Tex told me about when he was gambling in Paris, France?'

'I don't give a bugger about his gambling, I want a fight and I want it soon, Ed.'

That night, Freedom felt Evelyne's belly, and they both agreed it was going to be another boy. They discussed names, and Evelyne decided she would like to call him Alexander. Freedom muttered that it was a name for a woman, and she threw a pillow at him. He would have let her call the baby Freda if she'd wanted to.

The sun had tanned Evelyne's pale skin and lightened her long red hair. He had never seen her so beautiful. The good life suited her, and he was determined it wouldn't stop – not now, not ever.

He slipped from the bed and lifted the blind. The night was dark and the sea was lit by a perfect, brilliant moon. He clenched his hands, his frustration was building to bursting point. He couldn't sleep at night, and he spent all day waiting, always waiting.

At breakfast the following morning, Freedom had already been up for hours, running himself into exhaustion. He ate in silence, and the atmosphere grew tense. Ed was eating the most enormous platter of sausage and pancakes, and his paunch was growing as fast as Evelyne's pregnancy.

'Be patient, fings is goin' just right.'

That was it. Freedom banged his fist on the table. 'Sittin' around eatin', mun, you call that going just right? I came here to fight, so far I done nothin' . . . maybe it's not just Sir Charles out of his depth, mun, maybe you don't know what *you're* doin' . . . Get me a fight, that's all I want.'

As if on cue, a Western union boy rang their bell and handed over a telegram. Rickard had requested another meeting.

Ed and Freedom departed with the usual crashing of gears, Ed refusing to speak to Freedom until he apologized. Evelyne sighed, Freedom's moods were getting to them all, apart from Freda, who spent most of her time with her nose in the fridge eating all the goodies she had discovered on their trips into town.

'I'll take Edward down to the beach.'

'Freda, what if he loses? If he gets a bout and loses, we are all here, living in luxury – who's paying for it?'

Freda sat down at the table with her raspberry ripple ice-cream. 'Don't talk that way. Of *course* he will win, don't ever speak like that.'

But Evelyne couldn't rid herself of her foreboding. She knew Freedom was getting dangerously impatient. Freda waved her spoon at Evelyne. 'Maybe today they'll know about a fight, and you must not let Freedom see you are worried, promise me . . . have some raspberry ripple.'

Evelyne shook her head, collected the bucket and spade and, with Edward pulling excitedly at her hand, went down to the beach.

Ed drove through the gates of the luxurious ranch-style villa. This time Freedom hardly gave a second glance, already bored by Ed's non-stop description of all the Dempsey fights. Only when a servant led them into a gymnasium did he perk up. Everything was geared to boxing – a ring built in the centre of the vast, sprung floor. The servant showed them the dressing room, gesturing to Freedom to help himself, and then bowed out, leaving him to stare at the rows of gloves, robes and boots.

'Go on, get a work out, I'll take a stroll round the stables. I got a surprise for you, you wait. Go on, get dressed.'

Freedom was hammering hell out of a punchbag when the gym doors swung open. A tall, elegant man in a pale cream linen suit, his black hair slicked back, leaned on the doorframe. A large diamond ring glittered on his little finger.

'Carry on, son, let's have a look at you. Go on, hit that bag.'

Puzzled, Freedom blinked. Ed appeared behind the man and stared in adoration, near tears. As the man moved into the centre of the room, Freedom looked at him again and realized who he was. He wore a perfectly tailored suit and shirt with a silk tie, and a handkerchief placed just so in his breast pocket, but no amount of fancy tailoring could hide his muscular body. This was none other than Dempsey himself.

Dempsey's polished shoes made no sound on the pine floor. 'How ya doin', Freedom, glad to meet you.'

The hand was like a rock . . . so this was the 'Manassa Mauler', the iron man. Ed clutched Dempsey's hand, and for one awful moment it looked as if he were going to kiss it. Dempsey began to peel off his jacket, his perfect white teeth gleaming. 'Let's go to it, son, I need a work out.'

It took quite a lot of persuasion for Dempsey to get Freedom into the sauna, as Freedom had never been in one and didn't like it at all.

'Sweats out all the impurities, all the rage over here, they'll get to England in about twenty years. America's the place, this is the land, here, I love this goddam country.'

He poured pine essence on to the bed of hot coals and sat on one of the benches. His body was flabby, but still in better shape than most men of his age. He thumped his belly and roared his deep, bellowing laugh.

'This is the good life, I earned it, I earned it and now I'm living, really living . . . hey, you married?'

They both wore short white towels wrapped around their hips, and Dempsey seemed very proud of his 'manhood'. He snorted when Freedom told him he was married, and said marriage was the worst contract he had ever got himself into.

'An' that toff with the enlarged eyeball, your – what?'

Freedom smiled at his reference to Sir Charles, and said that he was his so-called promoter.

'They'll have him for dinner, you stayin' ta eat? Good, I'll make us a barbecue, one you won't forget, an' we'll have something wet to go with it.'

He was referring to the prohibition order, and when they were dressed they made their way to the patio for the barbecue, passing a very well-stocked bar. Prohibition hadn't, it appeared, affected the ex-world champion.

Ed was grinning like the Cheshire cat, his tête-à-tête with Tex Rickard had obviously lasted all afternoon. Dempsey made no reference to Freedom's fights, but they had worked out hard together in the afternoon and Freedom had been aware of the close scrutiny he had been under.

Dempsey heated the coals on the open grill, and some Mexican servants brought chops, steaks and sausages, already prepared for cooking.

'You ever eaten an American hamburger, Freedom? Hey, what kind of a hell of a name is that, Freedom?'

Tex poured drinks and said that it was a name that would look good in lights, on posters, and then Freedom knew that something must have been settled.

The whisky hit the back of the throat like a fireball, and Ed whistled. Dempsey grinned and said it was the best around these parts, he had the best contacts. The men lit cigars and watched as the food went on to the open grill, while Dempsey, in his shirtsleeves and with his cigar stuck in his mouth, wielded the fork like a fencer, jabbing and inspecting the meat. A table was set on the patio, and soon they were joined by Sir Charles and Jack Kearn. They were greeted with a bellow from Dempsey, who wanted to know where the hell they had been. Kearn poured himself a generous measure of whisky and, gesturing to Sir Charles, said that he was going to make a first-class pilot.

Suddenly there was a silence, the sort of silence they say means an angel is passing over, and Freedom knew instantly that something had definitely been decided. Rickard looked at him. 'Right, son, if all goes to plan – as you know, there are the big three, Risco, Schmeling and Sharkey. Right now you can't get a bout with any one of 'em, but we want you to start ploughing your way through a few smaller bouts – get some good publicity, get your name known. Then, if all goes well . . . it's Risco first, then the German, then the main contender, Sharkey. We've seen all their managers and it will be up to you to show us your worth . . . We want the Sharkey fight in Miami, that way Jack don't have to travel too far.' They roared with laughter, and more drinks were served. Freedom was beside himself. If they'd asked him to fight anyone then and there he would have been up on his feet.

Freedom was never to discover exactly what the financial arrangements were, he left that to Sir Charles. They were very relaxed, the conversation centred entirely on boxing, and Freedom ate like a horse while Dempsey held the floor. He was a great raconteur and made everyone roar with laughter at the stories of his days on the 'tank town' circuits. The subject of the forthcoming bout did not arise again and Freedom had no idea when it was to take place, but he was sure Ed would tell him everything on the journey home. In the meantime he enjoyed himself for what seemed the first time in months.

The following morning, Freedom and Ed received a visit from Sir Charles. He drove up to their villa in a car almost as long as the villa itself. The three men went into the front room and closed the door.

Ed was surprised to see Sir Charles was as hung over as himself and Freedom. His face was a greenish colour and he accepted black coffee gratefully. 'Right, now then, it's not quite as easy as those fellas made it out to be. They want you accepted as a real contender, so I have drawn up the eliminator bouts. If you come through, as I am sure you will, then they'll come in with their promotion for the last three – Risco first.'

Ed was sweating. He mopped his brow. 'Who does he take on first, sir, and where?'

Sir Charles paused a moment, then coughed. 'It's the Dane, Knud Hansen.'

Ed was tense, gripping his cup and saucer to stop them rattling. 'Next, who's after the Dane?'

'Monty Munn . . . first fight takes place in Cleveland, at the St Nicholas ring.'

'Where's Cleveland, local is it?'

'No, Ed, it's in Ohio, so get packing and be prepared to leave first thing in the morning.'

Freedom was beaming from ear to ear as Ed showed Sir Charles out.

'I don't know what you're so bleedin' 'appy about, you seen the size of this ruddy Dane? He's over six feet four, a fuckin' Viking.'

Freedom laughed and stood up, raising his arms. 'So am I, so what?'

'His bleedin' Lordship didn't mention yer might 'ave ter take on the friggin' French feller. Just two fights. Well, don't fink they're easy, you're up against it, and wiwout much time in between bouts if yer do win . . .'

Freedom rumpled Ed's thin, frazzled hair. 'That's what I like about you, mun, give me confidence, encouragement . . .'

Ed grinned and punched Freedom good-naturedly on the arm. 'You'll take 'em easy, lad, just don't want yer finkin' yer don't 'ave ter train.'

Freedom went into the kitchen to give Evelyne and Freda the news. Left alone, Ed's good humour dropped like a stone, and he muttered to himself, 'Christ almighty, 'e's got 'is 'ands full.'

The following morning they were packed and ready. Ed wouldn't even hear of Freda or Evelyne accompanying them. 'You'll both be there for the championship fight, but in the meantime me an' my lad's got our work cut out. We don't want you two slowin' us down.'

Evelyne was relieved. The thought of travelling all over America with little Edward, and pregnant at the same time, was daunting. Freedom was happy, confident, and couldn't wait to get started. But when they had gone the villa felt empty without them, peaceful.

Freda carried two milk shakes on to the patio. 'Banana, try it – have you ever had a banana?'

Evelyne shook her head and sipped the milky yellow drink, then smiled approval. Edward clambered on to her knee and grabbed the drink with both hands while Evelyne struggled to prevent him spilling it all over the table. At the same time she asked Freda what she thought about the forthcoming fights.

'Oh, darlink, first it's just a little one, with Knoot somebody, then a few more to get the Americans familiar with Freedom's name. You don't worry, Ed's not worried, and he knows . . . look, Edward – see, this is a straw, and you suck up your drink like so . . .'

She demonstrated sucking through the straw. Edward couldn't quite get the hang of it and blew instead. Freda turned to Evelyne with banana milk shake dripping down her face. She laughed, saying it was for her sunburn.

Ed and Freedom travelled to Ohio by train, while Sir Charles flew there in a private plane owned by Jack Kearn. He was even allowed to take over the controls, and began to think about acquiring one himself.

The gate for Freedom's fight with Knud Hansen was only fair, about four hundred people. Ed was confident Freedom could take the Dane with ease; the man punched wildly, and used an open-armed swing. He was enormous, weighing in eight pounds heavier than Freedom.

The crowd cheered them both, and as the gong went for round one their cheers turned to loud boos. Freedom was moving around, trying to assess his man, and had hardly thrown a single punch when he caught a wild right and was knocked clean out, to the fury of the crowd.

This was Freedom's first defeat, and he was totally demoralized and dejected, stunned at his own stupidity. However, with Ed always close by and confident that it was a fluke, they arranged a second bout fast. Although the press had been there, the fight hardly caused a ripple in the papers as they were all carrying banner headlines about a brutal killing, a blood bath that had taken place in Chicago.

The headlines ran, 'St Valentine's Day Massacre'. Only a small article, a single paragraph in the sporting section, reported the English contender, Britain's only hope for the Heavyweight Championship, had lost. 'Stubbs KO'd Round One by the Great Dane.'

Evelyne's heart stopped when the rotund figure of Freda charged down the beach, kicking up sand behind her. Evelyne jumped to her feet, panic-stricken. 'What is it? Freedom? Is he all right?'

'Ohhhh, oh, oh . . . it was on the radio, you won't believe it, but . . . they were murdered, all of them gunned down.'

Freda saw the horror in Evelyne's face and quickly gasped out the Al Capone story. Evelyne flopped back on the hot sand. 'Freda . . . oh, Freda, I thought something terrible had happened.' She sat up suddenly, stared at Freda. 'Al Capone? No, are you sure? It couldn't be right, he was so nice! He wouldn't do anything so terrible as shooting people, you must have misheard it, Al Capone?'

Freda was adamant. It had been on the radio, so it had to be true. Evelyne let a handful of sand trickle through her fingers. 'Was there anything about the fight?'

Freda shook her head, then screamed as Edward brought his spade crashing down on her head. Evelyne jumped up and grabbed him, taking the spade from his chubby fist. 'That was naughty, you apologize this instant to Auntie Freda! Edward, I mean it, say you're sorry . . . *Edward*!'

Edward pursed his lips and glowered.

'Right back to the house you go, my lad, and no more sandcastles today.'

Edward screamed and kicked at the sand in fury, his eyes black with anger. Evelyne chased him in circles on the beach until she eventually caught hold of him and dragged him back to face Freda. He wriggled free, then hurled himself into Freda's arms. He kissed her cheek, holding her face in his small hands. 'Kiss it better, kiss you better.'

Freda wrapped him in her arms, laughing. 'Oh, Eddie, you have lady-killer eyes, you have . . . It's all right, Auntie Freda forgives you, and I'm sure Mama will let you build another castle . . . Evie?'

Edward turned big, dark, innocent eyes on Evelyne and she gave a brief nod, then sat down next to Freda. They both watched him digging frantically, then he turned and gave them a wicked grin. Evelyne sighed. 'You spoil him, you know, he gets away with too much – and don't call him Eddie, I don't like it, his name's Edward.'

'Okie-dokie, whatever you say, darlink. He had such a look of Freedom, the image of his father – the eyes, oh, what eyes.'

'Well he won't take after him, that's for sure, I'll not have him fighting, he'll not be a fighter.'

Evelyne was staring, stony-faced, out to sea. She was so beautiful, her long red hair blowing in the breeze. Freda thought to herself, 'With a mother and father so handsome, the world could be little Edward's oyster.'

Ed had his hands full trying to keep Freedom's spirit up, as well as frantically trying to arrange a bout he could go on to immediately. Then they had a stroke of luck – the massive Dane was knocked out by the French contender, Pierre Charles. This left the contender Monty Munn available, so the fight was arranged.

Freedom received a call from Dempsey, who gave

him a talking-to. 'Listen to me, Stubbs, I been KO'd more times than I been balled. Pick yaself up, show us what you got, ya hear me? Go, boy *go*!'

Ed also kept up a steady, encouraging patter, assuring Freedom that if he won the Monty Munn fight he would take on the number three man, none other than Johnny Risco. 'They call him Rubber-legs. The man goes down and bounces back. Well, you get Monty down an' you'll bounce that Risco fella right outta the ring.'

Freedom went ten rounds with Munn, a tough fight, then got his famous punch in. Monty went down. Freedom's confidence was restored, and Kearn and Rickard were now convinced of his potential beyond doubt. They began to play a minor part in promoting Freedom, but they were still holding back. In a private meeting with Sir Charles they told him they both felt it was too early for Freedom to take on Risco, he was not ready. They also had an eye on the gates, wanting to build Freedom's name up.

The fight with Pierre Charles went ahead. This time Freedom had to go the full twenty rounds, and he won on points. Press reports began to feature Freedom Stubbs as a powerful contender for the title. The gates were also improving – money was coming in – and although deals had been set up between Sir Charles and the Golden Triangle, there was still a lot left in the purse for Freedom. But once again his hopes of getting closer to the championship were thwarted and another bout was arranged, this time in Chicago.

As always, Sir Charles kept his accounts with meticulous care, and all Freedom's expenses were deducted. The boat fares, the hotel, the train, the plane rides, nothing was left out. Then there were Ed's wages, taxes, the rent for the Miami villa, every dollar and cent was accounted for. Sir Charles, whose constant battles with the trustees of his estate made him only too aware of his cash flow, was miserly in many ways, but he astounded everyone by handing out huge tips. He would give with one hand and take with the other. Ed put it down to eccentricity, but Dempsey laughed, he put it down to his Lordship being 'just a goddam tight-ass'.

Whatever the outcome of the finances, Ed made sure Freedom's share was looked after, and to date they were, in his own word, 'flush'. Ed was holding more than five thousand dollars for Freedom, in large bills in a money-belt round his rotund stomach. Freedom never questioned Ed about finances. In truth, he didn't care. Being knocked out had marked him, and he was back in training with a vengeance. He never wanted to experience *that* humiliation again.

Ed had forgotten their problems in Chicago. In New York Freedom was accepted as a gypsy, but in Chicago they were again refused admission to any of the best hotels. Freedom grew moodier than ever, and twice Ed had to hold him back from physically assaulting hotel clerks.

Most blacks in Chicago resided in the area known as the South Side, ranging from 30th to 39th Street, and there was a famous hotel, the Du Sable, on the corner of 39th and Cottage Grove Avenue. The Du was one of the most popular hotels for the black élite, where great jazz musicians rubbed elbows with black politicians, judges and lawyers. Duke Ellington and Count Basie often stayed there when playing theatres in downtown

Chicago. The incongruous situation of being able to play there but not live there was a sore point. To Ed's shame, Freedom moved into the Du while he himself stayed at the Lexington with Sir Charles. Freedom had joked about it, saying he didn't give a damn what they wanted to think he was. Black or white, he was there to fight.

And he got a fight, not in the ring but outside a speakeasy. It started with Freedom and two black boxers he had met at the Du being barred from entering the speakeasy. The three boxers started slugging it out with the bouncers on the door, and the police were called. They were on a tough training schedule and Ed had assumed Freedom was resting, when he was summoned to the local police station. Along with his 'brothers', Freedom was put behind bars for the night. Sir Charles paid a heavy fine and made a large 'donation' to police funds to get Freedom released. Afraid of the bad press this situation was bound to cause, the venue was switched, and a hasty retreat to New York organized. In the end this proved beneficial because their luck was in. A contender removed from the running left an opening for Freedom in a fight scheduled to take place in Madison Square.

Freedom's arrest seemed at first to have no effect on him, but Ed detected a difference. He had often said that Freedom lacked the 'killer instinct' – now he saw an anger in Freedom that unleashed itself, but not necessarily in the ring. Ed warned him to keep his temper, at all cost they must avoid bad publicity. The old, familiar mask came down and he received that blank, hooded stare. Ed was told quietly but firmly that it was up to him to make sure that Freedom was never subjected to the insults his 'brothers' received.

Ed made a point of telling Sir Charles it was imperative to make the public aware of Freedom's Romany origins. If he were to be barred from any more hotels, there would be trouble and Ed doubted if he could control it.

From then on, Freedom made a point of mixing with black boxers in the gymnasiums and socializing with them in the bars and nightclubs. He felt an empathy with their segregation, and they in turn accepted him as one of them. They encouraged him and waited in line to act as sparring partners, and many of them should, by rights, have been put forward as contenders.

Ed sat in Freedom's sparse room in the run-down hotel. Freedom had pulled the mattress from his bed and laid it on the floor to sleep. He was stretched out on it now, his head resting on a grubby pillow. Ed knew he was exhausted, but all the attention he had been getting pumped him full of adrenalin.

Freedom felt Ed's eyes on him and turned with a smile. 'You got a big paunch on you, Ed. Want to run round the clubs with me, do the Black Bottom. That'll slim you down.'

'No I don't, and you shouldn't be out gallivantin' wiv all sorts. I'm not a stickler, I know you gotta let off a bit of steam now an' then, but keep it to a minimum. This isn't all belly, neither – this is our cash, son. I don't let it out of me sight fer a minute.'

Freedom laughed and told Ed he should take care on his way back to that posh hotel, joking that Ed might be robbed by some of his 'black brothers'.

'Never mind me, it's you I'm bothered about, you need to rest up.'

Freedom stretched his arms above his head and sighed. 'How many more times do they want me to show how good I am? I want Risco – I done my part,

I've proved myself, I want Risco. So you get that fat body round to his Lordship and tell him I'm through waiting.'

'I hear you, lad, but you remember I'm the trainer, don't get too big fer yer boots or you'll be leavin' 'em on the canvas ... An' stay in ternight, all right? No bloody Black Bottomin'.'

Ed clutched his belly all the way back to the hotel. He decided that perhaps it would be better if the winnings were put in the hotel safe. He counted all the dollar bills and stacked them in a neat pile. As always, Sir Charles had made Ed sign for the money when it was given to him. Ed now decided to ask him to arrange for its safekeeping.

That evening, Sir Charles watched as the money was put into the hotel safe. He suggested to Ed that he open a bank account, but Ed wouldn't hear of it. He had never had much to do with banks, he didn't even have an account back in England, having rarely had more than a pocketful of loose change to his name. Besides, most of the money belonged to Freedom. Another reason, which Ed did not mention to Sir Charles, was that Freedom was still barely able to write more than his own name. To give him a chequebook would only confuse the issue, and knowing his spendthrift ways it was better all round for the money to be kept out of generous hands.

Ed cabled Freda and Evelyne that all was well – more than well, they were inching closer and closer to the title. He did not mention that Freedom was becoming

562

hard to handle. He wanted to get Freedom out of New York. Even though he still worked out in the gyms, he was hitting the booze, and many a morning he was too hung over to train. At last Ed got a call to meet with the Golden Triangle. It seemed they had some good news for him.

The fight with Johnny 'Rubber-legs' Risco was on. Ed wanted Freedom to rest for at least a month, but Dempsey laughed at him, saying that in the days when he was in the booths he fought three or four fights a week, and he knew Freedom was raring to go. Against his better judgement, Ed agreed. The publicity campaign for the Risco–Stubbs fight was under way.

Freedom was working out when Ed told him the Risco fight was going ahead. He belted hell out of the punchbag, then clasped Ed joyfully to his sweating body. Ed did not mention the hours he had spent arguing with Sir Charles that it was too soon, that Freedom needed more rest.

Sir Charles had organized Freedom's match with Risco only three weeks after his win on points at Madison Square, but Ed gave Freedom no hint of his misgivings. Right now, Freedom was confident, even over-confident. 'This is it, I get through with Risco, there's just Sharkey and the German to go, that title's getting closer.'

'Yeah, yeah, I hear you. Just remember Sharkey's still number two contender. He's already wiped out Risco, so he'll be watching you like a hawk.'

Freedom went back to the punchbag with renewed energy. Ed sized him up. He reckoned Freedom could take Risco, but Sharkey would be another matter. Sharkey was lighter than Freedom, but he was said to be unstoppable. He would fight the winner of the Stubbs–Risco bout and, if Freedom won, he would be a very tired boxer.

Sharkey's only obstacle to the vacant throne was the big German, Max Schmeling. He was Germany's international champion and a formidable contender. Schmeling was already at the top in the betting. He and Sharkey had noted the meteoric rise of the gypsy fighter and, as Ed suspected, both men calculated that Freedom would be a very tired man. They booked ringside seats for the bout, which was to take place in Chicago and was already a sell-out. Rumours began to circulate; the Golden Triangle had an interest in the gypsy – tired he might be, but he was beginning to draw crowds. Freedom, at first a rank outsider, now featured in the last lap for the vacant throne. The running was still Schmeling first, Sharkey second, Risco third. Having done extremely well, Freedom was now placed fourth.

Freda and Evelyne felt cut off, waiting for the results. Both understood the importance of Freedom's fight against Johnny 'Rubber-legs' Risco. Evelyne would stand at the gate of the villa for hours on end hoping the Western Union boy would bring her a message. She couldn't sleep for worry.

Freda, who usually tried to keep Evelyne calm, almost induced a miscarriage by screaming at the top of her voice. 'He's here? He's coming! *Evie, Evie, he's got a telegram*!'

Evelyne's hands were shaking as she tore open the envelope. She read it, then closed her eyes. 'He's won, Freda, he's *won*!'

*

It had taken sixteen rounds for Freedom to get Risco down on the canvas. Down and unable to bounce back. Freedom was tired but jubilant, and Ed was beside himself. The throne was closer – his boy was now placed third.

Sharkey and Schmeling were impressed, but Sharkey was still more than confident. If the gyppo was tired before the Risco fight, now he would be exhausted. He put pressure on his promoters to push his fight with Freedom forward.

Dempsey and his partners celebrated when they received the news. Rickard increased the publicity with Sir Charles right alongside him and not afraid, as Dempsey joked, 'to get his hand outta his pocket'. Having been unsure to begin with, they now all believed there was a chance. They brought out the 'big guns' and set about designing posters. Their boy, they were sure, had the 'Golden Glove'.

CHAPTER 24

E D WAS unusually quiet on the flight back to
Miami. Freedom sat next to him, wearing dark
glasses, his head resting on the back of his seat.
He was exhausted.

Poor Ed had lost even more hair during their travels,
forever worrying, and now he believed he had a gastric
ulcer. Out of the corner of his eye, Freedom watched
him take out a cigar, roll it in his fingers, put it back in
his pocket and then take it out again. Fidget, fidget . . .
Freedom laid his hand on Ed's arm and quietly asked
him the important question, 'How long have I got,
Ed?'

Ed stared out of the window, his stomach churning.
He wasn't sure whether it was the fight that caused it,
or the realization that they had barely a month to
prepare. Freedom hesitated only a moment when told.
'Well, I said I wanted to fight, looks like Kearn and
Rickard are coming up trumps.'

Ed was too much the professional to get excited. He
knew it was too soon. Freedom needed more time to
rest. 'I think those two think they're goin' ter make
another Golden Triangle with you at the apex instead of
Dempsey. They'll be behind this razzmatazz. You think
you'll be fit enough, lad?'

Freedom laughed, punched Ed's shoulder and said he was ready. 'Sir Charles'd step in if I wasn't, wouldn't he? He wouldn't let me fight if I wasn't up to it, don't worry, Ed.'

'Sir Charles, lad, blows with the wind, that's all I know. Right now he's all over those two big Americans, talking of buying his own plane, God help us if he wants to take the controls.'

They strapped themselves into their seat belts as the pilot shouted that they were about to land. Ed's face turned green. 'Gawd, this is the bit I hate. S'all right getting up, an' while yer up there, but comin' down's horrible.'

'Yeah, it's like fighting, Ed, no fun when you're down.'

They landed safely and Ed fussed about their bags, worried they would lose the precious sets of gloves. Freedom shouted, 'Ed! Ed, look, will you look at that, well I'll be goddamned if that ain't a sonofa-bitch!'

He was pointing to a huge billboard God only knew how many feet high. 'STUBBS VERSUS SHARKEY.' 'Jeez, ain't that a goddam thing?' He had already picked up a lot of American slang and everything was 'Jeez, Ed' this and 'Jeez, Ed' that. Ed muttered that he'd got it wrong, it wasn't 'Jeez' but 'gee', like in 'gee whizz'. Freedom continued to get it wrong, and in the end Ed also found himself saying, 'Jeez, will you look at that goddam billboard, you could be a movie star.'

Tex played on Freedom's uncanny likeness to the film star Rudolph Valentino to the hilt. He also made much of Freedom's long hair and gypsy blood. On many of the boards, in huge red letters, were the words, 'The Gypsy King'; another favourite was 'The Wild Man'. All of them, like circus posters, were in brilliant colours, showing Freedom with his gloved hands held up, his hair flying out behind him.

The hired limousine was piled to the roof with gifts, many of them toys for Edward. Ed had tried hard, but in the end he had given way and let Freedom have some of his winnings, more than he would dare tell Evelyne. Freedom had gone on one of his wild spending sprees – suits, hats, coats, dresses, jewels, and, of course, a rocking horse, a drum and miniature boxing gloves for his son. For once, Ed had also been spending money like water and was loaded down with gifts for Freda. Also, both of them had bought the lightweight, light-coloured suits that were all the rage.

The elegance and superb tailoring of the clothes Sir Charles had had made for him were rejected for the flashy style favoured by their idol, Dempsey. They both sported loud floral silk ties with matching handkerchiefs and dark glasses.

Sir Charles' new-found friend, Jack Kearn, had taken him to an airstrip, where they inspected a second-hand light plane. Kearn was amazed to hear the usually thrifty Englishman giving instructions for the plane to be elaborately fitted out in red leather. He also wanted certain improvements on the control panel. Kearn paled when he heard how much it would cost, but Sir Charles was ecstatic, and they departed in high spirits. Kearn puzzled over the Englishman's eccentric behaviour, one moment fussing over five or ten dollars and the next spending thirty thousand as if it were no more than a couple of bucks.

*

All day Evelyne and Freda had waited, running to the gate every few minutes, eager to see their men. The car eventually drew up outside at five in the afternoon, and Ed and Freedom hopped out with all their bags and boxes of gifts.

The reunion was feverish, everyone talking at once, unwrapping their presents with shrieks of delight, and Freedom throwing his son up in the air and catching him.

Evelyne sensed that Freedom was slightly evasive, kissing her lightly without removing his dark glasses. She felt uneasy with him, knew there was something wrong.

When Freda and Ed went for a walk on the beach, Evelyne said, 'I think the boxing gloves are a bit big, we'll put them away until he gets bigger.' She was reluctant to tell Freedom that she didn't want Edward to be encouraged to fight.

'I see you're bigger now, how you been, all right?' Freedom asked.

She felt a distance between them. She was aware of how fat she had become with the baby, and felt unattractive, even ugly. She always forgot how tall he was, how handsome. His presence filled the room and made her self-conscious. She picked up all her gifts and thanked him.

'You see all the posters of me, then, love?'

Evelyne hadn't; as neither she nor Freda could drive they had hardly left the villa. She studied Freedom. The pale linen suit, she thought, was not too bad, but the silk tie with the painted flowers was utterly tasteless. 'You look very fancy.'

She could have bitten off her tongue as he looked into the mirror with a hurt expression and examined his tie.

'Not to your liking? Well, you can use it as a bandanna.'

She wished he would take the glasses off, not seeing his face unnerved her. She reached out to take them off, but he backed abruptly away from her. She withdrew her hand, her feelings hurt, but as he slowly removed them himself she understood why.

Both his eyes were bruised and swollen, and beneath his left eye was a gash with fresh stitches. The bridge of his nose was swollen and his cheek was puffy. The sight of him made her feel faint, and she steadied herself on the edge of the table. She knew she mustn't let him see the effect his injuries had on her, and she forced a smile. 'I'd better see if we've got some steak in the icebox, that's what they use, isn't it? Now, come here and let me have a good look at you.'

She could feel the relief in him, feel him relax, and as she took his face gently between her hands she couldn't stop the tears coming into her eyes. She kissed his bruised, hurt face softly.

Freedom gathered her into his arms and returned her kisses, murmuring that his face was fine, and he was just desperate for her. He laid her down on the bed and loosened his flowered tie. She unbuttoned her blouse, and he could see her breasts, swollen but still beautiful. He pulled his shirt open to reveal heavily strapped ribs. His body, like his face, was marked with deep, dark bruises. He sat close to her and helped her off with her blouse, and she kissed his chest, touched the tape.

'It's nothing, just to keep me standing straight.'

He oiled Evelyne's belly and asked if it was all right for him to make love to her. She smiled up at him, loving him for his consideration, and held him tightly. She felt him flinch slightly as she touched his bruised ribs.

He treated her so gently that it was she who urged him on. Again and again he took her until they lay back, sweating and exhausted. Leaning on his elbow he touched her face, brushed a strand of her wonderful long hair aside and kissed her neck, his voice husky and shy. 'There's never been a woman like you, *manushi*, you take me to a place so high up I'm flying. No woman but you can ever take me there, you know that? I love thee, worship thee, and to know you're here waiting for me, fills my soul.'

She looked up into his adoring face, and in her shyness could not tell him that he made her clumsy body feel as light as the day they first made love on the mountain. She felt beautiful again under his gaze, and she glowed.

That night the four of them ate a celebration dinner. Freedom was in high spirits, laughing and playing the fool, showing Freda some new dance steps. Ed put his arm around Evelyne, his eyes shining as he watched Freedom with total adoration. He just loved the lad to death. 'He's done well, Evie love, not just fighting, and he's near nine thousand dollars richer – you're looking at a wealthy gent.'

Evelyne gasped with astonishment. 'Nine thousand? But that's . . . why, Ed, that's . . .'

Ed laughed as she tried to translate dollars into pounds. 'Why, Ed, we're millionaires!' Suddenly she looked at Freedom, who was grinning broadly. He danced around the table with Freda, pausing briefly to turn the radio up even louder as he swung her in his arms.

'Ed, can I have a little word?' Evelyne asked quietly.

Puffing on his cigar, Ed walked with her to the

verandah. She looked over her shoulder and whispered, 'Ed, he's not got it all, has he? You know what a spendthrift he is . . .'

Ed chortled, 'There's no need to tell me, Evie love. Sir Charles keeps it in the hotel safes for us. 'E'll take care of it, 'cause we'll have taxes an' fings to work out before we leave.'

They could hear Freda insisting that Freedom try her banana and raspberry milk shake. She had taken to making elaborate concoctions in her new blender and, of course, feasting on them herself. She had gained at least eight pounds since they had arrived.

Ed turned his adoring expression on his little wife, 'My Gawd, she can certainly put the food away, what a woman.'

'Ed . . . will he win? Tell me, please – I can see his face, his body's all bruised, will he win?'

Ed assured her that, with rest and preparation, Freedom would win. There was nothing to worry about. 'He's goin' ter beat Sharkey, love, I know it.'

Evelyne planted a kiss on his shiny nose, then went into Freedom's arms. They danced around the room.

Ed's good-humoured expression faded quickly. Even from where he was standing, he could see Freedom's swollen face. He knew there would barely be time for it to go down before he went into the ring again. Ed didn't like it at all, especially with Freedom's bruised ribs. He sighed, turned to stare out at the ocean. He tossed his cigar away – it tasted bitter, he felt bitter. He muttered under his breath, 'Bastards, you bastards . . . some rest he's gonna get . . . bastards.'

Freedom took himself off to bed carrying his son high on his shoulders. Tired as he was, he wanted to bath the little fellow and spend some time with him because he had been away so long.

Freda and Evelyne washed up the dishes. By the time Evelyne went to bed Freedom was sleeping. In the crook of his arm lay Edward, who had crawled out of his cot and into the double bed. The child was fast asleep. With his thatch of dark hair and suntanned body he looked like a miniature of his father. Evelyne stood looking at them both, not wanting to disturb them, then slipped downstairs to lie on the settee. She felt her belly and knew that this time she would be there at the ringside, he would not be coming for another two months.

She slept fitfully, Freedom's bruised face floating in her mind's eye. She woke in the early dawn, cold, her body stiff. All around her lay the gifts, the child's toys, and she picked up the tiny boxing gloves. She would hide these, Edward would never have them, never have his face bruised and cut like his father's. Now they had the money she would be able to send him to a good school.

Evelyne smiled, hugging herself with pleasure. She could picture the house they would buy with the money, maybe even a pony for Edward. She would also take herself back to school – yes, she would pick up her studies. When she was qualified and the boys were grown, she could start teaching again. As the sun came up, Evelyne made notes on all the things she would do with the money, using one of the drawing books she had bought for Edward. She enjoyed writing and it had been a long time since she had written anything. She sighed as she looked at her handwriting. Perhaps with their new-found fortune she could persuade Freedom to learn too. Suddenly the thought of how much more they would take home when Freedom won the title made her gasp. She laughed out loud, then put her hand over her mouth, realizing how silly she must look.

She placed the notebook carefully in a dressing-table drawer, inching it open silently so as not to wake Freedom, then slipped into the warm bed beside him and their son. She sighed with happiness and found, to her amazement, that she could recall word for word Christina Rossetti's *The Dream*.

She laid her hand on Freedom's thigh. He turned towards her and, still asleep, pulled her to him. Cradled in his arms, with Edward asleep at Freedom's side, Evelyne felt happier than she had in her whole life. The future was rosy, glowing, and financially secure at long last. She fell into a deep, contented sleep.

CHAPTER 25

THE FIGHT was now only days away, and pre-fight fever made the villa a target for reporters. They photographed Freedom running along the beach, they tried to get to see him at the gym, and he was photographed with Dempsey. Ed finally had to ban the press completely so his fighter could concentrate on training.

Tension mounted in the house. Meals were worked around when Freedom was ready to eat, when he finished, when he slept. He kept himself apart from them all as much as possible, and had been sleeping in the spare room, as little Edward woke often in the night, and Freedom had to rise at the crack of dawn to train.

There was not a mark left on his face from his previous bouts. The small scar under his left eye had healed and he was in peak condition. As the day drew closer and closer, they read in the papers about the arrival of Jack Sharkey.

Every day Freda read the papers avidly, as there were so many articles about Freedom. She cut each one out and put them into a scrapbook. She would then display her cuttings and handwritten notes at breakfast. Evelyne started one, too, and the women would discuss the layout of their books together.

On a recent trip into town for groceries, Evelyne had bought two books and had taken to reading each afternoon on the porch. She loved the gentle, romantic, beautifully structured stories of Jane Austen.

Edward and Freda were making sandcastles on the beach. Evelyne could hear Freda screeching, 'Eddie! Eddie, that's far enough in the water . . . Eddie!' No matter how often Evelyne corrected her, she still called him Eddie. Evelyne sighed and tutted. Jane Austen would not have approved.

Far along the beach she could see Freedom running, no more than a small black dot. Ed drove the hired motorcar alongside, the exhaust leaving a trail of blue smoke in the warm air. Evelyne checked the time – she still had a few precious moments alone before the house would again revolve around Freedom. He ate early, a large steak, salad and fresh fruit, and drank a strange mixture that Freda spent ages mixing in her treasured blender. It consisted of raw eggs, milk, honey, and a vitamin powder Ed had been given by Dempsey. Freedom's training schedule ruled their lives, and now that Evelyne knew what was at stake financially, she made every effort not to disturb his rigorous routine. Mealtime and exercise charts hung all over the kitchen. The lounge was now used for Freedom's massage and as a place to discuss tactics, and the two of them spent hours closeted in there. In the afternoons Freedom went to Dempsey's gymnasium to work out on the proper equipment, returning for his long run, his massage, dinner and bed. The fight was drawing closer and closer, but if Freedom was nervous he took pains not to show it in front of the women. Ed was sharp-tempered if they were a minute off schedule, but neither Freda nor Evelyne argued. The fight was all-important.

Ed had taken Evelyne aside for one of their private

chats. Flushing with embarrassment, he forced himself to say what had to be said, 'Now, love, I know he won't tell you, so it's up to me – yer not to 'ave it away, not 'til after the fight.'

Evelyne smothered her smile and stared, poker-faced, at Ed, 'Have what away? I don't follow you, Ed.'

'Now, now, yer know what I mean! He's in the spare room and, well, yer see, one night's love-makin', Evie, is equivalent to about a six-mile run – d'yer understand me now? Conserve 'is energy.'

Evelyne repeated what Ed had said to Miss Freda. She patted her hair looking at her dumpy little husband, 'Well, I wish he'd do a bit of training. I don't know what's come over him of late, I think it's nerves, either that or he's been taking your Freedom's vitamins.' Ed, unaware that they were whispering about him, paced up and down. Evelyne kept her face straight as she looked back at Freda. 'I don't think it's vitamins, Freda. It's that floating nightdress with all the swansdown he brought you from New York, makes you look the image of Fay Wray.'

Freda giggled as Ed gave them a grunt, and walked out. 'Well darlink, if that's true, he's King Kong. Tonight I'll put my flannel nightie on, that'll finish him off, always has before . . .'

The two women giggled and looked through all the film magazines Ed had bought. Evelyne had to put her hand over her mouth as she caught Freda looking at herself in the mirror. She had made up her mouth with a cupid's bow and obviously thought she really did look like Fay Wray, or Clara Bow. She pursed her lips and batted her thickly mascara'd eyelashes. 'Oh, I just don't know what I am going to wear for the fight, have you thought about your outfit, Evie?'

Evelyne's good humour evaporated. Her stomach

turned over – just for a few moments she had forgotten about the fight. There were only three days to go . . . 'Oh God, Freda, it's not long now, not long.'

They both turned to the calendar where the dates were marked with crosses. Those few days slipped by fast.

On the day of the big fight Freedom left early with Ed. They all hugged him and wished him well. He kissed his son, and waved to them all as the car disappeared down the drive. The villa felt very quiet without him and Ed, and the day seemed to stretch endlessly ahead for Freda and Evelyne.

Jack Sharkey and Freedom faced each other at the weighing-in. Freedom had learnt fast – he out-stared Sharkey, glared for the press cameras and whispered that he was going to wipe the floor with Sharkey. He held up his fist for the photographers.

In the stiflingly hot dressing room, the thunder of the crowd could be heard. Ed bandaged Freedom's fists, and Dempsey came in, raising his clenched fist to Freedom in salute. Sir Charles, Tex and Kearn also made an appearance, Sir Charles bringing a crowd of visiting English aristocracy who all wanted to meet Freedom. Finally, Ed ordered everybody out and banged the door shut.

The seconds were sweating with nerves as they checked their equipment – the buckets, sponges, gumshield, plasters and towels.

Having finished bandaging Freedom's right hand, Ed gestured for him to lift his left. When he was wrapping the cloth tightly between Freedom's fingers, Freedom asked. 'They in their seats yet, Ed? Is she here?'

Ed gave the nod to one of the seconds to check that

the women were there, and he came back saying they were, and that the excited Edward was standing up in his seat waving a rattle. Having finished the bandaging, Ed started to massage Freedom's shoulders. He could feel the tension and kept up a steady flow of chatter, easing the stiffness from the muscles. 'Now remember the rules, Freedom. Make sure if 'e goes down you get over to the neutral corner fast as your legs'll carry yer. That's the law, they won't start the count until you're in the neutral.'

Freedom cuffed Ed good-naturedly on the chin. Before every single bout Ed went on like this, as if Freedom didn't know. Ed was keeping an eye on the clock – it was almost time. They waited for the referee to come in and inspect the bandages. At last he arrived and checked each hand meticulously, then patted Freedom's shoulder. 'I'll go over it in the ring, but I like to have a private word before the bout, understand me? Okay, you break when I tell you, no low punches, no holding. And remember, if either man goes down, you must return to the neutral corner for the count. I will not count until the fighter is in the corner – understand? We got judges each side of the ring, their decision is based on the effectiveness of your punches, they want nice, clean, forceful punches . . . Okay, right, we go in ten minutes, and good luck.'

Ed began to tie on the gloves, still talking in his soft, non-stop way. 'Remember yer get points for aggression, so go in there ter win. Sustain the rounds, don't pussy-foot up there, get in an' take 'im. This is the big one and the most important to date, so I want you in there ter win, you wiv me? You wiv me? Yer goin' ter knock 'im out, and yer goin' ter get that title, yes? Yes, yes?'

Freedom slapped Ed's open palm and yelled back, '*Yes yes yes!*'

There was a knock on the door and they were told to stand by. Ed pulled the robe around Freedom's shoulders and double-checked that the corner men had everything ready. After one last look, he winked and they went out through the door.

The stadium was packed to capacity and the thunder of the crowd's noise drowned out Ed's pep talk. At the opposite entrance stood Sharkey, hopping from one leg to the other, waiting for the signal to enter the ring. A fanfare started up and the audience rose to their feet as the band played the 'Victory March'.

Edward was jumping up and down in his seat, not really understanding what was going on but loving every minute of it. Evelyne's heart was thudding, and she felt the baby kicking inside her. The heat in the stadium was overpowering and the noise like thunderclaps overhead. Freda held Evelyne's hand tight, both their palms sticky from nerves.

The crowd roared as Freedom entered the ring, hemmed in by Ed and the seconds, with eight attendants to keep back the well-wishers' outstretched hands.

'Ladies and gentlemennnn . . . in the left-hand corner, the British Heavyweight Champion *Freedom Stubbs*, wearing the black shorts. Weighing in at two hundred and two pounds. In the right-hand corner, Jack Sharkey, from New York City, weighing in at one hundred and ninety pounds!'

Not a single one of the ringmaster's words about Sharkey was heard, the crowd rose with a deafening cheer, flowers were thrown and feet thudded on the wooden stands.

The two boxers met in the centre of the ring, while the band played first the 'Stars and Stripes', then 'God

Save the King'. The referee was introduced, to whistles and cheers, and the boxers retired to their corners.

'Ladies and gentlemen, there will be twenty rounds of two minutes each round.'

The judges took their bows and went to their seats, flowers and streamers were removed from the ring, and the gong was held up for display. Slowly the stadium grew quieter and quieter as they waited expectantly for the bout to begin.

Freedom glanced quickly over at Evelyne and smiled. She wanted to cry out, reach out to him and touch him. His hair, oiled to keep it off his face, was tied back in a leather thong, and his eyes, brows and cheeks were smeared with Vaseline. The gumshield was put into place and he sat poised and ready.

Sharkey delayed getting his gumshield in, talking to his trainer. The gong clanged loudly, and both men were up and moving to the centre of the ring. The seconds were out, taking the stools with them. Freda was shouting, 'Come on Freedom, come on Freedom . . .'

The boxers were well-matched, and it was not until round four that the crowd began to settle down. The two men were in close, jabbing, punching, trying to find each other's weaknesses. It was a good, clean fight when suddenly a punch that Evelyne didn't even see made Freedom's whole body buckle, and he fell to his knees. The crowd went wild. Ed waved his towel, screaming at the top of his voice, and climbed into the ring. There was almost a fight between Ed and the referee, two judges conferred and Freda was on her feet screaming along with everyone else in the front rows.

'*Foul . . . Foul . . . Foul . . .!*'

581

Freedom was helped to his feet by the ref, who looked into his face and turned, holding off Sharkey with his right hand. He was not counting. Sharkey, panicking, thought he had been disqualified, and turned to his seconds, who now got into the ring. The chant of 'foul' was taken up by a vast group at the back of the stadium, and the sing-song of 'low punch, low punch . . .'

The referee was holding Ed off, and Freedom backed, bent over slightly and shook his head. To everyone's amazement, the referee held up his hand and gave a two-minute respite to Freedom, throughout which Sharkey fumed and raged like a madman. Ed had to be hauled out of the ring, still insisting it was a foul, but the ref gave the signal for the round to continue.

The muscles in Freedom's left leg were seizing up, and it felt as if it were paralysed. For the duration of the round he fended off Sharkey's punches as best he could and at the end he limped back to his corner, which drew a series of loud boos and catcalls from the spectators.

Evelyne sat huddled in her seat. She couldn't understand what was going on, he was in pain and she knew it. 'He's hurt, Freda, he's hurt, he can hardly walk.'

In desperation Ed massaged Freedom's leg, at the same time yelling above the noise to Freedom, 'You want me stop the fight? Tell me, shall I stop the fight, can you move it, Jesus God, can you move your leg?'

The seconds could see that Freedom's old cut was an angry red, and they plastered it with grease . . . Ed had actually reached for the towel to throw it into the ring when the gong sounded for the round to begin. Ed knew his boy was hurt, it was obvious from his stance. This wasn't Freedom's style, he was a mover, and a fast one.

Freedom took a series of short, fast jabs to his face

and keeled over backwards, lost his balance and fell heavily out of the ring. Evelyne was on her feet, tears rolling down her cheeks. She couldn't stand to see it, see him hurt, she wanted him never to get back into the ring. The crowd around her were screaming like wild animals.

The referee started the count, holding Sharkey back as Freedom hauled himself back into the ring. The fall had cut him just above his left ear, and blood was trickling down on to his shoulder. Ed was at breaking point, but held back by the seconds. He wanted to throw in the towel; it was obvious Freedom couldn't stand properly. His left leg was dragging, useless. Freedom was taking his punishment, gritting his teeth to hold on until the round ended. It was taking everything he had just to stand with the agonizing pain in his left leg and the feeling that someone was hacking into his spine . . . Every movement made it worse.

Sharkey took every opportunity, spurred on by relief at not getting disqualified, and came on to Freedom with punch after punch. He was a short jab man, and Freedom was on the end of his hard rights time and time again. He felt his nose split open and stood dazed as the bell rang for the end of the round.

Ed concentrated on Freedom's face and begged him to throw in the towel. Blood was pouring from his nose, and the cut above his ear wouldn't stay shut. 'It's over, Freedom, it's over, he's mauling you.'

Sir Charles sat stiffly through the next round, not making a sound, and his companions went quiet as they saw his champion beaten. There was nothing anyone could say, the ring said it all, the crowds bayed for a knockout and Sir Charles knew they would get it at any moment. There was a flash of Freedom's old brilliance, but he stumbled and took a left hook to his jaw that lifted him off the canvas. No one could believe he would get up from it, but he did. It was tragic to see him swaying, blinded by his own blood, and for Evelyne and Freda it was a nightmare. Edward shouted, 'Daddy, Daddy,' and waved his rattle, thinking it was all a game. Evelyne hugged the child to her and sobbed; she couldn't bear to look into the ring.

At long last Freedom was down and out for the count, but there was none of the hysterical cheering. The crowd went quiet as they saw Freedom's terrible injuries and the pitiful attempts of his seconds to bring him round. His blood was all over the canvas, all over his opponent.

The referee held up Sharkey's hand as Ed was still trying to bring Freedom to. He lay face down, breathing in the resin, and eventually the two seconds managed to lift him back to his seat. From then on it was a blur to all those close to Freedom – the ride in the ambulance, the wait outside the hospital room for news. Ed wept unashamedly, but Freda had strength enough for them all. She chided Ed, saying he must put on a brave face for Freedom, Freedom mustn't see him like this. Evelyne cradled the sleeping child and was so exhausted she couldn't even cry.

The doctors took Ed aside and said that Freedom was going to be all right. He was semi-paralysed down his left side. They doubted that the paralysis would be permanent, and hoped he would recover the use of his leg completely. The blow to the side of Freedom's head caused much more worry, and although he had regained a semblance of consciousness he wasn't lucid. So they had taken X-rays of his skull and he was under sedation.

Ed went into the private room. Unable to speak he just stood looking at the still figure with the terribly swollen face and broken nose plastered up, and his heart broke. The room was silent except for Freedom's shallow breathing, and Ed touched his hand and had to hurry out before he broke down.

Ed tried to persuade Evelyne to go home with Freda, but he hadn't counted on her strength of will. She refused point-blank to move, insisting that Freda and Ed take the child home and return in the morning. Evelyne sat outside the room, quiet, alone, her eyes closed. She prayed for him, hand to her heart, and whispered his name over and over again.

Sir Charles was led past the waiting room. He could see her, her anguished face, as she waited. He followed the nurse down the corridor and into Freedom's room. The nurse hovered at the door.

'Thank you, I won't be a moment.' Left alone with the shrouded figure in the bed, surrounded by machines and intravenous drips, Sir Charles stood as if frozen. Slowly, without making a sound, he inched towards the bed, peered down into the distorted face with the swollen eyes and the thick bandages over the broken nose. He removed his monocle and his mouth twitched.

Freedom's hands were unmarked, his long, tapering fingers resting peacefully on the white sheet, making Sir Charles want to weep. Such fine hands, he had never really noticed them before. He looked towards the door, then reached out and touched Freedom's hand, as if afraid, then bent and kissed the tips of the fingers. Then he slipped from the room and walked back along the corridor to where Evelyne waited.

He looked embarrassed, he didn't know what to say to her, and he tapped his walking stick on the blue lino, making small indentations. She said not one word, but stared at him, her face tight and angry, her eyes cold.

'I'll make sure all the hospital bills are taken care of,

and, well, any expenses will, of course, be paid. I'm sorry.'

She wanted to strike him, smash his arrogant, stiff face, hit him so hard that his monocle would shatter on the floor. 'That's very kind of you, sir, what about his heart, can you pay for that, too? He'll not get over this and you know it.'

He coughed, shuffled his feet and said he would be flying to Chicago the following morning, and would no doubt see them on their return to England.

'He's just like one of your thoroughbreds really, isn't he, sir? Except when they break a leg you shoot them. Where's your gun? You're finished with him now, aren't you? Just like that, because he didn't win.'

Sir Charles went white with anger at her rudeness. 'Your husband never did anything he didn't want to. You of all people should know that. No one forced him into the ring and no one is to blame. He is a sportsman.'

Evelyne moved closer to him and her fists clenched. '*You* forced him and you know it, you never let him off the hook, did you? Because you owned him, from the day you first met him, you bought him.'

Sir Charles snapped that perhaps she would have preferred him to hang, as he most assuredly could have done without him.

'He repaid you, every penny you spent on that court case. How much have you made out of him?'

He pushed her away from him, his face ashen. His fury, usually so controlled, burst out. 'If there was anyone to blame, my dear, it was you, you who never let him be, you hung on to your meal ticket as he would have hanged from a rope. Do you think I don't know that?'

Evelyne slapped his face so hard that he reeled backwards. Taking out a silk handkerchief he dabbed at the

586

corners of his mouth, then replaced his monocle and reached for the door handle. He froze for a moment, his back to her, his voice choked, 'Forgive me, I should never, never have said those things to you. I cannot say how deeply sorry I am, I can only say that I am as distraught about what has happened as you are. You won't believe me, but it is the truth.'

Evelyne gave him a bitter smile, and he wouldn't meet her eyes, but he did turn towards her. 'I remember him from those early days, at Devil's Pit. I had such hopes for him, and they did not include you. I am sorry, perhaps I had a reason – you may call it jealousy, whatever you wish. But you have him now, he's all yours, and I feel sure your love for each other will be strong enough to overcome this sad situation.'

He wanted to leave but Evelyne caught his arm, and only his icy stare made her release him.

'They say he'll never fight again, do you know that? And I don't want him to, ever. Stay out of our lives, stay away from him, we don't need you.'

He gave her a brief nod, said his contract with Freedom was void as of that day. He opened the door, holding his back ramrod-stiff, and walked out. He said his last words to the corridor, not even directing them at Evelyne, 'You never needed me, my dear, never.'

Sir Charles walked slowly out of the hospital. His car drew up and he stepped in and leaned his head on the soft leather. He had a clear picture of the very first time he had seen Freedom, there at Devil's Pit, with his flowing hair and perfect body. How could those foolish people know, understand anything? No other man had had such care and attention lavished on him, but they believed it had been purely business.

'I wanted him, I wanted him.'

The chauffeur turned a puzzled look to Sir Charles,

587

they were still outside the hospital and he was not sure where he was supposed to take his passenger. Sir Charles opened his eyes and snapped that they were going to his hotel immediately; he had already made the decision not to return to Chicago, there was nothing there for him. He decided to go to Hollywood. Perhaps there he would find what he was always searching for but so afraid to make happen. Hollywood beckoned, the decadence, the freedom to love whom he chose.

Evelyne saw the limousine drive away and knew that an episode in her life, in all their lives, had closed.

At three o'clock the nurse came out with some hot tea for Evelyne and told her Freedom was asking for her. The nurse was worried, the woman looked heavily pregnant, and quietly warned her that he was not lucid, still under the effects of the drugs.

Evelyne walked to the bedside, and sat in the chair the nurse had placed there for her. Freedom's hands were still, lying on top of the folded white sheet. His face, so bruised and beaten, looked grotesque with the bandages over his nose.

'That you, *manushi*, that you?'

She took his hand and kissed it, whispering that she was there, she was there, and to go to sleep.

'I'm sorry, so sorry, *manushi*, sorry . . .'

The tears she thought had dried up flowed freely, dripping on to his hand, and he slept, holding her tight, afraid to let her go. In his sleep he was running through the fields, he was dragging the wild horse towards him and riding bareback through the clean, sweet, fresh air.

In the morning Ed came to find her still holding Freedom's hand, her head resting on the bed. He eased her away and she tried to argue, but he said it was not for her but for the baby, she must eat.

The villa's shutters were closed; Evelyne didn't want the sunlight, she wanted the dark to wrap around her and comfort her. Freda came and sat beside her, held her hand.

'Sir Charles was at the hospital. He said Freedom's contract was cancelled.'

Freda wanted to cry, but she kept herself under control. 'We'll go home, Ed says, as soon as Freedom's well.'

'How did Sir Charles come to have all that money? It doesn't seem right, the way he can pick people up, then drop them.'

Freda sighed and patted Evelyne's hand. 'Well, dar-link, he never even met any of his miners, but he treats them the same way.'

'What do you mean?'

Surprised she didn't know, Freda told her Sir Charles' family money was made from coal mining. She was taken aback when Evelyne laughed, a bitter, humourless laugh. 'My God, I should have known it. I hate him, Freda, I hate him so.'

'He has troubles, too, Evie. His trustees, so Ed tells me, always keep him short of money, he has to fight them all the time.'

'Keep him short? He wouldn't know the meaning of the word. My brothers worked the mines, their knees cut and their elbows bent, their backs torn to shreds. He wouldn't know what it felt like to go short, to beg for a crust of bread. I hate him.'

Freda saw the rage in Evelyne, the deep anger,

unleash itself. The violent movements of her hands emphasized what she was saying, 'I wonder how much he made out of him, how much? It'll be more than we have coming to us. Dear God, Freda, I hate that man so much I could go and . . . and . . .'

Suddenly Evelyne was sobbing, her shoulders heaving. Freda stroked her hair, knowing it was best Evie should cry, to release her anger. It wasn't really hatred for Sir Charles, it was her pain for Freedom.

Ed came home from the hospital, heavy-hearted. He laid his straw hat down. 'I dunno what's goin' ter 'appen, Freda, they tell me he's still paralysed down 'is left side. It must've 'appened when he fell outta the ring. I should've stopped 'im, Freda, I 'ad the chance first time 'e went down. I should've made 'im quit. But I wanted 'im ter win so bad . . . wanted 'im ter win, an' I failed 'im, I failed my boy, Freda.' He rubbed his head, held his hand out to Freda. He clung to her and sobbed, and she rocked him in her arms. Ed wasn't weeping for a fighter, the loss of the championship – he was heartbroken for his 'golden boy', his 'son'.

They could hear Evelyne moving around upstairs; she came down with her face set, pale and drawn from crying. 'Ed, will you drive me to the cab stand. I'll go back to the hospital, sit with him until morning.'

Ed wiped his tears with the back of his hand, afraid Evelyne had seen. He put his straw hat on at a jaunty angle.

'Right, then, let's be 'avin' yer.'

Sir Charles had been so silent, so preoccupied that Dewhurst crept around the hotel suite. 'I've packed

590

everything, sir, and we are ready whenever you wish to leave.'

Sir Charles gave him a small smile. 'Jolly good. I'll be flying, I know how you feel about planes, if you would prefer to travel straight back to the Grange I can arrange your passage.'

'Oh, that's very good of you, sir, but I have a great inclination to see Hollywood. They say there's a guided tour of the film stars' homes that's rather special.'

Sir Charles nodded, but seemed loath to leave.

'Will you be wanting to drive to the hospital before we depart, sir?'

He received no answer. 'May I ask how Mr Stubbs is, sir?'

Sir Charles stood up, straight as an arrow. He placed a long finger on the centre of his forehead as if he were in pain, and his voice sounded strangled, ''Fraid he's not too good, old chap, will you make sure they have their passages arranged, the boat, will you do that?'

He swallowed, still pressing his finger to his head, then took out a silk handkerchief and blew his nose.

'Will you be looking for a new fighter, sir?'

Sir Charles tucked his handkerchief back into his top pocket, making sure the folds were sitting exactly as they should. 'No, there'll be no more fighters, Dewhurst. Er! Well, hurry along and I'll meet you at the car.'

As the door closed behind Dewhurst, Sir Charles stared around the room. Crumpled in the waste basket was the fight programme, Freedom's face twisted and torn. The wondrous face, the long, flying hair, the 'Gypsy King' . . . He picked it up, took it to the table and tried to press out the creases, but they would not be smoothed. The beautiful face was cracked, crumpled, and Sir Charles tore it into tiny fragments. But the face was still there, in front of him on the polished table. He

591

felt as if Freedom were in the room with him and it frightened him.

Freedom lay still, his breathing shallow, and Evelyne sat beside him. For a moment his eyes opened, and he murmured, 'Sir Charles? Did he come, Evie?'

'He's gone, darling, we're free of him now. There'll be no more fighting, it's over.'

Freedom's body trembled, he moaned softly. His lips moved as if he were saying something she couldn't quite hear. She leaned closer, but the words were in his own language, jumbled, strange, sighing words. The trembling grew stronger, his whole body shaking. He gripped her hand tightly, and the tremor ran through her, making her body feel electrified. He gripped tighter, tighter, until her hand hurt, but she couldn't release it. Then, just as it had started, the shaking ceased. Freedom sighed, a long, soft moan that continued for almost half a minute. Evelyne drew back her hand, afraid, but now he was relaxed, a sweet smile on his lips. The time was exactly twelve o'clock, Evelyne knew it was exactly on the hour because her wrist watch had stopped.

Sir Charles looked at the dials, the needles were swinging round and round, and the engine cut . . . without power, they were dropping from the sky, a dead weight. Dewhurst tried to unbuckle his seat belt to get to his master, but there was no time. It was over in seconds, the plane spiralling as it made its terrifying journey to the ground. Sir Charles tried desperately to regain power, and then he gave up. A face, blurred, floated in the clouds like a hand-coloured photograph, but it was cracked and torn. In the seconds before the plane crashed into the Nevada desert, Sir Charles Wheeler saw the face of Freedom Stubbs, not as he had been when Sir Charles had first seen him in the ring, like a wild animal at Devil's Pit, but bloody, beaten, crumpled like the programme in the hotel waste paper basket.

The search party found the wreckage from the sky. The black smoke curling up in a spiral, thick grey and red smoke clouding the air with black specks of charred dollar bills. All Freedom Stubbs' winnings, all Ed Meadows' hard-earned wages, all gone. The plane was no more than a shell when the rescuers came on the scene.

They knew exactly what time the plane had crashed. Sir Charles' fob watch had stopped at precisely twelve o'clock. The dials on the plane's control panel were cracked and broken from the heat and the impact of the crash. The clock on the panel had also stopped at twelve o'clock.

BOOK FIVE

BOOK FIVE

CHAPTER 26

THE STUBBS family returned to England with the Meadows. The news of Freedom's terrible defeat arrived ahead of them. The British Champion limped, and his face still bore tell-tale marks of the beating. He felt he had let everyone down, and was ashamed to look anyone in the face. He could not defend his British title; his boxing days were, as Evelyne had said, over.

News of Sir Charles Wheeler's death also preceded them, as well as the two bodies, which were flown from Nevada. Ed did not understand the full implications of Sir Charles' death until he contacted the Wheeler trustees. Freedom's earnings and his own had been in Sir Charles' keeping, and it seemed to Ed a simple matter. The solicitors replied to his letter cordially enough, but in legal language that took a long time to decipher. The gist of it was accounted for, and there was no indication that anything was due to the fighter or his trainer – quite the contrary. The receipts were there to prove it – Ed had signed for all the money he had received on his own and Freedom's behalf. Ed wrote back stating that he had given the money back to Sir Charles for safekeeping, after signing for it. The letters passed back and forth, until Ed became frantic. He visited the solicitors personally, only to be told again that there was no record of any outstanding debts, either to him or Freedom. He was even shown the notification from Sir Charles that the hospital bills and the fares for their return journey were to be paid, but there was no mention of any cash. They could only suggest that Sir Charles had taken it with him to Nevada and it was destroyed with the plane, but they could do nothing.

Evelyne wrote copious letters to the trustees and received similar, cordial replies. The Wheeler estate was in financial difficulties. Death duties had taken their toll, and The Grange was to be sold in order to meet the heirs' interests.

She took legal advice. They could, if they wished, take the Wheeler estate to court over the matter, but they would have to be prepared to meet heavy legal costs, and there was very little hope of success.

Only Freedom appeared to have very little inclination to recover what was rightfully his. His attitude infuriated Evelyne. One morning, after receiving yet another letter of refusal from the trustees, she flew into a rage. 'They're saying the estate has no money? My God, what do they take us for? What's no money to them is millions to us. Freedom, will you go to them, in person?'

Freedom shook his head. 'No, I'll not go begging. We've no need of them, best we forget it. Besides, he paid for our passage home, all the hospital bills.'

'And so he should have, it was him put you in there! Can you not see how our lives would be if we had what was ours? Oh, Freedom, *will you not fight?*'

The look on his face made her want to weep. He picked up his cloth cap, his face twisted with emotion. 'I did fight, Evie, but I lost. I wasn't good enough. I've no fight left in me now, so just let things be. I mean it,

598

girl, I want no more of these letters – it's over, let us get on with our lives, or what life I've got left.'

Evelyne wept as he limped out. He didn't even slam the front door, but closed it gently, as if he were closing an episode in their lives. In a way, he was.

The new baby was born in the winter of 1926, the same year the film star, Rudolph Valentino, died. They called him Alex, as Evelyne had wanted. He was not as heavy as Edward had been, but he was perfect. His hair was sandy-coloured, his eyes blue. Evelyne touched a dimple that had already formed on his chin. 'Well, if it's not Hugh Jones himself.'

Edward was led to the old cradle where his new brother lay, and he peeked over the edge. Mrs Harris had warned Evelyne that, with only two years between the boys, there could be trouble. Edward might well be jealous of the 'intruder'. So it was a touching sight when the small boy, clinging to the side of the cradle, looked with adoration into the big blue eyes. Gently, he reached out and touched the baby's face, then ran out of the room, returning in moments with his arms full of toys. 'For Alex, for my bruvver.'

Edward showed not a hint of jealousy where Alex was concerned. He was very protective, and even at two and a half he insisted on taking care of his brother. He helped to bath and dress him, and watched while he was breast-fed.

Freedom went out and got work at the docks, without any encouragement from anyone. When he came back he said simply that with another mouth to feed he had to work. But there was one moment of his old glory when he handed over his British Championship to the new titleholder. He received a standing ovation at the Albert Hall, wearing his expensive clothes and looking as handsome as ever, and no one noticed the way he dragged his foot.

Somehow Ed knew he would be feeling low, so after the occasion he took Freedom to the pub and they got well and truly drunk. At long last the locals were able to talk about the American bout and Freedom opened up, describing the United States and each of his fights. He had an avid, attentive audience, and he enjoyed himself. He felt more confident, less defeated. The other dockers had nicknamed him 'Champ', and Freedom began to adjust to everyday life.

Money was short, unemployment was at a terrifying level, and the mere fact that both Ed and Freedom were working was in itself a feat. Ed was now taking work as a trainer wherever he could get it, and he asked Freedom if he would help out at the gym. Freedom refused and Ed never pushed it, knowing intuitively not to ask again, and kept quiet about what he was up to until Freedom asked him.

Ed never forgave Sir Charles, even though he was dead. He wept privately when he read of the championship match between Jack Sharkey and the German Max Schmeling. Against Freedom, Ed knew, Sharkey had punched low, and should have been disqualified. Ed read with satisfaction that he had lost the world title because of another foul. Max Schmeling won the title on a foul – the title Ed still believed should have been Freedom's.

*

Out in the back yard of number twelve, the small square that backed on to the canal, the ex-heavyweight contender held a small white rabbit aloft. He shouted for his boys to come and see what he had brought them, and they ran to his side. 'That's it, be gentle – see, you two are a lot bigger'n 'im, and we don't want him afeared of you, now do we? So, gently does it, an' he'll get to know you and not be afeared, see his little pink tongue, and his wonderful eyes? Now then, his whiskers, lads, they're like his ears, and they tell him when danger is close. They're very sensitive.'

The two brothers, so different, one as dark as his father, with black eyes, the other with a shock of sandy hair and big blue eyes, listened to every word their beloved father said. In turn, they touched the small, white bundle of fur.

Both boys were big for their ages, both had big hands, and they would take after Freedom in build. They were usually dressed in similar clothes, and there was rarely a time when they were not together. When Evelyne took them out, there was always someone who remarked how handsome they were. Edward would always answer, proudly, 'We are brothers.'

By 1931 unemployment in Britain had reached over two million. It was a time of crisis. The Labour Government was split over how to deal with the economic situation and a caucus led by J. Ramsay Macdonald joined the Conservatives and Liberals. The result of the ensuing election in October 1931 was a disaster for the Labour movement, and the most hated of all measures introduced by the First National Government was the means test. After twenty-six weeks on the dole, no money was given until the relieving officer, commonly known as the 'RO' man, had visited your house to see what could be sold. In this way many treasured possessions went in order to buy food. Pianos and wireless sets, considered luxuries, were always high on the 'hit list'.

The Stubbs family lived at number twelve, then there was Ed's brother and his big family at number sixteen, and Freda and Ed had moved into a house two doors the other way. They were always in and out of each other's houses, and even though money was scarce and there was terrible unemployment, they still felt like a family unit. Mrs Harris, living only a few streets away, was a frequent visitor. They would all gossip, moan about shortages and their menfolk, their doors always open to visitors.

Beer was cheap and it was used like aspirin. The pubs were warm, and with others in the same predicament they found companionship, but often kids, sent by mothers, would be seen trying to haul their menfolk home.

Monday mornings were days of reckoning, when the publicans counted their profits and tallied up the 'tick'. Mondays would see the wives carrying bundles to the pawnbrokers to get a few shillings, and their men's Sunday suits were constantly in and out of hock. They even took their blankets off the beds to get a few coppers in the constant battle to cover debts simply to feed their children.

You could always tell the widows, who would suddenly appear in black from head to toe, and remain in black for the rest of their lives. Sometimes, however, the fact that they had lost their loved ones changed their circumstances for the better, because of insurance. Realizing that this would more than likely be the one time in her life when she would have an accumulation of money, the widow would set herself up as a moneylender. The interest was very small, but it still proved profitable, and often these widows became more than merry, for the first time in their lives better off than they had been with their 'other halves'.

Funerals were a common sight, the black horse draped in mauve velvet. The mortality rate was high, mostly due to pneumonia, and survival was down to the fittest. Somehow, God knows how, every family was able to raise money for their dead, as if having been so unimportant in life they had to be noticed in death.

The Stubbs family was surviving, and better than most, partly due to Freedom's work on the docks, but also due to Evelyne's frugal household economy. She bought well, and wasted nothing; she counted every penny, and would traipse miles to a market-stall butcher with fresh cheap meat rather than buy in the shops. She always went to market late on Friday nights, when the stall-holders flogged off their wares cheaply. There were no fridges or iceboxes, so food had to be kept cooled in larders or meat-safes outside in the yard.

Evelyne sewed, making most of the boys' clothes, cutting down Freedom's trousers, knitting, her watchful eye on the purse strings, and she wasted nothing. Twice a week she would go to two bakeries to do their accounts, for which she was paid one pound fifteen shillings. She never used this money, but put it in her post office savings account. Freedom had never so much as seen her treasured, small, folded book, he didn't even know of its existence. She was obsessive about it, forever totalling the figures. She had saved more than one hundred and twenty-five pounds over the years, which was a lot of money, but she wouldn't touch it. She would use it for her sons' education when the time came, although she kept a small float and had become the 'widow' in her street. She lent out a shilling here, half-a-crown there, and would make neat notes on exactly how long her customers took to repay the small loans, with interest. She had begun with five pounds, and after four years she still had her original stake, all the money she had earned having gone straight into the post office.

Of course, Evelyne was lucky to have Freedom. If anyone was late in paying it took only one visit from him for the money to be handed over. Freedom hated it and would do anything to get out of having to pay these visits, but Evelyne would fold her arms and ask him if he thought they were a charity, they needed the money as much as anyone else did, and as he was the man of the house he had to pull his weight. He would look at her as she stood there, tall as ever and neat as a new pin, her hair coiled in a tight bun, and shrug his shoulders. He often wondered who really was the man of the house, she was a right devil with her temper.

The whole street respected Mrs Stubbs. Nothing defeated her, nothing got on top of her, and everyone had to admit she kept her house spotless and her two boys immaculate. She was not a great mixer, although she would have the odd schooner of sweet sherry at the pub, but she never stayed long and didn't like to gossip. They all knew she had some stories to tell, about her time in America, about her husband when he was boxing champion, but she rarely if ever spoke of these times. Freda, on the other hand, regaled everyone with stories of when they had travelled on the boat across the Atlantic, and of Miami. Freda was very popular and would feed back all the gossip to Evelyne whenever she called round for a cup of tea. She soon learned that Evelyne didn't want to discuss the past or even remember.

Freda always recognized the signs in Evelyne. Her face would tighten up, her mouth clamp shut whenever Freda tried to talk of the past, of the days in America. Freedom's agonizing headaches were a strong enough reminder. Evelyne would make a vinegar and brown paper compress to put on his brow, and he would lie in a darkened room for hours. Freda eventually gave up mentioning America, she kept her stories for the snug bar at the local pub.

Freda had seen change slowly creep up on Evelyne. She was still handsome, but her face had thinned, the prominent cheekbones making her look gaunt, though not haggard. They ate too well for that. It was just a strange hardening. She was obsessively clean and neat, her kitchen spotless. Her small row of leather-bound books was dusted and treasured. Hers was still the only house in the street with carpet, still the only house with good furniture and a bed that had been brand-new when they first arrived. Evelyne Stubbs was certainly very houseproud.

No matter how Evelyne had tried to make everyone use Edward's full name, he was always known as Eddie. He had a thick cockney accent and was a handful for anyone, always up to something, and she had discovered that smacking him had no effect at all. The only way she could control him was by showing more affection towards Alex, his younger brother. That always brought him to attention. Eddie adored his little brother, so long as he remained just that. Any sign that Alex was considered more special would result in moody tantrums. Alex, on the other hand, was easy-going, always cheerful, and did whatever his brother told him to do. Seeing them go off to school, hand-in-hand, wearing their matching grey sweaters and shorts, made Evelyne feel that all the hard work was worthwhile. They were different from the rest of their school-fellows.

Their tea was ready on the table, and Evelyne stood on the front step, waiting for them. They were more than half an hour late so she wrapped her shawl around her and went down the road to search for them. As she turned the corner near the patch of waste ground, she saw a tight group of boys cheering and shouting. Eddie, his fists flying, was on top of another boy, holding him by the hair and banging his head on the ground. Evelyne rolled up her sleeves and dragged him off, boxed his ears and picked the howling child up from the ground. The other children ran like hell, leaving Eddie and Alex with their mother, and the weeping boy still in Evelyne's tight grip.

'What's all this about then? Come on, I want to know . . . Fighting in the street like common nothings – what's it all about?'

Alex shuffled and looked away, and the little boy with the bloody nose wriggled out of Evelyne's grasp and ran off. Eddie yelled after him, his fist in the air, and turned defiantly to his mother. 'The little bastard hit me and me.' He pointed first to his brother and then to himself, referring to Alex as 'me', as if they were one.

'Why did he hit you? Come on then, why?'

Eddie picked up his school books and glared at his brother to keep quiet, but Evelyne was adamant.

'I want to know what it was about. I'll be down at the school first thing tomorrow morning if you don't speak up.'

606

Alex burst into tears, and stuttered out that Johnny Rigg had called them 'gyppos'.

Mrs Rigg couldn't believe her eyes when she opened her front door. There was Mrs Stubbs, arms folded, and with such a furious look on her face that Mrs Rigg was scared stiff.

'I want a word with you and your son, and I want it now.'

Eddie and Alex flushed with embarrassment as Mrs Rigg made her son apologize to the Stubbs family. When the door shut behind them she belted the boy, which caused her husband, who was just arriving home, to ask what the hell was going on. Poor Johnny got another thrashing from his father, as the last thing any of them wanted was that bloody gyppo coming round. The Stubbs boys' father was a champion boxer, and the family lived in fear of repercussions for weeks afterwards. But Freedom's reaction was a roar of laughter, and he pointed his fork at Alex and told him that after tea he would take him out in the yard and teach him a few punches.

Evelyne banged on the table. 'There will be *no more fighting*!'

Behind her back, Freedom winked at his sons, knowing she would soon be going off to do her accounting at the bakeries. So that night, in the small yard with the rabbits and the two hens, Freedom made Alex put up his fists. Eddie sat on the wall and watched, then it was his turn. They often had these secret lessons, Freedom sparring with his boys, jabbing short punches at their heads. His light taps hurt like hell, but Eddie loved it, and was showing signs of becoming a fighter like his Dad.

They were all sweating when they went back in, and Freedom saw the fire had gone out so he ordered Eddie to bring in the coal to stoke it up. 'She'll be after me, lads, if she knows what we been doin', so let's keep it our secret. When she's out at her work, we'll have our boxing nights.'

The boys were sleeping when Evelyne came home to find Freedom sitting by the blazing fire, staring into space.

'You stoked up the fire, I see. Do you think we have money to burn?'

He sighed and looked at her, held out his hand for her to sit on his knee, but she was too busy checking a pile of socks and stockings, putting aside the ones that needed darning. 'I'll go up to the school in the morning. I want a word with the teacher anyway – are you coming to bed?'

He shook his head, and again stared vacantly into the fire.

'Your head all right, is it?'

He got up and slammed out of the kitchen, shouting that his head was just fine. He loved his boys, of course he did, but she seemed to think of nobody else but them. It was as if he was a lodger in his own house. Her penny-pinching and her constant scrubbing and cleaning got on his nerves.

He walked along the canal towpath and sat on an old crate, tossing pebbles into the murky water. The alley cats screeched, and in the distance he could hear voices laughing, floating out of the pubs. They didn't seem to laugh all that much nowadays, it was all work, but he supposed he should thank God that he was still getting it. His strength usually made him one of the first to be called. Even with his bad leg he could do the work of two men, and the management at the docks knew it.

Evelyne was tired, her eyes aching from the darning. She rubbed them, looked at the clock on the mantle. Freedom had still not returned. She stood up to prod the fire with the poker and became aware of Alex. He was hovering by the kitchen door, his teeth chattering with the cold. 'Mum, I can't sleep, Dad not come back yet?'

Evelyne shook her head, then gestured for Alex to come into the kitchen. She smiled at his hair, which was ruffled and standing on end. 'You look as though you could do with the basin round your head – I'll have a go at it tomorrow. It's all right, you can sit with me a while. Let me rub those feet, they look blue.'

'Where's me Dad gone? I heard him go out.'

'Not *me* lovey, *my* . . . he'll have gone walking – now don't you worry about him. Do you want a biscuit? Well, shush, you know what that brother of yours is like, he can hear the biscuit tin opening a mile away.'

Alex sat beside her and nibbled one of her home-made biscuits. She stared into the fire, gently stroking his thick, blond curls. She was almost surprised when he spoke, she was so immersed in her own thoughts. His voice was soft, 'Will you read to me, Ma? Not my school work, one of your books.'

'My books, are they? Now, you know everything here is ours, just that you're not quite old enough yet and they're well . . . they're special. That is real leather they're bound in, did you know that?'

She watched him as he solemnly chose one from the row of books and brought it back to her. She laughed softly, 'Well, well, it's my favourite writer you've picked out. Her name was Christina Georgina Rossetti, now there's a name for you.'

Alex opened the book, traced the inscription with his finger. '"To Evie, from Doris . . ." Who's that, Mum? Is she related to us?'

'No, lovey, she's no relation, but she was a very special friend to me. A long, long time ago now.' She told Alex about Doris, about the valley, and he listened without saying a word. His mother looked so beautiful, caught in the firelight, he was almost afraid to move.

'Oh, Alex, she opened up a world to me, a world that was out of my reach. And, for a while, just a short while, I almost . . .'

Alex hung on her every word. She looked down at his upturned face and cupped his chin in her big, worn hands. 'You know, sweetheart, there's a world open to you if you want it. It's all there, but you have to work hard, because you'll only be able to find it if you get qualifications.'

'Eddie's clever, Ma. He's always top.'

'So you're clever too, it takes all sorts. You're not Edward, you're Alex, and you're top in some subjects, too.'

He smiled and nodded, then laughed softly. 'Tell you one thing he's not, Ma – tidy! Never puts a thing back in its place.'

'Well, he's like his father. The pair of them think I'm just here to pick up after them. Now, my lad, you should be in bed.'

Alex hugged her, whispering in her ear, 'Can I come and sit with you another night, just you and me?'

Kissing him, she whispered back, as if they were playing a game, 'I'd like that, and maybe, no promises, I'll read my books to you. Would you like that?'

Beaming, Alex went off to bed like a lamb. Evelyne yawned and stretched her arms. The book fell to the floor, and she picked it up, looked again at the flyleaf.

Lovingly, she replaced it and drew her hand along the row of books, taking down a thick volume of Ibsen. It opened naturally in the middle, and there between the pages were sheets of her own handwriting. Leaves from a child's drawing book. The colouring book she had bought for Edward in America. Slowly, she read her own work, placing each page on the fire as she finished it, letting the flames eat her memories. Tears trickled down her cheeks, and she sighed. What would Doris think if she saw her now?

Freedom sighed, pulled his coat collar up, and wondered how he had come to this. He felt tied, bound to that spotless house. He had almost forgotten his old life – not the boxing times, but before that – the caravans, the wagons. He decided it was time to show his sons where their roots were, and the more he thought about it the happier he felt. Come Saturday he would take them on a trip, no matter what Evelyne said, they could spare a few shillings. He walked on along the towpath and decided he would take them on a trip to Brighton, to the sea.

The schoolteacher, Miss Thomas, was relieved to see Mrs Stubbs. She had been hoping for a word with her but didn't like the thought of going down their street. The Stubbs family lived in one of the toughest districts, and she was not sure how they would react to her paying a house call.

They sat in the headmaster's office and Miss Thomas poured tea. She couldn't help but notice how clean and well turned out Mrs Stubbs looked. At one time she must have been a beauty. 'I'm glad you came in, Mrs

Stubbs, I've been wanting to talk to you.' She paused briefly, then went on, 'Edward is far in advance of the other children in his class, Mrs Stubbs. I would like to put him into the class above. It will mean he's with boys two years older and he may find it difficult to adapt so I wanted to talk to you first.'

The pleasure in Mrs Stubbs' face when she smiled softened her whole appearance. Miss Thomas warmed to her, and continued, 'I think Edward is clever enough to win a scholarship to a good grammar school. I have a couple of schools in mind, but there could be a slight financial problem. The best schools require the uniform to be bought by the student's family, and it would mean Edward would have to take the bus every day.'

Interrupting her, Evelyne assured her very firmly that there would be no financial problems. Her son's education was of the highest importance and if he gained a scholarship he would have his uniform.

'There is another reason, Mrs Stubbs. I think it would be beneficial for Alex. He is dominated by his older brother, and I think he would find his own personality if they were split up into different schools. They are unusually close, Edward is very protective.'

This observation met with a stiff reply. They were brothers and that was just how it should be.

Evelyne dropped in on Freda to tell her the news. Freda hadn't seen her so happy in a long time.

'He'll be the first lad from these parts ever to get a scholarship to that grammar school, and I know he'll do it, I just know it.'

Freda had been suffering with rheumatism, and had gained a lot of weight. Evelyne noted her frizzy hair, with the assistance of henna powder, was a rather strange orange colour, but even without the grey she was beginning to look her age. She gave Evelyne two jumpers she had knitted for the boys, identical as always, and Evelyne paid her for her work. Freda would have liked to have given them, but times were hard and Ed was making nothing at the gymnasium. They were mostly charitable institutes and his earnings were a mere gesture.

'Your boys never go to the gyms, Evie, and Ed'd love to see them there. Why don't you let them go, just to see what a boxing ring's like?'

Evelyne jumped up, that tight, pursed look on her face, and put her coat on. 'My sons are not going into any boxing ring, Freda, and that's final.'

Freedom fetched the tin bath and began to boil water for the boys' bath. He whistled, and Evelyne looked up from rolling the pastry. 'It's not Saturday, love, you've got the days muddled.'

He came up behind her, gave her a hug, and said they were having a bath early, because on Saturday they were going on a trip.

'Oh, we are, are we? And where's this trip to, then?'

Freedom tapped his nose and concentrated on the stove. He was in a good mood for a change so she continued with the pastry.

'An' I want you all decked out tomorrow an' all, we're all goin' and I won't have a word against it.'

She trimmed the edges of the pastry and when he slipped his arms round her waist she gave him a quick peck on the cheek.

'I've got some good news. It seems our Eddie's doing well at school.'

Freedom seemed not to hear, but continued pottering around the kitchen.

'He could get into the posh grammar school, his teacher told me. What do you think of that?'

Freedom shook his head and asked where on earth they would get the money to send him to one of the posh schools.

'If he wins the scholarship, they pay for everything.'

Bath time was always fun for the boys, sitting in the tin tub in front of the roaring fire. Evelyne would scrub them both with a pumice stone and a big bar of carbolic soap. She scrubbed until their bodies were bright red, then rubbed them dry with a big towel. When they were dry they ate their tea in the cosy, warm kitchen.

'Your Dad's got a surprise for you both – we're going on an outing tomorrow, all of us.'

They looked up in glee, and when she told them they would be going on a train to the seaside, they were so excited that neither of them could sleep.

Sandwiches were made, lemonade bottles filled, and the family rode into the West End on a tram. The boys had never been out of the East End, and they sat spellbound by the sights and the traffic. On the train, they ran from window to window in their excitement. Freedom sat holding Evelyne's hand, tickled that he had arranged it all and as excited as the boys. Evelyne talked of the old times, of how she had been shopping in Swan and Edgar, how they had found each other again, and they behaved like young lovers.

As the train pulled into Brighton Station, the boys let out such screams of delight that some of the other passengers frowned, but nothing could dampen their spirits. When he saw the beach, Edward ran like a wild pony towards the water and he had both feet in the sea before Freedom could haul him away.

Alex, riding on his father's shoulders, pointed hysterically at a big Ferris wheel and the lights of the fairground, the music drifting across the beach towards them. Up ahead, Edward climbed over a small wall and disappeared among the rides as Freedom shouted to him to wait.

The two sticky-faced boys wandered around with their candy-floss, open-mouthed with amazement. They went from booth to booth, and Freedom won a teddy bear on a shooting range, which Alex cuddled. They stopped at a punching machine.

'Punch the bell, mate, punch the bell and win a prize, come along now, punch the bell . . . lovely prizes, take your pick, all you gotta do is ring the bell . . .'

Freedom stepped back and punched, the bell clanged and the man almost fell over. He'd not had anyone ring the bell in ten years and he reluctantly offered a prize. Edward jumped up and down as Freedom led him towards the display, and he pointed to a tin of soap bubbles with a small wire hoop. The fairground man handed the boy the prize and nudged Freedom, saying with a wink that he would bet a shilling that he couldn't do it again.

Evelyne pulled at Freedom's arm, she wanted to move on, there was a small crowd gathering.

'Go on, Dad, do it again!'

Freedom looked at the man and asked if he was serious about the shilling, then rolled up his sleeves and belted the punchbag. The bell clanged again, drawing a ripple of applause from the crowd, and Freedom turned and gave them a mock bow. Evelyne went to choose a prize and after surveying the array of cheap gifts, she pointed to a doll. She would give it to Mrs Harris' little girl.

'You not lost your touch, mun.'

Freedom turned, and there, lolling against the side of a booth, was Jesse. He wore a flashy suit and a red polka-dot neckerchief. His long, dark eyelashes were as thick as ever. He still wore his earring, but now he had a big gold watch and heavy gold rings on his fingers.

The pair sized each other up, and slowly they moved closer.

'*Auv acoi.*'

Jesse held out his arms. 'It's *buddigur duvus*, a good time for us, but you *jinned* we'd be here, mun, more likely in the fairground than furniture sellin'.'

Jesse felt the muscles of Freedom's arms, their eyes locked. Then they kissed each other's cheeks. Freedom held Jesse's head in his hands and kissed his lips. Evelyne felt chilled, and drew her shawl closer around her shoulders.

'Eh, boys, come and meet Uncle Jesse, say hello to your Uncle Jesse.'

Evelyne stared, wanting to call the boys to her side, but she said nothing. The two of them hung back slightly, but then Jesse reached forward and took a coin from behind Edward's ear, and the child gasped. Jesse kept finding coins all over Edward and the boy was completely hooked. Alex, who had drawn back to cling to his mother's skirt, moved forward.

'Well, now, lemme see if this young'un's got the magic . . . Ohhh, yes, will you look at this, the money's just falling from him. Come and see this boy, he's got the Midas touch.'

Evelyne smiled but remained aloof and watchful as Jesse patted the punching-machine man's shoulder and told him Freedom was a boxing champion so no need to worry, his machine wasn't out of kilter.

'Will you come to the wagon?'

Evelyne opened her mouth to say no, but Freedom was already following Jesse. The boys hung on every word Jesse said, looking up into his face with adoring eyes.

'You like my fair, then, do ye? Well, there's a fine thing, I'm doin' all right, mun, am I not? Come on, come on.'

He strode among the booths, waving and smiling to everyone, and they made their way to the far end of the fairground. On a large square of wasteland was a line of caravans. He went to the door of the first one and opened it, calling to someone inside that he had a surprise. He lifted first Edward and then Alex up into the wagon. As they went inside, Evelyne caught hold of Freedom's sleeve.

'We should be going, the train leaves in half an hour.'

Freedom shrugged and said they would catch the later one, and gestured for her to go inside. It took Evelyne by surprise. A lot had changed with the years, and it was like a real house inside. The walls were draped, the place was filled with ornaments, and there were two parrots in a cage.

'Rawnie? Rawnie, come on out and see what I've found.'

The curtains at the far end of the caravan were drawn aside, and Rawnie, like a ghost from the past, stood staring at them all. Evelyne was shocked at her appearance, she was so thin her skin hung loose on her bones. Her thick hair was greying at the temples and, although

617

she still wore it in two long braids, there was nothing youthful about her; she had to hold on to the sides of the wagon to move towards them.

'Freedom, mun, *auv acoi, acoi acoi*, it's been *bershor*.'

He held his arms out to her and she went to him, touching his face. She kissed him and then held her hand out to Edward.

'Well, *chavo chiv*, is he not *rinkeney*, then, will you gimme a *choom*?'

Edward went straight to her and kissed her as if he understood every word she'd said. She held his face and looked into his eyes, then laughed, giving Freedom a look. She held on to the table and eased herself into a chair, tapped her knee and held out a hand to Alex.

'Eh, eh, eh, they're real *tatchey* Romany, and dressed like a *rye*.'

Alex was more wary of her, but in the end he sat on her knee and played with all the gold bangles along her thin arms. The two men spoke Romany together, sitting on a velvet settee with their arms around each other. Rawnie stared at Evelyne, nodding for her to sit down. 'The eldest has Romany *yocks*, looks like his Da – big 'n' strong, the pair of them. Yer little 'un's gentle, and yer got one wild, ain't that right?' She began to cough, and her whole body shook so that Alex had to get off her knee. Evelyne moved closer, put her hand on Rawnie's shoulder and could feel the sharp shoulder blades heaving beneath her clothes as she tried to catch her breath. Jesse stood up and clapped his beringed hands together, said he would take his brother around the fair, they'd be back shortly. The two boys ran to Jesse, and after a moment he gave way and they were allowed to go with the men. Evelyne tried to catch Freedom's eye to tell him they must leave, but he was out of the caravan too quickly.

Rawnie rolled herself a cigarette, a *tuv*, and began to smoke, then pulled herself up and put the kettle on, showing Evelyne the gas taps which were linked to a cylinder outside. She said that, like Freedom, they were almost *kairengos* now, the caravan staying at the fair all year round.

'Your eldest, he has the *dukkerin* look. He could read well, I can feel it, and you, me love, you look well-fed.'

While Evelyne sipped the thick, spicy, hot tea, Rawnie was twice seized by such spasms of coughing that it frightened her. Someone tapped on the caravan door and two little girls peeped in, but Rawnie shooed them outside.

'They're Jesse's babes from Martilda, she lives yonder. He's got a fine boy up in Scotland and one down in Cornwall, both fine boys.'

Evelyne didn't wish to appear shocked, and Rawnie's obvious acceptance of Jesse's other women made it seem almost natural.

As Evelyne finished her tea, Rawnie reached over for the cup and stared into the tea leaves. She put the cup down and sighed, she frightened Evelyne. 'What did you see? Rawnie . . .? What is it?'

Rawnie would not meet her eyes, she sucked in her hollow cheeks.

'Remember all those years ago, that terrible night at the fair, you saw something in my hand then, is it the same?'

Rawnie kept her head bowed. 'Do I remember that night? Now there's a question, do you think I would forget? 'Tis not something you forget, bein' defiled, torn inside. Don't heal like a cut on the outside.'

'I'm sorry, that was thoughtless, but will you tell

619

me? You see, I always remember your words – you said "Beware of the birds in the sky", but I don't understand . . .'

Rawnie coughed again, her body shaking, her bangles tinkling and jangling. 'Ye'll know when they come, I can't say when, but they're big, big birds.'

Rawnie did not finish telling Evelyne what she could see, could not tell her that when the birds flew over Evelyne's head they would take everything from her, all that she loved. Evelyne would have persisted, but the caravan door was flung open by Edward. He demanded that Evelyne come with him, the fair was closing and they were going to have chicken cooked over a real fire.

All the men from the fairground had gathered around the wagons and a fire had been built in the centre. Behind them the Ferris wheel was still lit up, but the organ that piped out the music was silent. A fiddler was sitting on a beer crate, tuning up.

'Well, gel, it's a night to celebrate, is it not, we're all brothers here, and we're going to put on some entertainment for you.'

Evelyne could see Edward and Alex, their shoes and socks discarded, running like wild things round and round the caravan. The fiddler started playing and the girls began to dance and sing.

Rawnie sat at her caravan door, tapping her foot and clapping to the music. Evelyne sat with a group of women who were peeling potatoes for a big pot of stew. She knew the last train would have gone by now. There was nothing she could do or say – Freedom was standing drinking with a group of his brothers and had no intention of leaving.

620

Evelyne wished the night would end. They had eaten, and the men were getting drunker and drunker. The girls still danced and the fiddler still played, and the fire had been constantly fed so that it still blazed. The two boys were curled up beside three other children on a large straw mattress dragged from one of the wagons, their arms wrapped around each other in exhausted sleep. Rawnie beckoned Evelyne to her caravan and pointed to a bed she had made up. Evelyne was as tired as her sons so she didn't refuse.

'He looks happy, a happy mun, will you see?'

Evelyne looked out of the door. Freedom was the centre of attention. Someone had given him a bandanna, which he had tied around his head, and he was roaring with laughter. He was well drunk, and they were trying to pull him to the fireside to dance. He made excuses about his bad leg, but they would not hear and he gave in to the young girls that pulled him. The fiddler began a new tune and they all watched as Freedom stood, straightbacked, heels together, slowly lifting his hands above his head. He began to clap, short, sharp slaps, then clicked his heels, and there was no sign of his limp. The alcohol and the atmosphere made him unaware of the pain in his leg, and he danced to his heart's content, soon joined by three other men.

At one point Jesse looked over to where Evelyne sat with Rawnie and gave her a cold stare. She was an outsider tonight, not her children nor her husband, but she was and she knew it. She got up and went to lie on the bed. The heavy, oily perfume that Freedom had always worn swamped her, but this time it was Rawnie's perfume, it was oil from her hair on the pillows.

Evelyne fell into a deep sleep, and when she woke it

was fully dark, the blackness lit only by a warm, glowing light from the fire. No candles, no blinking lights from the fairground, nothing but the fire.

The voice was beautiful, clear, singing such a sweet, sad song, and she lay back on the pillows and listened. There was no fiddle this time, but a guitar being played well.

> *Can you* rokka *Romany,*
> *Can you play the* bosh,
> *Can you* jal adrey the staripen
> *Can you* chin the cosh . . .

The singing lulled her, the voice deep and soft. She felt the caravan rock slightly as Rawnie moved, and she opened her eyes.

Rawnie gestured for Evelyne to come to the door, and she crept forward. She wanted to weep – the singer was Freedom, and he was playing the guitar. She had never heard him sing like this, had not known he could play. 'Oh, Rawnie, sometimes he is like a stranger. I've never seen him play, heard him sing . . . he does it so well.'

Rawnie patted the step for Evelyne to sit beside her. She too was moved by Freedom. That wondrous face, singing with his eyes closed, his whole body seeming to shimmer in the firelight. All the people around him were hushed. His voice rose and fell, emotional but clear, with such ease that it reached their souls.

'I loved that mun, but you know, I loved him so.'

Evelyne was touched by the dying woman, and she slipped her arm around the wasted shoulders. She did know, perhaps she always had. 'He loved you too, Rawnie, he would have hanged for you.'

Rawnie's gnarled hand reached out, gripped Evelyne's

chin, and she looked into her face. 'So would every mun around the fire. It were not love fer me, gel, but honour. Gringos don't understand, cannot understand our ways, our love of the stars, the air, the land ... But we can hate, and we believe in revenge, an eye for an eye, a tooth for a tooth. This is our way, our law.'

Evelyne bit her lip. Rawnie knew revenge, hadn't she slit every one of those boys' throats? Or had it been Jesse? As if Rawnie had read her mind, she gave a chuckle. 'It were me, gel, me used the knife. Now I'll tell yer what yer man is singing.'

She whispered the meaning of the song to Evelyne. Freedom was asking if they understood the Romany tongue, asking if they could hold their own in a *lay-chingarpen*, an argument or a fight; he was asking if they could play the fiddle, if they were men enough to fight the music, to hear a prison sentence and do their bit without flinching: last of all the song was asking if they were qualified to earn their living as gypsies. If they could not in one way or another *chin the cosh*, they would never be successful on the road.

Evelyne clung to Rawnie. Now she could see her boys, the two little brothers, standing naked by the fire, hand in hand, looking at their father, their eyes fixed as though hypnotized by him. An elder knelt down beside them, and she saw the knife. Rawnie gripped her tightly so she could not move. The sick woman had more strength than Evelyne had given her credit for.

'Let him make their blood our blood, their father's blood, it is right, they are Romany.'

Neither child made a murmur as his thumb was cut, and the blood kissed by their father. Then they were wrapped in blankets and taken back to sleep on the mattress. Evelyne now knew that Freedom had planned this – not necessarily with Jesse and Rawnie – but she remembered that bank holidays were their big days for fairs right across England. He had known all along that some of his people would be at Brighton – his brothers as he called them. She returned to Rawnie's bed.

When the morning came, Rawnie gave each child a golden sovereign. They kissed her, eager to get on to the train, not to get away, but just because it was a train. Their night's initiation had had no obvious after-effects, and Freedom was preparing to leave. 'I'll come again to you, sister, we won't be parted as long again.'

Rawnie touched his face, tracing it with her fingers; it was still handsome, even with his battle scars. She traced his lips, and then stood at her caravan door to wave their farewell. Rawnie knew she would never see him again, she would be dead within months.

'Well, gel, it looks like our brother's come back into the fold, eh?'

Rawnie smiled. Jesse had never had the powers, he couldn't read what was in the air. The woman still had Freedom, and she was stronger than they were.

The train journey home was as exciting for the brothers as the one to Brighton, and they wanted to go back again as soon as they got to London.

'We're going home, and you've got to go to school tomorrow.'

Eddie started sulking, and had to be dragged along to the tram stop. He wanted to go back to the fair, he didn't want to go to school. Evelyne slapped him hard, pushed him ahead of her up the tram stairs.

'You'll go to school, my lad, and what's more you'll get that scholarship or you'll end up on a fairground

624

with no education and no place else to go. Now get up these stairs this instant.'

Evelyne received a mask-like glare from Edward, and he stomped up the stairs to the top deck. Alex, close behind him, slipped his hand into his brother's, and they went to the very front seats.

Evelyne and Freedom sat at the back, looking at the busy traffic below as they headed across London. Evelyne took out the doll for Mrs Harris' youngest, and checked that she had all their things. She looked up sharply when she heard two small voices singing from the front seats,

> Can you rokka Romany,
> Can you play the bosh,
> Can you jal adrey the staripen
> Can you chin the cosh . . .

Freedom smiled and nodded to his sons, slipped an arm around her shoulders.

'Well, gel, looks like we gotta pair of gyppos up front.'

CHAPTER 27

EDWARD STUBBS was awarded a scholarship to a grammar school, the first boy ever from his area. For one son to gain a scholarship was a cause for celebration, but for a second son also to pass gave rise to suspicion and jealousy, and set both boys apart from the children of the neighbourhood.

In their identical uniforms the boys travelled to school together, always together. Already closer than most brothers, they grew even more so. Eddie and Alex were both tall for their ages, well-built and athletic, excelling at all sports. In the classroom, however, although Alex was bright, he fell short of his brother's academic brilliance. Edward was the dominant one, and Alex accepted life in his brother's shadow without jealousy. Edward was his hero.

Unemployment was as high as ever. Dole queues were long and money short, and for the workers and their families times were hard in the reign of King George.

Proud of her boys, Evelyne Stubbs worked constantly, and kept her head above water while all around her others sank. Freedom worked at the docks most weeks, and when he was laid off he busied himself making rabbit hutches in the back yard and selling them.

Occasionally he would disappear for a few days to visit his friends, and those were the times Evelyne dreaded. He would return surly and bad-tempered, and found it difficult to get back into the day-to-day routine.

Rawnie had died of consumption, and Jesse had lost his fairground through gambling. He was serving a sentence for robbery in Durham gaol.

Miss Freda and Ed were in financial trouble and had taken in more lodgers. They now had a married couple and two single girls. The girls, it was suspected, were 'on the game', but Freda wouldn't hear of it. To her they were simply youngsters trying to make their way.

Ed's brother's family were even worse off, and although their kids were working they still lived on the breadline, always in debt. They invariably owed money to Evelyne, whose moneylending business was growing. Freedom collected the debts for her, and the boys helped him at weekends. The Stubbs family was secure, and the brothers went from strength to strength with their school work.

Evelyne later tried to pinpoint the turn of events, to recall exactly why things went wrong. She had to try to blame someone, but she knew in her heart that the trouble was within her own home.

Freedom was the perfect father when the boys were small, attentive and fair, and they obeyed him. But he couldn't make head or tail of their homework, he was so far removed from them academically that his frustration turned to anger, and they in turn realized that their father – the man they had always looked up to – was illiterate. They were too young to be understanding about it, to help him, and they turned against him and looked increasingly to their mother for guidance. The resulting bitter arguments usually ended with Freedom storming out to the pub.

Evelyne had cleared the table, tidied away the boys' books, and was about to start on the weekly wash when there was a hard rapping on the door. A policeman informed Evelyne that Freedom had been arrested for brawling outside the docks. He had knocked out the manager who was pressing charges for assault.

Ed and Evelyne hurried to the police station and found Freedom sitting gloomily in a cell. The fight had started because Freedom, who always expected to be given work, had been rejected for three days running. He had not told Evelyne, pretending he had been taken on. But on the fourth day he *had* been offered work, and that was the cause of it. One man who was turned away muttered something in Freedom's hearing about black bastards getting work before whites, and when the manager had tried to break up the fight Freedom had knocked him senseless.

At the hearing the magistrate reprimanded Freedom severely – a man with a history of professional boxing should never resort to fighting in the streets. Freedom was given a three-month suspended sentence. Evelyne never said anything, but her reproachful looks and above all her silence tormented him. If he had felt inadequate before, now things were far worse. Evelyne had arranged for a lawyer and paid him, and the more Freedom thought about it the more frustration he felt.

The appearance of Jesse on their doorstep was the kiss of doom. Recently released from prison, he was as cocksure as ever, with rings on his fingers and gold chains around his neck. He offered Freedom the chance to go into business with him, buying and selling furniture. Evelyne tried to persuade Freedom to have nothing to do with him. They were sitting at the kitchen table where the two boys were doing their homework. Evelyne tried to keep her voice calm, not wanting to get into an argument in front of them. 'He's no good, Freedom, he never was. You and I know just how far he will go. Don't go with him, please, you can do my debt-collecting full-time, we could do it together.'

Freedom banged his fist on the table and Edward's inkwell tipped over, spilling its contents on his exercise books. The boys scrabbled to pick them up and mop them, fussing around.

Freedom couldn't take it any more and he roared, 'Will you get out from under ma feet, mun, take yer readin' out of here, better still, go get work like the other lads around here.'

Edward stood up to his father, just as hot-tempered, but cocky and self-assured. He gathered his schoolbooks up and hurled them across the room. 'Right, I'll go out now and join the dole queue, just like you and every other sucker round 'ere. You call that work, do yer?'

Freedom struck him so hard that he sprawled on the floor. Alex sprang between them, trying to protect Edward. 'Dad, no, don't, don't hit 'im no more.'

Freedom lashed out at Alex in fury, trying to grab Edward, and now Evelyne pushed between her sons and Freedom. With her arms out she faced her husband.

'You'll have to hit me first, Freedom, I mean it. Just stop this nonsense right now or so help me God I'll take the rolling pin to you, I will.'

Freedom backed away. The three of them were against him, and he knew then that Evelyne would

629

choose her sons before him. She was like a lioness with her cubs, glaring at him so fiercely . . . He turned and beat his fist against the fireplace.

Evelyne shooed the boys from the room, but Edward held on to her. She shook her hand free. 'Get out, the pair of you, leave us alone. Go on, nothing's going to happen.'

They slunk out and closed the door behind them. Freedom gave her such a helpless look, filled with guilt and remorse. It was the first time he had ever struck his sons, and his voice sounded choked in his throat. 'I'd never have struck thee, Evie, God help me, never.'

She held him in her arms and comforted him, whispering over and over that she knew, she knew it. She felt remorseful herself, it was becoming obvious that she put the boys before Freedom. 'I'm sorry too, Freedom. I should never have gone against you. Sometimes Eddie needs a firm hand. Will you forgive me?'

They kissed, it had been a long time since they kissed as lovers, and she sat on his knee by the fire. 'What is it, my love, what's hurting you so?'

He buried his face in her chest, and she stroked his hair.

'It's the debt-collecting, Evie. It's hard for me to face them that owes you, going to them with me hand out for their shillin's. Some of 'em have nothin', and to stand there frightening the life out of them, wantin' money paid over, knowing they've not got it to give – it's no job for a mun, I can't do it no more.'

Evelyne forced herself to keep her mouth shut, although she could have asked how he thought she felt. How did he think they could have lived so well for so long without her moneylending business?

'Just don't do anything against the law, the boys are doing so well and I don't want people talking.'

That did it. He pushed her away from him and grabbed his coat.

'Always the boys, always them, when do you ever think of *me*? When it's *too late*!'

He slammed out of the kitchen.

Eddie came downstairs and slipped his arms around his mother, kissed her and patted her head. 'Maybe he's right, Ma, I'm fourteen, I could get work.'

She grabbed him and held him, shook him roughly. He was shocked by her tone, her expression. 'You think I *like* collecting money I lend out? Do you? Why do you think I'm doing it, working myself into an early grave, why?'

Edward backed away from her, and Alex came to stand at his side, as their mother marched around the kitchen, rolling up her sleeves as if she was ready for a fight.

'Both of you are going places, getting out of this slum, and you won't do it like your father, with your fists. You'll do it with your brains. So help me God I'll go out on the streets if need be, to make sure you both stay at school, now is that clear, clear to both of you?'

They nodded solemnly.

'Right now, get your work and I'll fix us tea.'

Alex ran into the hallway, but as Edward turned to follow him he felt his hair tugged, and Evelyne kicked the door closed. She hit him so hard on his right ear that his head spun.

'If I ever hear you talk to your Dad in that tone of voice again I'll beat the living daylights out of you. Now hop it.'

*

Freedom was gone for more than two weeks, longer than he had ever stayed away from home before. At the weekend the brothers went around collecting the debts, and a couple of times they had to get tough in order to be paid. When they returned, they got out the books and began to tally up as Evelyne was out shopping. Edward fiddled the figures and pocketed sixpence, and Alex saw him do it. He wouldn't eat the toffee bar Edward offered him later.

Evelyne went to Ed's brother's house. There was a showdown on the cards as they owed her two pounds fifteen shillings, which was long overdue. There was no way around it – she couldn't run her home and support the Meadows family. But the rent-collector had got there before her, and two bailiffs waited outside with a cart. The Meadows owed six months' back rent at eighteen shillings a week.

'We're on the street, nothing we can do.'

Evelyne didn't like the way the rent-collector shouldered her aside. The bailiffs hammered on the door and shouted that the Meadows had better pay up or get out, otherwise they would break the door down. They couldn't wait all day, they had another call to make.

Again Evelyne was thrust aside and the two bailiff's men forced their way into the house. She barred their entrance. 'Out, the pair of you, there's no one moving a stick of furniture from here. Bugger off, or I'll get my boys . . .'

They hesitated, looking for guidance from the rent-collector. Evelyne siezed her chance. 'Now, it's Mr Simms, isn't it?'

Mr Simms, the most hated man in the district, pursed his chalk-white lips and adjusted his bowler. 'Yes it is, and I know who you are – Mrs Stubbs from number twelve. Now I've never had any trouble from you, so let's not start now. I am within the law, so I suggest you just leave well alone. The only way round this situation is for the back rent to be paid.'

Half an hour later in the kitchen of number twelve, the situation was more than resolved, and the bailiffs left with the cart to call on their next poor victim.

Evelyne Stubbs bought the Meadows' house, and they now had to pay their rent to her. She calculated that the rent would cover the cost of the house by the time Edward was in his final year at school. Knowing Ed's brother's financial state better than anyone, she offered him a job. He would collect the debts, and she would deduct the rent from his wages.

Edward looked up from his homework, threw down his pencil and picked up his mother's accounts book. 'You know, Ma, if you could, it might be a good thing to get hold of Auntie Freda and Uncle Ed's place. It'd be about the same price.'

Evelyne smiled and told him she'd already looked into it, and liked the fact that he was taking an interest. 'You just do your homework, lovey, and I'll think about it.'

Alex came in with a box, saying the rabbit looked poorly. He sat the box down in front of the fire. The rabbit was panting, its eyes glazed. 'He misses Dad. When do you think he'll be coming home, Ma?'

Alex really meant that he himself was missing Freedom, but he didn't like to admit it. He was closer to Freedom than Edward was, and night after night he stood by the front window watching for his father. Evelyne sighed, put down her sewing and brought some water for the rabbit. She had no idea where Freedom was – she had had no word. She was worried, of course, but at the same time the house was running like clockwork without him. 'He's working with Jesse, he'll be home when the time is right. Don't fret yourself, Alex. Done your homework, have you?'

The next day, at school assembly, the headmaster announced that the King was dead. Rows of small faces looked up in awe, and some of the juniors whispered 'what king?', but the whole school cheered when they were told they were being given the day off. This was not the effect the headmaster had desired, but shouts for quiet went unheard as the boys streamed out gleefully.

Edward and Alex took the tram home, and finding the house locked they went down the alley and along the canal to climb over the back wall. It was January 1936, and King George was to be replaced on the throne by his eldest son Edward VIII. England went into mourning, but the Stubbs boys were thrilled that they had a whole afternoon to themselves.

Alex stood on Edward's hands and climbed over into the yard, while Edward stood on an old crate and followed. He found Alex in tears by his rabbit hutch. Not only had the King died, so had his beloved rabbit.

Evelyne was out working, collecting her rents and doing her bakery accounts. Freedom had still not come back, and when she let herself into the house she called his name, thinking he had returned. She was surprised to find the boys waiting for her. 'There's nothing wrong, is there? Why aren't you both at school?'

Edward searched through her shopping bag for something to eat. 'King's dead, we all got the day off – I'm starvin', Ma!'

She took the bag away from him, muttering that no one had told her about the King, but that must be why the traffic was so bad. 'You'd best both sit at the table and do your school work, then. And no moaning, you're both old enough to know better. Lads your age were already working down the mines . . . You all right, Alex, you're a bit quiet?'

Eddie told her that the rabbit had died, that they had buried it by the canal. 'I got a shillin' for its cage, Ma, here's sixpence for you to buy yourself something.'

Alex glanced at his brother. He could lie so well, not a flicker on his face, and Alex was ashamed.

Touched by Edward's gift, Evelyne kissed him and said that they could have threepence each, but no more rabbits.

Later that night, as Evelyne brushed her hair, she heard soft, muffled sobs. She peeked into the boys' room.

Edward was sprawled across his bed. The blankets were tumbled, and the bed was surrounded by books, football boots, and the clothes he had taken off and dropped on the floor. On the opposite side of the room was Alex's neat bed, with the sheets and blankets just so. His school satchel and books were stacked neatly on his bedside box. It was Alex who was weeping, holding his pillow over his face.

Evelyne crept over to him and gently lifted the pillow. His eyes were red-rimmed from crying. She put her finger to her lips, pulled the bedclothes aside and gestured for him to follow her to her own room.

'Now, my love, what's all this about? Nothing wrong at school, is there? You want to tell me about it?'

Alex gulped his tears, bit his trembling lip.

'Is it the rabbit? Come on, get into bed with me . . . come on, Edward won't know. And it's not cissy, you're still only ten.'

'Nearly eleven.'

'So you are, so you are.'

Alex snuggled close to his mother, and she kissed the top of his head. She asked again what was wrong.

'I miss him, every day I look for him. Eddie says he might never come back . . . Oh, Ma . . . where's me Dad?'

'Now, now, it's not *me*, it's *my*, and your Dad is just away working. Don't you pay any attention to Edward. I'll give him a piece of my mind tomorrow for telling you such things.'

'Oh, no, please don't. He'll know I've said something.'

'All right, I won't. Now snuggle up, and I'll read to you. I'll read my favourite poem, how's that?'

Alex was delighted, and with his arms wrapped around her he listened to her soft, lilting Welsh voice. She had tried so hard not to pick up the East-End accent. It had been difficult – everyone she worked and mixed with spoke the local dialect – but she prided herself that she spoke well.

'Remember me when I am gone away, Gone far into the silent land, When you can no more hold me by the hand . . .' Evelyne knew the poem by heart.

Alex sighed, slowly his eyelids drooped, and he slept curled up beside his beloved mother. Evelyne lay, unable to sleep, staring at the ceiling. Her eyes filled with tears as she wondered where Freedom was . . .

From then on, Alex often came to her bed after Edward was asleep. Evelyne found herself waiting for him, and over the weeks she read through her small library until he slept in her arms.

*

Months had passed with no word from Freedom. Freda seemed more concerned about it than the Stubbs family, she was worried that something had happened to him. 'He's with that Jesse, Freda, so the least said the better. How's Ed doing? All right, is he?'

Freda nodded. Now that he was working for Evelyne it made the world of difference to Ed, bringing in that bit extra every week.

'Darlink, we owe you so much. Poor Ed was getting so upset about the money troubles. It is easier now, thanks to you.'

Evelyne shrugged it off, and said she never wanted to hear a word about it. 'We're a family, Freda, and we should help each other out, that's all that has to be said . . . now, how are your legs?'

Freedom still had not returned when the street began to prepare for the coronation of Edward, hanging memorabilia in their windows for the big occasion.

On 1 December 1936, the Crystal Palace burnt down. It was the most spectacular conflagration ever seen in London in peacetime. The flames lit the sky, and many gloomy speculations buzzed round the streets and in the newspapers that the fire was a disaster, a portent that boded ill for the monarchy. The new king, Edward, was not long in proving them right. Sitting around the radio, Evelyne, the boys, Freda and Ed listened to the abdication speech at one fifty-two on the afternoon of 10 December. Edward VIII, forced to choose between the woman he loved and his country, opted for his lady.

*

That night Ed sat in the local pub with Freda and Evelyne. It was a hive of gossip. He downed his pint, shook his head. 'Hard to believe, ain't it, I mean, fancy givin' up the throne fer a woman what's been married twice, I mean, it's not on, is it? She don't even 'ave no 'igh society connections, beats me.'

Someone shouted across the bar, asking if Freda knew the American woman.

'When I was in Florida I passed this close, within inches, and I didn't think much of her looks. Small, piggy eyes, and a very large nose, and so thin! Oh, she is so *thin*!'

Evelyne couldn't help but smile, and the more port and lemons that came Freda's way, the more intimate details of the royal couple she remembered. 'Mind you, what worries me, darlinks, and I am sure it will worry everyone – his brother, George . . . Well, he's always been in his shadow, always the quieter one. I hear he has a stammer, too. Well, darlinks, a younger brother always suffers if he has such a charming and handsome elder brother, it is always the way.'

Royalty forgotten, Evelyne went home. She wasn't thinking of King Edward but of her own Edward, and Alex. She considered what Freda had said. In a way Alex did suffer from Edward's dominance – he was quiet, easily led.

Alex was still pining for Freedom. Every afternoon he would sit on the front doorstep, looking up and down the road, and his little face would be crestfallen when eventually he came indoors to do his homework. She continued to allow him into her bed, enjoying the closeness and looking forward to reading to him. For the first time in years, she had begun to take odd spare moments to read for herself.

One night she read Alex one of her own stories, and his astonishment when she told him that she had written it herself filled her with pleasure.

Evelyne had begun to feel angry with Freedom, angry at the way he had disappeared without even a letter. Then she would sigh to herself – she knew Freedom's writing ability was confined to little more than his own name.

Coming home from the bakeries one day, she opened the door and knew he was home, without even seeing him. She rushed into the kitchen, and had to put her hand over her mouth to stop herself screaming. She thought he was an intruder and it wasn't until he turned to face her that she knew it was Freedom. His hair had been cut short, shaved round his ears, and he was thin, almost gaunt. 'Dear God, man, what happened?'

The two boys were sitting watching their parents, wide-eyed, and Evelyne told them to go up to their room. She closed the door behind them, then opened it again to give Edward his marching orders, as he was listening at the door.

'They tell me the rabbit's gone. I'll get 'em another.'

Evelyne was trying to control her anger. 'Bugger the rabbit, where have you been all these months?'

The haircut told her all, of course, but she wanted him to say it, and she stood with arms folded, looking at him as if he were a child.

Freedom had served six months in Durham gaol for handling stolen property. Evelyne threw up her hands in despair. How could he do something like that, how could he be so stupid? 'Jesse got you into this, didn't he? You might as well tell me, did he get you involved in this?'

639

Freedom gazed into the fire and shrugged. He wore that mask-like expression, and he didn't even have to tell her, she knew.

'Jesse go to prison with you, did he? Don't even tell me, I can see by the look of you. He left you to take the rap just like he did all those years ago! My God, Freedom, sometimes you behave like a child. Had you no thought for us, for the boys? What do you think they'll say at their school if they find out about this?'

Freedom wanted her to hold him, give him comfort, he felt so ashamed, but he could do nothing because she was so strong, so far out of his reach. He felt helpless, and he sat with his head in his hands. She put her arms around him as if he were just as she'd said, a child. She told him everything would be all right, at least he was home for Christmas.

'We'll make it the best Christmas since that time you came back with your Championship belt – remember all those years ago, Freedom, the way you came home with a cartful of furniture? Well, it'll be just like that again.'

He held her and kissed her neck, and the smell of soap and her clean, scrubbed hands moved him so that he couldn't speak. They went up the stairs together, arm in arm, to their bedroom, to the big bed they had bought all those years ago.

Edward sat up in bed, listening, wondering what Freedom was doing to his Ma, she moaned so. He wanted to hit his father. It was better when he was away. Edward put his head under the covers to block out the sound of his mother's moaning.

Alex slept like an angel, a wooden carving Freedom

had made for him clasped in his hand. He was happy now, his Dad was back.

Christmas fever was all around, and in number twelve they looked forward to it with as much happiness as the two Meadows' households. They were all out of debt because of Evelyne, and they were closer and more like a family than ever before.

Evelyne had told them all that they were never to let on to Freedom about how she had covered their rent, or that they were working for her. It was bad enough for him to lose his job at the docks and serve a prison sentence, let alone to have his manhood taken away from him in his own home. But Evelyne underestimated Freedom's intelligence. He knew she was the provider and at first he was distraught, then deeply ashamed. He could still get no legitimate work, but he bought and sold odd pieces of furniture, among them the cradle he had bought all those Christmases ago. Evelyne wasn't sad to see it go, she was glad of the space. She prepared the food for Christmas Day and went shopping in the markets with Freedom to choose the boys' presents.

On Christmas Eve Freedom was very cheerful. He had a fistful of pound notes, and told Evelyne that he had done well on a couple of pieces of furniture. He was going out to buy Evelyne's gift and a surprise for the boys. Evelyne was thrilled that he had accomplished something, but when she went to her wardrobe she saw that her hatbox had been disturbed. Something was missing. She searched the chest of drawers, but she knew what Freedom had done. He had taken her pearl and gold necklace – that was where his new-found wealth had come from. She sat on the bed, wondering what to do, and decided to say nothing, at least until Christmas was over.

When the boys were asleep, she filled their stockings with oranges, apples, sweets – and a volume of Dickens and a book of poetry for Alex. Freedom had bought some cheap, bright toys from the market and she slipped them in as well. Hearing him come into the house, she crept down to the kitchen. He was grinning from ear to ear, and gestured for her to come into the yard to see the present he'd got for the boys.

Tethered to the gate was a bull terrier, white, snipe-nosed with pink eyes. At first she thought it was a pig, but on closer inspection she was so angry that she swore. 'Just take that bugger back where you got it from. I'll not have it in the house. Is it not enough with four mouths to feed, and you go and get another? Go on, take it back where you found it.'

Freedom's fists curled and he felt like hitting her. He'd chosen the dog so carefully, he'd even given him a name. Standing his ground, he said the dog would stay – he couldn't even take it back if he wanted to, the kennels were closed for Christmas. She knew she'd been hard on him, but the last thing she wanted was a dog. He would go back after Christmas she said, and walked into the house.

Edward was up at the crack of dawn, delving into his stocking, and when he had eaten everything he started on Alex's presents. Evelyne woke to hear them fighting and yelled for quiet. Freedom had not slept with her, he was in the kitchen. From the back window she saw Alex run into his father's arms and kiss him, and the joy on the boy's face as he saw the dog made her regret what she had said the night before. By the time she was dressed and in the kitchen, Rex was sitting eating sausages by the blazing fire.

'Ma, he's mine, Dad give him to me! He's mine an' we're calling 'im Rex – ain't he just lovely, will you look at his face, and watch, Ma, he's as clever as anything . . . Sit!'

Rex promptly sat, and he even held out his paw on command. Freedom looked at Evelyne over the ecstatic Alex's head, and said that he thought a moneylender ought to have some protection, especially if there was cash in the house.

Christmas went by without any further arguments, and Rex became part of the household. He guarded the front door with a vengeance, and no one could get in or out unless he allowed them to. Alex adored Rex and made it his job to feed him. The dog slept curled up on the end of his bed. But Edward was not interested, he was more studious than ever and, as he was taking exams, the house revolved around his hours of study.

Edward came to his mother's side and slipped a note into her hand. The school prizegiving and sports day was coming up, and Edward whispered in her ear, 'Don't let him come, Ma, please, I don't want him there.'

Evelyne slapped him, and told him he was not to talk about his father like that.

'He's done time, Ma, I know it, everyone in the street knows it, and he's always in the pub. You earn our keep, not him, he's no use to us.'

Edward got another box on his ear, and was sent out. He hadn't noticed his father standing at the kitchen door.

'His report all right then, is it?'

It was more than all right, he was top of his class in every subject, and the headmaster had requested a meeting with Edward's parents on the prizegiving day. They were invited for tea in the headmaster's study.

'I'll not go with you, I've business to do.'

Evelyne put down the report and took his hand, held him close. She said that he was their father, and by God they were going to be proud of him, he was going at her side no matter what. 'Besides, your hair's grown now, you look like everyone else, so you're coming.'

The headmaster rose to his feet as Evelyne and Freedom entered his study, and gestured for them to sit down in the two chairs opposite his desk. He could see where the Stubbs boys got their size from, and he remarked that they were fine, big lads.

'My husband was Heavyweight Boxing Champion of Great Britain. I don't suppose the boys told you?'

He was surprised that they had never mentioned it. He shook Freedom's hand and asked him if he would be good enough to give the sports prizes in assembly. Freedom was tickled pink, and he gave such a dazzling smile to Evelyne that she gave his hand a quick pat.

'Now then, Mr and Mrs Stubbs – about Edward. It must be obvious to you that he is a more than excellent pupil – he is our star pupil really, not that we like him to know that, but if it is permissible I want him to go into the sixth form.' He paused, peered at them for a moment, 'I am fully aware of how hard these times are for us all, but I think Edward might be a suitable candidate for Cambridge University. He cannot take the entrance examination until he is sixteen, more likely seventeen. I shouldn't be surprised, with the state the country is in, if war were declared. However, in special cases, and I believe your son is a special case, enlistment can be deferred.'

The headmaster was really feeling his way around the Stubbs family's financial situation. It was rare, nowadays, for families to be able to afford to keep their boys at school for the sixth form. However, Mrs Stubbs' reaction was immediate. She smiled, brimming with pride. 'He'll stay on, sir, and thank you very much.'

Freedom, not fully comprehending what the headmaster was saying, said nothing. He knew, as did everyone else, that war was imminent, so he presumed it was some sort of military training the head was referring to.

The assembly hall was filled to capacity, the boys lined up for their prizes and the school choir sang on the platform. Edward was up and down like a yo-yo as he collected prize after prize. Alex, in the lower class, had gained a special prize for endeavour, and one in maths. Evelyne applauded so often her hands were red. She couldn't help but turn to the parents sitting next to her to say, 'That's my son.'

The majority of the parents were very middle class, but the Stubbs couple only stood out because of their height. Evelyne wore a new hat and coat, and Freedom was in one of his American suits, altered for the occasion by Freda.

'Now, ladies and gentlemen, as you know, the school boxing team has done well this year, and the school's senior boxing champion has become the overall grammar school champion. We are very fortunate to have an

645

honoured guest to present the medal. I ask to join me on the platform, Freedom Stubbs, the ex-British Heavy-weight Boxing Champion.'

They met Freda and Ed as they arrived home with the prizes, and they listened as Freedom told them about how he had gone up on the platform to present the boxing prize to the school champion. Alex wanted photographs of Freedom's boxing days to show the boys at school, and Ed had them enthralled with stories of Freedom's boxing matches. When they left, the boys went along to bring Freda's scrapbook home.

Freda had saved all the newspaper cuttings and photographs taken in America. The boys were fasci-nated, and Alex wouldn't let Evelyne turn a single page until he had asked every possible question. He wanted to know who was who and where all the places were.

'Freedom, come and sit with us, you know all these people better than I do . . . come on.'

Freedom pulled up a chair. He had not seen many of the photographs himself, had tried to forget that part of his life. Now, after his success at the school, he was almost as eager as the boys to go over old times. He drew the book towards him. 'Now then, lemme see . . . ah, see this fella here, on the side of the picture, that's Jack Dempsey, the greatest boxer I've ever seen.'

Alex hung on his father's every word, and clung to him. Edward had read the article and tried to turn the page. Alex stopped him. 'Did you fight him, Dad?'

'No, son, he'd retired when I met him . . . Now, then, this man on his right was Jack Kearn, a promoter, and this was Ted Rickard, they were a famous team, known as the "Golden Triangle" . . . An' look, see, this is Dempsey's thoroughbred stallion, ain't it just lovely?'

Evelyne had relinquished her place at the table to Freedom, and she looked up from her sewing and smiled at the boys hanging onto their father's arms, shouting and clapping.

'Now, lads, this is a great fighter, Gene Tunney. I was to fight him for the title, but then he stepped down and left his throne vacant, see. So fighters from all over the world came to try for the belt. See this, it's a picture of the belt, an' it's solid gold, pictures hand-painted round the sides, see? Oh! An' will you look at this, this was the Danish contender, name of Knud Hansen, big fella, eh?' He turned the pages, animated, eager, 'And Monty Munn ... this chap's a Frenchman, can't remember his name. Here ... here's the villa where we stayed in Miami, Florida. You wasn't born then, Alex, an' you was just a toddler, Eddie.'

Evelyne came back into the kitchen, clutching her own scrapbook. It was immaculate; all these years it had been carefully wrapped in brown paper. Beneath each article was the name of the newspaper and the date, in her neat handwriting.

'I notice your Dad is not showing you himself. Now, you've not seen this, it's a really big occasion.'

The book was such a contrast to Ed and Freda's, as theirs was full of their own memorabilia, and very well-thumbed as Ed had taken it down to the gym at every opportunity.

'Now then, you're going to learn something tonight, boys. Take a look at this – it's a programme, but see the front. There were posters, twenty, maybe twenty-five feet high. As you came in on the plane, your Dad's face was the first thing you saw.'

The two boys gaped as she turned the page. Freedom had to swallow tears. He reached for Evelyne's hand and she gave him such a look it made his heart swell. He had never known about the book. It was so precious it touched his soul.

'See, he was surrounded by autograph hunters, he was more famous than a film star. There was not a street in Miami he could walk down without crowds gathering.'

Freedom laughed and said she was exaggerating.

'Oh, no I'm not, and this should be a lesson to you both. Your father was a champion, a very famous man, but you don't see him pushing it down people's throats like some people from around these parts who have never gone further afield than Brighton.'

The boys were agog, holding the book between them, shouting, vying with each other to turn the pages. And then there was the programme for the match between Freedom and Sharkey.

The boys fell silent, their eyes popping out of their heads. This was a man they scarcely recognized. The handsome face stared back at them, the hair long, the fists raised. Alex was close to tears of pride, touching the pictures, patting them. Edward looked at his father, then his mother. They were so close to the boys, had their arms around them, and yet it was as if they were alone. Evelyne bent to kiss Freedom, their eyes hungry for each other.

'What happened then? At the big fight, Dad, what happened?'

Freedom turned the pages, trying to change the subject. 'This man was Sir Charles Wheeler, he was my promoter, an English knight he was . . .'

Edward turned the pages back to look at the fight programme. 'Well, did yer beat 'im, Dad? Jack Sharkey?'

Freedom gave him a sad smile. 'No, son, he beat me, wiped the floor with me, knocked me out of the ring.'

Evelyne leaned over and pointed to the picture of Jack Sharkey. 'He punched foul, that's why, he punched low, and your Dad's leg got paralysed. Sharkey was never world champion either, because he fouled again at his next fight. You shouldn't run yourself down like that, Freedom! Your Dad would have won, but he had so many fights and not enough rest before the big bout . . . Your face had to have time to heal – there were cuts around his eyes, his ribs broken. No man in that condition should have been allowed to go into the ring. You ask your Uncle Ed about it.'

Again, Freedom reached out and held her hand. 'I dunno, suddenly your mother's an authority on boxing, she who hated the very thought of it, now will you listen to her?'

Evelyne laughed, and sat on his knee. 'Ah, well, I hate it, and that's the truth, but I'll not hear you tell of everyone else. You were a champion, not many can say that. But neither of you two lads will ever have to go through what your Dad had to, fighting for money is a terrible way to earn a living . . . Have you never wondered why your father limps the way he does? That's fighting for you . . .'

Edward leafed through the book and then opened a folded page of newspaper. 'What's this? Dad, what's this?'

Freedom glanced at it and flushed, looked up at Evelyne. He couldn't read it. Evelyne took it from Edward, bit her lip.

'It's the headline about Al Capone, Freedom.'

Freedom laughed and jigged Evelyne up and down on his knee. The boys whistled and started in amazement as Freedom told them about the St Valentine's Day massacre. Alex started jumping up and down. 'Dad,

649

Dad, there's films about him, they have guns, bab-bab-bab-b-b-b-b, real machine-guns that kill hundreds 'n' thousands at the same time.'

Edward continued to read the article, but Alex was beside himself. 'Tell us more, Dad, tell us more, Ma, make him tell us more.'

Evelyne slid off Freedom's knee and picked up the paper. Clearing her throat theatrically, she acted out her scene with the bell hop in the Chicago hotel. She did not mention that the trouble they had getting rooms was due to Freedom's dark skin, but went on to tell how she had met the man in the lilac suit. She switched to a heavy Chicago accent, ' "Well, Ma'am," he said . . .,' and mimed smoking a huge cigar. The boys clapped their hands. They had never seen their mother behave in this way. Freedom roared with laughter and applauded. 'We got sent flowers and fruit, and we'd never even heard of him. Then when Ed saw his name, well, he almost shit himself.'

Evelyne cuffed Freedom's head. 'And we'll not use any language like that! Well, come on now, let's clear the table. Who's hungry?'

Edward held up a photograph of Evelyne, dressed in all her finery, on board the *Aquitania*, 'Ma, is this you? This you?'

Freedom took it from him and turned to Evelyne. 'Yes, it's your mother, and she turned every man's head on the ship. Wearing her real pearls, she was.'

The boys stared from the photo to Evelyne and back again. 'Is that necklace real, Ma? The jewels, are they real?'

Evelyne ruffled Alex's hair and said they were, and she had to get on with the tea. Edward gave her a sly look, then a hooded glance at his father. 'You still got yer necklace, have you, Ma?'

Evelyne looked hard at Edward, but he had the masked look on his face so similar to his father's. Edward, who pried into everything, did he know? Had he seen her frantic search for her necklace that day? She couldn't tell. Freedom, uncomfortable, tried to change the subject, but Edward persisted, asking again and again to see his mother's jewels. Freedom stood up. 'Why don't you show 'em, Evie, go on.' He left the room, and came back downstairs a few moments later to show the necklace to the boys.

'Here you go, Alex, look at this. See, that was the time when I bought your Ma the very best.'

How had Freedom got it back? When? She didn't know, but Edward's frown told her for certain that somehow the boy had known something.

CHAPTER 28

3 SEPTEMBER 1940 – England had been at war for a year and the effect was shattering as the young men enlisted and went off to fight. Not that they noticed much difference in their streets, just that many faces were missing. Times were still hard, but as so many men were employed in the forces it left opportunities for work open to women. Hundreds of children were evacuated to safety in the country, but not Edward and Alex. Evelyne was adamant. They would remain in London and at school – they were not babes in arms and she and Freedom would keep their eyes on them. Edward, nearly eighteen years old now, was in the sixth form at the grammar school, taking his entrance exams for Cambridge University.

Freedom had been turned down when he tried to enlist, because of his age and his bad leg. He was furious and felt slighted, but he got a job as a warden patrolling the streets.

The bombs were hitting the East End and the dock areas worst of all, and blackouts every night was the rule. Buckingham Palace was hit in the same month, and the Queen announced publicly that she was glad, it made her feel she could look the East End in the face. The Royal Family committed itself to the needs of war with a zeal and conscientiousness that won the respect of the people.

Jesse made an appearance and roped Freedom into black market activities, and although Evelyne was against it from the start she had to admit that the food they obtained helped their meagre rations to go round. She still did the accounting at the bakeries and still lent money, but she also went to work in a factory on the morning shift. Planes flying overhead and bombs dropping became an everyday occurrence, which left gaps in the rows of houses like blackened skeletons. There was hardly a family that hadn't lost a relative in the fighting, and now they were being hit themselves they lived in constant fear of air-raid warnings. The raids usually took place under cover of night. Evelyne had seen families lose everything they possessed, and, always one to take care, she carried her savings book with her at all times, strapped around her waist under her clothes.

At the factory Evelyne hemmed army blankets on a machine, and one day when the sirens sounded during work, they all ran for the shelter. As they crossed the yard, one of the foremen looked up into the sky. 'Dear God, look at 'em, they're like big, black birds, the bastards. In broad daylight an' all.'

Evelyne was in the shelter before his words struck home, and she remembered Rawnie's words so many years ago. She screamed at one of the workers, shook the women. 'What day is it? What day is it?'

Thursday was the boys' half-day at school, where they had a good shelter, but on Thursdays they came home. She ran from the shelter, forcing her way past the boss, who tried to hold her back. She yelled to them that it was Thursday, then she was gone. She couldn't get a bus, they had come to a halt, and the whole area was bedlam. The planes were coming closer and closer, and looking up she could see them like big, black birds flying she knew, towards the city, towards number twelve.

She ran until she was so exhausted that she had to lean against a wall. She looked up as the drone of the planes passed overhead. There was pandemonium as people screamed and ran. The glue factory took a direct hit, and the overpowering smell of glue and the black smoke choked the few workers who escaped, and the firemen alike. Evelyne gasped for breath but pushed herself on and on, towards home. Twice she was held back by firemen but dragged herself away. 'My boys, my boys, lemme go.'

At long last she reached the corner of the street to find it a nightmare of flames and charred buildings. Fire engines were trying to get through the rubble. Stumbling and crying, calling her boys' names, Evelyne stopped in horror. Ed's brother's house was no more than a heap of rubble, and fire gushed from next door's wooden window frames. Screams echoed around, the thick black smoke filled the street, and Evelyne pushed her way through the dazed people wandering around calling for their loved ones. One of Freda's lodgers, one of the tarts, was sitting on the pavement sobbing, repeating over and over in a shocked, hysterical voice, 'Me new dress, me new dress, I just got it, me new dress.'

Evelyne could see Ed and Freda's house burning, the roof on fire, and as she pressed on she prayed over and over again that her boys were safe.

She saw Edward first, he was scrambling over the rubble calling out for Auntie Freda, Uncle Ed, his hands bleeding as he clawed at the bricks. A fireman tried to haul him away as burning timbers came crashing down. Evelyne ran towards him, and Alex appeared, black from head to foot, his tear-stained face hysterical with fear as he pointed back to number twelve, still gabbling as

Evelyne held him tight, tried to calm him down. An unexploded incendiary bomb was sticking through the roof of their house, and the firemen were trying to clear the street. It could go off at any time.

'Where's your father, *Alex? Alex?*'

Evelyne had to slap his face, he didn't even seem to know that he was in her arms.

'Get the bloody fool outta there, it's going up at any time.'

Knowing both her boys were safe, Evelyne headed for number twelve. A fireman grabbed her, shouting that the house would blow at any minute, everyone had to get back.

'He's inside, Ma, he went in for Rex, he's gone to get Rex.'

The hoses drenched her as she screamed out for Freedom. The smoke was so thick now that their eyes were red and smarting, and the fumes from the glue factory hung in the air like an overpowering cloud.

'Freedom . . . *Freedom?*'

As the roof blew, Freedom hurtled out of the house, clutching the terrified, snarling dog to his chest. Evelyne, her arms wrapped around her boys, almost collapsed with relief. They all stood together and watched the house blaze. Alex clung to her, holding his beloved dog at the same time. The hoses sprayed them as they stood in the debris of their street. Freedom went back to help with the fire.

Freda had been at her sewing machine, and Ed had obviously tried to warn her – his body was found in the passageway between the rooms. Ed's brother and sister-in-law and two of their children had been trapped in the kitchen. They had not stood a chance.

The realization of how lucky they were did not dawn until later that night as they lay in the underground shelter. They huddled together, clinging to each other. Alex whispered to his mother that Edward had known it would happen, he had known.

'What are you talking about, love, how did he know?'

Edward was sleeping, his filthy face resting on his arms. Evelyne wrapped the blanket closer around him, tried not to cry.

'He knew, Ma. We were out in the yard and there was no sound of the planes, nothing – no sirens even, an' as it was day we didn't worry, like – an' suddenly he grabbed hold of me and said go and warn Auntie an' Uncle Ed. The planes weren't even overhead.'

Freedom left the shelter and went off to do his warden's duties, and in the morning he was back and said they could return to their house. The roof was badly damaged and they didn't have a single window left, but at least it was still standing.

The sad, bedraggled group made its way home. The street was full of rubble, and the ambulances were still taking the bodies of the dead away. Firemen were digging in the bombed-out buildings looking for survivors, for bodies. The family kept their eyes down, not wanting to see Freda's frilly curtains, charred and sodden, lying in the gutter. They stepped over puddles, charred furniture, shattered glass, until they stood outside their house. Evelyne shuddered, it looked so derelict, so black, so deathly.

'Freedom, I don't want to go in, is there anywhere else we could go?'

He was carrying Rex in his arms, and he paused. Was she reading his mind? 'It's our home, and the way you look at it is, they hit us once, be a miracle if they get us again ... Come on, lads, let's make some tea and get the place cleaned up.'

Freedom could feel the horror, the house closing in on him, and he gasped for breath. The acrid stench from the glue factory hung in the air, burning his nostrils. He put his shoulder to the door and it crashed open.

The impact of bombs all round had made the house subside. The passageway was waterlogged and strewn with broken glass, and over everything was thick, black dust. It broke Evelyne's heart. Ordering the boys to search for what could be salvaged, Freedom began to clear away the ruined furniture. In the centre of the room was the scrapbook – not one page was left intact. He picked it up, and all he could think of was Ed, how he had looked with his warden's tin hat on the back of his head. He gritted his teeth and threw the remains of the book out of the back door along with everything else. But he couldn't get Ed's voice out of his mind, heard again the last words Ed had said to him, 'Now, look, lad, I'm not one wiv words, but I want you ter know somefink should anyfink ever happen ... I love you, like you was me own son, an' I'm depending on you ter take care of Freda. I've not much, but what I 'ave is yours, that includes all me memorabilia.'

Freedom felt the loss swamping him, overpowering him, and he hurled a chair out through the broken window with all his might. Edward started screaming, and Freedom's heart lurched. He turned in panic, to see Edward waving a telegram, his face shining.

'Ma, Ma, it's come, I've won a scholarship to Cambridge. I've won a place at Cambridge University ... I've done it!'

Before Evelyne could congratulate him, Freedom slammed his fist into the last intact pane of glass, shattering it into the yard. His fist bleeding, he turned on Edward, his face dark with rage.

'Don't you ever think of anyone but yerself, boy? There's Freda an' Ed dead, an' all you can scream about is that *you won a bloody scholarship! I'll knock that smile off your face!*'

Edward was taken aback for a moment, then he glared. 'You just try it – come on then, try it.' He threw a wild punch at his father, and Freedom blocked it with a swift movement of his arm. Edward tottered backwards, off balance.

'You better stay away from me, Eddie, I mean it.'

Edward charged, head down, and butted Freedom in the stomach, then swung his fists like windmills, but again Freedom threw him off as though he were a small child. This time Edward lurched backwards, striking his head on the mantelpiece. His face red, his mouth tight, he picked himself up. 'That's the last time you'll ever hit me, you bastard, you bastard.'

Reaching out, Freedom grabbed Edward and pulled him closer, slapping his face, the blows jerking his head back and forth. 'Don't try fighting me, sonny, you don't stand a chance. Go and join the army like the rest of the lads, like a man, instead of a nancy boy tied to your mother's apron strings.'

Edward dodged behind the table. 'Only nancy boy round this place is you, the great champion fighter, an' the army wouldn't even take yer.'

Alex ran from the room into the hallway, calling for his mother, 'Ma, Ma, come quick, Dad and Eddie are fighting!'

Panic-stricken, he ran up the stairs. Freedom kicked the door shut, and began to roll up his sleeves. 'You'll not have your Ma to help you now, son, you've been asking for this for a long time.'

Evelyne ran down the stairs, screaming at the top of her voice. 'Freedom, Edward, what's going on?'

Freedom stood with his back against the door and shouted for her to stay out of it. She tried to push the door open, but he slammed it shut. Rex ran to Freedom, whimpering, but he kicked out at the dog.

'That's right, kick the dog, he can't kick you back, can he? I can and I will. What you ever done for us, you with your big mouth an' even bigger fists? Ma's provided for this family, not you, it's never been you. *Go back to prison an' leave us alone!*'

Freedom clenched his fists, fighting for self-control, trying to keep his blind fury in check. Suddenly he was pushed forward as Alex forced his way into the kitchen. He grabbed Freedom's arm. 'Dad, Dad, don't, he doesn't mean it! Tell him you didn't mean it, Eddie, please, Dad, don't!'

'I meant every word, we were better off when he was in jail, at least Ma didn't have an extra mouth to feed.'

Evelyne came in and moved right between Edward and Freedom. 'I'll talk to him, just don't fight, let me talk to him.'

Freedom pushed her aside. 'No, Evie, not this time, you've always protected them, protected him. He's going to have to learn.' Freedom's voice was icy calm. He moved closer and closer to Edward. 'You're going down to that recruiting office right now, if I have to drag you there meself.'

Edward spat at him and ran round the room, ducking behind Evelyne. She put her arms out, pleading, 'Don't, Freedom, ah, don't, don't do something you'll be sorry for, please, please, don't.'

The belt slithered from Freedom's trousers and he wound it around his hand. Edward shrieked, suddenly afraid. 'I'm going to university, tell him Ma, tell him.'

'You're going to work, lad, we can't afford no university, not with the house burnt down round our ears. You are gonna earn your keep like every other lad around here.'

Evelyne made a grab for Freedom, shouting, 'That's for me to say, Freedom, it's *my* savings, *mine*!'

Deflated, Freedom turned a beseeching look on her. She ran out of the house, shouting for help. Heartbroken, Freedom watched her go. Once again she had taken her son's side.

Edward took that moment to open the kitchen drawer and take out the carving knife. 'Satisfied, are you? You bloody satisfied, you bastard?' He was hysterical, shaking, holding the knife like a dagger. Alex was the one to move towards his brother to try and take the knife, but Rex ran to him and he tripped over the dog, sprawled on to the floor. Freedom's face terrified Edward, the mask in place, no expression, the eyes black . . . He kept moving, coming closer and closer, unafraid, menacing, daring Edward to use the knife.

Evelyne was out in the street. Police and firemen were everywhere, clearing the debris. She screamed. 'Dear God, stop them, *someone stop them*!'

Freedom reached out to grip his son by the hair, and Edward brought the knife down in one single, stabbing thrust. Freedom remained standing. He looked into his son's face, his mask dropped, and his eyes full of anguish. Edward stepped back, stared first at his empty hand, then back at his father. Freedom made no attempt to remove the knife. He lifted his arms as if to embrace his son, then he fell forward, fell on to the knife, pushing it further into his heart.

There was a terrible silence in the room. No one moved. The colour drained from Edward's face and he swayed. Alex still held Rex's collar as the dog howled, trying to get to Freedom. Two policemen rushed in, kicking the door wide open, and took the situation in immediately. Rex barked furiously, his claws scrabbling on the lino to get to Freedom, Edward stood, stupefied, staring at his father. One of the policemen knelt down, slowly turned the body over. The blood had already formed a thick, dark pool, the knife in Freedom's heart right up to the hilt.

'Oh, Jesus God . . . right, you two lads, up against the wall, the pair of you, against the wall, now.'

Like terrified children, Edward and Alex stood with their backs against the wall. They watched in horror as their mother looked from the open kitchen door at the body. Her legs were shaking, the tremor running right through her . . . she pushed the policeman's helping hand away, stumbled to kneel beside Freedom. She cradled him to her, the blood oozing over her chest as she rocked him in her arms. She made not a sound. They could see the blood spreading over her pinafore, his blood, blood to blood, heart to heart. Without looking at his brother, Alex put out his hand, and they grasped each other tight, but made no move towards their mother.

The drone of fighter planes coming closer made one of the policemen swear out loud, 'Dear God, the bastards are coming again, and in broad daylight.'

The air-raid warning sounded for everyone to take cover. Edward's black eyes clung to his mother, never leaving her face as he watched her cradle the body. He had never seen such raw agony. His body felt chilled, icy, as if his own life were draining steadily away. The grasp of his brother's hand gave him assurance, but the voices of the police became distorted, unreal. 'There's an ambulance outside, we'll get him outside later, best get to the shelter. There's nothing we can do here until

661

after the bombing. You two lads come with us, come on, move it.'

Alex and Edward were herded roughly out of the door by one of the policemen, and the other bent down to Evelyne. 'Come on, come on Missus, the bombs'll be dropping any minute. There's nothing you can do for him now . . .'

Evelyne looked up and told him quietly that there was no need for the ambulance, he was dead . . . 'Leave me, please, leave me with him, please.'

The policeman realized it was pointless to argue. She was so calm, like ice, and he didn't want to waste any more time. The unearthly wail of the sirens continued, and he followed the others out. As he hurried to the shelter, he looked up. Broad daylight, the bastards had the audacity to come in broad daylight, like big, black birds in the sky.

The deadly bombs fell all around number twelve, but Evelyne couldn't hear them. She sat on the floor cradling Freedom's body in her arms, unable to cry. Her body felt wounded as if the blood were slowly dripping from her. Rex whimpered, crawling on his belly to lie beside her, licking the outstretched, lifeless hand.

Under the watchful eyes of the policemen, the brothers huddled in the shelter. Alex held Edward in his arms, and whispered to him, softly so the police couldn't hear. 'Edward? Listen to me, I'll say that I did it. No one saw, no one will know, can you hear me?'

Holding his brother tight, needing his warmth, Edward listened.

'I'm two years younger, they can't do nothin' to me, I'm a juvenile, they'll not send me to jail. You can go to Cambridge, you can still go.'

Edward shuddered and clung even closer, feeling the softness of his brother's skin. He kissed Alex's neck.

'See, it's what Ma wants, what she's dreamed of, so I'll do it, I'll say it was me that knifed him.'

Edward whispered close to Alex's ear. 'I didn't mean it, you know that, I didn't mean to do it . . . I'll make it up to you, I will, I give you my word I'll make it up to you.'

Alex seemed satisfied, patting his brother as if he were the younger of the two. Edward gave him a small thankful smile. 'You won't go back on your word, will you? I mean, you won't ever tell anyone, will you?'

Alex blinked back his tears. 'No, Eddie, I'll never tell no one else, not even Ma if you don't want me to.'

Edward gave him a hug, then peeked out of the shelter, said he thought the bombing was almost over. Alex looked at Edward, who no longer seemed to be distressed, no longer clung to him. Alex was shocked, confused, but it was too late, he had given his word.

The bombing had ceased and the all-clear sounded. Edward's voice was calm. 'Will you have to take my brother to the police station, sir? I should get back to our mother.'

The people who had sheltered with them lingered to watch, but they were moved on by another officer. Alex was taken away from Edward, and was led to the front of the house. The police officer took Edward aside. 'Now, lad, best take care of your mother. We'll have to take him into custody, understand? Tell her she can come down the station any time, but we have to get your brother's statement.'

'What'll happen to him, sir? It was an accident, he didn't mean it.'

That was not for the officer to say, but he gave

Edward permission to have a few words with Alex before they took him away.

Some of the neighbours stood on their front steps, whispering and nodding at the ambulance and the police. Two air-raid wardens joined the gathering, and they all watched with interest, but the police kept them at a distance.

Edward went over to the silent Alex, standing between two police officers. He looked unafraid, his chin up and managing not to cry. Edward couldn't say what he wanted, not with the officers standing so close . . . He caught Alex's hand and tried to hug him, but the sergeant broke them apart, and pushed Edward roughly aside. 'Don't start anything, sonny, go to your mother, there's a good lad. Let's get this over with as quietly as we can. The whole street's watching.'

Alex was led to a police wagon and helped up into the back of it. Edward called out to him that everything would be all right. He watched the white face staring from the back of the van as they drove off.

The policeman and the ambulance attendant stood talking at the front door, and Edward went to pass them to enter the house, but the policeman put a hand on his arm. 'She's in a bad state, and she won't let anyone touch him. We've been waiting for a doctor so they can take him up to the morgue.'

Edward couldn't face her. She sat in exactly the same position, with Freedom still in her arms. Rex still licked the lifeless hand.

'Ma, Ma, you'll have to let him go. They have to take him away.'

Slowly she turned vacant eyes towards him, and as if in slow motion she blinked. Prising her rigid arms from his father's body, he held her. She was covered in blood, and it had dried, hard. The police and an attendant moved in, wrapped the body in a blanket and carried it outside to the ambulance, where the doctor was waiting. Several people watched the body being lifted into the ambulance, and the doctor examined it briefly and told the ambulance crew to take it straight to the morgue, the hospital could do nothing. One of the spectators asked if bombs had dropped on this side of the street, if they had he hadn't heard them. 'I've got so that I don't hear 'em any more, was it a bomb done it?'

The policeman shook his head, said quietly that this was a murder. They shut the back of the ambulance, not noticing the white dog standing by the closed doors.

The truck drove off, the dog followed, followed until his paws were bloody from running on the broken glass and rubble. He knew his master was inside the wagon, and he wouldn't stop following it. In his exhaustion and the confusion of the traffic he began to follow the wrong vehicle, becoming more bewildered and confused, unable to find the scent, unable to find Freedom. In the end he lay in the gutter, chest heaving, tongue lolling, and his pink eyes closed as his heart gradually stopped.

Evelyne felt as if her heart had broken, it was so painful, she kept her hand pressed to her chest, to the dark, crusted stain. Edward made her some tea. She didn't speak, but she sipped it, slowly. At long last she appeared to thaw out, the hand that had remained pressed to her chest moved, and she stared at her stained fingers. 'Where's Alex, where's Alex?'

Edward bit his nails, looking guilty. 'They took him down the station, Ma, just to give a statement.'

Evelyne was puzzled, she rubbed her head. 'Why Alex, Eddie? Why have they taken Alex?'

Edward chewed his thumbnail down to the quick, he

couldn't face her. 'Because he did it. They said you can see him any time.'

She knew it was a lie and she felt sick. She had to hold the table-top tightly, or she would have fainted. 'Alex would never have touched him, Eddie, he worshipped the ground he walked on . . . *Don't ever lie to me, don't lie to me!*' She gripped his hand so tight it was like a vice on his wrist.

He sobbed, 'He said that he would say it was him, then I could go to Cambridge. He said it was what you wanted, Ma, what you dreamed of, you always said that.'

She stared at him, as if he were a stranger. He had sent his own brother to jail.

'He's still a juvenile, Ma, they can't do anything to him, but they could to me. I'm two years older . . . It's what you always wanted, isn't it? You want me to go to university.'

She walked out into the hall, feeling her way along the walls, clinging to the banister as she walked up the stairs. Edward followed and stood at the foot of the stairs. 'It's what you want, isn't it?'

She looked down at him, her eyes as cold as the North Sea. 'It's what *you* want. Well, you go, if Alex doesn't mind, you go.'

'I'll show you, Ma, I'll be somebody for you, I will, I'll not stop until I prove it was the right thing to do . . . *Ma? Ma?*'

The bedroom door had slammed, and he banged on the banister rail with his fist.

Evelyne undressed, carefully folding each garment, the blood-stained apron, the blouse. She sat on the bed, touching it, running her fingers along the carved posts. One son at university, one in jail, Freda and Ed gone . . . this was what Rawnie had seen in the palm of her hand. 'Beware the black birds in the sky. You will lose

666

all you love.' They were the planes, the German bomb-
ers, and it was true, she had lost Freedom, she had lost
her love.

The scream echoed down through the derelict house.
In the kitchen, Edward raised his head, looked up
towards the bedroom. She frightened him, the terrible
sound of her screaming, calling his father's name over
and over. At long last the screams stopped, and he heard
sobbing, it reverberated through the whole house. He
put his hands over his ears to try to block out the noise,
but it went on and on. He rocked in his chair. 'Stop it,
stop it, stop it . . .'

When he took his hands away the house was silent.
He didn't know when he had fallen asleep, but he sat
up sharply as he heard her calling for him.

'Edward, bring me up some hot water, I have to
wash.'

He carried up the big kettle, poured the water into
her bowl.

'I'll be down in a minute.'

He had a pot of tea ready for her in the kitchen, and
two slices of buttered toast. She was dressed in her best
clothes. 'I'll go to the police station, poor Alex must
think we've forgotten him. We'll have a lot to be getting
on with, there's everything to arrange for you to go up
to Cambridge, and then we'll need the best lawyer there
is.'

Edward was stunned – she was as calm as ever, but
when he went to kiss her she pushed him away. She
didn't touch his tea or the toast, just counted the change
in her purse. Edward would never forget the way she
looked at him, it released him, released him from her.
Her eyes were filled with such loathing – as if he were

no more than an animal. She never let him touch her again, never held him in her arms, and never spoke of Freedom. She even removed the photograph of Freedom from the mantelpiece, along with those of her two sons.

Evelyne buried Freedom, and the local people showed their love and respect for their dead champion, walking in silence behind the hearse. Ten high-stepping men wearing dark pinstriped suits, bright neckerchiefs and gold earrings appeared as if from nowhere. Somehow news had reached them that their fighter was dead. They kept a few yards back from the rest of the mourners, their heads held high – arrogant, black-haired men.

When the ceremony was over, Evelyne remained beside the grave. There was an air of aloofness about her, an untouchable grief that made it difficult for her friends and neighbours to comfort her. Even Mrs Harris couldn't take her in her arms. It was strange, but it was Jesse, who had brought the men from the clans, who stood alone with her when everyone else had gone. It was Jesse who sensed her need, her devastating loss. He held her gently, and she could smell the same musky oil that Freedom used to wear.

'We burn our dead's possessions so they take them with them, and in that way they rest and will not haunt the living.'

'They've already gone, Jesse, went in the Blitz.'

'Have you nothing he were proud of? He's a Prince, he cannot lie without a treasure, with no talisman.'

Evelyne remembered the necklace, how proud Freedom had been the day he gave it to her. She hesitated.

It was all she had left of him, all she had to remember the good times. Jesse seemed to know instinctively that there was something and his black eyes went darker than dark as he whispered,

'He loved thee, woman, more'n ye may know, but he was the son of a *dukkerin*, his blood was royal. He has strong powers. No church, no service will give him peace. You bury the gold tonight, place it at the foot of the cross and he'll rest quiet.'

Evelyne knew now, more than ever, how much of his past Freedom had given up for her, how much of his life she knew nothing of, as if in death he had returned to the wild, returned to his people.

'Will you sing that song for me. He loved it so.'

Jesse straightened his waistcoat, and in a clear voice that rang out across the graveyard, he sang,

> *Can you* rokka *Romany,*
> *Can you play the* bosh,
> *Can you* jal adrey the staripen,
> *Can you* chin the cosh . . .

Evelyne stared at her reflection, her face worn and pale, her naked shoulders as white as her shift. She carefully clasped on the gold and pearl necklace and then each earring. She searched her own face, her own sad eyes for the past, eyes brimming with glistening tears; they once again sparkled with youth and vitality. In the half-light of the small bedside lamp she was sure, sure he had entered the room. A small china figure was placed in front of the lamp and, caught at that moment, held in the beam of the light, it formed a lifesize shadow. Evelyne carefully inched the tiny figure forward until the shadow seemed to stand over her bed. She then lay down and lifted her arms and the shadow kissed and enveloped her, and she knew he would never leave her.

The police constable took Alex a mug of hot tea. The boy had hardly had a bit of food since his arrest. As the key turned in the lock, Alex looked up with a pitiful expression of expectancy on his face.

'Here, lad, get this down you, you'll feel better for it.'

Alex's hands shook as he cupped the tin mug. His teeth chattered against the rim, and his face crumpled. The constable felt sorry for him, and sat down on the bunk. 'He was buried today. Streets of people walked behind him to say goodbye. They gave him a champion's . . .'

He broke off to grab the mug from Alex. He had begun sobbing, his whole body shaking, and he was spilling the scalding tea on himself. All night he sobbed for his father, until he was exhausted, totally drained. The police officers heaved sighs of relief when at last the boy in their charge was silent.

Edward walked across the cobbled courtyard towards the main hall. Hundreds of black-gowned students milled around, shouting and calling to each other, joyously reunited with old pals. Cycles wobbled past, bells rang and everywhere the eye fell there were students. The excitement was contagious and exhilarating, even for the nervous first-timers, the freshmen who looked shyly to one another with small embarrassed smiles. Edward wanted to touch the stone of the walls, wanted to get down on his knees to kiss the cobbled quadrangle, he still could not quite believe he was here, he had done it, he was at Cambridge. He could not contain the feeling of achievement. It was bubbling inside him, bursting from his brain. He had made it. As he crossed the threshold into the main hall for his first assembly, he noticed the stone was worn, curving at the centre from hundreds of years and thousands of students' hurried steps. Now it was his turn, his time, and he would use every second, every moment. Edward knew that there would be many students who could match him academically, but doubted if anyone, bar himself, would have committed murder to cross this worn, hallowed step. This would be one accomplishment he would never think or speak of; if he did it would destroy him.

As Edward crossed the threshold into his new life he left behind the East End, his mother and his brother. He could not lose or forget as easily the last image of his father. This memory, like a clearly painted picture, was not of when he had seen his dead father cradled in his mother's arms, it was not of when he had turned to threaten him, it was not even of the smile he had on his face when Edward had felt the knife cut into his heart. The image, the clear, brilliantly painted picture that swept into his dreams and often into his waking hours, was of a man with flowing black hair – a handsome wild man with black angry eyes. The man was Freedom holding his bare knuckled fist up ready to fight, Freedom, the fighter from Devil's Pit, Freedom alive in the days before Edward had even been born, before he had married Evelyne.

Alex would dream of him too, and in his dream was a surreal mountainside where the grass grew green, the sky was a brilliant blue and the sun sparkled, glinting rainbow colours like a child's picture story book.

Alex saw himself, running towards the peak of the mountain. There came a thunder of hooves, ringing and echoing around the mountainside, and still he ran on, breathing the sweet, clean air as he jumped for joy . . .

Breaking through clouds with his raised hooves came a black, shining stallion. Astride him sat a man of magical ethereal beauty. A wild man, with flowing, blue-black hair, barechested, at one with the beast. Alex lifted his arms, crying, 'Don't go! Don't go!' But the rider passed him by, as if leaping over the very mountain. The thunder of hooves merged into a thunderclap, and the clouds closed like a grey curtain. Alex screamed, struggling to run those last few yards up the mountain, 'Freedom! Freedom! Freedom!'

He was too late, he was too tired. He collapsed to the ground, and from the earth came the last, faint sounds of the still-galloping horse, fainter, fainter . . . The skies opened and rain began to fall.

Alex woke, drenched in his own sweat, his body stiff and cold. He pulled the worn blanket around his aching body and closed his eyes again, hoping to conjure up one more glimpse of the rider. Unable to sleep, he comforted himself with the thought that one day he would reach the top of the mountain.

ROMANY CURSE

He must lie with his treasures, be they tin or gold,
Resting in finery, his back to the soil.
One wheel of his *vargon* must light up with fire,
In the flame is his evil, his pain and his soul.
But beware of his *taelizman* (talisman) carved out of
    stone,
If not in his palm, then a curse is foretold.

For who steals the charm of this *dukkerin*'s son,
Will walk in his shadow, bleed with his blood,
Cry loud with his anguish and suffer his pain.
His unquiet spirit will rise up again,
His footsteps will echo unseen on the ground
Until the curse is fulfilled, his talisman found.

EPILOGUE

THE TALISMAN follows the lives of the two brothers: Edward's meteoric rise to vast wealth, Alex's prison sentence and release.

To ensure they were never to forget their origins, Edward took from his mother's grave the necklace his father had given to her the night he had claimed his championship belt. He melted the gold to make two medallions, and had their names inscribed, so they would never forget. Unknowingly he had committed a Romany sin. By opening the grave he had taken from his father and his mother their treasure. He had taken his father's life, and now he ransacked his soul, ignorant of the old customs and the curses. Edward evoked the unquiet dead.

The Talisman introduces the brothers' women, their wives and their children, all of them inexplicably bound by ghosts from the past. The murder of their father, Freedom Stubbs, the Champion fighter, constantly draws them back to their Romany origins . . . they have his blood in their veins, and his death on their consciences. They have inherited the Romany second sight and, as they reach a phenomenally high pinnacle of both material wealth and power, attained deviously and vio-lently, one of them must now pay the debt. One must pay at last for the murder. It is the law of the Romanies, be it sons or daughters, wives or mothers, fathers or brothers, a debt must be paid. A tear for a tear, a heart for a heart, blood to blood, soul to soul . . .

TRIAL AND RETRIBUTION

This book is dedicated to Norman Black and all the members of the organization Support After Murder & Manslaughter (SAMM), who work so tirelessly to support those bereaved by violent crime. In sharing their experiences, knowledge and sometimes humour, they help others to survive their tragic loss.

ACKNOWLEDGEMENTS

I WOULD like to sincerely thank the following for all their generosity and assistance:

Jackie Malton, David Martin-Sperry, Jeffrey McCann, Liz Justice, Dr Roger Berrett, Dr Liz Wilson and Detective Sergeant Ron Turnbull at the Forensic Science Service, Dr Iain West and Dr Ian Hill at Guy's Hospital, Bob Greenwell at Fulham Mortuary, Manuel Pereira, Chris Rank and Deline Richards at Westminster Mortuary, Detective Superintendent Richard Bell, Detective Sergeant Geoff Sinnott, Detective Constable Rod Austin, Detective Sergeant Andy James, Inspectors Douglas and Skinner at Kilburn ID Suite, Sergeant Adrian Elgstrand, and Inspector Stan Tullett from TSG, Marc Berners at Essex Police, Peter Kemp of Westminster Health Authority, Mike Cobb from the Metropolitan Police Press Office, Jo Scarratt, Dr Prance at the Forensic Science Service in Huntingdon.

There isn't an actor in *Trial and Retribution* who didn't give a performance of the highest quality. Special thanks must go to David Hayman, Kate Buffery, Helen McCrory, Anastasia Hille, Rhys Ifans, Lee Ross, Colin Weland and Corin Redgrave.

The talented cast and crew were led by a wonderful director, and friend, Aisling Walsh, supported by the peerless skills of executive producer Steve Lanning. I thank all the cast and crew equally for their dedication and hard work. Thanks to Howard Baker and the editing staff Terry Warwick, Rosie Dowson, Adrian Bleasdale, and Nigel Parkin at YTV in Leeds, Howard Lanning and all the post-production team. To Clare Forbes, Susie Tullett, and Georgina Weatherill and all at JAC.

Sincere thanks to Vaughan Kinghan for all her hard work and her awesome legal mind.

To Nick Elliott, Jenny Reeks and Marcus Plantin at the ITV Network Centre for making it all possible. Keith Richardson at Yorkshire Television.

Thanks to my literary agent Gill Coleridge, and to Ian Chapman, Suzanne Baboneau and Philippa McEwan at Macmillan.

Many thanks to Sue Rodgers and Duncan Heath at ICM, my agents and friends.

To my own team for all their hard work, Liz Thorburn, associate producer, Alice Asquith, researcher, Ciara McIlvenny and Lucy Richer, script editors.

I would like to give my sincere thanks to the talented writer Robin Blake for his care and skill in adapting the film of *Trial and Retribution*.

CHAPTER 1

THURSDAY 5 SEPTEMBER. MORNING

IT HAD rained in the night, just as the television said it would, and water lay around in pools and puddles, making the asphalt of the estate's roads, walkways and playground shine. It was the only time the place looked halfway clean, just after a shower. Even better when the sun was out – nothing like a few rays on the wet ground to give a bit of sparkle. But even on a cloudy day, like today, the view from the sixth floor looked better in the eyes of Enid Marsh. The weeks of the summer heatwave, trapped in her flat, had seemed endless.

'Flat? Prison cell more like,' she muttered to herself, wiping the kitchen surfaces down.

Had she wiped them already? Couldn't remember. Anyway, soon Mrs Wald would be here with her meals on wheels. Got to lay the table.

She shuffled painfully into the lounge and stood for a moment in the middle of the room. The television murmured in its corner – something about a by-election. Her eyes slid past the screen on which a reporter was talking earnestly in front of a polling booth. Politics. Life's too short – and that's one thing the politicians will never tell you.

Enid blanked out the reporter's voice and looked

1

towards the window. The plate glass was rattling as a plane circled somewhere near. Noisy beggars. More and more, she noticed everything: planes, police sirens, heat and cold, close air, buzzing bluebottles in her room. There was nothing much to keep her mind off all that annoying background noise. Most people go through life hardly thinking about them, but Enid heard every crying child and barking dog, every thump the woman next door got from her chap and every swearword that they hurled at each other.

Enid was not a profane person. But she'd lived through the war, been bombed out, helped dig out her own dead sister from under the rubble even. You used to hear plenty of language and rough stuff then, just like you did living here. Had to take it in your stride.

She grasped at her zimmer frame. Stride! That was good.

An ambulance siren wailed. One day that would be for her. What was hard was not being able to put the noises into the background and forget them. It was like a pain you couldn't put away from you, a nagging tooth, or this beggar the arthritis. A little bit of deafness would be a mercy, she sometimes thought.

It was all on account of the arthritis. She could hardly move some days. It was a life sentence – her and the walking frame. Next time they took her out it would be in a stretcher or a box . . .

She clicked her tongue to snap out of this. It had rained now, and you had to be thankful for half a cup of anything. The damp wasn't much good for her joints, but pleasure's got to be paid for.

'*Ryan! Ryan! Come on, it's half-past twelve! Ryan!*'

The voice rose from the playground down below.

2

There'd be the usual gang of little ones down there now and a few mums having a gossip. There usually was, dinnertime.

Enid started to move towards the wide plate-glass window, her slippered feet never out of contact with the carpet. Like someone learning to skate, she always thought. She arrived at the door of her balcony, hobbled outside and leaned over her parapet. She could see half the playground from here, surrounded by its cage of wire mesh. A couple of eight-year-olds were on the round-about, pushing it on the run then skipping on and off it, squealing at the danger they could create for themselves. A slightly younger boy was taking penalty kicks with a stone against the concrete wall. If he should kick too high and a bit to the left he'd smash the glass in that stairway door.

And who would care? His mum, standing with a small group of women on the far side of the playground, certainly wouldn't and Enid could understand why. Half the doors and windows in sight were boarded with plywood and most of the rest had been splintered and starred by flying missiles. Enid had seen the TV newsfilm from Sarajevo during the fighting there. This place didn't look that much different, not to her. And they wouldn't be fixing any of it. The whole lot was coming down, so they told her.

'Julie! Don't you go in that puddle, you hear me?'

That would be the mother of the little blonde-haired one in the red anorak, calling down from her balcony. Four months gone with her fourth. They lived below Enid. What a pet she was, that Julie, not like her brother on the roundabout. He was a holy terror but she was a proper little angel. Goldilocks, Enid called her in her

3

mind. There she was, standing on the edge of a great lake of a puddle that had collected around a blocked-up drain, splashing the water with a stick.

'*Jason! Watch your sister! You got ten minutes ... did you hear me? Ten minutes and it's dinner.*'

Enid kept her eyes on little Julie, watching how the ripples she was making in the black and silver puddle twisted the scarlet reflection of her jacket this way and that. She leaned out and looked until she got tired. Then she began the long trek back inside. Where *was* Mrs Wald? Hardly ever late, that woman. Set your watch by her as a rule. And what was that TV programme last night? Enid had been dying to tell Mrs Wald about that. She knew she'd be interested. Oh yes, the cookery thing where you had to make a meal in fifteen minutes. Must get Mrs Wald to stay for a cuppa so she could tell her. Enid prided herself on her memory. Unlike a lot of pensioners she'd known, she was as sharp as a hatpin when it came to remembering certain things.

'Roll on next week and the start of term, that's all I'm waiting for,' said Anita Harris to her boyfriend Peter who was stretched out, legs splayed, under the kitchen sink. 'Those war toys of Jason's are all over his bedroom and I specially told him to tidy them away before he went out. Sometimes I could cheerfully kill that boy.'

'And he's *your* flesh and blood. Just think what *I'd* like to do to him. He needs unblocking, that kid, like this bleedin' pipe. Got a bucket?'

Peter was struggling with a heavy wrench, tugging the locking nut on the S-bend section. Anita looked down at him from the kitchen table, where she was mashing

4

potatoes, pumping the masher down strongly into the pan of spuds. She straightened up and sighed.

'If only he was like Julie.'

'He's a boy, 'Nita! Can't be like Julie.'

'No, I mean, if only he was good – well, better anyway. How are you doing? I want to use that sink soon.'

'Don't know. Reckon I'm going to have to unscrew the whole S-bend. Because I've tightened everything up and it's still leaking.'

He raised his head to see where the copious leak was coming from. A drip of greasy water splashed into his eye.

'Shit!'

Anita laughed. 'I told you. You want to ask whatsit – you know, from the newsagent. Got his card in the window. Plumber.'

She stepped over Peter to get to the cooker, where a pound of sausages whispered and spat on the gas. By the window near the cooker little Tony sat in his high chair. He'd got a teaspoon and was busy cramming it between his toothless gums, most of his hand following it. Anita prised his mouth open and extracted the spoon.

'Tony, don't eat this.'

She picked up a plastic toy of Jason's, some kind of caterpillar-wheel space buggy which had somehow got on to Tony's table. Inside was a plastic helmeted khaki figure with a backpack and automatic weapon raised in the firing position. She never looked at one of these things without thinking of Jason's dad. Not to mention the entire bloody British army.

'I wouldn't trust 'em,' called Peter, his voice muffled.

'Who?'

'Those cards in the newsagents. They're cowboys.'

'You should try putting one in there yourself then.'

5

Peter craned his head out. He was laughing. 'Har-har. bitch.'

'Can you get the kids up for me? It's dinner.'

'Yeah, in a minute. I can't do everything at once.'

As she stepped back across his recumbent body, Peter's hand shot out and up Anita's miniskirt, his finger and thumb cowbiting the inside of her thigh. Anita laughed and flipped on the cold-water tap. The sound of water splattering over Peter's head and shoulders was covered by his howl of surprise.

'I'm sorry, Pete. Did you say you wanted a bucket?'

Peter slid out, flicking the waterdrops from his hair and eyes. 'Bit bloody late for that. Look at the state of me.' He clutched at Anita, mock-biting her neck and she melted into him for a proper kiss. He let her go and turned to the child.

'Here, Tony! What you laughing at? Want a tickle from your dad?'

Tony threw his head back and gurgled in ecstasy as Peter's hands found his ribcage.

Despite laying just for one, Enid took more than ten minutes to arrange the table for dinner. It may be only a meal on wheels but she insisted on everything being properly served, with the appropriate tableware neatly set out beforehand. It was hard to do it and manipulate the Zimmer but at last she had it laid out entirely to her satisfaction.

But *where* was Mrs Wald? She moved painfully back to the balcony. No sign of Mrs Wald's white van. The parents had gone in to cook lunch in those microwave ovens they all had now.

6

She looked around. There was nobody, except – yes, little Goldilocks, backing into view from the other half of the playground. Shouldn't she be in for her lunch? Enid saw her throw back her head, laughing. Then the child lifted her hands to her face. With fingers interlaced she covered her eyes and peeked through them. *Peek-a-boo*. Who was with her? Must be playing with brother Jason.

Beyond the play area, a white van rolled into sight, negotiating the estate's speedbumps with care. And about time, thought Enid. I was starting to get hungry. She gathered herself to turn – turning was one of the most difficult manoeuvres for her – but as she did so she saw Goldilocks drop her hands. Another hand came out from the dead ground that was blocked from her view by the side of the building. This hand took one of the child's hands. It was an adult's hand, attached to an adult's arm, and its owner was leaning down. He was wearing an adult's long dark coat. And just before Enid started back inside she saw Julie's companion straighten up and begin to walk away, skirting the roundabout and the playtrain. The little girl went too, trotting contentedly along with him.

Going to get their lunch too, thought Enid. Hungry, like me.

Carrying her meal trays stacked, Mrs Wald pressed the circular stainless steel lift-call button and waited. A remote sound of clanking and whirring came down the lift shaft but the door did not slide open. She had five clients in this tower. Two of them were robust enough old folk, able to get down to the pub or the day centre. But she worried about Mrs Marsh – housebound, abandoned by her family, hardly ever saw anyone except the meals on wheels service.

The trays had begun to feel heavy as she waited. To distract herself she read the bold marker pen inscription on the steel door: SKANK CITY FC: TICKET-HOLDERS ONLY. She did not understand what it meant. Again she pressed the button, on which the same pen had drawn an A in a circle. She sighed when there was still no response. She would have to take the stairs.

She swivelled and then stared in surprise as a man plunged down the flight of concrete stairs she was about to climb – a youngish fellow, late twenties, shoulder-length hair and wearing a long dark coat. No doubt a perfectly nice-looking young chap, except that his dirty, greasy long hair practically hid his face. Bet it didn't get washed more than once a fortnight, if it was lucky. As is the way with chance encounters in the hallways of London's more desolate council tower blocks, their eyes didn't meet and no words were exchanged. The man simply hurried past, crashing through the swing doors that led to the outside.

When at last she reached Enid's, her final call in this block, it was almost half-past one, by which time the poor thing's meal must be practically cold.

'I'm late, love, I know. Sorry. But I can't stop.'

Enid was standing there expectantly, with a small metal teapot in her hand. Mrs Wald swept past her and into the kitchen.

'Better just pop this in the oven, warm it through, eh? Give it ten or fifteen minutes before you take it out. Don't burn yourself. Oh dear, I've been late all round today. It's way after one now – in fact it's . . . What is it?' She looked at her watch, squinting and tilting her glasses

8

to focus on the impractically small watchface. 'Dear, dear, it's one-thirty.'

Enid hovered anxiously, gripping her tea pot, attending to Mrs Wald with all the concentration of a coarse-fisherman watching her float.

'Got to be getting along, love,' said Mrs Wald, briskly returning to the flat's front door. 'Have a cuppa tea tomorrow, shall we? OK? Don't you worry, let myself out! Enjoy your dinner. Tarra!'

The door's clunk as she shut it behind her had a very precise finality about it. Enid stood looking at it for a moment, then zimmered over and lifted the safety chain back into its groove, running it along to the end with a suddenly impatient flick of her arthritic fingers.

In her van, Mrs Wald depressed the clutch and turned the ignition key. The engine clicked and then gave a whirr followed by a dry *whumph*. Nothing more. She did it again, with the same result.

She clicked her tongue, pulled out the choke, pumped the accelerator and the clutch pedals and even, in her frustration, heaved herself backwards and forwards in her seat, rocking the vehicle on its springs. Nothing.

Mrs Wald looked around for someone to ask. She could see no one except an ice-cream van away over by the road. She remembered about flooding the carburettor and, though she had no idea what it meant, she knew you had to wait once it had happened. A man in a long dark coat – he looked like the fellow she'd seen on the stairs – was chatting with the ice-cream man. Then a boy came running up to stand jiggling next to the long-coated man, his face turned up imploringly. He appeared to get short

9

shrift and by the time Mrs Wald turned back to her ignition to try it once more he had peeled off and was pelting towards her, his arms flapping.

Her engine hawked and spat into life at last, just as the boy, whose name (though she didn't know it) was Jason Harris, careered past her towards the tower-block entrance. She could see him in the rear-view mirror, through the puffs of smoke rising from her exhaust.

Jason was hungry now. As he took the stairs two at a time he knew his mum would nag him. And she did.

'I said ten minutes, not an hour and a half.'

She had rewarmed the sausages and mash. Now she put it down in front of him with an impatient flourish.

'And where's Julie? She with Peter?'

'Gone to get a plumber, he says.' Jason looked at his plate dubiously. 'Why can't we have chips?'

'Because we've got mash. Did he say how long he'd be? I wish he'd waited till after his dinner.'

Jason answered with an exaggerated shrug, picked up his fork and harpooned a sausage. What did it have to do with him, anyway?

Still having her appetite, which no one could deny, Enid finished the pudding to the last crumb of apple pie and smear of custard. Out of nowhere, it occurred to her that the chink and scrape of this spoon in this bowl made exactly the same sound as spoons had made on pudding bowls when she was a baby and just learning how to hold a spoon. Funny how the world can be so different from what it used to be – more like another planet, if truth be told – and at the same time stay just the same. You can be watching a programme about microchips and there'd be some sound from outside, didn't matter what, and inside your head you'd go straight back to the days of trams and stays and ocean liners and the Crazy Gang.

It was not much use, knowing that the past never truly went away. But it *was* comforting anyhow.

'Julie! Julie!'

There it was, that voice again, outside on the estate, calling and calling. Enid looked up, tuning in to it. It was a woman's voice. First it had come from below in the playground, but now it was further away, almost distant, carried faintly on the blustering wind that had got up since morning. She remembered her own mum calling her in for her milk and a biscuit.

'Enid! Enid!'

The rattling plastic washing line on Enid's balcony half masked the voice of Julie's mother as she went on calling. Where had that little Goldilocks got to now? Enid chuckled. Hope she's not in trouble with the three bears again.

'Julie! Joo-oolie!'

Enid reached for the TV guide and carefully turned to today's page. *Call My Bluff* was on at two. She looked at her mantel clock, which showed ten past. Pity. She'd missed the start, but never mind, she liked that programme. She settled in her chair and switched on. There was a burst of laughter from the studio audience and, as it died away, she could still hear the mother's voice coming and going on the wind outside.

'Joo-oolie!'

*

11

When Peter came in without Julie, Anita simply assumed she'd gone round to her friend Hillary's. She was in a world of her own sometimes, that kid. If she thought of something she just did it and she'd been prattling on about Hillary's new kitten all morning. She'd probably gone over there to see it.

Without a phone it meant walking over. The Collins didn't live in the tower, but in one of the tiny ground-floor flats at the back of the old shopping parade. So Anita took her purse and put Tony in the buggy, thinking she'd collect her daughter at the same time as picking up a few things from Ali's convenience store.

But, of course, when she got there and rang the bell, there was no one at home in the Collins place. Which was quite natural when Anita thought about it. Hillary's mum, Sam, worked, so she had her kids over in the school-holiday playcentre at the church hall during the day.

So where was Julie? For the very first time a seed of dread started to sprout inside Anita. She stood at the Collins' front door, rocking Tony in his buggy to keep him asleep, and looked up and down the curved terrace. Someone might have seen her if she did come over here.

Sam Collins's neighbour on one side was an old bloke she knew by sight. He came to the door in response to her knock wearing slippers and vest.

'What time was that, love? No, sorry, haven't seen no little girl round here, but I wouldn't have, see? Been watching racing on telly. Gone and fallen asleep, haven't I?'

The flat on the other side of the Collins was boarded up and as she walked along the terrace she found only three more places with curtains up to show they were occupied. No one had seen Julie. Anita's heart was beating – not faster exactly, but more heavily, as she suddenly had to accept the fact: it may be only temporary, it may be all over in one minute's time, but at this precise moment she didn't know where her little girl was. Every cell of her body was in revolt against this idea. What good mother couldn't account for the whereabouts of her children? And if she wasn't a good mother, what was she?

Anita turned and hurried back to the tower. Julie would certainly have come home by now. After all, it was *way* past dinnertime and she'd be starving. Had a great appetite, that little girl, when she didn't fill herself up with too many chocolate bars.

But Julie was not at home and it was nearly half-past two. Peter ran out to the shops, see if Ali or the newsagent had seen her, or the attendant in the launderette. Anita questioned Jason. Had he seen Julie with anyone else? When they were in the playground together, did she run off anywhere? And why, why, *why* didn't he keep an eye on her? Christ, he was eight years old now, she was only five. It was *his* responsibility.

Jason said nothing, just shifted from foot to foot, staring at the wall behind his mother's head. And Anita knew what a lie she had told him. It wasn't Jason's responsibility at all, never had been. She was Julie's mother. The responsibility was hers.

She went back out with Tony and the buggy and just walked around, calling Julie's name. She marched three hundred yards along the main road, then doubled back towards the water. Behind the estate was the Royal Albert Dock, a vast basin of deserted, disused water. Someone had once told her that in its heyday it had been capable of docking a ship as big as the *Titanic*. It had been fringed by great warehouses and massive cranes until a few years ago. Now most of the land around the dock had been levelled and was strewn with all the rubble of demolition: broken bricks, shattered concrete piles, haystacks of rusty girders. The waste ground was relieved by the odd building site – the next phase of London's dockland development was due to occur here one day. But, judging by the desolation Anita saw all around her, it was a far-off day indeed.

She approached the edge of the dock. The wind was getting stronger and a few drops of chilly rain spattered her face. Anita scanned the gunmetal-grey water, which was beginning to rise in little peaks under the increasing breeze. She put her hands to her cheeks, scanning the surface for anything red, anything white.

'Oh, dear God,' she prayed. 'Please let her not be here.'

But there was nothing to be seen afloat on that water, just a few sticks, bottles and drink cans.

'Oh, this is such crap,' she told herself. 'Your daughter would never have come here on her own. It's too far, woman. You're imagining things.'

But there was already an edge of desperation in her voice as she pushed Tony back to the tower block, still calling Julie's name. There was a small knot of residents standing near the playground, and they'd heard that Julie was missing. Well, bad news travels quick. Karen Hyam, Ivy Green, Ron Hall and a few others were there when she went up to them. They knew Julie and her blonde curls all right. But none of them had any idea where she was now. Peter ran up as she was talking to them. He'd drawn a blank at the shops.

Exhausted, Anita agreed to go back home while Peter

went on searching. She dragged herself and Tony up to the flat. The moment she was dreading most of all was almost upon them: the moment when they would have to call in the police.

CHAPTER 2

SKANK CITY FC – TICKET-HOLDERS ONLY
While they waited by the lift Police Constable Simon Phelps read the inscription on the door and wondered if he should make a funny comment. But something about Detective Inspector North's way of doing things made it difficult. She was the most poised woman copper he'd come across during five years in the job. Thirty-five, not by any means a dog, unmarried but living with her boyfriend (so they gathered at the station) and, on top of that, smart as a whip. She was definitely Premier League to his Leyton Orient. Not that Phelps meant to stay Leyton Orient for ever but, even so, the Detective Inspector inhibited him. So he kept stum, allowing Pat North to take the lead. She nodded at the graffiti.

'Got your season ticket then, Simon?'

'Not yet, ma'am.'

'Don't bother. It's hard to see a player in *this* club scoring. Anyway, they'll be on borrowed time. This estate's condemned. Coming down as soon as they can find somewhere to park the people.'

Phelps looked around at the hallway. It was bare and brutal. 'Not a very nice place to lose your kid in.'

'Say that again. And have you ever been here when the bloody lifts have been working? Come on – stairs.'

They began slogging up to the third floor, where she indicated flat number nineteen. Phelps rang the bell.

Jason Harris opened the door and led them to his mother, who stood in her kitchen with two plates of sausages and mash, one in each hand. She was holding them helplessly, as if they were stuck to her and she could not dispose of them. Pat North could see the congealed white fat streaking the outside of the bangers. These meals had been cold for hours but their continued existence was a potent act of denial: the food *would* be eaten by the persons it was intended for, and then everything would be back to normal.

As Pat North did the introductions, Anita deposited the meal plates deliberately on the laminated counter. With the automatically appraising eye that she had long ago learned to use on domestic visits, Pat clocked the kitchen. It was clean and well stocked. The microwave looked fairly new and so did the toaster. Nothing was more than five years past its sell-by. Nothing was out of an Oxfam shop or the local purveyor of house-clearance junk.

'We've searched everywhere,' she said. 'Peter's still round the back, looking over the building site and I've been knocking on everyone's door.'

Her voice betrayed her. She was still in control, just. But she was close to panic, the classic patterns Pat remembered from psychology class: articulating rapidly and unevenly and with an intonation pattern in which the stresses hit unnaturally high notes. Meanwhile genuine, high-decibel hysteria was supplied by the toddler who was sitting in his highchair and beating his skull against the padded headrest. His screams would have doubled for a circular saw getting to work on a tough piece of hardwood. Pat caught Phelps's eye, nodded at the two children, then glanced back into the lounge.

'Is there somewhere else we can talk, Mrs Harris?'

Anita ushered Pat from the kitchen as Phelps bent to pick up a plastic toy space-tank, which he presented to Tony. It went straight up to the child's mouth, efficiently cutting off the screams. Phelps beamed with satisfaction.

'Maybe she's just gone into someone's flat,' Anita said, following the policewoman into her lounge. 'She's ever so friendly.'

She began darting about, picking up toys and cushions and a stray pair of trainers that were strewn about. Pat North could hear Phelps in the kitchen, talking to Jason in what he hoped was the tone of a friendly uncle.

'So, Julie's your little sister, is she? Eh, come on. You're not scared of me, big lad like you?'

'No I ain't. But you give him my Bone-Breaka, you tosser!'

Anita didn't seem to hear any of this. She was pitching a handful of toys into a drawer. Pat sat down on the sofa. She had no children of her own – she could only imagine what Anita was going through.

'Why don't you tell me what happened, Mrs Harris? Just the bare facts. When did you personally last see Julie?'

'Oh, yes. All right.'

Anita stopped moving and pressed her fingertips into her closed eyes, concentrating.

'It was about twelve-thirty. She was there when I looked over the balcony. I remember calling out to her not to get her feet wet.'

'In the playground just below you mean?'

18

'Yes. She was playing by a puddle.'

'Do you know if anyone saw her after twelve-thirty?'

'I sent Peter out to get them. But he said he couldn't find them.'

'Them?'

'Yes. She was with Jason. Julie was. Their— I'd got their dinner on the table for them. I didn't know— I don't know if anyone saw them.'

The front door crashed and a moment later Peter came into the lounge, a glowering, unkempt figure in a tatty long overcoat. Anita ran to him.

'Peter! Haven't you found her?'

Peter looked sullenly at the police officer. She was plain clothes but obviously a copper. Peter didn't like the filth.

'No,' he said. 'I've been all over the estate. Nothing.'

Pat turned to the sideboard, where a large selection of carefully framed family photos were arrayed. She picked one up which was obviously of Julie.

'Mrs Harris?' she asked in a low voice. Having been in this situation a couple of times before, she knew it was the question that really scared the parents. But it had to be asked. This was a missing persons case and, at this stage, nothing more than a missing persons case.

'Mrs Harris, do you have a recent photograph of Julie we can use?'

From the squad car on her way back to Southampton Street, Pat North got on the radio to Sergeant Paul Donaldson at the station. She gave him the bare details of her interview with the Harris family and instructed him to set up an incident room and get a team together smartish.

There was no knowing how long this might take but one thing was clear: the search area was neither small nor perfectly formed.

It was typical of Skipper Donaldson's devotion to efficiency that a dozen faces were already assembled as North walked into the Incident Room at Southampton Street police station.

'Right,' she said, looking around to see who she had to work with. 'We have a missing child on the Howarth, a little girl called Julie Ann Harris, aged five. Photo's being copied now. She was last seen in the playground this morning, in full view of the tower blocks. There were other kids about but, unlike them, Julie Ann never came in for lunch. I don't need to remind you all of the possible implications, just that we want her found, and before dark. OK?'

Donaldson shouldered his way through the doors with a sheaf of stapled notes. The first page of each was a colour copy of Julie Harris's photograph. He began handing the notes round, alert to the change of atmosphere, a sudden sobering, as the officers studied the image of the gap-toothed little girl staring out of the snapshot with such beguiling natural confidence. If Julie was alive, and maybe lying injured from an accident somewhere, to find her quickly was a reasonable prospect. Even if the accident was more serious and she was dead, they should still find her. As for the other possibilities, they all knew them and nobody wanted to think about them – not until they were forced to, anyway.

North was tacking a copy of the photograph on to the board behind her when PC Bavesh Marik cleared his throat.

'We going to get any back-up for the search?'

North knew these uniformed lads were keen and

thorough, she had a lot of confidence in them. But she couldn't hope they were numerous enough to cover the ground without assistance. She'd already contacted the Metropolitan Police Territorial Support Group, the reserve of officers kept chiefly for public order duties. TSG could usually be relied on to provide numbers for large-scale searches in London. She might also need POLSA, the specialist search boys. They were nauseatingly gung-ho, most of them ex-military, but they tended to get into places other coppers couldn't reach.

'Yes. TSG are coming in, probably POLSA too. But in the meantime, we get things started. I want a full house to house. It's a big estate and, remember, she's only five years old. Skipper, who've you got?'

Donaldson straightened to attention to call out the names from a clipboard.

'Constables Brown, Phelps, Barridge, Henshaw, Marik and Maudsley. That's all we can spare immediately for the estate.'

'Not bad for a start. And who's doing family liaison?' North looked round. A pleasant-faced, neatly dressed woman of about thirty made a signal with her hand.

'Me. Er, PC Meg Richards.'

North pointed with her handful of notes at Richards.

'Good, I want you to get over to the Howarth Estate straight away. The mother's Anita Harris, aged thirty-four. She's pregnant, by the way – four months gone, she tells me. And there's a toddler, two years old and a boy, Jason, nine.'

Donaldson was frowning over his papers. 'Who's this Peter James?'

'Live-in boyfriend,' said North. 'Aged twenty-seven and unemployed – then again, down there who isn't?'

'Record?'

'We're checking the computer now. I've got a few more details on Anita. She was previously married to a Thomas Harris, divorced three years ago. He's in the army reserves in Ireland.' She looked up. 'Thomas Harris is the little girl's father. We have no reason to suspect he's anywhere but in Ireland as I speak, but we're checking on that too.'

A low buzz of conversation and speculation had begun in the room. North raised her voice.

'She's been missing five hours already, so let's get going.'

The officers began to leave the incident room in twos and threes. North called Sergeant Donaldson over.

'One thing I want to do right away – check on any residents with previous.'

Donaldson gave a sardonic laugh. 'That's half the estate.'

'Specifically sex offenders.'

'That's *still* half the estate – joke . . .' He held up his palms. 'Just a joke! But that place is a nightmare.'

'Don't remind me,' said North grimly. 'I was there less than an hour ago, remember? But at this moment it's Mrs Harris's nightmare and we've got to sort it for her.'

'What d'you make of the family? Flat a tip?'

The DI shook her head. 'No, *not* a tip. Very far from it. She's houseproud. Everything's clean, place smells of furniture polish, all the surfaces are wiped, carpets hoovered, beds made. She's not a slut.'

'Got a job?'

'No, housewife. And she *likes* the Her Indoors bit. But the second thing is – there's money coming in. New appliances, lots of videos and toys, good carpets, children

22

neatly turned out. Boyfriend looks a bit of a scruff but that's just him.'

'Where's it coming from? Chummy's on the dole.'

North shrugged. 'Needn't be more sinister than he's moonlighting. Plus her ex is in the army. He's probably generous with maintenance. It all adds up, and she's careful, no question. But there *is* one thing about that family which doesn't quite fit the Bisto commercial.'

'Oh?'

She strolled across towards the picture of Julie Harris, Blu-Tacked to the laminated board. 'It's the older kid, Jason. He's a tearaway, yeah?'

'What is he, eight?'

'Nine. And the point is, I saw his arms.'

'You saw his arms? Christ, Pat, not needle marks?'

North turned and grimaced at Donaldson. 'No, you berk, *bruises*. And, in my professional opinion, somebody's beating those kids up.'

CHAPTER 3

THURSDAY 5 SEPTEMBER. AFTERNOON

THE HOWARTH ESTATE was built in the 1960s on the wave of the nation's desire to be shot of old terraced slums and get as fast as possible into modern tower blocks.

The Howarth had two such towers, each of twenty storeys. They were made from prefabricated concrete sections bolted to a Meccano-like steel structure and clad in roughcast and plate-glass framed in aluminium. Their position overlooking the children's playground was deliberate. The architect's fancy was that the towers were two parents, standing guard over their children's play. Beyond the playground was a row of lock-up garages and, alongside these, a parade of shops. The shops, too, were an important part of the original scheme. At one end the local pub had been the pride of the East End's largest brewery chain, designed to serve ploughman's lunches and chicken-in-the-basket along with the beer. The shops, too, had seemed to offer variety – a Co-op food market, fishmonger, Post Office, children's clothes shop, bakery, hardware store, launderette, hairdresser.

But the Howarth Estate represented something more even than that. In the East End of thirty-five years ago, still with brick and slate back-to-backs by the square mile,

24

this was modern and it came packaged with a vision of the new good life, free of poverty, crime and ugliness. In this urban utopia the young could raise their families and the old live on in apple-cheeked sufficiency.

But history played a cruel trick on the Howarth: the vision was shown up as a delusion. In the era of glue sniffing and junk food, of daytime TV, catalogue shopping and snuff horror, it soon fell victim to poverty and human isolation.

Meg Richards noted the signs of degradation all around as she drove with PC Phelps on to the estate. Everywhere the concrete was stained and graffiti-painted, the hallways and stairs smelled of excreta and most of the shops were gone. The Co-op, its windows boarded up, was a low-grade carpet warehouse and all that remained of the others was the heavily fortified launderette, about-to-close Post Office, dodgy betting shop, off-licence and an Indian newsagent with a sideline in video rental. At the pub, if you asked for food, they threw a bag of crisps at you. The two towers, the lock-ups, the shopping parade were all earmarked for demolition. No one could say just when, or how, it had all gone wrong.

The Detective Inspector's instructions to the Family Liaison Officer hadn't been too specific – 'Get over to the estate' – but DC Richards knew what was expected of her. This was to play the sympathetic ear but also to open a line of communication, relay any necessary information to the home and bring back to the station her own assessment of that home. Most serious crimes – assaults, murders – happen within families and it has been known for a result to be gained from the work of the FLO alone.

As she entered the Harris flat she was struck by the essential decency of the place, at such odds with the surrounding environment. Now, as Anita painstakingly poured her a cup of tea, she noted the pristine tea service, the bowl of lump sugar, the milk in a jug.

'I keep going over and over everything,' the mother was saying. 'I keep seeing her in the yard. She's no trouble, never any trouble, not really. And she's friendly, you know? Very friendly.'

She put the tea pot down and dragged a wisp of hair back behind her ear.

'But of course, she knows not to go with strangers. We've told her I don't know how many times.'

The toddler was sitting on the floor screaming and the older boy, Jason, was shouting at him, his mouth right up to his ear: '*Shutup! Shutup! Shutup!*'

Richards sipped her tea, trying to block out the noise. 'And you don't think Julie's gone to the house of a friend or neighbour?'

'I've called round to everyone she knows. Now everyone on the estate's helping look for her. They're all so kind. They *will* find her, won't they? Do *you* think they'll find her? I mean, she could just have crawled into some place, got trapped or something. She's ever so inquisitive. Bit naughty like that, really.'

'Mrs Harris, we have uniformed officers doing house-to-house inquiries right now. In no time they'll have covered every single household on the estate and if we don't find her we'll move on to the surrounding area. We also have a large search team on its way, but there's every chance we'll find her even before they turn up.'

Four floors above the Harris's PCs Brown and Barridge were knocking on the doors of two adjoining flats. Each

26

had a copy of the electoral register but, as far as Howarth Estate was concerned, this seemed to be a largely fictional document. It was Brown who had the quicker response.

'Excuse me, Mrs—?'

'Yes? What's it about?'

'There's a missing child, Julie Ann Harris. Five years old, lives on the third floor.'

'I know her.'

'She was last seen this morning. I—'

'She was last seen by *me*. With my Ryan and some other kids playing on the roundabout.'

'When would that be, exactly?'

'Be about lunchtime.'

'Do you know the *exact* time at all?'

The woman still hadn't opened the door more than a crack. Brown could see that she had not unlatched the safety chain.

'Well, one-ish. I was getting my kids in for their lunch. That good enough for you?'

'And your name, madam?'

'Hyam. Karen Hyam. But you ask Ivy, my next-door neighbour, about that pervert – what's his name? Well, *some* people reckon he's a pervert. She's had words with him before now about him and the kids and that . . .'

But Barridge hadn't needed prompting. He was already prising the information from a mock-reluctant Mrs Green in the doorway of her flat.

'There's this bloke, see?' she was saying. 'Real alkie he is. And he's always messing about with the kids, know what I mean?'

'No. What *do* you mean?'

'I mean he gives them sweets. They go in there, watch his videos. Cartoons apparently.'

'He live locally?'

'Oh, yes.'

Barridge sighed, writing. 'Name and address?'

'Ivy Green, Flat number—'

Barridge held up his hand and coughed discreetly. 'No, I've got yours, Mrs Green. What's *his* name and address?'

'Oh! One of those ground-floor flats, down behind the shops. Howarth Parade, number twelve I think it is. Anyway, his name's Michael Dunn.'

Barridge was still scribbling in his notebook when Ivy Green touched him lightly on the forearm.

'I don't want *my* name mentioned, though. I don't actually *know* anything, know what I mean? I can't make a statement or nothing.'

Barridge nodded sagely. 'I understand, madam, but your help is much appreciated.'

On the next floor down, Brown was having one door slammed in his face whilst Barridge became Enid Marsh's second visitor of the day.

'Good evening, Mrs, er . . .?'

'Yes?'

'I am Constable Barridge, Southampton Street police. We're doing a flat-to-flat inquiry about a little girl missing from number nineteen on the third floor. Julie Ann Harris?'

Like most of the people Barridge had spoken to since he got here, Enid had opened the door with the safety chain in place. She peered anxiously at him through the crack, shaking her head. 'I don't know anybody here.'

Barridge placed a hand reassuringly on the door frame. 'But your balcony looks over the playground, doesn't it? Did you see anything at all today? About lunchtime?'

28

Enid froze for a moment. She was concentrating. Her memory . . . Then she shook her head, even more vigorously. 'Lunchtime? Mrs Wald was late. Late with my lunch.'

'Could I just have your name?'

'What do you want to know about me for?'

'Just to eliminate you from our inquiries . . .' He noticed the old lady stiffen, as if about to slam the door on him. 'I mean, to note down that we asked you a few questions, that's all. Are you, er . . .?' He squinted at the electoral roll. 'Are you Mrs Edith Shaw?'

'I'm Mrs Enid Marsh. I'm seventy-eight years old and I've lived here for . . .'

'Well, that's all I need, love. Thank you for your cooperation and I'm sorry to bother you. Thanks for your time.'

Brown wandered up to him. 'That's my lot for this floor. Electoral register's crap for this job. I've not got a resident off it yet. Any joy with you?'

Barridge shook his head. 'Nope. All dodging bloody council tax!'

Julie Ann Harris had now been missing for nine hours. The atmosphere in the Incident Room had grown more serious and urgent. Pat North's team were, almost imperceptibly, putting aside the innocent reasons for the child's disappearance and focusing on all the possible criminal explanations.

At nine p.m. Pat North conferred with Donaldson in the incident room.

'Are there any more addresses for uniform to check?'

'There's a few we couldn't get access to. But, by now, everyone up there knows she's missing, so those who don't cooperate can be treated as suspects.'

'I hope not formally,' warned North. 'Please, *please*, don't tell me you want warrants at this time of night.'

'No, don't worry. But telling 'em don't half scare them shitless.'

The DI and her sergeant laughed.

'Anyway, it doesn't really matter,' she said. 'For tonight we're going to assume she's outside somewhere. TSG and POLSA will be arriving on site about now. Might even have started covering the ground. It's pissing down but they're used to that.'

'Well, while we're on the subject of suspects . . .'

North snapped her fingers. 'Oh yes, *suspects*. I can't tell you how much trouble we've had over the father. He started whirling round in my head the minute we knew she hadn't popped round to watch a neighbour's videos.'

'What's been the problem? Wait a minute, don't tell me – army liaison?'

'You've got it. You wouldn't believe how cagey they are. In the end I got someone I know in the RUC to chase him up for me.'

'And?'

'Well, it seems that Thomas Harris – that is this little girl's real father – is in the clear. He's in Ireland with his regiment.'

Donaldson could tell she was disappointed. For Julie Harris to have been kidnapped by a father who loved her, however jealously, was preferable to almost all the other remaining possibilities. He said, 'About Peter James.'

'Oh yes. What you got?'

'He's on probation for – wait for it – handling stolen

30

bricks. Probably nicked them off that massive building site on the estate. Also he's got two previous and . . .' He paused for effect.

'Well? And what?'

'He was arrested in eighty-nine for indecent assault. Charge dropped.'

North's face tightened. She picked up her bag.

'Go and question Peter James. I'm going down to the search.'

It was Meg Richards who opened the door to Sergeant Donaldson. She had stayed in the flat answering the phone and trying to remain discreetly useful without entirely surrendering her dignity as a member of the Metropolitan Police investigating this serious disappearance. Tony had been very unsettled and she'd eventually picked him up and jiggled him about until he went to sleep. He was still slumped in her arms, his mouth jammed into her shoulder, drooling in his sleep.

'Hi, Meg,' said Donaldson. 'Peter James here?'

'Yes, just come in.'

'I got to have a word.'

'Must you?' whispered Richards. 'He's been trying to help with the search but he's knackered.'

Donaldson looked at her in surprise. 'Yes, I got to. DI North says.'

'Oh, all right. He's in the kitchen.' She stepped aside to let Donaldson move towards the kitchen.

As he did so he whispered, 'Proper little earth mother, you!'

Richards didn't react. She could hear Anita's voice from the lounge.

31

'Jason, what did I say? Get to *bed*!'

Before Richards could leave the hall the doorbell rang and she opened it again. A dark-haired, comfortable looking woman of about fifty stood there shaking out an umbrella. A small suitcase stood beside her.

'Yes?' enquired Richards.

'Oh, hello!' The woman's voice was hesitant, trembly as she went on. 'Are you one of the neighbours?'

'No, I'm a police officer, DC Richards, Southampton Street. Can I help?'

'Oh, I see. I'm Mrs Hughes – Helen. The little girl's gran?'

'Oh, Mrs Hughes, of course.' Richards stood to one side, swinging back the door. 'Please, come in. Let me take your case.'

Mrs Hughes ignored the hand which Meg had extended to take the case, and parked it in the small hall, propping her dripping umbrella against it.

'I came as quick as I could. Is there any news?'

'None. I'm sorry. We're still looking.'

'Yes, I saw the search party out there. Awful weather they've got, too. How's the boys? I see that one's taken to you. What about Jason?'

'He's asleep, or going to sleep anyway.'

'Those are two very different things to that boy. *Anita*? It's *me*.'

She pattered into the lounge where her daughter was standing alone and in a kind of daze. She turned slowly, her face sparking in recognition as her mother came in. Helen opened her arms and Anita walked gratefully into the hug.

'Oh, Mum. She's going to be all right, isn't she?'

The mother patted her daughter's back. 'Sssh. We've

32

got to stay calm and think if there's any place, or anyone, she might've gone to.'

Helen moved a step back from the embrace and held Anita by the shoulders, looking intently into her face. It was just what she used to do years before, when she sent Anita off to school. A single hair had come loose and was hanging down over Anita's face. Helen brushed it back with her fingers.

'They got a nice woman looking after Tony, anyway. And Jason – he's asleep?'

Anita made her hands into fists. 'I'd like to wring his bloody neck! It's his fault, Mum. I said to him, Jason, look out for Julie. Never listens to a word you tell him. Never.'

'You're going to make yourself ill, love. Try not to worry.' She nodded at Anita's swollen belly. 'And you don't want to start hurting the baby, now, do you?'

'But Julie, Mum ... *She's* my baby too. Oh God, please, don't let anything have happened to her! Please!'

There was an efficient tap on the door and Meg came in with a tray. More tea. Anita swung round.

'Where's Peter? He still outside looking?'

Richards smiled and placed the tray on the low coffee table.

'No, he's here. Just talking to Sergeant Donaldson in the kitchen. Mrs Hughes – some tea?'

Helen's mouth was crumpled, a film of tears beginning to form over her eyes. She shook her head, as if she hadn't properly understood the question.

In the kitchen Peter James and Donaldson were facing each other across the small formica tabletop. The Sergeant was stirring three sugars into his mug of tea. He had his notebook open in front of him. Peter was slumped forward on his elbows. His head with its lanky unwashed hair hung down.

'I've said all this,' he mumbled. 'How many times do I have to repeat it?'

Suddenly he jerked his head up and nodded at the window. 'I should be out *there*.'

'Come on, son,' said Donaldson. 'You've been out there all afternoon. Mrs Harris is going to need you here, you know.'

'Why?' demanded the young man. He was agitating his head frantically up and down as his eyes challenged Donaldson. 'Why did you say that, that she's *going to* need me? Do you know something?'

Donaldson shook his head slowly. 'You know we don't. But there's fifty men out there searching already . . .'

'I don't understand why everybody keeps making me go over and over it.'

Donaldson used this as a cue to pick up his notebook and study it.

'Now you said there was an ice-cream van . . .'

'Yes!' Peter was being overtly aggressive now. He didn't like coppers at the best of times. 'I went up to him, asked if he'd seen Julie.' He shut his eyes and jammed the heels of his hands against the closed lids. 'That's another thing. Everybody keeps on calling her Julie Ann. It's not. Ann was her second name. We just call her Julie.'

Donaldson was still staring at the notes he had made. He cleared his throat. 'It's just that we're trying to pinpoint the last time she was seen.'

Peter shook out a cigarette from the packet which lay

34

in front of him. 'One o'clock. I told you . . .' He leaned back in his chair and was rummaging in his jeans pocket. 'One o'clock,' he said. 'That's . . . *how* long ago is that?'

He pulled a butane lighter from his pocket, flicked the flame and applied it to the cigarette, inhaling viciously. 'What time is it? What time is it *now*?'

Donaldson glanced at his watch. 'Just gone half ten, Peter.'

'Ten hours . . . Nine and a half *fucking hours*!'

In the living room, Helen had switched on the television. There was a comedy on BBC 1, but you couldn't watch that, so she'd switched to the national news on ITV. She sat with her daughter on the sofa and watched it through to the 'and finally' and Trevor MacDonald's goodnight. Neither woman had taken much in but there was relief in the numbness of watching that rapidly moving screen, flipping from one bland political interview about the Berringham by-election to the next, from one remote foreign conflict to another – Chechnya in flames, American presidential candidates on the stump, a football team unexpectedly losing.

During the adverts the telephone rang. It was Thomas Harris, calling from Northern Ireland. Helen took the call. She liked Tom and had never blamed him for the break-up of his marriage to her daughter. He wanted to know what the hell was going on. He wanted to know if they'd found his daughter. He wanted to speak to Anita. But when Helen looked across at Anita she saw her face white and rigid with shock as she stared at the television screen. Helen herself looked at the screen and understood why.

'Tom,' she said as calmly as she could, 'Anita can't talk right now . . . Look, I've got to go. I'll call you back as soon as something . . . Soon as I can . . . All right. Bye.'

She hung up and moved back to the sofa. The programme was the local London news bulletin *London Tonight*. The first story was Julie.

Detective Inspector North was standing on the steps of her police station. You could see the traditional blue police light above her head, artfully placed in shot by the cameraman. A knot of journalists was jostling around her.

She was saying, 'Julie Ann is wearing a green pleated skirt with a blue and red anorak and she has curly blonde shoulder-length hair. She has blue eyes. We are asking anyone who has any information at all to contact either the Incident Room at this station or any police station. The number is . . .'

Anita and her mother looked at each other. Neither spoke for a long time. Then Helen reached for the remote control unit and switched off the set.

'Mum.' Anita's voice was a whisper. 'Mum, she said *is*. Julie *is* five years old, Julie *is* wearing an anorak . . .'

Helen took Anita's hand and carefully stroked the back of it, as you might reassure a frightened cat.

'I know, love. I know she did. Got to hang on to that, right?'

CHAPTER 4

THURSDAY 5 SEPTEMBER. NIGHT

FIVE VANLOADS of TSG officers had arrived, with a catering unit and a pair of motorized telescopic masts mounted with arc lights. Their powerful beams shone down from sixty feet, making the raindrops glitter like tracer bullets. And above these, the area helicopter circled, directing its own searchlights downwards through the sousing cloudburst. Every officer on the ground had a personal radio and a constant traffic of radio signals crackled on the air.

Using the classic method whereby a large stretch of ground is meticulously combed, the area around the Howarth Estate had been subdivided into a grid and seven search parties, with seven officers in each, were formed. Togged up for the driving rain in rubber boots and Gortex jackets and equipped with powerful torches, crowbars, probes and other tools, these parties were now patiently trudging in lines across the ground allotted to them, marking the terrain section by section as they went with plastic yellow tape and a waxy yellow waterproof crayon.

Barridge was with the other locals. They'd been formed into a single search party under PC Phelps and detailed to cover one of several demolition and building sites scattered around the area. In spite of the foul weather conditions, he felt excited. He was like a kid, a Cub Scout taking part in a field game. He hadn't really thought about the purpose of the search or what would happen if and when something was found. Barridge was that kind of officer. Enthusiasm, he had it to spare, but all too often he'd throw himself into an action without looking to see where it might lead or what it meant. As far as he was concerned, policing didn't feel too different from his kiddy days in Scouts – with added fast cars screaming up and down Victoria Dock Road on a Saturday night. Like every young policeman, he loved the fast cars. He also loved the rugby, the martial arts, the swimming galas. The slow, meticulous side of the job was not high on his list of favourite things.

He was paired with PC Marik tonight. They were in a half demolished building when all of a sudden Barridge found the rubble slipping away from under his boots. For a brief moment he was sliding downwards as his footing simply disappeared beneath him.

'Jesus Christ!'

He lurched sideways and immediately his hip and elbow found solidity and he came to rest. But his legs were dangling into empty space.

'There's a bloody great hole here! I nearly fell in.'

Marik shone his torch. Half concealed by a sheet of corrugated iron was an opening in the ground. He could see steps descending below Barridge's feet.

'Some kind of cellar. You all right?'

'Yeah, I reckon.'

Barridge scrambled up and directed his own torch beam into the hole. Stone steps, damp and slippery with lichens, descended into the earth. Gingerly he probed with his feet but realized the aperture was not big enough for him. He came out and both men grasped the corrugated iron and pulled hard. At first the sheet stuck, then slid free. As they tossed it aside, a small avalanche of bricks and rubble bounced into the hole. They heard it plopping and splashing into deep water. Edging down the steps they shone their torches into the now fully revealed cellar.

'Oh, shit,' said Barridge. 'It's flooded.'

It also stank of oil mixed with organic decay. Marik played his torch over the surface of the water, liquorice-black except where a patch of petrol showed up in rainbow colours. A few items of flotsam could be seen – a plastic bottle, a shoe, a shapeless bloated mass of fur which Marik prodded with his toe. It rolled in the water and the remains of a small face turned up to them – empty eye-sockets and grinning, pinlike teeth. Marik gagged.

'Oh, God, it's a dead cat. Get me out of here.'

They hustled back up the steps and out into the clean rain, sucking in air. At this moment Henshaw appeared in the broken doorway of the house.

'Found anything?'

'Cellar, flooded. Could be something in there. We're going to need some equipment. You two stick around and I'll go and ask.'

Barridge stumbled past Henshaw and went in search of Phelps, who was with PC Brown examining the contents of a skip.

Barridge ran up to report. 'We need waterproofs. The cellars are flooded and they stink.'

Phelps had been in the job five years longer than Barridge. The kid was an innocent and Phelps enjoyed winding him up.

'First on the scene were you, Barridge?'

'Cellars? Yeah.'

'Well, finders get wet, son. That's the rule. Go back and stop wasting time.' He snorted. 'Waterproofs indeed!'

Barridge turned and started to trudge back as Brown came round from the other side of the skip.

'Hey, don't be a bastard. Oi, Barridge!'

Barridge turned and Brown pointed in the direction of the distant arc lights. 'There's a TSG van parked on the edge of the estate. They're handing out the gear.'

He saw Barridge change direction with a cheerful wave of his hand. He was a good-natured lad, you could say that for him.

Many of the Howarth residents wished to play some part in the drama that had seized their community, even if only that of idle spectators. So, despite the rain and the late hour, a number had drifted out in their parkas, macs and plastic hats. The TSG's tea van, known to the policemen as Teapot One, proved an irresistible draw and now a knot of locals were standing around chewing on free sandwiches, sipping from styrofoam cups and speculating about the outcome of the search.

Among them were Ron Hall, and the two friends, Ivy Green and Karen Hyam, from the seventh floor.

'We had a kid missing before, remember? About five years back.'

'Oh, yes,' said Karen. 'That MacKenzie girl. But that was different, she was—'

'She's been brought back four times, that one, bloody little tart.'

'Yes, but she was fourteen. This one's only five.'

Ivy was remembering her exchange with that nice-looking constable. 'First place I'd look is that wino's flat.'

'Which wino?'

'You know – on the parade! Disgusting pervert, he is.'

Karen tapped her on the sleeve. 'And you tell me how *he* gets a council house and d'you know, my sister with two kids has been on the waiting list nearly three years.'

'That's terrible,' said Ivy, clicking her tongue. 'Mind you she wouldn't want his place, it's a tip.'

'I told her, I said she should ditch her husband, then she'd get one.'

'S'cuse me, ladies!' Having obtained a sweet tea and a cheese and pickle sandwich from the counter, Sergeant Donaldson was sidling through the group of residents. He spotted Phelps a few yards away, warming his hands on a cup of tomato soup.

'You'd think that lot'd give us a hand,' muttered Phelps. 'All they're doing is cadging drinks and sandwiches.'

'That kind of help's more trouble than it's worth. Should leave it to the professionals.'

Phelps laughed. 'Not short of advice, though, are they? Uh-oh. Here comes another one.'

Ivy Green was approaching, with Karen and Ron in close attendance. She spoke loudly, as if addressing them from a soapbox.

'You checked that corner flat on Howarth Parade? If you ain't, you should. Be the first place I'd look. He's a drunk.'

Brown appeared as Donaldson bent his ear towards Ivy.

'Corner house, Mrs, er—? What number would that be?'

'Twelve, I think. Proper pervert he is in there.'

41

'Have we checked that one out yet, Skip?' asked Brown.

Donaldson consulted a clipboard. It was covered with a plastic sheet and the rain snapped down on it. He ran his index finger down a list of names and addresses. 'Number twelve. Name of . . . Michael Dunn.'

'That's him,' said Ivy. 'I've told my kids to stay well clear of that animal. He's always messing with them, he is.'

Donaldson glanced at Brown and then back at Ivy. He was interested.

'*Is* he now? And we *haven't* yet checked him out, so it seems.'

Barridge had picked up a rope and some chest-high waders from TSG. When he got back to the cellar, Marik and Henshaw had gone.

He found them placing yellow tape around a stack of sewage pipes to show that they'd been cleared. Henshaw had just finished shining his torch into them. The ground all around was a morass of liquid mud.

'Come on,' said Barridge. 'We have to do that cellar. I got the rope and waders but I need back-up.'

'Leave it,' said Henshaw. 'We looked didn't we? Me and Marik had another shufti after you scarpered. There was nothing.'

'There was a shoe, floating. I saw it.'

'Since when did little Julie Ann take a man's size twelves? Since her fifth birthday?'

'It could still be significant. And anyway we got to look in the water, not just on top of it.'

42

'Needs a diver. One of them POLSA heroes should do that.'

Barridge started walking back to the cellar. 'What's the matter with you two? Finder gets wet – that's me. All you custard creams got to do is hold my string.'

Minutes later, now wadered up and wearing a rope around his waist which Henshaw and Marik paid out above him, Barridge was again cautiously descending the cellar steps. He reached the water's edge and tested the depth with a scaled wooden pole: three foot six inches. The stairs descended another six steps below the water-line. He planted a foot on the next one down, tested it, then transferred the other foot as well. Now standing in seven inches of water, he shone his torch into the interior of the cellar. Several things back there, which had not been visible from his previous position, now appeared. They were floating, half submerged, one of them looked like a basketball, red – no, red and blue. He took another step down, craning forward to see better. There was also a pop bottle and part of what might be a chair sticking out of the stinking water.

'*Shit!*'

A gush of liquid had flowed into his boot through a gash in the rubber. It was cold and, as he knew, absolutely filthy. He tried to lift his foot clear but, full to the brim, it was unexpectedly heavy. He wobbled.

Had Marik been keeping the safety line taut Barridge might still have been saved but it lay slackly on the cellar steps. Overbalancing with a theatrical wave of his arms, and with his mouth open to yell, he pitched sideways into the flooded cellar. Briefly the water closed over him. He kicked and flapped and surfaced, ejecting the oily,

43

brackish mouthful he'd taken in. Even before he'd found a foothold he was yelling.

'Bloody hell! Give me some light!'

His head bumped painfully into something floating on the water. It was his torch, which had gone out. He grasped it, working the switch. Dead as a kipper.

Meanwhile, somewhere above him in the dark, Marik was shouting, 'You all right?'

'Bloody get me out!'

As he thrashed around he realized Marik and Henshaw were hooting with laughter.

'Got your twenty-five yards badge, Barridge?'

'You been bitten by that dead cat or what?'

'Shut it you two! Just give me some *light*! It's freezing and I think I've swallowed some of this bastard water.'

'You'll definitely be needing a stomach-pump, then,' Henshaw managed to say between fits of laughter. They stopped laughing as they saw the terror in Barridge's face as he lost his footing again and went beneath the water. When his head burst to the surface from the stinking black water, his eyes were stark with terror.

'For fuck's sake, pull me *out*!'

Howarth Parade was where Anita Harris had looked vainly for her daughter at the Collins' place the previous afternoon. Number twelve was one of the same small ground-floor flats that had been built along the back of the parade of shops. Originally, each had had its own mini-patch of garden in front, an area now universally reduced to urban wasteground. The garden in front of Michael Dunn's address had been turned at some unspecified time into a dump for useless motorbike parts. Part of his front window was boarded up.

The flat was in total darkness. Donaldson stood back and watched Phelps hammering on the door. Brown was shining his torch in through the unboarded part of the window.

'Mr Dunn! Mr Dunn!' Phelps called, crouching to shine his torch through the letter slot. The flat remained dark and soundless. Phelps straightened up and looked back at the Skipper.

'It doesn't look as if anyone's at home.'

Donaldson shook his head. Dunn was beginning to interest him.

'That doesn't mean he's not there, does it? But there's nothing we can do if he won't open up. If he's as much of a piss artist as they say he might be sleeping it off. Now I think I'll go over to the Harris's place and see what they know about this Michael Dunn.'

The Harrises didn't know much about Michael Dunn but despite Richards's presence and Sergeant Donaldson's skilful exercise of tact, an atmosphere of untargeted hostility was building up on the third floor.

'Look,' Helen was saying, 'has this Dunn man got our Julie? Is that what you're saying?'

'No,' said Donaldson. 'I was just *asking* if Julie Anne knew him.'

Peter got up and advanced on the policeman. He pushed his face almost into Donaldson's face.

'*Julie*! Her name is *Julie*! Not Julie Anne! And I've had enough. I'm not staying in here, I'm going out. And you can't stop me.'

45

'No,' said Donaldson simply, 'we can't, Mr James. But it really is better for your wife that you stay here.'

But Peter had already pushed past him. In the hall he swept his coat from a hook. Anita caught her breath, as if hit by a twinge of pain.

'I want to go with him! Peter, wait, I'm coming too.'

Meg stepped forward but as she did so, caught Donaldson's eye. He gave a minute shake of the head and Meg stayed where she was as Anita half ran into the hall. They all stood still as the flat door slammed. There was a pause, followed by a hammering on the door. It was Anita.

'Just get *out* of there! All of you. Leave us alone!'

Paul Donaldson and Meg Richards exchanged another glance as the sergeant picked up his cap.

'I think,' he said quietly, moving towards the door, 'that we're going to have trouble with him.'

Barridge was in the TSG van, peeling off the wet overalls so when she looked in to ask what had happened Pat North found him sitting shivering with a towel around his waist.

'Oh! Sorry, Barridge.'

She looked to see if he was embarrassed but Barridge seemed more exhausted than anything else. So she came in.

'You all right? I hear you had a tumble.'

He nodded as her radio squawked.

'Ma'am? Some of the residents, they're talking about a Michael Dunn. You know?'

'Yes, I heard. Don't worry, he's being checked out.'

She was listening to the radio. Pat North felt tired too. This was a big operation – fifty-strong TSG party, POLSA

46

macho-men running around on the docks in inflatable boats and wet suits, estate residents up in arms. If she screwed up she couldn't expect any sympathy from the Super.

Tactfully she turned her back, occupying herself with her radio as Barridge pulled on some trousers. The Control Van was relaying a message from the chopper about Howarth Parade. Barridge continued.

'It's just that the winos from round here – they either hole up in one of the derelict houses if it's bad weather, or there's a park and like a gent's toilet. They meet up there, just across from the Job Centre.' He pulled on a sweater. 'Anyway, as this is Thursday, they'll have got their Giros, so . . .'

'Was Thursday. It's Friday now.' She spoke into the radio. 'OK . . . On my way. Over.'

She turned back to Barridge. He was decent. She said, 'We've got a crowd forming on Howarth Parade. Better go.'

She left Barridge feeling unsatisfied. He hadn't explained his thinking at all well. What he meant to say was that, if Dunn was really a wino, they should interview a few of the other people he hung around with, and that they'd maybe have taken shelter somewhere in one of the derelict places nearby. TSG had probably turned some of them up already.

Outside number twelve Howarth Parade a small mob had been gathering for some time as a growing number of residents converged on the place. Phelps and Brown stood guard in front of the door. The mood of the residents, as soon as they had begun to connect the scruffy toe-rag

Dunn with the disappearance of the golden-haired child, had turned ugly.

Peter James stood at the front, taunting the grim-faced officers. 'Break down the sodding door! What you waiting for?'

Other shouts were directed at Dunn himself. 'Bleedin' *nonce*. Where's little Julie? What you done with her, you bastard?'

Meanwhile three or four in the middle of the crowd began to chant, '*Break* the door! Smash it *in*! Break the bastard's fucking *chin*!'

They must have been the outflow from the pub: there was a noticeable slur in their voices. Donaldson arrived to the sound of their refrain, noticing that Julie's mother was standing at the back of the pack, weeping. A neighbour – the woman he recalled who'd first mentioned Dunn's name to the police – was trying awkwardly to hug her. A few seconds later Pat North joined her sergeant and together they forced their way to where the two constables were looking increasingly nervous.

A half brick bounced off the wall of the flat. Donaldson took PC Brown's elbow and pointed to Peter James.

'That's the kid's stepfather. Get him out of here, right?'

As Brown went to tackle Peter, Pat North said to the sergeant, 'What we got on Michael Dunn? You checked his sheet?'

'Yeah. Nothing apart from persistent vagrancy.'

She glanced again at the angry residents as another brick hurtled towards the flat. 'Well . . . They're throwing bricks. So that gives us a bloody good reason to check this flat – for damage?'

Donaldson looked at his guvnor and smiled. For once a modicum of public disorder was exactly what the police required. It would mean they could effect an entry to the premises without a warrant.

'Well,' he said, 'it's been over twelve hours now so maybe . . .'

'We're looking for a body, aren't we?'

'Right!'

That added up to two possible pretexts to enter the Dunn house without a warrant. The decision was down to Pat North. She hesitated, weighing up what the Super would say. Again a brick spun through the air and clattered against the plywood screwed to Michael Dunn's window frame.

Donaldson said, gently, 'Well, guv? What do we do?'

Pat snapped her fingers. 'All right, do it. Break down the door.'

It was Phelps who sprinted to the equipment van and collected a sledgehammer. When he returned three blows against the lock sufficed to crash through the door. Pat North led Donaldson into the dark interior, with Phelps bringing up the rear. He still held the hammer, as if believing it may come in useful again.

The hall was littered with bottles, boxes, cans and dirty clothes. Broken glass crunched underfoot.

'God,' said the sergeant, 'the place stinks.'

Moving gingerly forward Pat North called into the darkness: 'Mr Dunn! Michael Dunn! This is the police. Is anybody here?'

She paused, waiting for a reply, listening for movement, snoring, a television set, anything. There was nothing. She looked to her left and right and found a lightswitch. She flipped it down. Nothing happened.

'Electric's off. We're in the dark. Phelps, go and get some torches from TSG and in the meantime lend me yours.'

With a barely suppressed sigh, PC Phelps handed her his standard-issue torch and doubled back for his second visit to the equipment vehicle. Pat North shone the torch ahead. There were four doors leading off the hall. She entered the first on the left.

The dank smell of Dunn's sitting room was enhanced by a mixture of stale beer, vinegary wine and tobacco ash. The torch picked out tattered curtains hanging drunkenly over the boarded-up windows, a broken-springed and lopsided sofa, a television set piled with video tapes, a morass of bottles, cartons and takeaway containers strewn about the filthy carpet.

'Don't touch anything!' warned Pat North as Donaldson, wading into the room, crouched to examine the video titles.

'Hmm. Local rental shop might be missing a few videos. Here we have *Die Hard 1*, *Snow White*, *Die Hard 2* and . . . hello-hello, what's these?'

He peered more closely. '*Aladdin*, *Lion King*, *My Little Pony*, *Child's Play*. *Child's Play!* – oh my God.'

Pat North kicked a Corn Flakes' packet that was lying at her feet.

'Well, we can get him on theft. I doubt he's rented all that lot. And, talking of child's play, what do you make of this?'

She was standing beside the sofa, the beam of her torch directed downwards at a blonde Barbie doll lying on the bare and greasy upholstery. She wore only her underwear and one of her arms was missing.

50

CHAPTER 5

FRIDAY 6 SEPTEMBER

ANITA GOT up at five. For most of the night she'd lain awake staring at the curtained window. Tomorrow, wash day. No orange juice in the fridge and the milk's off. Got to fit in a supermarket shop. Jason needs new shoes for school. Julie's supposed to have that eye-test the Nursery thought she needs. Better cancel. No way she'll be able to go after staying out all night. That teething gel for Tony she'd been looking for yesterday – be in that other handbag. She had it with her last time the two of them went to Mum's. Random, sluggish thoughts about anything but what happened yesterday.

There were a few lapses into sleep but these had been gashed by intense, violent fits of dreaming. She'd awoken each time hag-ridden, her heart pounding, sweat seeping from her armpits and scalp. The last dream had been of a car crash. The image was still vivid. A screeching tear of metal, a reek of scorched rubber, spattered oil, burning upholstery. And then the car – was it a car, a truck? – rolling over and plunging through a bare landscape of slag heaps towards a lake of still, black water. Bursting into consciousness, she had twisted towards Peter's side of the bed, desperate to hug him like a lifebelt. But Peter wasn't there.

She rolled from bed, pattered to the bathroom and sat to empty her bladder. Then, dodging the mirror, she scrubbed her teeth and filled the bath.

For half an hour she lay, listening to the bubbles snapping around her stomach rising above the foam like an island. This was the best way she knew to take her away from herself. Lying in an envelope of hot water, surrounded by steam, hissing taps, the smell of soap and laundered towels, she forgot the problems of a grown-up person and was transported back into the raw sensations of a child.

In general, her own childhood had receded to dimness after she became a mother. Wound up in the lives of her children, for their sakes acting the adult, Anita lost contact with the little girl she had once been. Occasionally she wondered if that little girl had survived anyway, inside her. If so, it was a child held hostage and hidden away. It wasn't coming out to play unless the world became a very different place.

If she was truthful with herself, Anita knew she had put away her child-self even before motherhood. She had done it quite deliberately. Leaving aside the usual things that mark the stages into adolescence – getting spots, smoking ciggies down on the allotment, the start of her periods – there was one day that she would remember as the end of childish things. The head teacher had come into her class in the middle of a lesson. He'd put on a long face especially for the occasion. He asked if Anita would please come out of the room and down to his office. Waiting there were Anita's year tutor, Mrs Morris, and the school nurse, who was hovering around in the secretary's room. The nurse being there was always a sign something dramatic had happened.

'I'm afraid I have some bad news to tell you, Anita,' said Mr Passmore at last, in his thin, precise voice. He had one hand up to his neck, nervously smoothing the wings of his spotted bow-tie. With a sound halfway between a squeak and a cough he forced some phlegm to the top of his throat.

'There is no way in which I can soften it for you, so I'm going to tell you straight out.' He had shot a nervous, uncertain glance at Mrs Morris who nodded encouragement. He continued. 'Your father's been in an accident. I'm sorry to say, he's been killed. Nobody knows yet what happened, but it appears he stepped into the path of a lorry.'

Compassion didn't come easily to Passmore. Disapproval was more in his line: how inconvenient of her father to get killed – worse, to do it in the middle of double maths. That was why he had Anita's year tutor at his elbow. Mrs Morris supplied the necessary; she did compassion brilliantly.

'We're so terribly sorry, Anita, dear. This is a tragedy, a real tragedy.'

There was a moistness about Mrs M's eyes that Anita might have found touching, except that nothing *could* touch her just then. She had just felt cold to her very bones.

Back in her bedroom Anita dressed mechanically and, coming back through the lounge, stepped out on to the balcony. A few spatters of light rain, the remnants of last night's downpour, flew around on the wind. She looked down. In the area below the tower block, the roundabout and climbing frames were deserted and silent. It was where she had last seen her daughter. Further away a few police vehicles – not so many as at the peak last night – could be seen in the dawn light. Julie had not been found, but nor had hope been abandoned. Anita had been told they'd go on searching all day.

'Hey!'

She turned. Peter stood just inside the room, still wearing his long overcoat. He had a look that Anita had never seen on his face before. It was a mixture of exhaustion and fear. Her own face must look just the same.

'Oh, Peter,' she said. 'I had such shitty dreams.'

She went to him and they hugged tightly.

He said, 'I've just come in for a coffee and a wash, then I'm going out again.'

She pulled back and took his face between her palms. 'You'll crack up, Peter. Then where will we be?'

He shook his head and there was a staring intensity in his eyes. 'I got to keep going. Don't see how I can stop at the moment.'

She shook her head and kissed him. 'No. I know.'

Pat North had hardly more sleep than Anita. At six-thirty she was back in the station belling AMIP – the Area Major Investigating Pool – to find out at what point they'd be grabbing the wheel.

Wanting to find out wasn't some chippy thing. North was aware of the score: AMIP was the murder squad. Anyway, she really could do with a hand, because already this inquiry had eaten up close to five hundred man hours and hardly seemed to have advanced since the off. They hadn't found Julie. They hadn't found anyone who'd seen her after twelve-thirty, when the group of mothers at the playground had drifted away to dish up their kids' lunches. They hadn't even managed to find a drunken piece of low-life called Michael Dunn. What was she doing wrong?

Back in the Incident Room she joined Sergeant Donaldson and PCs Brown and Phelps. The two constables had been on shift all night. They'd just come back from an early visit to the Howarth, having interviewed the newsagent as he opened up for the early trade. Yes, he remembered Peter James all right, coming in at about 1.15 the previous day looking for Julie, and then returning in the next half hour, all in a panic, to ask a second time. But, like he'd told Peter James on both occasions, the shopkeeper hadn't seen the little girl at all that day.

'So. Has anything useful come in on the phones, Skip?'

Donaldson waved a sheaf of forms – phone-messages to the incident room and faxes from other police stations around the capital. It was the sum of the general public's responses to last night's television news appeal, and they did not make Christian reading. Every one of the messages assumed that Julie Ann Harris had been abducted by a predatory paedophile. Most accepted that she was already dead. By no means all were phoning or faxing to express their sympathy.

'Just the usual sick bastards,' grunted the sergeant. 'Nothing to follow up as yet.'

'Well, I was just thinking – I've got to talk to the Press Office in a minute. So what about another TV appeal, this time by the family? Do you think they'd do it?'

''Course they will. Wouldn't you?'

North checked her watch. It was 7.10.

'I'll get Meg back up there to speak to the parents about it.'

But Donaldson was remembering Michael Dunn and the spin they'd given his flat in the middle of the night. 'Maybe she should ask them if Julie Ann had a doll with her as well, yeah?'

The DI nodded and, lowering her voice, she said for Donaldson's ears only, 'Not looking good, is it? I've contacted AMIP. They're not keen to come in on this unless and until we've got a body. So I've asked TSG to stay put and do the area all over again this morning. But we'll keep our lads after Dunn. While he's still AWOL he's got to be a suspect. Agreed?'

In the cramped Harris kitchen, Helen was feeding spoon-fuls of Weetabix into her youngest grandchild's mouth while Jason drove one of his screeching battery-powered battle machines up and down the kitchen table.

'That's it, my pet, here's another one. Open wide.'

Anita came in, depositing an empty mug in the sink. 'Peter's been out all night, he's exhausted but he says he'll keep on.'

The telephone rang and Anita jumped.

'It's all right, love,' said her mother. 'Meg's here. She'll get it – probably for her anyway.'

Anita came to the table. 'Here, Mum, let me. He does it better for me. Come on, Tony, love. Open your mouth, there's a good boy. Jason! I told you – stop that!'

Jason was adding to the noise of the toy with his own

56

high-pitched impression of a badly shot gearbox. Anita leaned over and swatted his head.

'Oi, Mum!' Jason stood rubbing his head for a moment, then darted forward, lifted his fist and dealt a painful, knuckly blow to Anita's arm. Something inside his mother snapped.

'Don't you do that to me, you little shit!'

Anita raised her hand again, higher this time. Jason flinched, then dodged out of the kitchen. He cannoned off Meg Richards as she entered.

'You all right, Anita?' asked the policewoman.

Anita sighed and, still standing beside the high chair, shoved another spoonful of milky mush into Tony's mouth. 'Yes, yes. Sometimes he can be a real handful. Misses his dad, of course . . .' She looked at Meg a moment, questioning. 'He phoned but I haven't spoken to him . . . Jason and Julie's dad, I mean. They *will* find her, won't they?'

Meg unslung her bag and sat down at the table.

'Don't lose hope. And why don't you just sit for a minute, eh? There's something I want to ask you.'

Anita slumped in the nearest chair. 'What?'

'Do you know if Julie had any – any kind of toy with her in the playground? A doll maybe?'

Anita stared at Meg. Toys? Dolls? What was the woman talking about? As soon as she thought it she gave up the effort of working out how these coppers' minds worked. She merely shook her head. She couldn't remember, anyway.

Dressed in fresh clothes from the bedroom, Peter appeared. Meg was glad he was here. She wasn't sure Anita was concentrating hard enough to give a considered answer to her next question.

'Peter,' asked Meg gently, 'would you be prepared to do a television appeal?'

Peter looked pleased to have been asked. He didn't pause to consider it. 'Me? Yeah, 'course.'

'Inspector North spoke on the local news last night, but she feels it'd be good to do an appeal. It would be broadcast about the time of day that Julie Ann – Julie – was last seen. And it'd be good if it came from . . . from the family.'

'Fine, Meg. No problem. We'll do whatever you people want – eh, love?'

He leaned over and squeezed Anita's hand.

Arriving in a smart, recently registered hatchback, the Scotland Yard Press Officer met Pat North at the main entrance of the tower block two hours later. Her clothes were maybe a touch flashy, her weight was a pound or three over the optimum, but there was no denying the great hair, the brilliantly applied make-up and the fantastic teeth. They flashed and flashed again as regular as a lighthouse.

'Hi,' she said, pumping North's hand briskly. 'Terrible traffic. This where they live?'

'Yes. Let's go straight up. What time is the press conference?'

'Twelve, at Scotland Yard.'

'Any other press action?'

'We contacted all the radio stations and breakfast TV shows overnight and there's been coverage in their morning bulletins. Also, there'll be a photo in the early editions of the *Standard*. Sadly, it's too late for this week's local rags. What are the family like?'

58

North gave her the facts as they climbed the stairs.

Later, sitting around the low table in the lounge, Anita and Peter were told what they would have to do.

'It's important that we keep it very simple,' said the Press Officer. 'Your little girl is missing. This is what she looks like. Anyone who knows anything, phone this number. Here, I've written out a possible script, something for you both to say. Would you like to try it?'

She drew a sheet of A4 from a file and passed it across. Anita's face was expressionless as she read it.

An hour later they were on their way to Scotland Yard, leaving Tony and Jason in the care of their grandmother.

'I remember, I remember, the house where I was born . . .'

Midge was trying to remember the rest of the poem. Matted pepper-and-salt hair dragged down to the collar of the man's tweed jacket that she wore over a leather skirt and dirty white cotton tights. A can of Tennants Extra was clutched in one claw-like hand. The other held an unlit roll-up.

According to a now barely legible council sign which stood beside its gate, the scrawny patch of railed-in green across the road from the Job Centre had been officially designated Princess Elizabeth Park. But for as long as anyone could remember this well established haunt of schoolgirls on the game had been universally known as the Scrubbery. The bench Midge sat on was the last not to have been dismantled by unauthorized persons or set on fire.

Amateur prostitution being for hot nights in high summer, and with the weather already growing more realistic, the Scrubbery had become a game reserve for junkies, crack smokers and the local wino fraternity. They congregated here to be near the public convenience, a foul and swampy concrete facility, about as far from convenient as you could get without asphyxiation. The ambience suited them, it suited everybody, because nobody else would think of going into the Scrubbery unless it was to vandalize something or for their dogs to relieve themselves. And not even the dogs would go into the Scrubbery's toilets.

On one side of her sat old Bert and, on the other, young Terry. They too had cans of lager and were listening in a desultory way as Midge strained for the next line.

'Well?' growled Bert aggressively. 'How does it go on?'

Midge screwed up her face. 'Hang on! Hang on and I'll tell you. *I remember, I remember . . .*'

'You said that bit. You remember sod all, missus. And that's a fact. The piss has gone and taken away whatever wit you once had.'

'Do not interrupt,' said Midge in her grandest manner, taking another sip of lager and shutting her eyes. '*I remember, I remember, the house where I was born, The little something-something-something* . . . I'll get it in a mo. Y'know my Grandmama taught it us at the Big House when I was a child. S'where she lived, old dragon and s'where I was born too, matter of fact, s'why I still like that sloppy old poem. Didn' I ever mention she was a Lady and Daddy was an honourable?'

Terry groaned. 'Did you ever? You hardly ever mention anything else. Leeches on the body politic, your mob. "The rich may drink the blood of the people but they cannot sap our will." Leon fucking Trotsky said that.'

A squad car containing PCs Marik and Davies arrived at the end of the street, unseen as yet by the trio of drinkers. An observer might have said it was some sixth sense, or else simply a coincidence, but as soon as the car began nosing down towards Nightingale Park, Terry rose and slipped into the toilets.

Marik eased himself from the car and strolled over to the remaining two derelicts.

'You seen a Michael Dunn?' he said to Bert.

Bert wouldn't meet the policeman's eye. He kept his chin jammed against his chest and shook his head.

'You?' demanded Marik, addressing Midge and looking around to see if there were any others in the area. He saw no one. 'Do any of you know a Michael Dunn?'

Midge met the question with a broken-toothed grin. She raised her beer can in salute and shook her head.

In the Harris flat, the television was droning on about the cost of food or something. Jason was lying on the floor of the lounge. Behind him his gran was on the sofa with Tony in her lap. They were staring at the screen but Jason was preoccupied with a game. So he was surprised when, a few minutes later, he became aware of his mother's voice.

'Please,' she was saying, 'if anyone saw my little girl . . . if anyone knows where she is . . .'

Jason looked up, twisting around on the floor and looked towards the door. He saw no Anita so he turned back to the television and examined the screen. His mum was there. Her face was right in the middle of the picture and it was crying, real tears.

He was puzzled. He concentrated on what she was saying.

61

'Don't hurt her. If you know where she is, or can help in any way, please telephone. All we want is for her to come home.'

Jason rolled on to his side and curled up so he could see Helen. He thought for a moment. What was Mum talking about? And that was another thing. He hadn't seen Julie today but no one had said where she was. 'Where's Julie gone, Gran?' he asked.

At the very beginning of the day the decision had been taken to search the ground all over again, inch by inch, this time with the help of local volunteers and council workers. Men from the various construction sites had also been given leave to join the hunt. Children had taken the day off school. It was an impressive turn-out.

Patiently, and largely in silence, they moved line abreast across the ground, prodding and peering in and under everything in their way. There was little laughter, few smiles. Everyone knew that it could be a body they were looking for now, or clues as to a body's whereabouts. Inspector North had given them a mass briefing before leaving for the press conference, describing every single item of Julie's clothing. It had a sobering effect.

Barridge had hardly slept. After his ducking in the flooded cellar he'd gone home but, as soon as he'd changed, he walked out of his flat and returned to the station. While that little girl was still out there somewhere the idea of sleep was repulsive to him.

Now – still unshaven and buzzing with physical exhaustion – he was with a group of locals, trying desperately to concentrate on the task underfoot. Suddenly he stopped. A desire for all this to be over washed through him like a wave: he wanted done with it, but he could not be until they found the kid.

He scanned the ground ahead. In his path were sewage pipes, surrounded by a litter of wooden pallets and building supplies, which Barridge remembered had been taped off by Marik and Henshaw the previous night. He trudged forward, bending to pass under the yellow control tape. Then, with his first step inside the taped area, the sole of his booted foot felt something beneath it.

'Hold it!' he called, raising his arm to the others.

Barridge got down on his haunches and, using a gloved finger, hooked a little of the mud away from whatever he had sensed in the ground. Part of a black, shiny object appeared with the edge of some metal attachment also visible. Carefully, he removed another small bit of mud. It clung to his finger and he shook it off. The metal was stainless steel: a buckle. And next to it was the unmistakable rim of the upper of a small shoe. A child's shoe.

Barridge's heart lurched. Reflexively he reached for the shoe but, just in time, remembered not to pick it up. Instead he called out.

'What shoes was she wearing?'

Someone said, 'Black and shiny, wasn't it?'

Another added, 'With a T-strap.'

Barridge carefully gouged out some more mud until he could see the shoe clearly. He shut his eyes and opened them again.

'Well, I've just found one. A black patent leather-type shoe with a T-strap. Looks like a little girl's.'

The volunteers began to cluster round. One or two of them yelled and waved, bringing some officers over at the double. Barridge sat back on his heels and looked around. The shoe was about six yards from the sewage pipes, he tonly nearby place of concealment. But they'd been checked . . .

Then he saw what Marik and Henshaw had missed in the night. These pipes were laid horizontally but two did not lie flush and, in the gap between, recessed so that it would not easily be noticed, lay another pipe of smaller diameter.

He strode over, bending to take a closer look. Something was blocking the smaller pipe. He thought he saw something in there, or was he imagining it? A couple of officers who had followed him to the pipes came nearer.

'I'll do it. I can squeeze through!' shouted Barridge.

Barridge stripped off his Gortex jacket. You couldn't get through by standing upright so, on hands and knees, he began crawling between the pipes, a space no more than two feet wide. Barridge was not a fat man, but he was solidly built and a thinner individual would have done the job better, no doubt. But Barridge was not going to cede this job to anybody. Grunting with effort he forced his body into the dark tunnel, gripping his torch with his right hand, making progress by levering his weight forward with his arms. The points of his elbows glanced off broken bricks and lumps of jagged rubble but he didn't notice.

He reached the small, concealed pipe and shone his torch. 'Jesus!'

'Barridge. See anything? Anything there?'

'Move the pipe, the big pipe. I'll need to get round to the other end.'

The pipe to his right began to roll away so that he could crawl past it. As he did so the face of a TSG sergeant appeared in his line of sight. 'Anything in there, son?'

Barridge paused and looked at the older man. He blinked, then nodded his head. So far he had not seen much – pink skin and a scrap of white cotton. But it was enough.

It was not until he had reached the far end of the pipe and looked inside that it suddenly became real for him. He saw a foot with a white sock, another wearing a black, shiny shoe. Between them rested two hands reaching in front of her. Beyond these in the gloom he could see a tangle of golden hair round about where the knees must be. He froze. He looked but couldn't move. The child was bent double inside a pipe little more than a foot in diameter. One of her hands was stretched out and Barridge could have sworn he saw it twitch.

'Oh, God . . .' he whispered. It was not an exclamation but a prayer.

He tore off his gloves and leaned into the pipe as far as he could to grasp the hands. They were icy cold. Barridge pulled but she was wedged too tight. Afraid to tug hard on the frail wrists, he grasped an ankle, pulling harder. The blood rose to his neck and face with the effort which, as much as anything, came from trying *not* to pull too hard in his desperation to get her out of there.

She moved at first by fractions of an inch and then, as he continued the steady pressure, by inches. She had been three feet into the pipe and he had already dragged her a foot nearer to the open air when some hindrance was suddenly released and she slid forward smoothly, easily and alarmingly. Barridge fell back as the small body, naked but for a pair of cotton pants, fell out of the pipe and flopped on top of him.

Other officers leapt to help, to take the body. But

Barridge was already struggling to his feet, holding on grimly.

'It's all *right*!' he was shouting, cradling the child. 'I've got her. And she's all right. She's alive. She's *alive*!'

The other officers knew otherwise. The child's head dangled from her shoulders like a broken flower. They made a close ring around Barridge, which is instinctive behaviour by police officers. It comes not just from a desire to shield members of the public from the sight of death, but from an almost unconscious sense that this moment – the pivotal moment in any police inquiry, the discovery of a body – was one that belonged to them all. And a body so tiny affected every man deeply. It was something they would never forget.

Barridge had taken one of the hands and was rubbing the back of it against his cheek. He was staring into space, seeing again in his mind the image of that hand as it had reached towards him from the depth of the pipe. He saw that slight pudginess which is in all children's hands. The fingers were slightly bent and the nails were rimmed with dirt. The ink of a faded Biro drawing was clearly visible on the back of it, like blue veins arranged to make a smiling face.

'Put her down, son,' said the TSG skipper softly. 'Just put her down, won't you?'

Barridge reacted badly to the suggestion. He took a step backwards, his eyes staring.

'No!' he yelled. 'No. I just need an ambulance. An *ambulance*, right? She's OK and I've got her ... I *found* her ... ! She's alive!'

He hardly seemed to have noticed the blue and red plastic washing line that was wound around the little girl's neck.

CHAPTER 6

FRIDAY 6 SEPTEMBER

HOW DO YOU TELL someone their child is dead? North had been called upon to do it only three times before, and each time she had used the same formula – the usual formula. She made sure the parents were both present, if she could, and made them sit down. Then she said she was sorry, awfully sorry, but she had some bad news to tell them. Some very, very bad news.

That was enough, usually – only the most dense could fail to grasp that a death was involved. It merely remained to establish whose death. Sometimes a short guessing game took place. My mother? My brother, sister? My child? The child was the least thinkable option. It always came up last.

Unless, as in this case, that child was already missing.

Meg Richards was standing at the window when the DI and her sergeant arrived below the tower block on the Howarth Estate. North saw her Family Liaison Officer's face on the third floor, looking out. Richards would deduce why they had come. She would know it couldn't be good news, because that can be conveyed on the telephone.

No word had been spoken in the flat but, by the time

the officers reached the Harris front door and were let in by Helen, everybody present shared Richards's knowledge. The atmosphere was one of accumulated tension. Knowing and realizing are not always the same thing, and in these situations reality is suspended until something gets said. Only with the release of words into the air, does the unthinkable become a solid, shared fact.

North walked into the sitting room. All those present were already sitting, except Richards. Anita had an album of family snaps open on her knee. Peter was smoking. A plate of untouched sandwiches lay on the low table between them. Everyone was looking at her, waiting. She glanced at each of them first, a flicking glance.

'It's very bad news, I'm afraid.' Anita's pale face registered nothing, not at first. For a few seconds it remained oddly at rest, tilted to one side and looking nowhere in particular. Then slowly it crumpled and darkened, like cellophane on the fire. The album slipped to the floor.

'No.'

She was hugging herself now, rocking almost imperceptibly back and forth. The surrounds of her eyes tightened and creased.

'No.'

She took a long, sighing breath and gave out a hoarse, unearthly howl.

'*No!*'

In a technical sense, with the finding of a dead body, a missing person case is solved and goes away. But, in reality, it simply grows a new identity. Growing and mutating like a monster in a horror-film, it efficiently metamorphoses into a murder inquiry.

To a police officer, murder is the ultimate. It is *Hamlet*, Wembley, Mount Everest: the point at which your professional life peaks and every tough question you've ever been trained to answer will be asked. Murder is the most demanding and a child murder the least forgiving of all a police officer's enemies, an adversary who will take away your sleep if possible or, failing that, creep into your dreams; an enemy who is always there to spring another surprise, to knock you back, find you out. If, with murder, you get it right you can have the Commissioner's pat on the back and some brief media glory. Screw it up and screw you – straight back to car-pound duties.

From the moment that North called in to report PC Barridge's discovery, the Murder Squad – AMIP – waiting in the wings since late last night, started making their dispositions.

'Team'll be deploying into this station within two hours,' said the Station Superintendent to North. 'Of course they'll want an incident room. We can make some suitable space available, I take it?'

'Yes, sir. Conference Suite. No problem.'

'They're assigning Detective Superintendent Mike Walker to the case. You know him?'

'No, sir.'

'He's a good officer. And he wants to co-opt someone local who's familiar with the inquiry so far. I told him you.'

North must have looked alarmed because the Super leaned forward in his most reassuring manner. 'Your first murder?'

North shook her head. 'Oh no, sir!'

Not that she'd been on very many.

'Well,' the Super continued, 'your first child murder anyway, the worst kind. But you'll be fine. I wouldn't give you to Walker if I thought you couldn't cope.'

'Thanks, sir. I'll go up and see how they're getting on with clearing the Incident Room.'

The Super detained her with a gesture of his hand.

'Before you go, I ought to tell you that they're starting the post-mortem in half an hour. Walker may go straight down to the mortuary from wherever he is now. I expect you to attend. All right?'

'I've been to them before, sir.'

'Good. Off you go, then.'

On the first floor, Donaldson was supervising the removal of files from the local Incident Room to the ground floor. Officers Brown, Phelps, Marik and Henshaw were all on shift but these were far from the usual wisecracking men that North knew. The finding of the body had changed and sobered each of them.

She asked the Skipper what Walker was like.

'Used to work here, in Division.'

He plumped another plastic files' bin on top of the stack near the door. Then he scratched his head. 'I wouldn't call him the absolutely top drawer, if you know what I mean.'

North had the impression that the Skipper had more to impart but, just then, Brown appeared at her elbow proffering a file.

'Ma'am, we've traced a Mrs Wald – she's meals on wheels.'

North remembered that several of the old folk on the estate had mentioned meals on wheels being brought into the Howarth about the time of the child's disappearance. She took the file.

'That's good. Anything else?'

'Well, we've also traced Kenneth Poole – the ice-cream seller on the Howarth Estate.'

Opening the file to scan the details, she saw in the corner of her eye a slim male figure entering the room.

'Mr Poole's got a sheet!' she said to the Skipper. 'He's another one of the dirty mac brigade. It says here he was "concerned in the management of a disorderly house".'

Donaldson shook his head. 'So how, in God's name, does he get a job selling ice-cream to kids?'

North was watching the new arrival, who was looking around uncertainly. He wore a suit and his arms were clasped behind his back. She said, 'Beats me. Is this him? Must have left his mac at home.'

Donaldson swung round to look. He suddenly coughed and cleared his throat. 'Oh, er, Detective Superintendent Walker – right?'

'That's right! And you are . . .?'

'Sergeant Donaldson, sir.'

Suddenly Walker produced a raincoat from behind his back, brandished it and said in a soft Glaswegian accent, 'So where do I put this?'

As Donaldson took the Superintendent's coat, North let out a snort of laughter, covering it with her closed fist. She straightened her face as best she could under Walker's suspicious glance. To have confused him with the dirty mac brigade was a major error of judgement, but she couldn't help but find it funny. He was a lean man of less than medium height but with the most vital grey-blue eyes she had ever seen in an officer of his rank. They darted restlessly about, she thought, like target-finders.

'I've been told I've got one of the best from here to join my team. Any idea where—?'

North stepped forward and held out her hand. 'Er – it's me, sir.'

Walker shook North's hand slowly, looking her hard in the face. Before he could speak again, she said, 'Did you know – they're due to begin the post-mortem in fifteen minutes?'

Walker glanced at his watch and took the coat back from Donaldson. 'You can brief me on the way,' he said.

June was the assistant in the path lab and she had had her car broken into the previous night. Now, preparing the post-mortem area for the examination of the little child's body, she just wanted to vent her frustration on somebody, and who better than a police officer – Detective Sergeant Polk, the area lab liaison officer, who was waiting for the officers on the case.

'I said to them, I *am* insured, I've been insured with this company for ten years. Never made a single claim . . .'

She was rattling surgical instruments as she placed them on the tray – scalpels, clamps. Not for the first time Polk reflected on how the situation would look to anyone unused to it. Lying between them, under a sheet, was the body of a child about four feet long and probably weighing no more than three stone. And here was this woman, with her carefully groomed blonde hair and scarlet nail polish clearly visible through the surgical gloves, going on about *insurance*.

After a few moments the pathologist breezed in, already gowned and booted. This was John Foster, in his fifties, with hollow cheeks, prominent cheekbones and long bony fingers. He had a Walkman-size tape recorder and a mini-microphone clipped to his blue plastic gown. He looked around.

'Who've I got with me today? Ah, the lovely June. Your boy pass his exam?'

'Don't speak to me about that little sod.'

Walker and North were on their way. Gloving up, Foster chatted amiably across the body of Julie Harris. Her extinguished life seemed to mean little more to them than a switched-off light. Soon they would be cutting the body open and delving inside.

A fat, moustached man in a green gown looked in.

'Oh, Foster, Detective Superintendent Walker and that other officer are gowning up. Mind if I look over your shoulder on this one?'

Foster shrugged. Arnold Mallory was not a man you said no to unless you wanted a fight. 'All right by me.' He gestured to him for the benefit of June and Polk. 'This is Arnold Mallory of the forensic service. Apparently—' He grinned theatrically at Mallory. 'Apparently our friends over there are uptight about the police removing her from the site.'

Mallory approached the table where Julie lay. He looked at the sheeted shape, shaking his head. 'Too bloody right we are.'

'Well, I'm glad you're here, Arnold. You can take the stomach contents away with you. Save a bit of time.'

Mallory grunted and at this moment, Walker, North and a police photographer arrived. They took up stations around the table, near enough to see without being in Foster's way. The pathologist reached for the sheet and drew it back slowly. In that moment his manner changed. There was no exaggerated reverence, but he was now serious and committed.

'Well, little one,' he said in a soft, intimate voice which excluded the others present, 'let's find out what happened to you, shall we?'

The photographer's camera flashed and the post-mortem began.

Walker had instructed that the whole team assemble in the new Incident Room at five p.m. The preparation of the space was nearly complete, with phone lines and computers installed, desk space for a dozen officers, cabinets and display boards.

As he spoke to them Walker's body language, North noted, was assertively brisk. He wouldn't suffer fools or be much of a diplomat but, at the same time, she could tell he wasn't personally vain. There was no arrogant expectation that people should bow their heads before his person. He worked hard at his job and expected others to do the same.

'OK, listen up!' he called. The buzz in the room subsided to a hush. 'I have with me DI North and DS Donaldson, CID from this station. They'll be working alongside us together with back-up from uniform. We've just come from the post-mortem. And I should add the body has now been formally identified by the grandmother as Julie Anne Harris.'

He looked across at a dark-haired man over by a whiteboard, who was writing details of the victim along-side a photograph.

74

'Over there is DC James, our Office Manager. These two are DCs Soames and Harrolds and over here we've got Smith, Macklin, Morrissey and Grimes.'

The two local detectives nodded their greetings, trying to fix the names in their memories.

'Oh, and this is Detective Sergeant David Satchell, my right hand.'

A handsome, smartly dressed man in his early thirties came forward. He was half smiling, an expression that might almost be called smug. Warily North shook his hand – that 'right hand' of Walker's. Satchell looked as if he might be possessive. He might take a little handling.

'And finally, Reg Cranham, our Exhibits Officer.'

Cranham was black and as sharply dressed as Satchell. North thought they were either allies or rivals.

'OK, now! Tomorrow morning we have a Mrs Wald coming in who's meals on wheels. She *may* be able to help as she seems to be one of the few people who was around the estate after twelve-thirty. We also have an ice-cream seller who was parked up on the estate around lunchtime. Otherwise we are very short of leads. We are looking for a wino – am I right? – name of Michael Dunn?'

North nodded. 'He has a flat on the estate. At the moment he's AWOL.'

'Right. Keep chasing him. We'll know a lot more about time of death, et cetera, when the pathologist comes through with his results. Meanwhile forensics are looking at the shoes, the pants, the rope. But we need the rest of the clothes – that's *our* priority right now. OK? Those not on shift tonight, go home and get a good night's sleep.

It'll be the last you get. This inquiry starts, in earnest, tomorrow. Good night.'

Helen sat at the kitchen table, warming her hands around a mug of tea. Her eyes were shut and there was an odd sensation in her stomach, a flickering alternation of heat and cold. Her grief was like the paralysis of fear, a desire to run away combined with the knowledge that – even if her legs would carry her – this grief could never be given the slip. Anita was in her bedroom, trying to sleep. She'd taken some Valium. Helen knew, with a mother's certain knowledge, that Anita was beginning to feel the same way that she was. But Anita was still insulated by shock, going through the motions of ordinary life.

This afternoon had been Helen's second experience of a coroner's morgue. The first time was when Jim was killed and he'd been so badly damaged by the lorry that hit him, his face appallingly crushed on impact. Some of his workmates, for example, might not at first have recognized him, but she'd known him instantly by a hundred small, familiar things – the shape of his ears, his bitten nails, the liver spots on his hands, the old acne scars. It had seemed like Jim, even though he was horribly disfigured.

When the attendant pulled back the sheet this afternoon Helen had had to force herself to look really hard at Julie's face. It would be the last time she would ever see it. They told her they'd already carried out a postmortem and Helen tried not to think about what that had involved. Anyway, there was no sign of it on Julie's clean, hardly blemished face. Helen couldn't help thinking that she looked perfect, like the angel on Christmas cards.

Helen had assented with a simple quick nod. Yes, this was my granddaughter Julie. She had held back the tears somehow until this moment, but then they came in an unstoppable surge.

All the way back in the police car, and later sitting in the kitchen with a cup of tea, Helen had thought of the little girl alive. Her high-pitched scream of laughter, her skip as she walked alongside you, the squeeze she always gave when you took her hand, the frown and quick shake of those curls when she didn't care to do something. Who had taken this away? Who could possibly do such a thing?

Suddenly a violent noise exploded from the sitting room, the clang of guitars and the thud of drums. Helen jumped to her feet and almost ran into the lounge. Peter was lying slumped on the settee. He'd done almost nothing but drink beer since the body was discovered. Now he was swinging his head to the rhythm of whatever foul music it was he'd put on. She strode to the hi-fi unit and punched the off button. Peter reacted instantly.

'*Leave that on!*'

'No, I will not,' said Helen, shaking with anger and grief. 'What are people going to think? And if *you* don't care, at least let Anita sleep. Let the kids sleep!'

Peter pouted drunkenly. 'Everybody's running around making sure 'Nita's OK. What about *me*?'

'You? You're not pregnant. And she wasn't even your daughter, Peter.'

Peter looked at her menacingly. 'How long you meaning to stay?'

Helen stiffened. She defied him. 'For as long as I'm needed.'

Peter took a swig from the beer can in his hand. He

gave up the battle, as if it required a concentration he couldn't muster. He lowered his head.

'When they going to let us bury her? When?'

Helen turned away to face the sideboard, where family and school photographs were ranged in frames. Now she was crying again.

'I don't know. I don't know . . .'

The last thing Detective Superintendent Walker did before returning home to his family in Grays, Essex, was give a press conference. BBC News and the *News at Ten* teams were both there. He kept his statement very simple, confirming that, after the police's continued search this morning, the body of the missing child, Julie Ann Harris, had been found close to the Howarth Estate and he was treating the death as suspicious. He was pursuing various lines of inquiry. An information hotline had been set up for any member of the public who might be able to help the police.

As in all cases of child murder, the rat-pack was deeply interested. Walker hoped their fascination would be relatively short-lived, as long as he could make a rapid arrest. He had at first considered issuing a description of Michael Dunn, but discarded the idea. The time wasn't yet ripe. He parried the reporters' questions. Asked, inevitably, if she'd been sexually assaulted, he said he was awaiting the pathologist's report. Asked about the murder method, he declined to give details.

He had good reason for this. Crazies routinely telephone the police claiming to have committed such crimes and it's vital to be able to eliminate them with a few simple, circumstantial questions.

Getting into bed beside Maggie, he asked if she thought the press conference had gone reasonably well on television. She looked up from her book.

'Your tie looked awful. And your bald spot was shining.'

He laughed and rolled over on to his side. She was right to stick a pin in his pretension. At the same time he needed to manage the Press. The last thing he wanted was a series of hysterical stories in the tabloids about families that cowered in fear of a madman stalking the estates of East London.

He was hopeful, all in all. He had the rope, the clothes and a suspect who would surely turn up soon. These factors gave Mike Walker comfort as he closed his eyes to begin his nightly battle with insomnia.

CHAPTER 7

SATURDAY 7 SEPTEMBER

MRS WALD'S HUSBAND was an inspector on the buses. She was not exactly used to the inside of police stations, and certainly not their interview rooms, though she'd seen these places on *Inspector Morse*, naturally. They'd always struck her as disagreeably gloomy and dungeon-like but this room was a surprise. It was rather like the little carpeted cubby-hole where she'd recently seen Mr McKendrick at the bank about her mortgage.

Detective Superintendent Walker took her patiently through Thursday morning's meals round on the estate. It was a little difficult at first. Every day tends to be much like another doing meals on wheels and Thursday had already become tangled up with Wednesday, while bits of Monday, Tuesday and Friday also needed weeding out. The weekly roster of menus helped, of course: Wednesday was chicken and Friday fish fingers. On Thursdays the old folks got Irish stew, apple pie and custard. She concentrated on the smell of the stew and it brought some details back to her.

'I remember when I first arrived a young man came tearing down the stairs. He almost bumped into me. Long hair, long dark coat. I didn't really see his face

80

– he had no manners, never said a word of hello or anything.'

'Did you see anyone else around the stairs?'

'No, just my old people and they were all in their flats. You don't see many people around the stairs and corridors up there you know.'

'But did you see the young man again?'

'Yes, I think so. You see, I was late. Old Mrs Marsh wanted me to have a cup of tea and a chat with her, but I didn't have time. We're supposed to have the vans back at the depot before quarter to two, you know, they're very strict on that. Anyway I did my last delivery at one-thirty, that was Enid Marsh. I remember checking the time in Mrs Marsh's flat. Then I got back to my van after that . . .'

Walker cleared his throat. 'Yes, but I need to know the time as accurately as possible, Mrs Wald. You made your last delivery at one-thirty. What floor was that?'

'Sixth.'

'So then you went down in the lift—'

'Lift? You are joking, Superintendent. The stairs.'

Walker struck his forehead with the heel of his hand. 'Ah yes, I was forgetting. Stairs. You got to the bottom a minute later, then?'

'Superintendent, I'm not Linford Christie and I was carrying stuff.'

'Two minutes, then?'

She nodded.

'What happened next?'

'I got back to my van and it wouldn't start. I waited a few minutes to let it rest. I looked around in case I needed help and I saw that young man again near the ice-cream seller's van.'

81

'Are you sure it was the same young man you saw earlier when you entered the block?'

'Yes, I think so – he was a young man, long hair, long dark coat. But I can't remember his face.'

'Did you see anyone else in the playground area at that time?'

'No, it was empty.'

'So, the time when you saw him, while you were sitting inside your van, was about what?'

'One thirty-five. Not later than one-forty.'

The ice-cream seller's name was Kenneth Poole, a chain-smoker. Sitting slightly hunched in the interview room, he held his cigarette in a cupped hand, and took rapid, nervous drags. His typed-up statement – a brief paragraph – lay on the table. Walker and Satchell were taking him through it one last time.

'I was parked at my usual pitch at twelve-thirty.'

'You're absolutely sure about that?' asked Walker.

'Yeah, twelve-thirty. There was nobody around except this bloke.'

Walker and Satchell exchanged looks.

'Can you describe him?'

'Long hair, black coat. He came up and asked if I'd seen his little girl. I said I hadn't.'

Poole's eyes were darting around and he seemed anxious to go.

'And you didn't see any children in the playground?'

'Nope. I usually stay on the Howarth Estate until two, two-thirty. You know – get 'em before lunch and after. Then I move on to the pitch near the comprehensive school.'

There was a long pause. Poole looked uncertainly from Walker's face to Satchell's and back again. Walker stood up.

'Thank you, Mr Poole. If you would just sign your statement you can go.'

Poole seemed surprised as he took the pen proffered by Satchell.

'Oh, OK. Thanks. Thanks a lot. Sorry I couldn't be more helpful.'

Walker picked up the signed paper and examined the rapid scrawl of Poole's signature. 'There's just one thing I was wondering, Mr Poole.'

Poole looked up, his eyes wary again. 'Oh, yeah? What?'

'Are your employers aware of your criminal record?'

Poole looked down at his hand. He mumbled. 'Don't know.'

Walker strode to the door and yanked it open. 'Thank you, Mr Poole.'

He waited as Poole almost ran out, then turned to Satchell. 'Dave – get the sheet on Peter James, will you?'

Pat North had had several glimpses already of the ferocious energy that drove Detective Superintendent Walker. In the Incident Room he paced ceaselessly, smoked without stopping, constantly ripping off the filter and occasionally spitting it out as he bit it off. He asked his questions again and again. Where was Michael Dunn? Where were Julie's clothes? Where did she die? *When* did she die?

What was bothering him now was the disparity between the statements of Peter James, Mrs Wald and the

83

ice-cream seller, Poole, about James's movements that lunchtime. James said he went out about one; the meals on wheels woman said she saw a long-haired man, who could have been James, at one-thirty, whilst Poole was talking about some time after twelve-thirty that James came and asked him about the missing girl.

'Did Peter James give a description of what he was wearing when he went out looking for Julie Ann?'

North didn't have the answer. She flannelled. 'It's been tough to question Mr James. He's been under a lot of strain – very volatile.'

Walker was standing at the pin-board with its diagram of the relationships within the victim's family. He tapped it hard. 'Inspector, it may be difficult but let me remind you that in ninety per cent of these cases the offender is a member of the family. Doesn't matter how tough it is, they've got to be checked out in every detail.'

He swivelled round towards Satchell. 'You question him.'

'Yes, guv.'

'Meanwhile, Inspector North and I will confer with Doctor Foster.'

Satchell's face was wearing a smug grin as he caught North's eye. One-nil to the visitors.

Walker added before he slammed out of the room, 'And most important, find Michael bloody Dunn.'

Foster stood smoking beside a vertical lightbox. On the screen were fixed nine large transparencies showing close-up post-mortem shots of Julie's body. Walker and North stood like an audience, looking and listening.

'She was a well-nourished, healthy young girl of about

five years old. As you can see she has bruising and abrasions to her shoulder, upper arm, legs and buttocks. The abrasions on the limbs were sustained when she was pushed into the sewage pipe. But – this is important – there has been bleeding and bruising around the abrasions to the limbs. And look – there are petechial haemorrhages on the face and scalp.'

Another slide displayed small spots on Julie's skin. They appeared like a rash.

'These are minute leakages of blood into the skin.'

North and Walker looked more closely at the slide indicated by the pathologist. He showed with his pointer the discoloured skin.

'Bleeding, bruising – those are all vital signs. Blood flowed into and from the damaged tissue, which means her heart was beating when it happened.'

He paused, as if waiting for them to grasp the implication.

'She was *alive* when she was pushed in the sewage pipe?' said North.

'That's about it.'

'What about the rope around her neck?'

Foster dragged deeply on his cigarette and exhaled quickly. He was an impatient smoker.

'Oh yes, there was a piece of plastic-coated line ligated around the neck, but she didn't actually die from strangulation.'

'So what did she die of?' asked North.

'Suffocation. She'd probably been made unconscious with the ligature then forced into a folded position with her head resting on her knees like so. She was then literally crammed into the pipe which was too tight. Hardly any air. Died approximately two hours later, judging by the colour of the bruising and degree of blood coagulation. Quite a rare blood group, by the way – AB negative.'

'Was she sexually assaulted?' Walker wanted to know.

Foster consulted his typewritten notes – a transcript of the oral commentary he'd made for the tape during his examination.

'She has a ruptured hymen and extensive bruising to her genitals consistent with penetration with a blunt rounded object.'

'Such as?' asked Walker, then he coughed. 'I mean, apart from the obvious.'

'It may not have been the obvious.' He flicked a glance at North and then went on. 'I mean there are no obvious traces of seminal fluid, although there might be minute traces. We'll have to leave that to forensics. Otherwise, it could be something like the neck of a bottle. There was blood on her pants – her own blood. No traces of semen, as I said. Oh, and here's something else you should know . . .'

He pointed to another slide showing a section of Julie's arm.

'Some of the bruises to her body, such as this one here, are yellowish brown and diffuse – see?'

They looked as Foster stubbed out his cigarette on a saucer.

'It means,' he said, 'that, unlike these bruises here which happened on the day she died, these yellower bruises are a couple of weeks old. Quite severe ones, too. Not the normal knocks a kid gets playing around. Now – contents of stomach . . .'

He strolled over to his desk and flipped open a file.

'According to Mallory, our little lady had cereal and

orange juice for breakfast. The stomach also had traces of milk proteins and nuts – could be an ice-cream eaten some time before she died.'

Walker looked over Foster's shoulder, squinting at the report. 'Can't you give us a time of death, or near enough?'

'Death occurred between three and seven on Thursday, that's the best I can do.'

'Any chance of telling us if it definitely was ice-cream?'

Foster lit another cigarette and shook his head. 'You need to talk to forensics. But if she did eat an ice-cream and they had a wrapper or, even better, a stick, there could be some of her DNA on it, couldn't there?'

Barridge had been in turmoil ever since he'd found Julie's body. Flashbacks of her face kept exploding in his mind, and tears were never far away. He'd cried openly when they'd taken the child's body from him.

This afternoon he was with Brown and Phelps on the search for the child's clothing. It was a more dreadful, because less hopeful, task than the search they'd been carrying out yesterday. Now they were back at the row of derelict houses into whose flooded cellars he had got a ducking on the Thursday night.

He was wearing chest-high waders again as he inched his way through the water, examining every disgusting object that floated on the water. There was plenty of clothing. He thought the worst was the knitwear. It seemed to absorb the most stomach-turning smells and when you lifted it from the water it exhaled them into your nose. Or was he imagining this?

His torch started to flicker. He banged it against his

hand and it came on again. He flashed it into a corner of the cellar where a wardrobe was standing drunkenly askew. He saw a piece of air-filled clothing, floating half concealed behind the wardrobe. It looked red. Then his torch went off again.

'Can you bring some more light over here, in this corner?'

Brown and Phelps started to work their way towards him. They shone their torches at the wardrobe.

'What colour was her anorak?' asked Barridge.

'Red.'

Slowly, he began to force his way towards the soggy lump of red material bobbing in the black water.

The rest of Julie's clothing had turned up in the cellar and, with the anorak, it was bagged and sent down to the forensic science laboratory in Lambeth, where the shoes, pants and post-mortem swabs, as well as ground samples taken from the area around the sewage pipes were already undergoing tests.

Driving to the same destination that afternoon, immediately after their meeting with Foster, North was at the wheel with Walker alongside her. He was smoking and staring out of the window and hardly saying a word. The more the traffic on London Bridge impeded their progress the more fiercely he inhaled the smoke. Here was a man heading for a heart attack, thought North. But then, show me a senior police officer who wasn't.

Sweeping into the labs, Walker was told Arnold Mallory had left for the Old Bailey.

'Great. We come all this way and the man we want to talk to is attending court. Bloody great!'

The next most senior scientist working on the Julie Harris case was James Haggard. When he appeared, Walker demanded a report on the deposits on Julie's shoes. He needed to know where she went after the playground, he needed to know where she might have died.

'And what about the rope? Where did it come from? Are there any prints?'

Walker was like an impatient businessman, chivvying a sluggardly supplier for early delivery of an order and this, as it happened, was close to the truth. In these cost-conscious times, the forensic service is operated as a business, a profit centre. Every test carried out by them, every report printed out or appearance by an expert witness, was costed and charged to the account of the investigation – in this case, to Walker. And the Detective Superintendent constantly had to remind himself that the old profligate, scattergun days when an investigating officer simply ordered any test he wanted, were over. Now he had to work within a budget; he needed, in short, value for money.

Patiently, Haggard parried the questions as best he could. 'All in good time, you know, Mr Walker. We're pulling out all the stops.'

'According to Doctor Foster she was sexually assaulted. Can't you even give me anything on that?'

Haggard was a grizzled old scientist, close to retirement. He'd had all this a thousand times before – pushy detectives demanding instant results. He sighed.

'Detective Superintendent, you'll get all we get as soon as we get it. You know Mallory's heading the team. He's so anally retentive, nothing comes out of here before he's satisfied.'

He looked around a shade furtively. It was a cheerfully clinical room, with laminated tables ranged in rows. At one table, two forensic biologists were microscopically examining the clothing for blood and other stains. At another, chemists were analysing mud from the shoes and other environmental samples. Haggard set off for a corner where no one was working, beckoning the police officers to follow. The section of rope, which the detectives had last seen wrapped around Julie Harris's neck, lay flat on an unattended table. The scientist gestured down at it.

'It was wound round her throat twice and pulled. No knot was tied. Just what you see, a loop one end. The free end has been cut. No touching please.'

Going over to a pin-board with a display of photographs of the exhibit, he started fishing in his lab coat pocket. He tapped a close-up of the small loop and began unwrapping the sweet he'd taken from the pocket.

'The loop has traces of paint on the inside – layer structure, brown over green. It's as it would be if the rope had been attached to a post.'

'So? What are you saying?' asked Walker.

'Find the post—'

'And you can match the paint?'

Haggard popped the toffee into his mouth.

'Oh, yes – no problem there.'

Back in the Incident Room, Satchell was having a go at anyone who'd listen about the late finding of the clothes. Catching sight of Pat North he strode up to her.

'Somebody should give your lot a bollocking. That

cellar had been officially searched. We could have had those clothes yesterday. Bloody incompetence!'

Yeah, yeah, thought North. Local yokel plod. This was the type of thing that gave AMIP its name for abrasive elitism. She was just about to react when she heard Reg Cranham's voice, with a note of real urgency in it.

'Guv! Call just came in from a Mrs Enid Marsh – Howarth Estate.'

Walker remembered the name but he couldn't quite place it. 'And?'

'Well, she was questioned the night the victim went missing. Said she didn't know anything then – but now she's seen the TV news and, well—'

'Well, what? What?'

'She said she saw the victim, guv, with a man in the playground. She then described the clothes – exactly Peter James's appearance – long hair, long dark coat . . .'

'What time? Did she give a time?'

Cranham smiled, with a hint of triumph. He didn't like Peter James. 'Yep! Just after one o'clock, so she says.'

There was a momentary pause, then North murmured, 'So – it's the stepfather. Do we bring him in?'

'And call off the search for Michael Dunn?' Walker held up his hand to check the outbreak of chicken-counting. 'No. If we find Michael Dunn we still hold him.'

'On what?'

'Stolen videos. Come on, Inspector, let's go and talk to Enid Marsh.'

The old lady insisted on serving them with tea which, at her speed of movement, could not be done within ten minutes. Impatiently Walker and North sat on the sofa while the wherewithal was assembled on the low table in front of them. At last, Mrs Marsh was ready to tell her tale. And it was better than Walker had dared hope. Not only had she seen the child – she'd seen her with a man.

'The first time I saw her, it was like she was playing a game. You know, covering her eyes and peeping through. She was laughing. That was a quarter to one.'

Walker took a sip from his tea. It was a good cup, he gave her that. 'And did you see her again?'

'Yes, I did. At exactly five past one.'

She levered herself out of her chair and stood before them in something like a pose. Her sitting room had turned, for her, into a stage.

'He was reaching out, like that.'

She let go of her walking frame and demonstrated. Then she turned and began a long shuffle towards the balcony.

'But anyway, you know, I wasn't paying attention. I was looking for Mrs Wald, waiting for my dinner. I was hungry.'

She had reached the door and was leaning on the handle.

'I went outside. From my balcony I've got a view of a bit of the playground. I often look at the kids down there. And I . . .'

She paused and leaned forward with a small jerk. Her voice flipped up to a higher register.

'But look, that's him! That's him, down there.'

She opened the door and started to shuffle outside. Walker and North were beside her.

'Who?'

'The man. The man who was with the little girl!'

92

Down below the roundabout was revolving. There was not a child in sight, only a man of about twenty-five, with long matted hair and a shin-length coat of dark material. He had got the platform turning and was now standing dangerously on top of it, swaying and singing as loud as he could. In his fist he gripped a can of extra strong lager.

Detective Superintendent Walker moved like lightning, with Detective Sergeant Satchell at his side. Dunn seemed unaware of their presence until Satchell almost ripped his arms out of their sockets as he grabbed the iron rail to stop the roundabout. Dunn fell backwards laughing, the lager spraying from his can. Droplets spattered across Walker's face. He never lifted a hand to wipe them away. He never took his eyes off the drunk's face.

'Michael Dunn, I am arresting you in connection with the theft of videotapes.'

CHAPTER 8

SUNDAY 8 SEPTEMBER

I T BEING SUNDAY made no difference. At half-past five, like most mornings, Pat North left her boyfriend Graham in bed, still wrapped in several layers of sleep and snoring gently. He was unwakeable before seven-thirty – nine at weekends. Even then, he'd take an hour to come to, mooching around the flat like a wounded bear, slurping tea and growling at his post or the paper. It was better to be out of his way. She knew, if ever they should marry and have kids, this would be the most difficult bit for him – getting up in the small hours, the family breakfast, the carefully timed school run.

Night time was when Graham reached his best. The previous evening they'd gone out to the pub and she'd told him about the arrest of Michael Dunn that afternoon, how he'd fallen about and sung 'Bohemian Rhapsody' for hours in the cell. They'd been back at home in time for the news but there was no mention of Dunn's arrest and afterwards Graham was eager to speculate about the murder.

'Is it this Dunn character, though? Sure, he's a drunk and he's disreputable, so all the neighbours point at him. But is he the only suspect?'

Pat remembered the dressing-down Walker had given

in front of the whole unit, reminding her unnecessarily that about fifty per cent of child murders are committed by someone inside the family. She didn't elaborate, just mentioned the possibility of Peter James, Julie Ann's stepfather. Graham asked about the real father, and by now Pat was becoming loath to discuss it further, saying that Thomas Harris was a soldier in Ulster and had already been checked. To her irritation Graham continued to ask what evidence they had against Michael Dunn. It appeared almost as if he was siding with him.

'For God's sake, Graham. This isn't bloody *Cluedo*. A five-year-old girl is dead. She was molested. The man who did it will do it again unless we stop him. It could be Michael Dunn, it might not be. Our job is to find him. Which is why I need to go to sleep. You may not have to, but I'm working tomorrow.'

She'd gone straight upstairs, leaving Graham to his beloved *Match of the Day*. But what she'd said must have had some effect. He brought her a cup of tea, which she didn't really want. He set it down on the bedside table, leaning forward to stroke her head.

'Sorry. Didn't mean to sound like a prat, but you know sometimes it's good to talk about it. It was the only way I knew how to get you to open up. You may not even be aware of it, but since this little girl case started you've been on edge, biting my head off.'

He smiled, missing *Match of the Day*. She sat up and lifted her arms. It was a hug she needed, and caught in his arms she whispered, 'She was so tiny, Graham.' And the tears she would never allow any of the men or women at the station to see now gave her a much needed release.

*

Driving across London from west to east, she focused on the issue that would dominate the rest of her day. They had a suspect but not a crumb of evidence. They needed time for forensics to search his flat minutely, they needed time to question him. For this, a pretext was necessary, and the best they had was the stack of hopefully stolen videos found in Dunn's flat, which lay on the seat alongside her.

She drove on to the Howarth Estate and past the parade of shops until she came to the newsagent. She opened the passenger door and carried the videos inside. It was six-thirty. Mr Shah was organizing the newspaper boys, giving them their loads of Sunday papers. He glanced at the pile of ten video feature films, running his finger down the titles – *Aladdin, My Little Pony, The Terminator, The Lion King, Die Hard, Child's Play* – and checked for his security mark scratched on the plastic casings.

'Yeah, these were all mine.'

'We found them at the flat belonging to a Michael Dunn. You know him?'

'Yes. He—'

'He stole them from you? They *are* stolen, Mr Shah?'

Shah shook his head and smiled, with his eyes wide. 'I always like to help the police, Inspector, but I'm sorry to say these were not stolen.'

North was aghast. 'Not stolen? But you said they were yours.'

'*Were*. Michael Dunn did an occasional paper round for me. I was replacing or running down my stock of videos. Some of them had snowy pictures – *The Terminator*'s very bad. Customers were complaining. So I gave

96

them to Michael Dunn instead of money – for his paper round.'

'Did he say why he wanted the kiddies' films?'

'No.'

'Or the violent ones?'

Shah shook his head. 'People don't generally say anything about the films, you know. They just take them and leave.'

He shrugged and North briskly gathered up the tapes.

'Since they are not at the present moment yours, you won't object if I take these away again – right?'

As she walked into the AMIP Incident Room she could hear Skipper Donaldson giving Barridge a bollocking.

'You cocked up, you know that? Enid Marsh – house to house. Ring any bells? *You* questioned her. Now she's come forward as our identifying witness . . .'

Barridge blinked miserably. 'Sorry, sarge.'

But Donaldson was only just getting into his stride.

'Plus you were doing the search at the cellar. You only missed her clothing. *And* you missed her shoe by the pipes. How come, Barridge? If you'd been more diligent, we might have got to her sooner. You do know that?'

Barridge looked as if he might cry. 'I wasn't the only one there. I—'

'Don't answer me back, son. I'm telling you, you screwed up. She was alive in that sewage pipe for almost two hours.'

Barridge swivelled slightly, looking for support from others in the room. Detective Superintendent Walker was standing just behind him. In his panic, he appealed to the AMIP Superintendent.

'*Is* it Dunn, sir? I mean, Sergeant Donaldson says—'

But the Superintendent appeared not to hear. He was checking some names on a memo, then looked up to see if the constables in question were present. He pointed to Brown and Phelps and then Barridge.

'You two, and you, are on house to house inquiries.'

There was an audible groan from Brown. Walker shot a look at him that would have stalled the Wall Street Crash. He held up an index finger.

'I want you to check every washing line on that estate. *Every* washing line. We're looking for a match to the one found around Julie Ann's neck. It's there on the board, check it out. We want to know about any washing lines or similar plastic-coated rope that may have gone missing.'

He looked hard at PC Barridge. '*Don't* screw up this time – it's the murder weapon we're talking about, got it?'

Barridge's mouth fell open – so the Super had heard Donaldson's tirade.

'It wasn't my *fault*,' he muttered to Phelps. 'I wasn't the only one there. Bloody hell!'

Walker took North by the arm and guided her to one side.

'Dunn's still sleeping it off – Christ, it must have been some binge. Where'd he get the money? Anyway, it gives us more time to find something on him for Julie Ann. You seen the newsagent? Can we charge him for those videos?'

North shook her head. ''Fraid not, guv. They're all ex-rentals.'

'Dunn bought them?'

'No, Dunn did a few paper rounds and he took the videos instead of cash.'

'Shit! There must be something!'

Walker fished out a Marlboro, broke off the filter tip and stuck the ragged end in his mouth.

'Guv, you know how we got those videos, don't you?'

Walker made a face, removed the cigarette and picked a flake of tobacco from his tongue. 'Yeah, yeah. Pretext was checking for damage.' Walker reversed the cigarette and lit it.

'Well, there were a number of toys – kids' toys – there as well. One of them was a doll.'

Walker's eyes sparked. 'Doll? Haven't we followed it up with the family? Haven't we checked if it was the victim's?'

Satchell got up from his desk and joined them. He knew the boss, recognized the signs. Walker was working his way up through the lower storeys of a towering rage.

'Do you realize,' Walker went on, 'we've got Dunn in the cells and he's our best suspect and unless I get more – and I've got bugger all right now – I'm going to have to let the sorry bastard *OUT*?'

'Guv,' said Satchell, 'I've got a suggestion.'

'Glad to hear it, Dave. Shoot.'

'Put him in a parade. See if old Mrs Marsh can pick him out.'

Walker snapped his fingers impatiently. 'Christ's sake, Dave. I'm already working on that! But *you* know how long it'll take to find lookalikes. If we don't find something in the next couple of hours he's going to walk as soon as he wakes.'

He paused and sucked hard on his Marlboro.

'OK, I know what I want. I want a search warrant for Dunn's place. Pat?'

'It's a Sunday, guv.'

Walker found an ashtray and ground out the cigarette.

'Then let's deliver the local magistrate's *Sunday* bloody *Telegraph* for him, shall we?'

The warrant had been a push-over. The JP opened the door hurriedly, dressed for golf, and stood impatiently while Walker explained his business.

'Yes, of course, I've heard of this distressing death,' said the magistrate. 'And you are who, precisely?'

Walker produced his warrant card. 'Officer in charge of the inquiry – Detective Superintendent Michael Walker.'

'And this man whose home you want to search – is he a suspect?'

'That's right, sir.'

'In custody?'

'Yes, sir, but may be released shortly. In which case we are anxious to give his pad a spin – or rather, his flat a *search*, sir – before he can get home to do what he likes with the evidence.'

'You got the papers there?' The old man looked at his watch. 'I'm due to tee off at eight forty-five and you don't miss the chance of a slot at Sunningdale.'

'Of course, sir. It's all prepared. Just needs signing.'

'Come in, then.'

Driving back with the papers in his pocket, Walker laughed in relief.

'Thank Christ for bloody Sunningdale. Speeded things up a bit.'

They arrived at the Dunn flat at eight-forty where Reg

Cranham, the Exhibits Officer, was waiting for them. Before they could go in Barridge arrived on the run.

'Excuse me, sir!'

Walker waited for Barridge to catch his breath. 'What is it, Barridge? Those washing lines?'

'Yes, sir. One tenant said most of the residents use the local launderette. But there's a recently built housing estate across the road. Got gardens so they're more likely to use proper washing lines. Want me to . . .?'

Barridge gestured with his thumb in the direction of the new houses.

'No. Just report it in, lad. Sergeant Satchell will allocate some of my guys to cover the new houses.'

Walker knew that most of the balconies on the tower blocks would have washing lines. Whether these were ever used or not was beside the point – they had to be checked. Young rookies like Barridge were always looking for ways of cutting corners.

Inside the flat enough daylight filtered through the window boards to reveal the full squalor of Michael Dunn's damp and broken-springed home life. North showed Walker the one-armed doll which lay pink and sprawling on the settee. He bent down and looked carefully at it.

'My kid's got one of these.'

'It looks like a Barbie,' said North. 'Actually it's a cheap market-stall rip-off. Only costs about a quid, while a real Barbie costs—'

'Twelve ninety-nine,' said Walker grimly, picturing his daughter's glowing face on her sixth birthday as she tore off the gift wrap. 'And that's before you've bought the wardrobe. *Reg!*'

Cranham came in from the kitchen with a pained expression on his face. 'Breakfast anyone? I found a couple of sausages in the fridge – best before three months ago. Can't see no washing line anywhere.'

Walker pointed at the fake Barbie. 'Bag the doll. Seal, sign and log it and then test it for prints. Now what's the kitchen like?'

'It smells, guv.'

In the kitchen there were lumps of food adhering to the walls. The sink overflowed with unwashed plates. The floor was caked and tacky underfoot. What interested Walker the most was a small pile of waste paper in one corner – empty crisp bags and ice-cream wrappers. One brand of ice-cream in particular caught his eye: Gnut-crunch. He crouched down.

'Forensic said her stomach contents had maybe ice-cream and nuts – yes? Well, look at these.'

In the other room Cranham had been on the radio. He came back into the kitchen.

'Michael Dunn's awake, sir, but he's asked for something to eat. They can spin things out for a while longer.'

Walker straightened. 'Good. But I wish he'd had the decency to sleep through to lunch.'

He pointed to the wrappers. 'I want these listed and bagged.' He turned to North and pointed to the bagged Barbie. 'We'll take the doll to the victim's family.' He noticed her startled look. 'You got a problem with that?'

'No, sir,' said North and instantly Walker was talking to Cranham again.

'I want full documentation on bar codes and I want to know where he got them. Lolly sticks are vital. We'll comb the whole flat for more of them if we have time, but I want these two tested anyway.'

It would take a couple of minutes for Cranham to complete the bagging. Walker dialled a number on his mobile. 'Dave? I want you to go and talk to the newsagent – can you do it now? Check what he said about Peter James. Then find out what brands of ice-cream he sells. I'm partial to one called Gnutcrunch – yes, with a G – and also if he sold any of the horrible stuff to Michael Dunn. See you later.'

He snapped the phone off. 'Come on, let's see if we can find any more lolly sticks.'

Mr Shah the newsagent was checking a toppling pile of newspapers to see that each included a colour supplement.

'I mean I got to be right within five or ten minutes,' he was saying to Satchell. 'It's my busy time, lunchtime. Pete – Peter James – came in twice. Once to ask about a plumber and then, fifteen or twenty minutes later, he came back again.'

Satchell was looking into the freezer chest, noting down the names of the ice-cream brands.

'Did Michael Dunn come into the shop Thursday at all?'

'No – well, to be honest, I've barred him.'

'But he did the odd paper round for you, didn't he?'

'Yeah, but not for a long time. He couldn't be trusted. Last time I found half the bloody newspapers stuffed into litter bins. I never let him do it any more after that.'

'And you paid Dunn in kind?'

'Yeah – with ice-creams and crisps. That's all he wanted.'

'And videos?'

'Yes, and the videos.'

Outside the shop, Satchell switched on his cellphone.

103

'Guv? Newsagent's got Cornetto, Snickers, Gnutcrunch, Galaxy Dove, Twister, Wall's Chunky Choc Ice ... Crisps? Golden Wonder, loads of flavours – yes, prawn cocktail. And, guv, listen, Dunn used to be paid for this so-called paper round in ice-cream and crisps sometimes, as well as the videos.'

Satchell's findings had been interesting enough to put a spring in Walker's step as he and North strode towards the entrance to the tower block.

'When we get up there we'll make sure Julie Anne didn't have any ice-cream for breakfast. I told Dave to check with the labs, see if they've got any results in yet on the lolly sticks.'

'Bit soon, isn't it?'

Walker smiled thinly. 'I know. Just pawing the starting gates a little. I'm pinning my hopes on that little dolly right now.'

Anita herself came to the door. She was as pale as paper and the skin around her eyes had taken on the shiny, opalescent colours of grief and insomnia. Her pregnant stomach seemed more obvious too, affecting the way she turned and moved her body.

Walker said, 'Hello, Mrs Harris. I'm Detective Super-intendent Walker, I'm the—'

'Yes, I know who you are,' said Anita. She didn't even try to smile. 'I saw you on the box. Come through, won't you?'

Peter James was in the lounge, pacing around like a trapped rodent. 'All right?' he muttered.

Anita placed Walker and North on the settee and sat down self-consciously between them, as if she preferred not to look either of them in the face. The atmosphere in the place was coldly calm.

Walker started by sketching in the progress of the inquiry. He didn't mention Dunn by name – just talked about 'a man we are interested in'.

'How do you mean, interested?' said Peter James.

'I mean, he may be able to help us. He may have given your daughter something to eat. Could you just remind us what she had to eat on Thursday morning?'

Anita bowed her head and shut her eyes, trying to remember as accurately as possible.

'She had cereal, orange juice. That's it. She never ate much at breakfast.'

'You don't know if she had any ice-cream or any nuts?'

'No. Not here, she didn't.'

Walker turned and nodded at Cranham who was standing with his hands behind his back beside the door. The exhibits officer came forward and carefully placed the transparent evidence bag on the low table in front of Anita.

'Mrs Harris,' said Walker, 'I wonder if you could tell me – have you seen this doll before?'

Anita stared at the pink plastic flesh and tangle of yellow hair, the straight, elongated legs, the pert breasts and the hideous empty arm socket. Her eyebrows drew fractionally closer together. She was about to speak when Peter's voice, excited, broke in.

'Yes, that's her doll.'

He was leaning over, pointing. He was animated for the first time. 'It's Julie's, Anita. She always had it with her. Tell him, Anita. That's Julie's doll.'

Anita opened her mouth and at once her lips began to quiver. Slowly she covered her face with her hands. She nodded her head as her frame shook with sobs.

North looked at Walker's face as he skipped down the stairs a couple of minutes later. It wore a look that said, broadly, 'Got him.' It wasn't exactly happiness but, by the length of the Old Kent Road, it was the nearest she'd seen him get to happiness.

'Come on, you guys!' he called out, a flight of stairs in the lead. 'Don't hang about or that Custody Sergeant will be getting it into his head to let Michael Dunn go. And we can't have that, can we?'

Walker arrested Michael Dunn in the hallway of the custody suite just as Sergeant Johns was signing him out. Dunn had looked at him in hungover bemusement. His reaction to the words 'on suspicion of the murder of Julie Ann Harris' was bovine.

'Who? I've never heard of her.'

'You do not have to say anything,' chanted the Detective Superintendent, 'but it may harm your defence if you do not mention, when questioned, something which you later rely on in court.'

'I don't get it. I been here all night.'

'Anything you do or say may be given in evidence.'

Dunn held his arms away from his side, the hands palm upwards. He shrugged until his shoulders almost touched his ears.

'I don't know what the fuck you're talking about, you know.'

The accent was liltingly Welsh. The breath that delivered it smelt overpoweringly of breakfast and nicotine.

*

Barridge had felt in an extraordinary mood all morning, a kind of reverse high. It wasn't happiness, but a wave of inspired misery that he was riding helplessly. Once he saw Walker and Inspector North leaving the search area, he'd asked to be attached to the squad at the newly built houses and had been assigned to cover Ashcroft Close. Some intuition told him this was where the washing line had come from, so this was where he wanted to be.

For some time now, an inner voice had been talking to Barridge, telling him he had a privileged place on this investigation, a place almost of destiny. If he thought about it properly – if he'd been capable at this stage of detached thought – he might have agreed it was his own voice talking, that he was, in fact, just talking to himself. But, in his present state he thought of it as a voice of inspiration, telling him *he had been chosen for this*.

Who found the body? murmured the voice. Who found the anorak? Who first talked to Enid Marsh, the eye-witness? It was you, Colin. Ask yourself why. Never mind what the Skipper's been saying, this is fate. This is *meant*.

These new houses were small – for young couples, singles. Each was identical and each had an identical rectangle of garden bounded by lattice fencework.

He knocked on the door of number four. According to the electoral roll, it was the address of a Miss A. Taylor. Miss Taylor herself opened. She was a bony woman with bashful eyes, eyes that were always being dragged downwards to look at the ground, as if overwhelmed by gravity.

'Excuse me, madam,' said Barridge gently, 'we're inquiring into the murder that occurred over on the Howarth Estate.'

Miss Taylor's eyes glanced at the constable's face and then dropped to consider his boots.

'Oh yes, that poor little girl. How awful that was! I saw about it on the news. I can't believe it happened right here. How can I help?'

'We're just asking around to find out if any thefts have been taking place around here – thefts from gardens.'

Ann Taylor opened her front door wide and ushered Barridge in. 'Come through! I'll show you.'

As they walked through the house, Barridge noticed Miss Taylor's limp. Not bad enough to need a stick, but pronounced nonetheless.

'I wouldn't have come to live here if I'd known,' she said. 'I mean the level of crime is really bad.' Then she laughed, cupping her hand to her mouth and shifting her eyes from side to side. 'But, of course, you're a policeman. You know that!'

The garden was neatly, if unimaginatively, kept: border shrubs lining the perimeter, an oblong of grass in the centre, a creosoted garden shed with a felted roof standing on duty in a far corner.

'But anyway, you can't leave anything out at night. They come from the estate. I've had plants taken and a white urn from round the front. We've got Neighbourhood Watch, but it's not helped.'

Barridge noticed a washing pole, notched at the top. He looked from side to side. There were posts to which a washing line would normally be attached. But there was no clothes-line.

'Where's your washing line, Miss Taylor?' he asked.

CHAPTER 9

PAT NORTH found Detective Superintendent Walker sitting at his desk in shirtsleeves, his tie loosened and the telephone receiver tucked between his shoulder and ear. He was tearing the filter off another Marlboro as he spoke into the mouthpiece.

'. . . just wondering if you'd got anything on those ice-cream wrappers . . . Yes, I know . . . it's just that I'm about to interview—' Walker held the receiver away from his ear and looked at North with a thin, ironic smile on his face. 'Mallory!' he mouthed.

From the door she could hear most of the earful Walker was getting from his chief forensic scientist.

'*You'll have it as soon as I have it, Walker! The way you buggers reckon you'll get anything faster by pestering me is a bloody irritant . . .*'

Walker covered the mouthpiece with his palm. 'What does Dunn want?' he asked. 'A lawyer?'

'No, another breakfast,' said North. 'Guv, the Press Office have been on. It's getting about that we're holding someone and they're being inundated with calls. Do you want to put out a blurb – "helping police with inquiries" kind of thing?'

Walker nodded then, still listening to Mallory, he

raised his eyebrows as Satchell walked in. The Sergeant slid a few paperclipped pages of A4 on to the desk.

'Here's as much as we could get from records – three vagrancy charges, unemployed, on housing benefit. Phone cut off, single, no family.'

'Social services?'

'I'm still waiting on them. They've gone all "patient confidentiality" on us. It could be weeks.'

Walker clicked his fingers three times in rapid succession. 'Get the family liaison officer – Meg Whatsit? See if she can dig around for us.'

Suddenly he realized that Mallory's tirade had stopped. A rasping voice could be heard.

'Hello? Hello? Walker?'

Walker addressed himself to the phone again. 'Look, thank you, Doctor Mallory. I'll be waiting to hear from you. OK?'

Walker didn't just hang up, he mashed the receiver on to its slot. Then he rubbed his palms into his face. To be always waiting – waiting for other people to finish their work, for the law to grind, for something to turn up – that was the worst of the policeman's lot as far as Walker was concerned. He dropped his hands and looked hopefully at Dave Satchell, a man who could always be relied on to keep things turning over.

'Maybe we'll get lucky with one of the lolly sticks or the wrappers,' said the Sergeant. 'If she was in Dunn's flat and ate the ice-cream there, maybe we can prove it with DNA.'

'Yes, I know.'

Walker sighed. 'My kid virtually licks the design off. Shit, this is going to cost a fortune! We got ten wrappers, six sticks and half my budget's already gone to that lunatic

Mallory and his bloody shoe casts. Did you know he's had four plaster casts done – that's a couple of hundred quid *each* off my budget!'

He looked at Satchell, squinting. They'd brought Dunn in last night for theft. Now, having rearrested him this morning they'd got until exactly ten-o-five tomorrow morning to hang a charge on him.

'So. How do we stand re Mr Dunn? The bastard sober?'

Satchell laughed. 'He's had ten hours kip and two breakfasts. He's hung-over, certainly, but . . .'

Walker got up and adjusted the knot of his tie. Then he held out his fist.

'OK – you ready? Prepare, engage . . .'

'Account, closure . . .' replied Satchell, knocking the Detective Superintendent's fist with his own. They were reciting the mnemonic formula for the interview of suspects, something learned by all trainee detectives.

'And – evaluation!' capped Walker, pulling on his jacket and jamming the still unlit cigarette at a jaunty angle into his mouth. 'Let's go!'

PACE is the acronym for the Police and Criminal Evidence Act which since 1982 has regulated all the police's dealings with suspects. Designed as much to shield the police from charges of unfair treatment as to protect the public from oppressive police questioning, it has a bad name amongst serving officers for being cumbersome, bureaucratic and over-restrictive. Under the code of practice, Michael Dunn could be held for up to twenty-four hours without being charged. He could have a solicitor if he wanted and the benefit of a single phone call. If he needed medical assistance because of illness or injuries a local GP on the register of police surgeons would be sent for. The arbiter in all these matters is not the arresting officer but the station custody officer, in this case Sergeant Johns, who is God when it comes to the welfare of the suspect.

Dunn's questioning must be audiotaped in duplicate; in more modern stations it would also be videotaped. A copy of the tape should be given him on request. He must also be given a break regularly every three-quarters of an hour and a hot drink every two hours.

When Johns delivered him to the interview room Dunn looked appalling. The whites of his eyes were streaked with blood. His hair hung in rats' tails, his nose was snotty, his hands, face and neck were caked with dirt. Having removed his clothes for forensic testing they had dressed him in a white paper jumpsuit which rattled to the rhythm of his violent shaking. He shuffled through the door, his feet in police-issue plimsolls, two sizes too large and minus the laces. He hardly looked fit for questioning but Johns had seen colossal hangovers before. There was no call, he had judged, for the surgeon.

'Sit down, please, Mr Dunn,' said Walker, turning to the double tape recorder near his elbow and speaking into the mike. 'This interview is being tape recorded and may be given in evidence. I am Detective Superintendent Walker attached to Southampton Street police station, and the other officer present is—' he cocked his head towards Satchell, who was sitting alongside him – 'Detective Sergeant Satchell, Southampton Street.'

Walker went on, 'We are in interview room one at Southampton Street Police Station, and I am interviewing . . .' He looked at Dunn, who had sat down and placed a packet of cigarettes and a lighter on the table in front of him. He selected a cigarette and lit up. 'Say your name now, Mr Dunn.'

The suspect seemed far away. He roused himself and spoke in a croaking voice. 'Michael Dunn.'

'There is no other person present,' continued Walker. 'The time is ten forty-four a.m. and the date is the eighth of September. At the end of this interview I will give you a notice explaining what will happen to the tapes. Now . . .'

Walker relaxed, pressing himself back against the chair and looking closely at Dunn. 'Let me remind you that you are still under caution, and that you are entitled to free legal advice.'

'I don't want any,' said Dunn.

'Could you state your name and address and date of birth?'

'Er, Michael . . . do you want my middle name as well? It's Michael . . . Frederick Dunn and I live at—'

Dunn screwed up his face. He seemed to be trying to visualize the information, like a witness recalling a car number plate.

'Twelve, Howarth Parade . . . and I was born, er, sixteenth March in nineteen . . . sixty-nine.'

'Good. Do you understand why you have been arrested?'

But Dunn had lapsed once more into a state of torpor.

'Will you say yes or no, please?'

Dunn roused himself, aware of a sharper tone in Walker's voice. 'Yes, yes. I understand. It's OK. Ask me anything you like.'

'Where were you last Thursday lunchtime?'

'Well, I would if I could. I don't remember ... Thursday?'

'Thursday,' said Walker.

'Well, now, let's see ... I get my giro Thursday. I go down and collect it personal because it's always getting nicked.'

'So you do remember Thursday. Good.'

'Yes, like I said. I cashed my giro.'

'Where did you cash it?'

'Post Office up by the newsagent.'

'Uh-huh. And which newsagent would that be?'

'One near the estate, near where I live.' He suddenly began to giggle. 'He got a bit nasty with me, the newsagent. Well, he had reasons.'

'Oh yes?'

'Yeah!'

He was fully laughing now, hunching over, his head going down to the table. 'I stuffed most of the papers I was supposed to deliver in the bins. Especially on Thursday. Couldn't be bothered.'

Dunn's mirth had subsided to a snigger.

'What did you do then – last Thursday?'

'Got me money, went round to the off-licence.'

'Which off-licence is that, Mr Dunn?'

'One near the newsagent. Near where I live. Then I went to the park. I go there.'

'And what do you do there?'

'I drink, with me pals. I'd have been there Thursday.'

Dunn had taken off one of the shoes they'd given him and was feeling around inside.

'Can you name any of these pals?'

'Yeah, er, there's Midge, Terry Smith and, um, some other bloke . . .'

'Do you know what time you met up with your mates?'

Dunn sat without answering for a moment, looking without curiosity at the shoe.

Walker repeated the question. 'When on Thursday? You got your giro and then . . .?'

Dunn roused himself. 'After the off-licence opened, must've been.'

'And what time does the off-licence open?'

Dunn raised his head and said, in mock patience, 'After eleven o'clock.'

'So, tell me what you do before you go to the off-licence.'

Dunn shrugged. 'I get up and I wait – for the off-licence to open.'

'And then, do you stay with these pals all afternoon on Thursdays?'

'Yeah, unless we get moved on. Or the kids start hassling us.'

Walker's eyebrows arched. 'Kids?'

'Yeah, off the estate.'

'Any specific kids? How old?'

'Some about eight, some about sixteen. I don't know. All kinds.'

'Do you like kids?'

'Yeah. But not when they mess me about.'

'What do you mean by that?'

'Oh, nick things off me. Break into me flat.'

Walker was interested now and he wanted Dunn to know it. He leaned nearer.

'So kids go into your flat?'

'Yeah.'

'Girls as well as boys?'

'Yes, they're worse than the lads.'

'Oh? But the little ones aren't, are they?'

'No. They're OK.'

Walker shifted on his chair so he was closer still to Dunn.

'Do you like little girls?'

He let the question hang for one, two, three seconds and then, just as Dunn was about to say something, Walker went on.

'Did you ever play peekaboo with them? You know, hide your face behind your fingers. Did you do that last Thursday afternoon? In the playground on the estate.'

The room was hot, the air fouled with sweat and smoke, the walls crawling with condensation. Dunn was still holding his shoe, looking at it. Walker couldn't tell if he was thinking about the question or his mind had wandered off again.

Then Dunn said, 'No, no. I was with me mates.'

'Why have you got kids' toys in your flat?'

'For the kids ... Well, I mean, some of them, are theirs.'

'Which toys specifically belong to the children?'

Pulling a sullen face, Dunn shrugged. 'I don't know what I've got and what I haven't got, do I?'

'Any kids play in your flat last Thursday?'

'I don't know. I wasn't there.'

'You were with your pals, right? In the park?'

'Yes, they'll ... what's the word? Vouch for me, yeah.'

'What do you mean, vouch for you?'

'Well, you want to know where I was Thursday. They'll tell you.'

Walker sighed and looked at Satchell, then pulled out a cigarette, broke off the filter and lit up.

'OK. What do you do when it's not Thursday? Other days?'

'You mean, when I got no money?'

'Exactly.'

'Stay in me flat, play videos . . . Well, I did play videos, till my video got nicked.'

'Oh? How long ago was that?'

Dunn shook his head and examined his fingernails. Each had a sickle-shaped deposit of black dirt beneath.

'I don't know. Months.'

'And did you play videos for the kids?'

'Yeah. I like cartoons. So do they.'

'What about videos like *The Terminator*?'

'Great.'

'And *Child's Play*?'

'Yeah, that's brilliant.'

'And how do those videos – videos like those – affect you?'

Dunn frowned. He was puzzled.

'How d'you mean?'

'How do they make you feel?'

Dunn frowned, staring up at the corner of the room. 'Feel? Oh, well. Sometimes I get angry.'

'And what do you do about that?'

'Drink.'

'In front of the kids? Are you watching these videos with kids?'

Dunn smiled, a droopy movement of the lips. 'Yeah, I did sometimes.'

117

'Were you watching videos on Thursday?'

Dunn straightened his drooping spine. 'No!' he flashed, angrily. 'You're not listening to me. I said I got no video now.'

'OK. But when you *used* to watch videos, did you ever watch them with a little girl called Julie Harris?'

Dunn had lapsed back into his former torpid state. He appeared not to hear.

'Do you know who she is?'

Dunn was fiddling with his Bic lighter, looking at it with interest.

'What about her brother, Jason?' persisted Walker.

'They were just kids to me, off the estate,' Dunn mumbled. 'I don't know their names.'

Beside Walker's chair on the floor was an exhibits bag, a canvas holdall. Now he reached into it and drew out the doll taken from Dunn's flat.

'I am now showing the interviewee exhibit number RC3.'

He held it up and turned it. The artificial flesh showed through the transparent plastic like real skin. 'Do you recognize this, Michael?'

It was the first time Walker had called him by his first name. Dunn raised his head sharply, then looked away.

'Yeah, it's a doll.'

'I know that. But this particular doll, Michael, we got from your flat.'

Dunn gave that momentary glance again before returning to his examination of his feet. 'It's got an arm missing.'

Walker sighed and spoke slowly and deliberately. 'I am investigating the murder of Julie Anne Harris. A little girl. If you fail – or refuse – to account for this doll's having

118

been found in your flat, a proper inference may be drawn in court.'

Dunn raised his eyes and looked at the doll. Walker turned the evidence bag through ninety degrees in front of his eyes which, though not as blank as they had been, remained dull and unresponsive. Perhaps he was considering what to say. Perhaps his sluggish, abused brain was genuinely striving to remember.

'I found it,' he said at last.

'You found this doll?'

'Yes. Up by the derelict houses. I want to go to the toilet.'

Walker's face was intense now. He searched Dunn's face for the lie, for the flicker of fear, that would tell him Michael Dunn was a murderer.

'*When* did you find it?'

'What?'

'When did you find the doll?'

'Thursday. I found it on Thursday. Look, can I—'

'When on Thursday did you find this doll? It's very important that we know, Michael.'

Dunn opened his mouth to speak, then shut it again. The brain was working better now. He looked at Satchell, who thought he saw a moment, just a moment, of shrewd calculation. It was the look of an animal about to back out of a trap. Then Dunn turned to Walker again. His face creased into a smile. He leaned towards them and put a hand to the side of his mouth.

'I lied,' he confided in a whisper. 'I had it for ages.' He erased the smile and straightened up. 'I have to go to the toilet now.'

Walker leaned towards the tape machine. 'Interview

suspended at eleven fifteen a.m. to allow Michael Dunn to use the toilet.'

Outside the interview room, Walker and Satchell were intercepted by Pat North.

'Mallory called. Says the tests on Julie Anne's stomach contents are going to take much longer than anticipated. Ditto Dunn's clothes.'

Walker groaned and shut his eyes. He stayed like that for a moment, then snapped back into action.

'Get him a bloody solicitor,' he told North. 'In the meantime, we check out his so-called alibi.'

'What do you reckon, guv?' asked Satchell. 'Is it Dunn?'

Walker scowled. He looked as if he might spit. 'Yeah. We just don't have enough to charge him.'

North returned to the Incident Room to check the house-to-house reports from Ashcroft Close and the other owner-occupied houses which had been trawled earlier. Barridge's report was long and painfully detailed.

There have been a lot of thefts [she read] *including washing, pegs, lines, plants and pots. Residents have repeatedly complained to the Council, who have promised to raise the height of the garden fences, but so far there has been no action. A Neighbourhood Watch scheme has not proved effective in stemming the level of crime and residents are critical of the police . . .*

Christ – he'd written a dissertation. She skimmed through the visit reports until one caught her attention.

Number 17 Ashcroft Close: corner house. Owner occupier, Miss A. Taylor, reports that her washing line has recently been stolen. Post to which line was attached had also been recently painted.

Sergeant Satchell came bustling in. 'We've got a Belinda Sinclair, in reception. Duty solicitor for Michael Dunn.'

North frowned, trying to place the name. 'Sinclair?'

'Sergeant Johns says she's only been on the scheme a few months – correction, three weeks. She's fresh as a daisy!'

North held Barridge's report before his eyes. 'I'll take her through to him. Check this, it's Barridge's door-to-door report.' She laid the report against his chest in such a way as to give him no choice but to take it or let it fall. 'Seventeen Ashcroft Close. Get a Scene of Crime Officer on to the post, will you?'

Satchell looked nonplussed. 'What post?'

'Miss Taylor's post – Ashcroft Close.'

'And? What's it all in aid of?'

North had begun to move. She stopped and turned. 'The rope around the victim's neck had traces of paint. It's all in the MG dockets, Sarge, if you would only make time to read them!'

Belinda Sinclair was young and she was a rookie, which Walker knew before he met her. He'd provisionally marked her down as a pushover, but two things changed his mind when he saw her. Firstly, she looked him smack in the eye and the look had ambition written right through it like a stick of rock. Secondly, she was beautiful.

121

If Ms Sinclair really knew how to handle herself, the beauty would be an asset every bit as useful as a doctorate in law or a father on the Bench.

She'd been escorted into the interview room by North and was reading the casework file. She wanted to master the brief before facing her client. Walker, who'd followed her in, stood by the window, smoking, glancing at his watch, wishing this well-dressed woman would speed up.

'So the twelve videos turned out to be Mr Dunn's own property?' she said, coolly.

'Yes,' said Walker, flicking his ash.

'So you then arrested him in connection with the murder of the little girl, Julie Anne Harris?'

'Yes.'

'But you really have no other evidence . . .' Walker was about to speak but she forestalled him by holding up her hand. She turned the page. '. . . apart from a statement by this Mrs Enid Marsh.'

'Who identified Dunn as the man last seen with Julie Anne Harris. Mrs Harris also identified a doll found in Dunn's flat. It belonged to her daughter.'

'But you haven't placed my client on an identification parade?'

Walker let out a single ironic laugh. 'You haven't seen him yet. It's not so easy.'

She shut the file and smiled at him glacially. 'Well, Detective Superintendent Walker, I suggest you get a parade arranged. If you have a witness, it *would* seem the logical next step – wouldn't it?'

Walker had an urge to tell her what to do with her suggestion, but repressed it.

'I'd like to see my client now. And I'd like access to

the recorded interview *and* a copy of the custody report, which does not seem to be here.'

Walker preceded her to the door and theatrically opened it for her. 'Right away, Ms Sinclair,' he said, barely concealing the sarcasm.

CHAPTER 10

MAKING THE beds Anita was thinking about the word tragedy and she couldn't find any meaning in it. She'd been told her father's death was a tragedy and now they were throwing the word around about Julie. But papers also talked about a footballer breaking his leg as a tragedy, or a pensioner's missing budgie. Anita shuddered convulsively. You couldn't begin to think about who might have done those deliberate, spiteful things to her daughter. Just to call it a tragedy was too automatic, a way of forgetting it – and they must never, ever forget.

She heard the doorbell in the hallway ring once. Suddenly she hated the outside world, the way it came in and interfered and took things. A sudden wave of hatred battered her. There was a bitter taste to it that had seized her from time to time in the last few days. She put up with it. She was still awaiting the sweet release of pure grief.

Entering the lounge a couple of minutes later, Anita gasped and put a hand to her mouth. The tall man standing by the sideboard, with his short hair and impeccable turn-out, was Thomas Harris, her ex-husband. He turned round and she saw in his hand one of the framed photographs of his daughter – the one in which she was wearing a spotted dress and sat astride a blue playground cow.

She looked directly into his eyes, saw their icy clarity. His voice was low, subdued.

'They let me have compassionate leave. Flew in last night. All right, are you?'

Anita remembered Thomas's rages. The worst had been when she'd told him she could no longer bear the bitchy life in army married quarters and was leaving. The anger had always started with Thomas speaking very low, quiet, controlled, before building up to an intensity that was terrifying. He never hit or even touched her. He would simply turn into a different person. It scared her then and, she realized, it still did.

'I swear to God, Thomas,' she said, her voice trembly, 'she was only out playing ten minutes. Jason was with her.'

Thomas returned the photograph to the sideboard. 'I don't know what to say. I can't take it in. She was my baby.'

He bowed his head. At this moment, Peter came in from the kitchen. He looked at Thomas in a way that was at the same time aggressive and guarded. He said, 'They got someone, you know. That pervert, the one from the estate . . .'

Thomas shook his head from side to side. 'Well, I'd like to have ten minutes with him, that's all.'

Pushing past Peter, Helen appeared. As soon as she realized that Thomas had come, she started to weep. Thomas went to her, wrapping his arms around her.

125

'Hello, Mum. I couldn't get here sooner. Eventually they gave me compassionate leave.'

Finally, Jason came hurtling in and threw himself at his father.

'Dad! Dad!' Jason was so excited to see him; his body trembled and he was close to tears.

Thomas stooped and gathered his son up. Jason clung to him as if afraid to let him go, showing in that moment more affection to his real father than he ever had for Peter James.

Helen watched them hugging and said to Peter, 'Maybe you should leave them alone.'

It was her way of pointing up the difference between Thomas and Peter. Helen had never wavered in believing that Anita and the kids belonged with Thomas. If only they'd stayed with him, how different things might have been!

Peter swung towards her, snarling. 'And maybe you should shut up! Just keep your nose out!'

'Eh!' said Thomas, putting Jason down. 'Don't you speak to Mum like that. You hear me?'

'Oh, this is your house, is it? You pay the bills, do you?'

Thomas raised a finger, real menace in his eyes. 'Julie was *my* daughter. So leave it *out*.'

Peter's lip curled. 'Prick!'

Standing aside, as if accidentally detached, Jason watched the adults. He didn't understand exactly what was going on, but he appreciated his dad telling Peter to get knotted. Peter slunk out of the room then, and his gran and his mum both started crying. His dad wrapped his arms around his mum and hugged her, swinging her from side to side. She pushed her face into his dad's shoulder and just sobbed and sobbed. Jason wanted to be

126

a part of that embrace. He was jealous of her. He wanted to still be held by his dad. He knew that Julie was gone, which wasn't *his* fault. But having his beloved dad back was all right.

Belinda Sinclair and Michael Dunn made quite a contrast – he, in his white paper overall, unshaven for several days, filthy fingernails, matted hair; she, in a dove-grey designer suit and apricot silk shirt, her lips glistening with perfectly applied scarlet lipstick, her blonde hair catching the light from the mundane striplight and turning it to pure gold. She sat upright in her chair with a legal pad on the table in front of her and an expensive ballpoint in her hand.

'You must concentrate, Michael. This is very serious,' she was saying. She could see he had not taken very much of his situation in. He wasn't frightened, but listless, detached.

'You have given two different versions of how you got the doll. An inference can be drawn from that in court, you know.'

Dunn, already sitting bent forward on his chair, slumped against the table, covering his face with his hands. 'I want to get out of here. I want to go home. I need a drink.'

'Michael.' Belinda's voice was coaxing, almost seductive. 'You do realize I am your solicitor. I am not a police officer.'

Dunn raised his head. The red-rimmed eyes looked feverish and hunted. 'Why am I here?'

In frustration, Belinda dropped the pen onto the pad. There was a tap on the door and Dunn, startled, shambled to his feet. It was Satchell.

127

'You ready yet, ma'am?'

Belinda Sinclair's response was frosty. 'No, but I will inform you when I am.'

Satchell hung for a moment in the doorway, made as if to speak and then changed his mind. He raised his hand and left.

'Now, Michael, please sit down. We need to talk about this doll. And then there is a small matter of an identification parade . . .'

PCs Phelps and Brown had been detailed to pay a visit to the Scrubbery and pick up any winos in sight – and in particular the one known as Midge. They found her sitting in her customary place, singing 'Somewhere Over the Rainbow'. She said she'd be delighted to accompany Phelps to Southampton Street nick, or to any other destination he might care to name.

'I'd go anywhere with you, darling,' she told him as he assisted her towards the squad car. 'Lovely looking boy like you. Who's a lovely boy then?'

She leaned into Phelps's shoulder and slid her cheek along until her forehead clashed with the line of his jaw.

'Oops! 'Scuse me. Give us a kiss, then – go on. Give us a kiss, handsome.'

Meanwhile Brown had got hold of Bert O'Farrell, who was proving less cooperative.

'I'll bloody kill you! Cart me off in your meat wagon, would you, you bastards!'

'Please, Mr O'Farrell,' said Brown, as his cap flew off. He gestured to Phelps for assistance. 'Look, we only want to talk to you.'

'Slaughter me? I'll bloody slaughter the pair of *you*. Come on, then, come on. Try me. Put up your fists, you pair of fairies.'

Midge Parker-Brown sat in the back seat of the car, watching the tussling men benignly. A fragment of distant memory had entered her brain – a Parker-Brown limousine standing on a gravel drive with her, aged ten, sitting demurely in the back. The engine was purring, ready to whisk her off for a birthday visit to the cinema.

At last Phelps and Brown bundled Bert O'Farrell into the car beside her. As they drove away Midge began to sing.

'*We're off to see the Wizard, the wunnerful Wizard of Oz, because, because, because, becauuuuuse . . .*'

At the station, Phelps got Midge sitting down in the waiting area as a WPC walked past. She took one look at Midge and stopped.

'Hello, Midge. What they bringing you in for this time?'

'You know her?' said Phelps. He guided his colleague out of Midge's earshot. 'That AMIP Sergeant Satchell's going to question her about the Harris suspect. Dunn's named her for his alibi. Trouble is she's pissed as a fart.'

'Nothing new there. Same story on Thursday when I last saw the old bat.'

Phelps did a double take. 'Thursday? Where'd you see her?'

'St John's hospital casualty. Took her there in the morning, about ten, ten-thirty.'

'What happened?'

'She fell down some steps. Suspected concussion.'

'How long did they keep her?'

129

'Don't know. I left her there. I'll look in my notes and give you a firm time. And you can always phone St John's.'

Twenty minutes later Phelps gave Sergeant Satchell the good news.

'Dunn's alibi just blew away, Sarge. Hospital says the Triage Nurse assessed Midge Parker-Brown at ten-thirty and they didn't release her until six at night. Apparently they thought she might have brain damage. That's a laugh. Anyway, she can't have been with Dunn at all on Thursday, can she? Unless they had a liquid breakfast together.'

'No,' said Satchell. 'Dunn didn't leave his house till eleven, as far as we can tell. What about the other bloke you pulled – what's his name, O'Farrell?'

Phelps made a face and shook his head. 'Got a bad case of uniformitis. Thinks he's Mike Tyson at the moment but I doubt we'll ever get anything out of him.'

Satchell smiled. 'Good. About Midge, put it in writing for me, will you, Phelps? And let her go. I'll give the glad tidings to Mr Walker.'

Walker sat at his desk, thinking through the chain of evidence he was constructing against Michael Dunn, link by link. Dunn had been suspected by the residents on the estate. He'd given an alibi, of course, but even though it hadn't stuck, the residents' suspicions would be dismissed by a jury as pure prejudice, except for one thing. Enid Marsh had seen a man with the missing child and he fitted Dunn's description. She was a dotty old lady, which wasn't exactly to her credit as a witness. But it helped in another way because Enid was a recluse and not exactly tuned in to the prejudices of the estate. So she probably didn't know Dunn for the 'pervert' that the residents had tagged him as.

It all hinged on identification: would old Enid recognize Dunn as the long-haired man in the long dark coat who she'd seen in the playground. You never knew with old people. One minute they could name every Grand National winner since 1936 and the next they'd forgotten how to make toast.

But one thing was for certain. Either he'd have to let Dunn go or put Enid's colander mind to the test, and soon. That meant lashing together an identification parade before the end of the day and that wasn't even half as easy as it looked in cop films. They'd have to assemble eight men, each with a superficial resemblance to Michael Dunn, and keep them in one place while the old dear was trundled from the Howarth Estate all the way to the Met's ID Suite at Kilburn.

Walker dared not think what was going to happen to his budget by the time this investigation was over. It was already in shreds. He sighed, flipped open the notebook he used to keep track of costs and began rummaging in a drawer for his calculator.

By three o'clock, eight men who were like, but not too like, Michael Dunn had been found at Kilburn and kitted out in various styles of long coat. The lights in the Identification Suite were down and they stood in semi-darkness, talking in low tones as they awaited the star of the show.

Michael Dunn, now in prison-issue clothes and a long dark coat similar to his own, sauntered in between two officers. He seemed unconcerned.

'Which position do you want?' asked the escorting officer.

Dunn looked at him in foggy puzzlement. 'Eh?'

'In the parade.' He jerked his thumb at the dark-glass window on the wall opposite the line of men. 'This is an Identification Suite. You'll be eyeballed from in there. So where do you want to stand?'

Dunn glanced up and down, scratching his head, then stepped into a place, the other men shuffling to make room. Cards with printed numbers were fixed above their heads. Struck by solemnity in the presence of a possible murderer, they listened to their instructions. They were to remember their numbers and keep their expressions neutral. Dunn's was number three.

'Any questions?'

Nobody had any questions.

The ID Suite at Kilburn is, in the correct marketing jargon, a state of the art facility, with a viewing room behind one-way glass, remote control lighting and talk-back. Enid Marsh entered the viewing room in a wheel-chair, followed by a small retinue of officers, one of them pushing, another carrying her walking frame and hand-bag. Belinda Sinclair was the last to enter. She stood quietly by the door watching Enid closely. The old woman was fidgeting impatiently.

'You can stay in your chair, Mrs Marsh, if you like,' said the Identification Officer.

'No, no. I *can* stand, you know. I don't even have a chair of my own at home. It's just this arthritis.'

She gripped the arms of the chair and heaved herself

on to her feet. She stood for a moment with knees and back braced and slightly bent. Then she straightened, almost triumphantly. 'See?' Looking from face to face, as if expecting a round of applause, she was smiling broadly.

The officer touched a button and the room behind the glass burst into light. The halogen brightness made the men look uniformly pale and unhealthy. Enid scanned them eagerly. She felt rejuvenated, important.

'You want me to pick him out now?'

The Identification Officer cleared his throat and raised a clipboard. He frowned at the witness.

'On September the fifth, at about one p.m., you saw a man take a little girl by the hand in the playground beneath your window. That man may—'

He looked severely at Enid. She was nodding at him like someone keeping time to music.

' – or may *not* be on this identification parade today, but I would ask you not to make any decision as to whether you can identify him before you have looked twice at each member of the parade.'

Enid swallowed. She mustn't rush, that's what he was saying to her, though why he had to read it out like that she didn't know.

'Could they stand up?' she asked.

She examined the man on the end of the line, position number nine. Never seen him before. Number eight, same. And number seven. Where did they get these chaps from? Number six, number five, number four – never clapped eyes on them, though five looked like that nice lad in the fish shop. Number three . . .

'Just take your time,' said the policeman.

Enid's heart quickened. Number three! That was him.

Since she knew about the murder she'd kept an image of what she'd seen from her window fresh in her mind. Same shape of head, same hair, same coat. It was him.

She turned to the policeman. 'Number three,' she said, firmly. 'That's the man.'

Belinda tore out of the ID Suite, keying the office number on her mobile. She had been trying to contain her excitement, but this was news she had to tell someone. She got Jeremy Oxley, one of the solicitors she shared her office with.

'Jeremy? Guess what! ... No, you berk. My client's just been picked out of a parade. I've got myself a murderer! What was that?' She giggled. 'Of course, I meant an *alleged* murderer. He's called Michael Frederick Dunn.'

Walker was still juggling the overtime figures when Satchell came in with the news that another link in the chain had been forged.

'We going to charge the bastard now, guv?'

Walker sighed and shook his head. 'This is identification, Dave. Too many cases that hinged on the dodgy memory of a witness have gone down the toilet. I need something more, or the CPS won't be playing ball.'

And, to satisfy the Crown Prosecution Service, he knew what he needed was forensic evidence. But did he have the money? He looked despairingly at the column of figures in front of him. If only this wasn't Sunday. On bloody Sunday everything cost double – or was it triple? Oh well, the fuck to it.

'Get on to Sergeant Polk,' he said wearily. 'I want forensics down at Dunn's flat – yes, again! The whole team. I want the floors up. I want every piece of bedbug shit turned over. I want something that'll stick to Dunn like superglue and I want it today or, at the latest, tomorrow. We've got till ten a.m. or this investigation has gone to buggery.'

CHAPTER 11

'HEY, BARRIDGE! What's this? Mine was ham and cheese.'

Barridge swivelled back to the Superintendent's desk, where he'd just deposited a coffee and a bagged sandwich. 'Sorry, sir. I—'

Walker held up the paper bag. 'This is cheese and pickle.'

Barridge looked at the cardboard tray he carried. He picked up another sandwich and gave it to the Detective Superintendent. 'Sorry, sir. Sorry. Got mixed up.'

Walker softened. He'd seen the look of panic on the constable's face. 'Look. It's no big deal, OK? Just I don't like pickle.'

He tossed the unwanted package back to Barridge and opened the second bag. Barridge hovered, waiting to be sent on his way.

'You all right, son?' Walker asked in a low voice as he extracted the replacement sandwich. 'I know it was you that found her. Living with you, is it?'

Barridge tried to stand as upright as possible. 'I'm all right, sir.'

'If ever you want to talk about it, you can go to occupational health. That's what they're there for. I've been there, son.'

136

Barridge, who didn't think the Detective Superintendent had ever in his life so much as breathed the same air as an occupational health therapist, said, 'Really, I'm—'

'*Don't* bottle it up. Which reminds me – Cranham!'

'Yes, guv?'

The Exhibits Officer came over and helped himself to a sandwich pack from Barridge's tray.

'I want those empty bottles collected from Dunn's place and sent over to Mallory.'

Cranham nodded as he tore open the sandwich. 'I'll sort it, guv. I'm on my way over now.'

'Take PC Barridge with you. Dunn had a bit of a problem with recycling so you'll need some extra muscle.'

An hour later, with Belinda Sinclair beside him, the suspect was back in the interview room facing Walker and Satchell across a table on which there were two brands of cigarette, a lighter, full ashtray, disposable cups. On the wall was a water cooler. The recording machine whirred.

The police were like fishermen moving up and down a riverbank, casting for a rise, but so far the fish stayed locked to the bottom. After more than an hour of questioning, there had been no bites – nothing to enable Walker to charge Dunn.

'This doll . . .' Walker held up the nude plastic doll in its polythene evidence bag. 'Julie Ann had this with her when she left home. She was subsequently found dead. Now, I am asking you again Mr Dunn: why was this doll found in your flat?'

Belinda turned her eyes on Dunn. *Be careful.* But Dunn seemed hardly to be attending.

'My flat? I don't know, do I? I mean, it used to be quite nice when I moved in, like. But me pals wrecked it, and the kids . . .'

He was shivering in rhythm with the throbbing of his head. The white paper suit that he again wore rustled slightly in the hollow room. All sensation, but especially the perception of sound and light, seemed swollen and bruised to him. He reached for the white cup of water and gulped. It felt good except there was no sting of alcohol in his throat.

'You haven't answered the question, Michael.'

Trying to stub his cigarette out against the inside of the cup, Dunn was burning a hole in the styrofoam. 'I found it.'

'When did you find it?'

Still intent on extinguishing his butt, Dunn produced a tentative, truncated shrug. 'About a year ago.'

Walker leaned forward. '*Where* did you find it?'

Dunn had by now poked the cigarette all the way through the cup. He peered at the protruding tip in surprise. An acrid smell permeated the room.

'Will you please answer the question?'

'On the building site – that building site on the estate.'

'Are you sure about that, Mr Dunn?'

Dunn glanced sideways at his brief, who smiled encouragingly. 'Yes.'

Now he was applying the tip of the cigarette tentatively to the white paper of his overall.

'Do you like ice-cream?' asked Walker.

'No.'

'But you have a lot of ice-cream wrappers in your flat. Where do they come from?'

'I don't know. Lots of people, like, come and go.' Suddenly he was shouting and waggling his head. 'Ice-cream van – *Ding-dong, ding dong* . . .'

By now he'd burned a series of holes in his sleeve so that the pale, goose-pimply skin could be seen. Walker shook out a Marlboro and snapped off the filter.

'Did you see Julie Ann Harris last Thursday afternoon?'

'No. I was with my friends, see? Like I told you.'

'Yes – you have stated that you were with—' Walker put the unlit cigarette in his mouth and lifted up his notes. 'Terry Smith, another man you were unable to name, and a woman named Midge.'

'Yes, I was.'

Walker lit the little bush of tobacco that stuck out of the end of his cigarette. 'Well, I'm afraid, Michael, that Midge Parker-Brown was *not* with you last Thursday. We have established that. We know where she was, and it was nowhere near you.'

He studied Dunn intently. He was an angler again, scrutinizing the broken surface of the river. 'What do you have to say about that?'

Dunn was now mashing his cigarette into his arm, to stub it out once and for all. 'I don't know,' he mumbled. 'Must have been mistaken.'

'Mistaken? Can I just go back over that, Michael. You say you were mistaken. About *what* exactly?'

Dunn looked up from his sleeve, which had begun to smoulder. 'What? Sorry, what was the question?'

Walker opened his mouth to repeat the question but he was forestalled. A pale blue flame had appeared on the suspect's sleeve, rimming one of the worn holes he'd made with his cigarette. Then, abruptly, the fire took

139

hold, turning yellow as it licked at the folds of the suspect's sleeve. Dunn was on fire. He leapt up, screeching and pawing at the flame, his chair clattering to the floor behind him. In the same instant Satchell reached for his own water cup, leaned across and threw it over Dunn. With a truncated fizzle, the fire died.

For a few beats, no one spoke. Satchell couldn't, he was trying to control himself – Belinda Sinclair's face could have put a fire out. Most of the water had gone over her anyway. She ran a hand through her hair and cleared her throat.

'Superintendent Walker, I am suggesting a bathroom break.'

She smiled thinly at the interrogators. 'If my client doesn't require one, I most certainly do.'

'Right,' snapped Walker. Then, for the tape: 'Interview suspended at seven-oh-two p.m., to allow Miss Sinclair to take a leak.'

At the Forensic Laboratory, a junior scientific officer rubbed his eyes under his plastic protective spectacles. Sometimes he got called in on Sunday, but not usually for a long shift. Police couldn't afford it. Today, it seemed, was different and he could have done without it. Saturday's rugger match, the party in the evening at Notting Hill and his night with that girl from Streatham – what was her name? – had taken its toll and he was shattered. Still, Sunday overtime was something else on this job.

He reached a latex-gloved hand, holding a pair of laboratory tongs, into the black dustbin bag which stood beside his test-bench, drawing out a crushed and soggy cereal packet. He carefully prized it open to see if anything had been pushed inside. Sometimes at parties he described himself for effect as a Garbologist. Other people's rubbish may be one of the least pleasant, but it was potentially the most revealing, of the stuff that came in for lab examination.

He dined out on the story of when he'd found a set of false eyelashes in the bin of an international opening batsman and DNA testing proved that the cricketer had worn them himself. It actually had nothing to do with the case, but he had never been able to watch the guy play in a Test Match since then without wondering if he wore them on the field.

The cereal packet was empty. He placed it with a pile of discarded packaging and recorded it on his inventory, then tonged out a lump of cheese with a rich crop of furry grey mould growing all over it. Seven to eight weeks' worth, he estimated. He made a note of it and fished again.

The tongs connected with something which at first slipped from their jaws. He took a firmer grip and pulled again. The thing was mixed up with other refuse and he had to tug it free. When it came loose he could see what it was – a tangle of red and blue washing line. One end had a loop. The other looked cut.

He flipped back the pages on his clipboard to the case report, just to make sure: 'A piece of plastic-coated line ligated around the neck, resembling a clothes-line. Colour, red and blue.'

He left the desk and went looking for Arnold Mallory.

'I don't know about any rope!'

They'd been just about to resume questioning the

suspect when North had clattered down the stairs. She virtually ran at Walker and Satchell, who'd been about to follow Dunn and his brief into the interview room.

'Guv, hold it a second! Lab's found something . . .'

When she told him, his face tightened and he grabbed her shoulders, planting a kiss on her cheek. 'Yes!'

Back in the interview room, he told Dunn what he had found, then listened as the man tried pathetically to deny all knowledge.

'I don't know how it got in my bin! I don't!' he bleated.

Walker interrupted him, placing both palms flat on the tabletop and leaning forward to make sure he was clearly understood.

'Michael Frederick Dunn,' he said, 'I am now charging you with the murder of Julie Ann Harris . . .'

CHAPTER 12

A T LEAST an hour of Walker's insomnia that night had been occupied with the magistrate's impending decision on bail. It would complicate things badly if Dunn was released. Walker still needed unfettered access to his flat – with the unused section of washing line found there, more evidence had to be forthcoming. *Had* to be. But if Dunn was out and about – living in the flat, because for sure he had nowhere else to go – that would badly screw up the forensic effort.

It was deep within Walker's nature to lie awake envying his wife's snores and worrying about tomorrow, but in this case it was all unnecessary. Next morning, Belinda Sinclair put in a noticeably half-hearted submission, probably preferring to have her client in the Scrubs where she could always find him and he couldn't drink. Knew what she was doing, that girl, Walker had to admit it. The magistrate duly ignored her trite remarks about her client's good intentions and summarily denied bail. Sinclair didn't even appear disappointed; Dunn didn't look as if he knew the time of day.

A dark fog of bewilderment swirled through the accused's head as he sat in the cells beneath the Magistrate's Court.

Fresh as spring in her expensively labelled clothes, Miss Sinclair sat opposite him, pushing a small sheaf of forms and a Biro across the table.

'Some more forms for you to put your signature to, Michael. This one's the final Legal Aid document. That's so that we can be paid for defending you.'

Dunn stared gravely at the paper and picked up the pen. But he did nothing. Belinda got up and looked at the Prison Officer standing guard by the door.

'I just need to show him where to sign – all right?'

The screw nodded and she moved to Dunn's shoulder. He could smell the mix of different perfumes as she leaned nearer – shampoo in her hair, a scented soap maybe and who knows what else? It stirred him out of his lethargy and he aimed the pen towards the dotted line, where her varnished fingernail gleamed.

'Sign here – see?'

Dunn looked up and down the document. 'It's a blank form.'

'Yes – we'll fill it out later. Just sign.'

Dunn wrote his signature in a shaky, childish script.

'And here and here and finally here.'

Dunn kept signing until she was satisfied. She took the pen from his hand and moved back to her seat, opening a thick notepad. Dunn looked at her, squinting. He was not used to looking at beauty. It seemed to make his situation even more confusing.

'OK, Michael. Let's start with your parents' name and address.'

'I don't have any – parents.'

Belinda scribbled a note and said, 'So, where were you brought up?'

'Foster homes. I don't know if I can remember them all.'

She tapped the Biro against her perfectly white teeth and began to speak, but Dunn cut in.

'I don't want to talk about them.' He lit a cigarette. He was edgy, looking away into a corner of the room. 'I don't, er, remember a lot of things. They said it was me blanking it all out.'

Belinda waited, staring at her client. She gave him a few seconds, then said, gently, 'Blanking out what, Michael?'

Dunn's attention was still fixed in the room's corner. He seemed not to hear her.

'Blanking out *what*, Michael?'

Three dull blows on the door echoed around the cell. The Prison Officer turned and looked through the spyhole.

'That's the transportation. Sorry, Miss, we can't wait any longer.'

With a sigh, Belinda closed her notebook. Dunn looked at her. He was quite good-looking really, under all that crud. But he also looked touchingly lost and alone.

'Where are they taking me?' he asked, looking at her now. He had the eyes of an abandoned puppy.

'You'll go to Wormwood Scrubs, Michael.'

'Prison?'

'The Magistrate has denied your bail. You'll stay there until the trial.'

'What d'you mean? What am I going to do? What's it going to be like?'

Sinclair may be a rookie, but she knew something about what it was going to be like. It was going to be hell in a box. Persecution without end, bawled at day and night, cut up in the showers, your food spat into. Nobody had a

worse time inside than a man who might have killed a child
– except for a man who actually had.

She stood up and said as softly as she could. 'You'll have
to be very, very patient, Michael. Do what they say, and
don't cause trouble. Will you do that?'

The Prison Officer swung the door open and moved to
stand behind the prisoner. He hooked his hand under
Dunn's arm and drew him to his feet.

Going through the day like a robot, Anita had spent a
lot of time waiting for the television news. There had
been a bulletin on BBC1 at eleven and, still in her
dressing gown, she watched it with close attention. The
case wasn't even mentioned and she felt bitterly disappointed. Was this what it all amounted to? Her little
girl's life worth a couple of days' media attention, and
then nothing?

After the news was over, she didn't move, just flicked
the picture over to ITV, a morning chat show. She knew
there was another news in an hour so she sat on, watching
the image on the screen whisk from face to face. She
couldn't have told you what they were saying.

Peter was sitting with a pile of music CDs on his knee,
sorting through them. He wanted to play something loud
and violent. He certainly didn't want to watch a bunch of
lottery winners and minor TV stars talking about their
philosophy of life.

'There wasn't anything about her on the news,' said
Anita.

Peter grunted.

She went on, 'Maybe there will be on the later one.'

Peter tossed a CD down and picked up another one.

'Great,' he said. 'Go on. You just sit there and wait for it. Whole place needs hoovering, but don't worry. You sit there. Nothing *else* to do, is there?'

Anita closed her eyes and rocked forward slightly across her folded arms. 'Oh, stop it, Pete. Just stop it.'

But Peter was just starting. 'There's no reason for your mother to stay either. I'm sick and tired of her bunking up in here.'

He put on a mimicking falsetto. 'Thomas this, Thomas that. You ask me, she fancies Thomas herself. And hasn't *he* been a pain in the arse? I'm glad he's gone back.'

'Maybe I need Mum.'

'And what about me? You don't need *me*?'

Anita looked at him. She seemed drugged, out of it. 'I didn't say that.'

'Feels like it.'

He crashed the heap of CDs on to the coffee table, picked up another from the floor and began impatiently dealing them down on to the table like a pack of cards. When he spoke again, she heard the sing-song of self-pity in his voice.

'I touch you and you, like, cringe away. Sleep as far from me in bed as you can. Don't cook any more. You bloody do nothing but sit in front of the TV, waiting for the news!'

She slid back against the chair, her body going limp. 'I'm sorry. I—'

'So am I.'

When Helen came in seconds later she found the two sitting in silence. She carried a tray which she placed on a low table. There were two mugs of tea on it.

'Here you are, love.'

She handed Anita a tea then took the other one and

147

subsided with a sigh into the vacant armchair. Peter looked at her murderously. Then, with a sweep of his arm, he knocked the CDs off the table, clattering them across the carpet. One or two hit the wall and bounced back. He jumped up, glared at the two women for a moment and slammed out of the room. A few seconds later they heard the flat's front door cannon against its frame.

Helen took an audible sip of tea, staring fixedly at the wall. 'Good riddance,' she observed.

Anita switched off the television and touched her mother on the arm. 'Mum. Maybe, you know, it's a small flat and I do appreciate you being here. I don't know what I'd have done without you, really. But . . .'

Helen looked. Her eyes and mouth were tight. 'My God,' she said quietly, through closed teeth, '*you* don't want me here for the funeral.'

It was a statement, not a question. Anita said, 'I just don't know when they'll let me bury her. It's all, it's all . . .'

'But that's not it, is it, 'Nita? You let *him* run your life. Why you ever broke up with Thomas is beyond me.'

Anita started to speak but her mother held up a hand.

'I'm warning you! I kept my mouth shut, I never said a word about it, but there comes a time—'

'A word about what, Mum? What are you saying?'

'About why Jason wasn't at school that Thursday – remember? About why you had to take Julie to the hospital, Christmas.'

Helen was staring hard at her daughter, challenging her. All she could see in response was exhaustion.

Anita shook her head slowly. 'For God's sake, Mum. Stop it, just stop it.'

A scream came from the kitchen. It was Tony, in his high chair. He hated being left alone. Helen got up.

'You'll have to be in court,' she said. 'So will Peter. But, well, if you don't need me, fine. I'll go.'

She went to attend to Tony. Anita folded her hands more tightly over her stomach and rocked in her chair. Never had she felt so alone. Now it was just her and the baby inside. Everything else was just a side show, a nothing.

Helen came storming back from the kitchen, pulling Jason behind her. 'He's just dragged Tony out of his chair again! Here, you talk to him.'

She hurried back to the kitchen. 'Jason,' warned his mother gently. 'I told you not to play around with him. He's just a baby.'

Jason pouted.

Anita got up and, wrapping her dressing gown around her, went into the kitchen. Helen was rocking Tony in the crook of her arm. She showed Anita a Gnutcrunch ice-cream, from the freezer.

'Can I give him one of these?'

'I'll do it, Mum. Give him me.'

Back in the lounge, Jason looked round to see if anybody was watching. Then he slipped across to the sideboard and selected one of the framed pictures of his dead sister. He looked at it closely, his eyes about four inches from the glass. He ran his finger over the image of Julie's face. Then he jerked his arm and threw the picture on to the floor. Then he began jumping on it, mashing the glass under his heel.

*

149

Walker returned from the remand hearing determined to get the budget sorted. He could never remember if the Forensic Lab charged a flat rate for a black sack of refuse, or whether they levied a fee for each article they pulled out. He'd already worked out a sheet based on £500 for a sack, but when he looked again at the faxed inventory of Dunn's rubbish, he thought they might be going to sting him for something like £25 an item – and there were thirty-four items on the list. He groaned. He'd have to recalculate.

The phone rang at his elbow.

'Walker? Mallory!'

'Oh, yes, sir. Anything new?'

Mallory spoke deliberately, in his usual pompous manner. 'On the matter of the material recovered from the dustbin of the suspect in the Harris case.'

'Accused.'

'I'm sorry?'

'The accused, sir. He's been charged. He's on remand.'

'I see. Well, I hope that's not solely on the basis of what I have in front of me.'

Walker sat up in his chair, his eyes wary. 'What have you in front of you, sir?'

'I have in front of me, Walker, one blue and red washing line. And yes, it is the same type of rope or washing line as was tied around the little lady's neck. But it is not *the* rope. I think you'd better come and see me.'

Walker all but slumped forward across the budgetary calculations on his desk. *Not the rope?*

PC Barridge was in the Incident Room when Walker burst from his office and shouted to DI North.

'Pat! I've just been talking to Mallory. It's not the rope! Come on, let's go!'

Not the rope? Barridge walked across to the pin-board, where a picture of the ligature used on Julie was displayed. Looking at it always hurt but he forced himself to do it.

At the lab, Mallory showed both lengths of line to Walker and North. They looked identical and Walker said so.

'Yes,' said Mallory, taking the cut end of the murder rope in one hand and the end of the sample found in Dunn's bin in the other. 'As I said, they're the same type of rope but—'

Slowly and theatrically, he brought his two hands together until the cut ends of the lengths of line met.

'These ends don't match.'

Walker tried hard to control himself. 'So – what *have* you got from the flat?'

'We're working on Dunn's clothes. But so far, I regret, there's nothing for you. We've taken up almost all the carpet but the problem here is, it's hard to find an area without stains. There's more than three hundred of them.'

'You're going to test them all?'

'We've done most of them already.'

He consulted the file, which lay open on his desk. 'Semen, blood, soup, alcohol, chocolate, tea, coffee – you want one?'

The police officers looked blank.

Mallory said, 'A coffee?'

Walker shook his head. 'No, thanks. What about the bottles I sent in? Foster said she might have been penetrated by . . .'

'We've got numerous prints from the bottles, mostly Dunn's, which is not surprising. Nothing to connect them to the victim, though. Now, what else? Oh, yes . . .'

He went to the door and called out, '*Jimmy!* Shoe casts!'

Haggard joined them, dressed in a lab coat, wearing a mask and latex gloves and carrying a muddy, down-at-heel shoe. He looked from Walker to North.

'Oh, ah! Hello, Superintendent, Inspector. You heard about the rope, that it's not—'

'Yes, we heard,' said Walker crisply.

Haggard removed his mask. 'Right, well. Shoe casts. We've cleared the backlog on the shoe casts. Eliminated twenty-four as officers' footwear but this . . .' He held up the shabby shoe. 'This was taken off the suspect, right?'

Walker nodded.

'Well, a good selection of ground deposits similar to the terrain we are interested in – brick dust, soil, cement dust – turned up on it. Plus, the ground near where the victim was hidden in the sewage pipes contained a high percentage of clay, so any footwear with all four samples matching means we can be pretty certain he was by those pipes. It's just that we have no shoeprint in that ground for this particular shoe.'

Walker nudged North and put on his coat. They turned to leave but Mallory called after them.

'Hang on, Walker, it's your lucky day after all.'

Walker turned round, his lip curled. He looked as if he might say something he would later find regrettable, but he curbed the impulse. Mallory was holding up the rope used in the murder.

'You haven't let me finish,' he said, mock-wounded. 'The section of line around the little girl's neck *can* be matched to something after all. In fact, I know exactly where it came from – from a Miss Taylor's back garden or, to be more specific, the post she used to hang her washing line from. Is that any help to you?'

It wasn't until they were in the car and on the way to Miss Taylor's that he remembered he'd forgotten to ask Mallory about the cost of tests on the refuse sack.

At the Harris's place, Jason was playing. He lay on the floor, as near as he could to the action he was creating with the small plastic-moulded figures. His mouth made the explosive noises he imagined would come from their weapons as they fired. It was a dangerous ambush, led by his dad's platoon against an attacking enemy force, riding in on their tank. Jason was so absorbed he never noticed Peter coming in.

'Jason! How many times have you been told not to mess around with Tony?'

Jason exploded the attackers' battle tank. The enemy assault party went flying in every direction. It was satisfying.

'You *hearing* me?'

Jason pulled himself up on his elbow and scowled at Peter.

'You're not my dad. And you're not Julie's dad either.'

Peter was standing with one hand behind his back. He kicked at the plastic tank, which skidded over the carpet and smacked the wall.

'I know I'm not. Because I'd never produce a snotty little bastard like you.'

He produced his concealed hand. It held the smashed photograph.

'Did you break this? *Did you?*

153

Jason cowered. He knew what was coming next.

'*Get up!*'

'No! I bloody won't. You can't make me.'

Quickly he began to wriggle under his bed. Peter tossed the broken picture on to the bed, grabbed and missed. He crouched, trying to fish the child out from the narrow space. His hand cast around but he couldn't reach far enough in to get a fistful.

'I know you did it. I know!'

'Stay away from me! You bastard!'

Jason was crying now, snivelling and crooning, like a trapped animal. 'I hate you. Julie hates you too!'

Peter got up. He stood for a moment over the bed. His voice suddenly became calm and cold. 'You got this room all to yourself now, Jason. And you're going to stay in it today, all day. And all night, too. *You hear me?*'

Jason crammed back into the furthest, darkest corner. He felt something digging into his back but so long as Peter didn't start pulling out the heavy bunkbed, he reckoned he was safe. Then he knew he was, at least for the moment, because he heard Peter slam out of the room. He twisted round and got a hand to whatever it was he had felt. He pulled it out and put it in front of his eyes – Julie's bloody Barbie doll. Yeuch!

He pushed the doll back into the darkest corner under the bed, slid carefully out into the room and began reassembling the enemy force. There was be a renewed assault and no mercy on either side.

CHAPTER 13

ANN TAYLOR was a surprise to Pat North. The disabled parking space outside her house on the new brick-built housing development next to the estate, the spinsterish 'Miss' on Barridge's visit report, the prissy, fanatically neat interior of the house all seemed to indicate someone in her sixties. But the woman who opened the door was only a little older than herself.

'Yes?'

Walker showed his warrant card. 'We're police officers, Miss Taylor. We are following up the house-to-house inquiries made by our constable yesterday. May we come in?'

North and Walker were escorted into the lounge with a ritual apology. 'Sorry about the mess. If I'd known you were coming . . . You'll have some coffee?'

Walker looked around with raised eyebrows at the incredibly tidy room, cheaply but carefully furnished. 'It's about this washing line. May we see your garden?'

Ann Taylor was surprised. 'The washing line? Oh, yes. I'll show you.'

She took them through the kitchen and out the back door. Walker inspected the posts from which her washing line had once hung. He walked around the perimeter of

155

the lawn and peered in at the windows of the garden shed. A small padlock secured the door.

Back in the lounge, she brought in coffee.

'I thought you were investigating the murder of that poor child.'

'That's right.'

'But I don't see how that's connected to my washing line?'

Walker took a token sip of his coffee and put the cup down.

'We're trying to establish one. Now, Miss Taylor, when you mentioned to our constable that your washing line had been stolen, was that the first time you reported it missing?'

'Yes.'

'So you never reported it stolen – officially I mean?'

'No. I didn't think it was worth it. I'm sorry – should I have?'

'No, no. Don't worry, it's just that there'd be a record if you had, you see. So, when exactly *was* it stolen?'

'One night, just after the fence had been painted. About two weeks ago. Only there wasn't anything on it – washing I mean. Or they would have stolen that as well, wouldn't they? Biscuit?' She offered a plate of custard creams.

Walker shook his head. 'No, thank you. Now, do you know Michael Dunn?'

Ann Taylor's eyes were fixed on the carpet. 'I know who he is, yes. It was in the papers – that he'd been arrested.' She twisted her hands together in her lap, the fingers of one gripping those of the other. 'Er, he used to come round knocking on doors to do odd jobs.'

Walker seemed indifferent to this information. He simply asked, 'When did you last see him?'

'Oh, a long time ago. More than nine months, maybe a year. He looked terrible. Unwashed, filthy dirty. I didn't open my door. Just told him to go away.'

'And?'

'He just walked off.' She looked nervously to Walker then clasped her hands. 'They've been to take tests on the fence. Will they be coming back? I mean it was only a rope.'

Walker got up suddenly, slightly knocking the table on which stood his barely touched coffee. The cup rattled. 'Thank you for your time, Miss Taylor.'

North took a hurried gulp of coffee as Walker moved towards the hall. She got up to follow him. 'Lovely house, you have. You live here alone, Miss Taylor?'

'Yes – since Mummy died.'

The woman hesitated, flicking a glance at North's face, then looking down at her hands. There was something more to this, North was sure of it. But Walker was impatient to be on his way. He was already standing by the front door, his hand groping in his coat pocket for cigarettes.

Miss Taylor smiled wanly. 'I'll show you out.'

On the way to the car, North spoke her mind. 'Bit abrupt, if you don't mind my saying so, sir.'

But Walker was having none of it. 'In case you've forgotten, Inspector North, we have a meeting with the Crown Prosecution Service tomorrow. And I can tell you exactly what they're going to say – we don't have a case. So I don't have time for small talk, OK?'

North decided not to push her luck.

Within five minutes of their arrival back at Southampton Street, Arnold Mallory was on the line. His voice was triumphant. 'We've got what I believe you would call a result from the shoes.'

'I know,' said Walker. 'You said four matching samples. But, as you also pointed out, as Dunn lived there he was likely to walk across the building site.'

'Four matching samples would be good, Walker. But five is very hard indeed to get out of.'

'Five? You're talking about Dunn's shoes?' Walker was taking the call in the Incident Room. As members of the team picked up on the conversation, the area fell into an expectant silence.

'Dunn's shoes – yes. I said we had soil, clay, brick dust and cement, right? All from the area around the pipes. But now I'm also talking about the victim's shoes too.'

'Yes?'

'And your suspect and the little lady walked in the same dog shit. Do you understand what I am saying to you, Walker? Traces of the same turd are on both shoes!' Mallory guffawed, 'You found the post for the washing line, all you've got to do now is find the dog that dropped the load!'

Walker attempted to join in with Mallory's frivolity, and to everyone gathered in the room it sounded like a bark, but no one laughed. Walker's eyes were like chipped ice. Deliberately Walker replaced the receiver. He remained still for a moment, then started walking jerkily around the room in a kind of muted dance of celebration. He was clicking his fingers.

'Yes! Yes-yes-yes! We've got him. We've bloody *got* him!'

There was a low cheer from members of the team. It

died away as Meg Richards, of Family Liaison, came hurrying in looking for Walker.

'Sir, I've got a Mrs Gillingham in my office. I think you'd better come and see her. She says she fostered Michael Dunn.'

Walker was enjoying the moment. His eyes were shining, the crows' feet laughter-lines etched into his temples. He rubbed his hands together.

'Better and better. Lead me to her!'

Mrs Gillingham was dressed in sweater and jeans under a brown car coat. Walker immediately had her down as a middle class liberal, a teenager in the sixties who now got by on charitable work and reading the *Guardian*. She also happened to be very tense, sitting bolt upright in the chair with her hands laced so tightly there was no blood in the knuckles.

Walker positioned himself on the edge of Richards' desk. 'Now, Mrs Gillingham, I believe you know Michael Dunn.'

'Yes – I read you had arrested him so I—'

'I'd appreciate anything you can tell us about him. Anything at all. He doesn't communicate much with us, you understand?'

'All right, well, let me see. Michael was an orphan, Superintendent. He was shuffled round various foster homes, adopted once but returned to an orphanage. He was too much of a handful apparently. But at the home he was subjected to, well, sexual and emotional abuse. Over a period of years. He made no less than three suicide attempts and . . . Well, we didn't know all the facts about

159

his past when we – my husband and I – agreed to foster him. We only found out afterwards . . .'

She stopped, but she had a lot more to tell. Richards looked at Walker warningly and he took the point. This was a witness you didn't push too hard. He simply nodded encouragingly and waited for the woman to go on.

'He was fourteen when he came to us, a very quiet, unassuming boy, and we felt he was really benefiting from being in a stable family environment.' She paused and cleared her throat.

Coming to the difficult bit, thought Walker.

'My daughters were then aged five and seven . . . We trusted him, you see. We did.' She swallowed. Her voice had gone shaky. 'And we left him to babysit one time and he, well, he abused both my daughters, you see.'

Walker blinked. He couldn't quite believe his luck. 'Did you report this?'

'No. No, I didn't.'

'Why not?'

Mrs Gillingham looked pathetic now. Guilt leaked out of her like battery acid.

'I – we – didn't want to subject the girls to any further distress. We just had him taken away – the social workers agreed at the time that nobody's interest would be served by a prosecution or anything like that.'

Richards leaned forward and said, quietly, 'Did he *sexually* abuse them?'

The woman had controlled herself now. Her voice was a little shaky, the emotions discernible but contained. She would make a good witness.

'He did not actually have sex with either of them. But he . . . touched them, you know. Fondled them. According to the presumption of the doctor, and the counsellors we spoke to subsequently, his own sexual abuse could have made him impotent.'

Richards had brought her visitor a glass of water and now she gulped three quick mouthfuls before placing the cup carefully on the desk.

'I wanted to tell you this because I was feeling guilty. Perhaps if we had taken this matter further, not simply returned him to care, then this tragedy – this murder – would never have happened.'

'Mrs Gillingham,' asked Walker, 'would you be prepared to make a statement?'

'Yes. Yes, I would.'

'And would your daughters?'

'Superintendent, I can't speak for my daughters. They are now eighteen and twenty years old. You must ask them.'

'I shall have to do that, Mrs Gillingham. I hope you understand. Do they both still live at home?'

'Yes.'

'Then may I make an appointment to come and see them?'

Michael Dunn's head had not stopped pounding all day. Now it felt cold as well, because those bastards had shaved off his hair. Said he was lousy, the pillocks. They'd spent ages taking his particulars, giving him bedding and suchlike. Now he was being marched through the prison and it was unbelievable how the inmates already knew about him – who he was, why he was here.

As he walked past the locked doors of cells, he could hear catcalls and wolf howls and the snarling of imaginary animals. He was called nonce and child killer and he was threatened at every step with the particular names of the bits of him these men wanted to cut off and make him eat. Michael Dunn was terrified.

The screws marched him into an empty cell, where there was a bed with the mattress folded.

'Make up that bed, Dunn. Wing governor'll be along to see you shortly. Behave yourself.'

The steel door closed with a horrible finality and the prisoner looked at the door with its spyhole. He sat down on the bare bedsprings.

'I'm innocent.'

His voice was a whimper in this bare box, where there was no one to hear him. He covered his face with his hands.

'I didn't do it. I didn't do it.'

CHAPTER 14

WITH HIS decision to prefer a charge of murder against Michael Dunn, Walker kissed goodbye to his control of the case. From now on the Special Casework Lawyer of the Crown Prosecution Service, and not Det. Supt. Walker, would call the shots.

But Walker's team couldn't pack up and go home just yet. The job of collecting evidence and processing paperwork went on uninterrupted, but now more sedately. The first few days had been a race against time, Walker driving his team like the devil in pursuit of the damned. Now, under this new driver, the wheels of investigation slowed to walking pace.

A murder trial is a demanding taskmaster. Everything taken from Dunn's flat had to be processed by Mallory's staff. The doll was followed up – its manufacturer in China established, its importer traced, the shops that stocked it itemized. Dunn's past was raked over with archaeological thoroughness and the key witnesses in the case were re-interviewed, their remarks double- and triple-checked against the statements they'd already made. For the Crown there must be no unnecessary weakness in the chain of proof. And above all there must be no surprises at the trial.

163

The man who now controlled the case was Clive Griffith – the Special Casework Lawyer. His word actually was the law in relation to the prosecution of Michael Dunn. He was a bureaucrat-lawyer, always with one eye on the bottom line. It made him, in a joke he liked to make to his golfing chums, a conviction lawyer: to him, every acquittal was a threat; the only word he wanted to hear was 'guilty'.

Griffith's obsession with convictions made his weekly casework conference a form of Chinese water torture for Walker, as the details of his case were examined drip by pessimistic drip.

'Ah, Superintendent Walker, Inspector North,' said Griffith, hurrying in to the conference room. He was followed by the stick-thin figure of his caseworker, a tall, black stunner called Jennifer Abantu, who carried two thick files. Whenever the atmosphere became too rancid, Walker would secretly refresh his eyes by glancing at Miss Abantu's fabulous body and flawless, sphinx-like face.

'I'm sorry to be a little late. Now, where are we? Ah, thank you, Jennifer.'

Miss Abantu had dumped her files on the table. She slid one of them towards her boss. Griffith reached for the file.

'Look, Superintendent, I have to tell you I'm really afraid the Dunn case is running out of petrol. I'm seriously thinking about pulling the plug, before we get in too deep.'

Walker was staggered. All that bloody work down the toilet! The plug had been pulled on him before, of course – several times in fact. And every time he had been staggered.

'We're in deep already, aren't we? And we haven't had

the final forensic report yet. I'm due over there later. So you're not telling me we won't go to trial?'

'Well, I am under a statutory duty to enter a discontinuance if there is no reasonable prospect of securing a conviction. I do feel these circumstance come close to falling into that category.

'Are you serious? Are you really saying—?'

'The fact is, you haven't established he harmed her in any way. The rope to, er, coin a phrase is pretty ropey.'

Walker shot a glance at North and deliberately drew his chair nearer to the conference table. He cleared his throat. 'Mr Griffith, Michael Dunn is a known drunk. He hadn't washed either himself or his clothes for months. Do you think any jury is going to believe that he went to the trouble of stealing a washing line because he had a lot of laundry to hang up?'

'You can't prove he stole the rope. And there is no mechanical fit between the end of the two bits you're offering in evidence.'

DI North interrupted. She had never thought much of Mallory's dismissal of the rope found in Dunn's rubbish bin. 'Mr Griffith, what if he cut the rope twice?' she said. 'that would explain why the ends don't fit.'

Griffith licked his thumb and finger and began leafing through the file. Walker watched him for a moment, then said, 'I wouldn't be pushing this so much if the type of rope wasn't the same. Not similar – identical!'

Griffith was perusing a page. He got out his pen and jotted a note in the margin. 'Hmm. Tell you what – we'll solicit an opinion on the rope from Treasury Counsel.'

'It's not just the rope. There's Mrs Gillingham's statement.'

'What page is that on?'

165

Walker's own file was tagged with post-it notes. He found the right place. 'Twenty-four.'

'Ah, yes – the foster carer.' Griffith scanned the statement, tapping his teeth with the Biro. 'Well, it's hearsay from the mother, this. You'll have to get statements from the Gillingham girls that Dunn molested them.'

Walker and North exchanged another glance. They'd been trying to get statements from the two Gillingham daughters for the past month. At last it looked as if this might happen tomorrow, but there was no way Walker was going to tell Griffith that now. He'd be told when those statements were in the can.

Griffith had finished reading Mrs Gillingham's statement.

'The only way we'll get this allegation into evidence is under the similar facts rule. It's going to have to be very close to what was done to Julie Anne – same age bracket and the use of some sort of instrument.'

North smiled emolliently. 'Well, we don't know what they're going to say until they say it, do we, sir?'

'No, Detective Inspector, we do not. So let's not waste any more time, shall we?' He turned another few pages. 'Now, another matter that is concerning me is your identifying witness. Mrs Enid Marsh.'

Walker's eyes narrowed. 'Why? She picked him out first time. She was in no doubt.'

'Yes, but number one, she says she'd never previously met Dunn. That weakens her position, though I admit it doesn't demolish her. Number two, and worse, she's old, her sighting of Dunn was brief and it was from high above his head. The judge will have to give the Turnbull Direction, no question.'

Walker scowled. The Turnbull Direction – the warning that judges issue to juries whenever they think a particular piece of identification evidence is not absolutely straight-forward – is detested by the police. Defence counsel, of course, adore it.

Walker made a fist of his right hand and hammered it into the palm of his left. 'She picked him out in the parade!' he cried. 'She was alpha-bloody-positive it was him!'

Griffith smiled in that superior way of his. 'What? A forgetful old lady who lives alone and doesn't get enough attention from the big wide world? Dunn's counsel won't just make mincemeat of her – he'll be going for the whole mince pie, Superintendent.'

For some reason North thought Griffith's smile made him look like a duck as Griffith added, 'Look, we're on course for the committal hearing next week, yes? We won't make a final decision until we cross that hurdle.'

Walker stood up and tucked the file under his arm. He tapped the file. 'And bear in mind, please, we still have more forensic to come, with any luck. I'll be in touch about that – oh, and the Gillingham girls also.'

Defending a client doesn't have to be a crusade. Belinda Sinclair may have been a rookie, but she had her task in proportion. It shouldn't really matter to her if Michael Dunn was innocent or guilty – under the so-called adversarial system of British justice there could be no trial without a defence and, win or lose, Belinda knew she could do herself a lot of good if she didn't mess things up.

Filthy, lousy and with his faculties corroded by drink, Dunn had certainly not been a pretty prospect when she'd met him at Southampton Street. But later, at Wormwood Scrubs, Belinda was pleasantly surprised by his changed appearance and now, making her third call, she'd grown used to the new Michael. His hair was cropped short. He was polite, more or less alert and, above all, clean. He had a winning smile when he felt like showing it and Belinda was even beginning to believe that her young man was incapable of doing this dreadful crime. If only he could be persuaded to make more use of that shy Welsh charm, the jury would surely be brought round to the same way of thinking.

The purpose of today's visit was to go through his proof of evidence.

'Mrs Enid Marsh says she doesn't know you, Michael. Is that true?'

Dunn didn't answer. He was standing casually, half turned away from Belinda, his hands sunk in his overall pockets. Although he'd come through alcoholic withdrawal after three days, he still found it hard to concentrate for long. Belinda tapped her notepad.

'Michael, you must pay attention. I am trying to take your proof of evidence.'

Dunn collected himself. He spoke quietly. 'She saw me when I did the paper round.'

'When exactly did you do the paper round, Michael?'

'Can't remember. Summer, I think. Not last year, the one before.'

'And how many times did she see you?'

'Well, a good few times – just on her doorstep, you know. In the mornings.'

'Did you talk to her at all? Did you say good morning?'

168

Dunn screwed up his face, trying to visualize the scene on Mrs Marsh's doorstep. He shook his head. 'No.'

Belinda Sinclair scribbled a note and murmured to herself, 'Good.'

'Oh, and I remembered something else!'

'Yes?'

Dunn pulled out a chair and sat down.

'Terry Smith, the bloke, you know, that was with me. Well, he may have gone home.'

'Home, Michael?'

'Yeah, Wales. Where I come from.'

The lawyer was writing in rapid shorthand. 'Seems to be all coming back to you today, Michael.'

And then that smile broke on his face. Belinda thought, bit of a heart-throb this boy could have been, if the breaks had been different. It was a cold and purely analytical thought – not what she herself felt, but what a jury could be made to feel.

She said, 'It makes it so much easier for me to do the absolutely best job I can.'

Dunn opened his eyes wide. 'Doing all right, then, am I?'

She nodded, looking at her watch. 'Yes. Yes, you are. But I have to leave it there, I'm afraid. Got to go. But I'll see you again on Wednesday.'

He watched her as she gathered her papers, making no movement. Then she stood up and extended her hand for him to shake.

'Goodbye for now, Michael.'

The hold he took on her hand was light, shy and – well, she thought, the only word for it was innocent. Then he said, out of nowhere, 'You've got lovely eyes. You're a very pretty woman.'

Belinda gave a tiny lift of her head. 'Well, thank you, Michael. Is there anything you need?'

'No, thank you very much. I'm fine here. Like to get out, but really I'm fine.'

'What about your treatment? Prison officers, other inmates?'

Dunn suddenly, and for the first time today, became tense and wary. But he shook his head. 'Fine, nothing. Really I'm OK. It's no problem.'

Like hell it is, thought Belinda. But she didn't pursue it.

Outside the CPS, Walker and North separated. She returned to Southampton Street, from where she would telephone to confirm tomorrow's appointment with the Gillingham sisters. He went on to Lambeth and the Forensic Laboratory. He knew that Mallory's team had come to the end of their tests but Arnold Mallory had kept him in the dark as to their progress and given not a hint about what he might have found.

The scientist was sitting at his desk and contemplating with evident satisfaction a sizeable patisserie carton which sat on his blotter.

'I've got excellent news for you, Walker,' he said without looking up. 'Excellent *epithelial* news.'

He picked up a laboratory scalpel and, after a moment's further thought, sliced delicately through the tape which secured the lid of the box. He then heaved his bulk backwards to allow space for the drawer of his desk to open.

'Shall I spell that for you? E-P-I-T—'

Walker cut him short. 'I've seen the word, yes. Epithelial.'

Mallory's habit of treating all policemen like they were missing a chunk of their brains was infuriating and Walker's nerves were in knots already after spending half an hour with Griffith. He didn't know exactly what epithelial meant, but sure as hell he'd rather look it up in *Black's Medical Dictionary* than be patronized by Mallory.

The scientist gestured at a sheaf of stapled A4. The top sheet had Walker's name highlighted on a circulation list.

'It's written in the report. Epithelial cells from the little lady's mouth, found in samples taken from the lolly sticks.' He was rummaging through his desk drawer.

Walker said, 'Are those the lolly sticks found in Dunn's flat?'

'Exactly. That's just bullet point number one. Point number two: one of her hairs recovered from suspect's carpet.'

'Just one?'

'Just the one. It's enough. And no question it's hers. Point number three: fibres. Blue and red cotton/polyester mix, recovered from the couch. These are consistent with the child's anorak.'

'No better than consistent?'

'No – they're common as muck.'

Mallory shut his drawer and stood up. Going across to a four-drawer filing cabinet, he started delving into it, coming out at last with a plastic spoon. 'Some bugger's always pinching the forks. But we also have bottle-green acrylic, consistent with the skirt. This is also a common type – but the combination of the two fibres, that's your evidence.'

Mallory shut the drawer, returned to his desk, tipping open the lid of the cake box. Walker, on the other side of the desk, couldn't see what it contained until Mallory had plunged his spoon in and come out with an overbalancing hunk of chocolate *ganache*. He hurriedly plugged his mouth before the cake could plop on to the desktop.

'No blood transfer?' asked Walker.

Mallory shook his head. 'Nnnh.'

'What about Dunn's clothes? Anything on them at all?'

Mallory's jaws worked over the mouthful of cake for another ten seconds and then, with a convulsion of his throat, he swallowed. 'His own blood. That's all. Now, what else?' He fingered the report, flipping over three of four pages. 'Ah, yes, the doll. Sorry, but the finger-print boys have found nothing on it that belongs to the kiddie. A few smudges only – so it could have been wiped.'

'And the bottles? Nothing on them?'

'His prints, that's all. If he did use a bottle to abuse our girl, we don't have the item.'

'Well, that was a waste of money!' Walker lit his cigarette and sucked the smoke in hard.

'You'll have to learn to be more selective. Do you want some cake? Home-made – at least, local bakery-made. No charge to you.'

Walker exhaled, shaking his head impatiently.

'But to get back to Dunn's clothes,' said Mallory, spooning another dollop of cake between his teeth. He didn't so much chew as pump with his mouth on the food. 'No fibres,' he said at last. 'But if there had been, you'd have lost them. He'd been shedding for over twenty-four hours when you finally collared him.'

'Shedding?'

With his finger, Mallory shifted a crumb of cake from the side of his mouth to his tongue, then sucked the fingertip clean. 'Like an Angora rabbit. His cloth coat was shiny – not a very adhesive substrate. And that, my dear Superintendent, is your lot.' He shut the lid of the cake box and rapped it with his fingers. 'That's all you're going to get out of this office. And don't look so down in the mouth, man. It's all in the report. Tests, double-checked by different operatives, prove beyond peradventure that the child was in Dunn's flat, guzzling his lollies. What more could you want?'

Walker got up, snatched up Mallory's report and strode to the door. 'That's easy. I want proof that he killed her. Goodbye and thanks. I'll keep you in touch with developments about the trial.'

At the offices of Clarence Clough, Solicitors, Belinda was greeted by her two colleagues, Jeremy Oxley and Stephen Cookham, with a familiar patter of jokes and badinage. Beneath, and partly because of, the high spirits of these two young men in her presence she discerned their unspoken fascination for her. The fact that it was a shared, but competitive, infatuation made it easy to keep them both at an equidistance from her.

She sat down at her desk, placing her shorthand notebook in front of her. Stephen came and stood behind her chair.

'And is the notorious Beastman of Beckton keeping well?'

She switched on her desktop computer.

'As a matter of act, Mr Dunn is not as brain-dead as I thought he was.'

Stephen leaned forward, his nose near her spun-gold hair. He inhaled ostentatiously.

'I bet he likes your perfume. It must make such a change from the persistent stench of urine that pervades each and every one of Her Majesty's establishments.'

He suddenly straightened as the door swung open and Derek Waugh walked in, his glasses glinting menacingly. Without missing a beat, Stephen snatched a memo from Belinda's desk.

'And I'll have *this* right back to you!'

'Hey!' she said, trying to grab it back. 'You can't take that!'

The senior partner stood surveying the room suspiciously as Stephen returned to his seat, suddenly all eagerness and efficiency. Waugh crooked a finger at Belinda.

'Belinda – a word, please. And Stephen – affidavits drafted yet?'

'Almost done, Derek.'

'Good. Bring them in when they are. Let's go to my office, shall we, Belinda? There's some fresh coffee.'

They left and Stephen and Jeremy looked at each other.

'Guess what?' said Stephen.

'I think she just lost her Beastman,' said Jeremy.

Waugh looked Belinda up and down as she sipped her coffee. She was certainly decorative. He regarded himself as a bit of a connoisseur of beauty – he personally bought all the original paintings that adorned the office walls. Hiring Belinda, as against the two or three ambitious young chaps who were in competition with her, had been a decision made in the same way as he made a bid at an auction at Phillips. She wasn't expensive, she was more than competent and she'd brighten the place up.

'As you know,' he was saying, 'we've been wanting to get more high-profile criminal work, to complement our extremely successful chancery and commercial divisions. So the Dunn case will have great significance for the firm. But we must also consider what is fair to you Belinda. There will be considerable – con*side*rable – professional interest and the media is always ready to seize on any irregularity, any pitfall into which inexperience may lead you.'

Belinda put down her cup and straightened her skirt across her thighs.

'I had thought I was managing reasonably well, Derek. I mean, especially with your support, and, er, supervision.'

She wasn't going to give Dunn up without a fight. But she knew that to confront Waugh with anger or weakness would be fatal.

'Was there anything in particular that I've not done right?'

Waugh smiled thinly. 'No, no, Belinda, assuredly not. You've done very creditably. We would be horrified – *horrified* – to think that you might read any hint of criticism in the decision. But that decision has been made – and it is that a partner should now act for Michael Dunn.'

Oh *shit*, thought Belinda. That's it. I'm off the case.

'Now,' Waugh was continuing unctuously, 'if you could just bring in the file, we'll go through it together – all right?'

*

175

The Incident Room at Southampton Street had kept going and now, after a quiet lull towards the end of September, it was busy again. The committal hearing was almost upon them.

Walker strode in and took a cigarette from Dave Satchell. He snapped off the filter and lit it in almost a single movement.

'What's the story?' asked Satchell.

'Short and sweet,' said Walker. 'Nothing for us on the doll. DNA on the lolly sticks all right – the victim's on some of them. But sweet FA on his clothes.'

Cranham came forward. He felt the disappointment on the governor's face as keenly as everyone else.

'But isn't it true we got her hair and fibres on the couch and the floor?'

'They're not denying she's been in the flat. They know she was. But it could have been three weeks or even three months before.'

'What fibres did he get?' asked North.

Walker shook his head. 'Possible anorak and skirt. Bloody useless.'

Dave Satchell said. 'Well, it should do us some good. She's not likely to have gone around three months later wearing exactly the same clothes.'

'I wouldn't bet on it,' Walker growled. 'Doubt there's a lot of money for clothes in that house.'

North, by the noticeboard, knocked on one of the snapshots of Julie Anne. 'She's wearing the same skirt in this photograph.'

Walker had whipped out his notebook and was scribbling something. 'Well, let's check with her mother – find out how new that anorak was. I'm away home now. Goodnight.'

He left a pall of depression over the room.

Satchell went and stood by North in front of the board. He stared at the picture of the golden-haired little girl, riding a bike with stabilizers.

'We don't have a case, do we?'

North turned to him.

'Don't let him hear you say that, Dave. He may be wondering – but there's no plus points for us if he's right. And it's the committal hearing next week.'

CHAPTER 15

As HE strode into Wormwood Scrubs, a pleasant, unaccustomed trickle of excitement told Derek Waugh he was alive and ready for a challenge. In his youth he'd done a fair amount of criminal work, though nothing very world-shaking. And then, during all those years of contracts, patents and other lucrative, boring spokes in the wheel of commerce, he'd often wondered how he would perform behind a top QC in a high-profile murder trial. Someone like Robert Rylands, he thought to himself.

This made it all the more disappointing that the client was fool enough to cling to the skirts of Belinda.

'Look, who are you? What is this?' Dunn was demanding. He wouldn't even sit at the interview table with Waugh. 'I'm very satisfied with Miss Sinclair. I don't want anyone else.'

Waugh cleared his throat. He must have put it too baldly. He'd assumed the lout would jump at the chance of getting a senior partner on his team.

'Naturally, there is no intention of excluding Miss Sinclair completely, Michael,' he lied. 'We were merely concerned to secure for her the benefit of a more seasoned—'

The empty chair clattered and skidded across the floor as Dunn kicked at it, his face contorted.

'Is it *my* fault? I don't want anyone else. I don't want anyone but Miss Sinclair.'

He pointed at Waugh. The attendant Prison Officer looked on, his mouth a slight twist of amusement as Dunn's spittle flew in Waugh's direction.

'I don't want *you*, anyway! I don't like you! I want Miss Sinclair, get it? Understand? Miss Sinclair or nobody!'

As Waugh left the Scrubs the feeling in his stomach had changed to the slight nausea of an adrenalin hangover.

Of course, when he told her back at the office, he made it sound like his own decision.

'I was on my way down there on the tube,' he told Belinda, 'when suddenly I thought to myself Lady Preece's estate is almost as much of a bitch as the woman herself, and then there's the Greenways-Benton thing and the Alphastrom litigation, so personally I'm going to have my hands pretty full over the next few months. Anyway, in the end I managed to persuade Dunn that his best interest would be served if you continued to handle the case.'

'Oh, well, thank you, Derek. Thank you very much.'

'Of course, we'll support you fully from the wings. There's absolutely no question, obviously, of your being exposed to any risks of a professional kind.'

Belinda thought, what on earth could the pompous prick mean? But she didn't dwell on it. She was filled instead with exultation and would have kissed Michael Dunn if he'd been in the room.

'Who's going to be leading counsel on it?' she asked, winking at Jeremy Oxley as he came in with a sandwich from Pret A Manger.

'I'd like Robert Rylands, if we can get him.'

'Rylands? He's the best there is! It'd be fantastic to work with him.'

Waugh was moving towards the door now. He said, sourly, 'I'm sure. So I think it would be politic to find a junior out of the same chambers and get him on board asap – OK?'

Waugh made his exit and Jeremy Oxley could hardly believe what he'd heard.

'Belinda! You've still got the case?'

'Yes, Jeremy, I have. But sadly I don't think we shall need the impressive Mr Rylands.'

'Oh? Why not?'

'Because I'm going to get it thrown out at committal – I think Michael Dunn's innocent. Now tell me, who's the clerk at Ryland's chambers?'

A quartet of builders working next to the Howarth Estate wandered out of the site-hut with mugs of tea. Sitting on breeze blocks, they set about unwrapping their sandwiches. After looking around, Jackie Brown nodded towards the stack of sewage pipes, about fifty yards away.

'Another of them prats having a gander.'

A dark-coated man was standing motionless near the pipes. Ron Corrigan, the site foreman, bit deep into his fried egg bap and chewed noisily.

'Police ought to put a stop to this. Nosy, sick bastards.'

Ron had tried to persuade his bosses to let him take the pipes away, or at least move them. His men thought the child's death would prove a hoodoo and all these sightseers, buzzing like blowflies around the place, seemed to confirm their fear. The employer told him to leave the pipes where they were.

'Perverts,' agreed Jackie. 'Nothing better to do than gawp.'

Ron put down his bap and stood.

'Yeah, and nick stuff too. They've no right to be down here at all – it's a hard-hat site.'

He stumped across to speak to the lone pilgrim. Jackie and the others watched the brief exchange without comment.

'It's all right,' said Ron, returning to the circle and picking up his bap and his steaming mug. 'It's that young copper was here when they were out looking for her. Police are keeping a watch, like.'

The four men resumed their lunch, staring without further comment at the unmoving, solitary figure of PC Colin Barridge, standing like a sentry over the killing ground.

Anita, too, had seen the gawpers from her bedroom window and she too wished the builder would move his pipes. It was just another reminder of the disaster that had carried away her happiness. With Helen gone, she'd hoped Peter would at least make some effort, but he was hardly ever in. And when he did come back he was drunk and foul-mouthed, lashing out at her and the children on any provocation, breaking ornaments.

She asked herself who was now – today – the worst victim of this crime? Not Julie – she was beyond all that now. Was it poor uncomprehending little Tony, whose father hit him when he spilled his food and shook him when he cried? Young Jason, wetting his bed at night, sullen and withdrawn in the day, hardly going near his school? Or Peter, drinking most of the night, sleeping in his clothes on the sofa, unable to communicate, unable to be tender? Anita looked at their lives and thought: how could she have imagined there was anything binding them all together? Why had it taken the death of little Julie to make her see that everything about their so-called family life was a sham – cheap, hopeless and meaningless?

She went shopping and saw people begging on the street, and she thought: we're not homeless. So why do I feel I haven't got a home any more?

She wouldn't say any of these things out loud, not to her mum and certainly not to Peter. A few days before, the vicar of the nearby church had come round. Thank God, Peter hadn't been there. She gave the vicar tea, though he tried to protest.

'No, no, Mrs Harris. I didn't come here to put you to any trouble!'

Then why did you come? she thought.

'I'm not a ... I mean, I don't go to church or anything, I'm afraid,' she had said.

'Oh, it isn't going to church that counts, is it?' he told her, his bald pate gleaming. The voice was painfully earnest. 'I always feel it's a matter of values, really. And when a tragedy like this strikes, well, it's hard not to feel those values have let you down.'

When he said 'values' he'd accidentally found just the right word. But she never told the vicar this. What could he do to help her? She hadn't believed in God since her father was killed and she certainly wasn't going to start now. But Anita *did* feel let down by the values she'd based her life on – not God and religion, but home, family, decency and prosperity.

When she looked out from the flat and saw that grey heap of sewage pipes, she thought automatically of her dead daughter, lying in the cold morgue, her body cruelly opened and roughly stitched up by the people who owned her now, who wanted to use her for their evidence. Looking down like this, twenty, thirty times a day, Anita wanted her daughter's body back. More than justice, more than revenge, she longed to take Julie, lay her to rest, say goodbye.

It was the last value left, her grief.

CHAPTER 16

TUESDAY 8 OCTOBER. 4 P.M.

BELINDA RETURNED to Wormwood Scrubs feeling like a winning athlete on her lap of honour. Her adversary had been swept away and the field was hers.

'Good news – great news, Michael. We've got your junior counsel on board, Mr Sampara, from Robert Rylands's chambers. That means we might well get Rylands himself if we have to go to trial. He's a top-flight silk.'

Dunn blinked. Why's he called a silk anyway? he thought idly. Something to do with his underwear, probably. At such moments, listening to her voice, he would forget he was a client. He just let the legal terminology wash over him as if he didn't care, as if he was only a detached observer. Being in Belinda's hands felt good, as long as it lasted. But, in his experience, nothing nice ever did last.

'What about that other man then? Mr Waugh? I didn't like him, he tried to get rid of you.'

'Well, thanks to you he didn't.'

Dunn watched the creamy skin of her throat ripple as she laughed. He felt something abrupt ripple through him, too, like an electric shock. She appeared to him like the promise of a new existence, a life in the public eye where fame and money were the means and pleasure the end. She made him unearth those deeply buried fantasies of glamour and fame, the Hollywood dreams that survive even the worst of poverty and human degradation.

'Michael, I think there's a good possibility we can have this dismissed at committal,' she continued, brisk and businesslike again. 'That'll be the next hearing, Michael. The next time you're in court.'

She had told him about committal, although she wasn't sure if he'd retained the explanation. 'It's when they decide whether they have a sufficient case against you and whether your case will be taken to court and a full trial. I don't think they have.'

'You think they'll throw it out?'

She noticed how his mouth puckered, the lower lip trembling. Was he about to burst into tears?

'Well, I don't want to raise your hopes too high, but that's our initial opinion.'

'So there'll be no court, no . . . trial?'

'If all goes well. We're waiting for their papers now.'

Dunn was staring at her. Not at her face or her tits, but at her throat. Suddenly his face broke into a smile and transformed itself. Not the lost and lonely child, but the personable young man. He said, 'That's wonderful.'

And it was.

The papers Belinda had referred to were the contents of a large ring file which now lay on the table at the offices of the Crown Prosecution Service. The solid, outspread hand of Senior Treasury Counsel Willis Fletcher rested on them. Griffith and Walker sat anxiously awaiting his conclusion.

The fingers of Fletcher's other hand idly stroked his beard. 'Well, Superintendent,' he said, 'I've been through the committal papers.'

Fletcher's baritone voice was low-key but convincing and Walker found himself warming to the man. He spoke to you as an equal. His self-assurance was earned, not borrowed. Griffith was sitting bolt upright, eager to get to the question-time of this discussion.

'And what's your view of this rope in his bin? It's just a piece of rope. I don't think it's evidence against him.'

Fletcher opened the file and turned to a yellow-tagged page. 'Can't see why not. It's an identical type to the one that was round the girl's neck. And what else was he doing with it – hanging up his smalls?'

Walker felt the tension in his body ease a fraction. Fletcher was OK. He might even be prepared to take a few risks, stick his neck out. He looked at Griffith, whose mouth was slightly open, ready to pounce with another interjection. But Fletcher was having none of it. He held up his hand.

'The forensic evidence can place the child in Michael Dunn's flat all right. But its value is reduced by the fact that Dunn doesn't deny she visited the flat at other times. That's a card in the defence's hand. But – a major card in ours is that he didn't say so in his first interview. According to the transcript, let's see . . . Yes, Dunn didn't reply when asked if he knew her, then said he didn't know whether he did or not.'

Griffith got in as Fletcher paused for breath. 'Of course, *a fortiori*, the doll proves that she was, in fact—'

But Fletcher shut him firmly down. 'Yes, first he lied about where he found it, then became agitated and admitted the lie in his second statement. But his solicitor had got it all tuned up and running sweetly the second time out, hadn't she?'

'What about the Gillinghams?' asked Walker.

'Mmm, well, it's difficult. This evidence is of indecent assault on two girls thirteen years ago, never reported and it's only hearsay in the form we have it at the moment, the mother's statement . . . unless you have a development there?'

'The young women are being interviewed now.' Walker hoped to God it was true. The Gillinghams had been giving them the run-around for weeks.

Fletcher nodded. 'Good.'

'Well, look,' Griffith put in. 'Can I ask you for an overall view at this stage, Mr Fletcher?'

Fletcher raised his large frame slightly from the seat and then resettled himself comfortably. 'Yes, all right. The forensic evidence may not be direct, Mr Griffith, but the *cumulative* weight of the evidence is strong. I think it'll get past half-time all right.'

Derek Waugh discovered the committal bundle on Belinda's desk during her lunch hour. It had been delivered in her absence by the CPS. When she came in, she found the senior partner sitting on the side of her desk leafing as if casually through Mallory's forensic reports.

'Is that the committal bundle?' she asked. She was miffed that Waugh was wrapped round the prosecution's case before she'd even had a chance to read it. Bloody cheek.

'Yes, you don't mind? I've had a look through. I understand you've been having some discussions about getting Dunn's case dismissed at committal.'

He didn't like the idea – Belinda could hear it in his voice. What was the bloody man playing at?

'That's right, Derek,' she said icily. 'I think we could argue that there's no case to answer.'

Waugh turned a page of Mallory's findings and read a paragraph or two before answering.

'Mmm. But all they've got to do at committal is show there *is* a case to answer. And I think they'll succeed. You won't get it thrown out – and you will have very helpfully alerted the Crown to the weak points of their case.'

'But if we put a bit of effort into the committal, we might—'

'Work *smarter*, Belinda. Not harder.' He wafted the air with his hand. 'Let it go through. We don't contest anything.'

He wants the trial, thought Belinda. He doesn't give a shit about the outcome. He just wants the glory of an Old Bailey appearance. How pathetic. But then, a little bit of her wanted that too – quite a lot of her, if she was honest.

'Who's prosecuting?' She couldn't help letting her interest show.

Waugh smiled in a sickly way. 'Looks like Willis Fletcher. He's only cruiser-class as regards my personal naval estimates. Robert Rylands is in a different league.'

'Have we got Rylands then?'

By a few thin millimetres, Waugh's smile widened. 'He can't commit till we've got a trial date. But my informants tell me he's very interested.'

Pat North had driven down to the Gillingham's home in Kent with a single image in her mind. As she was getting ready to leave, the Incident Room fax had started spewing and Meg Richards had ripped it.

'What is it?' Pat asked whilst putting on her coat.

'One of Anita's catalogue shopping accounts. Julie Anne's anorak came from here.'

Richards was frowning as she ran through the rows of figures. North looked over her shoulder and found the coat's purchase date.

'Twenty-second of August. That's two weeks before the murder – too long. No good to us.'

'Yes, but, oh, God, look at this, Pat,' said Richards, running her finger under a payment made only the previous week. 'That little girl's been dead over a month, and they're still paying for her anorak.'

The Gillinghams lived in a tidy piece of Tudabethan suburbia, a place of black-and-white half-timbering and trim evergreen hedges. The hum of garden vacuum machines sucking away the fallen leaves could be heard as she threaded her way through the Acorn Drives and Beech Avenues looking for the address. There was money here but, more important, there was respectability, a way of life that regarded itself as traditional, a sense of self-belief.

Mrs Gillingham opened the door and took her into the living room. North asked to see the sisters separately and it was Madeleine, the elder, who was offered up first. At twenty, she was a slim, fair girl in a print dress. Her manner was tentative and nervous.

'I know this is difficult for you, Madeleine,' North began, 'but we need to know about Michael Dunn. Can you tell me what happened when you were seven and he was living here?'

'What happened?' Madeleine's voice was trembly and

soft, almost a whisper. 'Yes, I'll tell you. He frightened me. He used to touch me, you know . . .'

The voice trailed away. Pat gave it ten seconds before she prompted.

'Touch you? How do you mean? In a sexual way?'

Madeleine thought for a moment, then swallowed. She closed her eyes and clenched her fists together in her lap. 'Yes. Yes, that's what I mean. He touched me in a sexual way. And I didn't like it.'

By the time she had finished her story she was crying. The mother came in, all concern, and stood at the door while Catherine, the younger sister, pushed past into the room.

'Thank you, Madeleine,' said North. 'Thanks very much. You can go now.'

She smiled at the other girl. 'You must be Catherine?'

Catherine sat down. She was wearing denim Levis and an open-necked shirt. Her manner and movements were not like her sister's – they were decisive and confident.

'Would you like me to stay, dear?' asked her mother.

'No thanks. I'm perfectly capable of handling this, mother.'

Mrs Gillingham followed Madeleine out and shut the door.

'Can you tell me about Michael Dunn, Catherine? And what happened?'

Catherine lay back in the plump cushions of the comfortably upholstered armchair. 'I think it's been blown out of all proportion.'

'Oh? How do you mean?'

'With Michael. It was just affection, you know? I was never scared of him. He was so funny, always playing games.'

'Games?' asked North. 'What games, Catherine?'

The girl was completely still for a moment, staring at the ceiling, remembering. Then suddenly, she sat up, leaned forward and put her hand up to conceal her eyes for a moment, then jerked it away. 'Hide-and-seek!' she said.

CHAPTER 17

MICHAEL DUNN was duly committed for trial and, talking to her client on the phone, Belinda sensed his heavy depression, close to some crisis. The rope found in his bin was a grave problem and she went to the Scrubs specially to discuss it.

'I never put any rope in the bin, or anywhere else,' Dunn moaned. 'It wasn't in my flat, not before I left it, I'm telling you.'

'There's no doubt in your mind – maybe one of your friends brought it in?'

'I never saw it or touched it.' He sprang to his feet and walked in an odd, jerky manner around the room.

'All right,' she said. 'Calm down.'

Dunn came back to the table. 'I'm sorry, but one minute you're telling me my case is going to be dismissed and the next I'm going up for one hearing after another and now the police are planting stuff on me. That rope in my bin. I never had a rope in the bin.'

'You are to stand trial, Michael.'

He put his face in his hands, shaking his head.

'Do you know Ann Taylor?' she asked.

'Yes, I know her,' Dunn snapped. 'I did some work for her too. I've said this before.'

192

'I know, Michael. Just be patient. Go on.'

Dunn sighed. 'She paid me to do a few odd jobs. That's it.' He was slowly moving his head from side to side.

'Just how well did you know her, Michael? ... Michael!'

Dunn traced the edge of the table with his finger. He frowned. 'She wouldn't like this to get out. It just happened, see?'

'What happened?'

'I was clearing stuff out of her mother's bedroom. She'd died, you see, and Ann was . . . she was very upset. We had a few drinks. She was crying. I put my arms around her and . . . it just led to us being, you know . . .'

Belinda had to stop herself from gasping. She was having a hard time grasping this. She said, very slowly, 'You had a sexual relationship with Ann Taylor?'

He nodded. 'I promised I'd never tell anyone.'

Belinda's head cleared. What were the implications of this? Probably nothing. Ann Taylor had undoubtedly kept quiet about it and they would too.

As she left him, she said, 'We've got Robert Rylands for your defence.'

'He's good, is he?' asked Dunn.

She had smiled broadly at the understatement. 'Very good, Michael. In fact he's the best. And I'm bringing him to see you in two weeks time.'

THURSDAY 31 OCTOBER. 4 P.M.

In thirty years at the bar, Robert Rylands QC had made a considerable name as an anti-establishment barrister of principle, but these days he rarely had time to think deeply about right and wrong. Years ago he'd formulated a personal code that he applied to his practice with a degree of pragmatic flexibility. He wouldn't defend capitalists accused of fraud (he hated big fraud trials anyway: they were 'quagmires'). He would only represent celebrities in libel if he thought they'd been targeted by the puritan establishment. He'd steer clear of organized gangsters and drug cartels – at least, he wouldn't appear for them in open court. (Written opinions, outside the public domain, were perhaps another matter.)

What Rylands liked, and thrived on, were cases involving the little man – legal-aid cases, miscarriage of justice appeals, frame-ups. He enjoyed standing up for lone defendants, the weak, the deprived, anyone easily crushed by the juggernaut of the law. Cynics said that, for a man of Ryland's skill, such briefs were the perfect vehicle. If he won, his reputation soared; if he lost, few found the issue serious enough for comment. These days Rylands rarely lost a case he could have won, but nor did a loss cause him to lose sleep. He could turn in a stunning emotional act in court but no case ever touched his own emotional core.

He had read the solicitor's summary of the Michael Dunn case, and he'd talked about it to young Sampara. Child murder as such had obvious drawbacks for Rylands, in particular the public's revulsion. Some of it could always rub off on the accused man's barrister. On the other hand, it did sound as if the CPS and police were in a bit of bother over Dunn. A pathetic drunk with no serious form, he looked an all-too-easy collar. Rylands decided to take the case. He smelt a scapegoat.

Today, a fortnight after Dunn had been committed for

trial, the instructing solicitor, Miss Sinclair, was taking Rylands to a conference. So he'd got up early in the morning to read the brief. Now, with the papers in his hand, he wandered into the room that he shared with Willis Fletcher, finding the prosecutor at his wide mahogany desk hunched over *Halsey*.

'Are you prosecuting me for this little girl in the pipe?'

Fletcher straightened up. 'I have that honour.'

'Pleasant family party then.'

Rylands eased the door shut with his heel and strolled across to the mantelpiece. He leaned against it, studying the grim police photographs of Julie Anne Harris's body. He flashed them at Fletcher.

'Do you see any *particular* need for these to go in? There's nothing to see that isn't in the pathologist's report.'

Fletcher had returned to his research and was running his finger along a line of closely printed text. 'No, I suppose there isn't.'

'I don't suppose there's any question of keeping the mother out of things, too?'

Fletcher's finger stopped moving across the page. What was Robert up to? With his thoughts full of an entirely different case, he had to think for a moment to recall Anita Harris's testimony. Then he shook his head.

'Absolutely not, Robert. Unless you're prepared to admit the daughter left the doll in your flat.'

Rylands smiled. 'There's no question of agreeing the doll. In fact, I'll be objecting to the identification. The woman was distressed, emotional. They dumped it down in front of her first thing in the morning – it's like a leading question to my mind.'

Fletcher sighed. 'All right, I won't open it.'

'And the Gillingham girls – they're no good to you either, Will.'

Fletcher took off his half-moon glasses and looked warningly at his colleague, who was grinning at him wolfishly. 'Now look, Robert—'

'One says he touched her, the other – and *younger* – thinks it was good clean fun. The facts aren't similar enough, so you won't get it in on that count, will you?'

Fletcher closed *Halsey* with a sound like a distant explosion. 'So be it. Let's talk about you. You've got a drink problem, haven't you?'

Rylands smiled, motioning with the brief. 'Apparently.'

'There's no question of a sudden medical expert popping up to say you did it all in a daze?'

Rylands shook his head. 'No, absolutely not. I'm temperance now and I remember everything. I am quite certain I was having a long talk with my friend—'

There was a rap on the heavy oak door and it opened. A secretary showed Belinda Sinclair inside. Rylands instantly changed his demeanour, stepping forward with a hand extended. 'Ah! You must be Belinda Sinclair. I'm Robert Rylands. It's very nice to put a face to the name.'

They shook hands and Rylands indicated Fletcher. 'You've caught me fraternizing with the enemy. Do you know Willis Fletcher?'

Fletcher rose and Belinda shook his rather fleshier hand in turn. She was surprised.

'I didn't know you two actually shared a room here.'

Rylands laughed. He looked the sumptuous Miss Sinclair up and down.

Fletcher said, 'Oh, we huddle together for warmth, you know . . .' He picked up *Halsey* and replaced it on the shelf. 'Need the room? I can clear off now, Robert.'

'Don't bother. We're going.' He flashed a look at an expensive watch. 'We are taking tea with Mr Dunn.'

The wind gusted, making their unbuttoned coats fly as they waited for a taxi. Unsure whether it was the appropriate question, Belinda asked Rylands what he thought about their prospects, about the brief.

'Crown's on shaky ground with the doll.'

'Well, the mother's identified it very firmly, hasn't she?'

'I know. But it might be worth seeing if she can do so again.'

Belinda looked at him, puzzled. 'I'm sorry? I don't get it.'

Rylands showed no irritation. 'I feel that the dolly may have to appear in an identity parade all of her own. Can you get me a few similar dolls?'

Belinda nodded, smiling. 'I'll have a look in my toy cupboard.'

'Taxi!' shouted Rylands, jerking out his arm.

They settled into the back seat of the taxi.

'Wormwood Scrubs prison,' called Rylands, snapping open his briefcase.

'I have to say,' he went on, after he had perused some of the statements. 'I am a little concerned about the length of washing line in Dunn's rubbish bin. Has he anything to say about it?'

'*Has* he? When I saw him after committal, he got very exercised about that. Vehemently denied it had anything to do with him.'

'All right – but the washing line used on the child was from this Miss Taylor's garden – am I right?'

Belinda nodded.

'And also we know that Dunn knew Miss Taylor. But more than that, he knew her intimately, he had been in her house, in short, he had *slept* with her.'

'Well, actually, the way he tells it, it's quite a sweet story . . .'

Rylands looked out of the window – the Strand, Charing Cross, Trafalgar Square, the Mall – as she told him Dunn's version of his relationship with Miss Taylor. The barrister wasn't particularly impressed.

'Fletcher won't touch any of that, even if she's admitted it. Just – did she know him? – had he been in her house? – did he know there was a washing line?'

'Oh, yes,' said Belinda, 'that reminds me. There's something else you should know about it.'

'What? The washing line?'

'Yes. He didn't just *know* she had it, you see. He actually put it up for her.'

Rylands rubbed his chin. 'Hmm. Does he maintain they parted as friends?'

'He says their relationship ended on good terms, yes.'

'Did he? That's at variance with what she says. We'd better clear one or two of these things up, hadn't we?'

Dunn had been given a jam doughnut with his tea – a perk for the occasion of a QC's visit. He hadn't had anything like it for more than a month and he was putting off the moment when he would bite into it, tormenting himself a little. Meanwhile he listened to Mr Rylands, nodding. Nice guy, Mr Rylands, for a toff . . .

He was especially keen to know about Dunn's friendship with the kids off the estate. All seemed pretty straightforward to Michael. The kids came around. They treated him like a normal human being, unlike the rest of the estate.

'So would it, in fact, be true,' asked Rylands, 'that your flat was a sort of open house, where many people, including children, came and went?'

'Yes. My mates, you know, who I drank with, and the kids like.'

'And you said in interview that Julie Anne Harris had been to your flat. So when was the last time?'

Dunn picked up the doughnut. He lowered his nose to it and sniffed.

Rylands persisted. 'I mean before she went missing, Michael – roughly?'

Dunn put the doughnut down. 'Oh, I don't know. It's hard to say.'

'Would it have been a week, a month? Two months?'

Dunn brightened. He said, 'Tell you one thing, though. Her brother was always with her. He used to bring her with him.'

'That would be Jason Harris, yes?'

Dunn picked up the doughnut again. 'Yes, Jason. It was him wanted to come, see? Watch videos.'

Rylands seized on the point energetically. He looked down the schedule of video titles. 'But you *did* say that your video had been stolen some months previously. Right?'

Dunn nodded and replaced the still untasted doughnut on his plate.

'Do you know how old Jason Harris is?'

'I don't know. Nine, maybe. But he's well ahead of himself in years, that one.'

Rylands tapped his lower lip with a bent forefinger. 'In what way?'

The doughnut was back between Dunn's fingers now. 'Because he didn't come round to watch the Disney cartoons.'

As if to let the implication of young Jason's taste in videos sink in, Dunn now bit into the doughnut. As his teeth plunged gratefully into its mushy innards, he seemed not to notice that a large blob of strawberry jam had squirted out and stuck to his cheek.

In the Incident Room at Southampton Street, Satchell, Cranham, Harrold and Soames were dispersing after a briefing from Pat North when Mike Walker came in.

Walker was tired. He'd been sidetracked by Area into helping out with some new training films for the Met, and he'd spent the day sitting through a series of filmed interviews, on which he was expected to deliver his considered judgement. A waste of bloody time, but someone had to do it.

North approached him warily. 'They've got Robert Rylands – did you know?'

'Yes, bloody did,' growled Walker. 'He'll have his filleting knife out, going through our unused material.'

North spoke quietly, carefully. 'Guv, I've been going through the files myself—'

'You got your knife out too?'

'Not exactly . . .' She glanced at Satchell who was grinning and making knife-sharpening gestures. 'The point is, we still haven't pinned Peter James down for those missing twenty minutes on the day of the murder.'

Walker shut his eyes. 'Peter James, Peter James! We can't seem to knock that one on the head, can we?'

'I think it would be better to have another go over these times before we get to court.'

'Before Rylands makes bloody hay with them, you mean?' He considered. Then made up his mind. 'OK, we'll do it. We'll start from scratch on the timetable for the murder day. I'll see Mrs Harris – Meg! Where is that Liaison Officer? Family visit, please!'

He went off to find the file containing the Harris family statements. Returning through the Incident Room, he seemed to have renewed his springs of energy.

'You're getting to be a persistent woman, DI North.'

'Just keeping you on your toes, guv.'

'Oh, don't worry. I'll be a bloody ballet dancer before this one pans out. What is it, Dave?'

Satchell was at his elbow. 'Guv, it's the meals on wheels woman from the Howarth – Mrs Wald?'

'Wald?' Walker's mind took a moment to retrieve the detail. 'Oh, yes, I remember.'

'She's in reception. Something about Peter James.'

Jason opened the door to Walker and Richards but his mother came drifting along behind him. Her hair looked like a ball of straw and her eyes were half shut. The stomach beneath her dressing gown swelled unambiguously now.

'Oh! It's you!' she said half dreamily. 'I'm sorry, I was lying down. The doctor told me – you know . . .'

She placed a palm on her bulge. Richards smiled her sweetest smile. She wondered what tranquillizers the doctor had been shelling out.

'Sorry to bother you, Anita. We wanted a word with Peter.'

'He's not here. I don't know where he is.'

Richards swapped a look with Walker and looked over Anita's shoulder at Jason, who was still hanging around in the hall.

'Jason still off school, Anita?'

Anita was clawing at her son's shoulder, trying to get him behind her. 'Oh, school!' she said. 'He's got a rash on his legs. It's nothing, just a rash.'

Jason was wearing shorts. Meg and Walker looked at his legs, covered with red marks. They were beginning to turn blue in patches.

'Any idea when Mr James will be back, Mrs Harris?'

'No, I don't really ... There's nothing wrong, is there?'

Walker said, 'No, no. We won't keep you out of bed.'

He started to leave, but turned at the last minute. 'Oh, Mrs Harris. Just the one thing. What time did you say Mr James left the flat – that lunchtime?'

Anita didn't understand. She looked in panic from Walker to Meg and back again.

Meg said, gently, 'The day Julie Anne went missing, Anita.'

'Oh! I think ... around twelve-thirty, I think. Yes. Is that all right?'

'Yes, thank you, Mrs Harris,' said Superintendent Walker, jerking his head for Meg Richards to follow him.

North and Satchell's second interview of Mrs Wald was brief but informative.

'You see,' the meals on wheel lady told them, 'I just

202

phoned my husband and he thinks I should come back to you – he's an Inspector on the buses, you know.'

'I see,' said North. 'What have you come back about, exactly?'

'Well, the murder of that little girl of course. I gave a statement—'

'Yes, I have it here.' North picked up the statement and showed it to the witness. 'Was there anything you wanted to add?'

'Well, I think I should. You remember I said I couldn't remember the face of the young man I saw on the stairs that day? The long-haired man with the dark overcoat? Well, I was doing my rounds today, lunchtime, when I actually met him. It was on the stairs again – he was carrying a tin of beer and he looked dreadful. Anyway, this time I asked him. Are you the little girl's stepfather? I said. You see I'd been up just after it happened with a bunch of flowers. So I just said something about that and he said yes, he was the stepfather and he said thanks and went on his way. It was then I heard the chimes of the ice-cream van and that made me think . . .'

'So now you would like to amend your statement giving a positive identification.'

'Yes. On the day of the murder, I saw him coming out of the flats about quarter past one. Then I delivered the lunch and left Enid's at about half-past one. Then I saw him again at the ice-cream van.'

'The same man you had seen earlier on?'

'Yes. You see, I didn't really get a good look at his face. But now that I've talked to him . . . I mean, it was definitely him, the stepfather. Half-past one.'

*

203

'Mrs Wald has strengthened her statement,' Satchell told Walker when he got back from seeing Anita Harris. 'Made a positive ID of Peter James coming down the stairs at one-fifteen on 5 September.'

'Well, I've just been to the Harris's,' said Walker, sharply. 'Mrs Harris says she sent Peter James out at half-past twelve. And Poole says he parked his ice-cream van around the same time.'

North and Satchell shook their heads.

'The meals on wheels woman said *she* saw Peter James again at half-past one.'

'At the ice-cream van,' added Satchell.

Walker considered. 'So either she's got it wrong or the ice-cream man has.'

He started to pace – up to the window, then back to the noticeboard, where the timetable of the murder was written up.

'We know the little girl was taken at five past one. So, if Mrs Wald is right about the times, Peter James is in the clear – right?'

'But if Poole is telling the truth, he could still be our man,' added Satchell.

'And Anita bears Poole out, doesn't she? Why would she give a time that puts her boyfriend in the frame?'

A thought struck Walker, as he pictured Anita standing in her hallway, with young Jason hovering behind her.

'Could she just have been confused?' he speculated. 'Or could she . . .' He studied the photo of Julie on the board. 'Julie Anne had all these bruises on her body. And Meg says the marks we saw on Jason's legs today looked like strap marks.'

He turned and glanced round his team. His face was

hard set. 'Bring in Peter James, first thing in the morning. Pat, take Meg, talk to the mother again. Make it nice and easy, nothing confrontational – yet. We've got to get to the bottom of whatever makes that family tick.'

'You've been talking to the *police*!'

Peter's voice was hoarse from all the alcohol and smokes he was consuming these days. But he could still make the ornamental plates on the kitchen shelf rattle with his shouts.

Anita continued peeling a carrot. In the lounge, Tony started to cry. 'They came round here. I never said a word to them. I wasn't well.'

Peter walked to the window and looked out into the dark as Jason wandered in. 'Well, there's one of them bloody watching us. He's on the building site. He's been watching us for weeks, the brickies told me. Watching what we do and whether *he* goes to school.'

Anita gave Jason the carrot and started shaving another. 'I swear to you – I never said nothing. They want to talk to *you*.'

Peter swung round menacingly. 'What about?'

'I don't know. They just asked what time you went out looking for Julie.'

'Oh yes?' His voice faltered, the bluster leaving him. 'So what time did you say?'

Anita told him. Peter looked at her in disbelief, then started hammering on the window pane.

'No, no, no!' he shouted. 'That's wrong. That's bloody *wrong*, you stupid, stupid cow!'

*

Down below the flats a car nosed into the estate, moving at walking speed past the playground before drawing up opposite the now deserted building site. The engine and lights were killed. After a few seconds the driver emerged and walked past the site office towards the pile of sewage pipes. Some wire fencing had been erected around them, but he pushed his way through.

For more than an hour, Colin Barridge stood beside the pipes. He wasn't thinking of anything, he was as blank as a sentry. Inspector North had seen that his mind wasn't on the job so she'd told him to take a couple of days leave. But what she couldn't tell him was how to fill the time. Coming here seemed the only thing to do, a compulsion. He didn't know why.

Perhaps it was because it was the only place he could feel any kind of peace.

CHAPTER 18

'HE'S THERE again – see him?'

Richards and North were back on the Howarth, meaning to invite Peter James to Southampton Street to help them with their inquiries or to speak with Anita Harris if James wasn't there. But DI North was deflected by the sight of a lone figure standing at the place where the body of Julie Anne Harris had been found.

'Come on,' she said. 'Let's get this sorted once and for all.'

'He's no better then?' asked Richards as they started across the muddy, rubble-strewn ground.

'No, he's not. As you know, he found the body. Now he's suffered some kind of reaction. Flashbacks. Says he keep feeling her in his arms. Can't sleep.'

'What about occupational health?'

'Says he's tried that. Doesn't help. I told him to take a day or two off – Barridge!'

They had reached the young constable, who was standing ramrod straight like a guardsman. He was wearing his uniform.

'What the hell are you doing here?'

Barridge had been oblivious to their approach. He gave a start.

207

'Nothing, ma'am.'

His nose was red and he was trembling with cold.

'What d'you mean, nothing? You were here yesterday as well, so I heard.'

Barridge looked at his feet. 'I'm not on duty, ma'am,' he mumbled. 'I did as you suggested, got some time off.'

North opened her mouth. She was going to tell him she didn't do it so he could feed his morbid state by making sick pilgrimages to the site of his trauma.

But Barridge wasn't listening anyway. He was pointing at the ground. 'That's where I found her shoe. Just there.'

Pat touched his sleeve and said, gently but with a touch of exasperation. 'Go home, Barridge. Take off your uniform. Rest and stay at home.'

They watched as he began to walk back to his car, then set off towards the Harris's block. Trudging up the stairs, they heard a click and a mechanical whirr.

'Lift's working today,' said Pat.

'Stairs are better,' said Richards. 'Calves and thighs!'

Before they reached the Harris's floor and sounded the bell, Peter James had exited the lift three floors below and headed off into the grey morning.

Half an hour later, Satchell found Det. Supt. Walker splashing cold water on his face in the Southampton Street gents.

'Guv – Peter James. He's here. Walked in of his own accord.'

Walker roller-towelled his face then beat Satchell to the door. 'Come on then – let's get at him.'

*

208

'Anita told me you wanted to see me.'

They were back in the interview room – the eternal, unchanging interview room. Peter James spoke in flat, cautious tones.

'Yes, we did,' said Walker. 'Did she tell you why? We've been a little concerned about marks which the pathologist found on Julie Anne's body – bruises consistent with being struck, several days before the day she died.

Peter shifted in his seat. 'Well, yeah. She was quite a naughty little kid underneath them blonde curls.'

'You hit her?'

'Like I said, her mother and me found her a handful, sometimes.'

'Perhaps you and Mrs Harris have had a talk about this?'

Peter looked straight into the Superintendent's newly washed face, clenching his teeth. He felt rising anger. 'No, but I tell you what we *have* talked about. The fact that we can't even bury her.'

'I am deeply sorry about that, but it's completely out of my control. Detective Inspector North has gone over to yours today. She'll be explaining to Mrs Harris.'

'So how come no one's explaining to me?' He thumbed himself in the chest. 'You think it doesn't affect me? I bathed her, I told her bedtime stories, I took her to school. You sons of bitches are trying to twist everything round to make something sick out of it.'

'But you admit that you've had to discipline the children—?'

'Look – what *is* this?'

'In your role as stepfather, Peter? Are you denying that you've disciplined them physically?'

'No – because I have.'

'That's good,' said Walker, jabbing the air with his finger. 'Because you have hit the kids more than once, in fact?'

'Yeah, I have. We both have. That doesn't mean . . . *Look!* You charging me or what? I came here, nobody had to bring me in. So what are you trying on? I never – I swear before God – I never done nothing wrong!'

'OK, take me through it again. What time did you go out looking for Julie Anne on September the fifth?'

Peter James was shaking his head. 'I don't believe this. It was *after* one o'clock! Before that I was in the flat fixing the sink. Anita asked me to get the kids in. But she turned the tap on by accident and soaked me – I had to go and change my clothes. So I didn't go downstairs for fifteen or twenty minutes.'

Walker showed him a statement form. 'That's not what Mrs Harris says in her statement.'

'She doesn't *know* does she? She's confused. She had it wrong. She remembers things a lot more clearly now that she's calmed down. Listen to me – it was well after one o'clock. *Well* after.'

Walker stood up stiffly and sighed. 'OK. Thank you, Mr James.' He moved towards the door.

'Just wanted to get things straight,' said Peter in a soft, conciliatory tone.

'That is exactly what I'm trying to do, Mr James.' He waved Peter away. 'You can go.'

The corridor was busy with officers going about the normal business of the police station. Walker cannoned through them like a dodgem car towards the Incident Room. He urgently wanted to hear what the Harris woman had had to say.

North and Richards weren't back yet. Exasperated, Walker decided to kill some time by juggling a few figures on his budget sheet.

By the time the Inspector and Sergeant came in he was in a terrible mess, with debit and credit figures wandering into the wrong columns as if they had lives of their own. He hurled his pencil into a corner.

'You know something?' he said darkly to North. 'If I'd wanted to run a sodding corner shop, why would I have joined the job? It's a fucking joke!'

North put a handwritten statement, typed and signed, on his desk. 'Guv, this is Mrs Harris's new version. I also double-checked with some of the other residents – not that any of them can remember that Thursday. But they do say the ice-cream van is *always* parked just at the time Poole says it was then – twelve-thirty.'

'And we've had Peter James here – and he says he left the flat at just—'

'After one o'clock,' interrupted North.

Walker nodded. 'Fixing the sink, right? Had to change his clothes?'

'Yes,' confirmed Pat, nodding at Anita Harris's latest statement. 'Word for word.'

Walker shook his head. 'She's covering for him, isn't she? Christ!'

'There's something else, guv. She seemed a different woman this morning, there was something about her – much more together. She was cleaning the place up. Doing the washing. And she seems more clear-headed.'

Walker covered his ears with his hands. 'Give me some good news, for God's sake! Because if there isn't a case against Michael bloody Dunn, where are we going to go?'

On the way back, Peter stopped at the post office to cash his benefit cheque, then decided to treat everyone to a kebab. When he reached home, the flat looked neater than it had for weeks. The windows were open and there was a smell of furniture polish.

'Hi!' he called. 'Got you a shish kebab.'

He went through to the lounge. On the sideboard, flowers and cards were arranged neatly, as round a shrine, in front of the framed photographs of Julie. *Good-bye, sweet Julie. We missed you, darling* . . .

Anita was sitting on the sofa. Nearby, Tony rolled on the floor in a T-shirt and nappy but she was taking no notice. She looked pale and stunned.

Peter crouched beside her. 'You all right, girl?'

Jason appeared. He was sniffing like a dog, smelling the kebabs.

Anita said, weakly, 'Jason – go to your room.'

'Mum, I'm hungry.'

'Go on – do as I tell you.'

Peter looked at Jason, who seemed to flinch from the glance, but Peter handed Jason the take-away bag.

'Here, take it with you.'

Jason grabbed the food and disappeared. Tony went on rolling and mumbling.

Anita said, almost in a whisper, 'I found the doll.'

Peter froze. 'You *what*?'

She stood up. 'I swapped their mattresses over, Jason's with Julie's. And I found her Barbie doll.'

Peter said nothing for several seconds. He got up

and walked to the window. 'Did you give it to the police?'

She shook her head. 'No, I—'

'Where is it? Anita! I'm warning you, I've had all the hassle I'm prepared to take this morning.'

He advanced on her, his fist raised. 'Anita, if that bastard Dunn gets off, it's me they're going to charge, you know that, don't you? They're after *me* for it, I can tell. And I never touched a hair of her head.'

Anita's hands were clenched together, white with the tension. She had begun to weep.

He grabbed her arms, shaking her, pushing her backwards. 'Anita! I never touched her! *I never touched her!*'

He let her go. She simply stood there, weeping, her arms raised from her sides. She made no attempt to defend herself.

Peter was snarling. 'I *loved* her, *listen* to me . . . I *couldn't* have harmed her.'

In his bedroom, Jason was sitting on the floor with the kebab bag spread open in front of him. Slowly he was eating the food, stuffing chips and chunks of meat into his mouth in continuous succession. And as he chewed he counted every slap of Peter's hand against his mum's face.

CHAPTER 19

At CLARENCE Clough, Derek Waugh was sniffing around the Dunn case again, in spite of the complexities of Lady Preece's will and the horrific breach of contract liabilities faced by his client, Alphastrom Management Systems.

'Not found the alibi witness yet, I see,' he said, waving Belinda's report commissioned from a South Wales private investigator. 'If you don't track him down pretty soon, we're looking at a blank on the alibi, Belinda.'

He dropped the report back in her pending tray, where he'd found it.

She kept her eyes on the computer screen, controlling an urge to snap. 'There has been a *possible* sighting of Terry Smith at the Simon Community in Cardiff, Tiger Bay. And I'm just drafting an ad in the *Big Issue* in London.'

Waugh snorted. 'Last people who read that thing are the homeless. Now, I was thinking about something else. Aren't you going to need independent forensic confirmation that the little girl frequented Dunn's flat, so that those fibres could have been left there any time? All we've got at the moment is his word.'

'Well, Dunn did mention that Jason Harris, the brother, was always—'

'Keep away from the family, it's a public relations hornets' nest.'

Waugh strode to the door but stopped as he gripped the handle, as if seized by a further thought. 'Has Rylands been over any likely cross-examination yet with Dunn?'

'No, we're doing that today. We thought it would be better to get a bit of rapport going between them first.'

The senior partner twisted the doorknob and stiff-armed the door open. From the corridor he called back, 'Well, don't feather-bed him. The Crown aren't going to.'

The door slammed and Belinda made a snarling face.

At the CPS, Walker and North were winding up a progress report to Griffith. It was basically a 'no-progress' report.

'So,' said Griffith, 'there's nothing more on the forensic front?'

Walker frowned. He wished to God there was.

'No,' he said. 'And I think what we've got is all there is. Also there's a lot of pressure to release the body for burial and I think we should do that now.'

'Agreed?' Griffith looked from Fletcher to North. 'Agreed,' he confirmed when they both nodded.

Walker continued, very subdued, 'There's really nothing to add to the scientific evidence and I'm afraid we didn't get quite what we'd hoped from the Gillingham interviews.'

Almost distastefully, Griffith flicked through the pages of the evidence bundle, now bulkier than ever. 'I have a responsibility not to waste public money on a case which is going to fold up. And I have to tell you . . .' He stared at the two police officers over his half-moon glasses. 'I *have* to tell you, I am coming to the view that we should offer no evidence.'

Willis Fletcher sat beside Griffith, his eyes fixed on an open page of his own copy of the file. The barrister's face was grave but with a suggestion of humour somewhere in the corner of his eyes. Walker found some encouragement in that. At the other end of the table Jennifer Abantu's face was as impassive as ever – Walker had no idea if her opinion counted for anything with Griffith. But then, he had no idea what her opinion was.

'Dunn still hasn't come up with his alibi witness,' he said. 'I think there's a very good chance we'll be able to show he's served a false notice of alibi.'

Fletcher stirred in his seat. 'Well, that *would* be a help,' he remarked.

Griffith looked at him without appreciation and closed the file decisively. 'I shall take that into consideration when making my decision.'

'Hang on,' said Walker desperately. 'There's something else you should take into consideration. I'm sure the Director of Public Prosecutions doesn't want any *more* sensitive, national cases dropped for lack of evidence, leaving *more* grieving families to drag their private prosecutions through the courts.'

He was going out on a limb here, and he knew it. But he ground on. 'Sometimes it's important to try a case. Sometimes it should be *seen* to be tried.'

Griffith stood up, capped his pen and clipped it into his breast pocket. 'I execute policy,' he said darkly, 'I don't play politics. I'll let you know what I decide.'

In the car, Walker pounded the dash with his fist,

working out his pent-up aggression. 'Fletcher wants to proceed – I can feel it. Griffith doesn't, but surely he won't have the balls to drop it?'

'You're going to need yours, I reckon.'

Walker looked at her.

She smiled, braking sharply. 'That crack about the DPP,' she went on, 'it didn't go down at all well.'

Walker banged the dash again. 'I *still* put money on Dunn.'

'What about Peter James, though?'

He shook his head as she put the car into gear. 'No. I don't like him, but I don't think he's a killer.'

As they pulled away from the lights, Walker shook off the sense of despair. 'Tell you what – get Satchell to have another go at the ice-cream seller. Speak to his boss this time. If he's lying . . .'

North nodded. 'Peter James would be in the clear – yes?'

'He'd be laughing and so would we. If I'm reading Griffith right, the reason for why he doesn't want to go on against Dunn is he's afraid the real killer's Peter James.'

Robert Rylands, the inveterate defence brief, had a favourite performance in prison conference rooms – acting the prosecutor. It was part of his job to play the game of putting a client through his witness box paces, to test him with the difficult questions the Crown would ask and gauge his readiness and credibility. And Rylands played the game hard, turning the small prison interview room into a court, circling the client like an attack helicopter, pouncing on his uncertainties and inconsistencies.

At Wormwood Scrubs, with Michael Dunn in his

sights, he wondered, not for the first time, why he found this task so satisfying. Perhaps, after all, he should have been a prosecutor himself. He'd have been a bloody good one.

'Now you admit you let young children into your flat unchaperoned?'

'I'm sorry?' asked Dunn. 'Unwhat?'

'Unsupervised. Without any adult with them.'

'Yes, I suppose so.'

'And you showed them videos. Why?'

'Because they like them.'

'But why did you want them to come to your place?'

'Because . . . because . . . I enjoyed their company.'

Dunn looked nervously at Belinda. He couldn't understand the change that had come over Mr Rylands. He'd gone so hard. She nodded encouragement at him, gave him a smile.

'And what sort of videos were these?'

'Well, cartoons and—'

'And some quite unsuitable material – am I right?'

'I don't know.'

'*Child's Play 3, The Terminator*?'

'Yes, I had them. But my video was nicked and I couldn't show them films any more, see.'

'But children came to your flat after the video disappeared, didn't they?'

'Yes.'

'When was the last time there were children at your flat?'

Dunn shook his head, bewildered. 'I don't know, I can't remember.'

'Can you remember a specific day when Julie Anne was at your flat?'

'No. No, I can't.'

Rylands rubbed his hands, a gesture which seemed to show he was pleased, though neither Dunn nor Belinda could see why.

'All right, Michael, let's turn to your alibi for 5th September. You know what an alibi is, don't you?'

''Course I do.'

Rylands paced to the window and swung around, leaning with his elbows on the sill. He pitched his voice a few semitones higher, his most sceptical courtroom voice.

'You've named two men and a woman as alibi witnesses. Of the men, one won't cooperate and the other can't be found. The woman's never heard of you. How did that happen, Mr Dunn?'

'I don't know, I was confused. I couldn't remember exactly—'

'Because if you were *not* with those people, then it is possible that it was you whom Mrs Marsh saw from her window, you who took a little girl by the hand and led her back to your flat. Isn't it?'

Dunn was shaking his head pathetically. 'No, really. There was never any little girl in my flat that day.'

Rylands thought for a moment, looking at the ceiling. 'If you can't recall any specific day or date that Julie Anne was at your flat – how can you be so sure she wasn't there on 5th September?'

Dunn was frightened now. His eyes were wide with anxiety as he looked for support to Belinda, then back to Rylands. He said, 'She used to come all the time. All the time. Just ask her brother. Ask Jason.'

Rylands held his gaze for a moment, then relaxed, smiling, coming forward to the table. He began assembling his papers.

'That's all right, Michael. Just remember it's in their interest to try to make you lose control of yourself. Just answer the questions and keep cool.' He tapped a stack of papers against the table to straighten them. 'We'll leave it for today, OK? I will see you again before trial.'

On the way back to town, Rylands was whistling to himself.

'You seem pleased,' Belinda said.

'Moderately, moderately. I wouldn't put it higher than that. You?'

'I don't know. There's something Michael said that's bugging me. Ask Jason, he said. Do you think we could?'

Rylands shook his head. 'Tricky. Young child witnesses? Very, very tricky . . .'

Two hours later Peter and Anita's door opened and Helen let herself in. She carried a suitcase.

'Didn't know you had a set of keys,' Peter told her when he met her in the hall. He glowered at her.

'I've come for the funeral.'

'Well, you're not staying here.'

Hearing voices, Anita came through. She gave her mother a hug. 'I want you to stay, Mum.'

Peter simply swore.

CHAPTER 20

KENNETH POOLE lay naked across a sturdy refectory-style kitchen table of Norwegian pine. A young woman was walking her fingernails up and down the length of his spine while he licked a few last vestiges of the strawberry yoghurt that he'd spooned into her navel a few minutes earlier. And then the telephone was ringing.

Most of Poole's Sunday mornings were like this. Around nine o'clock, after a look through the *News of the World* and a breakfast at his Bethnal Green flat of two fried eggs, a fried slice and grilled bacon, he'd catch a bus out to Romford. It was from there, at a quarter to ten sharp, that his boss would leave his comfortable home for the office and keep reliably busy all morning completing the previous week's accounts. Poole found it intensely exciting to lurk in the bus shelter opposite the house, waiting for Frank Petrie's exit.

It was always the same pantomime, starting with Petrie's jaunty appearance on the path, buttoning his camel coat. Kenneth watched as the electronic key beeped open the Merc's doors, the door opened and closed with a soft cough and Petrie settled in the driver's seat, lighting his first Cuban panatella of the day and stroking the

221

engine into life. Then, at last, as the growl of the Merc's radials died away, Poole nipped across the road, slipped through the side door of the house and slid into the willing arms of the young and lovely Mrs Petrie.

Kenneth knew he would never have that expensive coat, that Merc – or even that panatella. But what he did have, by the gift of nature, was the equipment to make Michelle Petrie, from time to time, a very happy woman. So, between ten and midday, before he himself had to clock on at the depot to start his Sunday shift, he and Michelle would cavort around the house like a pair of bonobo chimps. They did it on the World of Leather four-seat sofa in the lounge. They did it on the hairy astrakhan rug in front of the ingle-nook fireplace ('ingle-nookie' as Michelle called it with a delicious giggle). They did it rolling around the smoked-oak parquet in the hall, on the Cumberland slate worktop in the kitchen, in the dusty intimacy of the broom-cupboard, in the bubbling cauldron of the huge Jacuzzi bath. They even, if they felt lazy, did it in the emperor-size bed with its five-speed vibrating mattress.

And so, for a couple of hours each week, Kenneth Poole thought he'd died and gone to heaven. It couldn't last, of course.

As the phone warbled, he paused in mid-lick but Michelle didn't miss a finger-step. Nonchalantly she raised the portable handset that was never out of her reach.

'Yeah?'

Kenneth strained to listen. He recognized Petrie's nasal twang coming fuzzily through the earpiece. Michelle was drumming her fingers on his shoulder blade.

'What they want then?' she asked.

Judging by his tone of voice, Petrie seemed upset. It was even more squawkingly petulant than usual.

'Oh, OK,' his wife said at last. 'See ya later, sugar.'

Michelle laid the phone down and began to writhe her limbs, those limbs whose God-given shapeliness could make Kenneth break out in a sweat just thinking about them. She was evidently manoeuvring to force Poole's mouth to make a lower contact on her body. But, for the moment, he declined the gambit.

'What did he want?'

Michelle went on wriggling. Then she brought one of her nicely shaped feet up to the tabletop to give herself purchase.

'Oh, nothing.'

'What did Frank *want*?'

'Just, the police are down at the depot, asking a lot of questions about some murder, so he's going to be late.'

'A *murder*?'

Michelle sighed and lay still a moment. 'Yeah, but it's nothing to do with Frank, it's nothing important. So come on big boy, forget about it and just—'

'Wait a *minute*, Michelle. I want to know. What murder?'

'That little kid over docklands, it was in the news. A while ago. One of our vans was nearby when it happened or something.'

'Holy buckets of shit!' said Ken, rolling off the table and scrabbling for his jockey shorts. 'I got to go.'

Satchell hated funerals. He sometimes had an inexplicable impulse to laugh, so he tried to stay away. Now, with the

Guv and Pat North in attendance at the Harris burial, he felt it was OK to miss it.

Checking on Poole's story, he'd been down to the depot at eleven to interview Frank Petrie, the ice-cream van king. According to Petrie the vans went out at twelve every day.

'We got a roster of calls for every unit,' Petrie told him as they stood in his office. He walked and knocked on a chart on the wall. 'I got eight vans at the moment – goes up to a dozen in summer. And this chart plots every site visited by every van, how long they stay and so on. That way, nobody doubles up and we don't get into no turf wars with the opposition. Used to be anarchy out there at one time.'

Satchell said, 'So you know exactly when Mr Poole arrived at the Howarth Estate on 5th September?'

Petrie's face took on a crafty expression. 'I know when Poole *should* have been on the estate. He should have been there at half-past twelve. But I don't know if he actually was. I've had trouble with that young man before. Wouldn't put it past him if he was getting into the knickers of some tart on my time.'

'What – *Confessions of an Ice-Cream Seller* type of thing?'

Petrie lowered his voice and said contemptuously. 'I wouldn't put it past him.'

Satchell glanced at his watch. 'Is he working today?'

'Poole? Yes – due on at twelve, as usual.'

'Would you ask him to come down to the station when he knocks off? I just want to take him through his statement again.'

Now Satchell was back in the Incident Room cross-checking through the door-to-door inquiries for references to the visit of the ice-cream van. A call came through from the front desk.

'Got a Kenneth Poole here for you, Dave.'

Poole was early – it was only half one.

'OK,' he said. 'Be right down.'

'I was scared, you know? Thought I'd lose my job because he's a right bastard and I'd had one warning anyway . . .'

Poole was gabbling through nervousness. And from his breath, Satchell could tell he'd been in the pub for a few stiffeners.

'I mean, I never thought it would matter – half an hour, like.'

'What did you think wouldn't matter, Mr Poole? Just spell it out, easy like.'

Poole swallowed. 'I didn't get to the Howarth Estate until gone one on the day the little girl was murdered.'

He was rubbing his hand through his hair.

'Oh, shit! I knew it'd all come out.'

'What? What would come out?'

'I was shagging his wife, see? She'd give me a few quid, you know, to cover for the ices I might have sold and . . . well, he knows now because I told him. I got the boot – said he suspected I was with a tart, so I told him exactly who the tart was!'

Dave Satchell's mouth was open. This was absolutely bloody choice. He couldn't wait till he told the lads. Leaning meaningfully forward, he tried to keep a straight face.

'Well, this is potentially serious—'

'Serious? You're not joking. I lost my job!'

225

'I mean we could have you for making a false statement. You know that?'

'Yeah, of course. Look, I'm sorry. Me and Michelle, well, we stopped meeting in working time after that. We thought of another time.'

'I'm glad to hear it, Mr Poole, but let's not get sidetracked. Now, I want you to make out a new statement about your true movements on 5th September, OK?'

Half an hour later, DS Satchell was standing inside the door of the church where the funeral of Julie Anne Harris was just beginning. If you'd paid him he couldn't have waited with this news.

'He who dies and believes in me shall live,' intoned the vicar. 'And he who lives and believes in me shall never die . . .'

Satchell spotted Walker, North and Richards sitting near the back so he slid into the pew immediately behind and leaned into Walker's ear.

'Guv, the ice-cream seller lied about the times. He didn't get to the Howarth Estate till gone one.'

Walker looked round. 'Did you—'

'Yeah, I just took a new statement. This puts Peter James in the clear, right?'

Walker couldn't suppress a smile. He hammered once with his fist on his right knee. If he'd had a Marlboro between his fingers he'd have snapped off the filter.

He whispered to Pat North. 'Hear that? Griffith can't pull the case now – can he?'

'And', whispered Dave, 'Michael Dunn still has no alibi.'

Pat kept her face to the front, but she too was smiling faintly. They were back on track. Meanwhile the vicar's voice echoed over their heads.

'. . . and in the midst of life, we are in death.'

Belinda knew it was the funeral today and had even considered attending but dismissed the idea, remembering her violent reception at the Harris's front door. So she'd come to work instead.

Working on a Sunday was nothing new to Belinda. The offices of Clarence Clough usually had a few lawyers in over the weekend and security there was round the clock. Not that she thought much of the security presence – a bunch of dozy old men.

She had been re-reading the forensic reports on Julie Anne's clothes when one of the security men confirmed her worst opinions. He rang her from the front desk.

'Er, Miss Sinclair? Man's just come in for you.'

'Who?'

'A man.'

'And this man's name?'

'Oh, I see. Sorry, miss. There's only me on the desk, see? I must've forgot to ask him.'

'Well, ask him now.'

'You'll have to ask him yourself, miss. I've sent him up.'

'Did he say what it was about?'

'No, miss. Just that it's important.'

'Well, really! I've already had threats against me working on this case. And now you've let some strange man walk straight past you and up the stairs.'

'Well, like I say, miss, there's only me on the desk, it being Sunday.'

She hung up and called out to see if there was anyone in the next office. 'Stephen! Jeremy!'

There was no one and, as she heard the tread on the stair outside, she realized she was on her own.

In the church they were singing one of those funeral hymns that make you feel like crying even if you didn't know the deceased. At the front of the church, Helen was weeping copiously, but silently. Anita was bent forward in her pew, trembling and heaving as she breathed. Peter grasped her hand, his face taut with strain. Jason sat in the pew behind, the only impassive figure in the church. He was sitting next to his dad.

> Gentle Jesus, meek and mild
> Look upon a little child
> Pity my simplicity
> Suffer me to come to Thee.

Thomas Harris, in his dress uniform, sat rigidly to attention, his eyes brimming with tears that he just managed not to shed. And, at the very back of the church, in newly pressed uniform, was Colin Barridge. He stood, equally to attention, but for him there was no will to suppress the grief. Fat, frank teardrops coursed down his cheeks while rivers of dilute mucous poured from his nostrils. And when at last it was time to leave the church for the graveside, Barridge found himself stumbling around blindly among the cohorts of press and camera crews. He couldn't see his colleagues, until Meg Richards came up and gently walked him over to the rest of the funeral group.

The man was burly with a boxer's face. He was wearing a well-worn leather overcoat, blue jeans and red neck-scarf and Belinda was considerably taken aback by the way he looked around at the comfortable furniture and fittings of the office. He did this with undisguised contempt.

'Huh,' said the man in a marked Cardiff accent. 'Lawyers! Fat felines. Pampered pussycats.'

'Excuse me,' she squeaked, 'would you please state your business?'

She felt somehow that a show of extreme formality might protect her and certainly the man's manner did change. He had a rolled-up newspaper, somewhat battered and torn, in his hand and he pointed it at her in the same way, it occurred to Belinda, that you aim a gun.

'You Belinda Sinclair?'

'Yes, I am. What do you want?'

Then he changed suddenly, became business-like, unrolling the paper, which he opened and spread out on the desk between them. His movements were quick and precise but his breathing was laboured, with an intermittent smoker's crackle. The clothes smelt musty but somewhere there was an underlying scent of soap.

He said, 'It's just that I understand you're looking for me.'

She glanced down at the paper and up at him. She had recognized the title but anxiety made her slow-witted and she didn't see the clear connection. He stabbed one of the small ads with a nicotine-stained finger.

'It says in here that you want to see me. My name's Terry Smith.'

Her coffin was white and so small that Thomas Harris had picked it up and carried it by himself, across his arms like an offering, to the graveside. Now the vicar was reciting the ancient formula about ashes and dust.

Helen did not hear it. She was attending to Anita, because something bad was happening even worse than this terrible grief that she felt, Thomas felt, and which, she knew, was tearing at Anita's guts.

Anita had pulled free of Peter's hand. She was clinging on to her mother's arm, bending and swaying as she stood there, her breath coming in gasps.

'Mum,' she whispered, 'promise me you won't leave Peter alone with the kids.'

'What do you mean? What is it love?'

Anita looked up at her mother, her face white and pleading. And then it clenched, every muscle seizing up as a blaze of pain raked through her. Anita dropped her hand from her mum's arm and bent over her swollen belly. Her hands were braced now against her thighs and she was making sharp hiccuping sounds. Then Helen understood.

'Oh, my God, no! Anita, no!'

The vicar was still praying when Peter set off, hurdling across the graveyard as he yelled desperately for a car. They got Anita inside it but by this time she was bleeding. The press were running after them, clustering around the car, their questions muffled and distant but the flash of their cameras harsh and piercing, like the pain itself.

*

'So, Mr Smith, how can you be so sure of what you are saying?'

Belinda had made a pot of tea and she poured for them both.

'I mean, you did a lot of drinking that day, and—'

'I did a lot of drinking *every* day, miss. I'm an alcoholic, I admit that. But it doesn't mean I'm completely ga-ga. And anyway, now I'm off the booze completely – one day at a time, of course – my head's clear as crystal.'

He sipped from his mug and mildly smacked his lips. 'I didn't know which was more important to me, drink or politics. But, now I've got my head straightened out, I know.'

'So which is it?'

'Politics, miss. The Revolution – that's my only stimulant now. Better to die on your feet than live on your knees – a great Spanish revolutionary said that.'

Belinda nodded wisely, wondering how she was going to get Smith back on track. But she needn't have worried.

'Anyway, I can remember it all. We got together in the Scrubbery – you know, that little park place near the benefit office – after the office opened, about eleven o'clock. We started off there, then went to the chippie, then back to the park—'

He was interrupted by the door swinging open and the entrance of the senior partner in Sunday mufti, beige cardigan and Hush Puppies. He looked at Smith in surprise.

'Ah, Derek,' said Belinda. 'Do come in, join us.'

Feeling a sudden rush of triumph over Waugh, she didn't bother with introductions but carried straight on talking to the witness.

'So, Mr *Smith*' – she shot a quick glance at Waugh to

231

clock his astonishment – 'you read our advertisement in the *Big Issue* and you remember spending the whole day with Michael Dunn – right?'

Smith nodded.

'But how can you be certain it was that particular Thursday, the 5th September?'

Smith snapped his fingers. 'Easy. The Berringham by-election, fifth of September. Bloody Spartacist knocked our fellow out.'

Belinda scribbled a note. The by-election certainly rang a bell, and the date was easy enough to check.

'Good,' she said, 'very, very good.'

After Smith had left Waugh paid her a gruff compliment.

'Well done, Belinda. Fellow seems a good witness, though a bit of a Trot which we shall have to watch. That surprised me, actually. I thought Terry Smith was supposed to be a wino.'

'He was,' said Belinda. 'He's reformed. So you see, Derek, there's hope for us all.'

She was enjoying herself enormously. She would enjoy even more telling her client that his alibi had been confirmed.

CHAPTER 21

FRIDAY 15 NOVEMBER

THE MOOD of elation amongst Michael Dunn's defence team could not be too publicly celebrated. There was a need for secrecy. As Waugh told Belinda – and for once he was right – there was no requirement for the defence immediately to tell the CPS that Terry Smith had been found. In the interests of their client – of his more effective defence – they would keep their alibi witness under wraps until just before the off.

So it was that, only four days before Dunn was due to appear at the Crown Court to answer the charge of murder against him, Belinda Sinclair picked Terry Smith up from the hostel where he was living and brought him east to Southampton Street to make a sworn statement.

The scenes in the Incident Room were of consternation.

'Why the bloody hell couldn't *we* find him?' stormed Satchell. 'Bunch of incompetents are we, or what? Bunch of dozy bastards fit for nothing but touchline duty at Leyton Orient? Christ!'

'How did they find him, then?' asked Phelps. 'I can't believe their luck!'

'They advertised, didn't they?' said Satchell. 'Bloody

advertised! Well, of course, that's the difference, isn't it? We got no bastard advertising budget.'

'He was living in a hostel drying out,' put in Henshaw. 'Apparently he's obsessed with Lenin.'

'What – the Beatles?' asked Marik.

'Pillock!' said Henshaw, swiping Marik round the head with his copy of the *Daily Mail*. 'Len-*in*. He's political. A leftie.'

'Didn't know there was any of those no more,' retorted Marik. 'Could be good for us, though. Expose him as a Trot, a troublemaker. Discredited witness.'

Pat North heard this as she came in.

'I'm sorry, Marik, but it's more likely to harm us. Lefty's not much of a bogeyman any more. My guess is he'd come over as bright and serious, and a little bit of a romantic, you know? One of a dying breed.'

'Yes, but he might start mouthing off in court, have a go at the judge or the legal system,' said PC Brown hopefully. 'That would be good, wouldn't it?'

'I don't think, somehow, Rylands is going to allow that to happen,' said Satchell. 'But if he does, we'll know he's losing his grip big time. Is Smith here now, guv?'

Pat North was removing papers from a filing cabinet.

'Yes. Mike and I are about to take his sworn statement. Wouldn't it be nice if we could just make him disappear instead?'

She smiled all round and swung smartly out of the room to meet the man who might just extract Michael Dunn from a life sentence.

Walker smoked his amputated Marlboros more or less continuously during the interview and he let Terry Smith have free access to the packet as well. It wasn't generosity. Walker was so angry he was having a hard time concentrating so he just didn't notice the witness helping himself. Sitting beside Smith, Belinda, though she hated the smoke, saw it as a fair sign of how rattled the police were.

Walker had Smith's printed-out statement in front of him. He'd been over the statement again and again, but there was nothing he could prise from it, nothing of any use to his side. All that was left was for Smith to sign it.

'So, Mr Smith, you and Michael Dunn started talking about politics at eleven o'clock on that Thursday did you? Until when?'

'All day, like it says,' said Smith.

'What on earth was there to talk about *all day*?' said Walker incredulously.

There was a tap on the door and Satchell put his head in to beckon to Pat North. She left the room while Smith expanded.

'We were talking about whether the desire for property is natural to mankind. You see the Russian peasants before the revolution used to have little plots of land . . .'

Walker flicked a glance at Belinda who was clearly having to suppress a smile. He scowled but Smith was just getting into his stride.

'These guys were called kulaks, you see, and when it came to dealing with them, Lenin formulated a plan about which there has been considerable controversy over the years—'

'Yes, yes, yes. I get the gist,' said Walker. 'This isn't the Evening Institute. And you say this all-day drinking session didn't affect your memory to any material extent?'

Terry Smith smiled. Everything about him was so open and honest it made Walker cringe.

'No, I had a tolerance for it, you see. I'm telling you, I'll stand up in court and say it: Michael Dunn was with me all day on September the fifth. All day long, until six, seven at night.'

'He didn't leave at any time?'

'No. He didn't leave.'

Again Walker looked hopelessly at the statement, his eyes going this way and that over it as if casting about for comfort and finding none. His expression was bleak. He slid the statement on to the table, face up in front of the witness.

'Right, Mr Smith, I thank you for your co-operation in this matter. Would you like to read and sign the statement?'

Pat North returned to the room and stood near the door while Smith read rapidly through the text and, taking a pen from Belinda, scribbled his signature at the bottom. He handed the paper back to Walker like a bailiff serving a writ.

Belinda said, sweetly, 'There you are, Superintendent. All right if we go now?'

Walker couldn't bring himself to speak. He nodded.

After they'd left, he almost spat. 'Like the cat who got the cream, isn't she? What did Dave want?'

'Anita Harris has been released from hospital, guv,' said Pat.

'In time for the trial. Poor woman.'

'Yes. Buries one, miscarries another. Hard even to contemplate what she must be feeling right now.'

'I tell you one thing I'm feeling. More bloody determined than ever that Michael Dunn killed that child. And

I want to nail him. I want to hammer in those nails personally.'

'There's a bloke down there in the playground,' observed Karen Hyam, looking idly out of the staircase window in the early afternoon, as she and her friend Ivy Green hoisted the black bin bag down the stairs. 'He's going round on the kiddies' roundabout.'

She had caught a glimpse of the play area, deserted during the lunchtime of a school day. The man was sitting on one of the tubular bars which divided the revolving platform into four sections.

'Some men never grow up,' said Ivy Green drily, forging ahead of her friend up the stairs.

Ivy and Karen had volunteered to help get Enid Marsh to court on the Tuesday, properly dressed and in good shape to give her evidence. As a preparation for the big day on Tuesday, they'd decided to go down to her with some possible clothes for her outfit. The poor old dear had nothing much of her own, so they'd been round their friends – and their friends' mothers – on the scrounge.

When they arrived they saw that Mrs Wald, the meals on wheels, had been in half an hour earlier and the remains of Enid's lunch were still on the table.

'Come on, dear,' the practical Ivy had said, picking up the plates and bustling through into the kitchen. 'We've got you in some things to try on. For the trial.'

'Oh!' shrilled Enid. 'But there's no need for that. I've got plenty of things to choose from in my bedroom, I have.'

'No, you've not, petal. I've looked. It's all too old.' She caught the look of dismay on Enid's face. 'I'm not saying they didn't look brilliant in their day, but the moths have got at them. Now me and Karen have searched out a few pieces for you to choose from. Make you look exactly like a super model. It's only right – with you the star witness. Go on, Karen, back me up.'

'Oh yes, Enid, we've found some lovely things,' said Karen encouragingly. 'Near enough Paris fashions, some of it.'

As she watched the two neighbours, younger than her by decades, pulling skirts and blouses out of the bin bag, Enid Marsh started to get used to the idea. It was true she hadn't had on any of her really good clothes for a long time – not since the Silver Jubilee, probably. Spent most of her time in her old cardigan and jumper – never had the occasion to dress up. Moths – yes, it was very likely the good stuff was full of holes. She brightened. New clothes to try on. Come to think of it, that *did* sound nice.

Half an hour later she was sitting on her sofa with clothing strewn around her. She was wearing a powder blue sunray pleated skirt which looked like something Dame Vera Lynn might have worn. It *was* a tiny bit too big for her, but Ivy and Karen thought they could tuck it in at the waist and make it look very smart. The effect was topped off by the white nylon blouse with a frilled jabot, found at the bottom of the bin bag by Karen.

'Everybody's been so kind,' Enid was saying, looking at a portion of herself in the small portable mirror propped up on the table. 'Before all this happened, I never saw a soul.'

She twitched the skirt to arrange the pleats closer to the vertical. 'You don't think it's a bit bright?'

Ivy came over and considered for a moment. She had

238

her hand to her mouth and was pinching her lower lip between finger and thumb. 'Looks lovely, Enid, dear. But Mrs Kingsley says she's got a Jaeger suit if you want it.'

Karen, standing by the window, was pulling Enid's net curtains aside. 'Here, that man's still down there. I reckon he's staring up at this window. Bit of a toff.'

Enid shuffled across to join her, peering down. He was a well-dressed, well-preserved man in his mid-fifties, wearing a dark-grey woollen overcoat. The three women watched as, seeing their heads looking down, he turned away and bent to pick up his briefcase.

'I think I'll try the jacket now,' said Enid without further comment. 'And that mauve skirt – I haven't had that on yet. And what was you saying about a suit, Ivy, love?'

That afternoon Anita was also trying on clothes. Ten days after the miscarriage and she still had a fat stomach. She had even thought of going to court wearing the black maternity dress she'd bought for the funeral, but Helen told her no: it wouldn't look right.

'But nothing fits me,' Anita complained. 'I still look as if I'm pregnant.'

I still *feel* pregnant too, she thought. Three times before in her life she'd given birth and each time, once the baby was out and feeding, Anita had felt feather-light. Never had a day of post-natal depression either. This was her fourth, except it wasn't. Birth is all about life, that's why it's called *giving* birth. So she went on feeling heavy and burdened because she had given nothing, nothing had happened. The baby was dead.

In hospital she couldn't cry. Until they'd found her a

private room the second night she'd been stuck in a post-natal ward, full of other mums sitting up in bed nursing their little bundles, a cot next to every bed except hers. Anita was simply withdrawn. She hardly responded when anyone spoke to her. She stared straight ahead and talked silently to herself. The baby was dead; giving birth's about giving life . . .

'You should go out and buy something, love,' said Helen now, flicking through the dresses and jackets that hung in the wardrobe on their wire coat hangers. Truth be told, there was little enough here. 'You've got all those donations and I don't suppose anybody'd begrudge you.'

'It's too late now. I haven't got time. I can't go out and buy something, just like that.'

'Well, be warned. Peter's dipping into them all the time. Taking himself off to I don't know where.' She sniffed. 'I've hardly seen him – sober, that is.'

Anita touched her mother on the arm. 'Hey! Don't, Mum. Just don't get into that. Anyway I'm better off without him around.'

Helen took down a dark-blue jacket that looked OK, though it needed taking to the cleaners.

'A white blouse under that'll look nice in court, eh, my girl.'

Anita pushed her arms out behind to let Helen slip the jacket on for her. Turning this way and that in front of the mirror, she was trying to remember when she'd last worn it.

Darkness had fallen but the figure of a man in white shirtsleeves could be seen crossing the road and making for the sewage pipes. He carried a bundle in his arms.

It had been wet the last few days and the trench dug for the pipes was flooded. He stood on the edge of the trench, watching the reflections from the site security lighting wobble as the water was troubled by the wind. He was thinking of another flooded area not many yards away, where a dead cat had floated and he had fallen in. Put off doing a proper search because he swallowed some water. Stupid and unprofessional.

Barridge felt a heavy weight in the pit of his stomach. It was the weight of responsibility, the weight of guilt. For a long time during the investigation he had believed that finger was on him – like that lottery advert, it could be *you*. It was a pleasant feeling, a light feeling. He had trodden on air for a while, a man specially chosen who could do no wrong.

But doing *that* – well, he shouldn't have. That was wrong and Colin Barridge knew it. He'd have to come clean, he'd have to tell. And then they'd kick him out.

With a groaning sigh he raised the bundle in his arms and tossed it into the water of the trench. His uniform tunic gradually soaked up the water, then opened out, arms spreading, the chrome buttons catching the light.

CHAPTER 22

ROBERT RYLANDS was studying the list to see which judge had been allotted to the case. Barristers, solicitors, witnesses, police and officers of the court bustled through the lobby behind him as the Crown Court's working day began to unroll.

'Good morning, Robert. Alone and palely loitering?'

He turned. It was the solid figure of Willis Fletcher who, like him, had yet to robe. Behind Fletcher, in a little knot, were the Crown team – Griffith, Jennifer Abantu and Rylands's junior, Tom Jolowicz. They all hefted large tagged bundles, deep ring-files and thick law books.

'It's Winfield,' said Rylands, tipping his head back towards the list on the board behind him. 'Did you know?'

'Yes, I've seen the list. He's decent enough.'

'Babbles like the bloody brook, though. I'd have thought—' He broke off as the figure of Derek Waugh pushed eagerly through the crowd.

'Robert – it's delightful to see you again.'

Fletcher winked at his chambers room-mate and, stepping back, rejoined his team. Rylands looked down on the shorter man as if inspecting a dead fish.

'Very nice to see you, too, Derek. Show of solidarity by the firm?'

242

'Yes – ah, I thought I might just pop down. Belinda's with our friend downstairs.'

Rylands was only half listening – he was scanning over Waugh's head at the crowd. At last he saw Noah Sampara, his junior, struggling towards him laden with papers and carrying a plastic bag, out of which straggled several locks of beautifully permed nylon hair.

'Ah, Noah!' said Rylands heartily. He nodded at the carrier bag. 'Brought your friends with you? Good!' He glanced at his watch. 'Look, I'd better go and get clobbered up. See you both shortly.'

He turned to leave, then checked and tapped Sampara on the arm. 'It's Winfield, by the way. Neutral choice, I would think.'

Then he left them and walked smartly to the Queen's Counsel's robing rooms where he dressed carefully in his silk jacket and gown.

In the holding cells below the court, Belinda was doing a rapid repair job on her client's face.

'Dear God, Michael. How did this happen?'

'I just, bumped into something.'

'Oh, yeah?'

He had a large bump near his right eye, to the right, and another on the cheek, where it had also bled. She had a pot of pancake make-up and was smearing it over the damaged tissue.

'It's all right,' he said, wincing.

'No, it isn't. I told you to keep out of trouble.'

'Sorry.'

She screwed the lid back on the pot. 'Now, don't be frightened to look at the judge and the jury. But don't, whatever you do, stare at them. Just don't look as if you are avoiding their eyes. You're innocent, remember?'

'That's right. I got nothing to hide.'

'And don't smile, Michael. I want you to look serious – all right?'

He nodded. There was a rap on the door. It was time.

'Right,' she said. 'We're on. Ready?'

In the hierarchical and clearly mapped space of the courtroom, everyone has an allotted position. In some ways it is like an old-fashioned church, with the Judge sitting at his massive desk, as if planted in a great High Altar. Above him, suspended from the wall, is a resplendent royal coat of arms; below him is the Clerk of the Court at his desk with the stenographer and then the bar of the court like a communion rail, separating the officers of justice from those who have come in search of it.

The wood-panelled court is an easygoing place full of quiet conversation until the judge takes his seat. Like wedding guests, divided according to their allegiance and waiting for the arrival of the bride, the prosecution sits on one side and the defence on the other. They occupy ranks, the barristers to the fore and solicitors behind. Here, awaiting the arrival of Mr Justice Winfield, were Rylands, Fletcher and the other briefs in their gowns, bands and wigs. Rylands signalled with his finger to Fletcher and shifted a few seats towards the Prosecution side.

'You up for a game of tennis? Thursday night?'

'What time?'

'Court's booked for seven-thirty. I've got Roly and Bill on-side. Think you can make it?'

Fletcher flipped open a pocket diary and jotted a note. 'Certainly. Already looking forward to it, Robert.'

'Good. Should be a good game.'

He slid back to his place, next to which Sampara was checking the post-it notes he'd placed in their deposition bundle. Waugh was glancing at the crossword. Behind the lawyers were benches for the police and any other interested officials connected to the case. Even further back, and to the side, was a cramped area reserved for the press and media. And along the side wall, bridging the fore-and-aft division of the court, was the enclosure for the jury of twelve ordinary men and women, chosen at random from the electoral roll. At this stage of Regina vs. Michael Dunn the jury box was empty.

The public, too, were set apart, confined on a gallery perched above the court, as if in a kind of purdah and policed in officious style by ushers. They were present strictly on sufferance. And at the very back of the court, slightly raised, stood the dock, which would soon be offering up its prisoner for judgement.

At ten o'clock, before the clock on the tower had finished striking, the elaborate formality of the murder trial began.

'Be upstanding in court.'

Having arrived just ahead of the judge, Belinda hardly had time to take stock of Winfield before he started speaking. She had asked around about him and been told he was dry but decent. With judges it is always difficult at first sight to see the man under the wig, but he seemed a shrewd individual of about sixty, hurrying into his seat as if wanting to have the trial done and dusted with efficiency and speed. He nodded to the Clerk whose job it was to dock the prisoner.

'Put up Michael Dunn,' called the Clerk.

Dunn appeared at the back of the court flanked by two security guards. There was a palpable hush as the court registered his presence, followed by a rustle of whispered comment. Belinda turned to look at him, trying to catch his eye. Leaving him a few minutes earlier, she had felt sick with anxiety, but Dunn was calm and seemed almost at ease. So did he now. In suit, shirt and tie – bought by arrangement with social services – he looked nothing like the dirty, drink-ravaged social misfit that the police had arrested back in September. Searching the array of faces that had turned towards him, he found Belinda's. She smiled encouragingly and his mouth gave the merest twitch.

'Are you Michael Frederick Dunn?' asked the Clerk severely once the accused was standing in the dock.

'Yes.'

His voice came over as quiet, unassuming. It would lilt pleasantly when he gave evidence. Quite illogically, given that proceedings had not even begun yet, Belinda felt a surge of optimism. He was innocent and they would beat this.

'Please be seated,' said the Clerk. 'Jury panel, please.'

There was a renewal of the murmuring in the well of the court as fifteen men and women filed in, shuffling self-consciously until they all stood in a knot at the back of the court. Winfield, who had been writing and paying little heed to events so far, suddenly looked up, quelling all conversation. He turned without further ado to the jurors and cleared his throat.

'Ladies and gentlemen, this case involves events which took place on the Howarth Estate in East London. Without wishing to impugn the ability of any of you to apply your minds objectively to the evidence in the case, rather than to, er, any extraneous consideration, out of excess of caution I am sure you will agree that – if there *is* anyone here who has a close connection with the Howarth Estate, it would be better if you did not serve. Is there in fact anyone who falls into that category?'

The jurors looked sidelong at each other but no one spoke. Winfield nodded to the Clerk who turned to the accused and began to intone.

'The names you are about to hear are the names of the jurors who are to try you. If you have an objection to any of them you must say so before they come to book to be sworn, and your objection shall be heard.'

The Clerk turned to the panel of jurors. 'As your name is called,' said the Clerk, 'would you please answer and go and sit in the jury box.'

He had in his hand a pack of filecards. He shuffled the pack and picked up the top card.

'Sheree Granger?'

One of the jurors, a young woman, started slightly and said, 'Er – present!'

As the jury were being empanelled and sworn, Walker fidgeted. It wasn't the physical space of the courtroom that bothered him on these occasions, it was the way these trials inhabited the dimension of time – so leisurely, as if ritualized tedium was the essence of it all. It was like cricket – another of those English rituals that he, as a Scot, was baffled by. Five days to play a game that could be settled just as easily in an afternoon!

He looked at his watch then leaned towards Pat North's ear. 'Just going out for a smoke.'

Then he tiptoed out of the court.

*

Barridge had been anticipating the trial in a state of mounting distress. It was as if he was waiting for his own trial.

His uniform had been returned to him eventually. A building worker fished it out of the trench and they'd phoned Southampton Street from the site hut. The Super had called him in for a bollocking. Not a rap on the wrist: a right what's-got-into-you, it's-bloody-irresponsible, are-you-trying-to-make-a-laughing-stock-out-of-me type of bollocking.

Having been told, if he did it again, his size twelves wouldn't touch, he was fired into Mr Awad at Occupational Health. Awad meant well but Barridge had struggled from the off to communicate with him. The man had a habit of nodding and saying 'yes, yes, yes', as if hurrying him, when Barridge spoke about the flashbacks and the guilt and feelings about being chosen. It was so irritating that Barridge had never confided the most important and most secret details of all – the thing he had done. The unforgivable thing. After three appointments he had not felt like making a fourth.

At home, his dad never noticed a bloody thing, but his mum knew there was something very wrong.

'It's still that kid you found, isn't it? It's bugging you something terrible.'

'Don't know.'

'It is, Colin, I know you. And you're not sleeping. Well, if you won't go and see the doctor, what about that man at work, that Awad? You should go back to him again. Have another try.'

'Don't want to.'

'He might help, son. You got to do something. You can't just mope around here.'

Eventually he seemed to let himself be persuaded to go back to Awad. Privately he knew he would have to face him again anyway, and tell the truth. Today was the last possible day – the trial began this morning. Before it was too late he had to tell someone what he'd done – the thing they would call a perversion.

Fletcher opened for the Crown and from the first he showed his determination not to spare the jury.

'There are a number of things, members of the jury, which will not be in dispute: that Julie Anne was first strangled into unconsciousness by means of a rope ligated around her neck. That she was sexually assaulted and was then placed – alive – in one of the sewage pipes on a nearby building site. There are some photographs which I would like you to look at in the bundle.'

The jury turned to their copies of the site where the child's body had been found.

'As you can see,' said Fletcher, 'this is a pipe of narrow diameter and the position in which Julie Anne was placed forced her head down into her knees, restricting her breathing with the result that she died – some time later – of asphyxia or suffocation. There is no doubt, then, that Julie Anne was murdered.'

Walker had returned to his place before Fletcher got to his feet. Now he glanced at the public gallery – the grandmother was there and one or two of the Howarth Estate residents, dressed up as if for a charabanc-ride to Southend. Then he saw the stepfather come in, looking angry and unkempt, his eyes staring. Walker saw him favour Helen with a look of vicious hatred as he found a place in the row behind her.

'Now, members of the jury,' continued Fletcher, 'I would like you to view the evidence in this case as you would the pieces of a jigsaw. It may be that one or two of the pieces are missing – that there are some questions that will not be answered or details that will not be filled in. But enough of the overall picture will emerge for you to be certain that the person who murdered Julie Anne Harris in the way I have described is the defendant, Michael Dunn.'

Now Fletcher's glance met Dunn's eyes, which were fixed steadily on him. In Fletcher's experience, guilty men nearly always looked away first. Innocent men did too, sometimes. But it was a rule of thumb for Fletcher that guilty men never took him on in a courtroom staring duel. Dunn, it seemed, was going to be the exception.

'Michael Dunn did not deny in interview that he liked children – and, on the face of it, of course, there's nothing wrong with that. Children often visited Dunn's flat and he says that he used to watch videotapes, of various kinds, with them. He also kept toys there for the children's use. And he admitted in interview that he knew Julie Anne Harris.'

Fletcher stopped and drank from his water glass, still maintaining eye-contact with the jury over the rim of his glass.

'You will hear evidence,' he went on, replacing his glass on the desk in front of him, 'from a neighbour who says she saw a man, whom she later identified as being Michael Dunn, approach Julie Anne in the playground on the fifth of September, the day of her death. The Crown maintains that he took her from there to his flat. You will hear that genetic material of Julie Anne's, DNA contained in saliva, was recovered from a wrapper and

250

stick of an ice-cream bar which was found in Michael Dunn's kitchen. The Crown says that this is no coincidence.'

Fletcher remained still for a couple of seconds then brandished his index finger.

'Nor, the Crown says, is it any coincidence that fibres recovered from Michael Dunn's furniture are consistent with those taken from the clothes Julie Anne was wearing on the fifth of September. You must also consider if it is a coincidence – or something more significant – that the same sample of dog faeces was found on the footwear of both Julie Anne and Michael Dunn, as worn on that same day. You must consider what construction to put on these facts.

'One construction, and the Crown says it is the correct one, is that, on the fifth of September, Julie Anne Harris went out wearing the clothing from which the fibres would later be recovered, and there she trod in some dog mess; that Michael Dunn approached Julie Anne and, in so doing, trod on the same ground. He then took Julie Anne by the hand and led her to his flat, where she was indeed in contact with the furniture and the carpets. It may well be that she was encouraged there with the offer of an ice-cream, which she ate, leaving the wrapper and stick to be recovered later by police.

'It is possible that hair from Julie Anne's head, found on Michael Dunn's floor, was dislodged during the attack and sexual assault on her. We know that a rope was then used to strangle her until she lost consciousness – and it may not surprise you to learn that this rope, which was found around her neck by the police, was the same as one which Michael Dunn put up as a washing line for a neighbour – and which subsequently disappeared. Finally, on that day, Julie Anne was placed in the sewage pipe in which she died. Her clothing was found discarded in a nearby cellar. Significantly, a length of washing line of an identical type was discovered by the police in Michael Dunn's bin. The Crown cannot say how it got there, but if you come to the conclusion that Michael Dunn stole that washing line from his neighbour, you must ask yourself why? What did he want with it? What did he have in mind?'

With a piece of gentle, low-intensity mime, Fletcher held his hands out in front of him, as if lightly grasping some object, and drew them slightly apart.

'Was he experimenting in some way? The rope or line may well suggest to you, as it does to the Crown, that this was not an offence committed on impulse but that it was quite carefully pre-planned.'

Rylands had listened to Fletcher with his eyes half-closed, his face expressionless. But Belinda was worried. This was a highly confident start by the Prosecution. The jury were sitting up in their seats – marking every word, some of them nodding their heads or scribbling notes. By the time Fletcher was ready to call his first witness, Belinda found that her initial confidence was rapidly draining away.

CHAPTER 23

B ARRIDGE WAS well aware that some of his colleagues were inclined to deride the Metropolitan
Police's Occupational Health Service, and to scoff
equally at those who became its clients. It was known as
the Funny Farm or, more succinctly, Barking.

The idea behind the scheme is to offer counselling to
officers traumatized in the course of their duties, either
because of what they've seen or done in the line of duty
or because they have been physically injured and need
help in coming to terms with that.

The staff are professional counsellors, specialists in
post-traumatic stress, marriage breakdown, alcohol problems and other hazards of the job. Barridge had no idea
where his own counsellor, Awad, was coming from, but
he was highly reminiscent of a man who had taught
chemistry at Barridge's comprehensive school. Whenever
he sat opposite him, watching him nodding his head, he
couldn't help thinking about potassium sulphide.

The entrance to Area's Occupational Health Unit is discreetly placed in a side street – a small anonymous office
with total discretion assured. Barridge pushed his way in
and approached the reception desk, behind which a young
woman with brightly painted nails was talking on the phone.

'Yeah, I know,' she was saying, 'spent all that money at the hairdresser and all. Shame on him . . . That's what I say, serve him right. He'll never know what he missed . . .'

Barridge was trying to control the shakes. He looked around. Various posters about stress were pinned up.

> *Stress avoidance – a checklist of dos and don'ts: DO take plenty of physical exercise such as aerobics. DO set aside a period of time each day for silent relaxation. DON'T rely on alcohol, sex or drugs for relaxation. DON'T privilege your work at the expense of family and friends.*

There was nothing about going swimming with putrefying cats. There was nothing about finding what he'd found.

'Well, look, I got to go now,' the receptionist was saying into her phone. 'Yeah, same here. OK. Bye.'

She hung up.

'How can I help you?'

Barridge gripped the edge of her desk. There was a feeling of fatalism about him now.

'I'd like to see Mr Awad, please.'

'Oh! I'm afraid he's not in today.'

'Is there anyone else I can speak to? I've got to speak to someone.'

He was hyperventilating as the receptionist flipped through the appointments book in front of her. He pulled at the collar of his shirt.

'We-ell – there's Mrs Cheshire. But I'll have to ask her and she's busy right now.'

Barridge was sweating and his legs felt tingly, as if he were about to get an attack of pins and needles.

'I have to speak to someone.'

She gave him an odd, questioning look.

'All right, why don't you sit down in the waiting area and I'll have a word with her when I can. What did you say your name was?'

Barridge gave his name then wandered back to the door.

'I'll ... I need some air. I'll come back in ... ten minutes.'

The receptionist stared curiously at the swinging door then picked up her phone. 'Mrs Cheshire? I've had an officer in here, a PC Barridge. Seems in a very bad way. You couldn't see him, could you?'

Mrs Cheshire had a gap between appointments at ten-thirty. She had planned to nip out to the chemists but agreed to see Barridge instead. She was fortyish and far more like a school nurse than a science teacher, which Barridge found a little encouraging.

'So, how can I help you, PC Barridge – Colin?'

'Well, it's something I want to get off of my chest, see? It's hard. I don't know if I can come right out with it, like.'

'Uh-huh. Let me have a bit of background first, why don't you?'

This was one disadvantage of Awad's absence. He would have to go back over ground he'd already covered, otherwise Mrs Cheshire wouldn't understand. And he desperately wanted her to understand. So he started to tell her about the Howarth Estate case, and the missing child and the search in the rain and him falling in the water in that cellar and then finding the body and the terrible sadness and sense of waste and emptiness he'd had inside him every since the suspect had been arrested.

'Julie Anne, that's the little girl I found, I kept on seeing her face and I couldn't sleep.'

He was almost crying. He could feel the raw mass growing in his throat and the tears welling up. His voice wobbled and he had to struggle to control it.

'It was as if she was reaching out to me. They knew it was him . . . everybody knew. We knew it was him. I mean, we were certain, so certain. And the trial's started today. He's in the dock, and it's got to be stopped . . .'

The counsellor got up and went to where a water jug and some glasses stood on a shelf. She poured water, brought it back to her desk and placed it in front of Barridge. He was shivering, tipping over the edge into tears.

'You say it's got to be stopped? Do you mean you now think that this man might not have committed the murder?'

Barridge shook his head. 'I don't *know*,' he wailed. 'Maybe. It looks like him. But . . . it might not be.'

'Well, isn't that the purpose of the trial? I mean, surely the police officers have done their work – including you, Colin – and now it's up to the jury to decide—'

'That's it! Our work! That's what I have to tell you. It was my work, it was me wanting to be sure he'd be found guilty.'

The room felt very hot. Barridge's face was a deep red.

Mrs Chesire spoke very quietly. 'What did you do, Colin?'

'Do? I – I – well, I tampered with the evidence! I cheated.' He picked up the glass of water and drank.

Mrs Cheshire's eyes narrowed. 'You mean, in order to make it more likely this man would be convicted?'

He put down the glass and nodded his head. There, it was out. He'd admitted it.

'I see,' said Mrs Cheshire. 'And you've told no one about this?'

'No. No, I haven't. That's what I'm trying to tell *you*. That's why I'm here!'

'And what do you want me to do, Colin?'

'Get it *stopped*.'

Barridge felt the pins and needles again in his legs. He was sitting right on the edge of the chair. He reached for the waterglass again.

'He could end up with a life sentence for something he didn't do, if you don't believe what I'm saying.'

Mrs Cheshire was frowning, chewing the end of her Biro. She shook her head. 'I'm still trying to assimilate what you're saying.'

Oh, for Christ's sake!

Barridge hurled the glass down on the desk, scattering water all over Mrs Cheshire's papers. He was yelling openly now.

'*Look! I bought the rope. I cut it in two. And I put it in Michael Dunn's BIN.*'

He was snivelling, his head down again. 'I want the trial stopped because he might not have done it and, oh, *Jesus . . .*'

Mrs Cheshire said, 'Look, Colin, will you be all right?

Just while I pop out for a few moments. But I'll be back very shortly, all right?'

She whisked out of her office and went straight to reception.

'Denise – do you mind getting off the phone so I can use it, please? I think this is a bit of an emergency.'

CHAPTER 24

'ARE YOU Mrs Enid Marsh?' asked Willis Fletcher, when the old lady had completed her tortuous journey from the court corridor and was safely berthed in the witness stand. 'And do you live at number thirty-three, Howarth House?'

'Yes.'

Enid looked around. The stand was placed on the judge's left, across the court room from the jury box. In all her long life she had never entered a court of law. But she had seen Charles Laughton in *Witness for the Prosecution* many years ago and, ever since, she'd had quite a taste for courtroom dramas on television. For a murder trial, this was a smaller room than she had anticipated and less intimidating.

'And what floor is that on?'

'The sixth floor.'

'Please could you look at these photographs, Mrs Marsh?' He passed the photographs to the associate to take to the witness while Fletcher addressed the judge. 'If these could become exhibit one, m'lord?'

Enid looked at the numbered prints then placed them on the edge of the witness box and started fumbling for her glasses.

259

'Could you look at photograph number three, Mrs Marsh? Does it show what can be seen from your window?'

'Oh, yes,' said Enid as the picture came into focus. 'It does.'

'Just describe to us what you can see.'

'I can see the entrance to the flats and I can see the . . . the right-hand side of the playground.'

'Is there any particular time of day when you are in the habit of looking out of your window, Mrs Marsh?'

'Yes. I look out at lunchtimes. I wait for the meals on wheels every day.'

'Every day?'

'Yes.'

'Are you able to remember the day when Julie Anne Harris went missing? That was the day the police first called at your flat.'

'Yes – I remember it very well.'

The witness seemed to have shrugged off the uncertainty of her first replies. She was sounding positive and eager now.

'Tell the court about it, would you?'

'Well, I looked out at a quarter to one – I looked at the clock because she's usually brought my lunch by then. I mean, Mrs Wald, the lady who brings my lunch . . . And she – I . . .'

Enid had seized up again, unsure where her train of thought had started from. Gently, Fletcher brought her back on track.

'Yes, and what did you see when you looked out of the window?'

'I saw the little Harris girl playing on her own. I often saw her playing with the other children.'

There was a slight disturbance as the door of the court opened and Satchell came in. He slid along the bench beside where Pat North was sitting and began whispering urgently in her ear.

'Were you able to recognize that it was Julie Anne Harris at that distance?' continued Fletcher.

'Yes, I was. But you see, she was on her own. I thought she shouldn't have been left.'

'What did she do?'

'Well, she was playing and then she started covering her face and peeping out – sort of through her fingers, like this.'

Enid laced her twisted old fingers together and peeped girlishly through them at Fletcher.

'It was as though there was someone else playing with her . . .'

'Weren't you able to see that person?'

'No.'

'And did you see anything else unusual that lunchtime?'

'Yes. Well, I was looking out again at five past one for the meals on wheels, because it still hadn't come you know. And, anyway, I saw a man bend down and take the little girl's hand.'

'What did you see of that man, Mrs Marsh? Did you see his face?'

'Yes, I did. It was sideways on. But yes, I did, I saw his face.'

'Had you seen that man before?'

Enid shook her head. 'No. I didn't know him at all.'

'But did you see him again?'

'Oh, yes, I saw him again in Kilburn.'

Fletcher looked at her, questioningly. 'Kilburn?'

'You *know*, the parade thing – the identification parade. He was the one I picked.'

She made it sound like judging the supreme champion at Crufts Dog Show.

'Just one last thing, Mrs Marsh. I notice you are wearing glasses. Would you mind telling us if you always wear them?'

'Oh no, I only need them to read. I can see as well as anyone over a long distance. It's got better over the years.'

'Thank you very much, Mrs Marsh. Would you please wait there so that my learned friend can ask you a few questions?'

In the gap between Fletcher's examination of Mrs Marsh and Rylands's cross-examination, DI North and DS Satchell left the court. The door was still swinging as Rylands rose majestically to his feet and began to speak.

'Good morning, Mrs Marsh.'

She smiled uncertainly. 'Good morning.'

'It's very nice to see you again.'

She looked at him in his wig and black silk gown, a large and handsome but undeniably forceful figure. She frowned. 'I beg your pardon?'

Rylands propped a hand in the small of his back, looked down at his feet and up again at Enid.

'Don't you remember seeing me before?'

Enid hesitated again. Then shook her head. 'No. No, I don't.'

'Would this help?'

Rylands flipped his wig and his glasses from his head and got an instant reaction from the judge.

'Really, Mr Rylands,' expostulated Winfield.

'Please, m'lord—'

'I hope this is taking us somewhere.'

Pat North had crept back into court and was whispering to Walker. Winfield waved Rylands on.

'You *were* at your flat on Friday of last week at twelve-fifty p.m., were you not? And you were looking out of the window, at the playground.'

Enid did not reply. She scented some trap.

'Mrs Marsh, counsel often do go to the scene of a crime, as part of their preparation.'

'I saw a man in a blue suit,' said Enid hotly. 'He was carrying a briefcase and he was looking up at my flat. Was that you?'

'So you saw this man, carrying a briefcase? You noticed him and he was looking directly at you?'

'Yes.'

'Mrs Marsh,' said Rylands softly now. 'There will be evidence in due course that that man was myself. You saw me, you noticed me, you were able to describe my clothes and my superficial appearance. But, even though I was looking straight at you, you were unable to remember my face.'

'Oh, well, I . . . I mean, I'm sorry.'

'It's all right, Mrs Marsh, I am not offended in the least. Now, you identified a man at an identification parade as being the one you saw with Julie Anne, am I right?'

'Yes.'

There was another waft of air through the court and the sigh of the door as Walker and North left hurriedly. The judge frowned but said nothing, letting Rylands continue.

'Would you be so sure of your identification, if I told you that there was another man with long dark hair on the Howarth Estate around lunchtime on that day? Not the man you picked out but another of similar build?'

Winfield butted in firmly. 'I trust there is going to be an evidential basis for this.'

'There will indeed, m'lord. Would you like me to repeat my question, Mrs Marsh?'

He was as sweet as sugar to her now. He knew when not to crow over a witness's discomfort.

'Oh, no. I don't know . . .'

'You don't know if you *would* be sure?'

Enid shook her head despairingly. 'I don't know.'

Rylands hesitated, letting the import of the witness's confusion sink in. Then he swept back to his place.

'Thank you, Mrs Marsh.'

Winfield looked at Fletcher. Did he want a re-examination? Fletcher shook his head and the judge said to Enid. 'You may leave the witness box now, Mrs Marsh.'

Meg Richards came forward to help Enid down. All the fight had gone out of her, she seemed crumpled suddenly and, worst of all, disbelieved.

Winfield surveyed the court, looked at his watch and cleared his throat. He was hungry.

'I think this might be a convenient moment . . . er, if we come back at five past two.'

He rose and left the bench, scuttling through his private door into his chambers, where rather a fine *boeuf bourgignon* awaited him in the Judges' Dining Room.

During lunch, Belinda visited her client, who was brought up from the cells to one of the conference rooms. He seemed troubled.

'How are you feeling?' she asked.

'Been better.'

She saw the quiet confidence he'd had first thing in the morning was lost. Now he looked hunted; not yet scared but anxious and suspicious.

'Mr Rylands says to tell you that the beginning's always the hardest part, Michael. We've done well with the judge, too. He's the best we could have got.'

Dunn continued to appear doubtful.

'I don't know whether he likes our barrister,' he mumbled.

'What makes you say that?'

'Well, confusing that poor old woman like he did.'

'That poor old woman, as you put it, Michael, is one of the two principal planks of the Prosecution case.'

Dunn brooded for a moment and then suddenly laughed hysterically.

'Planks!' he said. 'That's good!'

By the time Walker and Satchell had driven from the court to Southampton Street, the tyres of the car were all but smouldering. Walker swept into the Incident Room baying for Barridge. All the way Walker had kept up a flow of invective.

'Wait till I see that bloody little pillock. I'll croak him. I'll have his nuts. Planting evidence. It'll probably stop the fucking case in its tracks. Don't these turniptops get any education at all? But I tell you what really turns me over – the stupid shitbag put his hands up. Don't they know Rule Number One about bent behaviour – never, *ever* own up? Jesus! It's unbelievable.'

Now he was sitting in his office with Barridge. The PC was sitting on a wheeled office chair, pushing himself backwards and staring at the floor. With every shuttle of his chair the wheels squeaked. Walker ripped a cigarette from its filter and rammed it in his mouth.

'What the fuck have you got to say for yourself, Barridge?'

The constable was sobbing unconsolably.

'I did it, sir. I'm so sorry.'

Walker lit up with exaggerated deliberation. He had regained control of himself after the fury he'd unleashed in the car.

'I have to tell you that I am suspending you from duty. You will have to surrender your warrant card. There is also the possibility that the defence may ask for you to be tendered as a witness.'

Barridge said nothing. He couldn't meet the Superintendent's eyes. He simply pushed his chair backwards and forwards in a kind of rocking motion.

'Do you understand, Barridge?'

Barridge nodded, streaming tears. When he spoke his voice was hoarse. 'If they want me to give evidence I'll have to tell the truth. I understand that – I've got to tell them the truth. I knew Dunn was the one. I wanted him caught.'

Walker sucked on his cigarette. Suddenly overwhelmed with tiredness he couldn't look at Barridge any more. He shut his eyes.

'So you planted the rope that was discovered at Michael Dunn's flat?'

'*Yes!* Anybody that hurts a little girl . . .'

He was choking on each word now, choking and shouting. 'Anybody who does that should hang. And if they ask me I'll say that too. I'll say it in court. They should *hang*.'

The surge of anger subsided as quickly as it had come and Barridge ran out of words. He shrugged his shoulders hopelessly. Walker watched the storm blow itself out then touched Barridge on the shoulder.

'You'll be all right, son.' He turned sharply to Satchell. 'We'll have to stop the trial,' he said. 'Come on – back to court!'

On the way in the car, Walker was talking into his mobile to the court.

'This is Detective Superintendent Walker speaking . . . Yes. I'm officer in charge of the case against Michael Dunn . . . no, no. Delta, Uniform, November, November. Dunn. Yes . . . It's started today in court one. Something very urgent indeed's come up and I need . . . No, no. I'm asking you: can you get Fletcher to wait for me before he goes into the afternoon session? What? What was that? No, Willis Fletcher, prosecuting counsel. I need to speak to him. Oh. Oh, I see. OK then.'

He disconnected as Satchell looked at his watch.

'It's after two.'

'I know. They've gone back in. Mrs Harris is giving evidence.'

CHAPTER 25

ANITA WORE black in the end. The skirt was maybe a little short, but it wasn't sexy or anything. And she'd been to the hairdresser yesterday for a trim. Helen thought her daughter looked much younger than she really was. A teenager, so you'd think. But she looked sensible, anyway.

Recently Helen had been having flashbacks of Anita as a little girl. It must have been because of Julie, and thinking about how her life had been snuffed out so easily and suddenly at five years old. Anita, too, had been five years old once, not so long ago actually. And now look at her, a grown woman even if she did look as young as she did. She was also, Helen knew, a good woman, a loving woman.

But some of the press had not been too kind to Anita. There'd been plenty of tabloid tears, of course, but Helen always thought they were much the same thing as crocodile tears. There had also been a lot of snide stuff about kids on rough estates being left to play out on their own, a prey to evil paedophiles. Well, what did they know?

Fletcher had given Anita a chance to settle comfortably in the witness stand after she'd been sworn in. His voice was gentle and supportive.

'Mrs Harris, are you Julie Anne's mother?'

268

'Yes, I am.' Anita frowned and added, 'Well, I was.'

Fletcher looked down at his notes. 'Mrs Harris, there is only one matter I want to ask you about. Did Julie Anne have any toy, or favoured object, to which she was particularly attached?'

'Yes, she had her doll.'

'Can you describe her doll for us?'

'Yes, well it looked like a Barbie, but it wasn't a real one. I bought it in the market for her. She always . . .' Anita took a deep breath to blow away the huskiness in her voice. 'She always carried it with her.'

'And did she have this doll with her on the day she went missing?'

There was a moment's hesitation, then, 'Yes, she did.' Anita's eyes filled.

'I am sorry, Mrs Harris,' said Fletcher caressingly. 'I realize this recalls a very distressing time. But did you see the doll again, after Julie Anne's disappearance?'

'Yes. The day after . . . the police . . .' She dabbed at her tears. It was hard to speak. 'I told them it was hers,' she managed finally.

The judge stopped writing on his pad, looking over his glasses at the witness. 'Mrs Harris, would you like a short adjournment?'

'No, no. I'm all right.'

She sniffed, then blew her nose as Fletcher said, 'Thank you, Mrs Harris. No further questions.'

Now it was Rylands's turn. Anita had not even considered him but, from the public gallery, Helen had. He was dangerous, that one. He was more powerful than Fletcher. Helen sent mental messages over to her distressed daughter. Don't let him trip you up, my darling. Keep cool.

269

The first thing Rylands did was signal to the usher to lay out the dolls which Sampara had brought in the carrier bag with two dolls found in Dunn's flat. Slowly and meticulously this was done on a table near the witness stand. Rylands waited patiently and then addressed the witness.

'Mrs Harris,' he said in a voice which, by comparison to Fletcher's, seemed dangerous and calculated, 'you last saw this doll that you have mentioned – the one the police found in Mr Dunn's flat, m'lord – first thing on the Sunday morning, which was the day after you learned of your daughter's death. The police came round and woke you up, is that right?'

'Yes.'

There was a minor disturbance at the back of court, where Dunn was muttering to himself.

'I found that doll. *Found* it.'

Belinda swivelled round and frowned at him. He shrugged.

'And do you feel certain,' continued Rylands, 'that you did not make a mistake in confusing one mass-produced doll manufactured by the thousand with another?'

'Yes, I do,' said Anita, positively. Yet she had seen the array of dolls on the table waiting for her and she was dreading Rylands's next move.

'Could you perhaps help us, Mrs Harris, by picking out Julie Anne's doll for us now?' He glanced at the bench. 'If the witness could perhaps step down for a moment, m'lord?'

Winfield assented and Anita stepped down to stand in front of the dolls. She remembered that the one the police showed her had one arm – but was it the right or the left?

She looked at these dolls and they were all one-armed. Looking closely at them it was obvious they were not identical, yet it was impossible to pick out any distinguishing characteristics in any of them because, unlike people, these were bland, generalized figures, with their frozen smiles and dazzled eyes.

Why had Anita told the police the Dunn doll was Julie's? Not because she'd particularly wanted it to be the doll. She really thought it *was* the doll. But it was too late to go back now. She looked among the dolls again, each of them with a paper tag tied around its ankle. She would have to make a choice.

'Oh, it's ... it was such a long time ago, I . . .' she said, and then cursed herself for speaking. She sounded an idiot.

'I appreciate that, Mrs Harris, please take your time.'

'I think it's that one.'

She pointed to one of the dolls which, if truth be told, she'd picked out at random. Rylands stepped forward and seized it.

'M'lord,' he said, 'could the doll which Mrs Harris has just identified become exhibit six?'

He picked up a second doll in his other hand and held it up for Winfield and the court to see.

'It's not exhibit five, the doll found by police in Michael Dunn's flat.'

Pat North was waiting at the entrance to the court when Walker and Satchell arrived.

'What's going on?' asked Walker.

'We've just lost our ID on the doll, guv.'

271

Walker's eyes bulged. '*What*? How come?'

'He tripped her up, the usual Rylands theatricals. What's the story on Barridge?'

North was feeling flat. It had not been a good day so far and it didn't promise to get any better.

'He did it. We'll have to try to get the trial stopped. The wheels are coming off one after the other. What's happening in there now?'

'Fletcher's got the pathologist, Foster, on the stand.'

'There was evidence of sexual assault,' Foster was saying in his carefully studied, neutral courtroom voice. 'The hymen had been ruptured with some blunt instrument, the defect measuring three centimetres.'

'And have you seen similar injuries in other cases, Doctor Foster?'

'Yes, I have. I have seen similar injuries which were established to have been caused by a bottle and I would say this could well have been the case here.'

Fletcher nodded. 'Thank you, Doctor Foster.'

Before Fletcher could hand over to Rylands, Walker and Pat North entered the court and, bowing to the judge, made for Fletcher. Griffith joined them in a huddle as they whispered together. After half a minute Fletcher, looking as if he'd just been mugged, spoke to Rylands and then addressed Winfield.

'M'lord, Could I ask m'lord to rise? A matter has arisen . . .'

Winfield sighed wearily like a schoolteacher dealing with a recalcitrant pupil. 'How long, Mr Fletcher?'

'Twenty minutes, m'lord?'

Winfield considered, glancing at the jury. Counsel

always underestimated the length of time they needed. 'Half an hour,' he said crisply.

In the bar mess Fletcher and Rylands conferred over cups of coffee. The fascinating thing for Willis Fletcher was that his friend didn't want the Crown to throw in the towel. Was he enjoying himself too much?

'OK, I'll tell you what. You'll have to make a clean breast of your rope trick. And live with it, I'm afraid. The jury may take a dim view given that you—'

'Opened with it?'

And so would you have, Fletcher was thinking. But of course the point was that he had presented a circumstance in his opening that was based on tainted evidence. If the trial was to continue the jury would have to put it out of their mind, or else the trial would have to start all over again with twelve new good men and true.

One step, ahead of his opponent, Rylands smiled. Fletcher, furious with the police for putting him in this position, could hardly raise his head, let alone a smile.

'You said practically nothing about it,' said Rylands. 'I'll object if you try to get the jury discharged.'

'Do you want me to tender the boy for cross-examination?'

'The policeman? Poor bastard's lost his marbles, hasn't he? I'm happy to leave him out of it.' He sipped his coffee, smirking mischievously. 'I'll draft a suitably damning admission which you will be happy to make – all right?' He sniggered with laughter as Fletcher winced.

'We'd better go and see Winfield,' Fletcher said gruffly.

But Rylands hadn't quite finished. 'And in the circumstances, I think we'll have woman-with-rope – brackets

NOT manufactured by basket-weaving policeman – down here in the witness stand, don't you?'

Fletcher walked glumly towards the door. 'If you mean, Miss Taylor, I'll call her in the morning. Satisfied?'

As soon as the adjournment was called, Walker had sent Satchell over to Occupational Health to see Mrs Cheshire and get a report on Barridge's mental health. At that stage there was still a chance Barridge might be called as a witness but, in any case, he was going to have to put in a disciplinary report. He might as well have all the facts.

Now, an hour later, Satchell was back. Hustling up the court steps he almost bumped into a nice-looking old bloke carrying a bag of golf clubs.

'Good afternoon,' said the man politely.

Satchell could have sworn he knew him. Three steps further on it clicked: Winfield! Going to the golf course!

He spotted Walker and North standing at the top of the steps, deep in conversation. Satchell joined them, pointing after the retreating golfer.

'That was the judge, wasn't it? So he's stopped the trial?'

North shook her head. She looked mystified. 'No.'

'What? You're kidding me?'

'Wish we were, pal,' said Walker, also shaking his head. The thought of what Rylands could do when proceedings recommenced didn't bear thinking about.

'But what about Barridge and the rope? They can't go on with it now, can they?'

'Yes they can,' said North simply.

'But it means the evidence was contaminated.'

Walker laughed grimly. 'Our man tried. But that

bastard Rylands is something else. The judge has adjourned until tomorrow and then it's business as usual.'

'I just don't believe it,' said Satchell.

A mobile phone rang and Walker reacted, patting his pockets. 'Where's my mobile? I couldn't take it into court so I put it down somewhere.'

North pulled the trilling receiver from her briefcase. 'You gave it to me, sir.'

Walker moved to the other side of the steps, switched on the phone and listened.

'Yes? Is this an emergency? . . . This is not an emergency and Daddy's told you never to . . . No, just listen to me! This is *not* an emergency. Put your mother on . . . Look, you'll have to talk to her. I've told her not to play near the conservatory. If she's broken the glass she'll have to pay for it out of her pocket money . . . No, all right – I'll tell her myself, I'm coming home. We've got the afternoon off.'

'So what happens next? Rylands is going to use this to get Dunn off,' said Satchell.

'We may not have a trial here this afternoon,' said Walker grimly, thinking of the glass of his conservatory, 'but I've got one at home.'

'What exactly does Fletcher think he's doing?' asked Satchell.

'He's going to look a fool,' observed North drily.

'We are looking even bigger ones,' Walker said, starting down the steps. 'They're calling Ann Taylor to give evidence tomorrow.'

And he set off to hear the case against his daughter.

CHAPTER 26

IT WAS a late start in court. The judge had required Rylands and Fletcher in his chambers at ten-thirty to go through the text of Fletcher's admission on the planted length of washing line. He had OK'd it and, after an eleven-thirty start, Fletcher was now nearly at the end of his scheduled grovel in front of the jury.

'. . . I must therefore emphasize to you again,' he was saying, 'that there is no question of the defendant being responsible for this piece of washing line. Its presence in the defendant's dustbin was entirely attributable to the actions of Constable Barridge. You must exclude it entirely from your minds.'

The jury had sat through this without showing any apparent reaction. Murder trial juries don't have much experience to draw on – everything is new and more or less unexpected to them. But what they would conclude about the strength of the Crown's case once they'd started to think about Barridge's rush of blood was anybody's guess.

Fletcher had finished. He turned to Rylands and fractionally lifted the sheet of A4 on which the admission had been printed. Rylands gave an almost imperceptible

276

nod of the head and Fletcher placed the statement with his other papers.

'Now, if I may continue with the case for the Crown, m'lord, I should like to call Ann Taylor, please.'

Ann Taylor appeared. She walked very hesitantly into court, looking around like a bird at the ranks of people, lawyers, the court officials, judge. Her head turned nervously in every direction except towards the dock.

She was sworn in and Fletcher began by establishing her address and knowledge of the defendant. Then he went on: 'Did Michael Dunn come to do odd jobs for you in your house?'

'Yes.'

'What sort of things did he do?'

'He did, well, different things. Six or seven times. Once he put up my washing line.'

A ripple of conversation washed around the court at this information and then died, quelled by Winfields' disapproving eye.

'Could you describe that washing line for us, please?'

'It was – it was blue and red. Plastic. I bought it in a local shop.'

'And when was that?'

But now the witness seemed to have frozen. So far Dunn had been looking at the rail of the dock throughout Ann Taylor's evidence. Now he raised his head and looked straight at her.

'When *was* that, Miss Taylor?'

She was flustered. She knew Dunn was staring at her. Suddenly she looked across the room and met his glance.

'Oh, um . . .' she wavered, her mouth trembling. She looked down and took a deep breath. 'It was quite a while ago. A few months. I didn't see him again for

. . . quite a while. In fact, no, I mean, I didn't see him at all.'

Anyone looking at Pat North as she watched these exchanges with intense concentration might have been surprised to see her sudden grim smile. Ann Taylor was proving an awkward witness for Fletcher. Her embarrassment was palpable – she was blushing uncontrollably – but what was its cause? Not just the shyness of a middle-aged spinster thrust into the limelight, surely.

Then suddenly she saw it. Of course, how could they have missed this when they'd interviewed her?

She nudged Walker, leaned sideways and whispered. 'Guv, you don't suppose she and Dunn . . .?'

But Walker had got there already. Without taking his eyes off the witness, he murmured. ''Course they bloody did.'

'And what happened,' asked Fletcher, 'to this length of line subsequently?'

'It was stolen. Um, towards the end of August, I think.'

'Thank you, Miss Taylor.'

Rylands stood up slowly and regarded the witness steadily without speaking. He went on doing so for slightly longer than was polite, but not long enough for the judge to call him for intimidation. Then he said, 'When did you move into your house, Miss Taylor?'

'Two years ago in April.'

'Have petty thefts of property from your garden been a problem ever since that time?'

She nodded. 'Yes, I've had a lot of things taken.'

'Did you ever find out who took any of them?'

'Only once. The police caught some boys on the estate with – a sort of urn.'

'Some boys. Thank you, Miss Taylor. No more questions.'

'Mr Fletcher?' asked the judge but Fletcher, with no further wish to expose his witness's confusion, shook his head. Winfield glanced at his timepiece. Despite the interest of the evidence, he'd caught himself thinking over the last half hour about the crackling on the loin of pork that was at this moment sizzling and spitting in the Crown Court judges' kitchen.

'Perhaps this would be a suitable time . . . Five past two.'

As the court started packing up for lunch, North watched Ann Taylor as she left the court, then stood up herself and pushed past Walker to get quickly to the exit.

'I'm going to have a word with her.'

North caught up with Ann Taylor in the hall. The witness stand had left her shaken and she was glad to spot someone she recognized. When North suggested they sit down, she accepted North's hand steering her towards a bench beside the wall.

'There was more to your friendship with Michael Dunn than you told us, wasn't there, Miss Taylor?'

'Was it so obvious?' She was calmer now – rueful rather than tearful.

'Yes, I'm afraid it was.'

'I felt so sorry for him when he told me what a terrible life he'd had – what had been done to him. Just a little boy when it first started, six years old. But then you must know that. He said the only kindness he'd ever known was when this family fostered him – but then they sent him back.'

She paused, biting her lip.

'That's why I never reported it. But I knew it was him that took the washing line. He took the sherry too.'

'The sherry? How can you be sure?'

'My mother didn't approve of drinking and I kept some hidden outside. He was the only person who knew where it was.'

Ann Taylor smiled and North caught a glimpse of the pretty woman who was normally masked by the bleak figure cut by this disappointed spinster.

'A pointless little act of rebellion, I suppose. I hardly ever drink myself. Forgot it was there most of the time, but he persuaded me to have one with him when I was grieving for Mother. I think we must have had more than one actually because, well, you know, it went further than it should have . . .'

North touched her on the forearm. 'It's been difficult, all this, hasn't it? You should go home and rest now.'

'Will it all come out, what I told you? Will I have to . . . tell the court?'

North wished she could tell her no. 'I don't know. It may not be necessary. Let's hope not, eh?'

In the Crown Court holding cells, Michael Dunn was as unhappy as Ann Taylor.

'I don't like the way he treats people, that Rylands,' he told Belinda while he waited for his lunch. 'I *told* you I didn't like the way he talked to the old lady. He got her all upset, and don't give me all that "planks" crap either! He shouldn't have asked Ann – Miss Taylor – all about—'

'Michael, calm down, for goodness' sake.'

'No! You lied to me. You said he would just ask if I worked for Ann. Not that other stuff.'

'It wasn't Mr Rylands who asked those questions, it was Mr Fletcher, the prosecuting counsel. I can't control his line of questioning.'

'She was nice to me, she was . . . She was a friend to me. And I won't have it. You tell him where he can stuff his planks. He shouldn't have upset her. Tell him I don't want any more of it – you hear me?'

Belinda fought to beat down the rising panic she felt. Dunn was verging on the uncontrollable. He might do anything in this mood – try to sack Rylands, make a kamikaze admission, anything. She had to take control back. She spoke as firmly as she knew how.

'Michael – Mrs Rylands is conducting your defence in the way he thinks best to secure your acquittal. You *must* trust him.'

'I did trust him – but he's messing me around.' Dunn thought for a moment, then upped the stakes a little more. 'I'm not going in the witness box to be messed around by him, that's for sure. No way. You tell him that, plank or no plank.'

There was a knock on the door – the defendant's lunch had arrived.

In the bar mess, Sinclair sought out Rylands and Waugh to tell them the bad news.

'We might have a problem here,' she told them. 'Michael's got upset about Ann Taylor. Now he doesn't want to give evidence.'

Ryland's face brightened – it didn't seem to be particularly bad news to him. 'Fine – it's just what I've been saying. We won't call him.'

Waugh frowned. He didn't like this. 'Robert, I think—'

But Rylands hadn't finished. He drew on his cigar and spoke through the gush of exhaled smoke. 'We shouldn't call any evidence for a defence. We don't have to. Their ID's worth virtually nothing. Their doll's gone out the window. We can explain all the forensic as innocent contact. Plus, they've had to admit police shenanigans. No jury's going to convict him on that!'

Derek was shaking his head. He looked like an old horse plagued by flies. 'We'll incur the adverse inference if he doesn't go on.'

'They'll do us just as much damage if he does. They'll be dragging him over the two alibi witnesses he couldn't find. Leave it alone.'

'I don't agree. Since they're trying to show a false alibi, we can show a true one. I honestly think I'd rather carry on according to plan – belt and braces and all that.'

Rylands released another stream of yellow Havana smoke into the atmosphere. Belinda looked at both men, wondering if they were going to ask her opinion. Not a chance.

'Well, you're instructing me, Derek,' said Rylands. 'But I think you're courting a risk here. That's my *considered* view.'

'I can't agree with you, Robert. I think they want to hear Michael Dunn deny it from his own lips.'

'As you wish, Derek.'

Waugh turned to Belinda. She could tell he was excited at having beaten Rylands into submission. She could almost hear him saying it, crowing about it back at the office: not many people could say they'd done *that*.

'Warn our boy, Belinda. Try to get him settled down.'

'Derek, I don't know, he was very upset.'

She looked at Rylands for support, but the silk had already mentally begun to work on how he would tackle Dunn on the stand.

'Nevertheless,' Waugh said firmly, 'he'll be giving evidence tomorrow.'

CHAPTER 27

THURSDAY 21 NOVEMBER

PETER HAD slept with Anita the previous night. They'd not made love, but at least they'd shared the bed. They began to feel again like a couple who loved one another.

Peter said nothing about Anita's evidence in court until the next morning. He'd come in from the newsagent with the papers and a carton of milk and found her out on the balcony, leaning against the rail, staring down at the playground.

'You got the doll wrong,' he said.

It was just a statement of the fact.

'Yes, I know, I'm sorry Peter.'

'So am I.'

She flicked a glance at him, a fearful glance. She steeled herself. Was this going to be another shouting match, another rough house of bitterness and blame? But Peter's voice was unexpectedly soft.

'I'm sorry about the way I've been. Really. But losing Julie and then the baby, well . . .'

Anita stared at him. She opened her mouth and thought about saying to him: you? How do you think *I* feel – their mother!

She didn't say it because, incredibly, Peter was crying

and for the first time he was revealed to her as being as vulnerable as anyone else. She put her arms around him.

'It's going to be all right,' she whispered, stroking his hair. '*All*, all right. That's right. Better now.'

Later, when he'd cried all his tears and he felt lighter than he had for weeks, he said, 'Hey, 'Nita. Let's not go to court today, eh? I just can't face having to listen to them trying to get that filthy pervert off.'

The Thursday afternoon had not been quite sufficient for Fletcher to wrap his case, so the evidence of Arnold Mallory, his last witness, was heard first thing in the morning. As ever, the scientist put up an impressive performance, taking the jury through the evidence of the fibres and the ice-cream wrappers, showing them DNA profiles and enlarged microscopic prints of various fibres, all of which proved beyond peradventure that Julie Anne had been in Michael Dunn's flat.

There had been one moment of comedy, when Rylands cross-examined on the dogshit.

'Would you say, Professor Mallory, that there is a lot of dog faeces lying about on the Howarth Estate?'

'I wouldn't know. I haven't studied that question.'

'Well, would it surprise you to know that, when I visited the area last Friday, I myself came away with some on my shoe?'

'No, it wouldn't.'

'Why not?'

'Because I would say that stepping in faeces was a hazard of your profession, sir.'

The press gallery had cracked up at this and even the

jury seemed entertained. If Winfield, too, had rather enjoyed the jibe, he concealed it.

Mallory's evidence had concluded Fletcher's case and now, without any interruption, Rylands rose to present his defence.

'I call the defendant,' he boomed. 'Michael Dunn.'

The element of serenity, evident in his appearance on the first day, had deserted Dunn. His face looked sullen as he was sworn in on the Bible and afterwards, awaiting Rylands's questions, he glowered ill-temperedly down at the court. Rylands, whose ability to read a court's atmosphere was legendary, felt the tension and expectation of the entire room feeding back at his client in a loop of anxiety and resentment. He decided to get straight to the meat of the thing.

'Where were you during the day of the fifth of September last year? That's the day before you were arrested by the police.'

'I was drinking in the park with a friend of mine – Terry Smith.'

'Which park was that?'

'The Scrub—, er, Princess Elizabeth Park. It's near the estate.'

'Were you alone there, the two of you, or was there anyone else with you?'

'There was another man there, I ... I can never remember his name.'

'How long were you there, the three of you?'

'All day, from eleven o'clock until early evening.'

'What did you do there?'

'Well, we were drinking, mainly, and talking. We were talking, er, politics like.'

'How much did you have to drink?'

Rylands was keeping it simple, his voice moderated if not exactly gentle or over-sympathetic. He wanted to present his man as a victim of prejudice and circumstance, a factual matter to which he hoped the jury would respond without emotion.

'Oh, quite a lot. Lager and vodka mainly. I wasn't drunk, though. I remember it quite well now.'

'In a pig's arse you do,' thought Pat North when she heard this. But would the jury think that? Dunn was beginning to come around under Rylands's businesslike approach. He was starting to look sympathetic again.

'Did you leave the company of Terry Smith and this other man at any time between eleven and the evening?'

'No, sir, I didn't. We bought some chips and some drink, but we went together to get that.'

Rylands took a drink of water and turned over a sheet of his notes. 'Now, did you know the little girl who was killed, Julie Anne Harris?'

'Yes, I did. That is, I didn't exactly know her. I knew her brother. He brought her round to my flat a few times.'

'Was it a common occurrence for children to play in your flat?'

'Yes, there was kids there all the time. I used to leave the door open. I didn't care who was there when I was drinking.'

'Did you see Julie Anne Harris at any time, even for a few moments, on the fifth of September?'

Dunn looked at the jury. He was innocent. He hadn't done this. He was telling the truth. 'No, I didn't.'

'Are you quite certain about that, notwithstanding the fact that you were drinking on that day?'

'Yes, I am, sir.'

'Did you not, for example, see her in the playground and bend down and speak to her or take her hand?'

Dunn shook his head. 'No, I didn't. I never saw her at all.'

Rylands glanced at his notes and then at the Court Associate. 'Could I ask you to have a look at the child's doll which has been referred to as exhibit five in this case?'

The doll was handed to Dunn, who took it in his hand and turned it over a few times as he looked at it.

'Do you recognize that doll?'

'Yes, I do. I had it in my flat. I found it on the estate . . .'

By the time Rylands sat down, he felt things hadn't gone too badly. He had broken through Dunn's initial resistance to the idea of giving evidence and the brisk, factual approach had played well. Now, after a brisk forty minutes or so, it was Fletcher's turn.

Willis Fletcher was not the Crown Court diva that Rylands could claim to be but, when he turned it on, he could be severe. He decided in advance that, in this cross-examination, he would go for the jugular as soon as it presented itself.

'Is it true, Mr Dunn, that you told police in interview and subsequently instructed your solicitor that you were with three friends, not two – two men and a woman – from eleven o'clock until early evening on the fifth of September?'

'Yes, but . . . I was confused then.'

'Were you confused about the people present, or were you confused about the day?'

'It was the people I got wrong. I got mixed up.'

'Unless of course . . .' Fletcher looked at the jury and then back at Dunn. 'Unless you weren't confused at all but were in fact telling untruths about your movements on that day.'

Dunn's mouth dropped open in surprise at the sudden accusation.

'I never said anything that wasn't true. I was with Terry Smith the whole day.'

'That's not right, is it Mr Dunn? You were *not* with Terry Smith for all of that time. And you *did* see Julie Anne Harris on that day.'

Dunn mustered all his reserves of sincerity. 'I didn't, sir. I never saw her.'

But Fletcher had his prey's neck between his teeth now. He decided to start applying pressure. 'You took Julie Anne Harris from the playground. You took her back to your flat. You then—'

'That's not *true*!'

'You then assaulted her sexually and took a rope which you'd previously stolen from a lady, er, acquaintance of yours and you—'

'No, no, no. Not at all. That's rubbish. I would *never* have stolen anything from Ann—'

He pulled up short, looking around. The court was suspended in silence, its attention riveted by his outburst. He set about trying to repair the damage. 'I mean, from Miss Taylor.'

There was a further moment's silence while Fletcher waited. Sometimes it paid to let distraught witnesses have their outbursts. He cocked his head to one side as he regarded Dunn, inviting him to continue and he did.

'I mean, I worked for her. She trusted me. She knew I was somebody she could . . . you know, trust.'

The last word came out as a mumble. Fletcher cut across it.

'And you then placed that rope around Julie Anne Harris's neck and you strangled her.'

'No, no. I didn't. I never *saw* her.'

'After which you took her unconscious body to a building site and you rammed it – you *rammed* it – into a sewage pipe like a bundle of rags. And you left that little girl to die there . . .'

His mouth turned down in revulsion at the acts he was describing, he stared at Dunn who simply stood before him, drooping.

'Didn't you?'

Stunned by the ferocity of Fletcher's attack. Dunn realized at last that his mouth was open but no word was coming out. He had to reply – but what *could* he say?

'*Didn't* you, Mr Dunn?'

At last, after what seemed an age, Dunn managed to shake his head and whisper the word, the one word that his thick, dry tongue had been groping for. 'No.'

'No more questions,' said Fletcher and sat down. Immediately a rustle of speculation and comment filled the court. Dunn had not cut a convincing figure in the witness box and the public gallery was beginning to wonder if there were to be any further twists in the unfolding of this trial. The buzz died away only as Rylands once more took the stage.

'I call Terry Smith, m'lord,' he said.

Smith walked into court looking dignified and confident. He was wearing a suit, not new exactly but even if it had come from Oxfam it was clean and pressed.

He took the oath with a touch of swagger in his bearing that did not escape Rylands's notice. It was OK, even quite attractive, for a witness to display a hint of independence, but it would have to be watched. Juries hate blatantly arrogant witnesses.

'Now, Mr Smith, you are an acquaintance of the defendant?'

'Yes.'

'A friend, even?'

'We used to drink together, yes.'

'And is it true that you, like Mr Dunn, used to have a problem with alcohol?'

'Yes, I did,' said Smith, loudly. 'I am an alcoholic.'

Rylands almost stopped in his tracks. 'You are—? Do you mean you are still addicted to alcohol?'

'Yes.'

'But you're not . . . not drinking to excess at present?'

'I'm not drinking at all.'

Rylands was rarely at a loss, but at this moment he came close. 'Forgive me, Mr Smith, but if you say you *are* an alcoholic—'

Rylands was floundering when a voice from the bench came to his rescue.

'I think what the witness means,' said Winfield, amused at the chance to air his knowledge of the operating principles of Alcoholics Anonymous, with which Robert Rylands was clearly not familiar, 'is that addiction to alcohol is considered a lifelong condition, which can be managed only by total abstention.'

He looked down at Smith who smiled cheerfully up at him.

'That's right, your Honour.'

Rylands bowed submissively and said, with only the barest suggestion of amusement in his voice, 'I'm *very* much obliged to your Lordship. So, Mr Smith, you now follow a regime of total abstinence from alcohol?'

'I do, sir. I gave up last month, sir. There's no other way.'

'I see. Now, I want to ask you about the fifth of September. Do you remember that day?'

'Yes, I do, sir.'

'And did you have a lot to drink on the fifth of September?'

'Pretty much the usual. I had, um, four cans of lager, then three more. Then half a bottle of vermouth and then some vodka.'

Smith was casting his eye around the court, clocking the jury, the benches for police and lawyers and the public gallery. Finally his eye rested on the dock. He seemed to be looking at Dunn strangely, as if he was trying to remember something.

'But that wasn't an unusual amount for you. You feel your perceptions and recollections of that day were more or less normal?'

'Yes, they were. I had a tolerance for drink then, you understand.'

'And who were you with on the fifth of September?'

'I was with Michael Dunn.'

As he spoke Smith's head turned back to the dock and he pointed at Dunn dramatically. 'And I think *that* bloke was there too. He had long hair then but it was definitely him. He was there.'

Rylands's train of thought jumped out of gear. What the hell was this? Who did Smith imagine Michael Dunn was? Winfield was slow to clamp down on the buzz of talk in court. He was equally mystified.

'Er, Mr Smith,' he said eventually, pausing in his note-taking, 'let us just be clear about your evidence at this point. Did you say that that man there was with you *as well as* Michael Dunn?'

Smith looked puzzled. Had he said something wrong? 'Yes, your Honour.'

'So the man you see here in court is not the man you have referred to up until now as Michael Dunn?'

Smith shook his head. 'No, your Honour. Michael Dunn – he was the other one. At least, that was my understanding.'

The court stirred like a carpet of leaves in a gust of wind. Rylands turned to Belinda Sinclair and whispered to her urgently, '*What the hell is this?*'

She merely shook her head helplessly, the pit of her stomach turning over. She'd never shown Smith a photograph of Dunn. Stupid? No, it was bloody cretinous.

'But that bloke was there as well,' Smith was saying now. 'I remember him. He's Welsh. We were there in the park, just by the gents toilet.'

Rylands turned back to the witness, smiling tautly, and took a deliberate flyer. 'Perhaps it doesn't matter, Mr Smith, by what name the defendant was known to you, if your evidence as to his presence is the same – yes?'

Rylands was decidedly not enjoying this. He'd been forced into breaking rule one in the code that governs the examination of witnesses: never ask a question to which you don't know the forthcoming answer. He wondered if Winfield was going to let him get away with it.

He shouldn't have wondered.

'Yes,' said Winfield impatiently, 'if it *is* the same. Now, Mr Smith. Was that man also with you continuously all day?'

Smith nodded, blinking ingenuously. 'Near enough,

293

your Honour. He went off I think a couple of times when we ran out of drink. He was the one brought us back the sherry, as I recall. I remember the sherry particularly because the bottle was made of blue glass.'

Walker murmured to North, 'What did Ann Taylor say?'

'Dunn took a bottle of sherry, guv.'

Walker nodded and pulled out his notebook. He was scribbling a note as Winfield was saying, 'Do you have a clear recollection of how long he was absent for?'

Smith pushed out his lips. 'Not long. About . . . half an hour, forty minutes each time. Round lunchtime.'

Walker passed the note he'd written to Fletcher who read it, nodded and conferred with Griffith.

Winfield said, 'Mr Rylands, is there anything else you would like to ask this witness?'

'No, m'lord.' Almost dumbfounded, Rylands sat down.

'Has the Crown any further questions to put to this witness?'

Still holding Walker's note, Fletcher leapt to his feet. 'Mr Smith – that bottle of sherry. Do you recall what became of it?'

'Yes,' said Smith, looking pained, 'as it happens I do. It got bust before we ever touched a drop.'

Before another question was asked, Walker and North were on their way.

CHAPTER 28

THURSDAY 21 NOVEMBER. LUNCHTIME

THE TYRES squawked in protest at Walker's aggressive braking as he brought the unmarked car to a halt beside Princess Elizabeth Park, also known as the Scrubbery.

'We'll never find it,' said North as they strode towards the bench near the public toilet. 'It's been months.'

'Well, I'm going to have a bloody good try,' said Walker. 'Nobody's cleaned up here for a lot longer than that – years.'

There was rubbish scattered right across the park, but especially among the leafless bushes and shrubs. They started poking around in the bushes. The whole area stank of urine.

'Jesus,' said North, making a face. 'Why can't they go in the loo? It's just over there.'

'Not open all the time. Look at that – we'll have to go through the lot.'

He gestured at the litter of glass, some of the bottles intact but mostly broken, that was scattered around amongst the dead leaves.

They could hear car doors slamming and the running feet of Satchell, followed by Cranham who had been plucked from the quiet of the Incident Room. Satchell called out even before he reached them.

'I spoke to Ann Taylor. The sherry bottle was blue glass all right. She can't remember the make.'

'Right,' said Walker, as Cranham, Phelps and Brown arrived panting from their exertions, 'we are searching this area for a blue bottle or fragments thereof. If we find it, it will need to go to forensic, so handle carefully. Got it everybody?'

In court Rylands had called Mrs Wald to the stand. His performance as he questioned her was downbeat, as if still affected by the stun grenade that had been tossed into court by his previous witness.

'. . . and what did he look like, this man who you saw at five past one in the Howarth Tower – by the way, was he coming in or going out?'

She was giving her evidence with a primness bordering on the fastidious.

'I'm afraid I cannot remember if he was going into the building or coming out. But he was certainly wearing a dark overcoat and he had long hair.'

'And did you on that day see the defendant, Michael Dunn, in or around the playground?'

'No, I did not.'

'Thank you, Mrs Wald. I have no further questions.'

Nor did the Crown have anything to ask Mrs Wald so Rylands rose again and said to Winfield, 'M'lord, that concludes our case.'

Winfield beamed benevolently up and down the court. 'Thank you, Mr Rylands. Shall we adjourn for five minutes before speeches? No, fifteen minutes – to allow the jury time to muster their fullest concentration.'

'I don't understand why Smithy didn't recognize me,' said Dunn to Belinda, fretting. 'He knows me perfectly. Bastard.'

Belinda soothed him as best she could.

'It was a bit of a surprise, I'll admit. But don't forget, you couldn't remember the name of the other man yourself – and *he* probably thinks you're Terry Smith. So it seems everybody's mixed up all round.'

'So what's going to happen now?'

'There'll be closing speeches by Mr Fletcher and Mr Rylands, and then the judge will sum up. That's why you see him writing notes during the evidence: he has to summarize what's been said in court by both sides before he sends the jury out to decide.'

'But they will find me innocent, won't they? I mean it's gone well, hasn't it?'

Belinda considered. Had it gone well? Not half as well as they originally hoped. The alibi had been a near disaster, and it had been her fault. But, self-protectively, she said nothing of this.

'It's gone very well, Michael. And another thing. Mr Fletcher will close tonight but there's every chance our side will be held over till tomorrow. That's good because Mr Rylands's words will be much fresher in everybody's mind than Mr Fletcher's.'

She left him then. Michael Dunn shut his eyes. He didn't think he could bear to sit through another session of blame and denigration from that Fletcher man. Why should he? He was just a scapegoat, a sacrificial victim. The filth had only picked him up because everybody on that estate hated him.

Why should he have to put up with listening to Fletcher's lies and sneers? He was innocent, wasn't he? This whole thing was a nightmare and he couldn't wake up.

'On Tuesday,' Fletcher reminded the jury, 'I asked you to consider this case like a jigsaw puzzle. You are now in possession of the available pieces and I trust you are also in a position to fit them together to form a true picture. It is a picture of a man, Michael Frederick Dunn, living alone, who admits to holding open house for children in his flat. Dunn is a heavy drinker – a very heavy drinker indeed, one might say – and he is also a man who harbours a tendency to anger and violence which, in his pathetic way, he dares to turn only against those very children who come so trustingly to his house.

'But there is another figure in this picture, a very tragic figure. This is a little girl of very appealing appearance, five years old, whom Michael Dunn knows. But even more significantly this little girl, Julie Anne Harris, knows Dunn for she has been to his house and watched cartoon videos there. These are the people in the picture. Now let us turn to what is happening in this picture . . .'

Fletcher went on to spell out the timetable of Julie Anne's death – between her last sighting and her finding the next day, ignominiously stuffed into the sewage pipe. He recalled Enid Marsh's evidence and her positive identification of Dunn at the parade. He ran through the

298

pathologist's evidence of strangulation and sexual assault. Lastly he laid out the forensic evidence – the footprints, the dog faeces, the soil samples, the clothing fibres, the washing line, all of which, he said, compellingly placed Michael Dunn, the rope and Julie Anne together on the day of her death.

'So much for the truth,' he declared. 'Now we must turn to the big lie: the defendant's alibi. He claims he was with Terry Smith throughout the day, and Mr Smith gave evidence that he was indeed drinking – heavily – with Michael Dunn on the fifth of September. But – and here is the crucial piece of our jigsaw ladies and gentlemen – Michael Dunn was *not* continuously with Mr Smith all day. He absented himself for two separate periods.

'When did Mrs Marsh see the defendant? At lunchtime. When did he absent himself from Mr Smith and the other man? At lunchtime. If you accept the evidence of Mrs Marsh and Mr Smith, Michael Dunn has not only *lied* to the police, as was admitted – you will remember what he said when he was first interviewed about the doll – but he has *lied* here today, on oath in front of you. You must ask yourselves what motives Michael Dunn might have for telling these lies. And it is my contention that his only possible one is that he killed Julie Anne.'

Fletcher took a drink of water and approached nearer to the jury for his final flourish.

'A jigsaw puzzle, ladies and gentlemen, often has a few pieces missing but, as I said at the outset, the overall picture can be clearly distinguished. A clear picture has, I believe, emerged from the evidence you have heard in this case, and it is one which points conclusively to Michael's Dunn's guilt.'

He sat down and immediately Winfield, as Belinda had predicted, called a halt for the day.

'We shall resume at ten-thirty tomorrow,' he decreed.

Jason wet the bed earlier than usual that night. He woke up at half past ten in a pool of his own urine and came out of the room crying for his mum.

She gave him fresh sheets and pyjamas while Peter stood with the damp undersheet, trying to dry it out in front of the bar fire in the lounge.

'Don't bother drying it,' said Anita, coming in after tucking the child back in. 'I'll put it in the washbag for tomorrow.'

'Did you get that rubber sheet like I told you?'

Anita shook her head. She took the sodden sheet and wrapped it around the pyjama bottoms. 'I meant to, I—'

Peter came up to her and held her hips. He said, very gently, 'You thought about what I said? This.' He nodded to the wet bundle. 'It's every night now. It would be better for him. They know how to handle this kind of thing.'

Anita looked at him sadly. 'You'd know, would you?' She sighed. 'Well, I spoke to Mum, but she couldn't take him.'

'Look, 'Nita. It would give you some rest. I'm only thinking of you. They've got special homes for kids like Jason. The way things are—'

'I don't want to talk about it.'

Anita suddenly turned away and walked out of the room with the sheet and pyjamas. She felt hot, suffocated. Peter stood there without moving, his fists clenched in frustration. A few seconds later Anita came back and moved over to the sideboard where the shrine to Julie was. She started to rearrange some of the photographs.

'It would only be for a short while?' she said quietly. The fight had all gone out of her. 'I mean – not for ever?'

''Course not,' said Peter. 'Just so you can get yourself back to . . . you know.'

'Normal.'

'Yeah. Normal.'

Anita was drifting out towards the hall.

'I'll call them . . . in the morning.'

In the dark at the Scrubbery the work went on under arc lights. The ground had been carefully squared off in a grid made of string, each grid sifted and any debris bagged. So far there had been no blue glass found.

But Satchell had raised a drain cover that had been hidden under a thick pelt of dead leaves. As the one with the longest arm, he was lying down, trying to search the inside of the drain.

'I can't reach any further. Should we start digging it up?'

'Yes,' said Walker decisively. The rest of the ground had turned up nothing. The drain looked their last hope.

'You sure?' said Satchell grunting with effort. 'We're talking about going into the drains now, guv. It'll be a big job and it's way past midnight . . . Hang on! I've got something. Glass.'

He pulled out a sizeable shard of glass. Eagerly Walker shone his torch on it.

'Shit!' said Satchell.

It was green glass.

'Is there a chance of more in there?' Walker asked.

'Sure, guv.'

Walker nodded grimly at the fragment in Satchell's glove. 'Well, call me colourblind, but in this light I'd swear that this piece of glass is from a blue bottle.'

A quarter of a mile away, a builders' security fence rattled slightly and, with a grating sound, a section of the galvanized mesh was pushed aside. A shadow slipped through and became a silhouette as it crossed a patch of ground lit by security lighting, then a shadow again as it passed into the gloom surrounding a stockpile of building materials.

Anita was wearing leggings, a sweatshirt and strapless sandals. She had come out on impulse, a sudden feeling that the funeral, the trial, were not enough to bring an end to the terrible event that had come along like a careering truck and smashed into her life. Out here in the dark and away from people and the bits and pieces of everyday life, there was one part of it at least that could be finished.

It was not a cold night. A breeze rustled the plane trees near the parade of shops. The remote drone of London's unceasing traffic came from almost every direction. The black rectangles of the two tower blocks, with a few lit windows, could be seen rearing up in the almost clear sky. Looking back, Anita could see her own bedroom window, from where a low light shone. Perhaps Peter was going to bed.

A dog barked and she crouched down. She knew there was a security presence on the building site now and she didn't want a big Doberman leaping at her throat. After the barking stopped she waited for a few seconds then walked rapidly towards her objective, stumbling here and there on broken bricks and chunks of hardcore. Finally she reached the pipes. But which one was it? No one had told her which particular pipe Julie Anne had died in. She hadn't known how to ask.

She fumbled around, a pallet nearly slipping on top of her as she disturbed its precarious balance. She knew only that she was looking for a narrow pipe – couldn't be the larger diameter ones at the outside of the heap. What about this one, tucked away in between? At this moment, high above Anita, a nearly full moon chased clear a bunch of cumuli and a silvery light caught the end of the pipe. Anita saw the remnant of yellow police tape on the narrow pipe and knew this was the one.

She huddled down and felt in her pocket, pulling out the small blue teddy bear that Julie had had in her bed every night of her life. Thomas had bought it at Woolworth's on his way to the hospital on the day she was born. Anita pressed her nose to the cheap artificial fur.

Reaching forward, smelling dampness and earth, she placed Julie's teddy inside the pipe and stayed crouching there, watching over the tiny object as it lay in the near darkness.

'Bye, bye, Julie,' she said. 'Bye, bye, my darling.'

Quite suddenly a wave of pain crashed through her. She may have thought she'd grieved for her daughter but she hadn't, not truly. Now, as grief mowed into her, she started to sob uncontrollably. It was like a racking physical pain crossed with terror – like the sudden cramps of sickness, the contractions of childbirth.

The moon slid behind the clouds once more. The teddy bear could no longer be seen. And Anita's low, mewing, inarticulate voice, like that of some sorely wounded animal, mingled with the sounds of the night.

CHAPTER 29

FRIDAY 22 NOVEMBER. MORNING

WALKER HAD been on to Griffith's home number as soon as he realized there was probably more glass in the drain. It couldn't be investigated at night – they needed daylight and proper equipment to excavate. They needed time.

'So will you get on to Fletcher first thing in the morning and ask him to request an adjournment? New evidence with an important bearing on the case, et cetera.'

'OK, Walker,' said Griffith drowsily. He'd been asleep for an hour. 'I'll ask but don't hold out too much hope.'

When Winfield heard in the morning that there would be a request for adjournment he immediately sent the jury out.

'M'lord,' said Willis Fletcher, 'I wonder if I might ask for a day. Some portions of a blue bottle have been discovered and there is at least the possibility that this might be the bottle mentioned by Mr Smith in his evidence. There is the further possibility that this was the bottle used to assault Julie Anne Harris.'

North, tired and dishevelled after being up all night,

was the only one in court from Southampton Street. Walker had sent her down specifically to get Winfield's reaction when Fletcher made his request. She watched him considering it, turning back a few pages of his notes to refer to some piece of evidence, probably Smith's. North saw Rylands turn to Belinda Sinclair and confer urgently. The judge cleared his throat.

'Mr Fletcher, what exactly are you asking me for?'

'A day's adjournment for the police to carry out further investigation.'

Winfield played with the pages of his notes for a few more seconds. He was no fool. North guessed the judge knew the police would want to fingerprint the glass they'd found and try and prove it was Ann Taylor's sherry bottle. But, even if they came up with Dunn's prints, what more would that prove? Everyone accepted that Dunn had used the Park. North watched closely as Winfield made up his mind. She just wished Fletcher had mentioned DNA in his request for an adjournment, to underline that they hoped to find a trace of Julie Anne on some piece of the bottle. But it was too late now. The judge was thinking in terms of the accused's traces.

'I am sorry, Mr Fletcher,' Winfield said at last. 'I imagine a person addicted to alcohol may handle a great many bottles in any one day, and I can't see any real justification for delaying the trial at this stage. We shall continue with Mr Rylands's closing speech. Ask the jury to come back in please.'

The scene at the park was now one of intense and concerted activity. TSG had been brought in with the intention of opening up the entire underground conduit

305

while other members of Walker's team were searching the open ground and undergrowth of the rest of the park.

'I want this drain opened up. I want the pipe smashed open so we can look inside.'

'Guv, the Borough Surveyor's got to give the go-ahead.'

'Well? Where is he? He should be here.'

'Guy on the phone says he's off sick and—'

But Walker had left him to meet North, who was almost running towards them.

'He won't adjourn,' she gasped. 'They're going on and Rylands is closing now.'

'How long have we got?'

'Till lunchtime, at least. Robert Rylands would listen to himself all day – right?'

Wrong. Rylands had drastically curtailed the closure he had originally planned. He knew that Walker had got on to the scent of something. He also knew that, once Winfield started his summing up, there was not much chance of him allowing whatever that something was to be given in evidence – and none at all once the jury had begun considering their verdict.

'I said when I got up that I would be brief, ladies and gentlemen,' Rylands was now telling them. He had been on his feet all of fifteen minutes and had, to his own satisfaction, if with considerably more abridgement than was ideal, exposed Fletcher's argument on the forensics, identification and alibi to ridicule. 'You may now feel that, far from having been presented with what the Crown would say is a clear evidential picture, you have in fact been presented with a ragbag of unrelated fragments.

'And you may feel, too, that the full truth has not been heard from anyone in this case – juries, I am sorry to tell you, often do. But you must keep in mind that Michael Dunn is not charged with telling untruths. He is charged with *murdering* a little girl.

'Even if you do not believe that everything he has said, every word of the story, is true you must *not* – without more proof – convict him. For Michael Dunn himself need prove nothing. It is for the prosecution to prove their case and to satisfy you so that you are *sure* Michael Dunn murdered Julie Anne Harris.

'The evidence you have heard, you may think, falls far short of that. In fact, it falls short by such a long way that the only verdict which is in good conscience open to you is one of "not guilty". Thank you.'

As he sat down it was apparent that even the judge had been caught on the hop by Rylands's unaccustomed brevity.

'Well,' he said, 'since Counsel have been so particularly succinct, I shall begin my summing-up now, without an adjournment. And I hope I shall follow their admirable example as to clarity and conciseness.'

''Nita, get a bucket. We're going to get rid of this little bastard once and for all.'

Peter was standing in the kitchen, holding Julie's doll in his hand. Anita produced a plastic bucket and showed it to him.

'Not that one – the galvanized one. I'm going to cremate the bloody thing. Burn it.'

He started pulling the limbs off the doll, unpopping the socketed legs, arms and head and yanking until the rubber ligaments snapped. He dropped the parts into the bucket which Anita had placed on the floor and rummaged in a drawer. Somewhere he'd got some firelighters left over from that barbecue they'd had last summer.

'When they come for him, it's best we've got rid of it. You know his big mouth.'

Anita was peering into the bucket where the dismembered doll lay in a heap, half covered by its gleaming blonde coiffure. Peter had found a firelighter which he'd broken up and was dropping fragments into the bucket. She struck a match and dropped it on the hair, which began to burn, frizzling as the flame ate it up.

'You – get out of here! Get out!'

It was Peter yelling at Jason, who had smelt the burning nylon and come wandering in.

'Don't you touch him, Peter!' Anita yelled. 'They'll be here any minute. Jason, get your bag. Jason!'

But Jason wasn't listening. Jason had been told he was being taken away and put in a home and he wasn't listening to anything any of them said. He went up to his mum and punched her as hard as he could. His fist bounced off her arm. He struck her again in the stomach, his face distorting with fury. She tried to fend him off, flailing with her arms, but the boy hit his mother two or three times more before Peter yanked him away.

And then the firelighters caught and Julie's little doll, the one she always had with her, the doll she wanted a wardrobe of party dresses for, burned. First the hair caught light, then the pink plastic body began melting and the kitchen began to fill with toxic black smoke.

*

The TSG officers, using sledgehammers and a drill, cracked the side of the drain four feet from the raised access cover and managed to open a jagged aperture a good eighteen inches long. There had been no permission from the Borough Surveyor, the water company, the environmental health or anybody else. Walker had just told them to do it and to blazes with the consequences.

A TSG officer was now lying down, his arm inserted into the pipe up to the armpit. He had already dragged out the remains of a dozen crisp bags, cigarette packets, leaves and other debris, which lay sodden and putrid in a mound by his side. Now he was grasping some polythene waste, a carrier bag perhaps. He drew it out and held it up. Walker saw a large plastic food bag, the sort used in freezers. Its neck had been tied. It was filthy, with decayed leaves and dirt stuck all over it, but everyone could see that the contents included some broken pieces of blue glass.

'Yes! That's it!' yelled Walker. 'That's it, what we're looking for!'

The officer handed up the bag very carefully and its glass contents clinked as the sour, nutty smell of a long-spilt Amontillado sherry met their nostrils.

'The issue is not what sort of a person the defendant is, or whether he is always truthful, but whether he is guilty of the very grave offence with which he is charged.'

Winfield took seriously the injunction that, when summing up, the judge should risk monotony rather than to allow emotion to enter his voice. His own voice, solemn and deep, had little problem complying, for it scarcely fluctuated in pitch.

'It is only if you feel that his reasons for lying tend to show he committed the offence – that he has lied out of guilt and a fear of the truth – that you should consider the fact that he has lied as relevant at all . . .'

While remaining admirably impartial, the style of delivery made the speech a little difficult to concentrate on. There was a lot of coughing and shuffling in court and not a few suppressed yawns.

Walker sent the bag under police escort to Arnold Mallory and, while it was still on its way, phoned the professor with the plea – no, the demand – that he drop everything just for this one day.

'So, what is it you're sending me?' Mallory wanted to know.

'Broken bottle. Found inside a polythene bag in a drain. It just might be the one Dunn used to assault the child. You got to do dabs and DNA.'

'Do try not to tell me what I've *got* to do, Walker. I'll do what I can.'

And by the time Walker, North and Satchell arrived at the lab, Mallory and his team had already done a considerable amount. They had in fact reassembled the broken bottle.

'We're good at jigsaws here and most of the glass survived.'

He showed them the object, clamped to a stand. The fault-lines where it had shattered were traced by the pale adhesive. The only missing piece now was the neck, which Mallory slotted into its place as they watched.

Mallory then took a sheet of filter paper and folded it in four. His face set in a mask of concentration, he moved the bottle aside, then with a fine pair of tweezers he picked up the rim they had removed from the bottle. Holding this in his left hand he used the pointed corner of the folded paper and prodded at a tiny, dark clot of matter that was stuck to the rim. A little of it came off on the paper.

Carefully, Mallory opened the paper and laid it flat on a glass petri dish. He opened a bottle of liquid chemical and, with a dropper, allowed a single drop of the chemical to fall on the sample. A colourless, circular, damp stain spread out around it. Replacing the stopper and returning the phial to its rack, he selected a second phial and repeated the procedure. This time the dampness instantly turned a bright pink.

Mallory released his breath in a wheezing exhalation. He glanced round the circle of expectant police officers.

'It's blood,' he declared.

Walker took a moment to register. Then he was patting his pockets as if for a cigarette but, in fact, for his mobile phone.

'I can't tell you yet,' continued Mallory, 'whether it's the girl's blood or not. The next step is to establish a blood group . . .'

Walker looked at North. He must have left his mobile in the car.

'Get me through to the Crown Court – quick! They'll have to adjourn now. We can't try him twice. We got just the one shot at him.'

At about the time that the pink stain appeared on the filter paper in Mallory's lab, Winfield wrapped up his speech and invited the jury to retire. As North's message

311

came through for an urgent word with Clive Griffith, one of the ushers was being sworn in as jury bailiff.

'. . . I shall not myself speak to them, nor suffer any other person to speak to them, save to ask them if they have reached their verdict.'

Griffith read the note and slipped out of court. But by the time he had used his phone, he knew it would be too late.

North snapped her mobile shut and returned to the lab bench. Mallory had just completed a test on a second sample from the bottle.

'Look – same blood group,' he said. 'AB negative. We're getting there!'

'Too slowly, I'm afraid,' said North grimly. 'I've just spoken to Griffith. Jury have retired. We're too late.'

'Shit!' Walker clenched his fists. 'What's been going on down there? Rylands must have been going for the fastest fucking closing speech on record.'

He was patting his pockets again and this time pulled out a packet of Marlboro. He said to Mallory, 'You will finish the tests, won't you? Whatever happens, you will do the DNA?'

Mallory smiled. He was a selfish man but towards this impassioned policeman he felt as near as he ever would to kindliness.

'Yes,' he said, 'I'll finish them. We all want to close the book on this, don't we?'

At the Howarth Estate, Enid Marsh's curtains twitched. She had no idea what was happening today at the trial. Television had an item on the news at dinner time, all

312

about closing speeches, summing up. But for all she knew it was finished by now.

On the back of Enid's door, the outfit she'd worn hung waiting for Ivy or Karen to come and claim it. When they did, Enid had planned a little tea party. There were some ginger nuts she could put out. It'd be nice to have a cuppa and a chat. But nobody had been near Enid since Wednesday except Mrs Wald and she didn't know any more than Enid about the trial. All the rest of them had stayed away.

She looked out across the estate. There were some people making their way out of the tower block below and going away towards the car park. One of them was that boy Jason, little Goldilocks's naughty brother. He was being almost dragged along by his fast-walking stepfather, Peter James. Enid knew him, she'd seen him in court.

Looking back she saw the boy's mother coming along behind them, accompanied by a stranger. This was a woman with short grey hair, a pale mac and a shoulder bag. She had social worker written all over her. The mother carried a suitcase. Where were they going?

Enid watched on. At the edge of the playground, the mother handed the suitcase to the social worker, who nodded her head and set off after Peter James and the boy, catching them up just before they reached the corner. She must have said something because Enid saw the kid twisting round, turning and trying to catch a glimpse of his mother. He called out, 'I want my dad! I want my dad!'

Enid could see Anita standing there, watching the departing group with her arms folded. What Enid could not see was that Anita was weeping. 'Taking the little bugger away,' Enid thought. 'Good riddance, he'd always been trouble.'

Anita didn't call out. She just watched as Jason was helped into a car. At length a car engine started and Enid saw the young woman, the mother, give a solitary wave. Peter James came back, took Anita in his arms, and walked her back to the tower block and out of Enid's sight. She never heard the mother, who had lost not one, but two of her babies, but was now sending a third away. Never heard the plaintive cry, 'I love them.'

CHAPTER 30

FRIDAY 22 SEPTEMBER. AFTERNOON

COLIN BARRIDGE sat on the bench in the Dockland Light Railway station, impervious to the trains going by. An hour ago, when he had walked out of Southampton Street in his civilian clothes, he had ceased to be the bearer of Her Majesty's warrant. He no longer stood – or sat – in the office of a constable. He was no longer, even, in possession of the uniform of the Metropolitan Police.

This was what suspension meant. It also meant hanging, didn't it? If this was the old days, it could be Michael Dunn who was going to be hanged, not him.

The jury were out on Dunn. He knew that. They would probably decide the guy's fate before the day was out. His own fate would take weeks to resolve. There would be a disciplinary hearing, evidence, admissions, severe words, tears. His dad would tell him I told you so. His mum would cry and cry and not be able to face the neighbours.

Barridge didn't want to go home to his mum and dad. He wanted to stay here. He was drained of all desire, all need, all ambition. Once he wanted to be a Detective Inspector in the Flying Squad. Now he watched train after train go by without feeling the need to move at all.

Belinda Sinclair went down to sit with her client in the holding cell. She didn't actually have to do this but, then again, there was no one else to do it.

There wasn't much conversation. Dunn was staring at the wall, humming to himself and smoking a roll up.

'How long's it been?'

'Fifty minutes.'

'Oh.'

He went on humming tunelessly.

Looking back on the trial, Belinda saw that her original faith in Dunn's innocence had been rather dented by Smith's failure to recognize Dunn in court. But this damage to her belief in the case had been mitigated by her own sense of responsibility for the cock-up. If only she had shown Smith a photograph of Dunn . . .

Michael had been terrible in the witness box yesterday. She couldn't understand it. He seemed so bright and personable, now that he'd got the booze completely out of his system. But as soon as Fletcher started to question him about things that happened on the day of the murder he'd fallen to pieces. Started looking shifty and, then, guilty.

Fletcher had been bloody good, better than flash-Harry Rylands, if truth be told. Their brief had been a little *too* brief in his closure, to her way of thinking. Then she remembered that Rylands's advice had been not to call Dunn at all. God, how she wished they'd taken it.

'How long now?'

'An hour.'

'Christ! How long's it going to take them to realize the police case is a load of shit?'

'An hour is nothing, Michael. Sometimes the longer they stay out the better.'

Was that true? In an apparently cut-and-dried case a long jury deliberation would be interesting. But was this such a case? Once she had thought it was.

'But you do think they'll acquit?' asked Dunn. He sounded pathetic now, forlorn, but that was hardly surprising in view of the fact that the sword of Damocles hung about an inch from his cranium. She remembered the last thing Rylands had said to her outside the court.

'We've got him off, Belinda, never fear.'

She replied, 'Or you'll eat your wig, Robert?'

But Rylands had just smiled enigmatically before waltzing off to the bar mess. Instead of telling Dunn about this exchange, she just said weakly, 'I sincerely hope so.'

He was kicking the leg of the table now, swinging his foot against it rhythmically. She wondered what would happen if she asked him to stop, but he stopped of his own accord anyway. There was something he wanted to ask her.

'Could I . . . well, let you know how I get on . . . afterwards?'

She looked sharply at him. What was he asking?

'Yes, of course,' she said guardedly. 'You have the office address.'

'Yes, I know. But you might leave, get married or something. So I thought . . .'

Jesus, she thought. He's asking if we can meet.

Before Belinda could cut him short or devise a reply, there was a sharp rap on the door. A voice called, 'Jury's back!'

She looked at Dunn, wishing he would hurry. His eyes were saucers but she was oddly unmoved.

He said, 'I'm ready now.'

'Come on, then.'

It was a long wait for the jury and all the time a long, long private prayer by Helen that they would find him guilty. She wanted it over and it wouldn't be, for any of them, until then.

Helen was the only member of the family who'd been at the trial every day. Some of the estate people had come in for the first and last days but, out of the relatives, even Thomas hadn't showed up for the verdict. Surely they'd have given him compassionate leave if he'd wanted it?

Helen understood why Anita stayed away, but she was adamant about her own presence. There had to be someone the same flesh and blood as little Julie present at the—
She nearly thought the phrase 'at the death'. The end.

What had been hard, especially, was listening to the pathologist and then that fat scientist telling what happened to Julie. They used that clinical, soulless language. From time to time, in the middle of it all, Helen had been flooded with memories of Julie alive. Sitting alongside her on the bus, bouncing on the cushion and talking away to herself, or to complete strangers.

'My dad's a soldier,' she'd tell them, 'but he hasn't got a gun.'

And at Helen's house after television: 'I'm going to be a dancer on *Top of the Pops*, I am. I can do disco, granny, look.'

And at bedtime, when Helen babysat one time: 'I love you best, granny.'

In court she'd had to listen to how her granddaughter's tongue had protruded in death through clenched teeth. How her neck had been injured, the ligature indenting the neck tissues. How she had been bruised, how she'd been penetrated . . .

'I love you best, granny.'

Helen studied the members of the jury as they filed in. They knew the verdict but you couldn't read anything in their faces, just seriousness. Michael Dunn never glanced at them. He stood in the dock, staring at the floor. Everyone in court could see how he was shaking.

'Would the foreman please stand?' asked the Clerk.

The woman who had led the jury into court rose to her feet. She was middle-aged and seemed to Helen educated, intelligent.

'Madam foreman, answer this question – yes or no. Members of the jury, have you reached a verdict upon which you are all agreed?'

The woman glanced at the judge then back at the Clerk. She nodded her head. 'Yes.'

A perceptible thrill of anticipation flickered through the court then died to a profound silence. The Associate gave a slight cough.

'Do you find the defendant guilty or not guilty of murder?'

There was a second's pause in which nobody breathed. Then the jury foreman herself took an intake of air so that she could speak up.

Helen continued to hold her breath.

*

Peter and Anita sat in their living room. Tony, his nappy a little sodden and its adhesive tabs coming adrift, was crawling around the floor with a long string of drool dangling from his mouth. Anita was impervious. She stared at her fingernails.

'Come on, love, we talked it through. I know it's hard but it's best for Jason, it really is. *They* even said so.'

He lapsed into silence when she didn't reply or react. He sat watching Tony, who was trying to stuff a plastic block into his mouth. There would be a time to talk about Jason but this wasn't it.

The phone rang. Peter looked at his watch and then at Anita and she was looking at him now with eyes wide. They both knew.

'This is it,' he said.

He went out to the hall and picked up the phone. Anita heard his responses, very quiet and short. She bit into a fingernail and it gave way with a loud snap. She heard Peter ring off.

He didn't come back instantly but lingered in the hall. She waited, holding the fragment of nail between her tongue and teeth. What was he doing?

Then Peter was standing at the door. His pose was easy, casual, leaning on the door frame. He was smiling when he gave her the news.

'It's guilty.'

Anita covered her face with her open hands and leaned forward to rest her head on her knees.

Belinda was shocked and Rylands too, perhaps, though he didn't show it. There was no one in court to boo or hiss the verdict. In the public gallery they celebrated.

Rylands was on his feet. Winfield raised an eyebrow.

'There is nothing I wish to say, m'lord.'

Rylands knew there was no point in mitigation, as Winfield was about to underline. The judge nodded to the associate who told Dunn to stand.

'Michael Dunn,' intoned Winfield, 'as I am sure you know, you have been convicted of an offence for which the sentence is fixed by law. There is only one sentence I can pass and I sentence you accordingly to life imprisonment. In this case, I recommend that the minimum term to be served should be no less than twenty years. Take him down.'

In the bustle and disturbance of the courtroom that followed the verdict. Belinda Sinclair had the odd feeling that she was in a kind of bubble of silence. It wasn't shock or disbelief – she'd always known this reverse could happen – but a sense of detachment. She'd done her best but it hadn't been enough and the jury had gone against her. Who was she, even silently, to criticize them?

She felt a tap on her arm and it was Detective Superintendent Walker. She looked at him without warmth.

'Miss Sinclair, I would like you to know this. We found something, a blue glass bottle. Tests carried out today have shown that traces around the neck of that bottle are blood – the same group as that of Julie Ann Harris – AB negative. It's a rare group. The bottle was found in a drain in Princess Elizabeth Park.'

She listened to what the policeman had to say. And as soon as she heard it she realized that she already knew this. At some point, in the last twenty-four hours, she had unconsciously changed her mind about Dunn. And she realized that, if she had been a member of the jury, she would have found him guilty too.

321

It was her duty to go down and see her client now. She made her way into the basement and was shown into Dunn's cell, where she was told she had a couple of minutes. The transport was about to leave.

He was sitting slumped at the table. Belinda took a packet of Silk Cut out of her bag and lit a cigarette, dropping the almost full packet on the table in front of him. He raised his head and looked at her. There were traces on his face of very recent tears.

'What happens now?' he asked. He looked more lonely, more pathetic than ever, but it didn't touch Belinda even remotely. Not any more.

'New evidence has apparently been found by the police, Michael.'

She looked steadily at him. She accused him with her eyes and he shrank away.

'But I didn't do it. I didn't. I *swear*. I'm innocent. I didn't do it!'

A security Guard hammered on the door – the transport was ready to take him. Belinda stood by the door as it swung open, then swivelled just for a moment.

'Yes, you did, Michael,' she said. 'Oh, yes, you did.'

And she went out to look for some fresh air to breathe.

Walker was not a man to go fishing. He liked an occasional day at the races or a football match with his boy. But even then he never truly relaxed. On the day after the trial was over he'd managed to get some tickets at Spurs for the Newcastle match, but the whole ninety minutes he was thinking about Mallory and what the DNA would turn up next week.

Dunn was safely banged up but Walker knew in his

heart that they'd been lucky. There had been as many defensive mistakes as he was watching out there on the White Hart Lane park. Barridge's own-goal should have finished them completely but then Rylands put Dunn in the witness box and the Crown got one back. Fletcher was brilliant. Terry Smith's failure to recognize Dunn was important too, but in the end it probably came down to the jury's intuition.

Which is why he still needed that DNA. The very last thing Walker wanted was a rematch at the Appeal Court with Rylands. Or a book exposing a so-called miscarriage of justice. Or – God forbid – a *Rough Justice* TV documentary.

He'd told everybody to take a long weekend but he himself was back at Southampton Street on the Monday, trying to disentangle the chaos that was the budget for this investigation. The station Super wanted the Incident Room packed up by the end of the week, before which he had to make sure all the reports, statements, notes and audio tapes were tagged, docketed and filed along with car logs, overtime sheets and all the other paper palaver that had to be placed these days in long-term storage. Then there was the Barridge disciplinary to deal with. He'd spent all Sunday morning writing his report.

Now Soames, Harrold, Macklin, Grimes and the others were humping files out to the AMIP van in the loading bay, while he furiously double-checked Mallory's invoices. He was cursing forensic's meticulous paperwork, with every procedure, even the most minute, timed and charged for, when the phone at his elbow sounded. It was the man himself on the phone.

'I thought you'd like to be the first to know, Detective Superintendent,' boomed Mallory.

'You've got the DNA tests?'

Walker signalled to North, Satchell and anyone else within earshot. They instantly stopped what they were doing and gathered round. The room fell silent.

'I have indeed,' said Mallory. 'I have carried out the tests you requested on the blood deposits found on the bottleneck from Princess Elizabeth Park.'

'And?'

'They prove without doubt that it was Julie Anne's blood on the bottle. Congratulations, Mr Walker. You got the right man. There'll be no books by leftie journalists trying to make a name for themselves. There'll be no shouting about a miscarriage of justice. You'll have my full report in the morning. Goodbye.'

Walker hung up and told his team. The cheer rattled the Venetian blinds and somebody's cap crossed the room like a frisbee. Walker went up to Pat North – he knew Satchell too well to say anything to him. He shook Pat's hand.

'Congratulations, Detective Inspector,' Walker said. 'I look forward to working with you again.'

Pat North smiled. Yes, she thought, it's been a hell of an experience, and some of it was just plain hell. But she was glad she'd done it.

CHAPTER 31

DUNN KICKED at the hard-backed solitary chair, then he picked it up and threw it against the wall. He tore the mattress off the bunk-bed. He tried to rip it apart, then he couldn't get his breath. He kept on clawing at his shirt where the tie they had given him had been. Even the open collar felt as if it was throttling him. It was the terrible rage of his own guilt slowly surfacing, and he began punching himself, slapping his face, ramming and hitting his head against the wall as the rage consumed him in agony. It was the same rage that had swept over him when she, Julie Ann, had begun screaming, she'd almost bitten his fingers as he closed her mouth. No one had heard his screams, so she had to be silenced, just as his abusers had silenced him. A rope round her neck, not too tight, only to frighten her, then he would carry her some place, hide her, as they had hidden him. There was nothing wrong. He hadn't done anything wrong. He had done nothing that hadn't been done to him. He was innocent. He didn't do it. His voice screeched into a howl. Spittle formed in globules at the edge of his mouth as he repeated over and over again: 'I didn't do it. *I didn't do it.*'

His own voice sounded hollow and empty, as empty as Belinda Sinclair's beautiful eyes when she had left his cell.

'I didn't do it. *I didn't do it.*'

There had been such pain, such disgust in her soft, musical voice. It had cut through his brain like a jagged knife.

'Yes you did, Michael. Yes you did.'

Michael Frederick Dunn was guilty but he was also a wretched, tragic young man who had learned as a child that if he did cry out no one would listen. No one had ever been punished for their crimes against him. He had never understood that what had been done to him was wrong . . . until it was too late.

LYNDA LA PLANTE

The Talisman

Pan Books

1945–1980

The sequel to the bestselling *The Legacy*

From the mineral mines of South Africa and the fashion houses of Paris to the boardrooms and brothels of London, *The Talisman* completes the vast and compelling saga that began with *The Legacy* as the long, dark skein of the romany curse runs down to the fourth generation . . .

'A torrid tale of love, intrigue and passion . . . packed with glamour, big business and big, big money'
Daily Express

LYNDA LA PLANTE

Bella Mafia

Pan Books

A classic crime thriller from TV's most popular author.

Following a terrible, bloody Mafia retribution, five women are all that remain of the Luciano clan – seemingly helpless after the murder of their husbands and the brutal destruction of their inheritance.

Their rivals thought they had eliminated all danger. They were wrong.

The Luciano widows. Vengeance will be theirs . . .

LYNDA LA PLANTE

Entwined

Pan Books

In the newly-liberated streets of modern Berlin two women, a pampered, beautiful Baroness, losing control of her mind, and a fearless wild animal trainer, facing the greatest challenge of her career, are drawn together by a series of tragic and extraordinary coincidences.

When a man is found brutally murdered, their lives become entangled by an investigation that uncovers a web of darkness and opens up secrets that have long been condemned to silence . . .

Who were they, all those years ago? What nightmares did they share? And what is the truth about the undying nature of their love?